Discovery Guide to
Egypt

by Michael Haag

Other *Discovery Guides* cover Cairo, Jordan and the Holy Land, West Africa, Zimbabwe, Vietnam, Rajasthan, Aegean and Mediterranean Turkey, Eastern Turkey, etc.

Please send for our complete list:
Discovery Guides
Michael Haag Limited
PO Box 369
London NW3 4DP
England

Discovery Guide to Egypt, fourth edition, September 1990
Text and photographs © 1990 by Michael Haag

Cover photographs by Michael Haag; cover design by Colin Elgie

Typeset in 9/10pt CG/Monotype Times by BP Integraphics, Bath, Avon

Printed in Great Britain at the Bath Press, Lower Bristol Road, Bath BA2 3BL

Published by Michael Haag Limited, PO Box 369, London NW3 4DP, England

ISBN 0 902743 75 9

CONTENTS

Practical Information sections follow most chapters and there are indexes at the rear.

DISCOVERY GUIDES

Discovery Guides take a fresh and original look at both the familiar and the less familiar places of the world. This *Discovery Guide to Egypt* recognises that it is not enough to describe, to list statistics of age and size. It must also explain the significance of what is seen.

The monuments of Egypt tell a story. The Pyramids created the Egyptian state; the desert monasteries transformed Christianity; the mosques of Cairo recount the struggles of Islam; the High Dam at Aswan is changing the ecology of northern Africa. Their stories are as fascinating as the monuments themselves.

In Egypt too there is the sheer vastness of a 5000-year history to come to terms with. And though the country is pervaded with an impressive sense of permanence and duration, the Nile and the deserts on either side have also witnessed the changing spectacle of successive dynasties, religions and foreign rulers, with numerous exemplars amongst them: Zoser and Ptolemy Philadelphos, Akhenaton and al-Hakim, Ramses II and Saladin, Moses and St Antony, Alexander and Amr, Cleopatra and Shagarat al-Durr, Mohammed Ali and Nasser — some names better known than others, but even then the traveller may be uncertain of their place within the Egyptian jigsaw.

And so the intention throughout has been to hear what stories the monuments have to tell, to link people with places, and to build up a comprehensible portrait of Egypt as you go along. Though for example there are step by step descriptions of great temples which you need follow carefully only on the spot, this guide is in large part a narrative designed to be read through at any time, or dipped into now and again.

The main text of the chapters contain this narrative, and the descriptions. An outline chronology is provided in the *Background* chapter to help you get your bearings. This introductory chapter also provides the information you need before you go and explains in general terms what you can expect when you arrive. At the end of most chapters are *Practical Information* sections with details on accommodation, eating places, travel, etc, within the area.

Changes inevitably occur and improvements to this guide are always possible. Readers are invited to contribute additional material or help update existing detail by writing to the *Discovery Guide to Egypt, Michael Haag Limited, PO Box 369, London NW3 4DP, England*. Thank you.

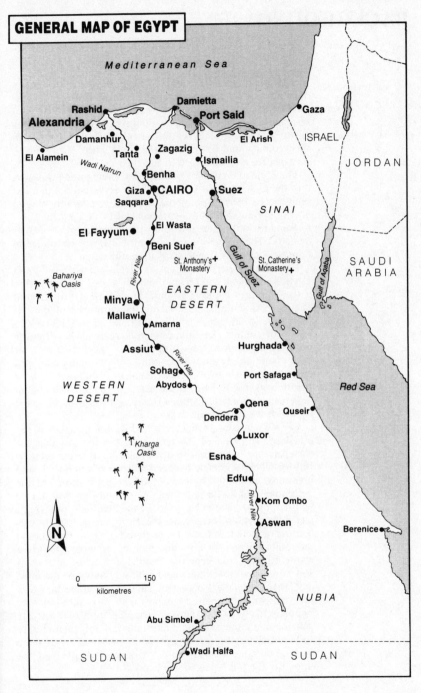

GENERAL MAP OF EGYPT

Mediterranean Sea

Damietta
Rashid
Alexandria
Port Said
Gaza
Damanhur
El Arish
ISRAEL
El Alamein
Tanta
Zagazig
Wadi Natrun
Ismailia
JORDAN
Benha
Giza **CAIRO**
Suez
Saqqara
SINAI
El Fayyum
El Wasta
SAUDI
ARABIA
Beni Suef
St. Anthony's
Monastery ✝
St. Catherine's
Monastery ✝
*Bahariya
Oasis*
*EASTERN
DESERT*
Gulf of Suez
Gulf of Aqaba
Minya
Mallawi
Amarna
Hurghada
Assiut
River Nile
*WESTERN
DESERT*
Sohag
Abydos
Port Safaga
Red Sea
Qena
*Kharga
Oasis*
Dendera
Quseir
Luxor
Esna
Edfu
River Nile
Kom Ombo
N
Aswan
Berenice

0 — 150
kilometres

NUBIA

Abu Simbel

SUDAN
Wadi Halfa
SUDAN

5

BACKGROUND

In pharaonic times the people of Egypt believed the sun was daily born of the goddess Nut and travelled westwards across the heavens until swallowed by her at day's end, to be born once more the following dawn. And they believed the waters of the Nile rose from beneath the firmament, flowed through their country and out beyond the Delta where they sank to their source and then rose to run their course again.

The cycle and continuity of natural events was translated into the philosophical basis of ancient Egyptian politics and religion. In hieroglyphics the name of a pharaoh or god always appeared within a cartouche, an oval ring that represented the unbroken, unending, unchanging power of ruler or deity. The order of natural events in Egypt continues to impress a sense of timelessness upon the country.

Herodotus described Egypt as 'a gift of the river', and Egypt's gift, like a great river of time, has been to carry within it the presence of the pharaonic, Hellenistic, Christian and Islamic periods, all embraced by the cartouche of the fellahin's millenial toil. Egypt's endurance and stability in a region of conflict, flux and immense creativity has been its outstanding contribution to the world. Egypt itself has not been exceptionally innovative; it did not give mankind mathematics, philosophy, science, medicine, Judaism, Christianity or Islam. But Egypt was essential to each, offering an impetus or a home, sometimes stamping them with the shape by which we know them today.

Egypt's sense of permanence and duration makes it par excellence the land of the past, and it is for this that the traveller usually comes, too often ignoring its living present. But for all the spectacle over the millenia of migrations and invasions, probably 90 percent of its population are the descendants of its ancient inhabitants, and they will not be ignored. I first came to Egypt to see the Pyramids, but what I met with greater force were the Egyptian people. It was because of them that I cared enough to explore as best I could the totality of their history and their experience. They are a warm, friendly and generous people; ambitious, intelligent and proud; naive, religious and fatalistic; and also the most indefatigable hustlers on earth. They are all these things in such an open and sometimes importunate way that the novice visitor is likely to find himself swinging from one extreme reaction to another within minutes. But it is only their vitality you are reacting to, for though their conditions are extreme they are not an extreme people. If you enjoy people, you will enjoy the Egyptian people especially.

The desert hare represents the verb 'to be'

The Egyptian Condition
About 10,000 years ago a dramatic change in climate caused the once fertile lands of northern Africa and the Middle East to turn to dust. Rock drawings in the Sahara depict ancient man hunting herbivores where now there is only sand. The inhabitants of this great belt of arid land migrated towards the few remaining rivers.

The river of life   The Nile provided water and its annual flood covered the fields with rich alluvial soil. The ancient Egyptians called their country 'The Black Land', and the Nile valley and the Delta is still today the most fertile land in the world. Were it not for the existence of the Nile, no part of Egypt would be capable of agriculture. But it was not entirely a gift. The river had to be regulated, swamps drained, canals dug, fields planted and irrigated, the entire complex system maintained. To this task the fellahin gave their unremitting labour, and the state provided direction.

During the Ptolemaic period Egypt reached a level of prosperity and population that it was not to enjoy again until the 19th C when the dynasty of Mohammed Ali reversed the country's long decline under Arab and Turkish rule. In 1882 Egypt's population stood at just under seven million — equivalent to the number of Cleopatra's subjects. But since then, the nine-fold increase in population has worked against economic advance.

7

Though Egypt is larger than any European country except Russia, 93 percent of its area is dry and barren desert where only a few oasis-dwellers and nomadic Bedouin can survive. In pharaonic times Egypt was likened to a lotus plant. The river was the stem, the Fayyum the bud, the Delta the flower. Within this figure of fertility today lives 95 percent of the nation's population, its density one of the highest in the world.

Since the construction of the Aswan High Dam in the 1960s the Nile no longer floods. Instead the river flows evenly throughout the year, the harvests have multiplied, deserts have been brought to life. And Egypt gained the energy that would lead, it was hoped, to wholesale industrialisation, releasing the fellahin from their drudgery, the nation from its poverty.

But as fast as the High Dam has helped bring new land under cultivation, other land has been swallowed by urban expansion. Fellahin seeking a better existence have been abandoning their diminishing plots in the desperate hope of a better life in the cities, which now hold half Egypt's population. In the 1970s Egypt was self-sufficient in food and even had a thriving export trade; now at least 60 percent of foodstuffs are imported.

Egyptians had put much faith in the fruits of peace. 'In war', I was told in the 1970s by a Luxor doctor, 'if you win, you lose something; if you lose, you lose everything. We want peace to build. The Egyptian people are used to living on very little. But we want a future, we want something for our children'.

Population explosion

But Egypt's children are being born at the rate of one every 24 seconds. The population numbers close to 60 million and is increasing by a million every nine months. Though the birth rate has been falling, it has not been falling fast enough: only 30 percent of married women practice birth control, and the earning potential of additional children is seen as a way of augmenting family income and providing for parents in old age. Meanwhile, the death rate has fallen even faster, a reflection of improved health services. The strain that rising population puts on Egypt's food supplies, housing, jobs and services is a part of the country's problem.

Attempts by Nasser and succeeding governments to alleviate social injustice brought new problems. The lands and wealth of pashas and foreigners were redistributed, but the creation of new wealth was neglected. Industry and commerce were nationalised. Free education was given to all and every university graduate was guaranteed a government job

Economic policy failures

by law. The result of these measures has been a collapse in investment and a bloated, inefficient bureaucracy. The wait for a guaranteed job is six years and getting longer; the proportion of the population in employment is falling; the stan-

8

dard of teaching is now so low that in some places free education is not worth having; and there is a grave housing crisis, illustrated by those three million Cairenes who live in the city's necropolises amongst the dead.

Many people are lucky to earn $250 a year; the average income is well under $1000 a year; a general in the Egyptian army earns about $2500 a year. Around 90 percent of the population depends for its survival on subsidies, mostly in the form of cheap food, fuel, travel and electricity, and depends too on rents held at 1950s levels. The consequences can be as absurd as they are wasteful: a litre of petrol costs less than a litre of bottled water; rents are so low that buildings cannot be maintained and fall down; bread is so cheap that it is fed as fodder to animals, while Egypt, once the bread basket of Rome, is the world's third largest importer of wheat after the Soviet Union and China.

Agriculture remains the basis of the Egyptian economy, and its main crops are cotton, sugar cane, maize, rice and wheat, while the raising of cattle and poultry is increasing. But the country's main foreign currency earners are oil, Suez Canal fees, remittances from Egyptians working abroad and tourism — and all these are peculiarly sensitive to political conditions in the Middle East. Of crucial importance are World Bank, International Monetary Fund and foreign government (principally United States) loans, on the repayments of which Egypt routinely defaults. And then there is foreign aid; for example Egypt is the second largest recipient of United States foreign aid (Egypt gets 19 percent, Israel 21 percent).

Egypt has a free press, partial freedom for political parties — the Nasserists and the fundamentalist Muslim Brotherhood are banned — and free elections under laws that are biased in favour of the ruling National Democratic Party. But while surrendering the dictatorial powers of the Nasser regime, the government does not yet enjoy full democratic support, and so lacks the authority and confidence to implement the radical and painful reforms necessary for Egypt's prosperity and stability. Apart from slowing the population increase, what is required, as is happening in Russia and Eastern Europe, is a reduction in subsidies while increasing productivity through encouragement of the private sector. Any sudden reform, however, would mean the further impoverishment of the poor and massive job losses — with the likelihood of political unrest, exploited by and benefiting the fundamentalists.

Cautious reforms   The government is cautiously increasing the price of bread and energy, imposing heavier taxes on marginal items, and attempting to replace across-the-board commodity subsidies with cash subsidies targetted on those most in need. The IMF and the United States continue to reschedule Egypt's debts,

9

and the oil-rich Arab states that turned their backs on Egypt after its peace treaty with Israel have now revised their attitude.

When I first went to Egypt in 1967 I was struck by the prevalence of disease, blindness and crippled beggars, by the dimness which fell with night in the cities and the utter darkness of the villages throughout much of the valley and the Delta where there was no electricity, and I was struck too by the sufferings of war. There have been great changes, though perhaps those changes under other policies could have been greater.

Tourist Information

Tourist information may be obtained from Egyptian tourist offices abroad. In Britain it is the Egyptian State Tourist Office, 168 Piccadilly, London WI (Tel: 071–493 5282). In the United States they are called Egyptian Government Tourist Offices and they are at 630 Fifth Avenue, New York, NY 10111 (Tel: 246–6960) and 323 Geary Street, San Francisco, California 94102 (Tel: 781 7676). There are tourist offices also in Montreal, Paris, Geneva, Frankfurt, Rome, Athens and Tokyo. The headquarters of the Egyptian General Authority for the Promotion of Tourism, Ministry of Tourism, is at Misr Travel Tower, Abbassia Square, Cairo (Tel: 826016) and the principal Tourist Information Office is at 5 Sharia Adli, Cairo (Tel: 923000).

Another organisation very much worth contacting is Misr Travel, the state-run tourist company. They are in business for themselves and so their advice is not necessarily impartial, but they are certainly helpful. Misr Travel is the largest tourist company in Egypt and operates hotels, coaches and limousines, and can make bookings for domestic air and rail services or for just about anything else. In London Misr Travel is at Langham House, Regent Street, WI (Tel: 071–255 1087), and there are offices in New York, Los Angeles, Paris, Frankfurt, Stockholm, Rome, Jeddah, Kuwait, Tokyo and Sidney. Misr Travel's head office is at 1 Sharia Talaat Harb, PO Box 1000, Cairo (Tel: 3930010).

Otherwise, Egyptian embassies and consulates, and also offices of the national airline Egyptair, may be able to provide basic information.

Climate and When to Visit Egypt

In the leisured days of travel it was often the custom to spend an entire winter, from November to May, in Egypt. This was 'the season', climatically, socially, and for those in search of dry mild conditions conducive to relief from asthma, chronic bronchitis, rheumatoid arthritis, gout, Bright's disease and other diseases of the kidneys. The late 20th C visitor is unlikely to come to Egypt for medicinal reasons, nor to stay so long.

Late autumn through early spring is still the most comfortable period within which to visit most of the country, particularly Cairo and southwards into Upper Egypt, though the reverse is true of Alexandria.

Only a thin strip of the northern coastline shares in a Mediterranean climate, giving Alexandria an annual rainfall of 18 centimetres, most of this from December through March when the city experiences cool, blustery and often stormy weather. This is true inland to Damanhur and Tanta in the Delta. But generally temperatures along the coast are moderated by the sea throughout the year, and are neither too cold nor too hot, except that Alexandria can become very humid in July and August. Farther inland Egypt is within the arid zone, with rainfall throughout most of the country well under 2.5 centimetres a year.

Temperatures increase as you travel south, though in Cairo during December, January and February it can be chilly. Cairo can be very hot from June through September, though the heat is often relieved by breezes from the north. It is hotter yet in Upper Egypt where summer can be reckoned from May through October, but peak temperatures are to some extent compensated for by extremely low humidity. From Cairo southwards at any time between March and May you may experience the *khamasin* (fifty), a hot dust- and sand-laden wind from the southwest which can be very unpleasant and can seem to last for 50 days. Everywhere in Egypt at any time of year, but mostly in the deserts, temperatures can fall off sharply at night.

Year-round destination
But not too much emphasis should be laid on season, for a variety of reasons. Cairo and Upper Egypt are most visited from November through April and there is pressure on accommodation. From May through September prices are lower in Upper Egypt. Air conditioning is general in the new hotels and in the better older ones. It can be very hot in Egypt, especially Upper Egypt, during the summer, but seeing the sights early in the morning and late in the afternoon, and the extraordinary dryness of the air the farther south you go, can make your stay more agreeable. The proof is that Egypt has become a year-round destination.

Table of Temperature °C	January min./max.	February min./max.	March min./max.	April min./max.	May min./max.	June min./max.
Alexandria	9.3 18.3	9.7 19.2	11.2 21.0	13.5 23.6	16.7 26.5	20.2 28.2
Aswan	8.0 23.8	9.4 26.1	12.6 30.4	17.5 35.0	21.1 38.5	24.2 42.1
Cairo	8.6 19.1	9.3 20.7	11.2 23.7	13.9 28.2	17.4 32.4	17.9 34.5
Dakhla	4.6 21.5	6.1 23.9	9.7 27.9	14.4 33.0	19.6 37.4	22.4 38.8
Hurghada	9.6 20.6	9.9 20.9	12.3 23.0	16.1 26.0	20.7 29.6	23.5 31.4
Ismailia	8.2 20.4	9.1 21.7	11.0 23.9	13.6 27.6	17.3 32.1	20.2 34.8
Luxor	5.4 23.0	6.8 25.4	10.7 29.0	15.7 34.8	20.7 39.3	22.6 40.7
Mersa Matruh	8.1 18.1	8.4 18.9	9.7 20.3	11.8 22.7	14.5 25.5	18.2 27.8
Minya	3.9 20.6	5.4 22.5	7.8 25.4	11.7 30.2	16.7 35.4	18.8 36.3
Port Said	11.3 18.0	12.1 18.7	13.5 20.2	16.1 22.6	19.6 25.8	22.4 28.5
Siwa	4.1 19.7	5.7 21.8	8.2 25.0	12.1 39.9	16.8 34.3	19.2 37.1

Table of Temperature °C	July min./max.	August min./max.	September min./max.	October min./max.	November min./max.	December min./max.
Alexandria	22.7 29.6	22.9 30.4	21.3 29.4	17.8 27.7	14.8 24.4	11.2 20.4
Aswan	24.5 41.2	24.7 41.3	22.2 39.6	19.3 36.6	14.5 20.2	9.9 25.5
Cairo	21.5 25.4	21.6 34.8	19.9 32.3	17.8 29.8	19.9 24.1	10.4 20.7
Dakhla	23.0 39.0	22.9 38.9	20.7 36.1	17.4 33.0	12.0 28.0	6.7 23.0
Hurghada	24.8 32.6	25.0 33.0	23.2 30.6	19.7 28.5	15.5 25.7	11.9 22.4
Ismailia	22.2 36.4	22.5 36.5	20.7 33.9	17.8 30.7	13.9 26.6	10.0 21.5
Luxor	23.6 40.8	23.5 41.0	21.5 38.5	17.8 35.1	12.3 29.6	7.7 24.8
Mersa Matruh	20.2 29.2	21.0 29.9	19.7 28.7	16.8 27.0	13.3 23.4	10.0 19.7
Minya	20.2 37.0	20.5 36.6	18.6 33.4	15.9 31.2	11.5 26.6	7.0 21.7
Port Said	24.1 30.4	24.9 30.9	23.9 29.2	21.8 27.4	18.4 24.0	12.7 19.9
Siwa	20.7 38.0	20.7 27.8	18.3 35.1	14.9 31.7	10.1 26.3	6.0 21.3

For conversion to Fahrenheit, see the *Weights and Measures* section below.

What to Take

The clothing you take will depend on where you go and the time of year. In winter you will need at least some light woollens and sweaters; in summer light cottons. In spring and autumn some combination of both is advisable against warm days and cool nights, and the possibility of changeable weather. Even in summer, however, at least one sweater or knit is likely to come in handy: at night the deserts can be cool, and Alexandria is freshened by strong sea breezes.

Clothes should be light in colour to reflect the sun and should be easily washable and drip-dry. In summer, anywhere in Egypt except Alexandria, you can wash a suit at night and have it bone dry in the morning.

Conservative dress
Although more liberal than most other Arab countries, and tolerant too of foreign habits even when not shared by the local population, Egypt is nevertheless conservative by Western standards and if anything has become more conservative over the past ten years or so. Your dress should allow for this. This is especially true if visiting mosques, churches and monasteries, where shorts or short skirts should not be worn, nor anything too revealing. Egyptians are less conservative on beaches and around swimming pools, however, and the briefest swimwear is acceptable, certainly at all hotels and resorts — not only on visitors, but on Egyptians.

Egyptian cotton is famous for its quality; clothes and shoes are inexpensive. Rather than overpack these things, it would be better to buy them once you are in the country.

There is too much dust and dirt for sandals to be generally useful; bring comfortable walking shoes. Sunglasses (preferably with polarised lenses) and a broad-brimmed hat will keep out the glare of the sun.

Egypt increasingly manufactures foreign-brand shampoos, soaps, toothpastes, razor blades and other toilet items, or otherwise imports them. All such things are readily available at the better hotels, but will be cheaper in local shops where you will also find less expensive Egyptian brands.

The same applies now to suntan lotions, insect repellents, batteries and film. But bring your own contraceptives and tampons. Also, if you think your requirements might be slightly out of the ordinary, bring those items too: they may not have the high-screen suntan lotion, for example, or the contact lens solution and the eye drops you want (good for dust), or precisely the size battery you need for camera or flash; and extremely high-speed colour film or almost any black and white film can be difficult to obtain. Anyway, these items will be cheaper abroad than in Egypt.

Bring an initial supply of toilet paper, or at least steal a roll from the first hotel you stay at, and then keep yourself stocked with it as you travel — amazing how useful it can be and how often it is not there. A universal-size bath and basin plug may also come in handy.

A flashlight is invaluable for exploring tombs and other nooks and crannies. Binoculars are also useful, especially if you are cruising along the Nile, but also for examining the details of gargantuan ruins.

You may need a travel plug adaptor; Egypt has Continental-style double round pin sockets, 220 volts AC.

If you like alcohol, bring some duty-free drink with you; it is very expensive in Egypt.

Entry Regulations

Visas All visitors to Egypt require a visa. To obtain one, your passport must be valid for at least three months following your arrival in the country. Visas (for a single visit or mutiple, ie three, visits) can be obtained in person (allow 24 hours) or by post (allow at least two weeks) from an Egyptian consulate abroad. You will need to present your passport, one passport photograph and pay the appropriate fee. Often tour companies will take care of this for you. It is also possible to obtain a visa on arrival. Visitors visas are valid for one month. Extensions and re-entry visas can be obtained in Egypt (eg at the Mugamaa, Midan el Tahrir, Cairo, near the Nile Hilton).

With the exception of those with pre-paid package arrangements, anyone staying in Egypt longer than 72 hours must purchase on arrival $150-worth (or the equivalent) of Egyptian pounds at a recognised bank of exchange (of which there are several at airports). You should also declare your currency on arrival; you are then allowed to leave the country with the amount of money you originally declared minus the sums you have officially exchanged and used during your stay in Egypt. (There is no longer a black market worth bothering about; see *Money* below.)

Within seven days of your arrival you must register your presence with the police, obtaining a triangular stamp in your passport (hotels or tour operators usually do this for you automatically).

To hire a car in Egypt you will need an International Driving Licence. This will be needed also if you are bringing your own vehicle, along with a carnet de passage (both obtainable from your motoring organisation at home), special insurance (obtainable on arrival) and either a deposit or some form of guarantee against road tax and customs duties. The deposit is refundable on departure. For further details, contact the Egyptian State Tourist Office or your motoring organisation. *Note that diesel vehicles are not allowed entry into Egypt.*

Cholera and yellow fever certificates are required if arriving from an infected area.

You may bring into Egypt, exempt from duty and other taxes, all personal effects, used or new, including camera equipment, radios, recorders, typewriters, word processors, jewellery, etc, provided these are listed on the customs declaration form.

Also exempt are 400 cigarettes, or 250 grams of tobacco or 50 cigars, and one litre of alcohol. Note that at Cairo Airport there is a duty-free shop for *arriving* passengers, though the selection is not as extensive as at foreign airports. (Oddly enough, there are duty-free shops before you pass through customs, but also one after you pass through customs and emerge into the arrivals hall, where it is quite possible to purchase still more duty-free goods — you will be asked only for your ticket, not whether you have already tanked up.)

Departure Regulations

When leaving Egypt you will be allowed (eg at the airport) to take with you the amount of money you declared on entry minus the sums officially exchanged and used during your stay. It has been known (very rarely) for travellers to have foreign currency confiscated because they have attempted to leave with more than they could possibly have under the above formula. More importantly, the amount of Egyptian pounds you will be allowed to change into foreign currency is based on the amount you first officially changed into Egyptian pounds and can show bank receipts for, minus an assumed

Getting rid of your Egyptian money

daily spending rate at a fairly high level. The Egyptian government is trying to obtain and hold on to all the foreign currency it can (which it needs to pay for imports), and so it does not bend over backwards to give it back to you. The best thing to do is to have spent all your Egyptian pounds before you go and to forget the nonsense of trying to convert them.

There is no airport departure tax.

Getting to Egypt

By air. Most scheduled flights arrive at Cairo International Airport, though there are flights also to Alexandria and Luxor. You can save a great deal on the normal fare by purchasing an Advance Purchase Excursion (APEX) or other discounted fare ticket. Direct scheduled flights between the United States and Egypt are operated by TWA and Egyptair, while those between Britain and Egypt are operated by British Airways and Egyptair. (Note that Egyptair does not serve alcohol on its flights, but permits you to bring your own.) From Britain it is often possible to get a cheaper discount fare by flying indirectly, eg on KLM via Amsterdam, Olympic via Athens; you do not deal directly with the airline, however, but with a specialised agent. The best agent in Britain for discounted fares is Trailfinders, 46 Earls Court Road, London W8 (Tel: 071–938 3366).

You should also compare the cost of a flight to what the tour operators (see below) have to offer; even for independent travellers who do not wish a full-blown tour or any tour at all, they can sometimes offer some attractive deals.

By sea. Italy's Adriatica Navigazione operates a car ferry service between Venice, Dubrovnik, Piraeus, Heraklion and Alexandria. The British agent is Sealink British Ferries Travel Centre, Platform 2, Victoria Station, London SW1 (Tel: 071–828 1940). Khedivial Mail Line, Egyptian House, Piccadilly, London WI (Tel: 071–499 1506) also has sailings to Alexandria.

Two modern ferries operate in the Red Sea between Suez and Aqaba, Jordan, and between Suez and Jeddah, Saudi Arabia (agents: Menatours, 14 Sharia Talaat Harb, Cairo).

Overland. There are frequent buses between Israel and Egypt. A daily luxury coach service between Cairo and Tel Aviv is operated by Travco, 13 Sharia Mahmoud Azmi, Zamalek, Cairo (Tel: 3404308). In Tel Aviv there are several agents near the Egyptian Embassy, eg VIP Tours, 130 Hayarkon Street (Tel: 244181). Check also with Egged, the national bus company of Israel. If crossing from Eilat, once over the border at Taba in Sinai you can catch a service taxi or bus down the coast as far as Sharm el Sheikh.

Between Sudan and Egypt there is a notoriously unreliable train service between Khartoum and Wadi Halfa on the border, connecting with a twice-weekly ferry to Aswan. In Sudan, bookings can be made at the Khartoum railway station, or in Egypt at the Nile Navigation Company, Ramses Station, Midan Ramses, Cairo, or at the Sudanese Maritime Office on the corniche near the Tourist Office in Aswan.

Tour and cruise operators. These are legion, with some offering flight-only arrangements, others specialising in adventurous treks and felucca journeys down the Nile, still others zapping you in and out by Concorde or giving you the full Nile cruise with on-board Egyptologist. Your nearest Egyptian Tourist Office can supply a complete list along with a description of what each offers.

By way of example:

Kuoni Travel, 33 Maddox Street, London WI (Tel: 071–499 8636), is one of the best general operators; it offers a variety of packages, some simply based in Cairo or Luxor (with or without a tour), others including a Nile cruise, and still others flight-only deals into Luxor which can work out much cheaper than the most discounted scheduled ticket.

Thomas Cook, 45 Berkeley Street, London WA (Tel: 071–499 4000), long famous for its Egyptian tours and cruises, has offices throughout Britain and many parts of the world, and offers a good selection of packages to Egypt, with cruises in the 22-cabin *Nile Rhapsody*.

Abercrombie & Kent, Sloane Square House, Holbein Place, London SWI (Tel: 071–730 9600), and in the United States, 1420 Kensington Road, Suite 111, Oak Brook, Illinois 60521 (Tel: 800–323–7308), is an upmarket company with the good sense to cruise the Nile in small boats large on character, eg the 23-cabin *Sunboat*.

Classic Tours, 87 Regent Street, London W1 (Tel: 071–734 7971), has a range of imaginative theme tours which include 'Pharaohs and Christians' and 'Pharaohs, the Nile and Tanis'.

British Museum Tours, 46 Bloomsbury Street, London WC1 (Tel: 071–323 1234), has the advantage of the museum's expertise and world-wide reputation. Doors often closed to other operators magically open when 'British Museum' is mentioned, and sites in the process of excavation are visited and explained. British Museum lecturers accompany groups on intensive studies of the pyramid phenomenon, the deserts and oases, Nubia and Sudan, etc.

Swan Hellenic, 77 New Oxford Street, London WI (Tel: 071–831 1515), and in the United States, c/o Esplanade Tours, 581 Boylston Street, Boston, Massachusetts 02116 (Tel: 800–426–5492), offers cruises of varying extent aboard the 35-cabin *Nile Star*, each exceptionally detailed and accompanied by expert lecturers.

مصلى
Prayer Room

Modern hieroglyphics open to interpretation at Cairo Airport

Misr Travel (see *Tourist Information* above) might be able to tailor a package exactly to your needs.

For general comments on Nile cruises, see under *Travel Within Egypt*, Along the Nile, below.

A word to the handicapped and the faint of heart. I can do no better than quote from a reader's letter. 'We made our trip in somewhat unusual circumstances — my wife has a hip problem which limits her mobility for other than short distances and a few (low) steps and, consequently, we use a wheelchair for anything over a short walk to the shops. While planning the trip I contacted several tour operators, only to find they were unanimous in implying that our custom really would not be appreciated. Faced with this, and in view of our limited funds, I contacted Misr Travel and arranged a trip on our own. ... Our reliance on your guidebook was absolute. No guided tours, no coaches, we did it all ourselves and I doubt if we missed anything within our capabilities or a single pertinent fact. .... We can't say enough about the service given us by Misr Travel — it was invaluable. Moreover, the total cost for the two of us for 16 days was less than the two-week tours offered by tour operators. Note, we did not travel deluxe — we stayed at the Windsor, Old Cataract and Etap hotels, and spent three nights on the MS *Giza*. The most valuable service, to us, was the attendant and transport at each change of location — stretched Mercedes, and knowledgeable representatives who, in each case, refused a tip. .... For anyone with a walking handicap, we strongly suggest, for visits to the Valley of the Kings, etc, taking a taxi from the hotel onto the vehicle ferry. We were able to take and use the wheelchair at every location, with not too much difficulty, since our time was our own. It would have been impossible to keep up with a group. At the tombs we were limited due to the large number of steps, but we were able to visit that of Ramses VI. .... Two possible items of interest, perhaps: Egyptair, for our flight from Cairo to Aswan, put us on the plane using one of those food vans with the lifting box, right to the rear entrance. The second, a conversation with an Egyptian who spoke fluent English. When we told him how we felt completely secure on the streets, even at night, in every city, he said "You must realise that to us Egyptians, you tourists are sacred! Five million Egyptians depend on tourism for a living". I doubt if we will visit Egypt again but we will never forget it. Particularly the people. We met with nothing but courtesy and smiles, not a single adverse memory.'

Visiting a royal tomb by wheelchair

Travel Within Egypt

By air. The principal carrier within the country is Egyptair, with flights from Cairo to Alexandria, Luxor, Aswan, Abu Simbel, New Valley (Kharga Oasis) and Hurghada. Air Sinai flies to Hurghada and, in Sinai, to St Catherine's, El Tor and Sharm el Sheikh. Egypt's private sector airline, Zas Passenger Service, flies to Aswan, Luxor, Hurghada and St Catherine's.

Always try to make advance reservations. In winter it is advisable to make reservations as far in advance as possible for Upper Egypt, and especially to Abu Simbel; in summer ditto for flights to Alexandria.

By rail. Air-conditioned rail travel in Egypt is comfortable and inexpensive, and still more inexpensive for students in possession of an International Student Identity Card (50 percent discount, though no discount on the Wagons-Lits sleepers).

The varieties of railway experience

All first class and combined first and second class trains are air-conditioned; others are not. Local trains serving smaller stations are likely to be slow, crowded and uncomfortable, and they will not be air-conditioned — the experience can be interesting if it does not go on for too long.

Travelling aboard a non-air-conditioned train can be like sharing a room in a tenth-rate Arab hotel with scores of guests, the only difference between second and third class being the number of Egyptians per cubic metre. In third class especially it is to suffer an intimacy one would prefer to do without. No matter what class of train you are travelling on, bring toilet paper.

Almost all air-conditioned trains require reservations and you should book at least a day in advance; in winter try to book several days in advance for Upper Egypt if possible. You can try getting on a train at the last moment to see if there is any space (a bit of baksheesh to the carriage attendant would not go amiss). Note that when queuing for tickets, men approach the ticket window from the right, women from the left, taking turns. The women's queue is shorter and quicker.

By way of example, from Cairo the fare to Alexandria is about LE7 first class one way; to Luxor about LE16 first class; to Aswan about LE18 first class. Second class air-conditioned fares are about half. Snacks and meals are served at your seat for a few pounds.

There is a Wagons-Lits sleeper service between Cairo and Luxor/Aswan using modern if dull German rolling stock. Each compartment has a washbasin and two berths and is taken either as a single or a double. Meals are served in the compartments, and there is a club car for drinks and socialising — and this can sometimes be a lot of fun when a party atmosphere is got going by the exceptionally agile Nubian staff who dance across tables with stacks of drinks balanced on their heads. The one way fare, either to Luxor or Aswan, is about LE90 per person on a double-berth basis, one way, but more if the compartment is taken on a single-berth basis. Reservations are essential and should be made at least a week in advance if possible. Book through a good agent abroad or in Egypt, or go direct to the Wagons-Lits office at Ramses Station, Cairo.

On all services, children under four travel free; those from four to ten obtain a 50 percent reduction and on sleepers are expected to share a berth with an adult.

Clerks at ticket windows and station masters can be helpful in telling you when the next train is to wherever, or how to get to some less-trafficked place. But it is nearly impossible to inform yourself comprehensively, and the few published timetables available to visitors assume that you want only to travel between Alexandria, Cairo, Luxor and Aswan, and then only on certain trains. The more adventurous traveller should equip himself in advance with a copy of the *Thomas Cook Overseas Timetable* (useful also for principal bus services, Nile cruises, the Aswan-Wadi Halfa-Khartoum journey and Red Sea shipping), available for about £5.95 from all Thomas Cook offices in Britain or by contacting Timetable

Publishing Office, Thomas Cook Limited, Thorpe Wood, Peterborough PE3 6SB, England (Tel: 0733 268937), from whom you can order direct (postage extra) or determine your local sales agent wherever in the world you may be. In North America, contact Forsyth Travel Library, 9154 West 57th Stree, PO Box 2975, Dept OT, Shawnee Mission, Kansas 66201, USA (Tel: 1–800–FORSYTH, except from Kansas or Canada, in which case Tel: 913–384–3440), who can supply the timetable for about $23 inclusive of postage.

Note that trains usually depart from main termini (eg Cairo, Alexandria) on time, but rarely arrive anywhere on time.

By road. To drive your own car or to hire one (unless you hire a driver too) you will need an International Driving Licence, obtainable from your motoring organisation at home (eg AA, RAC, AAA), and be not less than 25 and not more than 70 years of age. Car hire is not expensive, and petrol is very cheap.

The joy of the open road

But one problem is that Cairo is a madhouse on wheels, agricultural roads in the Delta and along the valley are often busy with trucks and donkeys and camels, at night oncoming car and truck lights are either beamed in the wrong direction or are not on at all, and Egyptians are in any case very odd drivers. With little appreciation of the virtue of keeping to a lane or even to the right-hand side of the road, they meander and eddy about as though negotiating mudbanks in the Nile. The way to survive is to wander with them, which means needing eyes on the sides and the back of your head — or no eyes at all. But do not be put off: you soon get the hang of it, and having your own car gives you great freedom and flexibility, especially in discovering the less beaten paths and trodden sites of Egypt.

A word of warning, however. If you run somebody over outside a city, immediately get into your car and either await the police or drive off to find them. Do not hang about on a lonely country or desert road on your own, certainly not at night. The families of victims have been known to exact instant justice, especially if they are Bedouin.

You can still have the advantage of a car without any of the problems if you hire one with a driver (not very expensive) or hire a taxi (see service taxis below) — amongst several people it can be quite reasonable to hire a taxi, say, from Cairo to Alexandria, stopping at the Wadi Natrun along the way.

Long distance buses can be fast, cheap and comfortable. From Cairo there are regular runs to Alexandria (also from Cairo Airport) and Upper Egypt. There are good services too from Alexandria to Siwa and Damietta, from Cairo and Assiut to the inner oases of the Western Desert, from Cairo and the Canal cities to Sinai and along the Red Sea coast, also from Luxor to Hurghada and from Aswan to Abu Simbel.

Except between Cairo and Alexandria, where the service is so frequent that you can almost always get a ticket for the same day, you should buy your ticket a day, preferably two days, in advance. Sample fares: Cairo to Minya, LE5; to Luxor, LE12; to Dakhla Oasis via Bahariya and Farafra, LE14; to St Catherine's, LE17; Cairo Airport to Alexandria by luxury coach, LE12.

Service (shared) taxis run just about everywhere. They are fast and very cheap, and are good both for long-distance travel and for hopping from town to town, site to site. They operate on a first come first served basis and carry seven passengers. You can buy the seat next to you for greater comfort, or you can hire them for private use. Sample fares per seat: Cairo to Medinet el Fayyum, LE4; to Alexandria, LE5; to Ismailia, LE6. A day's hire of an entire taxi for an excursion from Cairo to the Wadi Natrun and back, or being dropped off at Alexandria, costs about LE140.

Hitchhiking is possible though uncommon and it can be difficult.

Tours. You can always package yourself by deciding to take a tour on the spot. American Express offers a number of quickie tours from Cairo: Alexandria or the Suez Canal or the Fayyum or Luxor or St Catherine's, each in one day flat; or two-, three- and even four-day tours of the Red Sea/Sinai resorts, Luxor, Aswan and Abu Simbel. Thomas Cook does the same sort of thing, but also offers more personalised tours for a few people at a time. See also Misr Travel under *Tourist Information* above.

Cruises along the Nile. Most likely you will have arranged a cruise before coming to Egypt (see *Getting to Egypt*, Tour and Cruise Operators, above). It may form part of an overall package, or you may be arriving as an independent traveller but wanting to include a cruise somewhere in your plans. It is possible to do both from abroad. But you can also, space permitting, book yourself onto a cruise once in Egypt.

Agencies like Thomas Cook, American Express and Misr Travel can make the arrangements, either in Egypt or abroad. Also the Oberoi, Hilton and Sheraton hotels operate cruises, which similarly can be booked through their hotels or reservations centres either in Egypt or abroad.

Prices are highest from October through May, falling by about 40 percent in summer, and include meals, sightseeing ashore, taxes and service charges. For a five-day cruise on one of the hotel boats, expect to pay about $1200 per double cabin during high season and about $700 per double cabin during low season. Local operators offer cruises at rates substantially lower than those of the international hotels, and often the fewer cabins a boat has, the better the ambience. The smallest boats have between 20 and 30 cabins, eg *Nile Rhapsody* (owned by Presidential Nile Cruises and used by Thomas Cook), *Nile Star* (owned by Eastmar Line and used by Swan Hellenic) and *Sunboat* (owned by Sunboat Cruises and used by Abercrombie & Kent). See the *Practical Information* section following the *Cairo: Mother of the World* chapter for the addresses of local operators.

The hotel boats, indeed 'floating hotels' as they are called, and others like them, are the behemoths of the Nile. Equipped with boutiques, bars, hairdressers and discos, you are not certain that you have ever left dry land. They can provide luxury, though much of it may seem to you extraneous, and because of their size you may feel lost in the crowd. The Sheraton boats are the largest, with 80 cabins, and are utterly lacking in style. The Hilton boats have only 48 cabins, and are trim, well-run vessels. In size the Oberoi boats fall in between, with 69 cabins and two suites; they are the most luxurious, the best-run and have the best cuisine.

There are now about 180 cruise boats on the river, with the overwhelming number plying between Aswan and Luxor, and calling on Esna, Edfu and Kom Ombo along the way. Some of these loop a bit farther north to allow visits to Dendera and Abydos. Generally you spend four to eight days on the boat, though for about half this time you will be tied up at Luxor and Aswan while you go off touring their local sights. When sailing along this upper part of the river, I prefer south to Aswan for the sense of threading one's way more narrowly through the encroaching desert, but in whichever direction you sail, the Luxor–Aswan run certainly covers the greatest concentration of sepctacular ancient sites.

However, there are also a few longer cruises between Aswan and Minya, and between Aswan and Cairo (in both cases taking in Amarna and Beni Hassan). These take 11 to 13 days. The schedule is less hectic and there is the cumulative impression that the Nile makes upon you.

There is the clear sense that you are travelling along a valley. By road or rail perhaps you do not see it, or fail to pay attention, or are rushing too much, but by boat it is plain. The Nile cuts through rock close by on either side, or it meanders between one cliff wall of the valley and the other. Sometimes the valley walls are distant and the sense is momentarily lost, but then the river swings back against the rock and reminds you of the work it has been doing throughout the eons. But valley is perhaps misleading; this is more a groove, a broad canyon. It is a cut through sandstone and limestone, and then filled with mud from Africa.

Along the lower reaches of the Nile there are fewer landing stages and fewer boats; sometimes you might tie up at a palm tree along an empty stretch of river. There are shallows and mudbanks and low lying fields where land and river mingle; there are reed hides, hunters and fishermen poling their boats through knee-deep water, animals grazing on half-sunken islands, and sometimes, instead of mud brick villages, scatterings of palm-roofed dwellings like seasonal encampments, tentative, suggesting the earliest settlements along the Nile. Huge flights of birds pass through the sky, bound for the Danube or Lake Victoria. It goes on like this for days and days and is the journey of a lifetime.

By felucca along the Nile. For the adventurous, sailing the Nile in a felucca is the thing. Sleeping bags may be necessary, though often blankets will be provided. Meals are usually included in the cost which varies with the number of people aboard and your bargaining powers. Make arrangements with boatmen at Luxor or (better) Aswan. The duration of the journey will depend on the strength of the winds.

Map. The best readily-available map of Egypt is the Kuemmerly & Frey 1:750,000. In Egypt it is published by the Lehnert and Landrock bookshop and is sold widely.

Accommodation

The number of hotels in Egypt has increased greatly over the past ten years, though mostly in the main centres and particularly at the upper end of the market. However, there has been some increase too of middle-category accommodation, in Cairo especially, while Minya and Assiut in Middle Egypt have at last acquired a few decent places to stay. Resorts in Sinai and along the Red Sea are developing rapidly. But the number of visitors has also increased, and if possible you should make reservations, especially if you have your heart set on a particular hotel. Pressure on accommodation is most acute in Luxor and Aswan during winter, and in Alexandria during summer.

Reservations can be made through an experienced travel agent, or you can contact the hotel directly by letter or telephone. The international chain hotels can be booked by contacting one of their hotels in your own country.

Hotels in Egypt are officially rated from 5-star (luxury) to 1-star. The rating system is not always evenly graduated, and you may find that a 3-star hotel is just as good as a 4-star one, or that two 4-star hotels charge markedly different rates. Nevertheless, the official system has been used in this guide, along with a description which should help you form your own preliminary judgement. As a rule of thumb, any 3-star hotel will do; below that you should have a look for yourself.

There are also hotels that have no star rating; very few of

these have been included in this guide as the standard is pretty low, though at a pinch they can be worth checking out. Youth hostels are generally not worth bothering with; they are often full and it is usually possible to find more congenial accommodation without damaging the most exiguous budget.

Survivors from another age

One of the glories of Egypt was its older hotels, cavernous places with louvred doors and mosquito nets over the beds, an atmosphere of worn elegance. Too many of these have disappeared, replaced by modern nondescript hotels. But I preferred them, whatever their condition; they were friendly, personal, and spoke of Egypt. Where they survive they have lost much of that Egyptian touch, but I mention them in case, along with visiting sites of remote antiquity, you would like to share my taste for what remains of the more recent past. Of my favourites, only one has survived in its full decrepitude, the Windsor in Cairo. Other survivors, now well refurbished, are the old part of the Mena House out by the Pyramids, the Cecil in Alexandria and the Old Cataract in Aswan. In Luxor the Old Winter Palace has been refurbished, but much of the heart has been torn out of it by the New Winter Palace tacked alongside, while the Luxor Hotel and the Savoy were still undergoing refurbishment when I last saw them so I am not sure how much has been saved or lost.

The rates that follow are indicative only and are for double rooms with bath. To these must be added service and tax which put about another 15 percent on top. Also, breakfast is often an obligatory extra. Single rooms or single occupancy of a double room costs ten to 20 percent less than the doubles rate. Rates in Cairo are the same year-round; in Alexandria and at the Red Sea and Sinai resorts they are about ten percent lower in winter; in Upper Egypt about ten percent lower in summer. Lower category hotels will also have some rooms without bath, and these will be cheaper; also other factors, eg a less favourable view, may mean a lower rate than indicated here.

Hotel bills must be paid either in foreign currency (the better ones will accept credit cards) or in Egyptian pounds accompanied by an exchange receipt from a bank. Hotels quote room rates in both US dollars and Egyptian pounds. For convenience they are quoted here in US dollars.

Cairo's rates, category for category, are higher than in the rest of Egypt:
5-star: $100–$160 per double room
4-star: $70–$100 per double room
3-star: $45–$70 per double room
2-star: $15–$45 per double room
1-star: up to $15 per double room

Rates in the rest of the country are:
5-star: $80–$120 per double room
4-star: $30–$80 per double room

3-star: $12–$40 per double room
2-star: $8–$20 per double room
1-star: up to $8 per double room

Food and Drink

Most hotels in Egypt, particularly the more expensive ones, cater to the tastes of foreign visitors by serving an international cuisine. In Cairo, as befitting a large cosmopolitan city, there are also many restaurants specialising in one or other national cuisine, eg French, Italian, Lebanese, Greek, Chinese, Indian. Alexandrian cuisine is Levantine.

Eating Egyptian style   Though the classic Arab–Turkish cuisine of Egypt is best encountered in private houses, you should venture forth to Egyptian eating places, spanning the gamut in price and sophistication, for a taste of Egyptian cooking. Dishes are usually savoury, neither too oily nor too spicy, and as only fresh ingredients are used the menu varies with season. Except in the simplest eating places frequented exclusively by Egyptians, restaurant menus will be available in English and French as well as in Arabic, and the waiter will speak English. In the simple Egyptian places, as at a Greek taverna, you can go into the kitchen, have a look, a taste, and then point to what you want.

Egypt's national dishes are *fool*, a bean paste; *tamaiya*, the same beans but pressed into a patty and fried in oil; *tahina*, a sesame paste; *babaganoush*, like tahina but eggplant instead of sesame; and *koushari*, a mixture of rice, macaroni, lentils and chickpeas, topped with a spicy sauce. Meat usually comes as kebabs and *kofta*, a spicy ground meat patty.

At cafés, the preparation of mint tea and coffee is a ritual. Thick and black, Turkish-style, coffee is ordered according to the amount of sugar: sweet (*ziyada*), medium (*mazboota*), bitter (*saada*). While sitting there, ask for a waterpipe, that is a *shisha* or *narghile*. The tobacco is mild and sweet (*masil salom*) and the smoke is even milder by the time it has passed through the water. You do not inhale. Payment is a few piastres.

Beer long antedates wine as the regional drink of the Mediterranean, so it is not so strange to find it reintroduced and very popular in Egypt. The commonest brand is Stella, in green litre bottles, unpredictable but usually very good. Stella Export is sweeter, of more consistent quality, more expensive and not as good. It is in smaller brown bottles. Both are lagers. Aswali is an excellent dark beer from Aswan, sometimes found elsewhere. Bock beer is available briefly in the spring and is referred to as Marzen (ie *Marzenbier*, March beer).

Egyptian wines are from ex-Greek vineyards near Alexandria, 'mobilised' by the government. They can all be described as drinkable and are inexpensive. Omar Khayyam is a

25

dry red, Cru des Ptolémées a dry white, and Rubis d'Egypte a rosé. French wines are also available at better hotels and restaurants but are very expensive.

Imported spirits are extremely expensive. Egypt does make its own: the gin is undrinkable; the brandy compares with the Spanish variety; while *arak*, the Arab equivalent of Greek ouzo, Turkish raki, French anisette, and often called *zibab* in Egypt, is excellent, whether neat, on the rocks, or diluted with water, which turns it a characteristic milky colour.

Beer, wines and, less readily, spirits can be purchased in shops, often small places few and far between. When purchased at hotels and restaurants, the markup is considerable. If you are particularly fond of spirits, make sure you bring your own duty-free bottle.

Though I have rarely met a middle class Egyptian who does not drink beer, wine or spirits, the small but vociferous minority of Islamic fundamentalists have ensured that even the international-style hotels do not always flourish their alcoholic drinks lists; but ask and you will receive. Aboard trains (Wagons-Lits excepted) only a rubbishy non-alcoholic beer is sold; on both domestic and international Egyptair flights, no alcohol is served, though you are permitted to bring your own. Some Egyptian governorates, eg Suez, are dry.

Western-style soft drinks, including Coca-Cola and 7-Up, are available everywhere. Egypt scores well on tropical fruit and cane juices; try also *karkodeh* (a drink made from hibiscus leaves); all are delicious and cheap.

Drinking from the Nile Finally, it is said that if you drink from the Nile you will be sure to return to Egypt. You might think you would drop dead instead. But I have drunk it while sailing on the river at Aswan where boatmen assure me it is better than the ice-cold drinks favoured by tourists, its temperature more agreeable to the stomach. It is fresh if somewhat organic in taste. I have survived and have returned to Egypt to drink from the Nile again. Tap water is heavily chlorinated and entirely safe. Bottled spring water is universally available. See *Health* below.

Health

Shots Cholera and yellow fever vaccination certificates are required when entering Egypt from an infected area, but it would be a good idea to have these vaccinations anyway. Recently in Cairo there have been outbreaks of what the authorities euphemistically call 'the summer disease' and which bears a remarkable similarity to cholera, though this is not admitted. Malaria is a problem in the Sudan but only rarely in Egypt; nevertheless it is worth taking precautions against this and both typhoid and polio. The rich, damp soil of the Egyptian countryside offers a fine breeding ground for the tetanus bacteria; if you are going to tramp about here, get inoculated. Obtain the advice of your doctor beforehand.

Bites of all kinds need the immediate attention of a doctor. The bites of carnivores can be rabid, or at least can turn septic as can camel bites. Snakes may be encountered when you wander off the beaten path, and you should avoid turning over stones. Most Egyptian snakes are not poisonous (their bite is recognised by a double row of teeth), but some are, especially the cobra and the viper. The smaller Egyptian cobra (*Naja haje*), 120 to 200 cm long, is normally a sandy-olive colour and is found throughout the country. The black-necked cobra (*Naja nigricollis*), 200 cm long, is darker and is confined to southern Egypt. Both are capable of displaying the characteristic hood; the black-necked cobra has a dark band on the underside of the hood. Cobra bites display a single row of teeth plus fang-marks. It was *Naja haje* that appeared as the uraeus on the pharaonic crown. It was the viper that Cleopatra used to commit suicide. There are several kinds, from 34 to 150 cm long, varying in colour from sandy to reddish, or sometimes grey. The most dangerous snake in Egypt is the carpet viper (*Echis carinatus*), 72 cm long, with a light X on the head. Viper bite markings are simply the two fang punctures. It is helpful when seeing a doctor if you can describe the snake.

There are two diseases associated with Egypt, trachoma and bilharzia, though neither need unduly worry the visitor. Trachoma is a contagious infection of the eye, specifically the conjunctiva and cornea, and causes a cloudy scar and hence blindness. Unfortunately, many Egyptians have suffered from it. If you notice any inflammation of the eyes, you should at once consult an ophthalmologist. Bilharzia (or schistosomiasis) is caused by a worm which enters the body, causing disorders to the liver, bladder, lungs and nervous system. The worm lives only in stagnant water, eg some irrigation channels and slow-moving parts of the Nile. The Nile is entirely safe for swimming and drinking between the Aswan High Dam and Esna where, except possibly along its banks, it runs swiftly. If you have ventured or fallen into stagnant water, you should get a check-up when you return home.

To repeat, there is little risk of the visitor contracting either disease. Both can be successfully treated.

Getting medical assistance If you are unwell, you should first seek advice from your hotel. They will be able to refer you to a doctor, dentist or hospital, and may even have a doctor on call. Your embassy will also be able to recommend medical assistance. Particularly in the major centres, the standards of medical care are high. Many doctors will have trained in Europe or North America and will speak English. More detailed information on medical care, and on pharmacists, will be found in the *Practical Information* sections.

27

Stomach upsets   Most likely the worst you will suffer will be a brief upset stomach. This is an entirely normal reaction to a change of diet and passes after a few days. There is no need suddenly to stop eating Egyptian food; on the contrary, after a pause, you should continue. An anti-spasmodic medicine can be taken; standard preparations are available at any pharmacy. The one rule you should observe when eating in Egypt is to be sure your food has been washed; provided even the simplest eating place has running water, there should be no problem. Drinking water is heavily chlorinated and safe, though you can always have bottled water if you prefer.

The sun can be hot at any time of year, and the temperature can fall off sharply at night. At both times it is wise to be appropriately covered. During the day you should wear a head covering and sunglasses. It is not advisable to drink spirits before sundown, nor to consume iced drinks during the heat of the day. A high-screen suntan lotion is advisable, factor 6 or more. Also insect repellent would be helpful.

And of course it can pay to be medically insured.

Money

The unit of currency is the Egyptian pound (LE, from *livre égyptienne*) which is divided into 100 piastres (PT, from *piastre tarifée*). Also, notionally, each piastre is divided into ten millièmes, so that there are 1000 millièmes to the pound. But while there are coins for piastre donominations, and notes for both piastre and pound denominations, there are no millième denomination coins. Nevertheless, prices may be expressed in pounds, piastres or millièmes, which can add an alarming number of digits to a bill (all the more alarming as Egypt follows the continental European practice of using a comma instead of a decimal point). So a bill in a modest restaurant for 20,550 should not send you into the kitchen to start washing the dishes, it is simply LE20 and 55PT. Usually common sense will tell you what is meant.

At the time of going to press the approximate rate of exchange was £1 sterling = LE4 and US$1 = LE2.50 (or putting it the other way round, LE1 = 25p or 40c). But inflation is high (35 percent) and the Egyptian pound floats almost freely, and so it is likely to devalue. Though occasionally you will be asked to change money on the streets, the black market rate (which exists not because the Egyptian pound is pegged above its value but because Egyptians have difficulty getting foreign exchange at their banks) is not worth bothering with. There are exchange banks at the airports and other points of entry and at major hotels throughout Egypt. American Express and Thomas Cook also exchange money. You should hold on to your receipts to show when paying hotel bills and in the event you need to change money back out of Egyptian pounds on departure.

Travellers cheques and Eurocheques can be exchanged at many banks. Credit cards are accepted at all major hotels, and also at some shops and restaurants, but generally you should count on being able to use them only in obvious tourist areas.

Baksheesh

Tipping is expected for all services, and often for no service at all. Too often tourists are absurdly ignorant or generous, which has led some Egyptians to believe, often rightly, that if they pull a sour face, even vociferously complain, they can milk you for more. The Egyptian term for a tip is *baksheesh* which means literally 'share the wealth' and helps explain why sometimes an Egyptian is not at all abashed at wanting something for nothing: you have it, he does not but feels you should pass it round. Baksheesh can be a plague, and you may find yourself pestered for it in the streets. The rule is obvious: offer baksheesh only in return for a service, do not pay until the service has been performed, and do not pay too much.

Photography

Taking photographs at museums and in tombs may be forbidden except on payment of a special fee. Often a flash may not be used under any circumstances. Therefore you should be sure to bring with you from abroad very high-speed film, eg 1000 ASA colour film (which in any case can be uprated) or 3200 ASA black and white film.

Carrying a variety of film

On the other hand the skies are blue, the sun is bright, and there is much reflected light off sand and water: for the best outdoor results use low-speed film.

I have never experienced any objection to taking photos in mosques or other Islamic monuments, nor in churches and monasteries, though you should be courteous and inobtrusive. By and large, people do not object to being photographed on the street; indeed, if you ask first, people often charmingly compose themselves — and then ask to be sent a copy. If someone objects, however, do not insist.

Occasionally you may meet with objections to photographing a street or village scene which seems attractive to you but which an Egyptian might think poor or dirty and thereby bringing shame on his country. Again, do not insist.

No doubt Egypt's enemies have more photographs of its airports, docks, bridges, dams and military installations than they know what to do with; nevertheless, photography of military installations certainly, and of the other items possibly, can mean having your film confiscated at the very least.

Electricity

Electrical current throughout Egypt is 220 volts AC. Sockets take the standard continental European round two-pronged plug. Plug adaptors and current converters, as well as dual voltage appliances, can be bought at home.

Weights and Measures
Egypt officially employs the metric system, though sometimes traditional weights and measures will be encountered.

Temperature

Fahrenheit	=	Celsius
122		50
113		45
110		43.3
107.6		42
104		40
102.2		39
100		37.8
98.6		37
96.8		36
95		35
93.2		34
91.4		33
90		32
87.8		31
86		30
84.2		29
80		26.7
75		23.9
70		21
65		18.3
60		15.6
55		12.8
50		10
45		7.2
40		4
32		0
23		−5
14		−10
0		−17.8

Fahrenheit into Celsuis:
subtract 32 from Fahrenheit temperature, then multiply by 5, then divide by 9.
Celsius into Fahrenheit:
multiply Celsius by 9, then divide by 5, then add 32.

Linear Measure

0.39 inches	1 centimetre
1 inch	2.54 centimetres
1 foot (12 in)	0.30 metres
1 yard (3 ft)	0.91 metres
29.37 inches	1 metre
0.62 miles	1 kilometre
1 mile (5280 ft)	1.61 kilometres
3 miles	4.8 kilometres
10 miles	16 kilometres
60 miles	98.6 kilometres
100 miles	160.9 kilometres

Square Measure

1 sq foot	0.09 sq metres
1 sq yard	0.84 sq metres
1.20 sq yards	1 sq metre
1 acre	0.96 feddans
1.04 acres	1 feddan
4201 sq metres	1 feddan

Weight

0.04 ounces	1 gram
1 ounce	28.35 grams
1 pound	453.59 grams
2.20 pounds	1 kilogram
1 ton (2000 lbs)	907.18 kilograms
0.99 pounds	1 rotel
0.45 kilograms	1 rotel
100 rotels	1 qantar

Liquid Measure

0.22 imperial gallons	1 litre
0.26 US gallons	1 litre
1 US gallon	3.79 litres
1 imperial gallon	4.55 litres

Opening Times
Most banks, shops and offices are closed on Fridays, while Christian establishments are often closed on Sundays. Government departments are closed on Thursdays and Fridays.

Shops are usually open from 9am to 1pm and from 5pm to late in the evening. Banks normally open at 9am and close at 1pm.

Major museums are open daily, though some may close early on Fridays. Other museums may close on Fridays altogether, with a few closing on Sundays or Mondays instead. Opening times vary, and some museums close earlier in winter.

During Ramadan, government, bank, office and museum opening hours are often reduced. Shops, however, often stay open as late as midnight.

Communications

Detailed information on mail, telephones, etc, will be found in the *Practical Information* sections, particularly at the end of the *Cairo: Mother of the World* chapter. Generally, the telephone system, both domestic and international, is good, but the post abroad is often slow. For best results, use hotel post boxes. Fax machines are appearing in more and more hotels and can be used for a fee.

Language and Numerals

No real language problem The language of the country is Arabic, but English is taught to every schoolchild and, with French a close second, is the foreign language most spoken by Egyptians. In particular, most staff at hotels, restaurants and travel companies catering to foreigners will speak English, probably French, and perhaps also German and Italian. So along the well-beaten tourist paths, language is unlikely to prove a problem. Even so, the purchase of a traveller's phrase book at home or in Egypt can prove useful, and knowledge of a few words and phrases is always appreciated. Here are some courtesies and simple questions and remarks to set you off on the right track. Note that the ' (*ain*) is a gutteral vowel sound, achieved by constricting the throat as far back as possible.

Hello/goodbye	*sa'eeda*
Please	*minfadlak* (if addressing a man)
	minfadlik (if addressing a woman)
Thank you	*shukran*
No thank you	*la shukran*
Yes	*aywa* or sometimes *nam*
No	*la*
I want	*'aayiz* (if addressing a man)
	'ayza (if addressing a woman)
How much?	*bekaam?*
Good	*kuwayyis*
Bad	*mish kuwayyis*

Used throughout this guide are the words *sharia*, street, and *midan*, square.

Note that there are several methods of transliterating Arabic into the Latin alphabet. For example, the town of

31

Minya can also be written as Minia or Minieh. Sultan (or Fort) Qaytbay can be written as Kait Bay, Qaitbai, Qait Bey, etc. So first, I apologise for any inconsistencies; and second, in consulting the index or looking for places on maps, bear in mind possible variant spellings.

As well as learning to speak (if not read) a few words in Arabic, it would be useful to be able to recognise the Arabic numerals. As in the West, units are at the right, preceded by tens, hundreds, etc, as you move left. Recognition will prove a great help when shopping, examining bills, catching numbered buses, boarding numbered train carriages and looking for your numbered seat, etc.

ARABIC NUMERALS

١	٢	٣	٤	٥	٦	٧	٨	٩	١٠
1	2	3	4	5	6	7	8	9	10

Religion

Islam. The principal belief of Islam is the existence of one God, the same God worshipped by Christians and Jews, whom the Muslims call Allah. Islam means submission. Muslim means one who submits to monotheism as interpreted by the religion's founder, Mohammed (AD 570–632).

The message   Muslims must hold six beliefs: that Allah exists, is unique and is omnipotent; that the Angels of Allah are his perfect servants, and intercede for man and are his guardians; that there is only one true religion and the Koran is the only tangible word of Allah; that there have been many prophets of Allah, among them Ibrahim (Abraham), Nuh (Noah), Musa (Moses), Isa (Jesus) and Mohammed who was the last, his message uncorrupted; that everyone will live in eternity and will be judged; and that whatever has been or will come has been predestined by Divine Will and it is forbidden to question or investigate this point.

There are five practical devotions, the five Pillars of Faith, that all Muslims must perform: pronounce publicly that 'I bear witness that there is no god but Allah and Mohammed is His Prophet'; pray at five specific times of day (noon, afternoon, sunset, night and daybreak); pay a tithe, which is then dispersed to the poor, to needy debtors, for the ransom of captives, to travellers, and for the defence of Islam; fast during the month of Ramadan; and at least once in a lifetime make a pilgrimage to Mecca.

In addition, Islam is based on laws found in the Koran, in

the *Sunna* (the actions of the Prophet), decided by the unanimous agreement of Muslim scholars (*Ijma*), and arrived at by reasoned analogy (*Qiyas*) — each of descending authority.

The Prophet Mohammed was a merchant in Arabia. He often contemplated in the desert and at the age of 40 had a vision of the Angel Gabriel who commanded him to proclaim monotheism to the pagan Arabian tribes. In Arabic, 'to proclaim' is *Qur'an*, and so the Koran is the word of Allah as given to Mohammed. The merchants of Mecca, concerned by the unsettling effects of this new religion, drove Mohammed out of the city in 622. His flight (the *hegira*, though literally this means 'withdrawal of affection') from Mecca to Medina, where Islam first took root, is the event from which the Islamic calendar begins.

Nearly 90 percent of the Egyptian population is Muslim, adherents of the Sunni sect (for discussion of the Sunni and Shi'a sects, see the *Bab Zuwayla to Khan el Khalili* chapter for Cairo).

Christians. The remainder of the population includes a few Egyptian Jews and a small and declining number of Armenian and Greek Orthodox. As a result of Western missionary work during the 19th and early 20th C, initially intended amongst Muslims (where it met with virtually no success), some former Orthodox Copts adopted varieties of Protestantism and Catholicism. But 94 percent of Christian Egyptians are Coptic Orthodox, and these represent about ten percent of the Egyptian population as a whole.

Copt comes from the Greek word for Egypt, *Aigyptos*, and those who remain Copts today, having never intermarried with later peoples, can lay claim to being the pure successors of the ancient Egyptians. But it is also true that 90 percent of Muslim Egyptians were once Copts, making it impossible to distinguish any physical difference between the two, though some Egyptians will say Copts have higher cheekbones or almond-shaped eyes. Copts may choose to distinguish themselves by wearing a cross around their necks, for example. Some, usually fellahin or amongst the lower urban classes, have a cross tatooed on the inside of the right wrist — to ward off evil spirits or, in the past, to commit them to their faith during persecution. One possible identifier is choice of name, eg George (Girgis), Antony (Antunius) and Ramses; though Gamal, Nasser and Anwar could be either Coptic or Muslim. And for both groups the mother tongue is Arabic. In fact the difference between Coptic and Muslim Egyptians is neither ethnic nor cultural, except that the Copts adhere to the old religion.

The old religion It is therefore all the more remarkable that Christianity has survived in Egypt; it is the only country in northern Africa where this has been so. The reason is that Christianity in Egypt was not merely the faith of a settler community, but early on penetrated to the native population. And there it found a people of ancient culture with a highly developed religious system which included notions of the afterlife. Osiris and Isis, Horus and Seth, have their resonances in Christian belief, while the pharaonic ankh, the cross-like symbol of life, appears in early Christian Egyptian work. Yet though religion distinguishes Copts from the rest of the population, there are areas of overlap between Christianity and Islam in Egypt. Islam has its five pillars of faith; the Copts have their seven mysteries: baptism, confirmation, penance, eucharist, orders, matrimony and unction of the sick. Fasting is common to both, Copts almost competitively, it might seem, fasting more than Muslims. At the level of folk religion the overlap is greater still (see Tanta), Muslims and Christians visiting each other's shrines, calling upon one anothers' saints, for cures, favours and to give thanks.

Both Copts and Muslims are proud to call themselves Egyptians, and have fought shoulder to shoulder against the Crusaders and more recent opponents. Yet the gulf between the Copts and the Western churches has often seemed unbridgeable. The West has incorrectly called the Copts monophysites and since the Council of Chalcedon in 451 to nearly this day has dismissed the Coptic Church as heretical (see the *Alexandria: Capital of Memory* chapter).

The Christian centuries   That Christianity was introduced to Egypt by St Mark is entirely legendary. Nevertheless it almost certainly was introduced during the 1st C AD and came from Jerusalem, appearing first amongst the Jewish population of Alexandria and then spreading amongst the Greeks of both the city and the country. There is evidence that at the beginning of the 3rd C Christianity had taken root amongst native Egyptians, and by AD 300 most of the Bible had been translated from Greek into Coptic (antedating the translation of the Bible into Latin by a century). With the end of the Roman persecutions early in the 4th C there was a sudden flowering of Christianity in which, as a walk through the Coptic Museum in Cairo shows, the soul of Egypt refound itself after 600 years of Graeco-Roman rule. Expressed in the form of monasticism (see the Wadi Natrun in *The Western Desert* chapter), Egyptian Christianity also made a deeply spiritual impact on the wider world.

But political and theological disputes between Alexandria and Constantinople facilitated the Arab conquest of Egypt during 640–42. For the Copts the development of Christian thought now gave way to the need for unquestioning faith and social solidarity, even as they slowly accepted a new culture. As Arab civilisation from Baghdad to Cordoba achieved its apogee in the 9th, 10th and 11th C, men of talent and

Anthropomorphic ankhs at Medinet Habu

35

ambition gravitated in its direction. Coptic artists began to serve the tastes of their Muslim patrons, and Arabic became the language of administration and learning. Sometime between the 11th and 13th C the Coptic language, repository of the demotic tongue of pharaonic times, ceased to be spoken and survives now only in church liturgy.

The Arabs ruled Egypt for the revenues they could exact, while failing to maintain the irrigation system on which the country depended. Soon both agriculture and population began the long decline which was not reversed until the 19th **Revolts and** C. But as revenue fell the subject Christians were taxed all the **persecutions** more harshly; some Copts began converting to Islam while others in the 8th and 9th C rose in vain revolt. However, Copts probably remained in the majority until the Crusades; the Latin capture of Jerusalem in 1099, the Mongol sack of Baghdad in 1258 and the internecine struggles of Egypt's Mameluke rulers from the mid-13th to the 16th C produced an atmosphere of insecurity and distrust which, combined with the growing impoverishment of the country, had sultans and mobs alike turning against the Christians. In the early 14th C fanatical Muslims looted and destroyed all the principle churches of Egypt. In revenge the Copts fired many mosques, palaces and private Muslim houses, whereupon Christians suffered wholesale massacre. Copts were expelled from official positions and subjected to a range of indignities — forbidden to ride horses or asses unless they sat backwards, forced to wear distinctive clothing, even to have a bell tinkling round their necks when entering a public bath. Mass conversions to Islam followed.

Egypt's contact with European influences in the 19th C improved the condition of the Copts, who went on to play an important role in and to benefit from the growing secular nationalist movement. Over the same period the Coptic Church has gradually reformed itself, initially to meet the challenge of foreign missionaries. Under the last two popes **Coptic** especially, Kirollos VI and Shenuda III, the Church has ex- **renaissance** perienced a renaissance, attracting highly educated young men into the monasteries and the hierarchy, and reaching out into the community with schools and welfare programmes. Today, though there are reports of some discrimination, Copts officially enjoy all civil, political and religious rights and occupy high posts in government, the military and in business.

It is not unusual when walking around Cairo or elsewhere in Egypt to come upon Christian celebrations, the streets festooned with decorations and lights, pictures and icons of Christ and Mary and the various saints. If you are in Egypt for the Coptic Christmas (7 January) or the Coptic Easter (moveable), it is worthwhile visiting a Coptic Church for midnight mass (arrive no later than 11pm) on the eve.

Time and Egyptian Calendars

Egypt is two hours ahead of Greenwich Mean Time. Noon GMT is 2pm in Egypt.

Egypt uses three calendars: the Islamic, the Coptic and the Western. Both the Western and Coptic calendars are solar; the Islamic calendar is based on 12 lunar months and therefore rotates in relation to the other two, each Islamic year beginning 11 days sooner than the last. The Western calendar of course dates from the birth of Christ; the Coptic dates from AD 284, the accession of Diocletian, during whose reign the most ferocious Roman persecutions of the Christians, particularly in Egypt, occurred (see the *Alexandria: Capital of Memory* chapter); while the Islamic calendar dates from the flight of Mohammed from Mecca in AD 622. (Because the Islamic year is shorter than the Western, you cannot simply subtract 622 from our year to determine the current AH year; AH 1412 begins in July 1990).

Another point worth noting is that a day in the Islamic calendar begins at sundown. A consequence of this is that Islamic festivals start on the evening before you would expect if going by the Western calendar, that evening assuming as sacred a character as the following waking daylight period (compare Christmas Eve and Christmas Day in Western usage).

The official calendar You will be relieved to learn, however, that in all official transactions in Egypt the Western calendar and method of reckoning the day are used. The Islamic and Coptic calendars only really come into their own at festivals.

The Islamic months are as follows:

First month:	*Moharram* (30 days)
Second month:	*Safar* (29 days)
Third month:	*Rabei el Awal* (30 days)
Fourth month:	*Rabei el Tani* (29 days)
Fifth month:	*Gamad el Awal* (30 days)
Sixth month:	*Gamad el Tani* (29 days)
Seventh month:	*Ragab* (30 days)
Eighth month:	*Shaaban* (29 days)
Ninth month:	*Ramadan* (30 days)
Tenth month:	*Shawal* (29 days)
Eleventh month:	*Zoul Qidah* (30 days)
Twelfth month:	*Zoul Hagga* (29 days, or 30 in leap years)

Important Muslim festivals include:

Ras el Sana el Hegira, the Islamic New Year, beginning on the first day of Moharram.

Moulid el Nabi, the Prophet's birthday, on the twelfth day of Rabei el Awal, marked in Cairo by a spectacular procession.

Ramadan *Ramadan*, a month of fasting from dawn to sunset. As the last full meal is taken just before dawn, working hours are usually cut short to reduce afternoon effort to a minimum. Nothing is permitted to pass the lips during fasting hours, and

37

so while visitors are permitted to eat, drink and smoke, you should not do so in the presence of fasting Muslims out of common courtesy. Interestingly, more food is consumed during Ramadan than at any other time of year, everyone making up at night for what they gave up during the day. Every Ramadan night, therefore, has the character of a festival. In 1990 in Egypt Ramadan began on 28 March.

Qurban Bairam, 10–13 Zoul Higga, the month of the Pilgrimage. For days preceding the 10th, sheep, goats, cows and buffaloes fill the streets waiting to be slaughtered; on the 10th they are killed and skinned throughout the residential areas of town — not for the squeamish.

Coptic festivals centring around Easter do not follow the Western (Gregorian) calendar. Other festivals fall on fixed dates: Christmas, 7 January; Epiphany, 19 January; the Annunciation, 21 March. A national holiday that is an important Coptic-pharaonic inheritance is *Sham el Nessim*, which falls on the first Monday after the Coptic Easter and during which the entire population of whatever religion takes a day off. This is a celebration of the advent of spring; families go out into their fields or gardens, or into the country, early in the morning and eat salted fish, onions and coloured eggs. The fish and onions are said to prevent disease, while the eggs symbolise life.

Chronology of Egyptian History

Pharaonic dynasties The following is a list of the royal dynasties ruling Egypt successively or, where dates overlap, simultaneously and so indicating periods of disunity. The priests drew up long lists of monarchs, attaching to the years of a pharaoh's reign the events they wished to record. An example is the list of Seti I's predecessors in his mortuary temple at Abydos. Working from such lists, Manetho, an Egyptian priest under the early Ptolemies, arranged all the rulers of Egypt from Menes to Alexander into 31 dynasties. Egyptologists have relied on Manetho's list, and have been able to confirm its essential correctness while sometimes improving upon it. The dates, however, are approximate, those around 3000 BC having a margin of error of 100 years, those around 2500 BC of 75 years, those following 2000 BC of 10 years, those around 1500–1000 BC of 10–15 years, while fairly precise dates are possible around 500 BC. This dynastic arrangement has historical validity, for Egypt's fortunes were closely linked to the rise and fall of the various royal houses. Throughout this guide the dynasty of each pharaoh is mentioned after his name so that his place in the scheme of things can readily be ascertained. Only the most important pharaohs have been mentioned below within their dynasties; where their reigns overlap, this indicates joint rule.

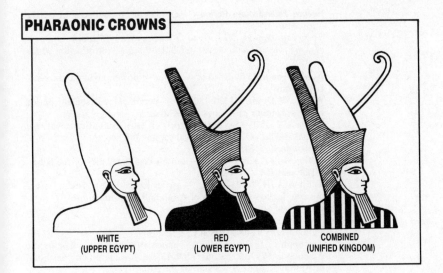

WHITE
(UPPER EGYPT)

RED
(LOWER EGYPT)

COMBINED
(UNIFIED KINGDOM)

First Dynastic Period (3100–2700 BC)
First Dynasty
Menes (Narmer) — unification of Egypt; capital at Memphis.
Second Dynasty
Old Kingdom (2700–2200 BC) — period of stability.
Third Dynasty (2700–2650 BC)
Zoser (2700 BC) — start of the Pyramid Age.
Fourth Dynasty (2650–2500 BC)
Snofru (2650 BC)
Cheops (2600 BC)
Chephren (2560 BC)
Mycerinus (2525 BC) — end of the Pyramid Age.
Fifth Dynasty (2500–2350 BC)
Unas (2375 BC) — Pyramid Texts.
Sixth Dynasty (2350–2200 BC) — period of decline.
Pepi I (2325 BC)
First Intermediate Period (2200–2050 BC) — collapse of central authority.
Seventh and Eighth Dynasties (2180–2155 BC)
Ninth and Tenth Dynasties (2155–2055 BC)
Eleventh Dynasty (2135–2000 BC)
Mentuhotep II (2060–2010 BC) — reunites Egypt; capital at Thebes.
Middle Kingdom (2050–1800 BC) — conquest of Nubia.
Twelfth Dynasty (1990–1780 BC) — royal residence moved to Memphis; major building works and hydrological programmes in the Fayyum.
Ammenemes I (1990–1963 BC)
Sesostris I (1972–1927 BC)
Ammenemes III (1842–1797 BC)

39

Second Intermediate Period (1800–1550 BC) — collapse of central authority.

Thirteenth through Seventeenth Dynasties (1780–1570 BC)

Hyksos rule in Lower Egypt (1730–1570 BC) — introduction of the chariot.

New Kingdom (1570–1090) BC — period of power, luxury and cosmopolitanism.

Eighteenth Dynasty (1570–1305 BC) — period of greatest contribution to the splendour of Thebes and Karnak.

Ahmosis I (1570–1545 BC) — expels Hyksos; establishes royal residence, and religious and political capital at Thebes.

Amenophis I (1545–1525 BC)

Tuthmosis I (1525–1495 BC) — burials begin at Valley of the Kings.

Tuthmosis II (1495–1490 BC)

Tuthmosis III (1490–1436 BC)— struggle with Hatshepsut; after her passing, he lays foundation of Asian and African empire.

Hatshepsut (1486–1468 BC)

Amenophis II (1439–1406 BC)

Tuthmosis IV (1406–1398 BC)

Amenophis III (1398–1361 BC) — apogee of New Kingdom opulence.

Amenophis IV (Akhenaton) (1369–1353 BC) — assault on priesthood of Amun; establishes worship of the Aton.

Smenkhkere (1355–1352 BC)

Tutankhaton (Tutankhamun) (1352–1344 BC)—return to orthodoxy.

Ay (1344–1342 BC)

Horemheb (1342–1303 BC) — military dictatorship.

Nineteenth Dynasty (1303–1200 BC) — restoration of royal power.

Ramses I (1303–1302 BC)

Seti I (1302–1290 BC) — new building work in Old Kingdom style.

Ramses II (1290–1224 BC) — prodigious builder, eg Rammesseum and Abu Simbel.

Merneptah (1224–1214 BC) — possible pharaoh of the Exodus.

Syrian interregnum (1202–1197 BC)

Twentieth Dynasty (1200–1090 BC) — dislocations as Egypt enters Iron Age.

Ramses III (1195–1164 BC) — defeats Sea Peoples; succeeded by incompetent rulers.

Ramses VI (1153–1149 BC)

Herihor (1098–1090 BC) — priest-pharaoh at Thebes; rival ruler at Tanis.

Late Dynastic Period (1090–332 BC) — period of decline; often foreign rule.

Twenty-first Dynasty (1090–945 BC) — capital at Tanis.

Twenty-second Dynasty (945–745 BC) — warriors of Libyan origin; capital at Tanis.

Sheshonk I (945 BC) — loots Jerusalem (I *Kings* 14, 25–26).

Twenty-third Dynasty (745–718 BC) — Ethiopian kings control Upper Egypt.

Twenty-fourth Dynasty (718–712 BC) — Ethiopian kings control all Egypt.

Twenty-fifth Dynasty (712–663 BC)

Taharka (695–671 BC) — Ethiopian king defeated by Assyrians who sack Thebes.

Twenty-sixth Dynasty (663–525 BC) — Delta rulers, their capital at Sais; Assyrians ejected with Greek help.

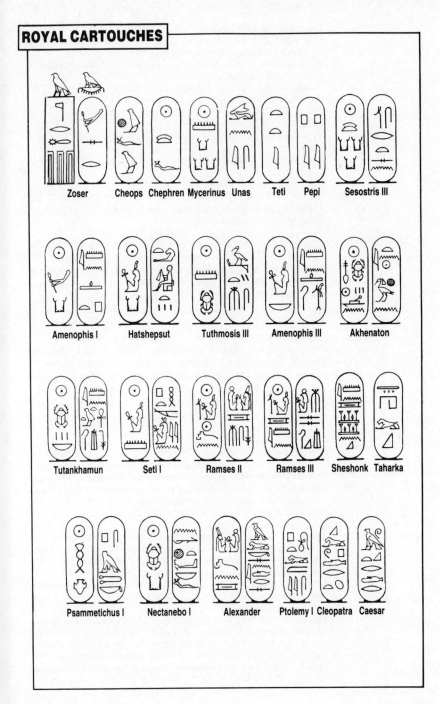

Zoser   Cheops Chephren Mycerinus Unas   Teti   Pepi   Sesostris III

Amenophis I   Hatshepsut   Tuthmosis III   Amenophis III   Akhenaton

Tutankhamun   Seti I   Ramses II   Ramses III   Sheshonk   Taharka

Psammetichus I   Nectanebo I   Alexander   Ptolemy I   Cleopatra   Caesar

Psammetichus I (663–610 BC)
Necho (610–595 BC) — attempts to link Red Sea and Mediterranean by a canal; circumnavigation of Africa.
Psammetichus II (595–589 BC) — Nubian expedition recorded in Greek at Abu Simbel.
Twenty-seventh Dynasty (525–404 BC) — Persian rule.
Cambyses (525–522 BC)
Darius I (522–486 BC)
Xerxes the Great (486–466 BC)
Twenty-eighth Dynasty (404–399 BC) — Persians ejected with Greek help.
Twenty-ninth Dynasty (399–380 BC) — Delta remains the vital centre of power.
Thirtieth Dynasty (380–343 BC)
Nectanebos I (380–343 BC) — great builder, eg at Philae.
Thirty-first Dynasty (343–332 BC) — Persian rule.
Alexander enters Egypt in 332 BC.

The Ptolemies   When Alexander died, his empire was divided between three of his Macedonian generals, Ptolemy taking Egypt. He established a dynasty which ruled the country for 300 years in the guise of pharaohs, albeit Greek-speaking ones, respecting the customs and religion of the Egyptians. The first three Ptolemies ruled ably, their greatest achievement Alexandria, which they adorned with Greek architecture and scholarship. In Upper Egypt the Ptolemies built archaic temples to please the priests, but otherwise they tied Egypt to the Mediterranean. Inevitably they encountered Rome, and through incompetence abroad and strife at home the later Ptolemies relied on the Romans for their very thrones. The last in the line was the great Cleopatra, who with Mark Antony attempted to create a new Hellenistic empire in the east.

323 BC: The death of *Alexander*.
323–282 BC: *Ptolemy I Soter* (Saviour). He added Cyrene, Palestine, Cyprus and parts of the Asia Minor coast to his realm, and at Alexandria, its geographical centre, he founded the Museion and Library.
282–46 BC: *Ptolemy II Philadelphos* (Lover of his Sister). To the shock of the Greeks, though with Egyptian precedent, he married his sister. He was a patron of poets, first invited the Jews to settle in Alexandria, and constructed the Pharos.
246–21 BC: *Ptolemy III Euergetes* (Benefactor). A soldier with a taste for science, during his rule Alexandria reached its height of splendour. In Upper Egypt he began the temple at Edfu. Abroad, he nearly reached India, and earned the title Conqueror of the World.
221–05 BC: *Ptolemy IV Philopator* (Lover of his Father). Setback in Syria, revolt at Thebes; he began construction of the temples at Esna and Kom Ombo.
205–181 BC: *Ptolemy V Epiphanes* (God Manifest). Child-king. Revolt at Alexandria, the interior in a state of anarchy, Epiphanes was placed under the protection of the Roman Senate, but by the time he came of age, Egypt had lost most of her overseas possessions.
181–45 BC: *Ptolemy VI Philometor* (Lover of his Mother). Seleucid invasion, Memphis captured, Egypt saved by Roman intervention.

GODS OF ANCIENT EGYPT

AMEN-RE   RE-HARAKHTI   ISIS   BASTET   HORUS   KHNUM

SETH   OSIRIS   MIN   PTAH   MAAT   THOTH

145–4 BC: *Ptolemy VII Neos Philopator.*

145–16 BC: *Ptolemy VII Euergetes II.* Also known as Physcon (Fatty): when he came puffing along the quay to greet Scipio Africanus the younger, the Roman sniggered, 'At least the Alexandrians have seen their king walk'. This Roman contempt applied to Egypt's sovereignty as well.

116–07, 88–80 BC: *Ptolemy IX Soter II.* Competed with his brother, Ptolemy X Alexander I, for the throne, both borrowing money from the Romans to raise arms.

107–88 BC: *Ptolemy X Alexander I.* To cover his debts he bequeathed Egypt to the Roman people, but as he had by then lost the throne his offer could not be accepted. But it was remembered.

80 BC: *Ptolemy XI Alexander II.* Forced by Sulla to marry his (Ptolemy's) elderly stepmother, he then killed her and was killed in turn by an Alexandrian mob.

80–58, 55–51 BC: *Ptolemy XII Neos Dionysos.* Also known as Nothos (Bastard), he rushed back from Syria so that the vacant throne should not attract Roman annexation, and bolstered his pedigree by adding Philopator to his official names. He was the son of Ptolemy IX and father of Cleopatra VII. He built at Dendera, completed the temple at Edfu and left his mark on Philae. His reign was briefly interrupted by internal disruption.

51–49, 48–30 BC: *Cleopatra VII.* Ruled jointly with her younger brother Ptolemy XIII who banished her (**48 BC**), but in the same year she received the support of Julius Caesar and Ptolemy was drowned in the Nile. Another brother, Ptolemy XIV, succeeded to the co-regency (**47 BC**), was assassinated (**45 BC**) at Cleopatra's instigation. Bore Caesar a son (**47 BC**), named Caesarion. He never ruled. Caesar assassinated (**44 BC**). Met Antony (**41 BC**). The battle of Actium (**31 BC**). Suicide of Antony and Cleopatra; Octavian (Augustus) makes Egypt a province of the Roman Empire (**30 BC**).

Roman and Byzantine periods

30 BC: *Octavian* (Augustus) incorporates Egypt into the Roman Empire. The Roman emperors followed the example of the Ptolemies in representing themselves to the Egyptian people as successors of the pharaohs and in maintaining the appearance of a national Egyptian state.

c. AD 30: Crucifixion of *Jesus of Nazareth* at Jerusalem.

AD 45: Legend has *St Mark* make his first convert to Christianity in Egypt, a Jewish shoemaker of Alexandria.

AD 98–117: Reign of *Trajan.*. The canal connecting the Nile with the Red Sea reopened (**AD 115**).

AD 117–38: Reign of *Hadrian.* Visits Egypt.

AD 204: Edict prohibiting Roman subjects from embracing Christianity. The Delta is studded with Christian communities.

AD 249–51: Reign of *Decius*; severe persecutions.

c. AD 251–356: *St Antony*; becomes the first hermit.

AD 284–305: Reign of *Diocletian.* His accession marks the beginning of the 'Era of Martyrs' from which the Copts date their calendar. Persecution of the Christians.

AD 312: *Constantine* becomes emperor in the West.

AD 313: Edict of Milan: Christianity tolerated throughout the Roman Empire.

AD 324–37: *Constantine the Great* becomes sole ruler of the Roman Empire. Converts to Christianity on his death bed. Founds Constantinople (**AD 330**).

c. AD 330: Founding of the first monasteries at Wadi Natrun.

AD 379–95: Reign of *Theodosius I.* Declares Christianity to be the religion of the Roman Empire (**AD 392**).

AD 395: Partition of the Roman Empire into East (Constantinople) and West (Rome). Notional date for the beginning of the Byzantine Empire.

AD 451: Council of Chalcedon declares monophysitism a heresy, effectively expelling the Egyptian (Coptic) Church from the main body of Christianity.

AD 476: Fall of the Roman Empire in the West.

AD 622: *Mohammed's* flight from Mecca, the *hegira*, from which the Muslim calendar is reckoned. His death (**AD 632**).

AD 636: Arabs defeat Byzantine army and take Damascus.

AD 637: Arabs destroy the Sassanian (Persian) Empire.

AD 638: Arabs take Jerusalem.

AD 640: An Arab force under *Amr* enters Egypt. Fortress of Babylon taken. (**AD 641**). Fustat founded; Alexandria surrenders and welcomes Arabs as liberators from Byzantine oppression (**AD 642**).

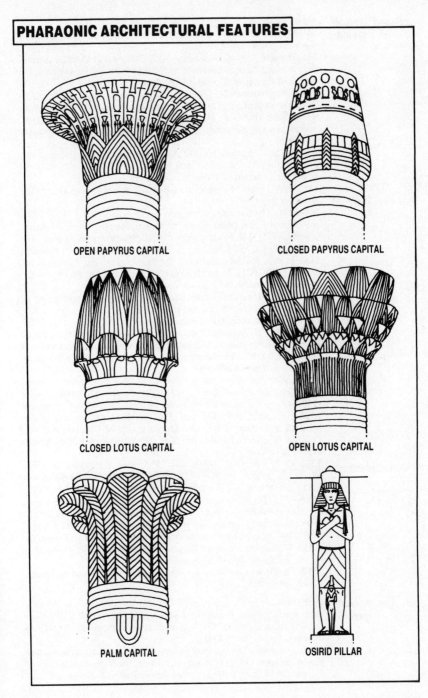

OPEN PAPYRUS CAPITAL

CLOSED PAPYRUS CAPITAL

CLOSED LOTUS CAPITAL

OPEN LOTUS CAPITAL

PALM CAPITAL

OSIRID PILLAR

Arab and Turkish periods

All dates are according to the Western calender (AD).
661: Murder of *Ali*, son-in-law of the Prophet; the caliphate passes to the Umayyads.
661–750: The *Umayyad caliphate*, with its capital at Damascus, rules over a united Arab empire stretching from the borders of China to the shores of the Atlantic, and up into France.
750–935: *Abbassids and Tulunids.* The Abbassids put a bloody end to the Umayyads in Syria and succeed to the caliphate, ruling the Arab world from Baghdad. *Ibn Tulun*, an Abbassid governor of Egypt, makes himself independent of Baghdad and establishes a dynasty **(870–935)**.
c. 820: The Copts, resentful of their Arab conquerors, rise in revolt several times during the 8th and 9th C.
909: Establishment of Fatimid caliphate in North Africa.
935–69: A Turkish dynasty, the *Ikhshidids*, seizes power through the governorship.
969–1171: The *Fatimid caliphate* in Egypt, which now follows Shi'a rather than Sunni Islam. Cairo, its capital, founded **(969)**. Al-Azhar founded **(971)**. The Fatimid empire reaches its peak under *Caliph Abu Mansur al-Aziz* **(975–96)**. He introduces the practice of importing slave troops, the forerunners of the Mamelukes. His successor, *al-Hakim* **(996–1021)**, is an all-powerful psychotic; the decline of the Fatimid empire begins with his death.
1055: The Seljuq Turks take Baghdad, leading to a resurgence of Sunni Islam in Iraq, Syria and Iran.
1099: The Crusaders take Jerusalem.
1171–1250: The *Ayyubids*; the dynasty of *Saladin*, a Kurd from Syria. He converts Egypt back to Sunni Islam. Drives the Crusaders from Jerusalem. **(1187)**. The Mamelukes rise to power during the rule of *Shagarat al-Durr* **(1249–59)**.
1250–1382: The *Bahri Mamelukes.* The most celebrated of these Mameluke sultans are *Baybars* **(1260–77)**; *Qalaun* **(1279–90)**; *al-Nasr* **(1309–40)** — the beautiful mausolea of these last two are on Sharia Muizz in Cairo; and *al-Hassan* **(1347–51, 1354–61)**, builder of the great madrasa bearing his name. During early 14th C, severe persecution of Christians who until this time are still perhaps half the population; mass conversions to Islam follow.
1382–1517: The *Burgi Mamelukes.* The most celebrated of these Mameluke sultans are *Barquq* **(1382–89, 1390–98)**, whose mosque is on Sharia Muizz, his mausoleum in the City of the Dead in Cairo; *Baybars* **(1422–38)**, whose mausoleum is in the City of the Dead; *Qaytbay* **(1468–95)**, known for his fortress on the site of the Pharos in Alexandria, and his mausoleum in the City of the Dead; and *al-Ghuri* **(1500–16)** whose monuments stand near Al-Azhar. *Tumanbay* **(1515–17)** was the last of the Burgi sultans; he was hanged three times by the Turks outside Bab Zuwayla in Cairo.
1517: The Rule of the *Ottoman Turks* begins in Egypt and continues, if only nominally, until 1914.

The modern period

1798–1801: *French occupation* of Egypt. *Napoleon* lands at Alexandria; Battle of the Pyramids; Battle of the Nile **(1798)**. *Napoleon* departs from Egypt **(1799)**. A British army compels the French to evacuate the country **(1801)**.
1805: *Mohammed Ali* becomes viceroy of Egypt and after massacring the Mamelukes **(1811)** becomes, effectively, the independent ruler of Egypt, establishing a dynasty that was to end with *Farouk*.

PHARAONIC ARCHITECTURAL FEATURES

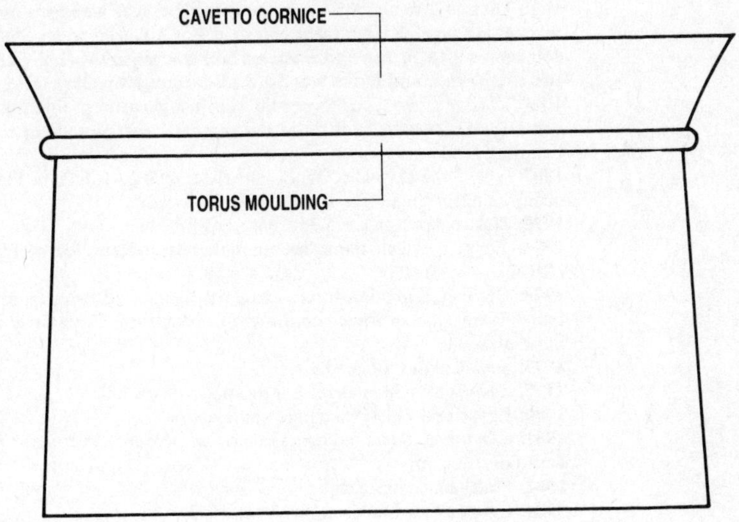

CAVETTO CORNICE

TORUS MOULDING

1869: Opening of the Suez Canal during the reign of *Ismail.*
1882: Nationalist uprising led by *Arabi. British occupation* of Egypt begins.
1883–1907: *Evelyn Baring (Lord Cromer)* is British consul in Egypt and effective ruler of the country.
1902: British complete construction of dam at Aswan.
1914: Britain declares Egypt to be a *British Protectorate.*
1918: *Saad Zaghloul,* nationalist leader, demands British withdrawal.
1922: British recognise Egypt as a sovereign state, but maintain an army in Egypt.
1936: Anglo-Egyptian Treaty, formally ending British occupation. British army withdraws, except from the Canal Zone.
1939–45: Egypt nominally neutral during the Second World War, but British Army invited to return to fight the encroaching Germans. Battle of el Alamein (**1942**); *Rommel* repulsed.
1948: End of British Mandate for Palestine. Establishment of the state of Israel. Arab-Israeli war; Arab debacle. Resentful of political corruption, *Gamal Abdel Nasser* (**1918–70**) gathers round him a group of dissident army officers.
1952: 25 January, British soldiers kill several Egyptian police in the Canal Zone. 26 January, rioting in Cairo at British action and Egyptian government's inaction. 23 July, *Nasser's* group stages a coup. 26 July, *King Farouk* abdicates and leaves the country.

1953: Egypt declared a *republic*.

1954: *Nasser* becomes head of state.

1954–56: British evacuate the Canal Zone.

1956: United States cancels loan to Egypt for construction of the High Dam at Aswan. *Nasser* nationalises the Suez Canal to use its revenues to pay for High Dam's construction. Israel invades Sinai in collusion with a British and French troop landing in the Canal Zone. Britain, France and Israel withdraw after international protest.

1961: *Nasser* introduces sweeping socialist measures, limiting incomes, nationalising banks and the cotton industry, further redistributing land.

1967: The June 'Six Day War'. Israel attacks and defeats Egypt, occupies all of Sinai. The Suez Canal is blocked.

1970: *Nasser* dies. *Anwar Sadat* becomes president.

1971: Egypt's official name becomes the Arab Republic of Egypt (ARE).

1973: October, Egyptian forces cross the Canal and drive back the Israeli army. Israeli forces continue to occupy the Gaza Strip and most of Sinai.

1975: Suez Canal reopened.

1977: *Sadat* visits Jerusalem in a dramatic peace bid.

1980: Egypt and Israel exchange ambassadors.

1981: 6 October, *Sadat* assassinated. *Hosni Mubarak* becomes president later that month.

1982: Israel evacuates Sinai.

1984: Egypt's first free elections since 1952.

Glossary

Abu: The Arabic for saint, whether Muslim or Christian. Holy man.

Archimedes' screw: An irrigation device introduced during the Ptolemaic period for raising water by means of an inclined screw.

Amun: God of Thebes; he was made a sun god under the name *Amun-Re* and became the national god during the New Kingdom. His sacred animal was the ram. Along with his wife, *Mut*, and their son, *Khonsu*, Amun was one of the Theban triad.

Ankh: The hieroglyphic sign for life, resembling a cross with a loop in place of the upper arm.

Anubis: God of the dead, associated with interment. His sacred animal was the dog or jackal.

Apis: The sacred bull of Memphis, buried in the Serapeum at Saqqara (see *Ptah*).

Apse: A semi-circular domed recess, most frequently at the east end of a church.

Aton: The sun's disc; the life force. Worshipped by Akhenaton, who attacked the priesthood of *Amun*.

Atum: The creator god of Heliopolis, represented as a man.

Azan: The Muslim call to prayer (see *muezzin*).

Ba: A spirit that inhabits the body during life but is not attached to it; at death it leaves the body and joins the divine spirit (see *ka*).

Bab: A gate, as Bab Zuwayla.

Basilica: A building, eg a church, in the form of a long colonnaded hall, usually with one or more *apses* at the east end, and a *narthex* at the west end.

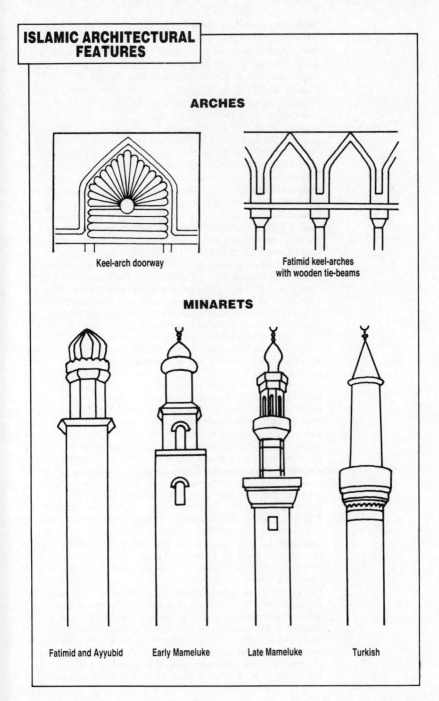

ISLAMIC ARCHITECTURAL FEATURES

ARCHES

Keel-arch doorway

Fatimid keel-arches
with wooden tie-beams

MINARETS

Fatimid and Ayyubid

Early Mameluke

Late Mameluke

Turkish

Bastet: The goddess of Bubastis, a goddess of joy. Her sacred animal was the lioness or cat.

Bes: A protective dwarf-god, averter of evil, helper in childbirth.

Bayt: A house, or the self-contained apartments into which Ummayad mansions and Abbasid palaces were divided.

Canopic jars: Containers placed within ancient tombs to preserve those organs and viscera thought essential for the dead man's continued existence in the afterlife.

Capitals: Pharaonic and Ptolemaic temples employed capitals decorated either with plant forms (palmiform, papyriform, lotiform) or other motifs (Hathoric, ie with the human face and cow's ears of Hathor; forms deriving from timber construction eg tent poles). (See illustration.)

Cartouche: In hieroglyphics, the oval band enclosing the god's or pharaoh's name and symbolising unchanging continuity.

Cavetto cornice: One of the most characteristic decorative features in ancient Egyptian architecture, a concave moulding decorated with palmettes. It was used along the tops of walls and *pylons*, projecting at front and sides. Below it would be a *torus* moulding.

Colours: Primary colours usually had particular applications and significance in ancient Egyptian painting. *Black* represented death: mummies, also Osiris as king of the dead, were commonly depicted in black. *Blue* was for sky and water, the sky gods painted this colour. *Green* was the colour of rebirth: Osiris, who overcame death and was reborn, often had his face and limbs painted green; also the solar disc was commonly painted light green on sarcophagi, instead of its usual red. *Red* was for blood and fire; men's bodies were depicted as reddish brown or brown; it also had a maleficent connotation: Seth was painted reddish brown. *White* represented silver and was the colour of the moon; it was also the colour of the garments of the gods and the crown of Upper Egypt. *Yellow* represented gold and was also used as the colour for women's bodies until the mid-XVIII Dynasty; thereafter the only women painted this colour were goddesses.

Columns: Like capitals, ancient columns followed certain decorative motifs, eg papyrus columns modelled after either a single stem and therefore smooth, or after a bundle of stems and therefore ribbed.

Crowns: The red crown of Lower Egypt was joined with the white crown of Upper Egypt to represent unification of the country (see *colours*). The blue crown or headdress was worn when riding a chariot; it appears after the introduction of the horse into Egypt by the Hyksos c. 1600 BC. No matter what headdress the pharaoh wore, he was always shown with the *uraeus* on his forehead.

Electrum: An alloy of gold and silver. The tips of obelisks were covered with electrum. In ancient Egypt, where gold was mined in abundance, both silver and electrum were more precious than gold alone.

Evil eye: The superstition that the envious glance of any passer-by, attracted by an immodest show of wealth, achievement or beauty, can harm or bewitch. Reciting certain verses of the Koran is one way of warding it off. *Uzait Horun*, the Eye of Horus, is meant to ensure safety and happiness and wards off the evil eye; it may be painted on cars, trucks and fishing boats, or worn as an amulet, particularly by children, who are especially vulnerable. Children also leave their handprints on walls to avert the evil eye. The probable value of the belief is as a social control, minimising at least the appearance of disparity in people's fortunes and so promoting solidarity.

Exonarthex: The outer vestibule of a church.

Faience: Glazed earthenware, often decorated, formed as pottery or in blocks or tiles as a wall facing.

Fellahin: Egyptian peasants. The singular is *fellah*.

Flagellum: A flail or rattle to drive away evil spirits, it could be used only by a pharaoh and so represented the royal authority in carvings and statues. In the other hand was the *crook*, another royal symbol.

Geb: Personification of the earth.

Hajj: The pilgrimage to Mecca that all Muslims should make at least once in their lifetime. When they have done so, they will often paint a scene of the event on their houses.

Hamam: A bath, public or private.

Hapy: God of the abundant Nile, represented as a man with pendulous breasts.

Harem: The private family (or specifically the women's) quarter in a house.

Haroeris: The elder *Horus*.

Harpocrates: *Horus* as child.

Hathor: The goddess of heaven, joy and love; the Greeks identified her with Aphrodite. She was the deity of Dendera and protector of the Theban necropolis. Her sacred animal was the cow.

Heb-Sed: The jubilee marking the thirtieth year of a pharoah's reign (see Saqqara).

Hegira: Mohammed's flight, or more properly his 'withdrawal of affection' from Mecca in AD 622. The Muslim calender starts from this date.

Herakhte: A form of *Horus*, 'Horus of the horizon', often combined with the sun god as *Re-Herakhte* and so worshipped at Heliopolis. The falcon was sacred to him.

Horus: The son of *Isis* and *Osiris*, and revered as the sun god. He was represented as the sun disc or a falcon, his sacred animal.

Hypostyle: A hypostyle hall is any chamber whose ceiling is supported by columns or pillars.

Iconostasis: The screen carrying icons between the main part of a church and the sanctuary or choir.

Isis: Sister and wife to *Osiris*, mother of *Horus*, the patron goddess of Philae. She was most highly revered at a late period. She is often shown with a throne on her head.

Ithyphallic: Denoting the erect phallus of a depicted god or pharaoh, most commonly the god *Min*. It was a sign of fertility.

Ka: A spirit that inhabits the body during life and may leave it in death, but requires the continued existence of the body (hence mummification or, by substitution, ka statues) for its survival. The ka was personal and individual, in a sense the ideal image of a man's own life. (See *ba*.)

Khan: See *wakala*.

Khnum: The patron god of Elephantine Island and the Cataracts. He fashioned man on his potter's wheel. His sacred animal was the ram.

Khonsu: Son of *Amun* and *Mut*; god of the moon. The falcon was sacred to him.

Kufic: An early style of Arabic calligraphy with angular letters.

Lily: The plant identified with Upper Egypt.

Liwan: A valuted hall (see *mosque*).

Maat: The goddess of truth, whose symbol was the ostrich feather. Maat is actually the deification of a concept which Egyptians strove for, both personally and for the state. As well as truth, one can attempt to define it as justice, correctness, balance. The best definition is the now rare English word meet.

Madrasa: See *mosque*.

Mashrabiyya: Interlaced wooden screenwork, used for example to cover street-facing windows in a house.

Mausoleum: A domed chamber with one or more tombs inside; though simple in form, these structures, characteristic of the City of the Dead, are sometimes of considerable beauty.

Mihrab: The niche in the *qibla wall* of a mosque, indicating the direction of Mecca.

Min: The god of the harvest, frequently amalgamated with *Amun*. He was *ithyphallically* represented. The Greeks identified him with Pan.

Minbar: The pulpit in a mosque from which the Friday prayer is spoken.

Monophysitism: Strictly, the Christian doctrine that the two natures of Christ (human and divine) are absorbed into one nature (the divine). Though this has often been said to be Coptic belief, that is not true: the Copts do not deny the continued existence of the two natures but stress their unity after the Incarnation. The Latin and Greek Churches emphasise the two natures of Christ, holding that they are unmixed and unchangeable even though indistinguishable and inseparable (Council of Chalcedon, 451); they are diophysite.

Mont: A Theban god of war, represented with a falcon's head.

Mosque: The first mosque was the courtyard of Mohammed's house at Medina, with no architectural refinements except a shaded area at one end. Indeed, the only requirement for a mosque is that it should demarcate a space in which people may gather for saying prayers, eg an open quadrangle marked off by a ditch. From this notion developed the congregational mosque, of which the Ibn Tulun is the most outstanding example. Among non-congregational mosques are two special types which are of Cairene inspiration and development, the cruciform madrasa and the sabil kuttab. The madrasa served as a theological college, introduced by Saladin to combat Fatimid Shi'ism. Later it became more complex, a tomb appended and the madrasa formed of four *liwans*, each opening into a central court, hence cruciform. The outstanding example of this type is the Hassan. This pattern was subsequently modified, the court covered over, the east and west liwans reduced to vestigial proportions, a Koranic school for boys (*kuttab*) added as a floor above, a public fountain (*sabil*) below.

Moulid: The birthday of a saint, Coptic or Muslim; it is often celebrated at the level of folk religion, a pharaonic deity transformed into a Christian saint who in turn resurfaces as a Muslim sheikh.

Muezzin: A crier who, as from a minaret, calls the faithful to prayer (see *azan*).

Mut: The wife of *Amun* and mother of *Khonsu*. Her sacred animal was the vulture.

Naos: The enclosed inner 'house of the god' (also *cella*), the central room of a temple, though sometimes referring to the entire temple. The sanctuary.

Narthex: The entrance vestibule at the west end of a church.

Nashki: A cursive form of Arabic writing, subsequent to *Kufic*.

Nephthys: Sister of *Isis* and *Osiris*, married to *Seth*; with outstretched wings one of the protector goddesses of the dead, guardian of the *Canopic jars*.

Nut: Goddess of the sky, often shown supported by *Shu*.

Okel: See *wakala*.

Osiris: Originally a vegetation god, later the god of the underworld. Murdered and dismembered by *Seth*, he was the husband and brother of *Isis* and father of *Horus*.

Papyrus: The plant identified with Lower Egypt.

Pronaos: A columned porch, leading to the *naos*.

Ptah: The patron god of Memphis and father of the gods. His sacred animal was the *Apis* bull.

Pylon: Arranged in pairs, forming a monumental gateway to a temple. Where there are several sets of pylons, each preceding a court, they descend in size as the sanctuary of the god is approached, while the floor level rises, creating a focussing or tunnelling effect.

Pyramidion: The capstone of a pyramid.

Qibla wall: The wall of a mosque facing Mecca.

Re: The sun god, usually combined with another god, eg *Amun-Re* or *Re-Herakhte*. His priesthood was at Heliopolis.

Riwaq: The arcade around a *sahn*, or a student apartment within the arcade.

Sabil kuttab: See *mosque*.

Sahn: An interior court, usually in a mosque.

Sakiya: An irrigation device introduced during the Ptolemaic period consisting of buckets attached to a wheel which lifts water to the fields and is driven by circling oxen.

Sekhmet: The lion goddess of war.

Serapis: A god invented by the Ptolemies, looking like *Zeus* but identified with *Osiris-Apis*.

Seth: Brother and slayer of *Osiris*, adversary of *Horus*, he became a god of war, though after the XXII Dynasty he was reduced to the god of the impure. His sacred animal was possibly the aardvark.

Shaduf: A simple lever device for lifting water to irrigate the fields. It is operated by hand.

Shu: The god of the air. He is often shown supporting *Nut*.

Sobek: God of the waters, patron of the Fayyum, the crocodile was sacred to him.

Squinches: Small arches or supports across the corners of a square, enabling the carriage of a dome.

Stele: An upright stone slab or pillar with an inscription or design, used as a monument or grave marker.

Thoth: A moon deity and the god of science. The ibis and baboon were sacred to him.

Torus: A convex moulding (see *cavetto cornice*).

Uraeus: The cobra worn on the forehead of a pharoah as both an emblem and an instrument of protection, breathing flames and destroying enemies.

Ushabti: A mummiform figurine, serving in the tomb as deputy for the dead man, carrying out his labour obligations.

Wakala: An inn for travelling merchants built around a courtyard, with stables and warehouses at ground level and living accommodation above. Other names are *khan* and *okel*.

Waqf: An endowment for the upkeep of a mosque, eg a nearby apartment house, or shops built into the street level of the mosque, earning rents.

Ziyadah: The outer court of a mosque.

Books About Egypt

The literature on Egypt is vast, and apart from pursuing your interest in libraries and bookshops at home there are several bookshops in Cairo worth visiting (see the *Practical Information* section following the *Cairo: Mother of the World* chapter). The American University in Cairo Press publishes a growing list of books on many aspects of Egypt past and present, including fiction, non-fiction and guides; their titles are widely available in Egypt and they have their own bookshop in Cairo.

A number of authors are quoted throughout the text of this guide, and you might like to pursue their books according to your interest. However, the following titles will provide introductions to various periods or aspects of Egyptian history and should prove readily available in Cairo:

An Introduction to Ancient Egypt by T G H James, British Museum Publications, London — the pharaonic period.

Egypt After the Pharaohs by Alan K Bowman, British Museum Publications, London — the Graeco-Roman period.

Alexandria: A History and a Guide by E M Forster, Michael Haag Limited, London — chiefly the Graeco-Roman and Christian periods, though with notes examining the city's most recent history and its literary associations.

Coptic Egypt by Barbara Watterson, Scottish Academic Press, Edinburgh — Coptic history and culture to the present.

Monks and Monasteries of the Egyptian Deserts by Otto Meinardus, American University in Cairo Press, Cairo — Coptic monasteries and monasticism, a guide and history.

The Arabs by Peter Mansfield, Penguin Books, London — a review of Arab history and the present situation.

Manners and Customs of the Modern Egyptians by E W Lane, East-West Publications, London and Livres de France, Cairo — the classic survey of early 19th C Cairo.

CAIRO: MOTHER OF THE WORLD

From the air Cairo is a city of circles and radiating avenues at the head of the Nile Delta, its houses and buildings dull brown as though camouflaged to blend with the impinging desert. The colour is of the local stone, but also the residue of sandstorms which sometimes dust the city. At sundown you can see a thin layer of sand clinging to the polished dome of the Mohammed Ali Mosque atop the Citadel, and as you walk along the cracked pavements the desert wells up from below.

Like a great lung the Nile breathes through the city, but away from the broad slow-flowing river Westernised Cairo can have a heavy, airless feeling, an architectural jumble of fake pharaonic, blocklike modern, unnoticed art-deco and oppressive Victorian. Yet farther east against the Moqattam Hills minarets like blades of tall grass rise against the sky, marking the old Islamic city of hidden beauty and palpitating energy which lends all Cairo its excitement.

In spirit Cairo remains as it began, an Arab encampment on the edge of the desert: hot, dry, the smell of dung, glowing coals and musk, lively with throngs of people. To this sprawling caravanserai come visitors from all over the Arab, African and Asian world, fantastically varied in colour, dress, characteristics, yet easily talking, mingling, bargaining like distant villagers meeting again in their market town.

For Cairo is the largest city in Africa and the political and cultural fulcrum of the Arab world. Its population is perhaps 15 million, a five-fold increase within a generation, and owes its recent staggering growth to Egypt's exploding birthrate, pressure on the land, and the fellahin's desire to transform their lives in a city which for all its seeming desperation still offers at least the hope of opportunity. At rush hours the buses threaten to burst or collapse with the pressure of Cairenes scrambling through doors and windows or clinging on outside for the long ride to or from the suburbs of Heliopolis, Maadi and Helwan.

But as the sun sets over the Nile the present slips away into timelessness, and from a high window over the river you can see the Pyramids at Giza glow gold against the Western Desert as they have done for one million, seven hundred thousand evenings past.

History of the City

Your orientation about the city is aided by a knowledge of its history, and its history, as with so much else in Egypt, is linked to the Nile.

Antiquity   In the Old Kingdom the capital of Egypt was at **Memphis**, 20 km to the south of present-day Cairo—but at that time the

Delta had not pushed as far north as it has today and Memphis stood closer then to the conjunction of the Delta and the valley, controlling Egypt to the north and south. In this strategic sense Cairo is heir to Memphis, for the Nile divides just to the north of the capital.

Ancient **Heliopolis**, its scant ruins near a modern suburb bearing the same name at the northeast of the city enroute to the airport, was once the religious centre of Egypt, and in pharaonic times there was a settlement, perhaps even a town, on the east bank of the Nile opposite the island of Roda, but Cairo cannot be said to have developed out of these, and even its connection with what is now called Old Cairo is tenuous. In Roman and Byzantine times when there was a fortress here, Old Cairo was called **Babylon in Egypt**, probably a Greek corruption of the ancient name of Roda, *Per-Hapi-en-Yun,* House of the Nile of Heliopolis. Fortress rather than administrative centre was sufficient role for the settlement, and Babylon never amounted to much. In the last centuries before Christ, Egypt was ruled by Alexander's successors, the Ptolemies, from their Mediterranean capital, Alexandria.

The Arab conquest

It was the Arabs, for whom the desert and not the sea provided familiar lines of communication, who developed the logic of the site. In AD 641, Amr arrived in Egypt at the head of a small army and both Alexandria and Babylon opened their gates to him. Amr was enchanted with Alexandria and wrote back to the Caliph at Medina that this should be the Muslim capital of the conquered country, but Omar replied, 'Will there be water between me and the Muslim army?' Amr returned to Babylon where only sand separated him from Arabia; the tent (*fustat*) he had pitched there before marching on Alexandria was still standing and a dove had nested in it with her young. On this spot Amr built his mosque, the first in Egypt and **Fustat**, the City of the Tent, grew up around.

Fustat was the first of several planned developments which over the centuries contributed to the growth of the medieval city. The Nile in those days lay farther to the east along what is now Sharia el Gumhuriya which runs up into Midan Ramses where the railway station is. All of what is now modern Cairo lay then on the west bank of the river, if not beneath it. And an ancient canal, once joining the Nile with the Red Sea, lay still farther to the east, along the line of Sharia Port Said, built when the canal, called the Khalig by the Arabs, was filled in during the 19th C. So the city developed along the narrow corridor of land between the canal to the west and the Moqattam Hills to the east, and extended northwards as successive rulers were intent on catching the cool summer breezes blowing in from the Mediterranean.

Bab Zuwayla, by David Roberts in the 1840s

The Tulunid city

When Ibn Tulun, Abbasid governor of Egypt, made himself virtually independent of the Baghdad caliph in 870, he built his palace, government buildings, a hippodrome and the famous mosque bearing his name to the north of Fustat. The **Mosque of Ibn Tulun** apart, little survives of his city, and still less of Fustat. The heart of what grew into the Cairo of today was established by the Fatimids.

Cairo founded by the Fatimids

On 5 August 969, with Mars in the ascendant, the first stone of the Fatimid capital was laid to the north of the Tulunid city. The city took its name, *al-Qahira,* The Triumphant, from the warrior planet. The Fatimids, of the persistent though minority Shi'ite sect of Islam, invaded Egypt from Tunisia where their caliphate declared its legitimacy through descent from Ali, husband of the Prophet's daughter Fatima. They imposed their Shi'ite doctrines (those same followed today in Iran) on Egypt which, apart from the Fatimid interlude, has kept within the orthodox Sunni fold. The **al-Azhar Mosque** dates from this period and is still the centre of Koranic studies for the whole Muslim world.

(Our name for the city, Cairo, derives from this al-Qahira found on maps, though as often as not Egyptians call it *Misr.* Of vague and haunting meaning, far antedating Islam, Misr is emotionally the more important name of the two and refers to both city and the country as a whole. An Egyptian abroad who says, 'I am going to Misr'. means he is returning to Egypt. If he says the same thing in Luxor, he means he is returning to Cairo. In either case, 'going to Misr' carries the sense of going home. For the fellahin, Cairo is *Misr um al-dunya*: Misr, Mother of the World.)

Saladin extends the medieval city

This walled city, centred on the popular market area known as **Khan el Khalili** and extending from the gate known as **Bab Zuwayla** in the south to **Bab al-Futuh** in the north, remains astonishingly intact both in structure and in atmosphere, the medieval city nonpareil in all the world. Its walls and area were extended by Saladin, a Kurdish general in the service of the Abbasid caliph in Baghdad. Foreign failures and the failure of the Nile itself led to the weakening of the Fatimid dynasty which trembled in confusion before the onslaught of the First Crusade. In triumphing over the armies of the West, Saladin established his own empire in Egypt and Syria and his own Ayyubid dynasty which ruled from 1171 to 1250. Orthodoxy was re-established and the Citadel begun, the redoubt of power and the centre of government throughout the troubled centuries of Mameluke and Ottoman rule.

Mameluke magnificence

Saladin's Ayyubid successors, however, relied increasingly on their slave militia, the Bahri Mamlukes. (*Mameluke* means white slave, while *bahri* means riverine and refers to their barracks on the island of Roda; these were mostly Turks and Mongols. The later Burgi Mamelukes, mostly Circassian, were quartered in the Citadel, hence *burg*.) The

Waterskiing on the Nile in Cairo

Mamelukes soon became an indispensable elite and successive sultans rose from their number, legitimising their authority more by the blood on their hands than the blood in their veins. The Mamelukes ruled Egypt until the Ottoman domination in 1517. In spite of the violent and repressive character of Mameluke rule, they enriched the city with their architecture, their most outstanding monuments the **Mosque of Sultan Hassan** and the **Mausoleum of Qaytbay**.

The Ottomans Around 1300 the island of Gezira was formed as the Nile shifted westwards but the city remained largely within its old boundaries right through the Ottoman period, its architecture following traditional styles with only a few baroque exceptions inspired by the mosques of Istanbul. As a province of the Ottoman Empire, Egypt was ruled by a Turkish governor housed in the Citadel who delegated most of his authority. Though no longer providing sultans, the Mamelukes perpetuated their slave aristocracy by levees of Christian youths from the Caucasus. But their power now was chaotic and rapacious. What the Turks did not take, the Mamelukes did, and Egypt suffered from famine and disease, its population falling to two million compared to eight million in Roman times.

Napoleon and the Westernisation of Cairo The brief French occupation of Egypt, from 1798 to 1801, was to have a profound effect on Cairo. Napoleon stayed in what was still then a country district, on the site where the old Shepheard's Hotel was later built, overlooking the

Ezbekieh lake, subsequently the Ezbekieh Gardens, only recently ruined by having a main street cut through the middle and flyover amputate one side. While reorganising the government, introducing the first printing press, launching a balloon and installing windmills on the Moqattam Hills, Napoleon also planned Parisian boulevards.

When Mohammed Ali finally massacred the Mamelukes in 1811, founding a dynasty which ended only with the abdication of Farouk in 1952, he proceeded with the Westernisation of Cairo which saw the canal filled in and the great swaths of Sharia el Muski and Sharia el Qalaa (formerly Sharia Mohammed Ali) mow down long rows of the medieval city. Fortunately, however, most of the modernising of Cairo — those circles and radiating avenues you see from the air — took place on the virgin land that the Nile provided when it settled in its present bed.

Orientation

It is in this newer, Westernised part of Cairo that we can start our orientation.

What now passes for the centre of town — for foreigners, anyway — is **Midan el Tahrir**, or Liberation Square, bounded by the Egyptian Museum to the north and the Nile Hilton to the west, with a madhouse of a bus terminus slap in the middle and a new metro station dug beneath. Hot, noisy, characterless and thick with exhaust fumes, Midan el Tahrir is among the more recent schemes to bring Cairo up to date. It was created after the 1952 revolution on the site of a British barracks, the Qasr el Nil, and at the same time powers of compulsory purchase were used to cut the **Corniche el Nil** through the many embassy and villa gardens to the south, the new roadway extending clear down to Maadi and Helwan.

South along the corniche to Garden city A short walk along the corniche are the Semiramis Intercontinental and Shepheard's — though the famous Shepheard's Hotel of the past, whose guest list included General Gordon and Sir Richard Burton and where anyone who was anyone was seen on the terrace drinking four o'clock tea, was located near the Ezbekieh Gardens and was burnt down by demonstrators in 1952. Farther south along the river is the convoluted pattern of **Garden City**, a pleasant residential district of treelined streets.

Immediately to the south of Midan el Tahrir is the Mugamaa, the suitably massive headquarters of the state administration, and next to it are the American University in Cairo and the National Assembly. Going east beyond the campus and the station you come to Abdin Palace, formerly a residence of King Farouk, now partly a museum and partly the offices of the President of the Republic.

North to Midan Ramses To the north of Midan el Tahrir, beyond the overpass leading to the new 6 October Bridge (named for the 1973 war), is the

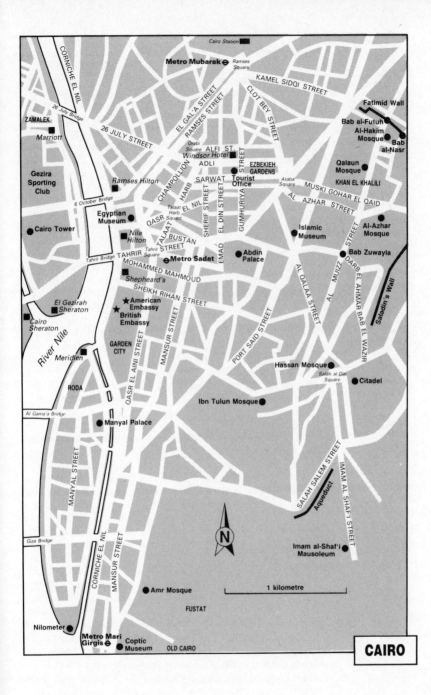

CAIRO

61

Ramses Hilton and past that the one-time slum districts of Bulaq and Shubra, now being redeveloped with skyscrapers along the river. On the corniche here is the Television Tower Building, housing radio and television studios and the press office, while the taller building beyond it is the new Ministry of Foreign Affairs. Sharia Ramses runs out from the top of Midan el Tahrir and turns northeast, leading to **Midan Ramses** with a colossal statue of Ramses II brought in 1955 from Memphis where his twin still resides. (A concrete clone has been erected on the way to the airport.) Here you will find the Mahattat Ramses or Bab el Hadeed, the main Cairo railway station for trains north to Alexandria and south to Luxor and Aswan.

Northeast to downtown

Around Midan el Tahrir and along the streets radiating out from it are numerous airline offices and travel agencies, and extending into the **downtown area** to the northeast several less expensive hotels. This downtown area is bordered by Sharia Ramses to the northwest, Sharia Tahrir to the south and Sharia el Gumhuriya to the west. Parallel to Sharia Ramses is Sharia Champollion; the Thomas Cook office is on the first street to intersect this, Sharia Mahmoud Basiony. Sharia Qasr el Nil heads more eastwards in the direction of the Ezbekieh Gardens, though not quite reaching that far; soon after leaving Midan el Tahrir you will find American Express on the right-hand side. Farther on, this street intersects several others at Midan Talaat Harb. Along Sharia Talaat Harb, beginning at Midan el Tahrir and ending at Midan Orabi, are numerous shops, cinemas and eating places — also along Sharias Adli and 26 July running east-west. This is the liveliest area of modern Cairo, particularly on a Thursday night, that is preceding Friday's day of rest.

Across Ezbekieh Gardens to Islamic Cairo

Until the creation of Midan el Tahrir, the **Ezbekieh Gardens** were the focal point for foreign visitors. The old Shepheard's Hotel stood on the corner of Sharias el Gumhuriya and Alfi at the northwest corner of the gardens, the Continental Savoy on el Gumhuriya overlooking Opera Square, which is immediately to the south of the gardens, is now a dishevelled reminder of those grand days of tourism. The Opera House mysteriously burnt down in 1971; it had been built in 1869, and the Khedive Ismail commissioned Verdi to write *Aida* to celebrate here the opening of the Suez Canal and Egypt's return to the crossroads of the world. In the event, *Aida* was late and *Rigoletto* was performed instead before a glittering international audience which included the Empress Eugénie, wife of Napoleon III. This area around Ezbekieh, though not what it used to be, is — along with the downtown area most adjacent to it — one of the best places to stay for anyone who is serious about exploring the city on foot. It enjoys the ambivalence of being on the edge of modern Cairo and within easy walking distance of the Fatimid city to the east.

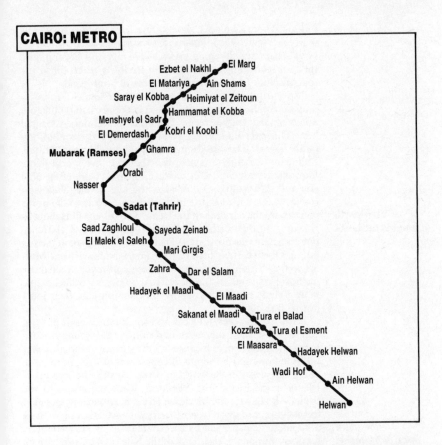

CAIRO: METRO

El Marg
Ezbet el Nakhl
El Matariya — Ain Shams
Saray el Kobba — Heimiyat el Zeitoun
Hammamat el Kobba
Menshyet el Sadr
El Demerdash — Kobri el Koobi
Mubarak (Ramses) — Ghamra
Orabi
Nasser
Sadat (Tahrir)
Saad Zaghloul — Sayeda Zeinab
El Malek el Saleh
Mari Girgis
Zahra — Dar el Salam
Hadayek el Maadi
El Maadi
Sakanat el Maadi — Tura el Balad
Kozzika — Tura el Esment
El Maasara
Hadayek Helwan
Wadi Hof
Ain Helwan
Helwan

The development and layout of the medieval **Islamic city** has already been outlined, and the details of its sights will be provided later. Suffice to say for the purpose of orientation that if you walk through the Ezbekieh Gardens you will come to Midan Ataba with its central post office, open 24 hours a day. From here you can press on into the heart of the bazaar area along Sharias el Muski or al-Azhar; or if instead you leave the square along Sharia al Qalaa (formerly Sharia Mohammed Ali and still called that by many) running south you come to the Islamic Museum at the intersection with Sharia Port Said, and still farther down you reach the Sultan Hassan Mosque and the Citadel. West of the Citadel is the Mosque of Ibn Tulun.

Gezira and the view from the Cairo Tower

Returning again to Midan el Tahrir for bearings, there is the Tahrir Bridge which crosses the Nile to the island of Gezira (*gezira* is in fact Arabic for island). The central part of Gezira is taken up with the Sporting and Racing Club, next to it rising in lotus motif the 180-metre **Cairo Tower**, completed in 1962. There is an open observation deck up top, and below it an enclosed coffee lounge and a restaurant of the revolving kind. There are sweeping views of the city and beyond, and this is a good place (easy too on the feet) to establish the topography of Cairo's outlying areas in your mind.

The north part of the island is called **Zamalek**, a mostly modern residential area, though with the occasional fine old home amidst leafy streets. The Marriott Hotel is located here. This part of Gezira can be reached directly from Midan Orabi along Sharia 26 July and across an old metal bridge. Following 26 July (named for the date on which King Farouk abdicated in 1952) across to the west bank of the Nile you see the suburb of **Embaba**, the site where Napoleon fought the so-called Battle of the Pyramids. Far to the north you can see the dark fan of the **Delta**. The suburb of **Heliopolis** is nearer, to the northeast, though the ancient site of Heliopolis is a bit to the north of it. There is nothing to see at the site but an Obelisk of Sesostris I (XII Dyn), and nearby at Matariya the Virgin's Tree, its predecessor much visited by medieval pilgrims in the belief that under its branches the Holy Family paused for shade before continuing their journey to Babylon.

View north towards the Delta

Below you, barges, feluccas and small motor craft pass up and down stream, the prevailing north wind giving the impression by the ripples it causes on the surface of the river that the Nile flows south though of course it is flowing north, one of the few rivers in the world to do so. At the southern tip of Gezira is the El Gezirah Sheraton, while the island to the south is **Roda** with the Meridien Hotel magnificently perched like a figurehead upon its northern prow. At its southern tip is a nilometer constructed by the Ummayads in 716. About as far down but on the east bank of the Nile is **Old Cairo** with its Coptic Museum, Coptic churches and a synagogue. Much farther south is **Maadi** (along with Zamalek one of the residential areas favoured by Cairo's foreign community), and farther on still the industrial town of **Helwan**, both on the east bank. The indiscernible remains of Egypt's ancient capital, **Memphis**, lie on the west bank opposite Helwan.

View south towards Memphis

Sweeping your gaze round to east and west you see how Cairo is bounded on either side by desert. The **Moqattam Hills** are to the east and beyond them the Arabian Plateau. On a spur of the hills is the **Citadel**, distinguished by the dome of the Mohammed Ali Mosque, and spread before it in dark sand-brown confusion is the old quarter of the city, as though lurking in past centuries behind the higher, more lightly dusted buildings of the new. The windows of the Nile Hilton cast a silvery cubistic pattern of setting sunlight on the river. Away to the west is the plateau of the Western Desert. Along the west bank of the Nile, opposite Gezira and south of Embaba, are the new suburbs of **Agouza, Medinat el Mohandiseen**

View east towards the Citadel

(Engineer's City) and, around the Cairo Sheraton, **Dokki**. Mrs Sadat continues to live in a villa here overlooking the Nile, just south of the hotel, once President Sadat's official residence. Sharia el Giza runs southwards from the Sheraton to the Zoological Gardens and Cairo University. This is **Giza**, here long before the suburbs began their sprawl along the west bank to the north and out towards the desert escarpment, obliterating the once extensive fields of the fellahin. From the Cairo Tower you can still make out some arable land but it is fast disappearing beneath the furious antlike progress all round you. It is best to be up in the tower at early evening as the sun sets over the Western Desert, the sharp outline of the **Pyramids** as ever marking the great divide between the distant haze of the void and the nearer ephemeral activity of the hive.

View west towards the Pyramids

Itineraries

Each of the following chapters offers an itinerary, though you might prefer breaking them down into shorter excursions or combining parts of one with another for variety. Cairo itself really deserves at least four full days of your time, and the great line of pyramids stretching along the verge of the Western Desert require another day or two. Therefore the traveller should allow himself a week in Cairo and its environs, but this may not always be possible and so under the *Practical Information* sections following each chapter the essential highlights for an abbreviated tour are listed.

PRACTICAL INFORMATION

ACCOMMODATION

If you have not already made a reservation, then on arrival at Cairo Airport you can go to the Tourist Information Office or Misr Travel and see if they can help. Or you can do your own hotel hunting, probably running no greater risk than having to visit a couple of hotels before finding something suitable. Often a hotel will volunteer, or can be prevailed upon, to phone ahead on your behalf, saving legwork and taxi fares.

The following is a selective list of hotels in the Cairo, Giza and Heliopolis areas:
Mena House Oberoi (5-star). Sharia al-Ahram, Giza. Tel: 855444. A historic hotel, originally a khedivial hunting lodge (converted to a hotel in 1869) and where Churchill and Roosevelt initiated

the D-Day plan. 11 km from Midan el Tahrir, linked by an infrequent free hotel bus service, the Mena House is convenient rather for the Pyramids (across the road). The old wing is magnificently decorated; it is here that you should make a point of staying, especially in a room overlooking the Pyramids — for my money, *the* place to stay if you do not mind the long journey into town. A garden wing was added in 1976, pleasant but without the old style and the dramatic Pyramid views — rates here are less than 5-star. All rooms have air conditioning and colour TV. Pool, tennis, golf, casino, nightclub, business centre, car hire, travel agent, etc., make the Mena House a self-sufficient resort on the desert's edge.
Nile Hilton (5-star), Midan el Tahrir, Cairo. Tel: 740777. Right next to the

Egyptian Museum and overlooking the Nile, this was the first international hotel built in Egypt (opening ceremonies in 1959 were attended by Nasser and Tito) and the first Hilton in the Middle East. It has become something of an institution. The Nile Hilton Centre, a 1981 extension, provides further rooms as well as a concentration of travel agencies, airline offices, banks, shops and business facilities in addition to those already in the main building. American Express, Avis and Egyptair are amongst those represented. It is in the main building with its larger rooms that you should try to stay, insisting on a Nile view. Pool, tennis courts, disco, nightclub, casino, sauna, plus numerous shops and a variety of eating places are amongst the facilities. The Ibis Café is open 24 hours; the Pizzeria is good; the Taverne du Champ de Mars, imported stick by stick from Brussels, is very agreeable. All rooms are air-conditioned and have colour TV.

Ramses Hilton (5-star), Corniche el Nil, Cairo. Tel: 758000. A 1981 tower, all rooms with balconies, many with a Nile view, the hotel is a short walk from the Egyptian Museum. The rooms are a bit small; all have air conditioning and colour TV. The best thing about it is its top-floor cocktail lounge with sweeping nighttime panorama. Pool, health club, casino, business centre, shops, Hertz, travel agent, etc.

Cairo Marriott (5-star), Serai el Gezira, Zamalek, Cairo. Tel: 3408888. On Gezira island overlooking the Nile, the public areas of the Marriott inhabit with effortless vulgarity an 1869 palace. The rooms are in new purpose-built towers, all air-conditioned, with colour TV. Pool, tennis courts, health club, casino, business centre, shops, car hire, travel agent, etc. Unless you like long walks, it is a taxi-ride to almost anywhere.

Cairo Sheraton (5-star), Midan el Galaa, Dokki, Cairo. Tel: 3488600. The first Sheraton in Egypt (1970), renovated in 1986, second tower opened in 1990, the hotel is located on the west bank of the Nile across the Tahrir Bridge, with upper-storey views either over the river or towards the Pyramids, all rooms air-conditioned and with colour TV. It is a lively

place, with a good nightclub; also 2 pools, health club, casino, business centre, many shops, a good 24-hour café and an Avis desk.

El Gezirah Sheraton (5-star), Gezira island, Cairo. Tel: 3411333. At the southern tip of Gezira, this circular tower offers wonderful views up and down the Nile and towards the Pyramids. The service however is poor and in summer the outdoor nightclub blasts every north- and east-facing room (the ones with the best views) until 4am. Nor are its facilities up to much. This is really a rip-off group-tour oriented hotel which does not give a damn about its guests.

Meridien Le Caire (5-star), PO Box 2288, Roda island, Cairo. Tel: 845444. Access is by private bridge from the Corniche el Nil, Garden City, to the north tip of Roda from where the hotel commands a sweeping view down the Nile. French flavour: boutiques and bidets; good coffee and pastries in the 24-hour café; its Champollion Restaurant is probably the best hotel restaurant in Cairo. Pool, health centre, well-run resort-style atmosphere. All rooms soundproofed, with Nile view, air conditioning and colour TV.

Semiramis Inter-Continental (5-star), Corniche el Nil, Cairo. Tel: 3557171. On the Nile, a short walk from Midan el Tahrir, this is one of Cairo's newest (1987) luxe hotels. Its cacophonic jumble of tiered reception area cum bar cum café is a good example of how not to design a hotel, but it has a high reputation for service and is particularly favoured by businessmen. Pool, health club, business centre, shops, travel agent, car hire, etc. All rooms air-conditioned, with colour TV.

Shepheard's (5-star), Corniche el Nil, Cairo. Tel: 3553800. This is not *the* famous Shepheard's; that was near Ezbekieh Gardens and was burnt down in the nationalist riots of 1952. This was built in 1956 and has recently been refurbished. Unlike the newer 5-star hotels, it is sedate, possesses some architectural charm, and has spacious rooms. The 24-hour café is very comfortable and the top-floor bar and restaurant have good views of the river. All rooms air-conditioned and have colour TV; the preferred Nile-side rooms have ceiling to floor picture windows and balconies. Shops, travel agent, car hire, but no pool. Prices are a bit lower than at the newer 5-star hotels.

Novotel Cairo Airport (4-star), Heliopolis. Tel: 671715. Frequent courtesy buses deliver you in minutes to the airport; this, plus soundproofed rooms, a reasonable price for its range, and good facilities (including tennis court, air-conditioned rooms with colour TV), make it a practical place to stay for those facing an early-morning take-off.

Manyal Palace (4-star), Roda island, Cairo. Tel: 844687. Run by Club Méditerranée but open to all, accommodation is in bungalows in the gardens of Mohammed Ali's palace. Beautiful setting, disco, pool, air conditioning.

Flamenco (4-star), 2 Sharia El Gezira el Wasta, Zamalek, Cairo. Tel: 3400815. At the northwest end of Gezira island in a residential area, this is a Spanish-run hotel, reflected in its café and restaurant cuisine. Shops, business centre, travel agent. Air-conditioned rooms with colour TV, some with Nile views.

Atlas Zamalek (4-star), 20 Sharia Gameat el Dowal el Arabia, Mohandiseen, Cairo. Tel: 3464175. Not in Zamalek at all, but just across an arm of the Nile in the west bank residential area of Mohandiseen. Despite its distance from the centre of town, it is a popular choice, with pool, sauna, a variety of eating places. Rooms with colour TV and air-conditioning.

President (3-star), 22 Sharia Taha Hussein, Zamalek, Cairo. Tel: 3413195. In a quiet residential area of many embassies and diplomatic residences on Gezira island. Rooms are simply furnished, large and clean; all have private baths, some have TV. Bar, restaurant, and the lively Cellar Pub in the basement.

Windsor (3-star), 19 Sharia Alfi, Cairo. Tel: 915810. This is one of my favourite hotels. Early this century Baedeker ranked it just below the old Shepheard's and since then it has not changed a jot: the character is literally peeling off its walls. High-ceilinged rooms for ventilation, much old wooden furnishing, a delightful bar/lounge/dining room hung with weird curios and damaged paintings, beers

served by berobed and long-dead waiters — this is the place to come for Cairo as it once was and if you are prepared to enjoy class in tatters and atmosphere in abundance. Towards Ezbekieh Gardens in downtown Cairo. Rooms with either shower or bath.

Cosmopolitan (3-star), Sharia Ibn Taalab, off Sharia Qasr el Nil, Cairo. Tel: 3923845. Tucked away in a quiet street downtown, this is an old traditional hotel nicely refurbished in 1983. Restaurant, bar, coffee shop and bank. All rooms are air-conditioned with bath.

Victoria (3-star), 66 Sharia el Gumhuriya, Cairo. Tel: 918766. A newly-renovated downtown hotel, with good food, a hairdresser and an Australian manager!

New Hotel (2-star), 21 Sharia Adli, Cairo. Tel: 3927065. Large simply-furnished and clean rooms — and clean bathrooms. Downtown.

Lotus (2-star), 12 Sharia Talaat Harb, Cairo. Tel: 750627. Opposite Felfela restaurant. Clean rooms, some with bath and air-conditioning.

Grand (2-star), 17 Sharia 26 July, Cairo. Tel: 757509. At the intersection with Talaat Harb, downtown. Clean, comfortable rooms, some with shower.

El Hussein (2-star), Midan el Hussein, Cairo. Tel: 918089. Right by the Mosque of Sayyidna al-Hussein on the edge of Khan el Khalili and with Fishawi's tea house next door, this is the best hotel for those wanting to be amidst the sights and atmosphere of Islamic Cairo. The restaurant on the roof offers a good view of the medieval city. Rooms are clean but very simple; all are air-conditioned but only some have bathrooms.

Garden City House (1-star), 23 Sharia Kamal el Din Dalah, Cairo. Tel: 3548126. Near the Semiramis Inter-Continental, this is good value for its price. From outside there is a small sign 3 storeys up; the rooms are there and on the floor above; you take the lift. The place is shabby, but clean and friendly, and the food good. Some rooms have baths, some face the river, most have balconies. There are not many single rooms. Half-board is compulsory.

Pensione Roma (1-star), 169 Sharia Imad el Din, Cairo. Tel: 911088. Near the intersection with Sharia Adli, downtown. Clean.

Hotel des Roses (1-star), 33 Sharia Talaat Harb, Cairo. Tel: 758022. Near the intersection with Sharia Sarwat, downtown. Clean rooms, some with showers; try for an upper-storey room with views.

Hostel and campsite:
Manyal Youth Hostel, 135 Sharia Abdel Aziz el-Saud, Cairo. Tel: 840729. Near the Manyal Palace on Roda island. From Midan el Tahrir, take bus 8 or 900; from Midan Ramses take bus 95. Get off at Kobri el Gamaa (University Bridge). Tolerably clean, about LE1 per night, often full up.

Camping Salome at Harraniyya, 3 km along the canal road from Giza to Saqqara. Harraniyya is the village where the late Ramses Wissa Wassef established his famous tapestry-weaving school, so the way will be well-known. Toilets, showers, meals. Camping costs about LE1.50 per night.

EATING PLACES
You can spend a fortune or a few piastres on a meal in Cairo, and choose between the world's cuisines. Not only restaurants, but coffee shops, tea rooms and snack bars are included here.

Western style food is served at all the hotels, regardless of category. Only the restaurants at a few major hotels, however, are worth going out of your way to dine at. The best is the **Champollion** at the Meridien; also worth trying are the **Rotisserie** at the Nile Hilton, **The Grill** at the El Gezira Sheraton, the **Ambassador's Club** and **The Grill** at the Semiramis and **Asia House** at Shepheard's. All are expensive. Western style meals (French International, to be exact) are also to be had at the following non-hotel restaurants:

Justine, 4 Sharia Hassan Sabri, Zamalek. Tel: 3412961. Part of the Four Corners Restaurant, the atmosphere is formal, the cuisine is nouvelle. Probably the best and most expensive restaurant in Cairo.

La Charmerie, 110 Sharia 26 July, Zamalek (set back a bit from 26 July, opposite Margaret's Boutique). Tel: 3403424. Stylish and pricey.

Don Quichotte, 9 Sharia Ahmed Heshmat, Zamalek. Tel: 3406415. Some Middle Eastern specialities. Expensive.

El Yotti, 44 Sharia Mohl el Din Abul Ezz, Mohandiseen. Tel: 3494944. Moderately priced.

It is significant that Cairo's better and newer Western style restaurants like those above are outside the downtown area which generally is deteriorating. However:

La Chesa, 21 Sharia Adli, downtown. Tel: 3939360. Operated by Swissair Restaurants, this is a haven of Swiss cleanliness, excellent food and a very good cake and pastry section.

Specialty restaurants offer one fare, with variations, though alternatives may be available:

Naniwa, Ramses Hilton Annex. Tel: 758000. Japanese in a pleasant atmosphere. Expensive.

Fu Ching, 28 Sharia Talaat Harb. Tel: 3936184. Inexpensive Chinese. Located in a passageway off Talaat Harb, downtown. Does take-aways.

Il Capo, 22 Sharia Taha Hussein, Zamalek. Tel: 3413870. Italian. Inexpensive and casual. Does take-aways. Near the President Hotel.

The Farm, 23 Maryutia Canal off Sharia al-Ahram (Pyramids Road) — signposted. Rustic setting, though fashionable. The speciality is roast lamb. Food and service are excellent. Reservations recommended. Tel: 851870. Moderately priced.

The Nile Pharaoh, a cruising restaurant got up like a pharaonic sailing barge. Lunch and dinner. Oberoi Hotels for reservations. Tel: 738855 or 738914. Expensive.

Pizzeria, Hilton Hotel, Midan el Tahrir. The atmosphere is pleasant, the food good and moderately priced.

Taverna, 3 Sharia Alfi, near Midan Orabi. Principally Cypriot, though other dishes too. Their speciality is shrimp. Inexpensive to moderate.

Oriental restaurants include the most simple peasant Egyptian through to the Levantine which can be a mixture of

Egyptian, Turkish, French and other cuisines. The Meridien's **Le Roof** is the best of the big hotel Oriental restaurants, and is of course expensive. But you should make a point of going to local places for the local atmosphere.

Arabesque, 6 Sharia Qasr el Nil. Tel: 759869. This is an elegant downtown restaurant with a small bar; adjoining it is a gallery of Egyptian artists. The cuisine is Egyptian, Lebanese and European. Prices are moderate but imported wine will make it expensive.

Felfela, 15 Sharia Hoda Sharawi, just off Sharia Talaat Harb. Though popular with tourists and foreign residents, it is also a favourite of Egyptians and the food is certainly good and inexpensive. Tree trunks serve as tables. The specialty is fool in all its varieties of preparation, but the menu extends to meat dishes, ice creams, etc. Try the Shakshouka Felfela, a blend of ground beef, egg and spices in tomato sauce, with rice.

Al Omdah, Sharia Al-Gazair (off Sharia Gameat el Dowal el Arabia), Mohandiseen. A few doors along from the Atlas Zamalek Hotel, the restaurant sign is in Arabic but features a man looking vaguely like Mark Twain. Large bowls of koushari. Cheap.

Lux, Sharia 26 July, near the intersection with Sherif, downtown. I think this was the first place I ever had an Egyptian meal. Kousharis cost next to nothing.

Khan el Khalili, 5 Sikket el Bedestane, the main east-west street, running through the centre of Khan el Khalili. Run by Oberoi hotels and has an outdoor sitting area for coffee and tea while inside amidst Oriental decor meals and mezes are served. Fairly expensive.

Abu Shakra, 69 Qasr el Aini, at the south end, about 3 km from Midan el Tahrir, near the bridge crossing over to Roda at the Manyal Palace. The epitome of its type, in marble and alabaster — also a strict Muslim establishment, serving no alcoholic beverages and closed Fridays and during Ramadan. The specialities are kofta and kebab, though sometimes pigeon and grilled chicken are also available. Usually (though not always) the food is excellent. Inexpensive to moderate.

Coffee shops, tea rooms and drink and snack bars abound, convenient for resting, cooling off and perhaps a light meal during the day:

The cafés in the major hotels have the advantage of being open 24 hours; also, they are air-conditioned. There is a minimum charge. **Le Café** at the Meridien is marvellous for its Nile views; the **lounge at Shepheard's** is a comfortable and civilised place for afternoon tea; while the Nile Hilton gets credit for its **Taverne du Champ de Mars**, a fin de siècle Brussels tavern, dismantled and reconstructed on the ground floor of the hotel. Beer, spirits and snacks are served from noon to 2am, and a reasonably priced buffet meal at evening.

Cairo Tower, Gezira island. Coffee, tea, beer, a snack are all available up top, at a slight surcharge for having got it up there, but the atmosphere is pleasant, the views wonderful.

Brazilian Coffee Shop, 38 Sharia Talaat Harb and 12 Sharia 26 July. Open from 7am to midnight, this is where to come if you care about coffee. The beans are freshly ground (unground beans can be taken away), the espresso, cappucino, café au lait — or almost any other way of drinking coffee — are excellent.

The Indian Tea Centre, off the passageway at 23 Sharia Talaat Harb. An inexpensive place where snacks are also served, though this is principally a tea room, with imported Indian teas and Indian-style pastries.

Groppi has three branches, at Midan Talaat Harb, on Sharia Adli, and in Heliopolis. It is **Garden Groppi**, as the one at the Midan el Opera end of Sharia Adli is called, that was so famous amongst British servicemen during the Second World War, and its outdoor café remains a pleasant place to sit by day or evening. There is a delicatessen here too, selling cold cuts, pastas, jams and bottles of wine.

Lappas, 17 Sharia Qasr el Nil, is a Groppi-like place of Groppi-like vintage, popular amongst those who do not want to be disturbed.

Café Riche, on Sharia Talaat Harb near the midan and next to the Brazilian Coffee Shop at No. 38, with a nondescript indoor restaurant (very cheap) and an outdoor café, frequented by Cairo's literati and where Nasser, Sadat and other officers met while planning the 1952 coup.

In wandering around the streets, either in modern or Islamic Cairo, you will encounter numerous simple establishments for having a snack, even a meal, and certainly a refreshing mint tea. There are also peripatetic street vendors, good for drinks though perhaps less so for food which may not be particularly clean. In buying anything to eat, always be sure the place has running water — if so, a modicum of hygiene can be counted upon. Forget the Cokes and 7-Ups for a change; instead pause for fresh guava, mango, orange, sugar cane or strawberry juice (after you have drunk it you scoop the strawberries from the glass with a spoon).

Finally, the café to go to when wandering round Khan el Khalili is the famous **Fishawi's** in a small alley near the Sayyidna Hussein Mosque. Here you sit on cane chairs at marble-topped tables in a narrow passage lined with mirrors, and as coffees pass by on brass trays you are propositioned with a shoeshine, a device for making catcalls, a woman's song accompanied by a tambourine, and necklaces of jasmine flowers, their scent thick on the night air.

ENTERTAINMENT

For up-to-date listings of entertainments in Cairo, get a copy of *Cairo Today*, the city's monthly English-language magazine.

Nightclubs in the main international hotels usually offer a programme of both Oriental and Western acts, eg a first-class Egyptian belly dancer followed by some unemployed London showgirls pretending to be from Las Vegas or Paris. Fifi Abdou, however, usually puts on a one-woman show, one moment the most graceful and subtle of belly dancers, the next moment a typhoon — it is well worth finding out where she is appearing.

Some other nightclubs, like those along the Pyramids Road (Sharia al-Ahram) and a few downtown will stage a more purely Egyptian programme, and these, even if sometimes second-rate, can be de-

lightful. A belly dancer or two will be followed by an Egyptian singer and several variety acts: human contortionists, laid back finger-cymbal players or a dull Lebanese riding a bicycle across a wire 2 metres above the stage. There is something in this of the Arab patronage of the popular mysteries, and one place to try is the **Scheherazade** at the Midan Orabi end of Sharia Alfi, downtown.

At **discos** you skip live entertainment, Western or Oriental, and twitch instead to the vibrating recorded music. Some of the best places for this are **Jackie's** at the Nile Hilton and **Regine's** (of Paris, London and New York fame) at the El Gezirah Sheraton (but both of these are open only to members or residents and their guests); also the **Saddle Room** at the Mena House Oberoi, and **After Eight**, at the end of a passageway at 6 Sharia Qasr el Nil, downtown. The food here is very good. Closed July and August.

Casinos (admission only to non-Egyptians) are found at the Meridien, the Marriott, the Mena House, the Hiltons, the Cairo and El Gezirah Sheratons, and the Heliopolis Movenpick Hotel. Play is in US dollars, free drinks for punters, doors close at dawn.

Many events with a Western content in the **performing arts** are arranged by foreign cultural organisations:
The British Council, 192 Sharia el Nil, Agouza. Tel: 3453281.
The Goethe Institute, 5 Sharia Abdel Salam Aref. Tel: 759877.
The French Cultural Centre, 1 Sharia Madraset el Huquq el Fransia. Tel: 3553725.
The American Center, 4 Sharia Ahmed Regheb, Garden City. Tel: 3549601.

These can tell you about films, theatre and dance productions, concerts, etc, in which they are involved or know something about.

A few Egyptian activities worth knowing about:
The National Troupe and the **Reda Troupe**, both folk dance troupes, who perform regularly at the Balloon Theatre, Sharia 26 July at Sharia Nil, Agouza. Tel: 3477457.

The **Arabic Music Troupe**, Tel: 742864, which performs at the Gumhuria Theatre, 12 Sharia Gumhuria, downtown.

The **Folkloric Orchestra of Egypt**, which performs with ancient Egyptian instruments, may be found at various venues. Tel: 735153 for information.

Note that with the recent opening of the **new Opera House** (The Egyptian Education and Culture Centre) at the Gezira Exhibition Grounds on Gezira island, some of the above activities and certainly many others will now be taking place there. Contact the Tourist Office for general information.

Cinemas are mostly located around Midans Talaat Harb and Orabi, and several are likely to be showing English-language films, subtitled in Arabic. The *Egyptian Gazette* carries listings. The problem is that the Egyptians, being able to read the subtitles, do not have to listen to the dialogue. Instead the audience chatters throughout the film, which often has its sound turned down anyway, so that you will be lucky to hear much of it — perhaps not so important when considering the entertainment potential of the audience. Tickets are cheap, and all seats are reserved. You should buy your tickets several hours in advance of the performance you intend seeing, as seats go very quickly.

It is the **popular mysteries** — the man staging a backstreet show with a snake and a guinea pig or a marriage procession of loud cries and ribald song strolling down the middle of a road — that are most entertaining in Cairo. Two fixtures appealing at this level are the **Egyptian National Circus**, a good one-ring affair usually found at Agouza by the 26 July Bridge (check with the Tourist Office for details); and the **Cairo Puppet Theatre** in Midan Ataba, at the southeast end of Ezbekieh Gardens, its season from October to May, with nightly performances at 6.30 as well as Friday and Sunday shows at 11am. The puppet shows are in Arabic, which hardly matters as it is easy to follow the action, and which anyway adds to the enchantment of the productions, appealing to adults and children alike.

It is probably best to approach the son et lumiere at the Pyramids on this level too, therefore so much the better if you go to the Arabic programme, not an English-language one. The **Sound and Light** show (say this to a taxi driver and you will be taken straight there) is presented twice nightly, at 7.30 and 8.30:

Monday: English/French
Tuesday: French/Italian
Wednesday: English/French
Thursday: Arabic/English
Friday: English/French
Saturday: English/Spanish
Sunday: French/German

Seating for the Sound and Light is facing the Sphinx; if you do not go by taxi, you can take the 800 or 900 bus from Midan el Tahrir, terminating at the Mena House Oberoi, and then backtrack on foot through the village at the edge of the escarpment, a 15-minute walk — though you can shorten the hike by getting off the bus along the Pyramids Road when you see (on your left) the sign for the Sound and Light, about 1000 metres before the Mena House Hotel.

After all that high- and low-lifing, you might like some effortless recreation. It is very pleasant, especially at evening, to sail up and down the Nile in a **felucca**. These can be hired by Shepheard's Hotel and at the Meridien.

SHOPPING

While shopping at the bazaar stalls is a matter of haggling over prices, shops and department stores in the modern part of Cairo sell at **fixed prices**. Except in shops found in the arcades of major hotels, prices are usually marked in Arabic numerals, and are often stated in piastres (100PT = LE1). So an item priced at 1000 is likely to be 1000PT or LE10. Usually, common sense will tell whether piastres or pounds is intended.

Opening hours for most shops are from 9am to 1pm and from 5pm till 8pm or later, though some may remain open continuously throughout the day, particularly in Khan el Khalili. Some shops will close on Fridays, others on Sundays. During Ramadan, shop hours are likely to be from 9.30am to 3.30pm and from 8 to 10pm or even later.

In the bazaars, price is usually what you agree on after a bout of **bargaining**. A stallkeeper will always ask more than he expects to get; the traditional response is to offer half as much. After several minutes, perhaps half an hour, a price midway between the extremes is agreed. That is the traditional way, but the visitor's impatience or foolishness can spoil the market, traders asking for and getting far more than their goods are worth. This is particularly true of hawkers at places like the Pyramids, and every now and again it is worth making a ridiculous counter-offer, perhaps only one-tenth of the asking price ... and finding it immediately accepted.

Hawkers at tourist sights are taking advantage of their isolation and yours in demanding exorbitant amounts. The virtue of a bazaar is that there is plenty of competition. In Khan el Khalili you will find all the copperware, all the spices, all the wood and mother-of-pearl inlay, etc, in the same area, and you should browse around, examining the goods, asking the prices, getting a feel for the market. Try to be dispassionate; the more you want something the more you are likely to pay for it. A good technique is to bargain first over something you do *not* want and then casually to start bargaining over what you do want — almost as though you did not want anything and just bargained for the sport. It *is* a sport and there are rules as well as tricks of the game. Your first extreme counter-offer will be laughed at and you may feel silly; do not worry, this is part of the game. After a few offers and counter-offers, walk out. If the shop or stall owner stops you, it means he thinks there is still a deal to be made; if he does not you may have learnt you are aiming at too low a price — go back later, or go to another shop, with an adjusted view of the item's worth. The essence of a bargain, of course, is not to arrive at some formula fraction of the original asking price, but to feel that you have paid the right price, a price you could not have bettered elsewhere, a price that makes the item worth it to you.

Clothing will be found in the hotel shops, shops in the downtown area (Sharias Talaat Harb and 26 July, for example), boutiques in Zamalek, Heliopolis and downtown, and in the big department stores: **Chemla**, 11 Sharia 26 July, where low prices are more important than quality; **Cicurel**, 3 Sharia 26 July, for quality and higher prices; **Omar Effendi**, a good department store with several branches — on Sharia Talaat Harb on Midan el Tahrir, on Sharia Adli near Sharia Talaat Harb, and also at Heliopolis and Dokki. Sizes are continental.

Shoes are found in the plethora of shoeshops along Sharia Qasr el Nil, Talaat Harb and 26 July.

The **galabiyya**, the full-length traditional garment of Egyptian men, is popular with both male and female visitors as comfortable casual wear. Fancier versions can also serve as evening wear for women. There are three basic styles: the *baladi* or peasant style, with wide sleeves and a low rounded neckline; the *saudi* style, more form-fitting, with a high-buttoned neck and cuffed sleeves; and the *efrangi* or foreign style, looking like a shirt with collar and cuffs but reaching all the way down to the floor. Several shops sell galabiyyas along Sharia Talaat Harb between Midan Talaat Harb and Sharia 26 July, and also the department stores. Fancier ones are at **Ammar**, 26 Sharia Qasr el Nil, and at **Atlas** in Khan el Khalili. Both are fixed price. Atlas is on Sikket el Badestane, the main east-west street through the bazaar.

Fabric, either for galabiyyas (Atlas and other good stores will tailor-make them for you, either from their own or your fabric) or to take home, is found in variety and quality at **Omar Effendi** (see *Clothing* above); **Salon Vert**, Sharia Qasr el Nil; or **Ouf** in el Mashhad el Hussein — heading south along Sharia Muizz and approaching Sharia al-Azhar, take the first right after Sharia el Muski/Sharia Gohar el Qaid and the first left; Ouf is on the right down this alley. Each of these stores also sell off-the-peg galabiyyas.

Weavings, carpets, tents and tapestries require further adventures if you want the best. In fact, Egypt is not particularly well-known for carpets, and if you are going to Aswan you should look around there first for small rugs and weavings. Old rugs are from time to time auctioned off, and you should look in the *Egyptian Gazette* for announcements. Carpets and rugs are found in Khan el Khalili and at **El Fatarani** and **Kazarouni**, both on Sharia Qasr el Nil.

Tent-making, on the other hand, is a Cairene speciality, and you should go to the **Street of the Tentmakers** immediately south of Bab Zuwayla. There are 6 or 7 workshops along this covered section of medieval Cairo's major north-south street, creating beautiful applique tents used at mosques or street festivals (and funerals). Some are decorated with scenes of pharaonic or Islamic themes, but the best have abstract arabesque designs or intricate calligraphy. Not that you have to buy a tent; they are made in sections and you can buy a piece about big enough to serve as a pillow cover.

Two villages outside Cairo are centres of the best tapestry-weaving in Egypt. **Harraniyya**, about 3 km along the canal road from Giza to Saqqara, was developed by the late Ramses Wissa Wassef; he taught the children how to card, dye and spin their own wool, and weave it into tapestries of their own design, usually village scenes, primitive and boldly coloured. Harraniyya's tapestries are now world-famous, and the workshop, on the right of the road, continues to be run by Wassef's wife. Tapestries cannot actually be bought here, however; for that you must go to **Senouhi**, 54 Sharia Abdel Khalek Sarwat, 5th floor, in downtown Cairo. This is also one of the best places to buy jewellery and (genuine) antiques. The other village is **Kardassa**, about 3 km off Sharia al-Ahram (turn right several hundred metres before the Mena House at the Pyramids, at the sign for Andrea's Restaurant). Here you can buy tapestries, and also bedspreads, rugs, shirts, dresses and black Bedouin dresses with bright cross-stitching — usually old, with a patchwork look after repairs, and becoming quite expensive and rare.

There are numerous **jewellery** shops in Sharia Abdel Khalek Sarwat (near Garden Groppi) and in the small street leading off it, Sikket el Manakh. And of course, there are numerous jewellers in Mouski and Khan el Khalili. By and large, Egyptian jewellery is disappointing, much of it mimicking the more obvious pharaonic motifs (cartouche, ankh, Eye of Horus), and those of Islamic motif showing little popular imagination — hands and eyes for warding off evil, or as pieces inscribed with 'Allah'. It may seem at first exotic but is limited and grows tiresome, while anything outside these two motifs is usually conceived in bad taste. **Senouhi**, 54 Sharia Abdel Khalek Sarwat, 5th floor, will have the finest selection.

Brass and copper work has long been a Cairo tradition, the standards still high today. The best place for it is in Khan el Khalili along or just off Sharia Muizz, south of the Madrasa of Qalaun. Small plates intended as ornaments and candlesticks, gongs, lamps, mugs and pitchers are the easiest to carry off — though be sure that anything you intend to drink out of is coated on the inside with another metal, like silver, as brass or copper in contact with some substances can be highly poisonous. The finest items, however, are the big brass trays which can serve as table tops (wooden stands are available).

Inlay of **wood and mother-of-pearl**, and also **leatherwork**, are also plentiful in the bazaar. Egyptian leather is not the best, however. The most common items are handbags, suitcases and hassocks. Also, more interesting than useful or comfortable, are camel saddles (for buying a camel, see below). Wooden trays, boards (including backgammon and chess boards) and boxes inlaid with mother-of-pearl and coloured bits of wood are not quite as good as those made in Syria, but are intricate and beautiful enough. Mashrabiyyas, those intricate screens found in old Cairene houses, made from bits of wood fitted together without nails or glue, occasionally come on sale in the bazaars.

Muski **glass**, usually turquoise or dark brown and recognisable by its numerous air bubbles, has been handblown in Cairo since the Middle Ages, and is now turned out as ash trays, candlesticks and glasses. It is inexpensive, but also very fragile. Try Sayed Abd al Raouf, 8 Khan el Khalili. Tel: 91466. The best **nargilehs** (hubblybubblies) will have glass, rather than brass, bottoms. For these, try around the Street of Coppersmiths, south of the Madrasa of Qalaun.

Alabaster statuettes, also vases and scarabs, are produced and are cheapest in Luxor; **baskets** made of palm fronds are best bought in the Fayyum, though platter-shaped basketry, woven in brilliant colours, should be sought in Luxor or Aswan. **Aswan** also is excellent for woven fabrics, for ivory, ebony and spices, and indeed it has the best bazaar outside of Cairo.

Antiquities offered to you on the street are bound to be fake. Which is not to say there are not any genuine pharaonic, Coptic and Islamic artefacts around, but they will cost a lot of money and your only guarantee of their authenticity is to buy them from a shop displaying a **licence from the Department of Antiquities**. The shop will also give you a certificate of authenticity. There are several such shops in modern Cairo and in Khan el Khalili; the best is the already-mentioned **Senouhi**, 54 Sharia Abdel Khalek Sarwat, downtown. There are more shops in **Luxor**, with prices lower than in Cairo.

One of the most enjoyable excursions, whether you intend to buy or not, is to wander through the **spice market** which lies off Sharia Muizz between Sharia el Muski (Sharia Gohar el Qaid) and Sharia al-Azhar. There are bottles of perfume essences, boxes of incense and bags of herbs and spices. Also there is kohl, a black eye cosmetic. The fragrances, and the quality of the light in awninged alleyways, awaken sensation.

A similarly enjoyable excursion (though the fragrance is not the same) is to the **camel bazaar**, northwest of the city just beyond Embaba. In Arabic it is the *Souk el Gimaal,* where camel herders from the Sudan bring their animals for sale, and farmers bring their horses, donkeys, goats and other livestock. The market is every Friday and starts very early: get there by 7 or 8am. You cross over to the west bank of the Nile and head north along the corniche (Sharia el Nil), going past the 26 July Bridge until you come to a square. Here you turn left, away from the river,

following Sharia Sudan for several kilometres. After a housing estate on your left (built for felaheen pouring into Cairo), a road goes off to the right across railway tracks. Take this, and immediately after crossing the tracks turn left. You will parallel a walled-in area on your right and soon meet up with people and animals heading for the market. Eventually, a road to your left crosses railway tracks again; take this and then immediately turn right. The market entrance will be on your left.

Books on Egypt and Egyptology, but also light holiday reading in paperback, are found in the major hotel bookshops, which also sell magazines and newspapers. There is also the shop in the **Egyptian Museum**. Other bookshops around town are: **Reader's Corner**, 33 Sharia Abdel Khalek Sarwat, downtown (with a branch at the Nile Hilton), has English, French and some German books, as well as old and reproduction prints (eg by David Roberts). **Lehnert and Landrock**, 44 Sharia Sherif, near Sharia Adli — English though principally German books on Egypt, while magazines and paperbacks are almost all German. They also sell (under their own imprint) the excellent Kuemmerly & Frey map of Egypt. And they do a map of Cairo, somewhat better than the one issued free by the Tourist Office, and with the virtue of a street index. **Madbouly**, Midan Talaat Harb, with English, French and some German books downstairs. Books about Egypt published by the American University in Cairo Press are obtainable at all the above shops, but you can also visit the **AUC Bookshop** at the university, 113 Sharia Qasr el Aini (entrance through Mohammed Mahmoud Gate), not far from Midan el Tahrir. Tel: 3542964.

INFORMATION

There are **Tourist Information Offices** at the airport (Tel. 966475), downtown (head office) at 5 Sharia Adli, at the Ezbekieh end (Tel: 923000) and at the Pyramids on Sharia al-Ahram (Tel: 850259). They can provide brochures, a good free map of Cairo (with practical information on the reverse) and copies of *Cairo by Night and Day,* filled with listings of hotels, restauants, entertainments, travel agents, embassies, etc.

The people working at their offices are charming and helpful (most helpful is the head office), but they are used to tourists going to the obvious places by the slickest means, and so have to be pressed for alternative information. If you do not want a tour, do not want to take taxis everywhere, then make it clear that you do not mind taking the local bus or train to Memphis, Saqqara, Meidum, etc, and they will come up with the information you require.

The **Tourist Police** are found browsing about ports of entry, in the bazaars and at tourist sights, and are recognised by a small blue strip on their left chest and a green armband with 'Tourist Police' written in Arabic and English. Otherwise they wear the normal police uniform, which is black in winter and white in summer. They usually speak at least 2 foreign languages and are helpful with information while doing their best to ensure that tourists are not fleeced. They are based at the airport (Tel: 965239), at the Midan Ramses railway station (Tel: 753555), at the Pyramids near the Mena House (Tel: 850259), in Midan el-Hussein on the edge of Khan el Khalili (Tel: 904827) and downtown at 5 Sharia Adli, towards Ezbekieh Gardens (Tel: 912644).

A useful source of information, as well as a brief up to date review of the news, is the *Egyptian Gazette* (published as the *Egyptian Mail* on Saturdays), Cairo's daily English-language **newspapers**. (In French there are 2 dailies. *Le Progres Egyptien* and *Journal d'Egypte*.) The *Gazette's* 'What's On' columns will tell you of current and forthcoming concerts, gallery shows, films, etc, while its 'Round and About' columns list opening times at museums and tourist sights. There are also cinema, restaurant, nightclub and travel advertisements; and television and radio listings. Also useful is the monthly English-language **magazine**, *Cairo Today*. This contains listings for entertainments, restaurants, sights, etc, while the articles will give you an in-depth look at various aspects of Cairene life. It has listings too for Alexandria.

Your own **hotel desk** or those at the major hotels, as well as such **travel agents** as Thomas Cook and American Express, and your own **embassy** can all be useful sources of varied information.

TRAVEL

The general information here on Cairo travel is supplemented by further details in subsequent chapters.

Though it is possible to get a public bus or minibus **from Cairo Airport (Matar al-Qahira) into town** (see below), for speed, comfort and convenience (not to mention your first hair-raising experience of driving in Egypt) it is close to infinitely preferable to take a limousine or taxi. Taxi drivers will be lurking in the background somewhere and it is usually possible to get a better price out of them; but you will first be presented with a rank of limousines (Mercedes and Volvos in fact) whose drivers will demand at least LE20 to anywhere in town, more to hotels out by the Pyramids. (The taxi fare *out* to the airport from town should be no more than LE15.)

Taxis, which are black and white Fiats or Peugeots usually, and have meters, are in theory a cheap way of getting about within Cairo. But Cairo taxi drivers hold to an opposite theory when giving rides to tourists. Occasionally you will get into a metered taxi and the driver will actually turn the meter on, in which case you will be amazed at how cheap it is, amazed at the man's innocence, and can leave it to your conscience whether you will pay him according to the metered reading. More often than not the driver will 'forget', or say his meter is broken, or simply refuse to turn it on. You have the right to insist. In fact you will soon learn not to bother arguing or even raising the matter, and will instead devise your own rule of thumb. If say from Midan el Tahrir you go to Zamalek, Khan el Khalili or Midan Ramses (2 to 2.5 km), pay LE3. From Midan el Tahrir to Old Cairo (5 km), pay LE5. And from Midan el Tahrir to the Pyramids (11 km), pay LE10. You can feel generous in knowing you are paying well over the proper fare. Your driver of course will have a fit. You then make noises about calling the police. Your driver will calm down, but even if he does not, ignore him. Taking taxis in Cairo is like bargaining in Khan el Khalili; you will soon get a feel for arriving at a fare acceptable to both of you.

There are also unmetered **limousines** (Volvos and Mercedes usually) operating from the major hotels. Their fares are posted in the lobby and are fixed. Though these fares are what you are bound to pay the limousine when leaving the hotel, they can serve as a guide as to how much *less* you ought to pay the taxi driver who brings you back or takes you from one point to another during the day.

The cheapest way of getting about within and around Cairo is by **public bus**. There are the **large red and white or black and white buses** which rarely cost more than 15PT a ride. Their major terminus is in Midan el Tahrir directly in front of the Nile Hilton. They are crowded, uncomfortable, difficult to get on, even more difficult to get off, and the main value they hold for the visitor is the entertainment derived from watching Cairenes embark and disembark through the windows. Some routes from Midan el Tahrir (indicated in Arabic numerals on the front of the bus): 8 and 900 to the Pyramids, 16 to Midan Dokki and Agouza, 400 to the airport (24-hour service on the hour), 174 to the Citadel, 600 to Zamalek.

Also there are the **small orange and white minibuses** at about 50PT a ride. Their major terminus is also Midan el Tahrir but over towards the Mugamaa, ie near Tahrir Bridge. They are comfortable and never crowded as standing is not allowed. 24, 27 and 35 all go to Midan Ramses, while 27 goes to the airport, 54 goes to the Citadel, and 82 goes to the Pyramids.

There are **river buses** too, making frequent runs from Maspero Station (on the Corniche in front of the Television Tower Building which is just north of the Ramses Hilton) clear down to Old Cairo, with stops at either side of the river along the way. There are also boats from Maspero Station north to the Nile barrages from 7am to 5pm daily.

But the great boon to visitors (not to mention Cairenes) is the completion of the new **Metro**. It is the first underground railway in Africa or the Arab world and it is excellent. For about 30PT and up, according to distance, you can travel quickly, cleanly and in comfort between important points like Midan Ramses (Metro station Mubarak), Midan el Tahrir (Sadat) and Old Cairo (Mari Girgis). Two further intersecting lines are planned.

If driving extensively in and around Cairo and farther afield, it could be worthwhile **hiring a car**. You need to be at least 25, must have an International Driver's Licence, and should have a sense of adventure: Cairenes, you will have observed, meander from one side of the road to the other as the fancy takes them, and the only way to survive is to meander with them. Both international and local car hire firms are represented; most of the major hotels will have agency desks. Avis is at the Meridien, Nile Hilton and Cairo Sheraton; Hertz at the Ramses Hilton; Europcar at the Marriott; while all these plus Budget and Inter Rent have desks at the airport and offices in town. It is worthwhile checking that everything essential actually works (like brakes) and that note is taken beforehand of any dents, etc. It is advisable to book a day in advance.

The alternative to public transport or car hire are **tours by car or bus with guide**. There are morning, afternoon and evening tours to the Antiquities Museum, the Pyramids and Sphinx, Memphis and Saqqara, Islamic Cairo, Old Cairo, Cairo by night with nightclub, etc. **Thomas Cook**, 17 Sharia Mahmoud Basiony, near Midan Talaat Harb (Tel: 743955), has a comprehensive list of tours by car with driver/guide. The more passengers, the less expensive per person. **American Express**, 15 Sharia Qasr el Nil, a short walk from Midan el Tahrir (Tel: 750444), and with branches at the Meridien, Marriott, Cairo Sheraton, and the Nile and Ramses Hiltons, does coach tours which for 1 or 2 people will work out about 40% cheaper than Cook's tours. These companies also offer **tours throughout Egypt by rail or air**.

Possibly cheaper and more comprehensive is Egypt's own tourist company **Misr Tours**, 7–9 Sharia Talaat Harb (Tel: 750010 or 750032), with an office also at 43 Qasr el Nil, and branches elsewhere. They are efficient, and can arrange accommodation, cruises, tours, and air, sea, road and rail travel.

Long-distance bus services are operated by various companies and depart from various termini according to destination.
Alexandria: The Super Jet luxury service (about hourly from 6am to 1am) departs from the airport, from Midan Ismailia in Heliopolis, from Midan el Tahrir (by the Nile Hilton) and from Midan Giza (not far from the Cairo Sheraton).
Alexandria and Mersa Matruh: The West Delta Bus Company service departs from Midan el Tahrir (by the Nile Hilton) and from Midan Ismailia in Helopolis (for Alexandria only). Daily 7.30am departure to Mersa Matruh in winter, several morning departures to Mersa Matruh in summer. Hourly departures to Alexandria from 5.30am to 6.30pm (winter) and 9pm (summer).
The Delta and the Canal Towns: The East Delta Bus Company service (about hourly) departs from al-Kulali terminal off Midan Ramses.
Upper Egypt, Fayyum and Red Sea: The Upper Egyptian Bus Company service departs from the Ahmed Helmi terminal across the tracks (north) from Ramses Station. Several departures daily to Upper Egypt and Hurghada, every 15 minutes to the Fayyum.
The Inner Oases: The Upper Egyptian Bus Company service (at least once a day) departs from the al-Azhar terminal, 45 Sharia al-Azhar at Sharia Port Said.
Sinai: The East Delta Bus Company service (at least once a day) departs from the Sinai terminal in Abbassia, 2.5 km east of Midan Ramses.
  All services (except the most frequent, eg to Alexandria, the Fayyum, the Canal) should be booked a day, preferably two days, in advance.

Long-distance service taxis also have their different termini according to destination.
Alexandria: al-Kulali terminal off Midan Ramses.

The Delta: Ahmed Helmi terminal immediately north of Ramses Station.
Ismailia, Suez and Sinai: al-Kulali terminal.
Red Sea: Ramses Station and Midan Giza (not far from the Cairo Sheraton).
Fayyum: Midan Giza.
The Inner Oases: al-Kulali, Ahmed Helmi and Midan el Tahrir.
Upper Egypt: Ahmed Helmi (change at Assiut for points south).

Cairo's main train station is **Ramses Station** (Mahattat Ramses) at Midan Ramses. From here there are trains north into the Delta and to Alexandria, and south to Upper Egypt, eg Minya, Assiut, Luxor and Aswan. **Limoun Station** (Mahattat Limoun), adjacent to Ramses Station, handles departures to the Canal towns.
  Wagons-Lits carriages operate overnight to Luxor and Aswan and tickets can be bought at Ramses Station; otherwise the reservations office for Compagnie Internationale des Wagons-Lits is at 48 Sharia Giza. Tel: 3487354.
  Wagons-Lits sleepers should be booked a week in advance. All first class travel should be booked at least a day in advance.
  Students with an ISIC, and YHA members, can obtain a 50% reduction on rail fairs (except Wagons-Lits).

Overland travel between Egypt and Israel is by daily luxury coach; contact Travco, 13 Sharia Mahmoud Azmi, Zamalek; Tel: 3404308. Tickets for the **Sudan** ferry can be purchased at the Nile Navigation Co office inside Ramses railway station (see *Aswan*).

Most **airline offices** are in the vicinity of Midan el Tahrir, eg:
Air France, Midan Talaat Harb (Tel: 743516).
Air Sinai, Nile Hilton Centre (Tel: 743488).
British Airways, 1 Sharia Abdel Salam Aref, on the corner of Midan el Tahrir (Tel: 762914).
Egyptair, Nile Hilton (Tel: 750666).
El Al, 5 Sharia al Maqrizi, Zamalek (Tel: 811620).
KLM, 11 Sharia Qasr el Nil (Tel: 740717).

Lufthansa, 9 Sharia Talaat Harb (Tel: 3930366).
Olympic, 23 Sharia Qasr el Nil (Tel: 3931459).
PIA, 22 Sharia Qasr el Nil (Tel: 3924134).
SAS, 2 Sharia Champollion (Tel: 753546).
Sudan Airways, 1 Sharia el Boustan (Tel: 747398).
Swissair, 22 Sharia Qasr el Nil (Tel: 3921522).
TWA, 1 Sharia Qasr el Nil, on the corner of Midan el Tahrir (Tel: 749900).
United, 16 Sharia Adli (Tel: 3905090).

The time-honoured way of making a progress through Egypt is to **cruise along the Nile. Hilton, Sheraton** and **Oberoi** all offer year-round sailings between Luxor and Aswan, taking in Dendera and Abydos too, and usually lasting 4 nights, 5 days.

There are an increasing number of local cruise operators, offering similar short sailings but also the full Cairo to Aswan voyage, and at rates substantially lower than those of the international hotels. Try **Eastmar**, 13 Sharia Qasr el Nil (Tel: 753216), **Presidential Nile Cruises**, 13 Sharia Marashly (Tel: 3400517) and **Sunboat Cruises**, 5A Sharia El Bustan (Tel: 765432).

OTHER THINGS

The **Central Post Office** is at Midan el Ataba, near the Ezbekieh Gardens, and is open 24 hours daily. Other post offices are open from 8.30am to 3pm daily except Fridays. Most hotels can supply you with stamps for cards and letters. There is a good chance that post cards sent home will arrive after you do: air mail *can* take 10 days to Europe, more to the US. Mail is faster if posted at one of the luxe hotels.

To send a parcel out of Egypt requires an export licence. You must obtain this at the Central Post Office, Midan el Ataba. Go there with your parcel unwrapped; go to the third building on the left in the rear of the complex; here it will be inspected and for a small fee sewn into a cloth cover; for a further small fee you will be guided through the remaining formalities and paperwork. Your parcel must not weigh more than 20 kilos nor exceed 1.5 metres in any direction. If sending home fabrics

or souvenirs you have bought, ask first at the shop whether they will do it for you. Most shops catering to tourists have export licences and are reliable.

You can **receive mail** at your hotel or care of American Express (if you have their travellers cheques or card) or care of your embassy (the envelope should be marked 'Visitors Mail'). American Express will forward any mail arriving for you after your departure for LE3 or so.

Telegrams in English or French can be sent from the PTT offices on the north side of Midan el Tahrir (open 24 hours daily), or in Sharia Alfi or Sharia Adli — or from major hotels. Night letters (no service to London) cost about half as much as full rate telegrams.

Most 3- and 4-star hotels and all 5-star hotels have **telex** and **fax** services available to guests.

Local telephone calls can be made from some cigarette kiosks or from shops and restaurants — or from your hotel. **Long distance calls** can be made from major hotels or from Midan el Tahrir (north side), Sharia Alfi or Sharia Adli PTT offices. The one at Midan el Tahrir is open 24 hours daily.

To exchange money, go to Thomas Cook, American Express, or to the banks in the major hotels — all the 5-star hotels have 24-hour banks. For a full-scale commercial banking service, there is Barclays Bank International, 12 Midan el Sheikh Youssef (PO Box 2335). Garden City, Cairo. Tel: 3549415 and 3541408.

If you have Egyptian pounds which you want to convert back into foreign currency before your departure, you can go to any bank (eg the one at the airport) and show them a receipt indicating that you had previously converted at least such an amount from foreign currency into Egyptian pounds. They will then subtract what they reckon you should have spent per day, with the result that you will probably be stuck with a load of unwanted Egyptian currency. Moral: never change too much at any one time, and what you do change, spend.

For **medical care**, ask at your hotel. Most will be able to refer you to a doctor or dentist, while some of the major hotels will have a doctor on call. Most Egyptian doctors have been trained in Europe or North America and speak English. Your embassy can also recommend doctors and dentists. In an emergency, the following private hospitals are recommended: the **Anglo-American Hospital** near the Cairo Tower, Gezira (Tel: 3418630), the **Italian Hospital** in Abbassia, northeast of Midan Ramses (Tel: 821433), and the **As Salam International Hospital**, Corniche el Nil, Maadi (Tel: 3638050). All of these are modern and fully-equipped hospitals. But note that it is unusual for any hospital to accept medical insurance: not only should you be prepared to pay cash, but a substantial deposit will be required before you are admitted.

There are several **pharmacists** around Midan el Tahrir and downtown with a wide range of medications not requiring prescriptions — describe your symptoms and, if the ailment is minor, the pharmacist will prescribe on the spot. Both imported medicines and those locally licenced are heavily subsidised by the government. You will probably be able to obtain your favourite drug at a fraction of its usual price. Cosmetics, perfumes and toilet articles are also stocked.

Your **embassy** can assist you by acting as a mail drop, advising on emergency financial and medical problems, effecting emergency communications home, etc. Embassies also encourage visitors, especially those not travelling in large groups, to register with them. It should be noted, however, that embassies cannot lend money to **stranded travellers** — though they can find ways of helping you. If stranded, you can go to Thomas Cook, American Express, Barclays International or the Nile Hilton and have them send a telegram or telex requesting your bank or persons at home to arrange the transfer of money to you in Egypt. This can be accomplished in 2–3 days. Or you can go to an airline office and ask for a pre-paid ticket, the airline cabling whomever you suggest to pay for the ticket home. Authorisation to issue you with a ticket can be received back in Cairo within 2 days.

A full list of embassies can be found in *Cairo Night and Day*; a few are listed below.

Australia, Cairo Plaza, Corniche el Nil, near the Ramses Hilton. (Tel: 777900).

Canada, 6 Sharia Mohammed Fahmi el Sayed, Garden City (Tel: 3543110).

Ireland, 3 Abu el Feda Tower, Zamalek. (Tel: 3408264).

Israel, 6 Sharia Ibn Malek, Giza (Tel: 729329).

Sudan, 3 Sharia Ibrahim, Garden City (Tel: 3545034).

United Kingdom, 7 Sharia Ahmed Raghab, Garden City (Tel: 3540850).

United States, 5 Sharia Latin America, Garden City (Tel: 3557371).

There is no **airport departure tax**. There are **banks** at the airport where you can convert your Egyptian pounds back into hard currency (lotsa luck!). The **duty-free shop**, which is available to *arriving* as well as departing passengers, sells cigarettes, tobacco, liquor, perfume, etc, but will not accept Egyptian money.

If you want a **view of the Pyramids**, sit on the right-hand side of the plane.

THE NILE, OLD CAIRO AND FUSTAT

Old Cairo and Fustat are about 5 km south of Midan el Tahrir from where you can take the metro, though you can also catch a bus, water bus or taxi (see *Practical Information* at the end of this chapter). Also there are a few places enroute worth noting for those with flexible transport. In any case, Garden City and the northern part of Roda can form a separate excursion, enjoyed on foot.

Along the Nile

A river walk   The Meridien Hotel at Roda's northern tip can be reached across its own bridge from Garden City, and here you can stop for a drink and a commanding view of the Nile. Gardens run along the western bank of the island to El Gama'a Bridge which crosses over the Nile to the Zoological Gardens. From there you can walk back along the west bank of the river through Dokki, visiting the Papyrus Institute on the way, coming up to the Cairo Sheraton and so back to Midan el Tahrir via Gezira.

But a quarter of the way down Roda, its grounds overlooking the smaller eastern branch of the Nile, its entrance however facing the approach road to El Gama'a Bridge, is the **Manyal Palace**, built by Mohammed Ali. It is now a museum. On view is a reception palace, the palace proper, a private mosque and Mohammed Ali's private hunting museum, which includes a table made of elephants' ears and a hermaphrodite goat. That pretty much sets the tone of the place, which is bizarre kitsch. There is also a garden of banyan trees.

To the Nilometer   Coming down the corniche from Midan el Tahrir towards Old Cairo, at a point two or three blocks south of your view across to the Manyal Palace on Roda is a traffic roundabout called **Fumm el Khalig**. This is where the canal, now covered by Sharia Port Said and its southern extension, left the river. There is a large octagonal tower of stone here, once housing great waterwheels which lifted water from the Nile to the level of the Mameluke **aqueduct** which can still be followed almost all the way to the Citadel. At this end, the aqueduct dates only from 1505 and was an extension made necessary by the westward-shifting Nile; the main part of the aqueduct, further east, was built by al-Nasr around 1311.

A further few blocks south is the Malek al-Salih bridge crossing over to the southern end of Roda. At the lower tip of the island is the **Nilometer**, dating from the 9th C, though the superstructure with its Turkish-style conical roof dates from Mohammed Ali's time. The stone-lined pit goes down well below the level of the Nile, though the water entry tunnels have been blocked up and you can descend by steps. At the centre of the pit is a graduated column for determining whether the river would rise enough, not enough, or too much, so announcing the expected fertility of all Egypt over the coming year. A reading of 16 *ells* (8.6 metres) ensured the complete irrigation of the valley; then the Nile crier would broadcast the *Wafa el Nil* or superfluity of the Nile and the dam to the Khalig would be cut amidst great festivity. The Nile used to reach its flood in mid-August, but the High Dam at Aswan now regulates its flow and it keeps a steady level year-round.

Immediately north of the Nilometer is the former Monasterly Palace, now the Centre for Art and Life.

Old Cairo

Old Cairo (*Misr el Qadima* in Arabic) describes the general area, but specifically you want to arrive at the Roman fortress (known in Arabic as *Qasr el Shamah*, Fortress of the Beacon) opposite the Mari Girgis metro station. The section of wall and two towers here formed part of the Roman **fortress of Babylon**, first built in the time of Augustus, added to by Trajan and remodelled by the Byzantines. The technique of dressed stone alternating with courses of brick is typically Roman. The portal between the towers was a water gate and excavation has revealed the original quay 6 metres below present street level, but the Nile has since shifted 400 metres to the west.

Babylon in Egypt

The Coptic Museum. Now the towers mark the entrance to the Coptic Museum, pleasantly set in gardens. It is a charming building, decorated with wooden mashrabiyyas from old Coptic houses, embracing green courtyards, airy and light within, its spirit in keeping with its collection. The exhibits cover Egypt's Christian era, from AD 300 to 1000, and are both religious and secular, linking the art of the pharaonic and Graeco-Roman periods with that of Islam. The museum is arranged in sections, covering stonework, manuscripts, textiles, icons and paintings as well as decorated ivories, woodwork, metalwork, and pottery and glass. Often, as in stone carving and painting, the work is crude, though agreeably naive. High artistic achievement, however, is found in the textiles, and there are many fine chemises, tapis and clothes here embroidered with motifs of St George, or graceful women and gazelles.

The arrangement of the museum, and some highlights:
New Wing, ground floor:
   Room 1: Pre-Christian reliefs and architectural fragments, 3rd and 4th C. The themes are pagan gods, eg Pan and Dionysos.
   Room 2: Again reliefs and fragments, but of the 4th to 6th C and so early Christian. The cross is incorporated at every opportunity, often surrounded by flowers or backed by a shell

The joie de vivre of a Coptic tapestry, 3rd–4th C AD (Room 10, Coptic Museum)

forming the half-dome of a niche — see 7065, a shell with dolphins on either side. Technically the work is similar to the pre-Christian, but there is a sense of excitement at working with the new imagery — Pan and other pagan motifs had become so hackneyed.

Room 3: Reliefs and frescoes, 6th C. See 7118 showing Christ ascending to heaven in a flaming chariot. *Rooms 4 through 8* contain more of the same, including work from Abu Jeremias Monastery at Saqqara.

Room 9: Reliefs and frescoes, from the 6th through the 10th C. See 3962, 10th C Fayyum frescoes, showing Adam and Eve before and after the Fall. On the right they are naked, enjoying the fruit; on the left they clasp fig leaves to their genitals and Adam points accusingly at Eve as if to say 'You made me do it'.

Note throughout the museum the beautifully carved wood ceilings and beams.

New Wing, first floor:

Rooms 10, 11 and 12 all contain textiles, *Room 10* also displaying manuscripts and ostraca; note especially in this room, Case 4, exhibit 7948, the tapestry showing a musician and dancers (3rd–4th C), beautifully observed, fluid, rhythmic, happy. The Copts were at their best in textiles which they developed from ancient Egyptian tradition, adding to it

Graeco-Roman and Sassanid influences. Plants, animals, birds and human beings blend in sumptuous decorative patterns that have a liveliness that Byzantium itself could not rival.

Room 13 contains icons and ivories; *Rooms 14, 15 and 16* display metalwork (including armour and weapons); *Room 17* has objects and several striking frescoes from Nubia.
Courtyard:

You step out from the main museum building into a courtyard like that of a grand Cairo house, planted and with mashrabiyyas round the walls. Across the court is part of the Roman wall and a gate of Babylon; you can descend to the level of the seeping Nile and step along concrete gangways beneath great arches and vaults where once were prisons, stables and a grain mill.
Old Wing:

Entered through the courtyard, the rooms here contain items of wood, pottery and glass. Most agreeable are the mashrabiyyas, fixed together without glue or nails, admitting a diffused light through their intricate Christian patterns.

Coptic churches. The oldest Coptic churches sought security within the fortress walls, and usually they avoid facing onto the street and so are indistinguishable from neighbouring houses. Their main entrances were long ago walled up against attack, entry being through a small side door. Their plan is basilical, with a narthex or porch admitting to an aisled nave with an iconostasis placed across the sanctuary. In seeking out the five churches within the fortress precincts, and also the synagogue, there is interest too in the winding little streets, glimpses within windows and doors, the decorations of the houses, the domes of some as in Upper Egypt, and the atmosphere of remove, of an almost rural village.

Alexandria was the Coptic Rome. Old Cairo was never a city, never a place of monuments, and it is not a ghetto. Copts live throughout Cairo and all over Egypt, and are particularly numerous in Upper Egypt. But especially within these walls it is an old and holy place, to Jews as well as Copts, and although Muslims are in the majority in Old Cairo, there are tens of thousands of Copts as well as a number of Jewish families living in the area.

The Hanging Church

The **Church of El Muallaqa**, the Hanging Church, is so named because it rests on the bastions of the southwest gate into the fortress, its nave suspended above the passage. It is reached by going out from the museum grounds between the two great towers and turning left. Though the church claims origins in the 4th C, it is unlikely that the present structure, which in any case has been rebuilt, would have been built on the walls until the Arab conquest made them redundant. Certainly, it is known to have become the seat of the patriarchate when it was moved from Alexandria to Cairo in the 11th C. The interior of El Muallaqa, with pointed arches, cedar panelling and translucent ivory screens, is intricately decorated — the carved white *marble pulpit* inlaid with marble of red and black is the finest in Egypt. Services are held in the dead Coptic language and in Arabic. On the right, as you come in, is a 10th C icon of the Virgin and Child, Egyptian faces, Byzantine crowns. On the same wall is an ancient icon of St Mark, by tradition the founder of Christianity in Egypt. El Muallaqa is dedicated to the Virgin and is properly called Sitt Mariam, St Mary. Its central sanctuary is dedicated to Christ, its left sanctuary to St George, its right sanctuary to St John the Baptist, scenes from the saints' lives decorating their iconostases.

Now walk back out to the street and turn right so that you pass by the entrance to the museum. Atop one of the Roman towers is the circular Greek Orthodox **Church of St George** (Mari Girgis) rebuilt in 1909 after a fire. It is the seat of the Greek patriarch. Farther along, steps on your right lead down to a narrow street at the level of the early settlement. Walking along this, the Coptic **Convent of Mari Girgis** is on your left. Still farther along, you are obliged to turn left or right. If you turn left into the narrow lane you pass (right) the Coptic **Church of Mari Girgis**, built originally in the 7th C but burnt down in the 19th, only a 14th C hall surviving. The modern church is of no interest. At the end of this lane you come to **El Adra**, the Coptic Church of the Virgin, first built in the 9th C but destroyed and rebuilt in the 18th C. It is known also as Kasriyat el Rihan, meaning pot of basil, a favoured herb of the Greek Orthodox Church. Al-Hakim's mother had been of that faith and for the duration of his reign it was transferred to Orthodox use.

If where you turned left for Al Adra you had instead turned right, you would at once be at **Abu Sarga**, the Coptic Church of St Sergius (which can also be reached by steps down from the ticket kiosk in front of the Coptic Museum). This is possibly the oldest church within the fortress, thought to date from the 5th C, though it was restored and partly rebuilt in **Associations with** the 12th C. European pilgrims are recorded as visiting the **the Holy Family** church from at least the 14th C because of its associations with the Flight into Egypt; steps to the right of the altar lead down to the *crypt*, once a cave, where according to tradition the Holy Family found refuge after fleeing from Herod.

Abu Sarga is typical of early Coptic churches, being a basilica with aisles separated from the nave by two rows of columns which support a high timbered roof. One column is granite, the other 11 are marble, and some bear faded paintings of the apostles, probably dating from the 8th C. Paintings of saints, probably 11th and 12th C, can also be made out within the central apse. A usual feature of early Coptic churches was a basin set in the floor of the narthex, used for Epiphany blessings. It is now boarded over. The central altar screen, inset above with ebony and ivory panels, is 13th C, but a century or so older are the carved wooden panels depicting (right) three warrior saints and (left) the Nativity and the Last Supper, probably once the leaves of a door. There is an icon in the south sanctuary of the Flight into Egypt. The marble pulpit is modern; the original rosewood pulpit and the canopied altar are now in the Coptic Museum.

Turning right out of Abu Sarga and then right at the corner, at the end of the street you see **Sitt Barbara** (St Barbara's) to the left, a synagogue to the right. The Coptic Church of Sitt Barbara was built in the 7th C to a similar pattern as Abu Sarga and like it was restored in Fatimid times. The central screen is 13th C; the icons atop it are 18th C. The marble pulpit is very fine. The relics of St Barbara are in the right-hand sanctuary; she had the misfortune to be born into the 3rd C, daughter of a pagan father, who discovering that she was a Christian, turned her over to the Roman authorities to be tortured and beheaded. Off to the left, as though an annexe, is the separate **Church of SS Cyrus and John**, also beheaded in the 3rd C.

Synagogue of Ben Ezra. This is a neighbourhood temple whose neighbourhood has gone away — left the country or **Oldest synagogue in Egypt** gone to other parts of Cairo. It is a forlorn place, a forgotten outpost, yet it claims a more ancient history than anything else in Old Cairo.

The synagogue is the oldest in Egypt and resembles in its basilical arrangement an early Christian church. The Coptic Church of St Michael did stand here from the 4th to 9th C, but the Copts had to sell it to the Jews to pay Ibn Tulun's tax towards the erection of his mosque. Sources differ as to whether the original church was destroyed or its fabric remains in what the Rabbi of Jerusalem, Abraham Ben Ezra, at least renewed in the 12th C. But the Jews say the site has far older associations than that: here in the 6th C BC Jeremiah preached after Nebuchadnezzar's destruction of Jerusalem, and it was the presence of their community here, they say, that drew the Holy Family to Babylon. For the same reason, say the Copts, the apostles Peter and Mark came here, in proof of this citing I Peter 5:13: 'The church that is at Babylon elected together with you, saluteth you; and so doth Marcus my son'. The rest of Christendom argues that Babylon is here a metaphor for Rome; but there is the suspicion that this interpretation is ingenuous, serving to appropriate Peter to Rome in order there to crown him pope and martyr, legitimating the Vatican's claim to apostolic supremacy.

Ben Ezra's synagogue sits in a small shady garden, its exterior plain, a Star of David in wrought iron over the gate.

Inside there is an arch of ablaq masonry and a small stained-glass window towards the far end above the sort of intricate stone inlay work you would expect to see around the mihrab of a mosque. The synagogue is undergoing extensive restoration, paid for by the Egyptian government and foreign donors.

Nathan Abraham Moishe Cohen lives opposite, and is often found sitting outside passing the time with his friend Ahmed. Since at least 1967 when I first came to this synagogue, Rabbi Cohen (who must be a rabbi by default, as he is illiterate) has been selling charmingly awful postcards of himself at wickedly high prices. Buy one and he may show you exactly where pharaoh's daughter plucked Moses from the bulrushes (I would have mistaken it for a sewer), the Miracle Rock beneath which Jeremiah is supposed to be buried, and tell you how the synagogue once possessed a library of 100,000 books, all gone. Discovered hidden in a genizah in the walls at the end of the 19th C was an ancient Torah, now dispersed throughout the great libraries of the Western world.

Moses in the bulrushes

Turning right out of the synagogue gate, a lane passes an abandoned Jewish school on the right and leads into a **Coptic cemetery**, a complete town of bungalows for the dead.

Fustat

The first mosque in Egypt

Emerging from the garden of the Coptic Museum, or back up the steps from the warren of streets where you have been visiting churches within the fortress walls, turn right (that is walk two or three blocks north of the fortress with the railway line on your left) and you will come to the **Mosque of Amr**, so restored and expanded that nothing remains of the original built here in 642, the first mosque in Egypt and the point from which the country's conversion to Islam began. Except for its associations, the present mosque is without interest. Its dimensions date to 827 when it was doubled in size, and it has several times since been restored, and has recently been restored again. It is a pedestrian reminder of a cheaply won victory, and you pause to wonder what it would take to reverse the effect of Amr's 3500 men.

Behind the mosque extends what appears to be a vast and smoking rubbish dump. The curious should wander into its midst — and be amazed and rewarded with one of the most fascinating sights in Cairo. No smouldering heaps at all, but a **community of earthenware manufacturers** whose seemingly rubbish houses (you should be careful not to fall through their ceilings as you walk over them) stand, or settle, amidst a complete and complex process for the making of fine clay and the fashioning of narghile stems, drums, small pots, large amphoras and road-sized drainage pipes — indeed these people could equip a band, a kitchen or a city, and do probably meet the earthenware needs of a large part of Cairo.

Synagogue of Ben Ezra, Old Cairo

There are vats dug into the ground for mixing and refining clay, subterranean workshops where potters draw from shapeless lumps beautifully curved vessels with all the mastery and mystery of a fakir charming a thick brown snake, and there are enormous beehive kilns like Mycenaean tombs fired from below with mounds of wood shavings shovelled in by Beelzebub children.

At evening these mud-covered people wash themselves off, the women appear from out of their hovels in bright dresses, flowers are arranged in soft-drink bottles, a television — wired up to a car battery — is switched on, tea is made, chairs set out, and if you are there then you will be invited to join them in watching the setting sun.

The true beginnings of Cairo Beyond this potters community — or, more easily, by returning towards the fortress of Babylon but turning left up the road running alongside the cemetery wall — lie the dismal **remains of Fustat**, that is the foundations and lower walls of the first Arab city in Egypt, the true beginnings of Cairo. Once famous for its glassware and ceramics, with water supply and sanitation facilities far more advanced than anything in Europe until the 18th C, the city was destroyed and abandoned in 1168 rather than let it fall into the hands of the Christian king of Jerusalem. Fustat's destruction fell most heavily on the Copts, who had been the majority here and lost everything. When the threat had passed, the Muslims turned their attention to their new city of Cairo which you can see rising to the north and filled it with some of the greatest monuments of medieval civilisation.

PRACTICAL INFORMATION

Details for visiting Old Cairo and Fustat follow later, but first some information on points of interest **along the Nile** which can all be easily reached on foot from Midan el Tahrir.

The Cairo Tower on the island of Gezira rises 187 metres and offers marvellous panoramas from its 14th level restaurant, 15th level cafeteria and 16th level observation platform. Fee for the ascent.

The Ethnological Museum, Sharia Qasr el Aini, a few blocks south of Midan el Tahrir. Open 9am to 1pm daily, closed Friday. Free. A small museum with displays of traditional village handicrafts and costumes from all over Egypt.

The Manyal Palace on the island of Roda is open daily from 9am to 2pm. LE1 entry.

The Papyrus Institute, on a houseboat tied up along Sharia el Nil, is just south of the Cairo Sheraton in Giza. Open from 10am to 7pm daily, free. Founded by Prof. Hassan Ragab, this is a workshop, research centre and small museum demonstrating the manufacture and use of this first flexible writing material. Only *cyperus papyrus*, the same plant used by the ancients, is used here (the institute has several commercial imitators, but they use the modern *cyperus alopecuroides* of inferior quality). The institute grows at least some of its own papyrus, and exhibits copies of ancient papyri and sells others. (As you go down the quayside steps, notice on your left the plaque marking the highest level of the Nile during the flood of September 1887.)

The Agricultural Museum and the **Cotton**

Museum, next to each other off Sharia Abdel Aziz Radwan, near the exit of the 6 October Bridge in Dokki. Open from 9am to 2pm except Fridays when they close at noon; closed Mondays. Small fee. The Agricultural Museum displays all aspects of present Egyptian rural life, while the Cotton Museum concentrates on the country's single most important crop.

If taking a **taxi** to the Fortress of Babylon in Old Cairo, ask first for *Misr* (or *Masr*) *el Qadima*, ie Old Cairo, and then specify *Mari Girgis*, ie St George, and he will bring you right to the walls outside the Coptic Museum. By **Metro**, get off at Mari Girgis station; by **river bus** the landing stage is also called Mari Girgis.

The churches close at 4pm; the synagogue keeps irregular hours and usually Rabbi Cohen or Ahmed are there after 4pm to show you around. All are free but are anxious for donations.

The Coptic Museum is open from 9am to 4pm daily except Fridays when it closes between 11am and 1pm. LE3 entry **fee**. Bags and cameras must be checked (no fee), though you can take your camera in by paying a special fee.

An **abbreviated tour** of the places mentioned in this chapter should at least include the Coptic Museum.

TOURING ISLAMIC CAIRO

Islam in Egypt began at Fustat (previous chapter) and flowered into a great civilisation, many of whose most beautiful monuments survive throughout the medieval quarters of Cairo. The following six chapters tour this Islamic Cairo, progressing generally from south to north.

The method The Islamic monuments of Cairo, and there are hundreds of them, are each marked with a small green enamelled plaque bearing an Arabic number. These numbers are given after the name of each monument covered in the itineraries of the following chapters to ensure identification. Although these are historical monuments, they are often places of current worship and when touring this most conservative part of the city you should dress and act with decorum. Women should not wear short dresses or too-revealing blouses. Inside mosques you must remove your shoes, or shoe coverings will be provided. For this, and if you accept the services of a guide, or sometimes if you ask to be shown the way up a minaret, baksheesh will be expected. And there is also an entry fee to many of the monuments. In short, it is a good idea to carry around a lot of small change.

You may sometimes find yourself in a mosque at prayer time, and then, though visitors are otherwise welcome, you might be asked to retreat into an alcove or out onto the street. Normally though the atmosphere is relaxed, even to the point where many of Mohammed's precepts on mosque conduct are ignored. Egypt in this as in many other ways is more liberal than most other Muslim countries.

Comfortable walking shoes are recommended. Though you might rely on a taxi or other transport to get you to the beginning of the itinerary or to some of the major monuments along the route, walking is otherwise preferable for a sense of leisure and atmosphere, and also because some places are difficult to get at or to discover even once you are in the vicinity. There are numerous *kahwehs* along the way, that is places to sit—often just a few chairs beneath the shade of a tree or awning—for a coffee or more likely a refreshing cup of mint tea. Then there is immediate tranquillity; you give your feet a rest and let the city parade by before you.

The grandeur of Islam In the 14th C the great Arab historian Ibn Khaldun wrote that 'he who has not seen Cairo cannot know the grandeur of Islam. It is the metropolis of the universe, the garden of the world, the nest of the human species, the gateway to Islam, the throne of royalty: it is a city embellished with castles and palaces and adorned with monasteries of dervishes and with

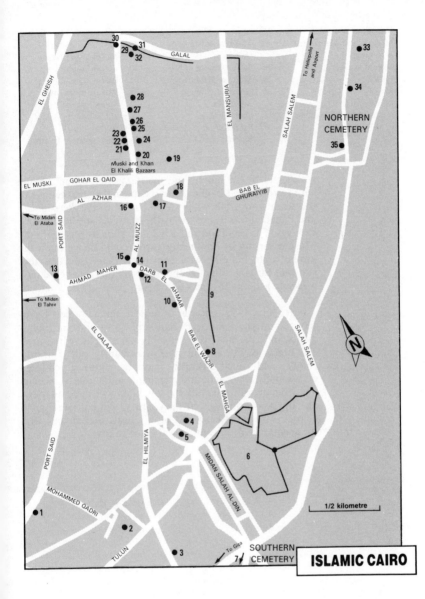

1.	Mosque of Sayyida Zeinab	4. Rifa'i Mosque	9. Saladin's Walls
2.	Mosque of Ibn Tulun and the Gayer-Anderson House	5. Mosque of Sultan Hassan 6. The Citadel	10. Maridani Mosque 11. Qijmas al-Ishaqi Mosque
3.	Tomb of Shagarat al-Durr	7. Mausoleum of Imam al-Shaf'i 8. Aqsunqur (Blue) Mosque	12. Mosque of Salih Talai 13. Islamic Museum and Egyptian Library 14. Bab Zuwayla

colleges lit by the moons and the stars of erudition'. Along with Cordoba and Baghdad, it was one of the great centres of the Arab world, but while Cordoba fell to the *Reconquista* and Baghdad was destroyed by the Mongols, medieval Cairo survives. The erudition Ibn Khaldun refers to was more the Muslim version of how many angels could dance upon the head of a pin, but otherwise many of the marvels he describes still wait for you, often so unobtrusively that you could pass a facade a hundred times and never guess at the grandeur within.

After sometimes centuries of neglect, there is a new Egyptian and international appreciation of Cairo's Islamic monuments, and a recent drive is very ably restoring these treasures. The streets may be ancient, narrow and dusty, full of strange colour and smell. People may be curious, children occasionally a nuisance and merchants in the tourist bazaars importunate, but generally the inhabitants of these quarters, like Egyptians throughout the country, will be friendly and helpful. This is the heart of Cairo, a heart that anyone with the least sense of adventure will come to love.

AROUND THE CITADEL

If you have time to visit only one Islamic monument, the
Mosque of Ibn Tulun (220) should be your choice. The
mosque can be reached by going east from Midan al-Sayyida
Zeinab at the bottom of Sharia Port Said or west from
Midan Salah al-Din below the Citadel. The area, though
not ancient, is poor and rundown, but behind its outer courtyard or *ziyadah* the mosque achieves an isolation which
heightens the dramatic effect of the inner courtyard's bold
simplicity.

Ibn Tulun was sent to govern Cairo by the Abbassid caliph
at Baghdad and the mosque, built in 876–9, displays strong

Congregational plan Mesopotamian influence. A congregational mosque with an
inner courtyard or *sahn* of parade ground proportions, it
strives to fulfil the ideal of accommodating all the troops and
subjects of the fortress capital for Friday prayers. Arcades run
round the sahn on four sides, deeper along the qibla wall
facing Mecca. Brick piers support the pointed horseshoe
arches which have a slight return, that is they continue their
curve inwards at the bottom, and the arches are decorated
with carved stucco (restored on the outer arches but original
on the others within the arcades), a technique Ibn Tulun
introduced to Cairo. The windows along the qibla wall (to
your left as you enter the mosque) have stucco grilles (the
fifth and sixth from the left are original), permitting a faint
light into this deeper arcade with its prayer niche or *mihrab*
and beautifully carved pulpit or *minbar*, 13th C restorations.
The roof, like the repaired stucco work, is owed to the efforts
of 20th C restorers. Original, however, is the Koranic inscription carved in sycamore running at a height round the interior
of the four arcades.

The effect as you enter the sahn is of severe simplicity, yet
these details of carved stucco and sycamore and returning
arches offer subtle relief. You should walk round the sahn
under the arcades to appreciate the play that is made with
light and shadows, the rhythm of the arches, the harmony of
the ensemble.

At the centre of the sahn is a 13th C fountain. All these 13th
C restorations and additions were undertaken by Sultan Lajin
who had assassinated the incumbent sultan and hid in the
then decrepit mosque. He vowed that if he survived to be
raised to the sultanate he would restore his hideaway, and to
him belongs an explanation also for the striking *minaret*
opposite the qibla wall. The original was Tulun's, in the
form of spiral, and there is a story of Tulun, normally of
grave demeanor, absentmindedly twiddling a strip of paper
round his finger to the consternation of his audience, excusing
himself with the explanation that it was the model for his new

minaret. In fact its prototype, still standing, was the minaret of the Great Mosque of Samarra in Iraq. But Lajin had to rebuild it and out of taste or for stability gave it a squared base. It succeeds in being extraordinary and along with the merlons along the parapets of the arcades, like a paperchain of cut-out men, it has the alertness of the surreal. You can climb the minaret right to the top, though as you round the spiral there is nothing to steady you and a high breeze adds to the vertigo. There is nothing much close by but tenements with views into bedroom windows, though to the west you can see the Pyramids, to the north pick out the major landmarks of the Fatimid city, and below you again the forthright plan of mosque.

At the northeast corner of the Ibn Tulun Mosque is the Bayt al-Kritliyya, the House of the Cretan Woman, though in fact it is two 17th C houses knocked together. It is better known as the **Gayer-Anderson House**, named for the British major who restored and occupied it earlier this century, filling it with his eclectic collection of English, French and Oriental furniture and bric-a-brac which can be disconcertingly anachronistic, but does give the place a lived-in feeling. Its tourist reputation must be founded on this, and its proximity to the Ibn Tulun, for otherwise it is not half as fine as the Bayt al-Suhaymi mentioned in a later chapter.

The harem   Overlooking its large reception room is a balcony enclosed in a wooden mashrabiyya screen from which the women of the harem could discreetly observe male visitors and their entertainments. Edward William Lane in his *Manners and Customs of the Modern Egyptians*, which describes Cairo in the 1830s, says the women 'have the character of being the most licentious in their feelings of all females who lay any claim to be considered as members of a civilised nation ... What liberty they have, many of them, it is said, abuse; and most of them are not considered safe unless under lock and key, to which restraint few are subjected. It is believed that they possess a degree of cunning in the management of their intrigues that the most prudent and careful husband cannot guard against'. Indeed, Lane believed that Egyptian women were under less restraint than those in any other country of the Turkish empire, with those 'of the lower orders flirting and jesting with men in public, and men laying their hands upon them very freely'. As for those of the upper classes: 'They generally look upon restraint with a degree of pride, as evincing the husband's care for them and value themselves upon their being hidden as treasures'. The only man allowed into the harem, that is the female domestic quarters, was the husband — and so the strictures worked against men, too, the only unveiled women they could see being their wives or female slaves.

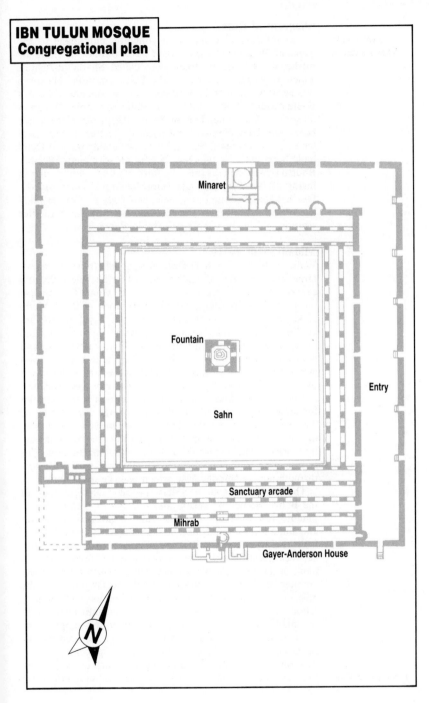

**IBN TULUN MOSQUE
Congregational plan**

Minaret

Fountain

Entry

Sahn

Sanctuary arcade

Mihrab

Gayer-Anderson House

N

Shagarat al-Durr

Those interested in making a romantic pilgrimage to the **Tomb of Shagarat al-Durr** should walk southwards along the medieval city's main street, here called Sharia al-Ashraf, which passes just to the east of Ibn Tulun's mosque. The tomb (169) is at the edge of the Southern Cemetery in one of Cairo's poorest areas. Built in 1250, it is small and simple, though in allusion to her name, Tree of Pearls, the prayer niche inside bears fine Byzantine-style mosaics of the tree of life inlaid with mother-of-pearl. She and a near-contemporary at Delhi have been the only two female Muslim sovereigns; Benazir Bhutto joined them as only the third Muslim woman ruler in history. It is a dangerous game and Shagarat al-Durr played it fast and loose, coming to a sticky end: only part of her body lies within her tomb — the rest was eaten by the dogs. Her story is told in the chapter *To the Northern Walls*.

Midan Salah al-Din

Walk to Midan Salah al-Din; to your left (north) are two large mosques pressed against each other like the walls of a canyon, Sharia el Qalaa cutting between them. The mosque on the right is the **Rifa'i**, a modern imitation of Bahri Mameluke style, where members of the late royal family, including King Farouk, are buried — and now also the ex-Shah of Iran. The best thing about the Rifa'i is its near-abutment with the Mosque of Sultan Hassan on the left, the canyon enhancing the massiveness of the latter. Both mosques are lit by orange lights at night, as though the light itself was old, not bright and white, and had been lingering on the facades for some long time until it darkened with age. But then in the darkness is the booming call to evening prayer, not mysterious but electrically amplified, saving the muezzin not only his voice but the long trudge up to the top of the minaret. This is one slip from fundamentalist practice, prevalent now throughout the Middle East, which is to be regretted.

The Mosque-madrasa of Sultan Hassan (133) is genuinely of the Bahri Mameluke period and was built — of stone (reputedly from the Great Pyramid), unlike the brick of Tulunid and some Fatimid mosques — in 1356–63. Its short distance from the Mosque of Ibn Tulun allows a ready comparison between these exemplars of the two principal forms of Cairo mosque. The purpose of the congregational is to gather in and architecturally the emphasis is on the rectangular and the horizontal. But the Sultan Hassan served as a theological school, a *madrasa*. The madrasa was first introduced to Egypt by Saladin as part of his effort to combat and suppress the Fatimid Shi'ites. Class and dormitory space required a vertical structure, most functionally a cube. The central courtyard remains a feature, but opening onto each of its sides are

four enormous vaulted halls or *liwans*, creating a cruciform

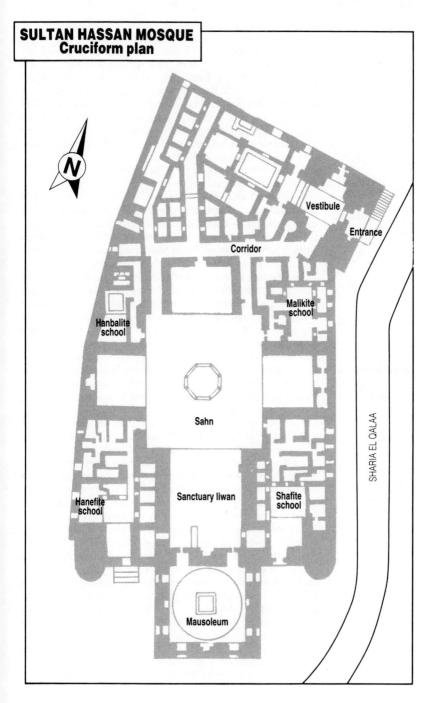

SULTAN HASSAN MOSQUE
Cruciform plan

N

Vestibule

Entrance

Corridor

Malikite
school

Hanbalite
school

Sahn

SHARIA EL QALAA

Sanctuary liwan

Shafite
school

Hanefite
school

Mausoleum

97

plan. The doctrinal justification for four liwans was that each served as a place for teaching one of the four Sunni, that is orthodox, Muslim rites (Shafite, Malikite, Hanefite and Hanbalite), though the origins of the liwan are found at Hatra in Iraq, an Arab city flourishing at least 400 years before Mohammed. But it was the Mamelukes who arranged them with magnificent effect in cruciform plan and who also added to their mosque-madrasas domed mausolea. Hassan's mausoleum is appended to the south end of the mosque but his tomb is empty; he was executed two years before its completion and his body disappeared.

There are many who regard the Sultan Hassan as the outstanding Islamic monument in Egypt, and certainly it vies with the Ibn Tulun. Though entirely different in type, the two mosques share a boldness of conception and clarity of execution, gathering still more strength in restraining decoration to the minimum necessary solely to underline architectural form. There is self-confidence, and at the Sultan Hassan even architectural insolence, but rarely indulgence.

The Sultan Hassan already impresses from the outside. Though it stands beneath the glare of the Citadel it holds its own, its great cornice and the strong verticals of its facade rising to the challenge. Notice how the broad surfaces along the east and west sides are relieved by blind recesses into which the paired arch windows of the dormitories are set. Height is especially emphasised as you enter on Sharia el Qalaa the towering *portal with its stalactite decorations* — a favourite Marmeluke motif. The portal is at an angle to the main east flank of the mosque and the west flank too is bent, though at first sight the building had seemed more regular. Earlier periods had enjoyed more space, but as Cairo grew and became more dense the Mamelukes had to squeeze their buildings in where they could, though they had a fetish for achieving a cubistic effect no matter how irregular the plot. The liwans had also to be cruciform regardless of the exterior and in the Sultan Hassan this has been neatly done, all hint inside of the irregularity of the outer walls suppressed except for the slight angle of the door in the west liwan.

The portal leads to a domed cruciform vestibule and you turn left into a dark angled passage. It empties suddenly into the north end of the brilliantly sun-filled sahn, certainly a deliberate effect and a preparation for the play of light and shadow, concrete and void, intended for the courtyard and its liwans. It is important that you do not come too late in the day, indeed it is best that you visit the Sultan Hassan in the morning when the sun lights up the mausoleum and west liwan and begins its long and rarely accomplished reach into the full depth of the sahn. Its depth is considerable, for the liwans lift about as high as the sahn is long. The sun soon passes, illuminating hardly more than the merlons by late

Mosque of Sultan Hassan: soaring liwans

afternoon, and much of the architectural effect of direct sunlight and strong shadows is lost so that the mosque can then
seem a disappointment. The stucco anyway is pasty brown
with sand and dirt, and other details need cleaning.

The gazebo at the centre of the sahn has been rebuilt in
Ottoman style and is used now for ablutions. The original
fountain is met later on in this guide at the Maridani Mosque.
Hundreds of chains hang down from the liwans, the glow of
their oil lamps at night a delight reserved for the imagination
as they are all gone, though some can be seen in the Islamic
Museum. The *sanctuary liwan* is opposite the entrance passage, a Kufic band running within it and an unfortunately
fussy marble decoration on its qibla wall. The columns on
either side of the mihrab are from some Christian edifice,
possibly Crusader — they do not seem Byzantine. Farther to
either side of the mihrab are doors leading into the *mausoleum*. The right-hand door is panelled with original bronze
inlaid with gold and dazzles when polished. The mausoleum
dome collapsed in the 17th C and was rebuilt in the 18th C in
the lofty imperial style of Istanbul, though it rests on the
original stalactite squinches. Rich though the restored decorations are, the atmosphere is sombre and Hassan's cenotaph,
surrounded by a wooden screen where women pray for the

sultan's intercession, is very simple. From the grilled windows there are views of the Citadel.

Visiting the Citadel

Returning towards the Citadel you once more enter Midan Salah al-Din, extended by clearances at the instruction of General Kitchener. It was here that the annual pilgrimage to Mecca gathered before winding through streets lined with thousands of spectators and leaving the city at the northern Fatimid gates of Bab al-Futuh and Bab al-Nasr. The long park to its south was a parade ground and polo field for the Mamelukes. Up a ramp at the front of the Citadel is a gate, closed to the public, **Bab al-Azab**. The crooked lane behind
the gate, enclosed by high walls, was the scene of the massacre of the Mamelukes by Mohammed Ali in 1811. Only one escaped, leaping on horseback through a gap in the wall into a moat. During the Ottoman occupation and even under Napoleon the Mamelukes had survived and were a power to be reckoned with. Mohammed Ali invited them to dinner at the Citadel, bidding them homewards via this cul-de-sac and cutting them down with their bellies full.

Massacre of the Mamelukes

The entry to the Citadel is round to the left, that is clockwise round its base. There is another entrance round the rear, off the Heliopolis and airport road. Much of the Citadel is off-limits, reserved for the military, an echo of its role as stronghold of the city from the time Saladin in 1176 built his fortress here to the reign of Mohammed Ali. For almost 700 years nearly all Egypt's rulers lived in the Citadel, held court, dispensed justice and received ambassadors. A succession of palaces and elaborate buildings thrown up during the Mameluke period were mostly levelled by Mohammed Ali when he built his mosque and **Bijou Palace** in their place. The palace, to the south of the mosque, is now a museum housing objects of its era and makes a pleasant visit if you have the time.

Turkish delight

The Mosque of Mohammed Ali, a Turkish delight on the Cairo skyline, proves disappointing close up — though perhaps not for those who have never visited an imperial Ottoman mosque in Turkey. Half domes rise as buttresses for the high central dome and the two thin minarets add an ethereal touch, more in tune perhaps with our Oriental dreams than the robust Arab minarets of Cairo. But the alabaster cladding, a gesture of baroque luxe, has cheapened with time, while the pretty courtyard with its gingerbread *clock* (given by Louis Philippe in exchange for the obelisk in the Place de la Concorde), suggests a folly rigged up for fashion and amusement. That could explain why the mosque is so popular with tourists, for also the interior is vast and agreeably cool, the dome huge and the decorations in opulent bad taste. Principally, though, the architecture is routine; there is no feeling of lift or weightlessness to the dome that you find in the better Istanbul mosques, nor an appeal to spiritual contemplation. Mohammed Ali, whose *tomb* is on the right as you enter, meant this more as a symbol of the Ottoman power he had snatched.

From the parapet to the southwest there is a good view of the mosques of Hassan and Tulun and a panorama of the city which will ·be more or less impressive depending on the cinereous haze that heat and Helwan together smother Cairo with.

Across from the entrance to the courtyard of the Mohammed Ali Mosque is the **Mosque of al-Nasr Mohammed** (143), not much visited, dating from 1318–35. Once the principal mosque of the Citadel, it was built in the congregational style with an arcaded courtyard, many of the columns re-used from pharaonic, Roman and Byzantine buildings. Plain though it is outside, it is beautiful inside, all the more so as Turkish vandals stripped it of its marble panels, revealing its simple elegance. The two minarets are unique for the pincushion shape of their tops and their Mongol-inspired faience decoration, of which only traces remain.

On leaving the Mosque of al-Nasr, turn tight and go round it, then take the first road to the right on the east side of the mosque. This brings you to a tower which stands over **Yusuf's (or Joseph's) Well** (305), also known as Salah al-Din's Well or Dir al-Halazun, the Well of the Snail for the spiral staircase leading 88 metres down the great central shaft to the level of the Nile. (The descent can be dangerous.) Yusuf was one of Saladin's names and the well was dug during his time by Crusader prisoners, providing a secure source of water in case of siege. The water reaches the well by natural rather than artificial channels, and was brought up by donkeys, the rock steps covered with earth to provide them with a foothold.

The Southern Cemetery

At this point you can interrupt your progress north with a visit to the Southern Cemetery, a vast, confusing and dilapidated Muslim necropolis stretching as far as Maadi. The Northern Cemetery generally offers the more impressive monuments and will be covered in a later chapter. But if you avail yourself of transport (or make the long walk there and back), the **Mausoleum of Imam al-Shaf'i** (281) in the Southern Cemetery would more than repay an excursion.

The mausoleum is most easily reached by heading south from the Citadel along the street bearing the Imam's name, a distance of about 2 km from Midan Salah al-Din. A descendant of an uncle of the Prophet, al-Shaf'i was the founder of one of the four rites of Sunni Islam and died in 820. The cenotaph was put here by Saladin and the mausoleum built by his brother-successor's wife who is also buried here. The mausoleum is covered by a large wooden dome sheathed in lead and is the largest Islamic mortuary chamber in Egypt. Inside, a couple of cats, some birds chirping, men lying about or reading the Koran, and above this the magnificent dome painted red and blue and gold, a pattern of flowers rising to the highest sound of birdsong. The original lighting system of lamps suspended from carved beams is intact — the only such in Cairo.

Magnificent dome

The spot itself is of significance: it was here that Saladin founded the first madrasa in Egypt to counter the Fatimid heresy, and it became a centre of Shafite missionary work, the rite predominant even today in southern Arabia, Bahrain, Malaysia and East Africa. The majority of Cairenes, too, are Shafites, and as the Imam is revered as one of the great Muslim saints (achieved by popular acclamation, as there is no formal notion of sainthood in Islam), the mausoleum is annually — in the eighth month of the Muslim calendar, lasting for a week from, usually, the first Wednesday — the site of great *moulid*, an anniversary birthday festival, in honour of Shaf'i. Atop the dome, like a weathervane, is a metal boat in which there used to be placed on the occasion of the moulid about 150 kilos of wheat and a camel-load of water for the birds. The boat is said to turn sometimes when there is no wind to move it, and according to the position it takes to foretoken various events, good or evil, such as plenty or scarcity, or the death of some great man.

PRACTICAL INFORMATION

To reach the starting point of this tour you can take a **taxi** or you can ride to Midan Salah al-Din (lying between the Citadel and the Sultan Hassan Mosque) on the **No. 174 bus** or the **No. 54 minibus** from Midan el Tahrir. All the monuments in this chapter are quite close together with the exception of the Mausoleum of Imam al-Shaf'i — to reach this take the **No. 405 bus** south from Midan Salah al-Din; it then turns left towards the Moqattam Hills and just where it does so there is a bus stop. You then walk down Sharia Imam al-Shaf'i a few hundred metres. Or take the **tram** from Midan Salah al-Din following the same route except that instead of it turning left it continues straight on, terminating just short of the Mausoleum.

Note that the tomb of Shagarat al-Durr stands within iron railings and is kept locked to prevent neighbourhood encroachment. To enter, permission must first be obtained from the Egyptian Antiquities Organisation, 4D Sharia Fakhry Abd al Nour, Abbassia. Tel: 839637.

The Ibn Tulun, Gayer-Anderson, Hassan, Rifa'i and the Citadel all charge a **fee** of LE1. (Your entrance ticket to the Gayer-Anderson is also valid on the same day for admission to the Islamic Museum.) There may be additional fees, or at least baksheesh, for shoe coverings. You should not assume that any of these places will remain open after 4pm. An additional fee of LE5 will permit you to take photographs inside the Gayer-Anderson.

For those with limited time an **abbreviated itinerary** should include the Mosques of Ibn Tulun and Sultan Hassan.

DARB EL AHMAR

Continuing our journey northwards, let us assume we are back at the Citadel. You should leave the Citadel by the northeast entrance (the one you entered if you came up from Midan Salah al-Din), turning left as soon as you pass through the gate. Down the hill you cross over the road which issues east out of the midan and you enter Sharia el Mahga. The road plunges downhill and soon becomes Sharia Bab el Wazir, the Street of the Gate of the Vizier, and later becomes Darb el Ahmar, the Red Road, as it runs up to Bab Zuwayla. This entire district is known as **Darb el Ahmar**, a name which nowadays epitomises a poorer, broken-down section of the city. At the Citadel end which is entirely residential the street is fairly quiet and fairly filthy; it becomes livelier, and you do not notice the filth so much, as you enter the bazaar area farther north. Apart from the ruins of many old houses and some fine intact monuments, you may also encounter the gaiety of a marriage procession, a great noise of motor scooters, car horns, tambourines, ululations, whistling, chanting and cries, an amazing public racket by no more than two dozen people escorting the bride and groom through the streets.

Along Sharia Bab el Wazir

Soon after setting off down Sharia Bab el Wazir you come on your right to the **Mosque of Aqsunqur** (123), better known as the **Blue Mosque** and much beloved for the wrong reasons by tour guides. It was built in 1347 but usurped in 1652 by the Turkish Governor Ibrahim Agha who slapped up the tiles that give the mosque its popular name. The best Turkish tiles were from Iznik; these were made in Ottoman factories at Damascus and are poorly decorated and often marred as well in the glazing. They are along the qibla wall and around the walls of Agha's tomb which you enter through a door on the right side of the courtyard. The worst thing about the tiles is their inappropriateness, for the mosque is otherwise charmingly simple. A stand of palms and other trees makes the courtyard an agreeable place to linger after the hot desolate sahns of other mosques. The pillars round the courtyard, and especially the octagonal ones of the sanctuary, are crude, but contribute to the rustic pleasantness of the whole. The finest work is the carved stone minbar, which is original. On the left before entering the courtyard is the tomb of Sultan Kuchuk, The Little One, a brother of Hassan who ruled for five months at the age of six, but was then deposed, imprisoned in the Citadel, and three years later strangled by another of his brothers.

A small strangling

From the street you can see behind the Aqsunqur a section

103

of **Saladin's walls** which extended from the Fatimid city in the north to Fustat in the south, the Mamelukes using a part of its southern section to carry their aqueduct. Across the street from the mosque is a **Turkish apartment building** from 1625.

Into Darb el Ahmar

Continuing north, Sharia Bab el Wazir becomes Darb el Ahmar and set at an angle to this street, on the left-hand side, is the **Maridani Mosque** (120). Built in 1339–40 in the early Mameluke period, it is one of the oldest buildings in the quarter which until the 14th C had been Fatimid and Ayyubid cemeteries.

Entering from the hurly-burly of the street you are soon absorbed into the restfulness of the Maridani, a monument, yes, but no museum, no entry fee, no one to ask baksheesh for shoe covers for there are none, and you leave your shoes inside the door and walk about in your socks. Not that you need worry about form, but as a matter of interest a Muslim will carry his shoes in his left hand, sole to sole (the left hand being for unclean uses), and he will put his right foot first over the threshold. If he has not already performed the ablution outside, he will at once go to the inner fountain. Before praying, he will place his shoes on the matting, a little before the spot where his head will touch the ground, and again, to avoid contaminating the mosque, he will put his shoes one upon the other, sole to sole.

Isolation from the outside world is as much a matter of tranquil ambience as it is of ritual cleanliness. The atmosphere attracts many who come not only for prayer: here I have seen men sleeping, boys doing their homework leaning up against the qibla screen, a dozen women talking and their children playing at the fountain (the one removed from the Sultan Hassan). Yet all of these things are against the precepts of Mohammed, and even though Lane reported, 150 years ago, eating, sewing and spinning as well, these activities ceased during prayers, though here, too, I have seen the hum of irreligion continue while men were on their palms and knees, submitting themselves to Allah.

Prayers are performed five times a day, though mostly at home, with better off people rarely visiting a mosque except for Friday prayers. But wherever they are performed, prayers follow the same procedure, which is quite involved. First the worshipper will stand, facing Mecca, and inaudibly propose a prayer of so many *rek'ahs*, or inclinations of the head. He then says 'Allahu Akbar', God is great, and recites the opening chapter of the Koran, followed by three or more other verses, again says 'Allahu Akbar' and makes an inclination of the head and body. Next he drops gently to his knees, places his palms upon the ground, his nose and forehead touching the ground between them, and during this

Removing shoes (margin)

Prayers (margin)

Fatimid keel-arches and tie-beams: Mosque of Salih Talai

prostration says 'I extol the perfection of my Lord, the Great', three times. Though still kneeling, he raises his head and body, again says 'God is great', and bends his head a second time to the ground and repeats what he has said before. This — and it is a simplification of the full litany — completes one rek'ah and will take about a minute, though several rek'ahs will be performed and there must be no wandering of the mind, no irregular movement and no interruptions, otherwise the procedure must be gone over from the beginning. Islam literally means submission and that is what the procedure achieves. The concentration required explains why mosques are often so austere: architecturally they should be conducive to prayer, but should not distract with decorations. That does not explain why, nowadays, and in some mosques, women should be chattering in the corner and children splashing in the fountain, yet it does all fit together most agreeably, and if you stand here in the open courtyard of the Maridani at evening, you may see a crescent moon hanging from the approving sky.

An easy rhythm of arches on slender columns runs round the courtyard, an inner and an outer series, a third and partial fourth (on either side of the mihrab) added to the qibla arcade. A wooden *screen* separates the qibla from the courtyard, a unique feature in Cairo, and, inside, the arcade is pleasantly dark. The mihrab and the minbar wall have had their mosaic decorations well restored. The dome above the mihrab is supported by two pink granite pharaonic columns. The merlons along the parapet of the courtyard are at intervals topped by curious pots. Try, if you can, to climb up the minaret for a more immediate view of the medieval city than you can get from the Citadel.

Another 150 metres up the street is the **Mosque of Qijmas al-Ishaqi** (114), built in 1480–1 during the Burgi Mameluke period. It has been squeezed into a triangular plot where a street joins Darb el Ahmar from the right, yet despite this the Mameluke fashion for rectangular illusion succeeds, at least at first glance. Inside, however, a sacrifice has been made in the cruciform plan: the north and south liwans are merely vestigal. So restricted was the space that the *kuttab*, the Koranic school usually part of the mosque, had to be sited across the street joining from the right; it is now derelict.

But the mosque itself has been very well restored and though around this period — only a few decades before the Turkish domination — Mameluke architecture began to deteriorate, there was a last bravado of decorative artistry with fine marble inlays and beautifully carved stone and stucco. Within this covered mosque is a feast of detail, yet all of it harmonious and restful; nothing jitters, jumps or jars. The east and west liwans are supported by arches with a slight return, the stonework in alternating red and white, the vaults very fine and the stucco windows excellent. The inlaid marble floor is covered with mats (the mosque is in daily use), but the keeper will lift these if you ask, the best section being the mosaic flooring of the east liwan. You can also ask to go up the minaret from which there is a clear view of Bab Zuwayla.

The tomb chamber by the entrance is plain and dignified beneath a lofty dome. But Qijmas, Master of the Sultan's Horse and officer in charge of the yearly pilgrimage to Mecca, died in Syria and is buried at Damascus; the chamber contains the more recent tomb of a 19th C holy man. Mamelukes and Turks of Qijmas' rank built not only for Allah or themselves, but also for the community, and a *sabil* or public watering fountain was often provided. This was in keeping with Mohammed's reply when asked what was the most meritorious act: 'To give people water to drink'. You can see its grille outside at what was a convenient height for drawing water 500 years ago, though now well below street level.

Outside the Gate of the Fatimid City
Darb el Ahmar now bends to the west, a surviving section of **Fatimid wall** concealed by the building on your right, and opens into a square dominated by **Bab Zuwayla** (see later chapter), the massive southern gate into the Fatimid city. The place has long had a reputation for being unlucky, perhaps because it led out to the cemeteries now built over by the Darb el Ahmar quarter, though also it was the site of public executions. Tumanbay, the last independent Mameluke sultan, was hanged here by the Turks. Twice the rope broke, the third time his neck.

Public executions

The street running directly south from Bab Zuwayla is the continuation of the principal Fatimid street to the north and extends all the way down, past the Mosque of Ibn Tulun and through Saladin's walls to the vicinity of the Mausoleum of Imam al-Shaf'i. This was the longest thoroughfare of the medieval city and along here amidst great festivity the Mecca pilgrims would begin their arduous journey. It changes its name several times and can be worth following for its own sake a little to the south where it is first the Street of the Tentmakers, becoming less colourful as the Street of the Saddlemakers before crossing Sharia el Qalaa.

On the corner of this street and Darb el Ahmar, facing the square, is the **Mosque of Salih Talai** (116), built in 1160 towards the close of the Fatimid period. A congregational mosque, perfectly rectangular in the Fatimid pattern, it is one of the most handsome in Cairo. A lower level of shops, again once at street level, was part of Salih Talai's *waqf* or endowment, as other mosques might have had fields or adjacent apartment buildings, the rents contributing to the mosque's upkeep. The facade, therefore, would have been higher, its effect still more imposing. Its five keel-arches, supported by

Classic Fatimid mosque

classical columns linked by wooden tie-beams, are flanked by sunken false arches or panels topped by stylised shell niches — the whole a perfect expression of the Fatimid style. The arches, however, form a *narthex* or porch unique in Cairo. Along its interior wall another set of panels, each one immediately behind an open keel-arch, runs in muted harmony. In its proportion and reserve the narthex is a fine composition in classical measure. The mosque interior is spacious, an agreeable rhythm of keel-arches and tie-beams running around the arcades.

PRACTICAL INFORMATION

To reach the starting point of this tour go to the Midan Salah al-Din (see the *Practical Information* section at the end of the previous chapter).

The mosques visited in this chapter are still very much places of worship rather than tourist sights and they are usually open throughout the day and into the evening. Nevertheless, tourists will often have to pay an entrance **fee** of LE1, and baksheesh should be paid for services, eg shoe coverings, being taken up a minaret.

The pleasure of this itinerary is the slow walk and the occasional pause at the mosques along the way — enjoyment of atmosphere. The person in a hurry might therefore wish to skip this chapter altogether, though the best advice is that he should not be in a hurry. An **abbreviated itinerary** should bring you to the square before the Mosque of Salih Talai and Bab Zuwayla; this could be combined with a visit to the Islamic Museum or with the walk from Bab Zuwayla to Khan el Khalili (see following chapters).

THE ISLAMIC MUSEUM

The Islamic Museum, to the west of the Bab Zuwayla, is at the intersection of Sharias el Qalaa and Port Said, its entrance on the latter through a garden to which you should return later. Of course the museum could be visited before you explore any part of Islamic Cairo, but for the neophyte, anyway, a visit at this point, halfway through the tour, might be best: you will already have seen enough to make you conversant with form and curious about detail, and you will explore the Fatimid city with greater appreciation.

A revelation, met especially here, is how much you miss human and animal representation in Islamic art and architecture. This is a museum without statues or paintings, where nearly every object is beautifully worked design. A different sort of attention is required, and perhaps you wish sometimes, more here than at other museums, that the exhibits could have remained *in situ*, admired as parts of a whole. But then the **Preservation of** collection began, in 1880, precisely because the monuments **Cairo's Islamic** from which they mostly came had suffered a long period of **treasures** neglect — it was only then, in part at European instigation, that the Egyptian government first seriously undertook preservation of Cairo's Islamic treasures.

The exhibits are well presented and lit and are arranged in 23 rooms which proceed chronologically for the most part, though some rooms specialise in examples of a single subject, eg textiles, from several periods. Though no guide book is available, the exhibits are numbered and labelled, often in English and French as well as in Arabic. A satisfying tour can be accomplished in an hour and a half. With one exception, all the rooms are on one floor. A brief outline follows, but note that some rooms may be closed and their contents either inaccessible or to be found in another nearby room.

Note that because the entrance used to be along the side of the building facing Sharia Port Said, the room numbers start from there; but because you now enter through the north garden (reached also from Sharia Port Said) you find yourself first in Room 7 and so should walk straight through rooms 7, 10, 4B and 2 in order to begin at Room 1.

A Tour of the Museum

Room 1 contains **recent acquisitions**, though also some permanent exhibits, including a magnificent lantern, 14th C, of bronze chased with silver from the Sultan Hassan mosque.

Room 2 deals with the **Ummayad** period (7th–8th C) whose art was representational and drew on Hellenistic and Sassanian (Persian) sources.

Room 3 is **Abbasid** (8th–10th C) and includes **Tulunid** (9th–10th C) works. Here there is greater stylisation, with the emphasis on decoration rather than representation, with great use of stucco, characterised by its slant cut. There are stucco panels from Samarra in Iraq, and tombstones, of which 3904, dating from 858, has fine Kufic inscriptions.

Room 4 displays works of the **Fatimid** period (10th–12th C) with examples of very fine woodwork, carved with human and animal figures and foliage. The Fatimids, who were Shi'ites, did not observe the Sunni prohibition on representation of high living forms, and were much influenced by the Persians, whose craftsmen they imported.

Room 4B, off Room 4, has fine wood, marble and stucco carving of the **Ayyubid** period (12th–13th C).

Before entering *Room 5*, note above the dividing arch the windows of openwork plaster filled with coloured glass (16th–18th C, Ottoman period). (The museum, incidentally, is not visited nearly as much as it deserves to be, so that you often receive personal attention. In this case, the attendant will turn off the main lights and illuminate the coloured windows for effect.) The room contains works of the **Mameluke** period (13th–16th C). There is a beautiful 14th C fountain sunk into the floor (the attendant will turn it on). Despite the bloody succession of Mameluke sultans, Egypt during much of this period enjoyed peace and the decorative arts flourished. A Chinese influence was felt in Mameluke ceramics and pottery. Soft woods were inlaid with ivory, bone, tin and ebony, usually in star-polygons, the Naskhi cursive supplanted the squat Kufic style of decorative inscription, and arabesque floral designs found favour. A 13th C wooden door (602) at the far end of the room shows both square Kufic and cursive Naskhi calligraphy. It is from the Mausoleum of al-Salih Ayyub.

Rooms 6–10 are devoted to **woodwork**, illustrating the development of the art. In *Room 6* on the far wall is a carved frieze originally from the western Fatimid palace, ie 10th C, showing scenes of hunting, music and other courtly activities rarely found in Islamic art. In *Room 7* are *mashrabiyyas*, wooden screens which preserved the privacy of the house from the gaze of the street while still admitting refreshing breezes. They were also used to screen off interior harem rooms from courtyards and reception halls. The projecting niches were for placing porous water jars for cooling. *Room 8* has examples of inlaid wood, while *Room 9* displays wood and bronze work.

In *Room 10*, off Room 9, you will be asked to sit down on a lattice-backed seat round a column fountain which will be turned on for you and illuminated. This is a restful and eye-filling place to linger: gaze up at the exquisite woodwork ceiling, carved and coffered, with three dome recesses, the centre one with windows round it for ladies of the harem to see below. The period is 17th–18th C.

Room 11 is hung with 14th C bronze chandeliers, and in the cases are various **metalwork** objects, eg a perfume brazier (15111, Case 7).

Room 12 contains armour and weapons, many of them chased and inlaid. In Case 7 are swords belonging to Mehmet II, who conquered Constantinople (4264), and Suleyman the Magnificent (4263). And another in the same case, opposite the windows on the right, which has had a remarkable history: the sword of Muradbey, commander of the Mamelukes, was taken by the French general Murat after he had chased the Mamelukes up the Nile, and was presented to Napoleon who in turn wore it when calling on the Directory shortly before seizing power on 18 Brumaire 1799. He had it with him also at Waterloo, and leaving it in his carriage which he abandoned in haste after the battle, it was presented to Wellington.

Rooms 13–16 contain **pottery** of various periods from Egypt and as far west as Spain, as far east as China.

Room 17 is up the stairs on your right as you enter from the garden. It displays textiles and carpets of various periods from Egypt and elsewhere in the Islamic world.

Leading off Room 19 is an outdoor court which is *Room 18* and is principally of Turkish headstones and tombs, but also other **stonework** objects, including a sundial and water level measures.

Room 19 is devoted to the art of the book with many illuminated **manuscripts**, mostly Korans. This may be a sign of these increasingly fundamentalist times. Until recently, pride of place was given to manuscripts of Avicenna on anatomy and botany, but these have been removed. He lived from 980 to 1037 and was one of the greatest physicians of the Middle Ages. Chaucer mentions him in *The Canterbury Tales*. He was an example of the way in which the Arabs passed on the medical theory of the Greeks, enriching it by practical observation and clinical experience. This room now illuminates merely the eclipse of their genius.

Room 20 exhibits **Turkish** art since the 15th C including tapestries, china and jewellery.

Between Rooms 20 and 21 are enamelled glass **lamps** which the attendant will illuminate, while there are more glass lamps in cases round the walls of *Room 21* and in the centre a fine Isfahan carpet that once belonged to King Farouk. The lamps are from mosques (and include some of those now entirely missing from the liwans of the Sultan Hassan) and are arranged chronologically from left to right from the 12th through the 15th C.

Room 22 contains **Persian** objects, mostly pottery, some of which (Cases 1 and 2) have been copied from Chinese models.

Room 23 is for **temporary exhibitions**.

The garden can now be enjoyed on your way out; there are welcome refreshments for sale in a flower-planted setting with a shaded gazebo, a fountain, columns and other large stone pieces. Particularly fine are the large marble panels bearing Fatimid figurative reliefs of plants, birds, fish and animals.

Story of the fountain   Concerning the fountain, there is a story that I have from a member of the Monasterly family to whom it once belonged. The fountain was in their palace on Roda. Its purpose was to run a stream of water through channels decorated with creatures of the Nile, the channels encircling a large dining table, the flowing water keeping the diners cool. The palace was sequestrated by King Farouk, but when Queen Marie of Romania announced her intention to pay the family a visit Farouk kindly let them have the use of the palace for one last dinner. By now, however, the fountain would not work; yet the water flowed, the guests were cooled — the old servants were brought back, my friend explained, and formed a human chain between the Nile and the back of the fountain into which they tipped bucket after bucket of water throughout the dinner. 'They so enjoyed it', my friend said of the servants, 'wasn't that *sweet*?' The Monasterly Palace is now the Centre for Art and Life.

In the same building but on the upper floor is the **Egyptian Library** with its entrance on Sharia el Qalaa. Containing over 750,000 volumes and a vast collection of manuscripts of the Koran dating back to the 8th C and, most outstanding visually, a collection of Persian manuscripts adorned with miniatures of imaginative conception and frequently employing living forms as distinct from the purely ornamental art of the Korans.

PRACTICAL INFORMATION

The Islamic Museum is at Midan Ahmed Maher, where Sharia Port Said and Sharia el Qalaa intersect. A **taxi** can take you here or to nearby Bab Zuwayla (the driver may know it better as Bab al-Mitwalli), or you can take the **No. 66 bus** from Midan el Tahrir.

The museum is open daily from 9am to 4pm except Fridays when it is closed from 11am to 1.30pm. There is an entrance **fee** of LE2 (LE1 for students with card) which is also valid on the same day for the Gayer-Anderson House.

Provided you do not use a flash, you may take unlimited photographs for LE5. With a flash, the fee is LE5 *per photo*.

BAB ZUWAYLA TO KHAN EL KHALILI

Entering the Fatimid city

We now turn to **Bab Zuwayla**, built at the same time (11th C) and in a plan similar to Bab al-Futuh and Bab al-Nasr to the north. These three are the last surviving of the 60 gates that once encircled medieval Cairo and which, well into the 19th C, were shut at night, enclosing the city's then 240,000 population. Except that Bab Zuwayla had long since found itself outflanked by the growth of the city to the south (where it was delimited by Saladin's walls), and in fact marked the city centre. The architects of all three were Armenians from Edessa, and the projecting round towers connected by a walkway and an arch repeating the curve of the gateway below show Byzantine rather than Arab inspiration. Springing from the massive towers are the elegant minarets of the Mosque of Muayyad, its serrated dome farther back seeming to rise between them.

The gate was named for the al-Zawila, a Berber tribe whose Fatimid soldiery were quartered nearby. But most inhabitants know it as the al-Mitwalli after El Kutb al-Mitwalli, the holiest man alive at any one time, who would assume a humble demeanour and simple dress, and station himself inconspicuously, even invisibly, at certain favourite places. Bab Zuwayla was the most famous of these in Egypt, though he could flit to Tanta in the Delta, or to Mecca and back, in an instant. His service was to reprove the impious, expose the sanctimonious, and to distribute evils and blessings, the awards of destiny. Into the earlier part of this century, passers-by would recite the opening of the Koran, while those with headache would drive a nail into the door, or sufferers from a recent toothache would fix their tooth to it as a charm against recurrence. Locks of hair, bits of clothing, would also be attached by the sick in search of a miracle — indeed they still are; and, it is said, the saint still makes his presence known by a gleam of light mysteriously appearing behind the west door.

Climbing the minarets above Bab Zuwayla

Passing through the gate, you should enter the **Mosque of Muayyad** (190) on your left, less for any intrinsic interest, though it is restful and has a garden, than for access to the top of Bab Zuwayla or even up one of the minarets. This is a view of medieval Cairo from its heart and it is splendid. The last of the great open courtyard congregational mosques, the Muayyad was built in 1416–20 by the Burgi Mameluke Muayyad Shaykh who had been imprisoned on the spot before becoming sultan.

Souks and Okels

This street running north from Bab Zuwayla is Sharia Muizz (named for the caliph of the Fatimid conquest), though over its distance between Bab Zuwayla and Bab al-Futuh it enjoys successive traditional names, each one demarcating a souk reserved to a particular trade or the sale of a particular type of merchandise — ensuring, subject to proper bargaining, price control by competition between neighbours. Alongside Muayyad's mosque, for example, the street is Shari'es-Sukkariya, the sugar bazaar. Competition, however, was not the only control on market prices: the Mohtesib, an officer on horseback, would regularly ride through the souks, preceded by a man carrying a pair of scales and followed by the executioner. If spot checks revealed short weights, a butcher, for example, or a baker would have his nose pierced with a hook, a piece of meat, a loaf of bread, suspended from it as the poor man was himself tied to the grilled window of a mosque and left to endure the heat of the sun, the indifference of passersby. One butcher who sold short was deprived of that much flesh from his own body, while a seller of *kunefeh*, a sweet-meat made from that vermicelli pasta (*atayif*) you still see prepared along the streets at night, was fried on his own copper tray for overcharging.

Continuing up to the intersection with the modern Sharia al-Azhar, you find yourself between two Mameluke buildings, the **Madrasa of Sultan al-Ghuri** (189) on the left and his **Mausoleum** (67) on the right. Al-Ghuri was the penultimate Mameluke sultan and the last to reign for any duration (1500–16). A keen polo player into his seventies, a grandiose builder, an arbitrary despot, a torturer, murderer and thief, in short no less than what you would expect a Mameluke sultan to be, he inaugurated his madrasa in May 1503 with a great banquet attended by the Abbasid caliph and all the principal civil, military and religious officials, the souks down to Bab Zuwayla magnificently illuminated and decorated. But though agreeably exotic at first impression, with strong lines and bold *ablaq* (that red and white pattern of the minaret with its curious topping of five small bulbous domes) on closer inspection there is lack of elegance in the details, and in climbing up to the roof you see that the ablaq is not contrasting stone but crudely painted on.

Mameluke sunset Across the street, the mausoleum dome, now collapsed, had to be rebuilt three times during al-Ghuri's reign, and as though shrewdly realising that this might be an unsafe place to be buried, he got himself killed outside Aleppo in a losing battle against the Turks. His luckless successor, that same Tumanbay who was hanged three times at Bab Zuwayla, is buried here instead.

Heading east along Sharia al-Azhar you come after about 100 metres to the **Okel of al-Ghuri** (64) on your right, unmistakably Mameluke with its ablaq masonry and strong, square lines. Built in 1504–5, this is Cairo's best preserved example of a merchants' hotel, the animals quartered on the

The medieval city near Bab Zuwayla: an atmosphere still of the Arabian Nights

ground floor and their masters above. The courtyard would be the scene of unloading aromatic cargoes, with buyers and sellers sitting round and bargaining. This okel was built just at the time that the Portuguese were dealing a blow to Egypt's overland trade with the East by their discovery of new routes round the Cape to India. Even so, as late as 1835 there were still 200 okels serving Cairo's bazaars.

The Religious Heart of Islamic Cairo

The famous **Mosque of al-Azhar** (97), 'the most blooming', is 100 metres east of al-Ghuri's caravanserai, the first mosque of the Fatimid city (completed in 971), the oldest university in the world and the foremost centre of Islamic theology. Its age and importance have caused it to be rebuilt and added to many times, the result confusing and unremarkable. The court and arcades are basically Fatimid, but their interest lies in the people gathered here, students and teachers at lessons, some pacing back and forth, mumbling to themselves, memorising religious texts, others dozing.

Throughout the millenium of its existence, al-Azhar has offered free instruction and board to students from all over the Islamic world, from West Africa to the East Indies, its courses sometimes lasting 15 years. *Riwaqs* or apartments are set aside around three sides of the court for specific nationalities or provinces of Egypt, and here students have traditionally studied religious, moral, civil and criminal law, grammar, rhetoric, theology, logic, algebra and calculations on the Muslim calendar which is based on the moon, its festivals changeable but always advancing against the secular solar calendar. The Chapel of the Blind at the eastern angle of al-Azhar accommodates blind students, once notorious for their outrageous behaviour. Fanatical in their belief and easily thinking themselves persecuted, they would rush out into the streets, snatching at turbans, beating people with their staves and groping about for infidels to kill.

Oldest university in the world

Al-Azhar's religious curriculum has remained unchanged since the days of Saladin, who turned al-Azhar from a hotbed of Shi'ism to the home of orthodoxy, though Nasser obliged the university to include, too, schools of medicine, science and foreign languages, so that now in many ways it is competitive with other institutions of higher education in Egypt. The modern university buildings are behind the mosque proper.

You enter the mosque through the double-arched Gate of the Barbers (the only one open to visitors) where formerly students had their heads shaved, and for a bit of baksheesh can ascend the *minaret of Qaytbay*. Passing into the courtyard, on the left is the *library*, worth a visit, and to the right a 14th C *madrasa* with a fine mihrab. The *sanctuary hall* directly opposite the entry gate is very deep, though in Fatimid times it did not extend beyond the fifth row of columns (that is five rows beyond the two of the east arcade), and the original mihrab remains. These columns were taken mostly from early churches. The sanctuary was extended to eight rows in the 18th C and a new mihrab placed at its farthest, qibla, wall.

Leaving al-Azhar and walking north, you pass under the busy Sharia al-Azhar and stand before the **Mosque of Sayyidna al-Hussein**, a modern structure with slender Turkish-style minarets built on a Fatimid site. This is the main congregational mosque of Cairo and the President of the Republic comes here on feast days for prayers, while the open square before it is the centre for popular nightly celebrations throughout the month of Ramadan — well worth seeing.

The Hussein, named for a grandson of the Prophet, is supposedly forbidden to non-Muslims, though I have several times been invited inside. Hussein's head, brought to Cairo in 1153 in a green silk bag, is in the mausoleum (it is also said to be in the Great Mosque in Damascus), a relic of one of the most critical events in Islamic history, the schism between the Sunni majority and the Shi'ites.

The Sunni-Shi'ite schism
Mohammed was more than a prophet, he organised the Arab tribes into an enduring political and military force that within a hundred years or so of his death in 632 advanced as far west as Morocco and Spain, as far north as Poitiers and as far east as the Indus. But Mohammed died without naming a successor. His son-in-law Ali, husband of the Prophet's daughter Fatima, advanced his claim but after some argument Abu Bakr, one of Mohammed's companions, won acceptance as *Khalifat rasul-Allah* or Successor to the Apostle of God. Abu Bakr was succeeded by Omar who was succeded on his death by Othman, an old, weak and vacillating man, but a member of the powerful Umayyad family of Mecca. Tribal tensions within the ever-expanding Arab empire led to revolt and his murder in 656. Again Ali put himself forward as the natural inheritor of the caliphate, for not only was he related to Mohammed through Fatima, but he was a man of considerable religious learning and sincerity, while his supporters claimed the Umayyads were no more than power-seeking opportunists. To some extent both sides cloaked political and economic aspirations in religious arguments. Ali however was opposed by Aisha, who had been Mohammed's favourite wife, along with her Umayyad family and many of Mohammed's surviving companions. He took to arms and won his first battle, but later saw his authority dissolve when rebels advanced on his army with copies of the Koran fixed to the points of their spears and his troops refused to fight. Ali was assassinated and the Umayyads were installed once again in the caliphate.

The real wound to Islam occurred, however, when Ali's

son — no mere in-law of the Prophet but of his blood — led a revolt against the by now overwhelming forces of the Umayyads and after a fanatical struggle was slain with all his men. In a sense the Prophet's own blood had been shed — excusable, said the Ummayads, for Hussein was no more than an outlaw; martyrdom, replied those who had supported Ali and Hussein. It was on this matter of succession — divine right versus might — that Islam was riven, for the partisans or *Shia* of Ali refused to accept as caliph any but Ali's descendants, while the *Sunni*, followers of the *sunna*, The Way, barred the caliphate to the Prophet's descendants for all time.

In fact, the Shi'ites went on to win some notable victories as when the Fatimids took Egypt, and to this day one-tenth of all Muslims (Iranians, most Iraqis and significant numbers in Yemen, Syria, Lebanon and eastern Arabia) still hold to the Shi'ite conviction that with the deaths of Ali and Hussein the greater part of Islam was stained with betrayal. All the same, this division within Islam is much less important than the doctrinal rifts within Christianity, and it is remarkable that it is here in the old Fatimid city, by the mausoleum supposedly containing the very head of the Shi'ite martyr, that the president of thoroughly Sunni Egypt should come to pray.

Muski and Khan el Khalili

The bazaars

Muski and Khan el Khalili are used interchangeably by both foreigners and Egyptians alike to describe what are historically two different bazaars. **Muski** lies astride Sharia el Muski, a street of Mohammed Ali's period running east from Midan Ataba, pots, pans, plastic bowls and other prosaic wares sold at its western end but blending with the Oriental atmosphere of Khan el Khalili which it joins to the east.

Khan el Khalili is the larger and older of the two, and grew round a khan or caravanserai built in 1382 by Sultan Barquq's Master of Horse, Garkas el Khalili. It became known as the Turkish bazaar during the Ottoman period and has always attracted foreign merchants — Jews, Armenians, Persians and non-Egyptian Arabs — and so it is not surprising that today, along with the Muski, it is Cairo's tourist bazaar, selling souvenirs, perfume oils, jewellery, leather goods and fabrics. Of course the sight of so many tourists invites relentless importuning, but there is adventure all the same. Escape down back alleyways where an artisan sitting in his hole in the wall may patiently be making beads one by one from rough bits of stone, turning them on a spindle by means of a bow. Or start in bargaining and then break off — an accepted, indeed the expert pattern — and instead sip a proffered glass of tea, idling for hours if you like upon a pile of carpets without there being any sense of the need for business. Or go into Fishawi's, the famous café just off Midan Sayyidna Hussein. Here you can have the chance of easy conversation

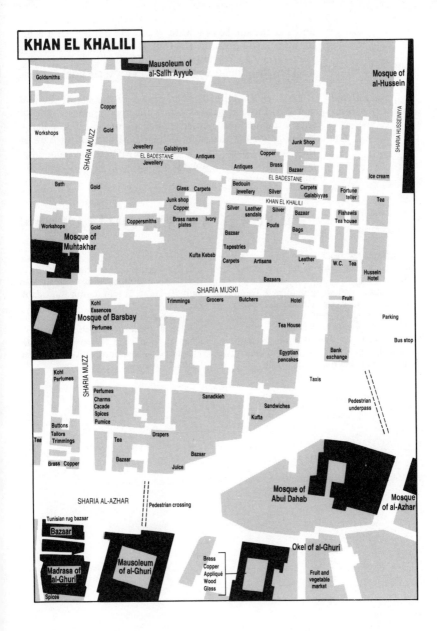

KHAN EL KHALILI

Goldsmiths

Mausoleum of
al-Salih Ayyub

Mosque of
al-Hussein

Copper

Gold

Workshops

SHARIA MUIZZ

SHARIA HUSSEINIYA

Jewellery Galabiyyas
EL BADESTANE
Jewellery

Antiques

Junk Shop

Copper

Brass

Antiques

Bazaar

EL BADESTANE

Ice cream

Bath

Gold

Glass Carpeta

Bedouin
jewellery

Silver

Carpets
Galabiyyas

Fortune
teller

Tea

Junk shop

KHAN EL KHALILI

Copper

Silver Leather
sandals

Silver

Bazaar

Fishawis
Tea house

Coppersmiths

Brass name
plates

Ivory

Bazaar

Pouts

Bags

Workshops

Gold

Mosque of
Muhtakhar

Tapestries

Kufta Kebab

Carpets

Artisans

Leather

W.C. Tea

Hussein
Hotel

Bazaars

SHARIA MUSKI

Kohl
Essences

Trimmings

Grocers

Butchers

Hotel

Fruit

Parking

Mosque of Barsbay

Perfumes

Tea House

Bus stop

SHARIA MUIZZ

Egyptian
pancakes

Bank
exchange

Kohl
Perfumes

Taxis

Perfumes
Charms
Cacade
Spices
Pumice

Sanadkieh

Sandwiches

Pedestrian
underpass

Kufta

Buttons
Tailors
Trimmings

Tea

Tea

Drapers

Bazaar

Brass Copper

Bazaar

Juice

Mosque of
Abul Dahab

Mosque
of al-Azhar

SHARIA AL-AZHAR

Pedestrian crossing

Tunisian rug bazaar

Okel of al-Ghuri

Bazaar

Madrasa of
al-Ghuri

Mausoleum
of al-Ghuri

Brass
Copper
Appliqué
Wood
Glass

Fruit and
vegetable
market

Spices

and a gentle smoke of a water pipe ('Do not inhale, it is not hashish.'), and open the pages of *Midaq Alley* or *Children of the Gebelawi* by Neguib Mahfouz, Egypt's Nobel Prize winning novelist, who found the settings for these books around this area.

The Fatimid palaces   Khan el Khalili extends in part over the site of the now vanished Fatimid palaces which covered an area of 400,000 square metres and housed 12,000 domestics. The palaces, al-Muizz on the east side of Sharia Muizz and al-Aziz on the west, loomed like mountains when seen from afar; near to, they could not be seen at all, so high were the surrounding walls.

PRACTICAL INFORMATION

Instructions for reaching the start of this itinerary are the same as for the Islamic Museum.

Remember that there is often a **fee** of LE1 at mosques, etc, classed as Islamic monuments. Also you will need small change for services performed.

The Okel (or Wakala) of al-Ghuri serves also as a permanent exhibition of fellahin and Bedouin folk crafts, and those of Nubia and the oases. Folk music and dancing troupes sometimes perform in the courtyard. Open from 9am to 5pm daily (9–11am, 2–4pm during Ramadan). **Fee LE2.**

An **abbreviated itinerary** should at least involve a stroll from Bab Zuwayla to Khan el Khalili for the passing flavour. This could be combined with a visit to the Islamic Museum.

TO THE NORTHERN WALLS

Street of the Coppersmiths

Sharia Muizz, as you leave the awning-covered alleyways of Khan el Khalili and walk north along it, is the Street of the Coppersmiths, some bashing of metal, much flashing of sunlight. Some reminders of the Fatimid period survive, though mostly the monuments are Mameluke. There should be a mosque on every street, it is said. Here mosques fight for every corner, their domes and minarets bunched like palms in an oasis grove. The scene is still that of the *Thousand and One Nights*, ostensibly set in Baghdad, though Baghdad by then had been razed by Tamerlane and it was the Cairo of the Mamelukes that was described. Sweet juices, cool water are sold in the street, the waterseller with a large flask slung under one arm like a bagpipe, round his waist the cups. He leans forward to pour, and for a moment you imagine this an obeisance to a passing sultan, and in the sweep of robes, the clattering of donkey carts, the bursts of reflected light from the coppersmiths' stalls, you easily imagine a triumphal entry, a parade of state, singers and poets preceding the royal appearance, celebrating the achievements of his reign. You see fluttering banners of silk and gold thread, then carried before the sultan himself the jewelled saddlecloth, symbol of his sovereignty, and above his head a parasol of yellow silk surmounted with a golden cupola on which perches a golden bird, this held aloft by a prince of the blood, a band of flutes, of kettledrums, trumpets and hautboys passing now, their music mingling in the clamour of the street and then lost.

There is spectacle enough in Sharia Muizz, and behind its facades, to remind you that this was a city of beauty and mystery. Ruthless for power, cunning in government, brutal and barbarous often, the Mamelukes at their best were resourceful and vital, with an incomparable flair for architecture. Their grandiose designs, bold, vigorous and voluminous, were gracefully decorated with the play of arabesques, the embroidery of light through stained-glass windows.

The Story of Shagarat al-Durr

You come first, on the right, to the Mausoleum and Madrasa of al-Salih Ayyub, diagonally opposite the Maristan of Qalaun. Where the street now presses its way was once, in Fatimid times, a broad avenue, so broad it served as a parade ground, the great palaces looking down upon it from either side. Throughout the Fatimid and Mameluke periods, this was the very centre of Cairo.

The **Mausoleum and Madrasa of al-Salih Ayyub** (38) need to be searched for. You turn right off Muizz into a lane — there is a tiny teashop on the corner with some round brass tables outside (an agreable place to sit for a while). A short distance

121

along the lane is an arch set into a facade with a Fatimid-style minaret rising from it. This is the madrasa, and you enter what remains of it by turning left into what is now used by neighbourhood youths as a playing field, liwans to east and west. The mausoleum is reached by returning to the Street of the Coppersmiths and turning right. You will see the dome on your right, and the door will be locked, but ask (or gesture to) anyone nearby for the key: they will find the keeper.

The interest of this place is historical, for it marks a political and architectural transition. Al-Salih Ayyub was the last ruler of Saladin's dynasty. His wife, who completed his madrasa and mausoleum after he died in 1249, was Shagarat al-Durr, a beautiful Armenian or Turkish slave girl who ushered in Mameluke rule. While it has Fatimid elements, the madrasa was also the first to provide for all four schools of Sunni Islam, and was the first also to link madrasa and mausoleum — in short, it was the prototype for the Mameluke mosque-madrasa-mausolea to follow. Throughout the Mameluke period it was used as Cairo's central court (the schools teaching, amongst other things, law as at al-Azhar), and the street outside, Sharia Muizz, served as the place of execution.

Tree of Pearls

Shagarat al-Durr, whose name means Tree of Pearls, shares with Hatshepsut and Cleopatra that rare distinction of having been a female ruler of Egypt. She rose to power at a critical moment, when St Louis at the head of the Sixth Crusade seized Damietta in the Delta. Ayyub, dying from cancer, was too weak to dislodge him, and St Louis was content to await the sultan's death and what he imagined would be the collapse of government and all resistance to Christian occupation of the country.

But Shagarat al-Durr was of independent nomadic stock, a society in which women went unveiled and were the equals of their men. She hid her husband's corpse in the Mameluke barracks on Roda while pretending he was merely ailing, and for three months ruled Egypt by appearing to transmit orders from Ayyub to his generals.

Egypt played for time and offered the Crusaders Jerusalem if they would abandon Damietta. St Louis refused. But meanwhile in the heat, and fed bad fish by the Delta people, the Crusaders became sick with scurvy and plague. St Louis then accepted the offer of Jerusalem, but it was the Egyptians now who refused, and the Mameluke general Baybars fell

The capture of St Louis

upon the Crusaders, capturing St Louis, who had to buy his freedom with a vast indemnity and the renunciation of all claim to Egypt.

Shagarat al-Durr now openly proclaimed herself sultana and for 80 days was the only female Muslim ruler in Middle Eastern history, but the Abbasid Caliph refused to recognise her, quoting the Prophet who had said, 'The people that

Minarets of Qalaun, al-Nasr and Barquq along medieval Cairo's main Fatimid street

123

make a woman their ruler are past saving'. So she married the leader of her Mameluke slave-warriors, Aybak, ruling through him, but when she heard he was considering another marriage she hired assassins to murder him in his bath. Hearing his screams, seeing his body hacked at with swords, at the last moment she tried to save his life, but the assassins went on: 'If we stop halfway through, he will kill both you and us'.

When the murder was discovered, Shagarat al-Durr offered to marry the new Mameluke chief, but she was imprisoned instead and is said to have spent her last days grinding up all her jewels so that no other woman should wear them. The Mamelukes had discovered their power to make and unmake rulers; in future they ruled themselves. Shagarat al-Durr was turned over to the wife she had made Aybak divorce who instructed her female slaves to beat her to death with bath clogs. They tossed her naked body over the Citadel wall to be devoured by dogs. Her few remains were deposited in her tomb on the edge of the Southern Cemetery not too far from the Mosque of Ibn Tulun.

Qalaun, al-Nasr and Barquq

A splendour of domes and minarets Looking up and across Sharia Muizz you see on its west side the splendid cluster of domes and minarets that are the Madrasa and Mausoleum of Qalaun, the Mausoleum of al-Nasr, his son and successor, and the Mosque of Barquq. Qalaun — the name means duck and has an absurd ring in Arabic — was one of the ablest, most successful and long-lived (1220–90) of the notoriously short-lived Mameluke sultans, who moreover founded a dynasty lasting nearly 100 years. His name suggests Mongol origins, and he is known to have been brought from the lower Volga region, ruled at the time by the Golden Horde. It was al-Salih Ayyub, buried across the street, who first began importing slaves from there, employing them as bodyguards. Qalaun served the country of his purchase well: Damascus and Baghdad had fallen to the Mongols, Egypt and Arabia the sole remaining bulwarks of Islam; Baybars checked the threat, Qalaun eliminated it, and then marched against the Crusaders at Acre, their last stonghold in the Holy Land, but died enroute. An outstanding builder, his tribute to his Christian enemies was the adoption of Romanesque elements in his complex here, the **Maristan, Madrasa and Mausoleum of Qalaun** (43).

First you go through the gate and down a wide tree-shaded walk, the heat and noise of the Street of the Coppersmiths falling away behind you. At the end is a modern hospital, built within the vaster limits of Qalaun's **maristan** or hospital and insane asylum — a hospital has stood on this spot for 700 years. Three great liwans of the original remain, the windows of the east liwan still displaying their carved stucco surrounds. The north liwan, it seems, is now used as a dump for surgical dressings.

Islamic enlightenment Islam was a wonder of enlightened medical care at a time when the ill, especially the mad, were pariahs in Christian Europe. From Spain to Persia, hospitals flourished, were divided into clinics, surgery was perfected, such delicate operations as the removal of cataracts were performed, musicians and singers entertained the sick, and upon their discharge patients were given sums of money to enable them to live until they could again find employment.

Returning now to the street and turning left, the wall on your left-hand side is that of Qalaun's **madrasa**. At the far corner the line of the building then retreats and you come to what was the original entrance to the maristan. The entrance opens onto a corridor, blocked at the far end, which runs between the mausoleum on the right and the madrasa on the left. During recent reconstruction of the madrasa the opportunity was taken to excavate for clues to the Fatimids' western palace which stood here. The plan is a courtyard with a liwan at either end, the sanctuary or eastern liwan suggesting a north Syrian basilical church, with three aisles and classical columns. The stucco work farther in from the arch is original.

Qalaun's **mausoleum** is off the other side of the corridor. The plan has been influenced by the Dome of the Rock at Jerusalem, well known to the sultan: an octagon approaching the circular within a square, the arches supported by square piers and classical columns. The dome has been restored. The structure perhaps does not seem light enough, the decorations too rich, and the mashrabiyya screen obstructs a total view (the best is from the entrance) — though it also has the effect of making the relatively small interior seem endless. But there is splendour all the same, in carved stucco, the stone inlay, the wood ornamentation, slowly revealed as your eyes get used to the filtered coloured light from the stained-glass windows — those high, double round-arched windows with oculi above, framed (from both inside and out on the street) by deeply recessed pointed arches, Qalaun's borrowing of the Romanesque.

On your way out through the corridor, have a look at its beamed and coffered ceiling, which is marvellous. The street is just before you, yet in this complex all has been private, cool and quiet, birds chirping, trees and shade and shafts of sunlight. The buildings and their purpose reveal a dignity and humanity; they provide the peace by which you recognise an unexpected civilisation.

The next building along, that is continuing north on Sharia Muizz and on the left, is the **Mausoleum of al-Nasr Mohammed** (44), now ruinous except for the facade with its Gothic doorway, removed from the Crusader Church of St John when al-Nasr completed his father's work and took Acre.

Al-Nasr's reign marked the zenith of Mameluke civilistion; his principal monuments are the mosque on the Citadel and the aqueduct bringing water there from the Nile. He is in fact buried next door in Qalaun's mausoleum.

The third of this group is the **Mosque of Barquq** (187), the first Burgi Mameluke sultan. It dates from 1386, about a century later than Qalaun's buildings, and the change in style is evident; the minaret, for example, is octagonal and, compared to the square blocks of Qalaun's, slender, while here is the high monumental entrance topped with stalactite decorations, seen also at the Sultan Hassan, which became typical of Mameluke architecture. This mosque-madrasa, in cruciform plan, was in use until this century and has been well maintained and restored. This portal is of black and white marble, the doors of bronze inlaid with silver. The sanctuary liwan is flat-ceilinged, not vaulted like the others, and receives support from four pharaonic columns of porphyry quarried in the Eastern Desert. The exquisite domed tomb chamber with marbled floors and walls of varying colours, painted ceiling, latticed and stained-glass windows and ornate wooden stalactites in the corners, contains the grave of one of Barquq's daughters — he was removed to his mausoleum in the Northern Cemetery.

Some Grand Cairene Houses Along the Way

Nearby are two houses of the Bahri Mameluke period. The **House of Uthman Katkhuda** (50) is in the street running east from Sharia Muizz, opposite Qalaun's mausoleum. It is about halfway down on the left-hand side. The doorway is entirely ordinary, but knock, or go to the apartment up the stairs, and someone will appear to show you round. (When soliciting local assistance, baksheesh is expected — usually demanded; but you should avoid paying until you have seen everything you want to, otherwise the demand for baksheesh will be made again and again, at each stage.)

Katkhuda was an 18th C lieutenant governor of the city who made what in fact was a mid-14th C palace into his home. Only a part of the whole remains, but it is an impressive example of Mameluke domestic architecture. Suddenly you are in a narrow hall of enormous height, its bare stone walls rising to the support of a wooden dome, distant sunlight streaming through the windows of its octagonal drum. This was the reception room, and guests sat in the raised area at the south end. The walls were once wainscotted with marble; the woodwork remains, though the consoles within the arches date from the 16th C. Ask to go up to the roof for a view of the quarter, and look at the *malqaf* or ventilator, a rectangular scoop common to old Cairene houses and always facing north to catch the Mediterranean breeze. One of the best things about this place is that you will almost certainly be the

Traditional air conditioning

Fatimid keel-arch portal of al-Aqmar mosque

only visitor, and its fresh bareness invites pleasing, undisturbed thoughts of moving in and where to put the furniture.

The other house, even more so a palace, is the **Qasr Beshtak** (34). This is back on Sharia Muizz, just to the north of Barquq's mosque and on the right-hand side. The entrance is the second door along the little street of the north facade — and again you will have to find someone, with some difficulty this time, who has the key.

The Emir Beshtak was married to the daughter of al-Nasr and was a man of great wealth. He built his palace on part of the foundations of the eastern Fatimid palace and it once rose to five storeys, with running water on all floors. You pass though a courtyard, up some stairs, and enter the harem reception room, vaster yet than Katkhuda's with mashrabiyya screens along the galleries. From these there is a perfectly medieval view of the streets below.

Koranic school and fountain

The **Sabil Kuttab of Abdul Katkhuda** (21) was built in 1744 by Uthman Katkhuda's son and is one of the most charming structures in Cairo. It stands on a triangular plot, causing a fork in the street, the kuttab's porches overhanging the roadways on either side, the great grille of what was the fountain at its base facing south towards you as you approach. The kutab is still used as the neighbourhood Koranic school, while the rest of the block is taken up with a renovated 14th C apartment building.

You continue along the left-hand fork and at last, on the next block, on the right-hand side, discover a rare surviving Fatimid structure in this Mameluke-dominated part of the city. The **Mosque of al-Aqmar** (33) dates from 1125 and displays a typically Fatimid keel-arch portal. The niche ribbing, used here for the first time, was to become a favourite Cairene motif. The medallion set into the niche ribbing is very finely executed. The recesses on either side of the portal have stalactite decorations, also appearing here for the first time and later taken up by the Mamelukes. The interior is original, but the slapdash minaret is modern. Aqmar means moonlit, so named for the pale stone — the Fatimids,who meant to stay, building in stone rather than the earlier brick and stucco.

The finest house in Cairo The **Bayt al-Suhaymi** (339) is not a palace and not a refuge for an English major's bric-a-brac. It is a merchant's house of the Ottoman period, built in the 16th and 17th C, and completely furnished to the age. It is the finest house in Cairo and wonderfully achieves the ambition of Islamic secular architecture — the anticipation of paradise. You reach it by taking the first right a block after the Mosque of al-Aqmar. The street is called Haret ed-Darb el Asfar and the house is at No. 19 (in case you do not notice the little green and white plaque) on the left-hand side. There is a broad wooden door. Knock.

There is nothing at the facade that prepares you for what lies within. The house consists of numerous rooms on irregular levels, mashrabiyya screen windows looking out onto the streets at one side, screened and latticed windows and arched galleries giving onto a garden courtyard on the other. You will want to wander, to enjoy the perspectives across the court from every possible angle and elevation, though you will probably be guided — by well-informed students. They will take you, for example, to the women's bedroom which faces the street but is closely latticed, to the women's chapel outside it, a malqaf 'air conditioner' above your head. You will then be deposited in the harem reception room overlooking the garden, its floors of marble, its walls covered with the most delicate green and blue plant-patterned enamel tiles, and with carved and painted wood decorations. Here you can rest and perhaps send out for tea, and begin taking it all in. For it is not the plan, not the details, but the ambience of the place that seduces you and you want time.

Though this house was built in later centuries, in ambience it cannot be different from Cairene houses of earlier times, and it becomes obvious why Crusaders crusaded — the East offered such a luxuriantly pleasurable life for those with the means, far exceeding anything back in Europe. Medieval Western architecture and certainly domestic living (with the possible exception of Provence) was crude in comparison and worst of all uncomfortable. In Europe there were the seasons of cold and wet to contend with; in Egypt the heat. But here in this house they so easily defeated heat and burning sun, creating shadows and breezes, bringing plants and birds into their home, embracing a nature they had made kinder.

The Mosque of al-Hakim and the Northern Gates

Return once again to Sharia Muizz and turn right (north). It becomes wonderful walking along this seemingly humble street, learning its secrets, its treasures offered in this guide still only a sampling of the many more that would require a far longer exploration. You are heading towards Bab al-Futuh and the walls which limit the Fatimid city. But first, on **Turkish minaret** your left, is the clean, pencil-like minaret of the **Silahdar mosque**, a Turkish-style structure of Mohammed Ali's time. Though centuries out of place for this quarter, the minaret is a graceful landmark that never fails to draw your attention as you pass by.

After about two blocks, the street broadens into a market area where garlic and onions are transported into the city and sold. The trucks which rumble in and out of Bab al-Futuh are painted with eyes as talismans against the evil eye. It is an appropriate place for superstition: on your right and leading to the Fatimid wall is the **Mosque of al-Hakim** (15), completed in 1010.

Al-Hakim was the third of the Fatimid caliphs who ruled with absolute political, military and religious authority. He was a paranoic who declared himself God and answered objections by inciting mobs to burn half the city while he lopped off the heads of the well-to-do, claiming the assistance of Adam and Solomon in angel guise. Jews he made walk about Cairo wearing clogs round their necks and Christians he made carry heavy crosses. He would spend his wary nights riding a donkey, in the company of only a mute slave, into the Moqattam to observe the stars for portents. Then exchanging clothes with his slave he would secretly descend into the city and mix with the people to learn their complaints, though assuming the role of a qadi to punish infractions with summary decapitations. One night, returning from the hills, he was assassinated — at the instigation, it is thought, of his sister Setalmulq, whom he had intended to marry.

Some say he survived the attack and retreated to the desert. The Copts claim that Christ appeared to him, and that he begged for and was granted pardon. Others say he withdrew to the sanctuary of Ammon at the Siwa Oasis deep in the Western Desert, where more than a thousand years earlier Alexander had heard himself declared the son of Zeus. There it is said, al-Hakim formulated his doctrine of a tolerant religion, similar to Islam, which was carried by Darazi, his disciple, to Lebanon where the Druze view al-Hakim's life as a kind of Passion, giving him his due as their messiah.

For centuries this mosque had an aura avoided by Cairenes who rarely used it for worship and let it crumble. It had been used as a prison for Crusader captives, as a stable by Saladin and as a warehouse by Napoleon. As recently as 1980 it was ruinous, its roofless arcades haunting, dominated by its massive brooding minarets in keeping with the Fatimid wall. These minarets proved unsound soon after construction and needed buttressing by great trapeziod bases that project out into the street, so that they seem like ziggurats (especially when viewed from outside the walls), with pepperpot domes, placed there by Baybars II at the begining of the 14th C. The mosque has now been entirely restored — perhaps over-restored — by the Indian-based Bohra sect of Ismailis who claim spiritual descent from the Fatimid imams. They will tell you that al-Hakim was not mad, that these are the lies of his enemies. And here certainly they have erased the darkness: there is the bright glitter of white marble and gold leaf, and at night the once forbidding arcades are illuminated by the warm glow of suspended glass oil lamps.

It was at **Bab al-Futuh,** the Gate of Conquests, that the great caravan of pilgrims returned each year from Mecca and then made its way along Sharia Muizz and Sharia Bab el Wazir to the Citadel. Nowadays the journey is made by jet, but in 1844 Gérard de Nerval, in *Journey to the Orient*, witnessed it like this: 'As many as 30,000 people were about to swell the population of Cairo. I managed to make my way to Bab al-Futuh; the whole of the main street which leads there was crammed with bystanders who were kept in orderly lines by government troops. The sound of trumpets, cymbals and drums directed the advancing procession; the various nations and sects were distinguished by their trophies and flags. The long files of harnessed dromedaries, which were mounted by Bedouins armed with long rifles, followed one another, but it was only when I reached the countryside that I was able to appreciate the full impact of a spectacle which is unique in all the world.

'A whole nation on the march was merging into the huge population which adorned the knolls of the Moqattam on the right, and, on the left, the thousands of usually deserted edifices of the City of the Dead; streaked with red and yellow bands, the turreted copings of the walls and towers of Saladin were also swarming with onlookers. I had the impression that I was present at a scene during the Crusades. Farther ahead, in the plain where the Qalish meanders, stood thousands of chequered tents where the pilgrims halted to refresh themselves; there was no lack of dancers and singers; all the musicians of Cairo, in fact, competed with the hornblowers and kettledrummers of the procession, an enormous orchestra whose members were perched on top of camels.

'Late in the afternoon, the booming of the Citadel cannons and a sudden blast of trumpets proclaimed that the Mahmal, a holy ark which contains Mohammed's robe of golden cloth, had arrived within sight of the city ... From time to time the Mahmal came to a halt, and the entire population prostrated themselves in the dust, cupping their heads in their hands. An escort of guards struggled to drive back the Negroes who were more fanatical than the other Muslims; they aspired, in fact, to the honour of being trampled to death beneath the camels, but the only share of martyrdom bestowed upon them was a volley of baton blows. As for the Santons, who are an even more ecstatic species of saints than the Dervishes and whose orthodoxy is more questionable, several of them pierced their cheeks with long, pointed nails and walked on, showered in blood; others devoured live serpents, while a third group stuffed their mouths with burning coals.'

Nerval was a precursor of surrealism; he enjoyed going over the top. But in this case that sober chronicler Edward William Lane (*Manners and Customs of the Modern Egyptians*), who observed the arrival of the caravan ten years before, is hardly less fantastic in his description, though he says the swallowing of serpents went out with the Mamelukes. The journey from Mecca took 37 days across rocky desert, the caravan moving at night. Not everyone survived: 'Many of the women who go forth to meet their husbands or sons receive the melancholy tidings of their having fallen victim to privation and fatigue. The piercing shrieks with which they rend the air, as they retrace their steps to the city, are often heard predominant over the noise of the drum and the shrill notes of the hautboy which proclaim the joy of others.'

Lane also mentions that the Mahmal was empty; its purpose was entirely symbolic, dating back to the reign of Shagarat al-Durr. She went on the pilgrimage one year, travelling in a magnificent *hodag* or covered litter borne by a camel, and for several successive years her empty hodag was sent with the caravan merely for the sake of state. The practice was continued by Egypt's rulers till 1927, when the puritanical Saudi king, on the pretext of objecting to the soldiers accompanying it, forbade passage of this 'object of vain pomp'. These days, alas, you wait in vain for pomp at Bab al-Futuh.

Along the walls   The gate is similar to Bab Zuwayla, with projecting oval towers, though the masonry is finer and the impression greater for the space outside it has been cleared and there is a magnificent view of the ensemble of **Bab al-Futuh, Bab al-Nasr** — the Gate of Victory — (to the east), the linking **Fatimid wall** and al-Hakim's minarets. The Fatimid wall extends to the west;

beyond that, where it retreats, and also to the east of Bab al-Nasr, the wall dates from Saladin. You can walk both within and along the top of the wall between the gates, and to do this you should make yourself obviously interested at either gate and eventually someone with the key will come along.

Re-entering the medieval city through Bab al-Nasr, the immediate area is noisy with metal workshops. On the right (west) against the east facade of al-Hakim's mosque is the caravanserai or **wakala of Sultan Qaytbay** (11) built in 1481. It is now inhabited by tinsmiths and their families; women scrubbing, washing strung across the courtyard, children beating a kitten and throwing it into the air.

PRACTICAL INFORMATION

To reach the starting point of this tour take a **taxi** or the **No. 66 bus** to Khan el Kahlili.

Entrance **fees** are payable at the Qalaun complex and the Bayt al-Suhaymi, and baksheesh should be paid for services elsewhere.

For those with limited time, an **abbreviated itinerary** should include a visit to the Qalaun complex, the Bayt al-Suhaymi and a walk along the walls between Bab al-Futuh and Bab al-Nasr — but above all visit the Bayt al-Suhaymi.

THE CITY OF THE DEAD

Burial ground of the Mameluke sultans

The Northern Cemetery or City of the Dead lies to the east of the Fatimid city. The Mausoleum of Barquq is 1.5 km from Bab al-Nasr, for example, and Qaytbay's mausoleum is a kilometre from al-Azhar. So a walk from Bab al-Nasr, visiting these two mausolea as well as that of Ashraf Baybars' — the three most outstanding buildings — and then back to al-Azhar, will cover about 3 km. You may prefer to make a separate journey of it, hiring a taxi.

You may already have noticed the City of the Dead as you drove in on the Heliopolis road from the airport; it did not seem inviting. It has the look of a bidonville — hot, dusty, dilapidated, with a quanity of domes. It is in fact the burial ground of the Mameluke sultans and of others who aspired to their end, and some of its mausolea are as wonderful as anything in the city of the living. Nor is the cemetery without life. There were monasteries and schools, part of the mausolea. And the poor have always made their homes here, and the keepers, while relatives visit the family plots on feast days for a picnic. This is reminiscent of the ancient Egyptian practice of feeding the dead, though it is practiced elsewhere in the Mediterranean, as in Greece where it is more a cheerful popping of the cork and celebration of life.

The Three Most Outstanding Mausolea

Follow the road that runs east outside Bab al-Nasr and on reaching the cemetery you will see ahead of you a broad building with two domes and two minarets. This is the **Mausoleum of Barquq** (149), completed in 1411. Its plan is similar to that of a cruciform madrasa, but the liwans are not vaulted, instead entered through multi-domed arcades. You enter nowadays at the southwest corner and pass through a corridor into the sahn, its vastness once relieved by a pair of tamarisk trees, now only by the fountain. On the eastern side is the sanctuary liwan with a beautifully carved marble minbar, dedicated by Qaytbay. At either end of the liwan are domed tomb chambers, Barquq (removed here from his mausoleum in Sharia Muizz) and his two sons buried in the left chamber, women of the family in the right. These domes are the earliest of stone in Cairo; the zigzag ribbing on their exteriors was to develop into the elaborate polygons of Qaytbay's domed mausoleum. From the outside, the domes are minimised by the surrounding structure, and so inside their marvellous shape and soaring height comes as a surprise.

Go back across the courtyard to the northwest corner and up the stairs. These lead you to the *khanqah* or Dervish monastery, its four storeys a warrren of rooms, cells and corridors. For some extra baksheesh the keeper will usually let you go up the

133

northern minaret for a sweeping view of the nercropolis itself and all of Cairo from Heliopolis to the Citadel.

The **Mausoleum of Sultan Ashraf Baybars** (121) — he is also known as Barsbey — is south down the paved but dusty road that passes along the front of Barquq's mausoleum. This building is less visited than the other two and finding the keeper may be more difficult; at any monument, here or in the city, apprehend the first child or lounger you see and make it known you want the key — the keeper will usually soon appear. Baksheesh is then of course expected all round.

This was originally planned solely as a khanqah and so is usually elongated; also it is recognised by its ungainly

Tombs in the City of the Dead, c. 1800

unminaret which too soon comes to a point. This Baybars, whose mausoleum dates from 1432, was a Burgi or Circassian Mameluke and is not to be confused with his namesake who held St Louis to ransom. He neither drank nor swore, though was martial enough and took Cyprus from the Franks in 1426. The appeal of the place is in its few but well-chosen elaborations — the polygonally decorated dome rising above the simple facade through which you pass by a doorway with trefoil arch. The tomb chamber is at the north end of the mosque, dimly illuminated by stained-glass windows subsequently introduced, though the mihrab of mother-of-pearl and marble mosaic is original. But really you have come for the interior view of the dome and its impression alone is sufficient: it ascends effortlessly upwards, almost losing itself to infinity.

A jewel of
Mameluke
architecture
It is a longer distance down this same dusty road to the **Mausoleum of Qaytbay** (99), completed in 1474 and a jewel of Mameluke architecture. First, from across the square, look at the ablaq masonry of the facade, the intricate polygonal relief on the exquisitely proportioned dome, and the slender minaret of three tiers (the Mameluke fashion), each tier ornately decorated with columned recesses or raised arabesques or stalactite clusters. Along with the Ibn Tulun and the Sultan Hassan, this rates as one of the great buildings of Cairo. Unlike them it is free with decoration, but like them it uses its decoration to the highest effect — the frequent play, for example, of filigree flowers upon star-shaped polygons which has been described as 'a song for two voices', a geometrical base with floral melody.

Along with al-Nasr, Qaytbay was the grandest of Mameluke builders, emblazoning his cartouche on buildings religious and secular throughout the Middle East, as well as in Cairo and Alexandria. He was also the last Mameluke ruler of strength. Meshullam ben Menahem, an Italian Jew, described him: 'He is an old man of about 80, but tall, handsome and as upright as a reed. Dressed in white, he was on horseback, accompanied by more than 2000 Mameluke soldiers ... Whoever wishes can have access to the sultan: there is in the town a great and splendid fortress at the entrance of which he sits publicly on Mondays and Thursdays, accompanied by the governor of the city; a guard of more than 3000 Mamelukes surrounds him. Whoever has been manhandled or robbed by one of the Mameluke princes or emirs can there complain. Thus the nobles refrain from actions that might carry condemnation'. He came up through the ranks, having been bought by Ashraf Baybars, and apart from al-Nasr ruled longer than any other sultan. The perfection of his mausoleum, however, like the splendour of his reign, marked the final apogee of Mameluke vigour. Decadence ensued; two decades later the Turks were in the city, Bab Zuwayla ornamented by the last Mameluke sultan, a rope round his neck.

Inside is a cruciform madrasa with vestigial liwans to east and west. The decoration of ceilings, pavings, arches, windows is breathtakingly variegated, yet overall it is measured and subdued. There is deliberate though sensitive contrast with the scale of the courtyard and sanctuary in the immense height of the tomb chamber, its walls drawn into the ascending dome.

Finally, from the sanctuary, you should climb the roof to enjoy at closer hand the tracery of stone carving, as delicate as previous periods had managed in wood and stucco, on the dome and minaret.

PRACTICAL INFORMATION

Apart from resorting to a **taxi, bus No. 500** goes from Midan el Tahrir to Midan el Barquq; the Mausoleum of Barquq lies not far to the southeast.

For those with limited time the temptation might be to leave out this long journey to the City of the Dead altogether, but even the most **abbreviated itinerary** should include a visit to the Mausoleum of Qaytbay, one of the finest enclosed interiors in the world.

THE EGYPTIAN MUSEUM

The Museum of Egyptian Antiquities, to give it its proper name, is on the north side of Midan el Tahrir, near the Nile Hilton. It was founded at Bulaq in 1858 by Auguste Mariette, the great pioneer archaeologist who first excavated the Serapeum at Saqqara, the Temple of Amun at Karnak, Hatshepsut's mortuary temple at Deir el Bahri, and the temples at Dendera and Edfu. The collection has occupied the present classical-style building since 1902 and has long since outgrown it. There are over 100,000 exhibits which could easily fill half a dozen museums this size, a unique storehouse of one of the oldest and grandest civilisations on earth.

Allowing one minute for each exhibit, you could see everything in the museum in about nine months. The average guided tour lasts two hours. The selection offered here would take one hard-working day to cover, though it would be better to break that down into two or three half-day visits.

The exhibits are numbered and some carry background notes in English, French and Arabic. The rooms are also numbered, as shown on the plans. The collection is arranged more or less chronologically, so that starting at the entrance and walking clockwise round the ground floor you pass from Old Kingdom through Middle and New Kingdom exhibits, concluding with Ptolemaic and Roman exhibits. The first floor contains prehistoric and early dynastic exhibits and the contents of several tombs, including Tutankhamun's. *Not every room is mentioned in the tour below*.

The Ground Floor

Immediately upon entering (from the south), you walk into a rotunda that is *Room 48*. Apart from the monumental Sphinx at Giza, the colossal head to the left (6051) of Userkaf (V Dyn) is the only large sculpture surviving from the Old Kingdom. The rotunda contains other giant works (out of chronological order), including three colossi (1, 2, 4) of Ramses II (XIX Dyn) and a statue of Amenhotep son of Hapu (3), architect to Amenophis III (XVIII Dyn).

The Old Kingdom   *Room 47*: Contains IV, V and VI Dynasty items. The walls are lined with sarcophagi. Most interesting are the figures in the central aisle cases, including, in Case B, statuettes of the dwarf (160), the man with a deformed head (6310) and the hunchback (6311), but also, in Case D, those of people grinding corn, kneading dough, preparing food (a goose about to be gutted and plucked).

Room 41: The V Dynasty bas-relief (79) with scenes of country life is particularly worthy of close observation. Farm tasks and crafts are carried on through a series of registers.

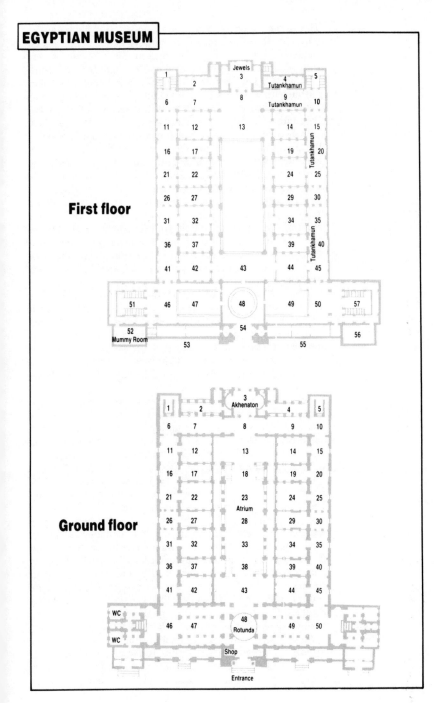

EGYPTIAN MUSEUM

First floor

Ground floor

The women wear ankle-length chemises, but the men wear only a cloth or are sometimes entirely naked. They are circumcised as was the Egyptian custom. There is also one episode of a malefactor being held and brought before a court.

Room 42: The very fine statue of Chephren (138) in black diorite with white marbling was found in a shaft at his Valley Temple at Giza where he built the second of the Great Pyramids. The falcon god Horus embraces Chephren's head with his wings, at once transferring the ka and protecting the pharaoh. The remarkably preserved wooden statue of Ka-aper (140) is vividly executed. You feel you would recognise the face in the original, and indeed when Mariette found it at Saqqara his workmen immediately dubbed it Sheikh el Beled because of its resemblance to their village headman. The living eyes are copper inlaid with quartz. It is said of some paintings that the eyes follow you; in this case it is uncanny how they fix you with their sure and level gaze when faced head on, but as soon as you shift even a centimetre they gaze off — not inert, but reflectively, into an internal dream world of their past.

Room 31: Outstanding here are the six wooden panels of the II Dynasty priest Hesire (88). This was the brief period in ancient Egyptian history when moustaches were fashionable.

Room 32: One gets so used to the rigid frontality of Egyptian sculpture that it is a surprise to see the wooden statue in the far right corner with its slight twist. At the centre of the room are the IV Dynasty statues (223, 195) of Prince Rahotep and Princess Nafrit, her skin painted yellow, his ruddy brown. He has short back and sides and sports a natty moustache. In his white waist cloth he looks all the world like an advertising executive taking a sauna. The group representing the dwarf Seneb, Chief of the Wardrobe, with his wife and two children (6055) deserves close attention. It is delightful, but also a puzzle. Despite his small size, Seneb is a man of importance; he looks pleased with himself, sure of his position, his family, his wife's proud affection. Notice his legs: they are too short to hang over the edge of the chair; instead his children stand where his legs would be — is this a mere compositional nicety or has it a symbolic intention? And look at the children, their right index fingers to their lips as though they were keeping a secret. The III/IV Dynasty 'Geese of Meidum' (136) are vividly coloured. The copper statues (230, 231) of Pepi I and his son are the first metal statues known, and that of Pepi the largest of its kind. He is a great striding figure, reminiscent of an archaic Greek kouros.

The Middle Kingdom

With *Room 26* you pass into the Middle Kingdom.

Room 22: Generally sculpture and stone monuments of the Middle Kingdom. At the centre is the burial chamber of Horhotep (300). The walls are painted with oil jars and offerings are closely listed. The decorated doors, like patchwork

Akhenaton (Room 3, ground floor): the glare of revolution

curtains, were for the ka to flit in and out at will. Around the chamber are ten statues of Sesostris I (301). On the sides of each throne are reliefs of the gods of Upper and Lower Egypt entwining the lotus and papyrus, symbolising the unity of the country.

The New Kingdom

With *Room 11* you pass into the New Kingdom. 400: a fine statue of Tuthmosis III (XVII Dynasty) in grey schist.

Room 12: XVIII Dynasty sculpture. The brightly decorated chapel built for Amenophis II or his predecessor Tuthmosis III once contained Hathor as cow (445, 446) — she now stands before it in a glass case. To the right is a pink granite statue (952) of Hatshepsut. Look also for the case containing a small statuette (6257), delicately carved out of Sudanese ebony, of Thay, a royal equerry.

Room 8: It is unusual for mud brick houses, even palaces, to survive, and so our impression of ancient Egypt is largely determined, often distorted, by rock tombs and stone mortuary temples. But the Egyptians did concern themselves with this world and at the centre of this room is a model of a typical house as excavated at Tell el Amarna, Akhenaton's brief capital on the Nile near Minya.

The Akhenaton Room

Room 3 contains perhaps the most astonishing works in the museum, from the reign of Akhenaton. Some find the Amarna style — particularly when applied in its most exaggerated form to Akhenaton himself — grotesque. I think it powerful and often beautiful. Staring down at you are four colossi of the pharaoh: the glare of revolution. Elongated face, narrow eyes, long thin nose with flaring nostrils and full, perhaps sardonic lips. The belly and thighs protrude like some primitive female fertility figure. These are from the temple he built, at Karnak, later destroyed, its blocks serving as foundations and pylon filler for others' works. In its own glass case there is a magnificent head, probably of Nefertiti, and this is not distorted at all — though examples of Amarnan distortion applied to Nefertiti are seen on the stele in Case F, and the centre stele in Case H. This distortion is sometimes called realism; there is a theory that Akhenaton was indeed deformed and that some of his family may have been also — and that the Amarna style was a mass acquiescence to this misfortune. But you might prefer to think that this style was deliberately experimental, calculated for effect, indeed to illustrate opposition, and as readily dispensed with (as with the bust of Nefertiti, above) when sheer beauty rather than shock value was desired. There *is* a note of realism, at least intimacy, in the centre stele in Case F. Instead of showing the royal family in formal adoration of the sun disc Aton, Akhenaton is seen playing with his eldest daughter Meritaten, while Nefertiti holds their other two daughters on her lap. This expression of family joy, or any personal feelings whatsoever, was seen never before and never again in depictions of the pharaohs. Note also the cuneiform tablets, the famous 'Amarna Letters', in Case A, and the representational masks, either models or perhaps death masks, eg 478 in Case D.

Coins *Room 4* contains a collection of Greek, Roman, Byzantine and Arab coins. Quite a few bear the head of Alexander, and on the left side of the first case on the right are several coins bearing the head of Cleopatra VII.

The Ramessids *Room 15*: Items from the reign of Ramses II, including a painted limestone statue of a XIX Dynasty queen from the Ramesseum (Case A).

Room 14: On the right is a statue (743) of Ramses VI (XX Dyn), unusual for its attempt at movement, dragging a doubled up Libyan by the hair. A painted sunk relief (769) in the left near corner shows Ramses II similarly apprehending three prisoners, one black, one red, one brown. At the centre (unnumbered, but catalogued as 765) is a unique freestanding coronation group sculpture, Ramses III at the centre, Horus on the left, Seth on the right. Though greatly restored, enough was found to determine that the figures stood on their own legs without supports.

The Late Period The New Kingdom, in any case tottering since the end of the XX Dynasty, ended with the XXI Dynasty. Objects from the Late Period begin with *Room 25*. One ruler of the XXV Dynasty, Taharka, left his mark at several sites in Upper Egypt, eg the remains of his kiosk in the Great Court at Karnak. Here you see his sculpted head (1185) with curled hair — he was from the Sudan (which the Greeks called Ethiopia). He enjoys the distinction of being mentioned in the Bible (II Kings 19:9). In *Room 24* is a green schist statue of the goddess Tweri (791) — finely finished, though an utterly ridiculous image of a pregnant anthropomorphic hippopotamus. Otherwise, the most interesting items are the Osiris, Isis and Hathor group (855, 856, 857) at the centre, and to the left 1184, an attempt at portraiture of the Mayor of Thebes.

Room 30: At Medinet Habu are the mortuary chapels of the Divine Adorers of Amun. Amenardis, in white stone (930), was one of these princesses, of the XXV Dynasty.

The Graeco-Roman Period *Room 34*: Note the colossal bust (1003) of Serapis. This god was an invention of Ptolemy Soter and combined Osiris with Apis, the bull god of Memphis, but with Greek features and dress.

Room 44: The contents of royal tombs of a Nubian people, the Blemmyes, who lived just south of Abu Simbel during the Byzantine period and were under the dominion of Meroë in the Sudan. Their aristocracy was strongly negroid. Long after Christianity came to Egypt, they worshipped Isis, Horus and Bes. The burial of kings and queens was accompanied by strangled slaves and servants, and gaily caparisoned horses which were led into the tombs and axed to death. Crowns, the skeleton of a horse, the caparisoned models of two others,

143

along with spearheads, jewellery, pottery and other artefacts form this fascinating exhibit. The artefacts of the Blemmyes have a strong, handsome look, similar to Celtic work — a fine brutality.

Room 49: An exceptional piece is the coffin of Petosiris (6036), a high priest of Thoth at Hermopolis (c.300 BC). The hieroglyphics are beautifully inlaid with stone and enamel. From Saqqara during the Persian Period is the stone sarcophagus (on the right, near the rotunda) of a dwarf dancer at the Serapeum Apis ceremony. He has been well rewarded: his true to life figure is cut on the outside of the adjacent lid, while on the inside of the lid and at the bottom of the sarcophagus is carved a sex-bomb Nut for him to lie on and stare up at for eternity.

The Atrium: large objects of various periods

On the ground floor there now remains only the atrium to visit.

At the centre of *Room 43* is the Palette of Narmer (3055), possibly the oldest record of a political event, the unification of Egypt, c.3100 BC. Narmer was probably one of the names of Menes, the founder of the I Dynasty, from which Egypt's historical period is dated. Writing was not yet able to convey complex sentences and this slate palette tells its story by means of pictures which are easily translated into words. On the obverse, Narmer is shown braining an enemy, and to the right is a complex symbol relating the significance of this action. The falcon is Narmer, holding a rope attached to the head of a bearded man. The head protrudes from a bed of papyri, representing Lower Egypt. Therefore the symbol reads, 'The falcon god Horus (Narmer) leads captive the inhabitants of the papyrus country'. Narmer came from Upper Egypt, as the crown he wears on this side shows. On the reverse, Narmer wears the crown of Lower Egypt as he reviews the spoils of his victory, which include the decapitated bodies of his foes. The centre panel shows two fantastic beasts, their necks entwined but restrained from fighting by bearded men on either side: Upper and Lower Egypt joined, if not yet altogether at ease. On either side of the room are two large wooden boats for solar sailing from the pyramid of Sesostris III at Dahshur.

Room 38 is really a stairway leading down into the well of the atrium and contains the rectangular stone sarcophagus (624) of Ay, at first an advisor to Akhenaton and later his successor. Four goddesses at each corner extend their wings protectively: Isis, Nephthys, Neith and Selket.

Room 33 displays various pyramidions from Dahshur, the capstones to pyramids. Under 6175 you can see the stone peg which slotted into the pyramid top. The sarcophagus (6337A) of Psusennas I, a XXI Dynasty pharaoh ruling from Tanis in the Delta after Egypt had split in two, has its lid (6337B) raised over a mirror so that you can see the lovely raised relief of Nut suspended from its underside. To the left, from the XVIII Dynasty, are the stone sarcophagi of Tuthmosis I (619), that of his daughter Hatshepsut made before she came to the throne (6024) and her final sarcophagus (620).

At the centre of the atrium (*Room 28*) is a painted floor with a river scene (627) from the palace of Akhenaton at Tell el Amarna.

In *Room 23* there are two interesting lintels, the one on the left (6189) showing the Heb-Sed of Senusret III (XII Dyn) very finely cut in sunk relief, while the one on the right is a tenth-rate copy by a later pharaoh.

Room 18 (the stairway leading out of the atrium well) has the colossal group (610) of Amenophis III and his wife Tiy with three of their daughters (XVII Dyn). They are serene, almost a portrait of Victorian contentment but for the play of a smile on their lips and the physicalness of their bodies. Despite the formality of the work and its size, there is a great sensuality to it. The reign of Amenophis was marked by luxury and a sudden eruption (or at least recording) of fashion consciousness: note particularly Tiy's full wig, the hair falling down to her breasts, a style associated almost exclusively with this reign.

Room 13: On the right is a fascinating document, a stele (599) inscribed on the reverse during the reign of Amenophis III with all that the pharaoh had done for Amun, but later inscribed on the obverse by Merneptah, pharaoh at about the time of the Exodus, with the sole known reference in Egyptian texts to the Israelites: 'Israel is crushed, it has no more seed!'

The *corridors* on either side of the atrium (allowing communication between Rooms 43 and 8 but not with the atrium itself) are lined with pottery, wall paintings and inscription fragments.

The First Floor

To see the first floor rooms in approximate chronological order you should start at Room 43 overlooking the atrium from the south and follow the corridors in a clockwise direction.

Old and Middle Kingdom tomb contents

Outside *Room 42* is a panel (6278) inlaid with blue faience, from Zoser's Step Pyramid at Saqqara. Inside the room you should spend time with the alabaster vase (3054) on the right, beautifully round and smooth and yet criss-crossed in raised stone with ropes from which it would have been suspended. In Case Q is the black Palermo Stone which bears a list of pharaohs from the I to mid-V Dynasties along with important events during the period and annual measurements of the Nile flood, thus adding to our knowledge of the Old Kingdom.

Room 37 is full of wooden coffins and sarcophagi of the Middle Kingdom. The coffin of Sepi (3101 in Case C), a XII

Dynasty general, is particularly well-painted. This is the oldest anthropoid coffin in the museum. See also the dismantled panels of his sarcophagus (3104 in Cases A and L), finely painted and extensively inscribed. Artefacts from the tomb of General Mesah at Assiut are displayed in several cases and include his sandals, mirror and neck pillow, and models of Egyptian soldiers (3345), black soldiers (3346) and a pleasure barge (3347).

In the corridor facing *Room 32* is a rare and astonishing wooden ka statue (280) of the Pharaoh Hor (XII Dyn) stepping out from its naos. It actually stands on a sliding base to demonstrate the wanderings of Hor's double — and that it is his ka is clear from the ka hieroglyph of upraised arms on his head, and his nakedness. Inside the room are models (Case E: 3246, 4347) of solar boats. The solar boats are unmanned, operating on autopilot. They are the abstraction of the other boats displayed: funerary boats for carrying the dead man on a canopied bier, or for transport of the living. There is a delightful model of a boat (3244 in Case F) with its mast down, its rowers pulling at full strength, one rower taking a quick sidelong glance at you as the boat shoots by.

Room 27 contains marvellous models (6077–86) from the XI Dynasty tomb of Meketre at Thebes, including a plantation owner reviewing a parade of his cattle and workers (6080); a carpenters' workshop (6083); a pleasure garden with pool, lined with sycamore-figs, at one end a columned verandah (6084); and two boats dragging a net between them, taking fish from the Nile (6085).

New Kingdom tomb contents

Room 22 contains many interesting small figures, including XII–XXX Dynasty ushabtis (Cases I and J: 6062–72), and women, perhaps concubines of the dead man, lying on beds (Case C: 9435, 9437). Cases O, P and R contain New Kingdom funerary gear, painted linen or woven cloth for covering the chest, body and feet, beautifully designed and all the more fine for being highly perishable materials that have survived.

Room 17 is particularly interesting for the papyri on its walls from the Book of the Dead.

Room 12 contains artefacts from royal tombs: a chariot of Tuthmosis IV (3000); the mummies of a child and a gazelle (Case I: 3776, 3780); a collection of priestly wigs and wig boxes (Case L: 3779).

Room 13 at the north end of the atrium displays furnishings from the intact Theban tomb of Yuya and Tuyu, parents-in-law of Amenophis III, with beds, chairs, whippet-like chariots, mummified food and time-serving ushabtis.

The north end of the first floor and all the outer rooms along its east side are devoted to Tutankhamun's treasures, but it is not easy to include their profusion in the middle of this tour. Come back to it later. In any case, more affecting are the burial exhibits in *Room 14*. These people, mostly

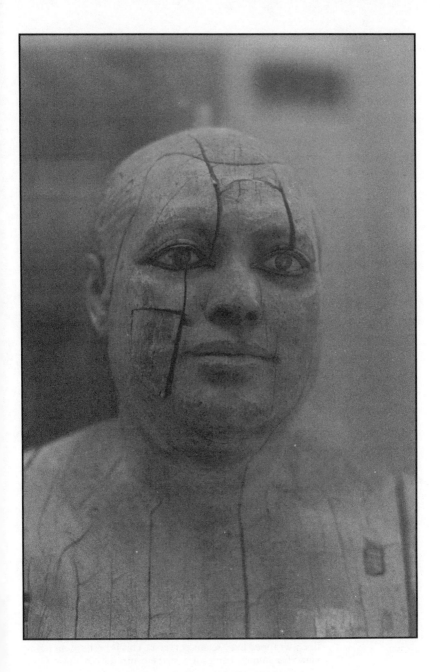

Sheikh el Beled (Room 42, ground floor): internal dream world

Greeks from the Fayyum, continued the Egyptian practice of mummification, yet from their portraits, so lifelike and modern, you cannot imagine they would have accepted the ancient belief. The encaustic portraits (colours mixed into molten wax) were bound onto the mummies — there are shelves of these. A collection of panels is against the south wall (4310): the technique is superb, with shading, highlighting and perspective, two or three of them qualifying as masterpieces in their own right. Those garbage bodies, yet these living faces in which you can read whole lives. All are marked by a seriousness, rarely pompous, occasionally sad, a faint smile on one man's lips. They have steadfastly faced the passing millenia and now look at you as you look at them as though suddenly we might recognise one another.

In *Room 19* are the gods of the Egyptian pantheon.

Room 24 is full of painted ostraka, limestone fragments.

Case 18 contains interesting representations of animals: a monkey eating, a man leading a bull, a lion devouring a prisoner, etc. People too: an intriguing picture of a woman relaxing and playing a stringed instrument. There is also, in the east doorway, a plan of a Theban tomb (4371), with what appear to be doorways shown in elevation.

In *Room 29* are further ostraka, but written on, and papyri — 6335 especially worthwhile: a Ptolemaic Book of the Dead in finest detail, showing the 'Weighing of the Heart' ceremony.

In the corridor outside *Room 34* is an Amarna toilet seat. Is this the loo on which Akhenaton sat?

Room 44 displays decorative details, most interesting the faience from palaces of Ramses II and III.

Room 57 is around the southeast staircase. The square red and green leather tent (3848) belonged to a XXI Dynasty queen and was used at her funeral.

At the centre of the south wings is *Room 48* with a model of a funerary complex, showing how a river temple linked with the pyramid on the desert's edge. There is also a cross-sectioned pyramid showing the internal buttressing. A case to the north contains beautifully worked statuettes from various periods.

Rooms 54, 55 and 53 are devoted to prehistoric and predynastic artefacts, eg pottery and tools, and are generally dull, except that in *Room 53* are mummified baboons, a dog, a crocodile and the skeleton of a mare — and these are disgusting. You can understand that the Egyptians, having convinced themselves of the efficacy of preservation, would wrap each other up. But to impose it on animals (look at their little linen-wrapped legs) seems perverse. This is perhaps an unfair view, for human beings are at the centre of our cosmology, animals only soulless lookers-on, while Egyptian religion grew out of animal worship, totemism, an admiration of their qualities (strength, swiftness, beauty), or a desire to appease; wild dogs, the 'Egyptian wolf', prowled the cemeteries by night in search of bones and bodies that the Egyptians hoped would remain unmolested, and so this predator of their eternal life was transformed into their funerary deity, Anubis. Animal cults proliferated towards the end of the pagan period and were extremely popular, religious societies collecting the sacred animals (from shrew mice to hippopotami) which died in the district, mummifying them and burying them in special cemeteries.

The Mummy Room

Room 52 is the Mummy Room where many of the mightiest men in ancient history lie naked and bird-boned in glass cases. Alas, since early 1981 visitors have been forbidden entry. The royal bodies of Amenophis III, Seti I, Ramses II and others are to be reburied either in their original tombs or in a chamber built for the purpose. This is meant as a gesture to Islam, also to national pride, yet I am inclined to agree with Jean Cocteau (*Maalesh, A Theatrical Tour of the Middle East*) that the pharaohs did not intend to hide away: 'The more I walk along, the more I listen, the more I move around the columns, the more do I experience the feeling of a dark world which fastens on to ours and which will not loosen the suckers through which it takes its life. Whatever it may cost, they find it necessary to confirm their existence, to perpetuate themselves, to incarnate, to reincarnate, to hypnotise nothingness and to vanquish it ... They did not hide themselves in order to disappear, but in order to await the cue for their entry on the stage. They have not been dragged from the tomb. They have been brought from the limbo of the wings with masks and gloves of gold ... Seti the First! How beautiful he is, with his little nose, his pointed teeth showing, his little face which belongs to death, reduced to one requirement alone — not to die. "I! I! I!" This is the word which the rafters throw back.'

Returning to the New Kingdom

You can now walk back to the north end of the first floor for the Tutankhamun exhibition which begins at *Room 7*. You pass through *Room 6* with a collection of scarabs. This black dung beetle, running everywhere about the desert sands, pushing a ball of dung before it, symbolised the self-creator, the morning sun.

Rooms 2 and 3, though leading off from the Tutankhamun exhibition area, are not properly part of it. In *Room 2* is a falcon-style coffin, very impressive in black with gold leaf design and gold bird's face (Case 4).

The Jewellery Room

Room 3 closes a quarter of an hour before the rest of the museum and is specially guarded: it contains jewellery from the I Dynasty through to the Byzantine period: necklaces, pectorals, diadems, daggers and much else in gold, silver and precious stones. The best workmanship is found in the jewellery of the XII Dynasty, and the stones are real (carnelian for red and orange, amethyst for purple and violet, lapis lazuli for blue, feldspar for green) — in Tutankhamun's time, as you will see in the following rooms, paste and glass were used instead and though the settings are gold it is mere costume jewellery. If I could walk out with any of it, you would find the VI Dynasty gold falcon head (Case 3: 4010) missing, and Mary Astor, Peter Lorre and Sidney Greenstreet hot on my trail.

The Tutankhamun Exhibition

Walking round the Tutankhamun exhibition, you occasionally notice a dust-free silhouette where a piece has been removed to join one of the Tut Tours around America, Britain, France, etc, and yet these absences hardly relieve the overwhelming impression of the whole. There is just so much, yet Tutankhamun was a minor figure who died young and was stuffed into a small tomb; imagine the impedimenta that Seti I tried taking with him. I have seen three Tutankhamun roadshows and have in each case preferred their careful choice and presentation to the jumble sale effect at the Cairo Museum. *Rooms 7, 8, 9, 10, 15, 25, 30, 35, 40 and 45*, and also *Room 4* (off Room 9) and part of *Room 13*, contain 1700 items in all. The eyes jadedly search for the highlights of the highlights, or otherwise fix on curiosities.

The gold mask

Tutankhamun's mummy, his outermost coffin of gilded wood and his granite sarcophagus are all in his tomb in the Valley of the Kings, but the second coffin of gilded wood and the third of solid gold are in *Room 4*, along with the gold mask. Each of these, placed one within the other like Russian dolls, in turn were placed within a gilded wood shrine — which again fitted within three more (*Rooms 7 and 8*). These shrines remind me of Wilhelm Reich's orgone boxes, a crackpot device for concentrating orgone energy around the human body: 'Quite unexpectedly the knowledge of the biological function of tension and charge led me to the discovery of hitherto unknown energy processes in bions, in the human organism and in the radiation of the sun... This energy, which is capable of charging non-conducting substances, I termed *orgone*... The orgone energy has a parasympatheticotonic effect and charges living tissues... The human organism is surrounded by an orgonotic field which varies according to the individual's vegetative motility' (*The Function of the Orgasm*). The ancient Egyptians, however, were born and died too soon to benefit from Reich's teachings, and employed these gold casings in part because gold was thought to be the flesh of the gods, and also because it warded off all outside contamination, presumably including, alas, orgone.

In *Room 5* is a curiosity other examples of which you may have noticed elsewhere in the museum: a vegetating Osiris (Case 93, 1064). It is a wooden silhouette of the god, his image again carved out within this and the depression once filled with earth from which grass would sprout with symbolic effect.

Among the finer or more curious items in the east gallery (*Rooms 15 to 45*) are a jewellery casket of gilded wood (*Room 45*, Case 54, 447) in the form of a naos with the figure of Anubis on top; a chest (*Room 35*, Case 20, 324) for the pharaoh's clothes decorated on the lid with a desert hunt, on the large panels with Tutankhamun waging war, and on the small panels with the royal sphinx trampling on his enemies; two life-size statues of Tutankhamun (96 and 181, at the entrance to Room 45 near the stairway) which guarded the entrance to the burial chamber; and the famous small throne (1), its back richly decorated with a scene of Tutankhamun's queen placing her right hand on his left shoulder, often interpreted as a relaxed domestic scene, though probably a gesture confirming his position, as she was after all the daughter — and possibly a widow — of Akhenaton, and the royal ka was transferred through the female line (explaining the frequent sister and daughter marriages of pharaohs). The armrests too are beautiful, the lovely shape of falcons' wings extending in protection, the birds' heads wearing the crown of Upper and Lower Egypt. As you leave the gallery, on either side of the doorway are statues of the two guards who were found standing in Tutankhamun's tomb. It was a job they quietly performed for well over 3000 years until Howard Carter caught them napping. In penance they must stand here in the Cairo Museum for a few more years yet.

Tutankhamun's throne

PRACTICAL INFORMATION

The Museum of Egyptian Antiquities is open daily from 9am to 4pm except Fridays when it is closed from 11.30 to 1.30. Entrance **fee** is LE3, or LE1.50 for students with card.

For sale at the ticket kiosk is *A Guide to the Egyptian Museum*, LE3. This is the official publication and is reasonably comprehensive though descriptions are perfunctory and it is arranged by catalogue number rather than by room which makes it a nuisance to use. It is probably of little value to the passer-through.

A fee of LE10 is payable if you want to take photographs inside. Otherwise bags and cameras cannot be taken into the museum. These may be checked free of charge (which does not stop the attendant, *sotto voce*, asking for 50PT).

There is a shop just inside the entrance selling books, cards, reproductions, etc.

THE PYRAMID AGE

Before taking the Giza road out to that desert escarpment where the famous Pyramids of Cheops, Chephren and Mycerinus stand, it is worth knowing something of the period in which they were built, and to know too something of that entire line of Old Kingdom pyramids which extends from Abu Roash to the north of Giza to Meidum near the Fayyum, a line that is 70 km long and numbers over 80 pyramids. This chapter will refer to the main pyramid clusters, and will explain why and how, at the very beginning of recorded history, these most prodigious and enduring monuments in stone were built. 'Everything fears time', wrote an Arab physician in the 12th C, 'but time fears the Pyramids'.

The First Pyramid

The struggle for unity

Around 3100 BC, Upper and Lower Egypt were united under Menes and the I Dynasty established. It is not certain that Menes was an individual; he may represent a conflation of early warrior-princes, and the conquest of the Delta may not have been a single campaign but a struggle lasting over generations. There is evidence of fighting and rebellion during the I and II Dynasties, and the energies of this period would have

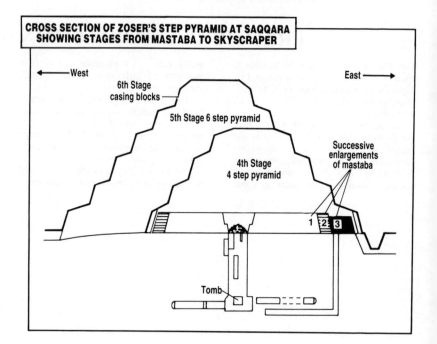

CROSS SECTION OF ZOSER'S STEP PYRAMID AT SAQQARA
SHOWING STAGES FROM MASTABA TO SKYSCRAPER

← West   East →

6th Stage casing blocks

5th Stage 6 step pyramid

4th Stage 4 step pyramid

Successive enlargements of mastaba

1 2 3

Tomb

been devoted to consolidation. Building was in mud brick and reed, though during the II Dynasty some stone was used underground in tombs.

Mastabas   Below ground these tombs were built like houses: rectangular and divided into chambers. Above ground they had a low, flat-topped form with sloping walls. This mud brick superstructure was sometimes faced with mud plaster and covered with white gypsum stucco. Mariette called them *mastabas,* the Arabic for those stone benches outside the shops and coffee houses of medieval Cairo.

The Old Kingdom   About 400 years after unification, that is c.2700 BC, Egypt entered into a long period of security and order known to us as the Old Kingdom and beginning with the III Dynasty. Awareness of the two Egypts, Upper and Lower, remained acute, as can be read from the ritual of Zoser's Heb-Sed festival at Saqqara, and the village and tribal units up and down the Nile continued to worship their local gods, that prolific pantheon that never disappeared but which eventually was overlaid by a few powerful national cults.

The III Dynasty: building in stone   During the reign of Zoser (III Dyn) there was a sudden use and mastery of stone at Saqqara. His mortuary complex of courts and chapels, 544 metres long and 277 metres wide and surrounded by a wall 10 metres high, was all of stone, beautifully detailed and architectured. And dominating the whole was the first pyramid, over 62 metres high, built in steps. Stone had risen from the darkness of the tomb into the confident light of the sun.

The explanation is not found in technology; stone was not new and tools and construction methods remained as simple as they had been in the past — the lever was used but the wheel and pulley were unknown. Rather there was peace and stability; there was a developing theocratic doctrine that invited the use of stone; and there was a man of genius who knew how to build with it.

The genius of Imhotep   That man was Imhotep, Zoser's grand vizier, chief judge, minister of agriculture and supervisor of building works. He was also high priest at Heliopolis. His range of accomplishment typified the opportunities and needs of a new civilisation, where everything was still to be invented and then organised. He was revered throughout pharaonic history, though recalled as a healer rather than as an organiser, statesman or architect, and he became a mythic figure, a demigod, and was eventually raised to unqualified divinity — but his contemporary existence is certain from inscriptions found at Zoser's complex.

The doctrine that begged the use of stone was that of the pharaoh's sole possession of the *ka*, the vital force emanating from the god to his son, the king, who could then dispense it to his subjects. The ka was eternal so long as it was linked to the pharaoh, and so it was essential that ka and king be given an indestructible container of stone.

Building the first
pyramid
Zoser was built a stone mastaba and this was twice enlarged. Then in three further stages, Imhotep made a qualitative leap, a sudden vertical thrust, and created the world's first skyscraper, the Step Pyramid. Political and cultural revolution in Egypt has always swept down through the valley, nomadic in inspiration. The mastaba belonged to the earthbound world of the Delta farmers; the pyramid and generally Egyptian architecture thereafter eschewed the enclosure of space and instead posed itself against the sun and the stars. Stone permitted it; Imhotep mastered the physics required; and yearning for the vast and timeless cosmos was its inspiration.

It is interesting and important, though, that Zoser's complex remains human in feeling. Zoser was the son of the god, and even if he was the god himself, he at least relished the life of man, for in the house-like arrangement of chambers beneath his pyramid, with their faience decorations imitating domestic reeding, there is the desire to project his present life into the hereafter. This sense never again appears inside a pyramid, and rarely at any mortuary structure of a pharaoh throughout Egypt's history. Instead the savouring of the everyday was excluded, divinity insisted upon, and ritual became obsessive.

The pyramid
revolution
So there was a first revolution, an eruption, in stone. But the second revolution was an adventure even more astonishing and led to the perfection of the pyramid form at Giza. We think of the vastness of Egyptian history and how slowly it must have unfolded, yet from Zoser's complex to Cheops' Pyramid no more time passed than our fast-moving age took to travel from the beginnings of iron construction to the Eiffel Tower — around 75 years in fact. What is more, the age of the great pyramids was over in 200 years. What explains its sudden coming and going, and the intensity, the phenomenal labour, with which it was pursued?

You see that in rushing out to Giza you confront the apogee, but you do not meet the answer. That is found to the south of Saqqara, at Dahshur and at Meidum.

The Pyramid Production Line

The collapse of
the Meidum
pyramid
The pyramid at Meidum is about 90 km by road south of Cairo and even without visiting it you can see it, if you are alert, from the left side of the overnight train back from Luxor soon after it passes El Wasta in the morning. Like all the pyramids, it stands beyond the belt of cultivation on the edge of the desert. It is an amazing sight: a steeply inclined tower rising from a low hill — and that is exactly what it was thought to be by early travellers. In fact it is a pyramid that collapsed. It did not slowly crumble over time; near the

The collapsed pyramid at Meidum

moment of its completion there was some catastrophe. Then or after a series of collapses only a part of the core remained clear of the mound of debris all around.

This was the first pyramid after Zoser's and it was conceived at first as a step pyramid. A second, larger stepped structure was soon superimposed and finally a true pyramidal shell was added, its smooth sides rising at an angle of about 52°. But there were serious design faults, including the badly squared stones of the outer casing which stood on horizontal limestone blocks embedded in compacted sand instead of on a bedrock foundation given an inward slope. The weight of the pyramid, instead of being directed downwards and inwards, was directed outwards; it was destroyed by its own lateral forces.

The mystery of Snofru's pyramids at Dahshur

This disaster leads to an explanation of the pyramid craze that marks the succeeding dynasty to Zoser's. An inscription at Meidum says it was built by Snofru (IV Dyn). But this has disturbed Egyptologists because Snofru was known to have built two pyramids at Dahshur. If the purpose of a pyramid was to provide an indestructible container for the pharaoh and his ka, why did Snofru need three? Snofru's inscription was explained away as a usurpation of his predecessor's pyramid: 'It cannot but seem extraordinary that one and the same king should have built for himself two pyramids of vast dimensions at no great distance from one another ... and

155

since it is hard to imagine that he erected three pyramids, the one at Meidum is now tentatively ascribed to Huny', wrote Sir Alan Gardiner, the noted Egyptologist, in *Egypt of the Pharaohs*. But that left the Bent and Red Pyramids at Dahshur. The Bent Pyramid was disposed of with the argument that it had been deemed unsafe and so Snofru decided to build another. One pharaoh, one ka and one pyramid to suit.

The Bent Pyramid rises for 70 percent of its bulk at an angle of 52°, the same as at Meidum. It then abruptly alters angle to 43.5°. The Red Pyramid rises at a constant angle of 43.5°. The lower angle of the Red would clearly be safer than the steeper initial angle of the Bent, but it fails to explain why the angle of the Bent should have been changed in mid-construction. If the steep initial angle of the Bent was thought to be unsafe, why not at once abandon the project? But if changing the angle was thought to make it safe, why build the Red Pyramid? Of course, one could argue that it was thought the change of angle would make the Bent Pyramid safe and that unhappily this proved not to be true — though the pyramid has stood safe and sound for nearly 5000 years.

Eminent Egyptologists have said that the builders of the Bent Pyramid suddenly tired of their task and decided to reduce the pyramid's volume, and hence their labour, by reducing its angle. It has also been said that the bend in the pyramid was predetermined and meant to express a 'double pyramid', that is two pyramids of different angles superimposed, and that this symbolised some unexplained duality. And it has been said that the architect lost his nerve, but one reason for this tantalising possibility — the collapse of the Meidum pyramid at a point when the Bent Pyramid was 70 percent of the way towards completion — has not been countenanced by Egyptologists because it would reintroduce the 'unpalatable conclusion that Snofru did possess three pyramids' (Gardiner). The key word there is possess, for it signals the insistence that pyramids were built for the sole reason of providing a container for the pharaoh's ka, so that Snofru had no business building what he believed at that point to be two perfectly good pyramids.

The Egyptologists' evasions could have gone on indefinitely as long as they could have believed that the pyramid at Meidum had belonged to Snofru's predecessor and had merely crumbled with time. But in *The Riddle of the Pyramids* and the *Journal of Egyptian Archaeology*, Kurt Mendelssohn, professor of physics at Oxford, has argued that Meidum, while nearing completion, came down with a bang as Snofru was already well advanced on his second pyramid — which only then, and for that reason, was continued at a bent angle. (Mendelssohn's opponents in the *JEA* argued well against a single bang, but some initial partial disaster seems likely.)

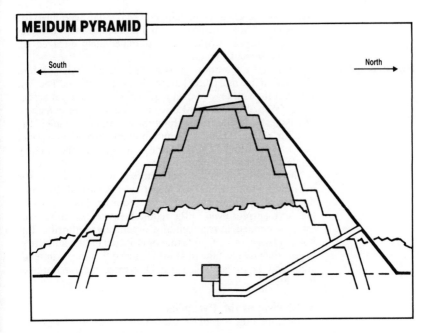

MEIDUM PYRAMID

South ← | → North

Overlap in pyramid construction

So why should several pyramids be built in overlapping succession during the reign of a single pharaoh? It is a fact that more large pyramids were built during the IV Dynasty than there were pharaohs to fill them. The answer is in the scale of the task. Herodotus says it took 20 years to build Cheops' Pyramid and 10 years to build the causeway and the earth ramps that served as a kind of scaffolding, with 100,000 men working a three-month shift. Modern calculation of the workforce required does not vary substantially from Herodotus' figure, though it is likely that several thousand men, highly skilled as stone-cutters, masons, surveyors, etc, would have been employed year-round, while the larger requirement for unskilled labour would have been drawn from the fields between July and November, the period of the inundation. All of these people needed training and organisation, as well as feeding, clothing and housing, and the logistics of the operation must have been formidable. It is not the sort of operation that is easily or efficiently mounted at the uncertain occasion of a pharaoh's accession, nor is the size of a pyramid and so the time it will take to build readily geared to the uncertain duration of a pharaoh's reign. The suggestion is rather that pyramid construction was continuous and independent of whether or not there would be enough pharaohs to fill them. And this is what the evidence of Meidum and the

157

Bent Pyramid suggests did happen, the overlap accounted for by the fact that as the first pyramid tapered towards completion, the surplus workforce was immediately engaged on starting a second pyramid.

Pyramids and the state

Whether by intention or as a consequence, this pyramid production line must have had two important effects. The first was that the vast levy of men required would have cut across the division of Upper and Lower Egypt and the parochialism of villages and tribes throughout the length of the valley, the breadth of the Delta. Pyramid building would complete, down to the fibres of society, the unification of the country begun by Menes by force of arms.

The second effect was that whoever was responsible for pyramid building would see their power enhanced. But production of pyramids surplus to the requirements of any one pharaoh, surplus even to the requirements of an entire dynasty, demanded a transcending organising authority. Imhotep's own career suggests the composition of that authority: in part the power of the pharaoh, but also that of the bureaucracy and the priesthood. Pyramids created the apparatus of the state.

Symbolism of the Pyramids

There is then the pyramidal form. One can see how constructionally the pyramids began with the mastaba, Zoser's pyramid in fact a stepped mastaba. The achievement in architecture of the pure abstract pyramidal form came, briefly, at Meidum, when before it collapsed its steps were being sheathed in planes. If anything, the disaster was a spur to the technical perfection of the pyramidal symbol. That symbol preceded construction rather than technology dictated symbol seems likely. In Egyptian creation myths there is a primal hill which rises above the waters, and from it ascends the sun. And until the High Dam at Aswan finally put an end to the annual inundation, that was very much the scene in Egypt: villages huddled on mounds to avoid the flood, then its subsidence and the sun drawing from the mud the harvest. This myth is referred to at Medinet Habu and Hermopolis; Helio-

The primal hill

polis also claimed a primal hill, the *benben,* a tapering megalith, a word whose root, *bn,* is bound up with the notion of shining, brilliant, ascending. It is depicted in II Dynasty inscriptions, that is before the pyramid age.

Variations on the pyramidal form continued to be popular throughout Egyptian history, as for example the obelisks whose points or pyramidions were sheathed in electrum, a mixture of silver and gold. Pliny the Elder described obelisks as petrified rays of sunlight, and more than one modern writer has remarked on the pyramid-like form of a burst of sunlight through the clouds after a rare Egyptian rain.

The building of pyramids then would have been no mere drudgery inflicted on the population by some megalomaniac pharaoh. The symbolism would have been appreciated throughout all levels of society, and it is quite likely that far from being built by slave-labour, as Herodotus claims, they were built willingly and with a shared sense of exalted purpose which at the time would have seemed far more important, and certainly would have been more conscious, than creating new political forms.

The end of the pyramid age But here the gods died sooner than the works of men. And those works included not only the pyramids, but the creation for the first time in human history of an organisational principle, the state, that was to serve Egypt until her absorption into the Roman Empire, and is the basis of human organisation to this day. Once the pyramid production line had achieved this, their symbolism could be carried on in lesser forms, such as obelisks; in any case, it was no longer politically necessary to build pyramids, and apart from some inferior examples in later dynasties, by 2500 BC the age of the pyramids was over.

THE GREAT PYRAMIDS OF GIZA

Approaching the Pyramids

Half a day should be allowed for the visit to the Giza Pyramids, though you should return again at night. They are approached along a broad straight road, originally built for that same Empress Eugénie who attended the opening night at the Opera House, so that she could cover the 11 km from Cairo in her carriage. This Sharia al-Ahram or Road of the Pyramids once passed across fellahin's fields which would flood with the rising of the Nile, but nowadays the entire route has been built up. There is therefore, at first, something ordinary about the approach, as though you were off to a funfair on the edge of town, expecting at any moment the distant screams of roller coaster passengers as they plunge down papier-maché mountains.

But even the Pyramids themselves initially conspire to deflate anticipation. One of the savants accompanying Napoleon described his approach: 'Seen from a distance they produce the same kind of effect as do high mountain peaks. The nearer one approaches, the more this effect decreases. Only when at last you are within a short distance of these regular masses is a wholly different impression produced; you are struck by surprise, and as soon as you have reached the top of the slope, your ideas change in a flash. Finally, when you have reached the foot of the Great Pyramid, you are

The Sphinx and Chephren's Pyramid

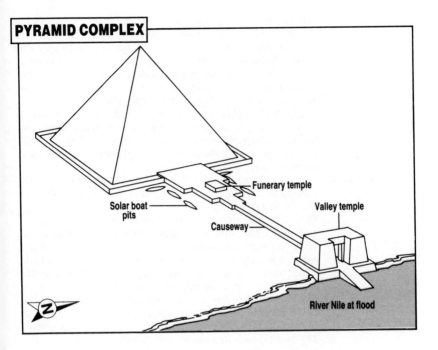

PYRAMID COMPLEX

Funerary temple

Solar boat pits

Valley temple

Causeway

River Nile at flood

seized with a vivid and powerful emotion, tempered by a sort of stupefaction, almost overwhelming in its effects.'

Even so, you might just as easily be overwhelmed by touts urging you to ride their donkey, horse or camel, and by numberless 'guides' and 'watchmen' who gather about you like mosquitoes, endlessly trying to lure you into ruined little temples with the promise of an undiscovered mummy or reliefs of pharaonic pornography. In the old days, visitors would come with a dragoman who wielded a big stick for which you are bound to develop the greatest nostalgia. Mark Twain, who led a party of tourists here in the 1860s, attempted escape by climbing to the top of Cheops' Pyramid but was pursued by an Arab whom he offered $1 if he could race to the top of Chephren's Pyramid and back to the top of Cheops' within nine minutes, in the hope that the man would break his neck. Three dollars later an exasperated Twain, now joined by the man's mother, offered them each $100 if they would jump off the Pyramid head first.

The best times to visit the Pyramids are at dawn, at sunset and at night when they form as much a part of the natural order as the sun, the moon and the stars. Flaubert recalled the view from the top of Cheops' Pyramid: 'The sun was rising just opposite; the whole valley of the Nile, bathed in mist, seemed to be a still white sea; and the desert behind us, with its

161

hillocks of sand, another ocean, deep purple, its waves all petrified'. My first visit was at night. I had gone to the son et lumiere, the Arabic programme, so that I could enjoy the play of lights to the eerie accompaniment of this booming, gutteral but poetic language. The programme over but some floodlights on, I walked up past the Sphinx and stood between the Pyramids of Cheops and Chephren. And then suddenly the lights went out. Black night. The great stones rising on either side, picked out by the moon and stars. The feeling, as Napoleon said here to his army, of 'forty centuries of history looking down upon us', feeling it in the most awesome way.

Statistics   The road arrives at the Mena House Hotel and then curves sharply to the left, mounting a gentle slope and finishing at the north end of the plateau, almost directly opposite the Great Pyramid, that of Cheops. This is the oldest of the group and the largest, and the others, Chephren and Mycerinus, stand in descending order of age and size along a southwest axis, each identically oriented 8.5° west of magnetic north; when built they were probably aligned precisely with the North Star, their entrance corridors aiming straight at it. At first the second pyramid, that of Chephren, seems largest, but that is because it stands on higher ground and retains its casing towards its peak. Its present height is 136.4 metres (originally 143 metres) and its volume is 2,200,000 cubic metres; this compares with a height of 137.2 metres (originally 146.6 metres) for the Great Pyramid of Cheops, which has a volume of 2,550,000 cubic metres. This pyramid was built of over 2,500,000 enormous blocks of limestone cut from the Moqattam and locally, though about 170,000 have been removed by Arabs and Turks since the founding of Cairo. Mycerinus is much smaller, rising only to a height of 65.5 metres, though it is still imposing, and it contributes to the satisfying arrangement of the group. Napoleon astonished his officers with the calculation that the stones from these three pyramids would be sufficient to build a wall 3 metres high and 0.3 metres thick around the whole of France.

But the Pyramids do not have this rocky ledge entirely to themselves. There are smaller attendant pyramids, some at least for royal wives, and suburban rows of mastabas for nobles and princes of the blood. There are the remains of temples and causeways; there are solar boat pits; and there is **A pyramid** the Sphinx. A pyramid was never merely a self-sufficient geo**complex** metrically shaped tumulus of masonry raised above a royal burial; it was the culminating point of a vast funerary area comprising, apart from the pyramid itself, three parts. First, near the desert edge and overlooking the cultivation so as to be accessible by boat in the inundation season was a modest *valley chapel.* From it led a walled-in *causeway,* as long as 500 metres, upwards to the *funerary temple* proper, this abut-

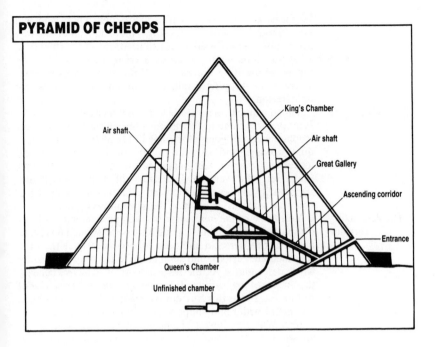

PYRAMID OF CHEOPS

King's Chamber

Air shaft

Air shaft

Great Gallery

Ascending corridor

Entrance

Queen's Chamber

Unfinished chamber

ting on to the east side of the pyramid, where a false door permitted the deceased pharaoh to emerge in order to partake of the offered feasts. Also, on several sides of a pyramid, set in pits, *wooden boats* have been found. Whether these were only symbolic or actually used is not known; some have supposed they enabled the pharaoh to follow the sun god across the skies, but as they have been found facing all four points of the compass they could as easily have been intended to enable the pharaoh to go wherever he desired. For convenience, however, they will be referred to here as solar boats.

The Pyramid of Cheops

Climbing the Great Pyramid

The polished casing to the **Pyramid of Cheops** (Khufu) is entirely gone and so you are presented with the tiered courses of limestone blocks, an invitation to climb to the platform at the top, 10 metres square. This used to be a fairly easy and entirely safe thing to do, as guides would simply haul you up, one at each arm, a third shoving from below. Climbing the Pyramids is now forbidden, however, which leaves the field open to the more adventurous or the more foolhardy to make the attempt unassisted. The ascent is best made at the northeast corner, each 'step' a metre-high block, and will take 15 to 20 minutes. The footing is more difficult on the way down; also you are more prone to tiredness and vertigo (you must now look *down*). Recently a young man who slept on top while awaiting the dawn fell out of bed, so to speak. There is no stopping a fall; he bounced only twice before obliteration.

Going inside

The squeamish might content themselves with going inside. Here the only thing to fear is fear itself, in the form of claustrophobia and difficulty for some in breathing due to inadequate oxygen, and also the possibility that you might get locked in, which in fact happened one night to my brother (more on the very real dangers of being sealed up, temporarily and even permanently, in ancient tombs when you read about Saqqara and the Theban necropolis).

The descending corridor

You *enter at the north face* through an opening made by Caliph al-Mamun in his search for treasure (though it is probable that this pyramid had been robbed as early as the First Intermediate Period), and soon come to the *original corridor* which descends for 100 metres to a depth of 30 metres beneath the surface of the bedrock. It reaches an *unfinished chamber* of no interest, and as this corridor is constricted (1.3 metres high, one metre wide) and slippery, it is not usually open to the public. Why this lowest chamber was never finished is not known; Herodotus said it was subject to flooding by the Nile.

The ascending corridor

Instead, about 20 metres from the entrance along the descending corridor you come to a block of granite designed to prevent access to the *ascending corridor*, though al-Mamun merely hollowed out the rock to the left and you soon find yourself crouching your way upwards (height again 1.3 metres, width one metre) for 40 metres. The gradient is 1 in 2, and so can be quite tiring, but arrival at the Great Gallery at least permits a stretch. Here there is a *shaft* (right) which winds down to the descending corridor — purpose unknown. There is also a *horizontal corridor,* again only 1.3 metres high for

The Queen's Chamber and Great Gallery

most of its length, which leads to the so-called *Queen's Chamber*, nearly square with a pointed roof of gigantic blocks. But best by far is the ascending *Great Gallery*, 8.5 metres high, 47 metres long, a marvel of precision masonry, of which it has been said that neither a needle nor a hair can be inserted into the joints of the stones.

The King's Chamber

This gives on to the principal tomb chamber, commonly called the *King's Chamber,* 42.5 metres above the surface of the bedrock, 5.22 metres wide and 10.44 metres long, that is a double square, aligned east-west. On the north and south walls, a metre above the floor, are the rectangular mouths of the two *ventilation shafts* which extend to the surfaces of the pyramid. The chamber is built entirely in pink Aswan granite and roofed over with nine huge granite slabs laid horizontally, and above these (seen by means of a ladder leading to a

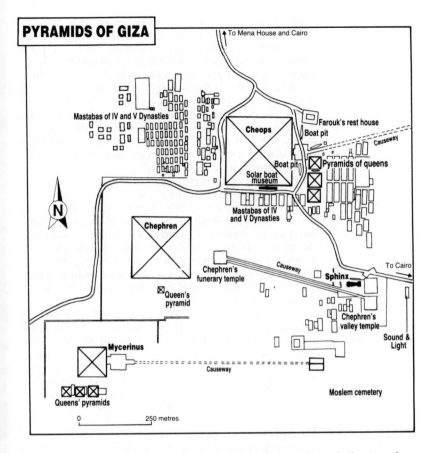

PYRAMIDS OF GIZA

To Mena House and Cairo

Mastabas of IV and V Dynasties

Cheops

Farouk's rest house

Boat pit

Causeway

Boat pit

Pyramids of queens

Solar boat museum

Mastabas of IV and V Dynasties

Chephren

Queen's pyramid

Chephren's funerary temple

Causeway

Sphinx

To Cairo

Chephren's valley temple

Sound & Light

Mycerinus

Causeway

Queens' pyramids

Moslem cemetery

N

0   250 metres

passage in the upper south wall of the Great Gallery) are four more granite layers, each separated by a *relieving chamber,* possibly meant to distribute the full weight of the pyramid away from the King's Chamber, though in fact this job is accomplished by the topmost pointed roof of limestone blocks. It was in these relieving chambers that the only inscriptions in any of the Giza Pyramids were found — the cartouche, traced several times in red, of Khufu, Cheops. His mummy, if it found its way to this pyramid at all, would have been placed in this King's Chamber; the sarcophagus is empty.

It is here that you might think about the great weight upon you. Over your head is 95 metres of solid pyramid, more than enough to squash you very thin for a very long time. Unlike the Meidum pyramid, however, the Pyramid of Cheops has been shown by Swiss engineer H. Roessler (1952) to be exceptionally stable. The building blocks are far larger than those used for earlier pyramids and they are precisely fitted together, while the casing blocks overlaying the basic step structure rest upon foundations slotted into the bedrock. The weight of the pyramid itself contributes to its stability, but not simply its dead weight; the stepped inclined buttresses throw much of this weight towards the centre. At every level the pyramid's horizontal thrusts are directed towards the central core, while 35 percent of the vertical thrusts are transmitted to the inner core (that is the line running from the top of the pyramid *through you* to the base), only the remaining thrusts being carried down into the bedrock. In fact the bigger the pyramid the more stable it becomes.

Coming out of the pyramid you can see on the north side, also on the east, the remains of the original *enclosure wall,* about 10 metres from the base. Backing against this wall on the east side is the basalt paving of **Cheops' funerary temple**, about all that remains of it, and only occasional traces too of the *causeway* that came up from the **valley temple**, which was discovered in 1990, 4 metres below street level in the village lying at the foot of the plateau. The **three small pyramids**, from 15 to 20 metres high, probably belonged to Cheops' queens or sisters.

Solar boat
museum

Three empty boat pits have been found near Cheops' Pyramid, but in 1954 a fourth pit revealed a dismantled **solar boat** of Syrian cedar. This magnificent craft has been reassembled and housed in its own specially-constructed museum on the south side of the pyramid. Video cameras lowered through drill holes into a fifth pit in 1987 discovered another boat perfectly preserved in 4600-year old air beneath the hermetic seal of 1.5-metre thick limestone slabs.

The Sphinx

An outcrop of hard grey and soft yellow limestone, useless as building material, was left standing in the quarry from which Cheops cut many of the blocks for his pyramid. His son Chephren had the happy idea of shaping it into a figure — lion's body, god's face, though perhaps Chephren's own, and wearing the royal headdress with uraeus. The Egyptians would have regarded it as a symbol of strength and wisdom combined, but the Greeks applied their word sphinx to it, recalling a lion's body but the breasts and head of a woman given to putting riddles to passers-by, and so this most famous **Sphinx** has acquired an air of mystery quite foreign to its intention.

Nevertheless, some mysteries are associated with it. Neither Herodotus nor any other classical writer until Pliny the Elder mentioned the Sphinx, presumably because it was buried in sand. Prints and photographs of recent times show its features looming from an engulfing sea of sand, but this is all too assiduously cleared today, some mystery swept away with it. The future Tuthmosis IV (XVIII Dyn) dreamt here that if he was to become pharaoh he must clear away the sands: his stelae between the Sphinx' paws commemorate this first known restoration. During the Turkish domination the Sphinx was used for target practice and its nose, which originally had been cemented on, fell off; 18th C drawings show that it was missing long before Napoleon was supposed to have done the damage. The uraeus has also gone, but the beard is being pieced together and should soon be struck back on. In the son et lumiere programmes, the Sphinx is given the role of narrator which it performs, as I have said, much better in Arabic when you cannot understand a word. This is in fact one of the best times for viewing it or, after the programme, having a drink on the terrace of the Pavilion of Cheops, for then it gains in perspective against the more distant Pyramids. It may not otherwise seem as large as you had imagined: it is 20 metres high and 48.5 metres long, much of its bulk crouched within the quarry so that only its head overtops the horizon.

Chephren's Pyramid Complex

Immediately in front of the Sphinx and associated with it is a IV Dynasty temple, one reason for believing the face on the Sphinx is a god's and not Chephren's, for the Egyptians did not build temples to their kings. Adjacent and to the south is **Chephren's valley temple**, facing east. This is the only IV Dynasty sanctuary to retain its grandeur, its exceptional state of preservation owing to having been buried in the sands and not discovered until 1853 by Mariette (though it may prove to be rivalled by Cheops' valley temple, now being excavated). The material is pink Aswan granite, majestically and simply assembled in strong verticals and horizontals, square monolithic pillars supporting massive granite architraves. It was here that Mariette discovered the magnificent diorite statue of Chephren (Room 42, Ground Floor, Egyptian Museum). The purpose of this temple is uncertain, or rather certain for some and contradicted by others. One view is that valley temples were used for mummification; others think the site too exposed and that embalming would have been done either at the pharaoh's Memphis palace or at the base of the pyramid, in the funerary temple. There is at least more general agreement that here was performed the 'Opening of the Mouth' ceremony at which the ka entered the deceased's body. The ka always required a secure residence, hence pyramids and immutable bodies, though it would also inhabit the mortuary statue of the pharaoh, such as that one in the Egyptian Museum, one of 23 that sat round the main T-shaped chamber.

'Opening of the
Mouth' ceremony

You should now follow if you can the traces of Chephren's *causeway* up to his **funerary temple** at the base of his pyramid. More of this temple survives than of Cheops', the walls formed of possibly the largest blocks ever used in building, one of them 13.4 metres long and weighing 163,000 kilos. To the south of the pyramid is a ruined small pyramid, probably of a queen.

The **Pyramid of Chephren** (Khafre) compares to Cheops' in size, seemingly exceeds it in height and is also capped with its original casing. But its interior is less interesting, while the outside ascent is much more difficult, requiring an hour to get to the casing, progress being very dangerous thence upwards because the smooth surface offers no hold. One of the earlier explorers and snatchers of antiquities was Belzoni, born in Italy but first achieving fame for his 'human pyramid' act on the stage of the Sadlers Wells in London. He was the first European to enter this pyramid (1818) and promptly emblazoned his name on the south wall of the burial chamber. When Flaubert entered the chamber 33 years later he recorded: 'Under Belzoni's name, and no less large, is that of a M Just de Chasseloup-Laubat. One is irritated by the number of imbeciles' names written everywhere: on the top of the Great Pyramid there is a certain Buffard, 79 Rue Saint-Martin, wallpaper manufacturer, in black letters; an English fan of Jenny Lind's has written her name; there is also a pear, representing Louis-Phillipe'.

When the Egyptians built their pyramids it was with a feeling for the sublime power of the plane, without reliefs, inscriptions or any detailing whatsoever. Once the polished limestone casings were set in place, the pyramids both literally and symbolically repulsed the touch of mortals — well, that was the idea, anyway. One of the high points of a visit to the Pyramids in Roman times was the spectacle of men from a nearby village shinning up from the ground to their very tips; while one Roman woman scribbled on a casing stone, 'I saw the Pyramids without you; sadly I shed tears here', a lament copied down by a 15th C pilgrim, when the casing was more extensive than now.

Antique tourists

Last of the Great Pyramids

The **Pyramid of Mycerinus** (Menkaure) has only one-tenth of the volume of the other two pyramids and effectively marks the end of the pyramid age. The last pharaoh of the IV Dynasty built a quite different sort of tomb at Saqqara, while the pyramids of the next dynasty were small and shoddy. Though last of the great pyramids, Mycerinus' was built well, with granite used for the lower courses and a casing that remained intact until the 16th C. An attempt was made by the caliph in 1215 to destroy all the Pyramids and his workmen started with Mycerinus'. After eight months they gave up. 'Considering the vast masses that have been taken away, it might be supposed that the building would have been completely destroyed, but so immense is the pile that the stones are scarcely missed. Only on one of its sides can be noticed any trace of the impression which it was attempted to be made', wrote the 12th C historian Abd el Latif. Though you can enter, the interior is not interesting. Opposite the south face are three small pyramids, while against the east are the remains of Mycerinus' funerary temple.

Mons Venus   Herodotus recorded a belief in Greece that this pyramid was in fact built by Rhodopis, a beautiful courtesan from Thrace who flourished in Egypt, charging a building stone for her services. The Pyramid of Mycerinus is built of at least 200,000 granite and limestone blocks. But it is not only for that reason that the story is untrue.

PRACTICAL INFORMATION

The *Practical Information* section at the end of the *Cairo: Mother of the World* chapter contains information on getting to the Pyramids and on the Sound and Light show. One of the most agreeable things you can do while out here is to have tea or a meal at the Mena House.

Although you can have a general view of the Pyramids and Sphinx at any time of day or night, **access** to the Sphinx, tombs and valley temples, and **entry** into the chambers of the Pyramids is from 8am to 4.30pm daily. The only fees are for seeing the solar boat in its glass-enclosed chamber (LE6, students with card LE2.50 — open 9am to 2pm daily, closed Tuesdays) and for entering the Pyramids (LE5, students with card LE2); tickets for the Pyramids should be bought at the kiosk at the top of the road coming up from the Mena House Hotel towards the north side of the Pyramid of Cheops. Con men may attempt to extort money from you for simply staring at the monuments, while others will press their services upon you as guides or try to sell you fake antiquities and other rubbish. All are to be ignored, and if necessary the Tourist Police invoked. You should accept assistance and agree a price only if you want help in climbing the Pyramids.

You can **ride on horseback or camel-back** across the desert from the Pyramids to Saqqara. The journey will take at least 3 hours in each direction, and spending just a little time at Saqqara means an 8-hour expedition in all. For this reason you should resist offers of hire by the hour and negotiate a price for the entire day. Camels will cost about LE25 and can carry two people, though that is not advisable; horses cost a bit less. There is some dispute as to which animal is better; most people prefer horses over longer distances. Either way, all but the most hardened rider can expect to end the day feeling pretty sore.

There are **Sound and Light** shows nightly at 7.30 and 8.30pm. English programmes are at 7.30 on Mondays, Wednesdays, Fridays and Saturdays, and at 8.30 on Thursday. Admission LE6 except for the Arabic programme which is LE1. Seating is on a terrace facing the valley temple of the Pyramid of Chephren, ie by the Sphinx. Bring a sweater; it can get cool on the edge of the desert, even in summer.

Almost any taxi driver will know what you mean if you say Sound and Light. Agree a per-hour or all-in rate if you want him to wait (thus avoiding any difficulty in getting a ride back, though you can walk over to the Mena House and get a taxi there); the hotel limousines have a set rate for this. Also there are buses, but these will take you to the Mena House Hotel and you will have to walk back down the

Pyramids Road till you reach the Sound and Light sign (on the right as you face Cairo) and then walk to the right, through the village on the edge of the desert escarpment. Or if you are alert you can alight at the sign (it is about 1000 metres before the Mena House Hotel), saving yourself some shoe leather. Another alternative is to take a tour, which will include admission and the ride out and back. This works out at about as much as it would cost one person to take a taxi and keep it waiting; for 2 or more people it is better to take the taxi.

MEMPHIS AND SAQQARA

Saqqara is 32 km by road from Cairo and 21 km south of the Giza Pyramids. The necropolis extends about 7 km north to south along the desert plateau and looks down over the palm groves that cover the site of **Memphis**, about 6 km to the southeast in the valley of the Nile. Memphis was the capital of the Old Kingdom, its palaces and shrines of that period built of mud brick for the span of the living and now vanished; Saqqara, built of stone to endure eternity, survives.

The Saqqara road is a left turn off the Road to the Pyramids at the traffic lights immediately after a canal about 1500 metres before the Mena House Hotel. It is a pleasant country road with glimpses to the right of the Libyan Desert and the V Dynasty pyramids of Abusir. (You can also ride across the desert by camel or horse from the Giza Pyramids in about three hours). You come first to the turning, on your right, for Saqqara; or you can carry straight on for the left-hand turning to the Memphis site. Alternatively, you can take the bus from the Giza Pyramids to Badrashein and can ask to be let off at Memphis. It is best to visit Saqqara early in the morning to avoid the heat, and so to call on Memphis afterwards. But for context, Memphis will be mentioned first.

Old Kingdom Capital

History of Memphis Memphis probably began as a fortress by which Menes controlled the land and water routes between Upper and Lower Egypt and kept the conquered inhabitants of the Delta in subjection. By the III Dynasty it must have become a sizeable capital, as the Saqqara necropolis suggests, but it may not have been fixed. The IV Dynasty pharaohs built their pyramids to the north at Giza and might well have had their palaces near there too. One can imagine Memphis developing in stages like Arab Fustat and its successors, decamping northwards. Whether it was the Mediterranean breezes that attracted, or the growing dominance of the sun cult at Heliopolis, so closely associated with pyramid development, is not known. By the VI Dynasty, however, the old site of Memphis had been reoccupied, its attraction the venerable sanctuary of Ptah. From the court of Pepi and its associated monuments came the name *Men-nefru-Mire,* The Beauty of King Mire (Pepi), later abbreviated to Menfe, in Greek Memphis.

Although no longer capital, in the New Kingdom Memphis rivalled Thebes in grandeur, embellished in particular by Ramses II's mania for building. During the 5th C bc when the Persians ruled Egypt from here and Herodotus visited the city, it was a great cosmopolitan centre, a foreshadowing of Alexandria, with many Greeks and Jews, Phoenicians and Libyans amongst its population, as full of

Oriental spectacle as Cairo is today. Herodotus, in his hydrology of Egypt, which fascinated him, wrote that 'when the Nile overflows, the whole country is converted into a sea, and the towns, which alone remain above water, look like islands in the Aegean. At these times water transport is used all over the country, instead of merely along the course of the river and anyone going from Naucratis to Memphis would pass right by the Pyramids ... The priests told me that it was Menes, the first king of Egypt, who raised the dam which protects Memphis from the floods ... On the land which had been drained by the diversion of the river, King Menes built his city and afterwards on the north and west sides of the town excavated a lake, communicating with the river.' As late as the 12th C, Abd el Latif could write that 'the ruins still offer, to those who contemplate them, a collection of such marvellous beauty that the intelligence is confounded, and the most eloquent man would be unable to describe them adequately'. But towards the end of the Mameluke period the dikes around Memphis fell into disrepair and at every inundation the level of the ground was raised.

Memphis today   Today the centuries of Nile mud have swallowed Memphis entirely, so much so that it is impossible to stand here and soliloquise on how the once mighty has fallen — there is, simply, so little to stir reflection. And even had the dikes been maintained, the more ancient stratas of Memphis would have been lost. Herodotus exactly describes those conditions, persisting until the building of the High Dam at Aswan, which annually drowned the valley and the Delta and gradually covered the past with mud, so that settlements built upon themselves, one strata upon another, to form what in Arabic are known as *tells*. The earliest mud brick houses, palaces and sanctuaries have long since disintegrated beneath the wash of the annual flood, explaining why so much is known of the Egyptian dead, who dwelt in stone on high desert ground, while so little is known of the living.

At Memphis there is a modern building erected for the sole purpose of roofing over a supine **colossus of Ramses II**, brother to the one outside the Cairo railway station. This Ramses is the victim of monumental indifference: the Egyptian government gave him to the British Museum — which failed to collect. He lies here with his right fist clenched, like a cataleptic Gulliver, bound down by brain seizure rather than ropes. Several smaller statues stand or lie in the grass beneath palms near the covered colossus. Otherwise the immediate area has been turned into a garden, and set up along the central pathway like a plaster gnome is a friendly alabaster **sphinx** dating from the New Kingdom. If you walk a bit beyond this, no more than 100 metres eastwards, you can survey the shapeless mounds that cloak the ancient city. The faint remains of the vast **Temple of Ptah** lie waterlogged beside the

The world's first building in stone: the Step Pyramid at Saqqara

village of Mit Rahinah. Or from the garden with its sphinx follow the road to Saqqara for 100 metres; off its north side are the alabaster **mummification beds** where the Apis bulls (see the Serapeum at Saqqara) were prepared for burial.

The Egypt Exploration Society is now excavating at Memphis; perhaps in a decade or so there will be more to see.

Saqqara

Touring the necropolis   The Saqqara site has a far more desert feel than Giza; the sands wash about your feet nearly everywhere. Also it is dotted with untended holes left by excavators, some of terrific depth and not always enclosed. It would be dangerous for children on the loose, and adults should mind their step. Many tombs, once discovered and examined, have been closed again and some even sanded over. The most comfortable way to explore the site is to go first to Zoser's funerary complex, visiting also the Pyramid of Unas nearby, and then to drive round to the refreshment tent (or walk across the sands to it) from where you can visit the Mastaba of Akhti-hotep and Ptah-hotep, the Mastaba of Ti and the Serapeum.

Saqqara, from Sokkar, the Memphite god of the dead, was a necropolis from the unification of Egypt through the Ptolemaic period, and it is the site also of a Coptic monastery destroyed by the Arabs c.960, so that discoveries here span 4000 years. In historical range and the quantity and value of

173

what has been found here — monuments, works of art, texts and vases — there can be few archaeological sites in all the world, let alone Egypt, to compare with Saqqara. Even so, serious examination of the site only began in the mid-19th C and what remains to be discovered is incalculable. Early in 1986 there was the most important find since Howard Carter broke into Tutankhamun's tomb; the discovery here of the tomb of Maya, a close friend of the famous boy-pharaoh. (It will not be open to the public for several years.)

Discovery   Except for Zoser's Step Pyramid, Saqqara was ignored, its revelations unsuspected, until 1851 when Auguste Mariette discovered the Serapeum. Even the funerary complex immediately surrounding the Step Pyramid went undiscovered until 1924, and its restoration, to which Jean-Phillipe Lauer has given a lifetime, continues to this day. Cecil M Firth's campaign of 1924–7 overturned accepted notions about the origins of Egyptian architecture in stone which, because of the gigantic blocks used at Giza, was thought to have developed from megalithic monuments. Instead, at Zoser's complex, one sees a stone architecture which replicates the use of brick in its size and courses, and which also is full of imitative references to rush matting, reed and wood forms. One of the greatest achievements of Egyptian civilisation was to sever stone from the rock and to make of it a building material unsurpassed to this day. It happened here, for the first time, at Saqqara, with some hesitancy in the new technology but astonishing artistic brilliance.

Zoser's Funerary Complex

Zoser's funerary complex, dominated by the Step Pyramid, is 544 metres from north to south, 277 metres from east to west, and entirely surrounded by a magnificent panelled and bastioned **enclosure wall** of fine limestone. It still survives to a height of 3.7 metres at some places along its south side, while on the east side, near the southeast corner, it has been rebuilt with stones found in the sand to its original height of 10.48 metres. This vast white wall in itself, once easily visible from Memphis, must have conferred enormous prestige on Zoser and his architect Imhotep. Lauer was himself at first an architect and was called in by Firth when it was realised that the complex could be accurately reconstructed using the original stones.

Though there are many *false doors* in the enclosure wall for the ka to come and go, there is only one *entrance* (1) for the living, at the southeast corner. The narrow passage is through a fortress-like tower and gives on to a vestibule where you can see on either side the leaves of a *simulated double door* thrown open, complete with hinge pins and sockets. Ahead of you is a *colonnaded corridor* (2), its columns engaged and ribbed in imitation of palm stems (the protective ceiling is modern

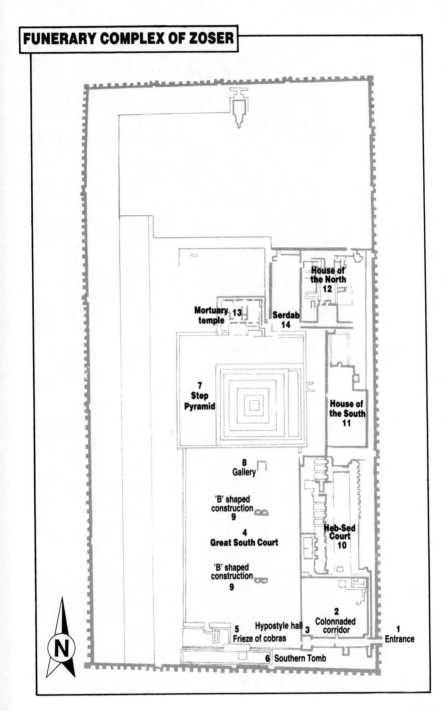

FUNERARY COMPLEX OF ZOSER

House of the North 12

Mortuary temple 13

Serdab 14

7 Step Pyramid

House of the South 11

8 Gallery

'B' shaped construction 9

4 Great South Court

Heb-Sed Court 10

'B' shaped construction 9

5 Frieze of cobras

Hypostyle hall

3

2 Colonnaded corridor

1 Entrance

6 Southern Tomb

N

concrete). At the far end is a broad *hypostyle hall* (3) with four pairs of engaged columns, and on your right as you enter the court a half open ka door. This is where the statue base bearing Imhotep's titles was found. Before leaving the hall, notice that the columns are comprised of drums seldom exceeding 25 cm in height, one of many details of the masonry which betray Imhotep's hesitancy in working with this new material, stone.

You now emerge into the **Great South Court** (4), and along the wall to your left is a section of rebuilt wall with a *frieze of cobras* (5). The cobra, *uraeus* in Latin, was an emblem of royalty and an instrument of protection, always appearing on the pharaoh's headdress and able to destroy his enemies by breathing flames. The cobra was worshipped in Lower Egypt, and so here in this early dynasty it also emphasises Zoser's mastery over the conquered peoples of the Delta. Near here is a shaft leading to Zoser's *southern tomb* (6), similar in its faience decoration to that beneath the Step Pyramid. There is a relief here of Zoser running the Heb-Sed race (see below). One explanation for two tombs is that early pharaohs thereby demonstrated their connection with the two Egypts, so a southern and northern tomb. Possibly the canopic jars containing Zoser's viscera were placed here, the body beneath the pyramid (where in fact a foot was found).

Zoser's Step Pyramid
The **Step Pyramid** (7) and its place in the development of pyramid building has already been referred to in an earlier chapter. Now you have a first-hand opportunity to examine its features. Despite its 62-metre height, it was built of fairly small limestone blocks, far smaller than those enormous blocks at Giza. Though working with stone, Imhotep was still thinking in terms of mud brick. But even in the enlargement of his monument from mastaba to pyramid you can detect signs of Imhotep's growing confidence in the new medium: at the southeast corner where the casing has come away you can see the smaller stonework of the *mastaba,* as you can if you walk along the east face of the pyramid. Also note how regularly the courses are laid, both of the mastaba and the pyramid as a whole, and how well shaped and fitted the stones are. In technique, Imhotep was without fault. The last enlarged mastaba measured 63 metres each way and a little over 8 metres high. Recall that the first pyramid erected over this mastaba rose four steps; the further pyramid of two additional steps increased the total volume by more than four fold. The entire monument was then sheathed in fine limestone from Tura, just to the south of modern Cairo, as were the Giza Pyramids.

Entrance to the pyramid
The original entrance to the Step Pyramid was at the north face, but in the XXVI Dynasty, known as the Saite period for its dynasty's origins at Sais in the Delta, a *gallery* (8) was dug from the Great South Court to the chambers beneath the

pyramid. Permission and keys will have to be asked for at the office of the Inspector of Antiquities to the northeast of the Pyramid of Teti. The Saites admired the works of the Old Kingdom and it is quite possible they tunnelled their way into the pyramid out of sheer archaeological curiosity. After 60 metres you come to the main central shaft from where there are impressive views up into the pyramid and down towards the *burial chamber* which is sealed with a huge granite plug.

Emerging once again into the Great South Court, you see two *B-shaped constructions* (9) near the centre. These marked the limits of Upper and Lower Egypt, the gap between them **The Heb-Sed** symbolically spanned by Zoser in the Heb-Sed race. (A *relief* **race** in the southern tomb shows Zoser in full stride, the two B-shaped constructions to the rear and fore.) The Heb-Sed race was one of the ceremonies during the five-day jubilee which occurred in the thirtieth year — that is at the interval of one generation — of the pharaoh's reign. It is possible that at some earlier period, power was granted only for 30 years, the chieftain then deposed, perhaps killed, to spare the land from decline because of his failing strength. This jubilee, therefore, was a renewal of the vital forces of the pharaoh and his ka, and so of all Egypt.

Also at his jubilee the pharaoh re-enacted his coronation, sitting first on the throne of Upper Egypt, then on the throne of Lower Egypt, each time presenting gifts to the various priesthoods before they returned to their provinces. Participation in the festival obliged the priests to recognise the supremacy of the pharaoh over their own local deities. These ceremonies, however, including the ritual race, would not **Significance of** have taken place here but at Memphis. The funerary complex **the Heb-Sed** was meant as a cosmic 'stand-in' for the actual jubilee site — **Court** it perpetuated the regenerating Heb-Sed in eternal stone. This explains the extraordinary film set quality of the Heb-Sed Court.

The **Heb-Sed Court** (10) in the southeast part of the complex is rectangular and flanked to east and west by *shrines,* each one representing a province. They are hardly more than facades, as in a Hollywood Western. Access to the offering niches is by circumventing a screen wall, disguising the lack of depth, for the tall buildings are mere dummies, filled with rubble. Half open doors with hinges, imitations of the wooden originals, receive immortality in stone. In actuality, these shrines would have been tents with wooden poles and cross-supports. The chapels are not uniform; some have a curved cornice, as though the underlying frame represented flexed wood; other roofs are horizontal with the outward curve of the cavetto cornice that was to become so familiar a feature of Egyptian architecture, and torus moulding. Drawing on earlier building materials, Imhotep here invented the language of stone architecture. Cornices, torus mouldings, stone corner posts and columns and a variety of capitals appear for the first time in history at Saqqara. All the more astonishing that the effect is so delicate and beautifully proportioned.

A stone *platform* at the south end of the court is probably where the two thrones of Egypt stood for the re-enactment of the coronation, while at the north end of the court, to the left, is a *base with four pairs of feet*, most likely those of statues of Zoser, his wife and two daughters.

North of the Heb-Sed Court is another spacious court and the **House of the South** (11) with engaged proto-Doric columns. These Doric-style columns were never popular in Egypt where planes and hence smoothly-rounded columns were preferred to the Aegean play of light and shadow. There is the peculiarity of the door being placed asymmetrically, owing to the prototype facade being no more than a curtain, the door therefore needing to abut a column for support. As with the shrines in the Heb-Sed Court, the House of the South and the House of the North would actually have had wooden frames. They may have been sanctuaries, or possibly they represent government buildings of Upper and Lower Egypt.

First tourist graffiti

Inside the corridor are the first known examples of tourist graffiti, written in a cursive form of hieroglyphics and dating from the New Kingdom. The visitors, scribes from Thebes, express their admiration for Zoser's achievement, though here and elsewhere some settle for the ancient equivalent of 'Kilroy was here', while one smug crackpot, taking exception to some illiterate graffiti he must have seen, scribbled: 'The scribe of clever fingers came, a clever scribe without his equal among any men of Memphis, the scribe Amenemhet. I say: Explain to me these words. My heart is sick when I see the work of their hands. It is like the work of a woman who has no mind.'

The **House of the North** (12) is similar to that of the South except here the columns have the form of a papyrus plant, the shaft the triangular stem, the capital the fanning head.

The **mortuary temple** (13) at the north face of the pyramid is largely in ruins. The original entrance to the burial chamber beneath the pyramid led from this temple. To the east of the temple is the **serdab** (14), as startling now as it was to Firth when he uncovered it. It is a masonry box, tilted slightly back and with two small holes drilled through its north face. A window at the side, put there by the excavators, allows you to peer in. And there is Zoser! A life-size painted *limestone statue* as you realise after the initial surprise, but for all the world

Pharaonic astronaut

like a strapped-in astronaut in his space capsule, his eyes fixed through the holes on the North Star, awaiting blast-off and immortality. The circumpolar stars and the North Star itself were 'those that know no destruction' or 'those that know no weariness', for they never set and so never died; this was the

Zoser awaiting blast-off

place of eternal blessedness for which Egyptians longed. And there is Zoser. It is absolutely convincing. It is this which impresses about the ancient Egyptians again and again, how they gave as well as they could mechanical effect to their illusions. They put California body-freezers to shame. Alas for poor Zoser, the unbelieving Mr Firth removed the original statue to the Antiquities Museum in Cairo; this is a copy. But then again, the substitution probably does not bother Zoser's ka, and it lives here still, and at dark of night it rockets starwards and mingles with the universe.

The Pyramid of Unas
Unas was the last pharaoh of the V Dynasty. About 350 years mark the distance between Zoser's Step Pyramid, the Great

179

Pyramids at Giza, and this heap of rubble that is Unas' pyramid. These monuments graphically portray the rise and decline of the Old Kingdom sun cult.

The Pyramid of Unas was approached by a kilometre-long *causeway,* part of which has been reconstructed, including a very short section of its walls and roof, for it was entirely enclosed. A slit in the roof allowed the sunlight to illuminate the inscribed walls which were lively with everyday scenes. On the north side several *mastabas* are arranged like village houses on either side of narrow lanes. The best is of Princess Idut (V Dyn) with ten rooms. On the south side of the causeway there are impressive *boat pits.* Also, about 150 metres to the south are the sanded over ruins of the **Monastery of St Jeremias**, founded in the second half of the 5th C and destroyed by the Arabs around 960. Practically all of its paintings and carvings have been removed to the Coptic Museum in Old Cairo.

The **Pyramid of Unas** looks like a pile of dirt, certainly when approached from the east. On the west side its stones are more evident, but are disarrayed. Even originally it rose only about 18.5 metres; its core was loose blocks and rubble, its casing alone in hewn limestone. Nevertheless, the pyramid has proved of immense historical importance, for when Gaston Maspero entered the tomb chamber in 1881 he found the walls covered with inscriptions, the *Pyramid Texts,* which are the earliest mortuary literature of Egypt. These are hymns and rituals that preceded and accompanied the interment of the body; prayers for the release of the *ba* or soul; another section listing offerings of food, drink and clothing for use in the afterlife. Until this time, pyramids had gone unadorned. Thereafter, funerary literature underwent considerable elaboration and embroidery, culminating in that collection — or rather genre, for no such definitive compilation existed — of New Kingdom literature known to us as the Book of the Dead.

Despite its exterior, the pyramid remains internally sound and you can creep down the 1.4-metre high corridor, entered from the north face, past three enormous slabs of granite meant to block the way. Unlike the New Kingdom texts which were full of advice on how to steer a course clear of the forces of evil, which in effect emphasised the dangers that preceded safe arrival in the afterlife and were the tools of the trade of a blackmailing priesthood, the Pyramid Texts celebrate eternal life and identify the deceased pharaoh with Osiris. Nevertheless, there is anxiety in the prayers. The confident era of the sun cult was waning; a personal god and a note of redemption marked the rising cult of Osiris. The state was weakening; the troubled times of the First Intermediate Period were approaching.

The Pyramid Texts

Visiting the Outstanding Mastabas

Refreshments and Mariette's house You can now trudge across the sands or drive to the refreshment tent which stands near the site of Mariette's house, where he stayed during those first serious explorations of Saqqara. The beer is cold and in the heat goes straight to your head. You can walk around the rest of the necropolis in a state of intoxication. When visiting the Serapeum, you may be grateful for that.

But first you can visit some mastabas. The **Mastaba of Mereruka**, with 32 rooms, is the largest at Saqqara. He enjoyed in death not only elbow room, but the prestigious company to which he had become accustomed in life. For Mereruka was vizier to the Pharaoh Teti (VI Dyn), whose pyramid is next door, and he married and was buried with the boss's daughter. The *entry passage* shows Mereruka painting a picture of the seasons and playing a board game to pass away the time, while the *first three chambers* are decorated with scenes of hunting, furniture making and goldsmiths at work. At the far end of the mastaba is a *chapel* with six pillars, containing a statue of the vizier himself. The scenes to the left of this are interesting: they show the domestication of gazelles, goats and hyenas.

The double **Mastaba of Akhti-Hotep and Ptah-Hotep** is to the southeast of the refreshment tent, along your way if you are walking between the complexes of Zoser or Unas or Mereruka's mastaba and a beer. Ptah-Hotep describes himself as a priest of Maat and he may have held other positions too. At any rate, he seems to have been a very important official during the reign of Djedkare (V Dyn), predecessor of Unas. His son Akhti-Hotep was vizier, judge and chief of the granary and treasury. Their mastaba is smaller than that of Ti's, which we come to next, but is more developed and is particularly interesting for the reliefs which are in various stages of completion.

Reliefs in progress You enter from the north and come into a *corridor.* On its left wall are preliminary drawings in red with corrections by the master artist in black. On the right wall are various stages of low relief. The background is cut away first to yield a silhouette and then the details are pencilled in and cut. In the lower registers, servants carry fowl in the arms towards Ptah-Hotep who stands at the far end of this right-hand wall. Though somewhat stylised, with his shoulders squared but with head and limbs in profile, the detailed musculature shows the artist's sound sense of anatomy.

At the top end of the corridor you turn right into a *pillared hall* and then left, passing through a *vestibule,* into *Ptah-Hotep's tomb chamber.* The ceiling imitates the trunks of palm trees while the mural reliefs, still retaining some colour, are the finest preserved of the Old Kingdom, surpassing even those in the more famous Mastaba of Ti.

Ptah-Hotep's tomb chamber; the finest Old Kingdom reliefs

On the *right wall* are two door-shaped stelae, representing the entrance to the tomb. Between them is Ptah-Hotep, depicted in the panther-skin of a high priest, seated at a cornucopian table of offerings, a goblet raised to his lips. In the upper register, priests make offerings; in the lower three rows, servants bear gifts. They are lucky to get off so lightly; during the I Dynasty they were sacrificed and interred around their master's mastaba. On the *far wall* Ptah-Hotep is again at table, this time with a stylised loaf of bread before him and copper basins and ewers alongside so that he may cleanse himself before eating. In the upper register women representing various estates bring him the products of his farms, while in the second register animals are being thrown and slaughtered. The reliefs on the *left wall* are the finest and most interesting, a catalogue of events in the life of the deceased. On the right, according to the text, Ptah-Hotep is inspecting the 'gifts and tribute that are brought by the estates of the North and South'; boys are wrestling and running, caged animals (lions, gazelles, hares and hedgehogs) are drawn up, and a cow is giving birth, a peasant guiding the calf into the world. The bottom register shows domestic poultry and the text claims that Ptah-Hotep possessed '121,000 geese of one variety, 11,210 of another variety, 120,000 small geese, 111,200 goslings and 1225 swans'. On the left of this wall Ptah-Hotep 'witnesses all the pleasant activities that take place in the whole country'. In the top registers, boys and girls are playing; there is one episode of two boys seated and facing each other as their friends vault over them. This game, called *Khaki la wizza,* is still played today by Nubians. The third register is devoted to aspects of viticulture; the fourth shows animal life (note the hare emerging from its hole with a cricket in its mouth); the fifth is a hunting scene, the cow tied as bait for the lion; the fifth and sixth registers show marsh and boating scenes.

Above the entrance is a faded mural, but you can make out Ptah-Hotep preparing for his day, a manicurist at his hands, a pedicurist at his feet, musicians entertaining him, greyhounds beneath his chair and a pet monkey held by his valet. The sophistication of this scene is all the more striking when you recall that it depicts daily Egyptian life, albeit at the very top of the social ladder, nearly 4500 years ago, that is when Europe and most of Asia were still in the Stone Age.

The purpose of tomb reliefs

The purpose of these reliefs was to provide food, indeed a complete experience of life, for the ka. They began during the IV Dynasty as it was realised that relatives and descendants did not always provide fresh offerings; the reliefs were imitative magic against default. But one can also imagine the great pleasure they must have given the tomb owner, an assurance that he was going to take it all with him, and to his relatives when they did gather in his tomb. I think of some of the more

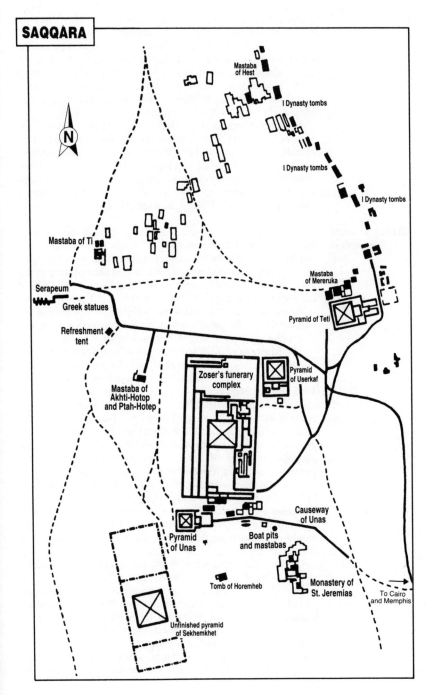

SAQQARA

N

Mastaba of Hest

I Dynasty tombs

I Dynasty tombs

I Dynasty tombs

Mastaba of Ti

Serapeum

Greek statues

Refreshment tent

Mastaba of Akhti-Hotep and Ptah-Hotep

Mastaba of Mereruka

Pyramid of Teti

Zoser's funerary complex

Pyramid of Userkaf

Pyramid of Unas

Causeway of Unas

Boat pits and mastabas

Tomb of Horemheb

Monastery of St. Jeremias

To Cairo and Memphis

Unfinished pyramid of Sekhemkhet

elaborate marble tombs in Greek cemeteries today; they are like small shrines with an inner chamber for the deceased and an outer chamber with seats for the living, and they are the cheeriest places, often attracting bountiful picnics. Unas, a generation later, was already worried about his relationship with Osiris; but here there is not a single god, no judgement, no doubt — afterlife follows on from life as assuredly as day follows day, and without even an intervening night.

Now returning to the pillared hall you turn left for the *chamber of Akhti-Hotep,* similarly though less finely decorated. A passageway leads out of the side of this and opening off it, on your left, is a chamber containing an *anonymous mummy.* The passageway leads back to the pillared hall and the entrance corridor; while negotiating it I tripped over a skeleton, perhaps belonging to a 20th C AD tourist who had got locked in.

Getting yourself entombed

I have already mentioned that my brother got himself locked into the Great Pyramid; at Saqqara a friend got himself locked into the Serapeum for half an hour with the lights off (an experience that would have turned me instantly into a skeleton); and I got locked into the Mastaba of Ti, and would have spent the night there but for a ladder left providentially in the open court. If you lack Ptah-Hotep's confidence in the coming day, make certain the keeper knows you are there and looks like the sort of fellow who would let you out.

The **Mastaba of Ti** is to the north of the refreshment tent and you can follow the road that leads to the Serapeum part of the way there. The mastaba was discovered by Mariette in 1865 and has been well restored by the Egyptian Department of Antiquities. It originally stood above ground but is now entirely sunk in the sand. Its reliefs rival those in Ptah-Hotep's tomb chamber and exceed them in variety. Ti was a parvenu and royal hairdresser during the early V Dynasty; he was also overseer of several royal mortuary temples and pyramids and controller of royal ponds, farms and stock from which he evidently enriched himself. His wife was related to the royal family and his children bore the title 'royal descendant', to which Ti himself was not entitled. Ti's wife and eldest son were also entombed here, but some later would-be arriviste made off with the goods and disposed of the bodies.

In plan, the entrance is from the north, a two-pillared vestibule leading to a spacious open pillared court at the centre of which a flight of stairs descends to a subterranean passage ending in an antechamber and the tomb chamber. Otherwise, a corridor leads out from the rear of the open court and passes a chamber on the right, arriving at the funerary chamber and the serdab.

Once through the open court, whose reliefs have been badly damaged by exposure, the walls of corridors and rooms are finely decorated with familiar scenes. The most interesting room, with the most beautiful reliefs, is Ti's *funerary chamber*. Through the slot in the far (south) wall you can see Ti (this is a cast of the original statue now in the Cairo Museum) staring vacantly northwards from his serdab, lacking, I am afraid, Zoser's look of adventure. Needless to say his hair, or rather his wig, is well done. Most enjoyable are the *reliefs on the near (north) wall,* all concerned with life in the marshes of the Delta. Look particularly at the central relief of Ti *sailing through the marshes.* This is a classic representation of a hippopotamus hunt; the hippopotamus, to the lower right, has seized a crocodile which, meanwhile, is desperately trying to bite the hippo's leg. Ti is shown larger than his huntsmen who, from another boat, are harpooning the hippo. Below the boats are fine Nile fish of different species, identifiable as favoured catches in the river today. On the right, in a small boat with a curiously truncated stern, a fisherman is about to club a large schal fish over the head. Above Ti, amongst the papyrus clusters, birds are being attacked in their nests by carnivorous animals, the reeds bending with their weight. In the register below is a line of *elegant female bearers,* their transparent coloured dresses surrendered to time, their nakedness and varied poses freshly pleasing.

Hippopotamus hunt

This relief is unusual for having two layers of meaning. Literally it is a hunt in the marshes; but symbolically it is Ti against the forces of evil and chaos. The hippopotamus was particularly feared and hated in ancient Egypt, but Ti together with a helpful crocodile is killing it. Fish and birds represented chaos, but here again man and animals are subduing them.

By way of making amends for having locked me in Ti's tomb, the keeper afterwards invited me to his little concrete hut for a glass of mint tea. It was clearly his eagerness to retreat here, out of the blistering heat, that caused my incarceration in the first place. We sat on a reed mat on the floor while he manipulated various soda cans over his burner — some of the cans for storing the water, one for boiling it, others for decanting the tea — and we smoked his hubbly-bubbly meanwhile. This he lit with bits of dried corncob he kept for the purpose and brought to a glow in the burner flame. The surrounding necropolis, my temporary entombment, the sand and heat were all forgotten in this humble private place where tea and tobacco were prepared and consumed with meticulous ritual. The keeper fussed and bubbled and tasted and grunted with the fullness of it all, and as we drank the thick sweet tea, so satisfying, and enjoyed the relaxation of the waterpipe, we looked out as from a serdab upon the desert wasteland and he called this tea and this tobacco his friends.

Tea in the desert

Tombs of the Apis Bulls

The Serapeum is the strangest place at Saqqara. A temple once stood here amidst the sands but what remain are the long underground galleries cut through the rock where the Apis bulls were buried. This was Mariette's great discovery in 1851 which began the serious excavation of Saqqara that has continued ever since. Entry is to the west of the refreshment tent; you follow the road which first bends right towards Ti's mastaba and then turns left. At this second bend was Mariette's house, and immediately by the roadside, on your left and under the protective roof, is the surprising sight of several Greek statues arranged in a semicircle. These and their unlikely connection with bull burial requires some explanation.

The huge tombs of these Apis bulls were previously known only from references to them by various writers of antiquity.

For instance, Herodotus wrote: 'The Apis is the calf of a cow which is never afterwards able to have another. The Egyptian belief is that a flash of light descends upon the cow from heaven, and this causes her to receive Apis. The Apis-calf has distinctive marks; it is black, with a white diamond on its forehead, the image of an eagle on its back, the hairs on its tail double, and a scarab under its tongue'. Apis thus miraculously conceived was considered to be an incarnation of Ptah, the god of Memphis. Worshipped as such during his lifetime within a special sanctuary in the Temple of Ptah, he was mummified after his death on those alabaster beds you can still see amongst the few surviving stones of Memphis. Then, identified with Osiris under the name Osiris-Apis, he was taken with great pomp to these underground galleries at the Serapeum and placed within a gigantic sarcophagus.

Sacred bull cults go back into the prehistory of Egypt, and during the I and II Dynasties a bull would wander across the field of the Heb-Sed race, symbolically fertilising the two lands. But animal cults enjoyed an astonishing popularity during the Late Egyptian Period as the old beliefs degenerated. Herodotus, attempting to demonstrate the madness of Cambyses, the Persian ruler of Egypt, records that 'the priests brought Apis and Cambyses, half mad as he was, drew his dagger, aimed a blow at its belly, but missed and struck its thigh. Then he laughed, and said to the priests: "Do you call that a god, you poor creatures? Are your gods flesh and blood? Do they feel the prick of steel? No doubt a god like that is good enough for the Egyptians; but you won't get away with trying to make a fool of me"', and he had the priests whipped and forbade the cult, but when finally Apis died of his wounds he was buried by the priests without the knowledge of Cambyses. In this instance, at least, Cambyses sounds quite sane, but it is understandable that the once mighty priesthood should cling to some tangible shred of belief as the old order was being attacked by foreign rulers. The Ptolemies were more shrewd and flattered the priesthood, encouraged their cults, built temples and ruled Egypt for 300 years.

The galleries of the Serapeum date from three periods, the earliest to the reign of Ramses II (XIX Dyn), enlarged by his son Khaemwas; a second to the reign of Psammetichus I (XXVI Dyn); and a main gallery to the Ptolemies. It was the Greek Ptolemies who encouraged an identity between Osiris and Dionysos, and Plutarch comments that 'as for what the priests openly do in the burial of the Apis when they transport its carcass on a raft, this in no way falls short of Bacchic revelry, for they wear fawn-skins and carry thyrsus-rods' — a staff tipped with a pine cone, in short a phallus — 'and produce shouts and movements as do the ecstatic celebrants of the Dionysiac orgies'. (Recall the sarcophagus of the dwarf in Room 49 on the ground floor of the Cairo Museum.) It is from the Ptolemaic period that the **semicircle of Greek statues** of poets and philosophers dates. Homer is at the centre, Pindar plays the lyre at the far right, and at the far left is a base inscribed with the name of Plato. They must be turning over in their graves.

Mariette was led to the Serapeum by recalling a quotation from Strabo (24 BC): 'One finds at Memphis a temple to Serapis in such a sandy place that the wind heaps up sand dunes beneath which we saw sphinxes, some half-buried, some buried up to the head, from which one can suppose that the way to the temple could not be without danger if one were caught in a sudden wind-storm'. Mariette had found one such head at Saqqara, and removing the sand in the area found an entire avenue of sphinxes leading to the Greek statues and to the Serapeum galleries. The avenue has since sanded up again.

Mariette's description of his discovery of the Serapeum

Saqqara can seem strange enough today. When Mariette was excavating here, he described the conditions in his house: 'Snakes slithered along the floor, tarantulas or scorpions swarmed in the wall crevices, large spider webs waved from the ceiling like flags. As soon as night fell, bats, attracted by the light, entered my cell through the cracks in the door and kept me awake with their spectral flights. Before going to sleep, I tucked the edges of my mosquito net beneath my mattress and put my trust in God and all the saints, while outside jackals, hyenas and wolves howled around the house'. Of entering the Serapeum, Mariette wrote: 'When I first penetrated into the sepulchre of the Apis, I was so overcome with astonishment that, though it is now five years ago, the feeling is still vivid in my mind. By some inexplicable accident one chamber of the Apis tombs, walled up in the thirtieth year of Ramses II, had escaped the general plunder of the monuments, and I was so fortunate as to find it untouched. Three thousand seven hundred years had had no effect in altering its primitive state. The finger mark of the Egyptian who set the last stone in the wall built up to cover the door was still visible in the mortar. Bare feet had left their traces on the sand strewn in a corner of this chamber of the dead; nothing had been disturbed in this burying-place where an embalmed ox had been resting for nearly forty centuries'.

A terrifying moronic force

My own impression was of a terrifying moronic force at work. You descend a ramp slipping under the formless desert surface and reach a *corridor* leading off to left and right. Down to the left it meets a *transverse gallery* and left into that, on the left, within a vault, is a massive *pink granite sarcophagus* with panels and across the top edge hieroglyphics — on the right an Apis bull is depicted with the characteristic black markings. The rest of this gallery is blocked off by a grate.

You now reverse direction, heading down a 150-metre gallery. On either side, in alternating succession, are more vaults, in all but one of which squats a monstrous black sarcophagus — bull-size. The *finest sarcophagus* of all is at the very end of this gallery, on the right, with carved decoration and polished to a glassy lustre. You can climb down into its pit and stand on a step at the back to peer inside.

Until a few years ago the Serapeum was lit only at lengthy intervals by dim yellow lights which in the murky darkness cast a greenish glow. At some places, the lights would have gone out and you had to walk through velvety blackness. In the silence and the dim light, the repetition of vaults and sarcophagi became like a bad dream you could not awake from, and you just walked on, with literally no light at the end of the tunnel. It was macabre, and with your capillaries shot full with beer you achieved enough perspective to find it utterly incredible that the Ptolemies, whose gallery this is, could have perpetuated anything so repulsive and outlandish. The lighting has now been greatly 'improved' — and perhaps also I have recovered from my first shock; but what was once the weirdest place in Egypt seems now to be only as discomforting, say, as walking down a corridor of Cairo's Marriott Hotel.

It was not here, but in the Rammesid gallery, now inaccessible, that Mariette found the one untouched Apis tomb, a mummified bull inside, and also in the gallery the mummy of Khaemwas, who had been appointed by his father Ramses II High Priest of Ptah. And there he found those ancient footprints. You notice footprints in the sand in this Ptolemaic gallery too, of more recent visitors, and they bring to mind, as so often encounters with Egypt's pharaonic past do, our own voyages into the cosomos, those footprints left in the dust on the surface of the windless Moon which may remain for millions of years undisturbed.

Retracing your steps from the end of the main gallery, turn

to the left and then to the right. An *empty sarcophagus* almost blocks the route. A little farther on is its lid. It seems to have been abandoned before the interment of the sacred bull, suggesting the cult was abruptly ended.

Other Animal Cults at Saqqara

The search for Imhotep's tomb

This account of Saqqara has covered only the most major points of interest to the layman. There is a search now going on for Imhotep's tomb which is thought to be to the northeast of the Serapeum and the Mastaba of Ti. In this area have been found the Anubieion, sacred to Anubis, with a gallery for dogs; the galleries of the Bubasteion, sacred to Bastet, filled with mummified cats; the Temple of Thoth, its galleries piled with thousands of mummified ibises, baboons and falcons; and the Isieion, the Temple of Isis, with underground galleries containing the sarcophagi of the sacred cows that had given birth to the Apis bulls. It is possible that these stacks of smaller mummified creatures were brought over hundreds of years by pilgrims as offerings to a favoured god, or as supplication by those seeking a cure. It is because of these associations with healing cults that Imhotep's shrine and tomb might be here; he was later worshipped as the god of medicine, the Egyptian equivalent of Asclepios. These cults continued into the Roman period and were only finally suppressed several centuries into our era by the victory of Christianity over paganism, when the fashion changed from dogs, cats, birds and baboons to collecting bits of martyrs' bodies.

Pyramids Farther South

The **necropolis of Dahshur** is a few kilometres to the south of Saqqara. Of its four pyramids, two date from the Middle Kingdom and are badly ruined — they are likely to be of interest only to the specialist. Snofru's **Bent and Red Pyramids**, already referred to in an earlier chapter, are the chief attraction. But this is a military area, and foreign tourists are not permitted entry. Instead you should stand on the southern ramparts of Zoser's funerary complex to see these great pyramids resting upon an endless plain confronting only the cosmos.

Much farther south is the **Meidum pyramid**, or what remains of it. This was the first attempt at a true pyramid (see *The Pyramid Age* chapter) and the lessons learnt from its monumental failure, if one accepts Mendelssohn's theory, led to the successful completion of those greatest pyramids of all at Giza. For that reason, but also for the spectacle of this abrupt tower on the desert's edge, the Meidum pyramid is as much worth visiting as any.

PRACTICAL INFORMATION

You can reach **Saqqara** by horse or camel from the Giza Pyramids (see previous chapter), though you will not be left with much time to explore the site, and a visit to Memphis would probably be out of the question. (You can, however, hire a camel *at* Saqqara for a little trot round the site.) There is also a bus to Badrashein, a village near Memphis; ask about it at the Mena House or the Tourist Police at the Pyramids. And there are tours or a taxi from Cairo. Refreshments and light meals are available at the Saqqara site. There is no **site fee for Memphis**. The **site fee for Saqqara** is LE5, or LE2 for students.

Dahshur is in the midst of a military area and is off-limits to foreign tourists. Specialists may be able to obtain permission from the Ministry of the Interior, Midan Lazouli, Cairo.

Tours do not include Meidum with Memphis and Saqqara. But ask, eg at Thomas Cook, if it can be included at an extra cost, or go to Misr Travel. If driving to **Meidum**, follow the road along the west bank of the Nile south towards El Wasta; the pyramid will appear on your right but you drive past it a bit until you come to a paved road signposted for the pyramid in English and Arabic. This heads off into the desert, at first passing south of the pyramid and then coming up to its northwest corner.

THE FAYYUM

The desert road to the Fayyum

The easiest, most direct approach to the Fayyum, and also the most striking, is by the desert road from Giza. You drive out of Cairo as though to the Giza Pyramids but before reaching the Mena House Hotel you turn right onto the desert road for Alexandria. Follow this for 500 metres and then turn left; you are now on a good fast road all the way to Medinet el Fayyum, capital of Fayyum province. Behind you, to the east, there is a wonderful view of the Pyramids across the untrammelled sand; like a departed shore they sink into the horizon as you commit yourself to the desert. After 76 km you approach the edge of the depression at Kom Aushim, the ancient Karanis, on your left. From here there is a fine panorama over the whole of the Fayyum, a surprise of green cultivation and blue lakewater surrounded by rocky hills and expanses of sandy desert. An excursion to the Fayyum can be accomplished in a day, starting early in the morning. For a longer stay it is most agreeable to overnight at Lake Qarun, though there is accommodation too at Medinet el Fayyum (106 km from Cairo).

The Garden of Egypt

'Cool are the dawns; prolific are the trees; diverse are the fruits; little are the rains.' This was how a Syrian emir described the Fayyum in the 13th C, comparing it to the luxuriant gardens which until recently have surrounded Damascus. A growing number of visitors, both foreigners and Cairenes escaping the oppressive heat and congestion of their city, are finding that the Fayyum still retains its charms.

Abundance and variety

The Fayyum is the cultivated area occupying the northern part of a much larger depression surrounded by those low mountains you see from the Giza road. Here vegetables, cereals, fruits and flowers grow in remarkable abundance, watered by 2300 km of capillary canals — equivalent to the entire length of the Nile through Egypt. The rich soil of the central Fayyum yields such crops as wheat, rice, melons and cauliflowers according to season, and in particular cotton, the main cash crop, which is planted in April and harvested in September. Around the periphery of the oasis where the soil is sandier, tomatoes are a favourite crop, as well as such medicinal and aromatic plants as camomile, mint, fenugreek and sesame. Palms, acacias, tamarisks and eucalyptus trees are loosely distributed across the level placid landscape. Groves of almonds, apricots, oranges, lemons, pomegranates, figs and olives screen the horizon. The vine and the olive have been cultivated here since ancient times. Classical writers mentioned the deep red roses for which the Fayyum was famous, 'so lavishly strewn at the banquets of Cleopatra' (as Baedeker floridly put it in 1878), though now you will find only a humbler, pallid pink variety growing wild along the roadsides. Geraniums are grown for their essence, used in perfumes.

Fish and birdlife   Lake Qarun, growing saltier with the centuries, is now nearly as saline as sea water and supports a dwindling stock of freshwater fish, notably a tastier version of the Nile bolti, but certain species of marine fish like sole, mullett, eel and shrimp are being introduced. At places muddy and marshy and not suitable for swimming, the lake appeals to a wide variety of migratory birds, including the pink flamingo, and in winter its pearly surface is blackened by thousands of ducks. As throughout Egypt, egrets are a familiar sight, often roosting en masse and seeming to fill the trees with a sudden display of white blossoms. But the most common bird of the Fayyum is the chicken; under factory conditions five million are produced every year.

The Hydrology of the Fayyum

Fayyum comes from the Coptic *phiom*, meaning sea. Yet the present-day lake clinging to the northwest edge of the cultivation is called merely Birket Qarun, literally Qarun Pond. For Lake Qarun, at 45 metres below sea level, is only a vestigial reminder of a once much greater expanse which stood at 40 metres above sea level. In that prehistoric time the lake was in free communication with the Nile, that is filling when the Nile flooded and then partly emptying itself back into the river when the Nile fell. For whatever reason — perhaps climatic or a change in the level or course of the Nile — by the New Kingdom the lake was only about 2 metres above sea level and no longer exchanged seasonal waters with the river. Much of the lake now became swamp and marshland, the sort of hunting ground depicted in the Saqqara tombs, rich in wildlife and particularly in crocodiles which were worshipped here throughout the pharaonic and Graeco-Roman periods.

Pharaonic environmental planning   Not until the Middle Kingdom did human agency really make an impression on the Fayyum, but then with massive effect. Ammenemes I (XII Dyn) widened and deepened the primeval channel between the depression and the Nile at a gap in the mountains near El Lahun. The river rushed through once more and the level of the lake rose to 18 metres above sea level. An immediate motive might have been to drain marshes along the western embankment of the Nile, but the grander conception was nothing less than to turn the Fayyum into a giant regulating reservoir which would moderate the effect on the Delta of high and low Niles. At flood the river would pour into the Fayyum; at other times the water could be refunded into the Nile to irrigate Lower Egypt. The regulator which Ammenemes I installed at El Lahun has its successor in the same place today.

Though water still enters the Fayyum through the Lahun Gap, it does so today via the canalised Bahr Yusef (River of Joseph) which sinuously parallels the Nile for over 200 km from Deirut, nearly opposite Tell el Amarna, where it is fed in turn by the 19th C Ibrahimiya Canal originating near Assiut. It is because of its ultimate dependency on the Nile that the Fayyum is not a true oasis. For 20 days every January the sluices at El Lahun are shut and the Fayyum's entire canal system dries up, 'to let the land rest' and to permit the clearing of waterways and the repair of bridges.

Rise and Fall

Succeeding pharaohs of the XII Dynasty developed an attachment to the Fayyum after Ammenemes I created Me-Wer (the Great Lake). Sesostris I built the pyramid at Lahun; Ammenemes III raised the colossi at Biahmu, and at Hawara he built both a pyramid and the famous Labyrinth.

The Greek oasis　　But it was the Ptolemies, 1500 years later, who developed the Fayyum as a major agricultural and population centre. The key once again was the level of Lake Moeris, as the Greeks called Me-Wer. Still at its Middle Kingdom level, it covered about three-fifths of the present cultivation. The Ptolemies now lowered Moeris to its Old Kingdom level of 2 metres above sea level, gaining a vast area of fertile land which was maintained by an elaborate irrigation system benefiting from such Greek inventions as Archimedes' screw and the sakiya. Ptolemy II named his new province for his sister-wife Arsinoë, and of all the provinces or nomes of Egypt, Strabo extolled the Arsinoite nome as 'the most remarkable of all, both on account of its scenery and its fertility and cultivation'. The settlers — Macedonians, Greeks and Jews — established new towns such as Crocodilopolis, Karanis and Dionysias, and the Fayyum became a centre of Hellenistic culture in Egypt. Later it was once of the early centres of Christianity, its relative isolation securing it against the extremes of persecution. Despite a large influx of Islamicised Bedouin following the Arab invasion it remained a significant Coptic redoubt into the Middle Ages, with 35 monasteries recorded in the Fayyum in the 13th C.

Long decline from Roman through Turkish times　　During the Roman period the variety of the Fayyum was sacrificed to the demand that it supply Rome with corn, and the harsh imperial taxes led to the neglect of the irrigation system. By the 5th C AD Lake Moeris had fallen to 36 metres below sea level, and the salinity of the water, no longer adequately refreshed by the Nile, increased. The desert crept closer and once flourishing fields and towns were abandoned. The process accelerated under Turkish rule; remote, vulnerable to nomad raids and visited no more than once a year by the cadi from Constantinople, the Fayyum's fortunes reached their nadir.

193

In 1874 a railway link tied the Fayyum once again to the Nile valley. Around the turn of the century the British built roads and revived the irrigation system, encouraging major land reclamation. Once again the Fayyum is one of the most productive provinces in Egypt, though it has not yet regained the prosperity of Ptolemaic times.

Entering the Oasis

If you have come along the road from Giza, you first come to **Kom Aushim** on the edge of the desert overlooking the oasis. A small **museum** is by the roadside to the left. It is well laid out and contains finds from the Middle Kingdom to the Christian period from throughout the Fayyum.

Remains of Karanis

Immediately behind the museum are the extensive remains of **Karanis**, once set amidst fields irrigated from the lake. Like other Greek towns of the Fayyum, it was founded in the 3rd C BC and abandoned to the sands late in the 4th or early in the 5th C AD. Once 3000 people lived here, on or near the shore of Lake Moeris; you can walk along their streets and lanes, between the walls of their mud brick houses, noticing the millstones and granite olive presses often lying within. There are two limestone temples, the larger **south temple** standing on massive foundations at the middle of the town. It was built in the 1st or early 2nd C AD and dedicated to two crocodile gods, Pnepheros and Petesouchus. On its east face are Greek inscriptions from the time of Nero. There is a good view of the town and the Fayyum from atop the temple, and of the second smaller though otherwise almost identical **north temple**, dating to the 1st C BC and dedicated to Isis and the crocodile god Suchos.

The long low building between the town ruins and the museum was the **villa of Sir Miles Lampson** (later Lord Killearn), the high-handed High Commissioner and then British Ambassador to Egypt from 1933 to 1946.

Continuing south from Kom Aushim on the road to Medinet el Fayyum, a turning off to the right (west) leads to **Lake Qarun** (50 km east to west, 10 km maximum north to south). The southest end of the lake is developed for tourism, and it is from the Auberge el Fayyum or the village of Shakshouk that you can hire a boat for **Dimeh el Siba** up a

Ptolemaic caravan station across the lake

steep 3-km track from the north shore. This was the Ptolemaic settlement of **Soknopaiou Nesos**, that is Island of Soknopaiou, a local variant of the crocodile god Sobek, but by the time of its founding the level of Lake Moeris had been lowered and the town in fact stood on a promontory. It now stands 65 metres above the lake; a 400-metre *processional way* begins at what was the ancient lakeshore and by steps passes through the city gate and past two ruined pylons to the **Temple of Soknopaios and Isis**. The limestone temple preserves a few reliefs, one of Ptolemy II praying before Amun, and

One of the famous Fayyum portraits (Room 14, first floor, Egyptian Museum)

is surrounded by its original high mud brick enclosure wall. There are several well-preserved houses in the vicinity. The settlement was a fortified caravan station; goods would have been transported across Lake Moeris and here final preparations made before the caravans set off across the Western Desert for the more distant oases.

(Dimeh el Siba can also be reached by desert track from the Kom Aushim museum, leading first to **Qasr el Sagha** (28 km), where at the foot of an escarpment there is a small unfinished **Middle Kingdom temple** built of irregularly shaped blocks, often cut at angles and fitted together like bits of a jigsaw. Nearby are the remains of an ancient quay. Soknopaiou Nesos is then a further 8 km south. Though this route is possible even without four-wheel drive, there is the danger of losing your way or getting stuck in the sand, and a guide is strongly recommended. Arrangements can be made through the museum, preferably the day before.)

Resuming the main road to Medinet el Fayyum, at 4 km south of Sennouris near the village of Biahmu is the site where Ammenemes III (XII Dyn) erected two **colossal seated figures** of himself. Herodotus saw these from a distance, rising above the flooded fields, and thought they must have been sitting atop pyramids. Originally they may have stood on either side of a lakeside harbour. Both colossi were still in place in the 13th C when they were seen by an Arab visitor, and part of one was seen as recently as the 17th C by a European traveller. They were apparently hacked down in an ignorant search for treasure. Though 47 pieces are held at the Ashmolean Museum, Oxford (where a nose is on display), here only the bases remain — the statues rose another 12 metres above these, which would have made them as high as the famous Colossi of Memnon at Thebes, erected 400-odd years later.

A further 7 km south lies Medinet el Fayyum.

Hub of the Oasis

Capital and market centre of the Fayyum, **Medinet el Fayyum** is also the point from which all roads radiate and where the waters of the Bahr Yusef are distributed throughout the oasis. The name mean simply Town of the Fayyum. The population of the entire oasis is about 1.6 million, of which about 400,000 live here. It is the antithesis of the surrounding countryside and is not an attractive place.

Nevertheless there are some points of interest within and near Medinet el Fayyum. As you enter the town on the Cairo road you pass the 13-metre **obelisk of Sesostris I** (XII Dyn) in the middle of a roundabout. This stood until the 18th C at its original site near the village of Abgig, but at the time of Napoleon's invasion of Egypt it was discovered lying on the ground broken in two. It has only recently been reconstructed and erected here.

Colossi of Ammenemes III

At the town centre, by the tourist information kiosk, is the large white Cafeteria el Medina, the obvious place to sit out at a table for something to eat — it all but embraces four **waterwheels** which groan like air raid sirens during the London blitz. The Fayyum is famous for its waterwheels, and there are said to be about 200 throughout the oasis. These are the heirs of those Ptolemaic sakiyas which brought the Fayyum to such a pitch of abundance. They are driven by the water itself, which because the oasis is higher in the south (26 metres above sea level) than in the north (45 metres below sea level), runs swiftly through its capillary canals, unlike the sluggish or stagnant canals of Upper Egypt and the Delta. Sitting here, you notice the Bahr Yusef flowing from east to west in front of you; the wheels carry a portion of its flow into the Bahr Tanhala which runs off behind you to the north, while a block to the west there is the Bahr Sennouris, which also flows north. At the far west end of town, the Bahr Yusef divides into six other distributory canals which wend their way throughout the oasis. If you follow the Bahr Sennouris on foot for about half an hour northwards, first on the west bank, then on the east, you will come to the **Seven Waterwheels**, a Fayyum landmark. The first is at a farm, then you see a lovely group of four against a screen of mangoes, palms and willows, and then a final pair by a rustic bridge. It makes a delightful country walk.

The waters distributed

Also northwards (20 minutes on foot), and now encroached upon by the town itself, is **Kiman Faris**, site of the original town, Shedet during the Middle Kingdom, Crocodilopolis or Arsinoë under the Ptolemies. This was the chief centre for the worship of the crocodile god Sobek, and in Graeco-Roman times tourists came from all over the Mediterranean to feed the sacred beasts with specially prepared food, a more exciting version of feeding the pigeons in Trafalgar Square. Now there is nothing to see but mounds beside the railway line, the occasional bit of mosaic, a fragment of sculpture, a foundation block poking out. Items of interest turned up by the recent construction of the Faculty of Engineering are in the Kom Aushim museum. But even before the mounds were built on, the *sebakhin* had made a mess of the site, an interesting example of how Egypt lives upon its past. In a land where wood is a rarity, animal dung has traditionally been used for fuel and so other fertilisers have been sought. One of these has been the debris mounds of ancient towns which yield a kind of earth, called *sebahk*, containing as much as 12 percent potassium nitrate, sodium carbonate and ammonium chloride.

Ancient Crocodilopolis

You will find some remains of Crocodilopolis inside the **Mosque of Qaytbay**, which stands on the south bank of the Bahr Yusef by the sixth bridge west of the Cafeteria el Medina. The mosque was in fact built at the end of the 15th C by Qaytbay's favourite concubine Khawand Asal Bay (by

197

whose name it is often known). In 1892 the greater part of it fell into the Bahr Yusef, and so much of it is new. The south entrance with its heavy double wooden doors ornamented with greenish bronze is very fine, the portion below the trefoil arch being original; Asal Bay is mentioned in the inscriptions here, and she gave to the mosque its superb gilded teak minbar. Many of the marble columns within are clearly ancient, and would have been taken from the ruins of Crocodilopolis.

Covered bazaar

At the fourth bridge west of the Cafeteria el Medina on the south side of the Bahr Yusef is the **souk**, a warren of narrow and occasionally covered streets known as el Qantara. Behind it is el Sagha, the street of gold and silversmiths, mostly Christians.

Excursions Around the Oasis

When in late Roman times the irrigation system of the Fayyum began to fail through neglect, a number of Ptolemaic towns around the periphery of the oasis were left abandoned to the advancing sands. Two in particular are worth visiting from Medinet el Fayyum, **Dionysias** (at Qasr Qarun, 36 km to the west) and **Narmouthis** (at Medinet Madi, 25 km to the southwest). A third, **Tebtynis** (at Omm el Borigat, 26 km to the south), can be visited if you have the time or as an alternative to Narmouthis.

Dionysias: Ptolemaic temple and Diocletian fort

Qasr Qarun (Dionysias) is at the western extremity of Lake Qarun. From here, caravans would set out for Bahariya Oasis in the Western Desert, and it was to secure this end of the route that a fortress of mud brick was built during Diocletian's reign, its walls now only a metre high, its interior filled with sand. 200 metres to the southeast is the most noticeable feature of the site, a sandstone Ptolemaic **temple** dedicated to Sobek. It is a maze of corridors, chambers, tunnels and stairways within, including secret chambers within the thickness of the walls where the priests presumably hid themselves and made oracular noises. On either side of the sanctuary spiral staircases lead to the roof, where there may have been a chapel similar in purpose to that at Dendera where the sun's rays revivified the cult statues, and from where you can enjoy far views over the oasis and the desert. Remains of the town in badly worn mud brick are evident, while here and there the shriveled branches of small, long dead trees trained up walls are reminders of a vanished fertility.

Narmouthis: rare Middle Kingdom temple

At **Medinet Madi** (Narmouthis) there is a XII Dynasty **temple** dedicated to Sobek and the serpent goddess Renenutet set in a sand-filled hollow. The work of Ammenemes III, it is one of the few surviving examples of Middle Kingdom religious architecture. Approached by a paved *processional way* lined with lions and sphinxes, the limestone temple consists of a pronaos with two papyrus bud columns and a sanctuary filled with hieroglyphics. Amongst the numerous temple reliefs, there is a fine one of Sobek as a man with a crocodile's head on the outside back wall. The Ptolemies extended the temple at its south end. To the southeast of the temple are the mud brick remains of the town, while just to the north of the temple is a raised embankment which runs northwestwards, a natural formation marking the storm beach of Lake Moeris when it was 23 metres above sea level.

Tebtynis

Omm el Borigat (Tebtynis) is similar to Medinet Madi, with an even longer lion- and sphinx-guarded processional way leading up to the Sobek temple. A square tank in the court-yard may have been home to the sacred crocodile. The enclosure wall of mud brick is virtually intact, but the temple has been almost entirely destroyed. It was probably Middle Kingdom; the vestibule however bears Ptolemaic re-liefs, and it seems that the Ptolemies refounded Tebtynis, which then remained inhabited into the Arab period.

History's debt to the crocodile

The site is best known for the treasure trove of papyri found here in 1899–1900 which did so much to throw light on Pto-lemaic Egypt. B P Grenfell, who excavated here, described the unusual circumstances of the discovery: 'The Arsinoite was the nome of the crocodile-god Sobek, who under various forms and names was worshipped in every village that could boast a temple of its own. In the Ptolemaic period, even after the extensive land reclamations from Lake Moeris, crocodiles must have still frequented the district in great numbers, and a pond or small lake full of the sacred animals was no doubt a common feature of the local shrines . . . The tombs of the large necropolis adjoining Tebtynis proved in many instances to contain only crocodiles . . . One of our workmen, disgusted at finding a row of crocodiles where he expected sarcophagi, broke one of them in pieces and disclosed the surprising fact that the creature was wrapped in sheets of papyrus. As may be imagined, after this we dug out all the crocodile-tombs in the cemetery . . . The most remarkable characteristic of the Greek papyri from crocodile-mummies is their great size. For enfol-ding crocodiles 3 or 4 metres in length small documents were useless, though they were employed as padding, in which case they had often not been unrolled or were hastily crushed together. For the outer layers the papyri used consisted of large unfolded rolls.' Our own times excepted, there is no period or place better documented and understood, right down to the smallest details of everyday life, than Ptolemaic Egypt — thanks very largely to the papyrus-wrapped crocodiles of the Fayyum.

The Road to the Nile

From Medinet el Fayyum the road southeastwards towards Beni Suef passes along the narrow corridor of cultivation which attaches like a stem the bud of the Fayyum to the Nile. From the village of Hawaret el Maqta (10 km) a track runs north (1 km) to the dilapidated mud brick **pyramid of Hawara** on the edge of the desert plateau. This was the tomb of Ammenemes III, and to its south are the remains of his once vast mortuary temple, now all but vanished at the hands of stone robbers, which so excited ancient travellers who knew it as the Labyrinth.

The Labyrinth: 'surpassing the Pyramids'

Herodotus, who saw the Labyrinth for himself in the 5th C BC , said 'It is beyond my power to describe', and then warmed to the challenge: 'It must have cost more in labour and money than all the walls and public works of the Greeks put together — though no one would deny that the temples of Ephesus and Samos are remarkable buildings. The Pyramids too are astonishing structures, each one of them equal to many of the most ambitious works of Greece; but the Labyrinth surpasses them. It has 12 covered courts — six in a row facing north, six south ... Inside, the building is of two storeys and contains 3000 rooms, of which half are underground, and the other half directly above them. I was taken through the rooms in the upper storey, so what I shall say of them is from my own observation, but the underground ones I can speak of only from report, because the Egyptians in charge refused to let me see them, as they contain the tombs of the kings who built the Labyrinth, and also the tombs of the sacred crocodiles. The upper rooms, on the contrary, I did actually see, and it is hard to believe that they are the work of men; the baffling and intricate passages from room to room and from court to court were an endless wonder to me, as we passed from a courtyard into rooms, from rooms into galleries, from galleries into more rooms, and thence into yet more courtyards. The roof of every chamber, courtyard and gallery is, like the walls, of stone. The walls are covered with carved figures, and each court is exquisitely built of white marble and surrounded by a colonnade'.

The Fayyum portraits

It was at a desert cemetery near here that Flinders Petrie uncovered the remarkable painted wax portraits attached to mummies of the Graeco-Roman period, the best and greatest number now at the Cairo Museum. They were painted in life and hung in the home until death when they were sent along with the body to the embalmer to be positioned over the face in the final wrapping. From observation of the mummies, Petrie thought that they were then kept in the house for a generation or two, where they were knocked about a bit and damaged like old furniture, until the descendants lost interest and gave them a perfunctory burial.

A further 9 km on is the small village of **El Lahun**, from the Coptic *Lehune*, mouth of the canal. It is here that the Bahr Yusef leaves the Nile valley and passes through a gap in the hills encircling the Fayyum depression; from the XII Dynasty to the present day there has been a regulator here to control its flow. A road turns north out of the village and in

3 km comes to the **Lahun pyramid** of Sesostris II (XII Dyn), its limestone casing blocks long ago stolen and its mud brick core exposed and rotting away.

If you have not already visited the **Meidum pyramid** from the north (Saqqara, etc), you can now look out for it towering in the desert to the west if you return to Cairo along the Nile valley road.

PRACTICAL INFORMATION

INFORMATION

There is a **tourist information kiosk** opposite the Cafeteria el Medina in Medinet el Fayyum where you can pick up a simple map and enquire about travel and accommodation.

TRAVEL

There are numerous one-day tours to the Fayyum, usually stopping at Karanis, the lake, Medinet el Fayyum and the Hawarat and Lahun pyramids. This amounts to the **abbreviated itinerary**. I am not aware of any that stop at Meidum, nor do they visit the Ptolemaic sites (Dionysias, Narmouthis, etc) around the periphery of the oasis or allow time to cross the lake to Soknopaiou Nesos. Even with your own transport, to cover the Fayyum as outlined in this chapter would necessitate staying overnight. Note that it can be slow going on the roads within the Fayyum, and that at least 6 hours must be allowed for the excursion by boat and foot from the south shore of the lake to Soknopaiou Nesos on the north shore and back.

Public transport to the Fayyum:
Trains leave Ramses Station in Cairo for Medinet el Fayyum via El Wasta and take 4 hours.

Fast air-conditioned **buses** depart from Midan Ahmed Helmi behind Ramses Station in Cairo every half hour from 6.30am to 6pm. 2 hours to Medinet el Fayyum. You should book in advance. Avoid Thursdays outbound, Fridays and Saturdays back.

Share (service) taxis depart round the clock from Midan el Giza on Sharia al-Ahram (Pyramids Road) — in Giza a few blocks west of the Giza Bridge from Roda.

Public transport within the Fayyum:
In Medinet el Fayyum there are **horse carriages**.

Most conveniently and ubiquitously, **service taxis** run along fixed routes from village to village. State where you want to go and you will be directed to the appropriate taxi.

Private hire taxis are found in Medinet el Fayyum on the north side of the Bahr Yusef, three bridges west of the Cafeteria el Medina.

From Medinet el Fayyum, three **train lines** radiate out into the oasis, one to El Wasta, a second to Sennouris via Biahmu, the third northwest to Abuqsah via Ibshaway.

There are **buses** too, going from village to village like the service taxis, but they are slow and crowded.

For a taxi to **the lake**, ask for *el birka*, though *Qarun* or *el Oburj* (ie Auberge el Fayyum/Auberge du Lac) will also get you there. Taxis are also recommended for visiting **Qasr Qarun** (though you could first take the train to Ibshaway), **Medinet Madi**, **Omm el Borigat** and the **Hawara and Lahun pyramids**. **Karanis** can be reached by the Cairo/Fayyum bus; ask for Mathaf (ie museum) Kom Aushim. The museum is open from 8.30am to 3.30pm daily. For the colossi bases near **Biahmu**, take the Sennouris train from Medinet el Fayyum; after c.15 minutes alight at the second stop, Biahmu, and walk 10 minutes north out of the village along the railway line. It is much easier to reach and find the site this way than by car.

ACCOMMODATION

In Medinet el Fayyum the best you will find is the simple but clean **Montazah**

Hotel (2-star), in the north part of town near the Bahr Sennouris. There are also numerous no-star places, probably the best of which is the **Abdel Hamid**, just west of the Cafeteria el Medina on the north side of the Bahr Yusef. There is a youth hostel at the extreme east end of town.

At the southeast corner of the lake:
Auberge el Fayyum (4-star), Lake Qarun.

Tel: (84)324924. The former Auberge du Lac and hunting lodge of King Farouk, now a small luxury hotel with swimming pool, tennis courts, health club, water sports, hunting and horseback riding, disco, etc.

Panorama (3-star), Shakshouk el Fayyum. Tel: (84)322653. On the lake, all rooms with bath and air conditioning. Water sports facilities.

THE VALLEY

The two Egypts   Lower Egypt is the Delta; Upper Egypt is the valley where the desert and mountains encroach on either side. But throughout Egyptian history the distinction has been as much cultural and political as geographical. In an ancient text the contrast between the two Egypts serves as a metaphor for the bewilderment of an Egyptian exiled to a foreign country: 'It was like a dream, as if a man of the Delta were to see himself in Elephantine, or a man of the northern marshes in Nubia'. Lower Egypt in the north has been more open to foreign influences, more cosmopolitan; but along the valley from the south, from Upper Egypt, has come the periodic flood of national regeneration.

Travelling Through Time
In terms of pharaonic history, by following the Nile southwards you are — as nearly as geography and chronology in
From the Old   Egypt coincide — travelling from the Old Kingdom into the
Kingdom into the   New. For the traveller flying from Cairo to Luxor, the
New   chronology is simple and abrupt. Less than 60 minutes intervene between the Memphite pyramids and your first glimpse of the sprawling Theban temples below. Along the way there is the amazing and beautiful sight of the long blue ribbon of the Nile snaking through the scorched desert bringing a few kilometres, sometimes only a few metres, of land to life on either side. A life fragile like the delicate green wheat which waves against vast sand plateaux, a life — if you were close enough to know it — heavy with the mass of fellahin whose survival has depended on the varying generosity of the river's annual flood and the constancy of their own unending field labours.

The traveller through time is isolated from the moment. From the air, this isolation seems no more than standing back from a charming tapestry to appreciate its overall effect. Travelling overland you are closer and you see the threads and knots; you long to feel for texture. If you are travelling by air-conditioned train, then outside the sealed windows, sealed against the sand, sealed against the heat, sealed against fragrance and life, Egypt passes in a series of tableaux vivants.

The pattern of older villages is a vestige of living 10,000 years with annual inundations: they sit on low mounds beyond the reach of a river which for three decades has ceased to rise. Their mud brick houses pack against and on top of one another, a dense metropolis in embryo. At first their roofs are flat like houses of the Delta, but as you run southwards you see the dome and barrel roofs of Upper Egypt which so admirably deflect the heavy fall of heat. Camels, carts, donkeys and women troop along the road, enduring the flame-

203

blue sky. An old man stands up to his knees in an irrigation ditch, washing himself, naked to the passing eyes and years, no longer ithyphallic Min.

These things pass beyond touch, beyond sound. You are an air-conditioned pharaoh riding with the sun, uncontaminated, unliving, kept company through eternity by wall paintings.

Off the beaten paths of history

But though it is true that the major sites along this valley journey lead you away from the Old Kingdom pyramids to the Middle Kingdom tombs at Beni Hasan and then finally to the New Kingdom temples at Luxor, in fact there are many non-pharaonic interludes along the way. The traveller with more time, and who enjoys getting off the beaten paths of tourism and history, might like to explore some of the eddies enroute. Not all are worth visiting; indeed at some there is nothing to see. But they are worth knowing about, to gain a greater appreciation of the many swirls and layerings of time in Egypt. There are quite a few Christian sites along the way, and you will notice also many modern churches, for the stretch of valley between Minya and Sohag in particular is a stronghold of the Coptic faith.

Christian Interludes

At the point where the valley is widest, 124 km south of Cairo, is **Beni Suef** on the west bank of the Nile. Celebrated for its linen manufacture in the Middle Ages, it continues as a cotton-spinning and carpet-making town, at once crumbling and jerking into new forms as modern factories and housing blocks go up. 15 km west on the east bank of the Bahr Yusef, near the village of Ihnasya el Medina, a huge area of rubble marks **Heracleopolis Magna**, founded early during the Old Kingdom and surviving through to Christian times. It achieved importance during the First Intermediate Period when its rulers governed most of northern Egypt. Opposite Beni Suef on the east bank of the Nile, St Antony first lived as a hermit before withdrawing deep into the Arabian or Eastern Desert. Today a road strikes out across the desert to Zafarana on the Red Sea, passing near St Antony's Monastery from where monasticism spread throughout Christendom. That is covered in a later chapter.

Oxyrhynchus may have been one reason why St Antony felt he was one Christian too many in the valley. It lies 75 km south of Beni Suef and 9 km west of Beni Mazar, and is today no more than a mound of rubble atop which the present Muslim village of Bahnasa stands. But in the 4th C Oxyrhynchus was a hive of Christianity, with 10,000 monks and 20,000 virgins, 'enough to turn the town into a kind of holy city', according to the *Historia Monachorum*, 'where monks congested the streets and seemed to outnumber everyone else and monkish songs were heard in every quarter'. The ancient

Monks and Virgins

temples served as monasteries and there were 12 churches; a large Roman theatre has been excavated. Most importantly B P Grenfell, who later learnt so much about Ptolemaic Egypt from the sacred crocodile wrappings of Tebtynis in the Fayyum, uncovered here vast quantitites of papyri which included 3rd C fragments of the gospels of Matthew and John, poems of Pindar and Sappho, and large portions of plays by Sophocles, Euripides and Menander, as well as summaries of the lost books of Livy. Oxyrhynchus declined during the Mameluke period.

A landmark you cannot fail to notice whether you are travelling along this stretch of the Nile by rail or road or best of all by ship is the almost cliff-like hill of **Gebel el Teir** (Bird Mountain) on the east bank of the river, just south of the west bank town of Samalut (223 km from Cairo). On the level summit is the Coptic **Deir el Adra** (Monastery of the Virgin), inhabited by monks until the 19th C, its *Church of the Holy Virgin* partly cut into the rock and said to have been founded by St Helena, mother of the Emperor Constantine, in AD 328. The legend has it that the Holy Family were sailing along the Nile when a rock nearly fell upon Mary and was only averted by the quick reaction of the child Jesus. 'This church is hewn out of the mountainside', wrote a 12th C Christian chronicler, 'and in the rock is the mark of the palm of the hand of the Lord Christ which was made when He touched the mountain'. Tens of thousands of pilgrims come here for the Feast of the Assumption on 22 August, mostly by felucca and from as far as Minya, Assiut and even Cairo. The doorway to the church is decorated in Byzantine style, and there are fine views over the Nile valley.

Into the Middle Kingdom and Beyond
Beni Hasan, Hermopolis and Amarna all lie near **Minya** (247 km from Cairo), a commercial town on the west bank, between the Nile and the Ibrahimiya canal, with an attractive and winding riverside corniche and a good range of accommodation.

Beni Hasan, on the east bank of the Nile, about 25 km south of Minya, is a Middle Kingdom necropolis of 39 rock tombs belonging mostly to XI and XII Dynasty monarchs. The excursion from Minya taking in four of the tombs most worth visiting, will take about half a day, but less if you have come by cruise ship. A path leads up from the Nile to the tombs cut into the cliff.

Exceptional Middle Kingdom tomb paintings

The tombs are exceptional for their architecturally refined columns, including a fluted style designated by Champollion as 'proto-Doric', but most of all for the excellence of their paintings, done on stucco. Unfortunately, many of the paintings have been either damaged or obscured, though the Department of Antiquities is in the process of cleaning them. Therefore, except for the specialist, only four of the tombs repay visiting, and there is a great deal of satisfying detail in these — Tombs 17, 15, 3 and 2 (this being the order in which you will encounter them, to your left, after you have ascended to the cliff terrace). Agricultural, craft, hunting and sport scenes are usual, and occasionally military scenes, for the princes of this nome were powerful in their own right.

Tomb 17 of Kheti (XI Dyn). Two of the original six lotus cluster columns with bud capitals survive and bear their original colouring. The stumps of the other four protrude from the ceiling. The left (north) and rear (east) walls are delightful for their painted scenes of small figures caught as though in the frames of a film at various stages of movement. On the rear wall men are wrestling; on the left wall the top register shows men hunting, the second register shows figures baking, and in the two registers below these, women and men dancing. At the rear end of the right (south) wall, Kheti is shown as high priest, wearing a leopard skin; closer to the entrance along the same wall Kheti is receiving offerings; while on the front (west) wall to the immediate right of the entrance he is shown making the final journey to Abydos — the symbolism of which is explained under Abydos.

Tomb 15 of Baket (XI Dyn). Baket was Kheti's father, and like his son was nomarch, that is governor of the nome. The tomb is very similar to 17 in decoration and proportion, but was intended to have only two columns, which are both missing.

Tomb 3 of Khnumhotep (XII Dyn). Famous for its finely drawn hunting, fishing and fowling scenes, this tomb has only recently been cleaned and the colours enhanced. The four interior columns are missing, but the antechamber is marked by two proto-Doric columns. At the rear (east) wall, on either side of the shrine chamber, are wonderful scenes of Khnumhotep standing on a reed boat in a papyrus swamp, fishing and fowling (left), and harpooning fish in the Nile (right). Note the stars on the ceiling. Apart from being local nomarch, Khnumhotep was also governor of the Eastern Desert; on the left (north) wall he is shown receiving gifts of eye paint from a caravan of Semites, gaudily dressed and with beards and non-Egyptian hairstyles, who have crossed into Egypt with their women, their children and their goats and asses in tow.

Tomb 2 of Amenemhat (XII Dyn). In plan this is very similar to Tomb 3, and it has three of its interior proto-Doric columns intact, and one nearly so. The antechamber is marked by two octagonal columns. The wall paintings too are similar to those in Tomb 3; there is a good scene here on the left (north) wall, top register, of an antelope hunt.

Hunting in the marshes: a tomb scene at Beni Hasan

On the way down from the necropolis you pass the entrance to a wadi on the left. About 500 metres along its south side is the rock chapel of Pakhet, the lioness goddess, assimilated by the Greeks to Artemis so that the chapel is better known as **Speos Artemidos** (Grotto of Artemis). Inside are scenes of offerings to various deities, but the chief interest of the shrine is the inscription over the entrance in which Hatshepsut (XVIII Dyn) implies that she has rid Egypt of the Hyksos invaders. That she certainly did not only heightens the belief that Hatshepsut desired to be seen as the restorer of stability and the old ways of the Middle Kingdom in her struggle against Tuthmosis III's imperial ambitions (see Deir el Bahri). As it extends deeper into the forbidding desert landscape, the wadi is cut with numerous other grottoes, once anchorite cells and early Christian tombs.

Also on the east bank, 10 km south of Beni Hasan at the village of Sheikh Abada, are the scanty ruins of **Antinopolis**. Antinous, the lover of Hadrian, accompanied the Emperor on his journey to Egypt in AD 130. An oracle foretold that Hadrian would suffer a heavy loss, and it was to fulfill this and thereby forestall some greater calamity, that Antinous drowned himself in the Nile. 'Everything

Lovers on the Nile

gave way; everything seemed extinguished. The Olympian Zeus, Master of All, Saviour of the World — all toppled together, and there was only a man with greying hair sobbing on the deck of a boat' (*Memoirs of Hadrian* by Marguerite Yourcenar). The young favourite whose features are known to us from numerous antique sculptures, was deified, with temples built and coins struck in his honour. Hadrian, according to Yourcenar, took Antinous, 'once so responsive', to the embalmers, knowing 'to what outrages I was submitting this body; but fire is horrible too, searing and charring the beloved flesh; and in the earth it rots. ... All the metaphors took on meaning: I held the heart in my hands. When I left the empty body it was no more than an embalmer's preparation, the first stage of a frightful masterpiece.' Afterwards Hadrian founded this city: 'A check to death to impose upon such a sinister land a city wholly Greek ... where his cult would be forever mingled with the coming and going on the public square, where his name would be repeated in the casual talk of evening'. Cities, like lovers, die, and the corpse of Antinopolis is not worth visiting. But it is a good story.

Hermopolis Magna near the village of El Ashmunein on the west bank of the river, lies off a secondary road between Minya and Mallawi. The remains of the Middle and New Kingdom cities here are no more than uncertain mounds of earth and rubble, though a 5th C **Christian basilica**, built with stones and columns from an earlier Ptolemaic temple, has been restored. It must have been of considerable size, comparable to the churches at Abu Mina and those of the Red and White Monasteries near Sohag, and was probably a cathedral, dedicated to the Virgin. The surrounding palm grove lends a picturesque effect. An early association with Thoth, whom the Greeks identified with Hermes, accounts for its familiar name. Originally known as Khmun, meaning city of the eight primordial forces, it was said to have been built upon the primal hill from which the sun first rose above the waters to create the world out of Chaos — though the same claim was made for Medinet Habu and Heliopolis. The primal name, if not the hill or city, has tenaciously survived: from Khmun derived the Coptic Shmun, whence the Arabic Ashmunein.

Tuna el Gebel, 7 km west of Ashmunein and beyond the Bahr Yusef, marked the western limits of Akhenaton's new city of Akhetaton. This side of the river was reserved for villages and farms. A boundary stela remains *in situ*, carved from the top of a cliff, showing the heretic pharaoh, Nefertiti and three of their daughters with upraised arms in adoration of the solar disc. A necropolis to the south is riddled with underground passages used by the inhabitants of Hermopolis for burying mummified ibises and dog-headed baboons, sacred to Thoth. The most important building here is the

Ptolemaic **tomb of Petosiris**, chief priest of Thoth at Hermopolis. It imitates the pronaos of a temple and is entered through a vestibule of four columns with floral capitals painted red, blue and turquoise though bleached where exposed to the sun. Inside, the reliefs portray traditional Egyptian themes but Petosiris and his family wear Greek clothing. (His coffin is in the Egyptian Museum, Room 49, ground floor.)

Akhetaton: Capital of the Heretic Pharaoh

The Amarna revolution

The beauty of Old Kingdom art and architecture lay in its restraint, in its simplicity and its confident mastery of form. There was a moment of discovery, of harmonisation and integrity, and if the First Intermediate Period had instead marked the termination of pharaonic civilisation we might now more eagerly respond to what had been lost. But the centuries rolled on and too often carried with them only the embalmed culture of the past, integrity reduced to repetition, mastery to facility, the spirit salved with interminable formulae, authority justified and reassured with bombast. Even when using the old forms, there were brilliant exceptions as will be seen here and there farther upriver. But the general impression of tedium weighs heavily on the traveller. The breathtaking impact, then, of the Amarna period is all the more powerful, the sense of something wonderful, tragic and lost all the more acute.

The sensitivity and delight, the reverence and forcefulness conveyed in the painting, reliefs, sculpture and hymns of Akhenaton's reign are probably best appreciated in museums and books, for at his capital city of Akhetaton very little of these things remain. Nevertheless, its site should be visited — in homage, perhaps; for the interest it does hold; and for its own beauty, spared the incursions of large numbers of

Akhenaton's city

tourists. Akhetaton, or **Amarna** as it is known, is on the east bank, 67 km south of Minya, 11 km south of Mallawi. Cruise ships usually land you at the village of El Till towards the north end of the site, as do most ferries (though there are smaller ferries to the village of al-Hagg Qandil 3.5 km to the south). The palace and temple area described below lies between these two villages and can easily be visited on foot, but to reach the tombs and other outlying sights there are donkeys and tractors to haul you round. Allow at least half a day for the visit.

Incorrectly known as Tell el Amarna, this conflates the name of a local village, El Till, and the tribal name of the Beni Amran bedouin who live here. In wrongly supplying Tell for Till it gives the impression that a mound created of centuries of human habitation and debris (*tell*) identifies the spot. It does not, and that is what makes Amarna achaeologically so interesting. It is all one layer, the largely mud brick remains of a complete royal city begun in the fourth year of Akhenaton's reign, his residence from about his sixth year, and abandoned for all time soon after his death in the eighteenth year of his reign.

The ancient name Akhetaton means 'Horizon (or Resting Place) of the Disc', so that just as Amun dwelt at Thebes, Ptah at Memphis and other gods at their favoured places the pharaoh Akhenaton offered this as home to Aton. On boundary stelae he inscribed: 'Akhetaton belongs to Aton my Father like the mountains, the deserts, the fields, the islands, the upper lands and the lower lands, the water, the villages, the men, the animals and all those things to which Aton my Father will give life eternally. I shall not neglect the oath which I have made to Aton my Father for eternity'. From a strip of palm-spiked fields along the Nile, a plain, 12 km from north to south, swells against a crescent ridge of the Arabian plateau. Sand fills the greater part of the arena, the remains of temples, houses and palaces trace upon it in bare outline. It is a lonely spot, of melancholy beauty, one of the most attractive in all Egypt.

Touring Akhenaton's City

From your probable landing place at El Till the ancient **Royal Road** runs southwards through the administrative centre of the city. (If instead you have landed at the village of al-Hagg Qandil 3.5 km to the south, you can pick up the Royal Road and walk north along it to the administrative centre.) Folk memory recalls the grandeur of this thoroughfare with the modern name Sikket-es-Sultan, Road of the Sultan. On your left (east) is a Muslim cemetery and traced in part beneath it is a vast rectangle, stretching 800 metres back towards the ridge, marking the **Great Temple of Aton**. It was deliberately desecrated and destroyed after Akhenaton's death and its foundations later quarried by Ramses II for his temples at Hermopolis Magna. Farther along on your left are the faint outlines of the temple's *magazines*. Then there are three excavated rectangles, again on the left. (Many of these features may be difficult to distinguish owing to a shifting veil of sand and broken stone.) The first was an extension of the royal palace and was the **Residence of Akhenaton** and his queen, Nefertiti. It was divided in to a *walled garden* (northwest quadrant), *private apartments* (southwest quadrant) and *storerooms* (the east half). Near the bedroom was found the celebrated picture now in the Ashmolean Museum at Oxford of Akhenaton and Nefertiti seated upon an embroidered cushion, face to face, surrounded by their six daughters. The entire residence was decorated with lively scenes, and the ceilings painted with ducks and other aquatic birds flying in all directions.

The royal residence was linked by a *bridge* across the Royal

The slight remains of Akhenaton's palace

Road to the **main palace complex** on your right (west). Set within the bridge was a Window of Appearances where the royal family showed themselves before the public, as often depicted on reliefs and tomb paintings. (Indeed it is to the detailed and realistic tomb paintings at Amarna that so much knowledge of the city's original appearance is owed.) The next rectangle to the east marks the **Sanctuary of Aton** used by the royal family, and the rectangle beyond it the *magazines* associated with it.

Along a parallel road to the east and immediately behind the royal residence stood the **Foreign Office** where the famous Amarna Letters, cuneiform tablets received from Asian princes, were found. If you walk from here south towards the village of al-Hagg Qandil you pass through the **residential quarters**. Much of this area has been sanded over and little can be discerned; however, here lived such dignitaries as General Ramose, Vizier Nakht (neither are to be confused with their namesakes in the Theban necropolis) and Panehsi (see Tomb 6, below). Also here were the workshops of the sculptor Tuthmosis where the exquisite bust of Nefertiti, now in the Berlin Museum, was found. There is a model of an Amarnan house in Room 8 on the ground floor of the Cairo Museum. Other quarters, palaces and temples are scattered throughout the plain, their seemingly aimless distribution probably dictated by available well water, but exploration is unlikely to prove meaningful without the company of an archaeologist familiar with the site.

Visiting the Amarna Cliff Tombs

The **necropolis** at Amarna is in the eastern cliffs. Unlike at Thebes, the tomb decorations do not concern themselves with the afterlife: the Judgement of Osiris, for example, is absent, while instead there are vivid scenes of the everyday. Many of the tombs were never finished and only a few reveal signs of burial, as if the collapse of the Amarna revolution outpaced mortality. Akhenaton's body has been vainly sought both here and at Thebes; one imagines him disinterred at the restoration of Amun and left to rot like Cromwell. The **royal tomb** lies far back in the wild valley, the Darb el Malik, dividing the north and south faces of the cliff. On founding Amarna, Akhenaton proclaimed: 'My tomb will be hollowed in the Eastern Mountain, my burial will be made there in the multitude of jubilees which Aton my Father has ordained for me, and the burial of the Great Royal Wife Nefertiti will take place there in the multitude of years'. Instead, like an ominous cloud on the Amarna horizon, it was their young daughter Makitaton who first died and was entombed here. Akhenaton and Nefertiti, joyful children of the solar disc, are shown on the walls of Makitaton's sarcophagus chamber in sad mourning. The tomb is closed to the public.

There are 25 tombs along the base of the cliff face, Nos. 1 to 6 to the north of the Darb el Malik, Nos. 7 to 25 to the south. Both to see the wall carvings and to avoid tumbling down the shafts leading to the burial chambers, a flashlight should be brought. The tombs are preceded by an open court, as at Thebes, and then usually run through two or three chambers, sometimes with papyrus-bundle columns, ending at a recess in the rear wall where a statue of the deceased (if it remains) stares in surprise at its infrequent visitors. The lyrical 'Hymn to the Sun' composed by Akhenaton is frequently incorporated into the decorations.

The tombs most worth visiting are No. 1 of Huya, superintendent of the royal harem and steward to the queen mother, Tiy; No. 4 of Merire, high priest of Aton; No. 6 of Panehsi, servant of Aton with responsibility for his granaries and herds and also vizier of Lower Egypt; No. 9 of Mahu, chief of police; and No. 25 of Ay, royal confidant, Akhenaton's scribe and successor to Tutankhamun as pharaoh of Egypt. The outstanding tombs are the last two.

Mahu's tomb (9) is one of the best preserved and is interesting for the detail it gives of his duties. He was responsible for certain desert frontier posts and is shown receiving a report of a nomadic incursion. Three offenders are brought before Mahu and the vizier for interrogation; the chief of police is true to his timeless type in accusing them of being 'agitated by some foreign power'.

Ay's tomb (25) is the finest in the necropolis. In one scene, Ay and his wife are shown receiving golden collars from Akhenaton and Nefertiti while guards and onlookers outside the palace react to the honour and excitement of it all. There are street scenes, closely observed and marvellously true to life, and peeps of palace intimacy, with a lady of the harem having her hair done, some girls playing the harp and dancing, while others prepare the food and sweep the floor. Also, on the right-hand side of the doorway is the most complete and probably the most correct version of Akhenaton's hymn. Here are some excerpts.

Akhenaton's 'Hymn to the Sun'

At dawn you rise shining in the horizon, you shine as Aton in the sky and drive away darkness by sending forth your rays. The Two Lands awake in festivity, and men stand on their feet, for you have raised them up. They wash their bodies, they take their garments, and their arms are raised to praise your rising. The whole world does its work.

The cattle are content in their pasture, the trees and plants are green, the birds fly from their nests. Their wings are raised in praise of your soul. The goats leap on their feet. All flying and fluttering things live when you shine for them. Likewise the boats race up and down the river, and every way is open, because you have appeared. The fish in the river leap before your face. Your rays go to the depths of the sea.

You set the germ in women and make seed in men. You maintain the son in the womb of the mother and soothe him so that he does not weep, you nurse in the womb. You give the breath of life to all you have created. When the child comes forth from the womb on the day of his birth, you open his mouth and you supply his needs. The chick in the egg can be heard in the shell, for you give him breath inside it so that he may live. You have given him in the egg the power to break it. He comes out of the egg to chirp as loudly as he can; and when he comes out, he walks on his feet.

Like the wall reliefs, the hymn portrays in remarkable detail and variety the cumulative incidents that give wonder to life. Convention, myth and abstraction are dispensed with, replaced by the sensate reality of Aton which creates, embraces and expresses existence.

213

The Counterrevolution

For a moment, Egypt was offered spiritual and philosophical renewal. Akhenaton broke with a past whose search for stasis was leading to sterility. The sun and soul were recovered from their long dark voyage through the underworld and set in brilliant transit across the horizons of this life. Whether it was monotheism is uncertain and probably irrelevant; the universe was alive again. More important is whether Atonism was ever anything more than a royal cult. Akhenaton's hymn, phrased in demotic, suggests his intention was to place his revelation before all mankind. Yet when he died, his religion was soon suppressed, and what is more, all mention of the heretic pharaoh was proscribed from the king lists and he went unknown until the 19th C of our era. Can it have been just a political reaction? Dynastic infighting led Tuthmosis III to obliterate all images and cartouches of Hatshepsut, but her memory remained. It seems as if Akhenaton offered something far more than a political threat — and more than the military and administrative failures he has been accused of. Possibly Egypt had so far lost its faith in life that it could accept no substitute for its long investment in death. That may explain the empty tombs at Amarna; cold comfort, for all their paeans, to a civilisation lost to the hocus-pocus of formulae and solar boats. It is significant that with the coming of the Ramessids, tomb decorations concentrated less on the quality of this life or the next but on the rigmarole of passing from one to the other.

Like Akhenaton himself, those pharaohs who followed him and had shared at some time in their lives in the worship of Aton — Smenkhkere, Tutankhamun and Ay — were proscribed from the king lists at Saqqara and Abydos, and from that of Manetho. Akhetaton was never built on again. Horemheb's reign marked the full force of the reaction and cleared the decks for Seti I's classical renaissance. Something of Amarna art is found, straitjacketed and reduced to mannerism, in the works of Ramses II, especially in the fluid beauty accorded the female form, a touch of Nefertiti's Florentine elegance in those portraits of Nefertari, Ramses' queen, on the tomb walls at Biban el Harem at Thebes and inside the Temple of Hathor at Abu Simbel.

Last redoubt of Atonism Nefertiti stayed on at Amarna after her husband's death. Living in exile at the north end of the plain, she had carved on the walls of her palace the names of Akhenaton and herself. And this **Northern Palace**, the foundations of which you can see 1.5 km north of El Till, she called without compromise the House of Aton.

The Coptic Nile

From about the 4th C AD until the Arab invasion in the 7th C Egypt was a Christian country which was then gradually

214

Christ with the four creatures of the Apocalypse, from Bawit, 6th C (Room 3, Coptic Museum)

Islamicised. In Upper Egypt the process worked slowest, the Nile valley being distant from the Arab centres of Fustat and Cairo and largely free from the wholesale settlement of Arab tribes, as happened in the Delta. Suffering less from persecution and with the moral and physical support of Christian Nubia south of Aswan, the Copts of Upper Egypt were probably not outnumbered by Muslims until the 14th C. Even today, as a proportion of the local population, Copts are most numerous between Minya and Sohag where they are about double the national average of around ten percent. So apart from early Christian sites along the Nile, you will also encounter the living faith.

10 km south of Amarna but on the west bank is **Deirut** where the Bahr Yusef, which waters the Fayyum, branches off from the Ibrahimiya Canal. 3 km north of Deirut is the village of Bawit, 1 km west of which are the ruins of the 5th or 6th C **Deir Anba Abulu** (Monastery of St Apollo) in the desert. There is nothing to see amongst the mounds of debris, but it is worth mentioning that it was from St Apollo that one of the most famous and magnificent paintings of early Christianity was rescued for display in Cairo's Coptic Museum (exhibit 7118, Room 3): Christ enthroned, the four creatures of the Apocalypse in his fiery wings, and supported by the Virgin Mary and the Apostles.

215

About 20 km south of Deirut is **Deir el Muharraq**, a large and functioning Coptic monastery built at what is by tradition the southernmost point of the Holy Family's flight into Egypt. 'But when Herod was dead, behold, an angel of the Lord appeareth in a dream to Joseph in Egypt, saying, Arise, and take the young child and his mother, and go into the land of Israel' (Matthew 2:19–20). A church, **al-Adra** (the Virgin), was built over the cave where the Holy Family supposedly stayed; the altar stone is dated AD 747 but the claim is made that this is the oldest church in Egypt. Next to al-Adra is a three-storey *keep*, built in the 12th C. Muharraq (meaning burnt) is unlike other still tenanted Coptic monasteries for being not in the desert but on the edge of the cultivation. It is reached by turning west off the main road at El Qusiya. Annually during the week of 21 June, upwards of 50,000 people attend the Feast of the Consecration of the Church of the Virgin.

'Arise, and go into the land of Israel'

Farther south on the opposite (east) side of the Nile from Manfalut and 5 km northeast of the village of El Maabda is the **Crocodile Grotto**, contemptuously dismissed in old Baedekers as 'hardly worth visiting, as practically nothing is to be seen except the charred remains of the mummies of crocodiles'. Not only crocodiles, but human mummies too, as Flaubert, crawling about through the oozing bitumen and cracking bones, discovered. He returned to France with a human foot and kept it in his study as he wrote *Madame Bovary*; one day his servant shined it up with shoe polish.

Flaubert's friend, Maxime du Camp, emerged with a head and a pair of hands and feet. Du Camp later wrote: 'When you are standing on this bed of corpses, precautions cannot be too stringent: a bit of flame falling from a candle could instantly set fire to the dry debris, full of inflammable material, and then flight would be impossible and even useless. About 20 years ago an American visited the grotto with his dragoman and a guide. Some time after he went down, a loud noise was heard, and then black smoke poured from the opening. Neither American nor dragoman nor guide was ever seen again; the fire lasted 18 months and burnt itself out; for several years no one dared venture into the dangerous cave' (*Flaubert in Egypt*).

Inflammable mummies

Assiut (378 km from Cairo), with a population exceeding a quarter of a million, is the largest town in Upper Egypt. Its importance, like its name (from the ancient Egyptian *Syut*), goes back to pharaonic times, though it never achieved political dominance. Its prosperity has been owed to its position in the midst of an extensive and fertile plain on the west bank of the Nile, and to being the terminus of the Darb el Arba'in (Forty Days Road) which came up from Darfur in the Sudan and from the oases of the Libyan Desert. These circumstances filled its markets with produce as well as such craftwork as

Largest town in Upper Egypt

marquetry and carved ivory — and a supply of slaves which until well into the 19th C made Assiut the largest slave market in Egypt. Nowadays the export of wheat, cotton and soda is the main economic activity, though a busy souk (carpets are the specialty) survives in the old town west of the railway line. The newer districts extend along the tree-lined Nile corniche. Assiut is a lively and airy place, but has few sights or facilities to detain the traveller for long.

The **barrage** at Assiut, built in 1898–1902, formed part of the British plan, which included the old dam at Aswan, for controlling the Nile. From here the amount of water entering the Ibrahimiya Canal is regulated for the irrigation of the valley right the way down to Beni Suef. Where Sharia Gumhurriya, the road leading from the railway station to the barrage, is about to cross the canal you will find the **museum** with a small but good collection of local finds. In the souk in the old town is the **Hammam el Qadim** (the old bath), dating from the earliest Muslim period. 2 km to the west of the city, cut into the hills, are a number of **Middle Kingdom and Ramessid tombs**, subsequently inhabited by Christian ascetics, but these are closed. Nevertheless, it is worth climbing up here for the view over the **Muslim cemetery** just below with its hundreds of domed mausolea, while from higher up, beyond a Coptic rock chapel, there is a magnificent panorama encompassing river, canal and desert.

Along with a large Coptic population, the Islamic university here, associated with the al-Azhar in Cairo, is the focus for Muslim fundamentalist activities. There is a sense of suppressed confrontation between the two communities, and in 1981 following the assassination of Sadat there were bloody battles between the fundamentalists and the police.

Plotinus (AD 205–270), the great Neo-Platonist, was probably born in Assiut: 'No one could find out for certain because he was reticent about it, saying that the descent of his soul into his body had been a great misfortune, which he did not desire to discuss' (E M Forster, *Alexandria*).

Monasticism in Upper Egypt

A road crosses the Assiut barrage and continues along the east bank of the river, but the main road and the railway follow the west bank with its broader cultivation and more frequent towns and villages. One of these is **Sohag** (470 km from Cairo), a small agricultural town; 5 km west along a country road to the edge of the desert hills is the White Monastery (Deir el Abyad), and another 5 km north of that the Red Monastery (Deir el Ahmar), two of the most ancient Christian monuments in Egypt.

Though monasticism began early in the 4th C when Antony's followers gathered near him in the Red Sea hills, the first monasteries of Lower Egypt, including those in the

Eastern and Western Deserts, were informal communities of individual hermits. No vow of obedience was taken, and the monks were free to develop their own way of practising the religious life. But in Upper Egypt monasticism was regulated from the start. Pachom, born to pagan parents at Esna in c.292, served in the Roman army during the reign of the emperor Constantine before converting to Christianity. In c.320, in response to a vision, he founded his own monastic community, followed by 11 more throughout Upper Egypt by the time of his death in 346. All were based on his military experience. Under the Pachomian rule, which with various modifications served as the model for monasticism in the West, the needs of the individual were subjugated to the requirements of the community, and the life of each monk was governed by a precise code of discipline. This coenobitic way of life, spiritually and economically self-sufficient, proved immediately popular.

St Shenute The screw was further tightened by Shenute (334–452 *sic*, though some sources place his death a bit earlier), in a sense the true founder of Coptic Christianity. He was a fierce nationalist, and had no time for Greek philosophy or theological niceties; and he was a scourge of paganism, condemning the folk superstitions of the peasantry. As in the old Osiris religion, he emphasised judgement and inevitable punishment for even the smallest sin, rather than atonement and redemption. In 385 he became abbot of the White Monastery (though the monastic church to which that name now attaches was not built until c.440) and instituted a far stricter regime than Pachom's over work, diet and prayer.

On joining the community, a monk made a compact: 'If I transgress that which I have vowed may I behold the Kingdom of Heaven and not enter in thereto. May God, in whose presence I have made covenant, destroy my soul and my body in Hellfire'. Not that Shenute left God with a monopoly on punishment: when he discovered that a monk had slipped a woman into the monastery, he flogged him to death in a rage. Yet Shenute was regarded as a great reformer. He was working against the abuses, the laxity and the ignorance found amongst the fellahin, and was determined to build an enduring native Church.

The White Monastery

'The noblest church in Egypt' As you follow the road from Sohag you see a startling sight — at the edge of the cultivation, with its back against the Libyan hills, what seems to be an intact Egyptian temple. The White Monastery (Deir el Abyad) is the most remarkable instance of resemblance between Coptic and pharaonic architecture. Massive white limestone **walls** (hence its name) slope inwards and are finished off with a cavetto cornice of white marble. Two rows of small windows, like loopholes set in the flanks of a fortress, run round all four sides; but these are blocked up, as are five of the six gates, their jambs of red granite. It is through the one open gate on the south side that you enter 'the noblest church of which we have any remains in Egypt, the chief monument of the Christians' (Somers Clarke, *Christian Antiquities*).

And church it is, White Monastery a misnomer, for this great edifice was only a part of a once vast monastery of 2000 monks, its remains beneath the adjacent mounds of debris. The church is dedicated to St Shenute, so that Deir Anba Shenouda (Monastery of St Shenute) is often heard, particularly locally, instead of Deir el Abyad. There is the medieval sight of tented stalls, a sprawling encampment pitched beneath the walls in the week leading up to the saint's moulid on 14 July. Thousands of pilgrims come then from all over Upper Egypt, and the night is filled with drifting laughter, the aroma of cooked foods, the sinuous sound of Egyptian music, counterpoint to the incense, prayers and chantings inside the church in honour of the severe Shenute.

Entering the church You enter a long **south hall**, which some authorities have thought housed the cells of the monks, but that assumes that the church was the monastery. Others say it was a refectory for the eating of the *agape*, the communal religious meal, literally love feast, of the early Christians. More likely it

Like a Ptolemaic temple, the White Monastery near Sohag

219

served as a secondary narthex, for the church was not reserved for the monks alone; Shenute opened it to the general populace on Saturdays and Sundays, and he invited people who could not make the pilgrimage to Jerusalem to look upon the church as a substitute. Along this hall to the right (east), notice that an architrave has made use of a block of stone bearing hieroglyphics.

You then enter the body of the church proper, a basilica in which broken columns of marble and granite mark off the *aisles* from the **nave**. Deep galleries above the aisles would have been reserved for women. Midway down the line of columns along the north side of the nave are steps which once rose to the *ambon* from where the scriptures were read. Much of the destruction you see before you can be dated to 1798, when both this church and Deir el Ahmar were fired by Mamelukes fleeing Napoleon's troops, though the timbered roof had already gone at least a century and a half before.

At the west end of the nave is the **narthex**, a *baptistry* at its southern extremity preceded by a vestibule, while at its northern extremity a *chapel* for first communion. Lord Curzon described this chapel in the 1840s: 'It is a splendid specimen of the richest Roman architecture of the later empire, and is truly an imperial little room. The arched ceiling is of stone; and there are three beautifully ornamented niches on each side. The upper end is semicircular, and has been entirely covered with a profusion of sculpture in panels, cornices, and every kind of architectural enrichment. When it was entire, and covered with gilding, painting, or mosaic, it must have been most gorgeous' (*Visits to Monasteries in the Levant*). The chapel has suffered greatly since then, yet the semicircular recess at the north end with its diagonal patterning of bricks and its circlet of five slender Corinthian columns, bare though it is, remains exquisite. It is a moment to notice how strangely the interior of the church is in classical contrast to its enclosing pharaonic walls.

At the east end of the nave a wall of stuccoed brick, built not long before Curzon's visit, transforms what was the **sanctuary** into an entire church. Usually in Coptic churches there is one haikal (apse) or three in line, but in the oldest (pre-7th C) there is sometimes a trefoil arrangement as here and at the Red Monastery, deriving ultimately from the throne chamber of the Byzantine emperors. The *paintings* in the semidomes, however, are 12th C. In the south haikal Mary and St John flank a large blue cross draped with a red cloth and set within an oval frame; it represents the Resurrection. The central haikal has a large Christ Pantocrator. The subject in the semidome of the north haikal is impossible to determine; the Dormition of the Virgin has been suggested. On the wall of this haikal is a painting of a bearded saint, possibly Shenute himself. Higher up, note the shell niche and

Remains of an exquisite chapel

Paintings in the sanctuary

the floral and vine frieze, favourite early Christian motifs adopted from pagan Graeco-Roman decoration.

The Red Monastery

The road north along the boundary between the cultivation and the desert brings you to a small village where patterns of crosses are worked into the otherwise plain brick facades of the huddled houses. Hiding behind these is Deir el Ahmar, the Red Monastery, itself built of red brick throughout. The monastery is smaller and in many ways less impressive than the White Monastery, which it closely resembles in plan and fortune. There is the same ruined nave and aisles, the same trefoil arrangement of the haikals now screened off by a wall to form a truncated church. You enter midway along the southern perimeter wall into what was probably a long southern hall, though only a suggestion of it remains at the east end. But whereas at Deir el Abyad this feature served as a supplementary narthex, an important difference between the two monasteries is that there is no evidence of a western narthex at Deir el Ahmar at all.

Built by a disciple of Shenute and dedicated to St Bishoi, the Red Monastery is also known as Deir Anba Bishoi. But the **Church of the Virgin**, built in the southwest corner of the enclosure, though ancient, is not part of the original foundation. Within the truncated church at the east end of the enclosure, that is the original **sanctuary**, the paintings in the semidomes are almost impossible to make out beneath the grime. But whereas at Deir el Abyad the sanctuary has been heavily plastered and whitewashed, here there is a richness of original decorative detail, with finely carved Corinthian columns, elaborate niches set into the semidomes, marble panelling and brick and stone inlay, and architraves and arches painted with curling patterns. It is in poor repair, but there is enough here to show what Curzon meant at Deir el Abyad by 'gorgeous'.

PRACTICAL INFORMATION

TRAVEL

Distances between major points in this and the following chapter are by rail and so are less than those for road or river travel. A voyage between Cairo and Luxor follows the Nile for 740 km; by road the journey covers 730 km; while by rail the distance is 676 km.

Boat. It is a rare and beautiful experience to sail all the way from Cairo to Aswan, normally a voyage of 11 to 13 days. Shore excursions below Luxor are usually limited to pharaonic and Ptolemaic sites such as Beni Hasan and Amarna (in this chapter) and Dendera and Abydos (in the next chapter); if you want to visit the monasteries, for example, you will probably have to strike out on your own, hiring a taxi when the boat ties up at Minya, Assiut or Sohag (though it is as likely to attach itself to a palm tree in the middle of nowhere for the night). See the *Background* chapter for further details.

Train. The railway keeps to the west bank of the Nile between Cairo and Nag Hammadi (which lies between Abydos and Dendera — see next chapter) before crossing over to the east bank to continue to Luxor and Aswan. The overnight sleeper or day express between Cairo and Luxor takes about 11 hours. The day train permits you to see the scenery enroute and is recommended in at least one direction. But rail travel is also a good way to see the valley in stages, overnighting for example at Minya and Assiut. For greater flexibility, rail journeys can also be combined with stages covered by service taxi or private taxi.

Road. The main road follows the railway (see above). There are also alternatives, a minor road along the east bank between Assiut and Nag Hammadi, and another along the west bank between Nag Hammadi and Edfu (see also the following chapters). The main road is good along the entire length of the valley; you can drive between Cairo and Luxor in as little as 12 hours, but if you want to explore anything along the way, you will have to make one or two overnight stops.

Long-distance buses are operated by the Upper Egypt Bus Company, and depart Cairo from Midan Ahmed Helmi near Midan Ramses, and from the al-Azhar station (towards the al-Azhar Mosque between Midan Ataba and Sharia Port Said).

Long-distance service taxis from Cairo to Upper Egypt set out from the Ahmed Halmi depot near Midan Ramses and normally go as far as Assiut, where you must change for destinations south.

Local buses, service taxis and private taxis operate throughout the valley. Service (share) taxis are particularly recommended as a quick, inexpensive and not uncomfortable way of getting from town to town. At Beni Suef, Minya, Mallawi, Assiut and Sohag (as indeed everywhere else along the valley), the bus and service taxi stations are almost next to or only a

short walk from the train station, as are most hotels.

Bridges and ferries. There are no bridges across the Nile between El Wasta and Assiut, and so to get to sites on the east bank (eg Beni Hasan and Amarna) means taking a boat across. There are regular ferry services at all towns and many villages. On the east bank you will usually have to continue on foot or by donkey or tractor.

MINYA: ACCOMMODATION AND EXCURSIONS

Etap (4-star), Corniche el Nil. Tel: (86) 326281 and (86) 326282. New hotel on the Nile, all rooms with balconies, colour TV, air conditioning. Restaurants, coffee shop, bars; pool, tennis court, shopping arcade.

Lotus (2-star), Sharia Port Said, 4 blocks north of the railway station. Air conditioned rooms, good restaurant.

Ibn Khaseeb (1-star), Sharia Adli Yakan, 1 block from the station towards the Nile.

The **Tourist Office** is in the Governorate building on the Nile corniche.

West bank sites such as **Hermopolis Magna** and **Tuna el Gebel** are easily reached by service or private taxi to Ashmunein. **Deir el Muharraq** can be reached by service taxi via Mallawi to El Qusiya from where there are occasional minibuses to the monastery; otherwise private taxi direct. East bank sites involve getting to the appropriate ferry landing.

Visiting Gebel el Tier. Taxi north to the ferry crossing, asking for *il markib li Gebel el Tier*, ie for the boat, which turns out to be no more than a canoe.

Visiting Beni Hasan. Private taxi south to the ferry crossing. Alternatively, take a service taxi (see Amarna, below, for directions) to Abu Qerqaz for a trifling sum, thence a pretty country walk of about 3 km (or a ride in a pickup truck) to the ferry. Donkeys can be hired on the other side.

Visiting Amarna. The simplest approach is to take a train south to Mallawi and a taxi, service or private, to the ferry landing. There is also a local train from Mallawi to Deir Mawas from where you can walk or take a pickup truck to the ferry. Otherwise, direct from Minya, you can either take a private taxi for the 1-hour journey, arranging for the driver to wait 3 or 4 hours, or go by service taxi (turn right out of the railway station and walk 500 metres south, following the railway tracks, until you reach a flyover coming in from the right). You can cross the Nile cheaply by felucca; the motor launch is much more expensive. On the other side you can hire a donkey or tractor.

To appreciate the magnificence of the site you must go out to the cliffs and climb up to the tombs. Perhaps the most enjoyable part of the excursion is to wander along the east bank of the Nile between El Till and al-Hagg Qandil, the path leafy and shaded, the air sweet, water buffalo tied to trees, and numerous vine trellises — these last an agreeable continuity, as it has been suggested that the square pillar bases of mud brick noticeable in the palace area might have supported grape trellises.

ASSIUT: ACCOMMODATION AND EXCURSIONS
Badr Hotel (3-star), Sharia el Thallaga, behind the railway station. Tel: 329811/2. Assiut's Western-style hotel, all rooms air-conditioned with colour TV. Restaurant and coffee shop.
Reem Hotel (2-star), Sharia Salah Salem, a block south from the station. Tel: 326235 and 327610. Air conditioning, colour TV, restaurant.

Zamzam Hotel, Sharia Salah Salem, opposite the Reem Hotel. Cheap and clean.

The **Tourist Office** is in the Governorate building at the corniche end of Sharia el Mohafaza, a short walk from the station.

Visiting Deir el Muharraq. Private taxi; otherwise service taxi to El Qusiya from where occasional minibuses run to the monastery.

SOHAG: ACCOMMODATION AND EXCURSIONS
If you must stay at Sohag, make it the Andalous Hotel opposite the train station, friendly, reasonably clean, with hot water, and cheap.

Visiting the White and Red Monasteries. During the moulid of St Shenute buses run out to the White Monastery, otherwise you will have to take a taxi.

Visiting Abydos and Dendera (see following chapter). Train, bus or service taxi to El Balyana (10 km to Abydos) from where service taxis and minibuses run out to the temple. Ditto to Qena (4 km to Dendera), whence service taxis and carriages to the temple. If arriving by boat, avoid your waiting tour bus if possible and enjoy the 1.5-km walk along a country road.

An **abbreviated itinerary** should include Beni Hasan and Amarna, and if you are interested in Christian sites, then the White Monastery.

ABYDOS AND DENDERA

Gnostic gospels

At **Nag Hammadi** (556 km from Cairo) on the west bank of the Nile, the river sweeps round in a great bend to the east and the main road and the railway both transfer to the opposite bank — the road passing over the Nag Hammadi barrage, the railway carried by a bridge. 10 km along the east bank 150 or so ancient tombs, later used by Christian hermits, are cut into the Gebel el Tarif — and in one of these in 1945 the now famous Nag Hammadi codices were discovered. These are gnostic gospels in Coptic dating from the late 4th C but translated from Greek originals of the early 2nd C. One of them, the Gospel of Thomas, might even date from AD 50 to 100 and therefore be as early as or even earlier than Matthew, Mark, Luke and John.

Gnosis is Greek for knowledge, in this case the intuitive process of knowing oneself and thereby to know human nature and human destiny, and at the deepest level to know God. In Judeo-Christian teaching the Creator and humanity are separate; in gnosticism the self and the divine are one. The Old and New Testaments discuss evil in terms of sin and repentence; the gnostics said the world was an illusion from which the escape was enlightenment. Jesus did not offer salvation by dying on the cross; he was a spiritual guide. 'If you bring forth what is within you', said Jesus according to the Gospel of Thomas, 'what you bring forth will save you. If you do not bring forth what is within you, what you do not bring forth will destroy you.'

Caravan Routes Across the Eastern Desert

Faw Qibli is 19 km northeast of Nag Hammadi on the 'east' bank of the Nile (actually on the north side of the river as it here runs east-west); just south of it was **Tabennese** where Pachom founded the first coenobitic monastery. At **Qena** (612 km from Cairo) on the east bank the Nile again bends sharply, resuming its flow from south to north. This part of the river is closest to the Red Sea and from Qena a main road rises through desert and mountain landscapes (beautiful during the second half of the journey) to Port Safaga on the coast, from where you can head north to Hurghada.

Flaubert journeyed by camel through the devouring heat to Quseir, to the south of Safaga, in four days; on returning to Qena he sank into a bath and then into the arms of a prostitute: 'Dark eyes, much lengthened by antimony; her face held up by velvet chinstraps; sunken mouth, jutting chin, smelling of butter, blue robe'. But the major starting point for caravans from pharaonic to more modern times was **Qift** (633 km from Cairo), the ancient Coptos. Expeditions such as Hatshepsut's (see Deir el Bahri) would have set out for the Red Sea from around here and then continued by ship to the land of Punt, while throughout antiquity and until the Portuguese found their way around Africa Coptos thrived on trade with Arabia and India. The Eastern Desert was once a busy place, criss-crossed by the Egyptians, and later the Romans, in search of **Luxury trade** gold, emeralds, granite and porphyry. The Romans turned it into a highway and maintained staging posts a day's march from each other along the way charging a levy which rose from 5 drachmas for an able seaman or shipyard hand to 108 drachmas for luxury traffic like prostitutes. The Suez Canal, which made transshipment between the Red Sea and Alexandria no longer necessary, dealt the final blow to Qift's fortunes. There is now nothing of interest or of licence to detain you, and from here it is only another 43 km to Luxor.

Shrine of Osiris

Along the way we have missed out Abydos (reached via Baliana, 40 km west of Nag Hammadi) and Dendera (6 km west of Qena), both on the west bank of the Nile. The express sleepers and shuttle jets between Cairo and Luxor spoil us, make it seem hard to explore the route described from Beni Suef, and so these famous temples are usually visited as day-trips by taxi or air-conditioned tour bus from Luxor, or as part of a river cruise. They are mentioned here for the sake of geographical integrity but will probably be footnotes to your stay at Luxor — and historically that is not altogether untrue.

The distinctive features of Seti I at Abydos

The local god of **Abydos** had been a patron of the dead and the identification of Osiris with him towards the end of the Old Kingdom was both natural and rapid. The crucial role Osiris played in the Egyptian conception of the afterlife soon turned Abydos into a national shrine. Rather like Mecca is to Muslims today, it became the goal of all Egyptians to visit Abydos during their lifetimes, or failing that, between death and burial. Frequently on the tomb walls at the Theban necropolis you see the mummy of some notable making the voyage by river to Abydos. Some were even buried here as Old, Middle and New Kingdom tombs testify. The appeal was to lie for eternity at that very spot where the head of Osiris was buried after Seth had cut him to pieces and scattered his remains (see Philae).

It is a measure of Akhenaton's assault on the established religion that not only did Aton supplant Amun but that the Judgement of Osiris did not appear on the tomb walls at Amarna. After Akhenaton and his successors were proscribed and Horemheb restored the old ways, the XVIII Dynasty was replaced by the XIX Dynasty from the northeastern Delta — by the brief reign of Ramses I and by Seti I who now had to consolidate. Ironically, Seti bore the name of Osiris' mortal enemy — his sensitivity on this point is demonstrated at Abydos where his cartouche reads Menmare Osiris-Merneptah rather than Menmare Seti-Merneptah — and both to remove any doubts about his loyalty to the past, and to identify his dynasty with the national god, Seti built a temple of fine limestone at Abydos. But Seti was more than a reactionary; he declared a renaissance, and in art he ignored both Ahkenaton's expressionism and the overblown style of the XVIII Dynasty empire. His bas-reliefs at Abydos are

finely formed and beautifully coloured Old Kingdom revivals — though perhaps a touch effete: it is these one comes to see.

The pylon of **Seti's mortuary temple** has collapsed and the walls of the first and second courts are reduced almost to foundation level. You enter the temple by the central door of seven (the three on either side were sealed by Ramses II) and pass through the first hypostyle hall, completed by Ramses and of inferior work, into the second hypostyle hall which was the last part of the temple decorated before Seti's death. The *seven doors* are explained by the unusual feature of *seven sanctuaries* lying beyond, dedicated, from right to left, to Horus, Isis, Osiris, Amun, Re-Herakhte, Ptah (with fine though bleak profiles of the god) and Seti himself. But it is in the *second hypostyle hall* that you should pause, for this contains the remarkable *reliefs*. Seti appears in distinctive profile, a stylised but close likeness to his mummy (now off limits at the Cairo museum).

Also unusual is the wing built onto the temple to the left of

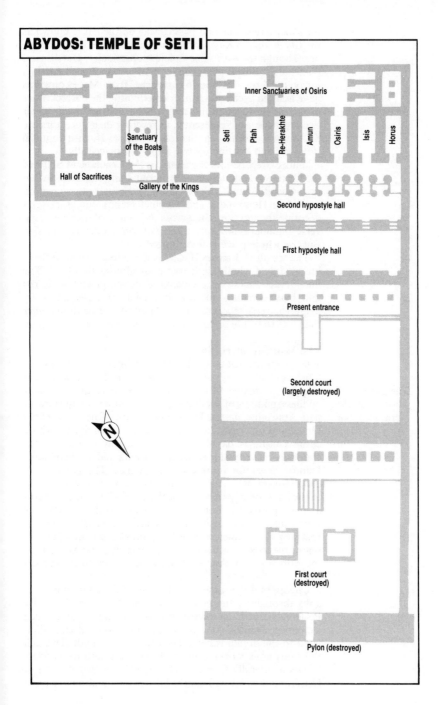

ABYDOS: TEMPLE OF SETI I

Inner Sanctuaries of Osiris

Sanctuary of the Boats

Seti

Ptah

Re-Herakhte

Amun

Osiris

Isis

Horus

Hall of Sacrifices

Gallery of the Kings

Second hypostyle hall

First hypostyle hall

Present entrance

Second court
(largely destroyed)

N

First court
(destroyed)

Pylon (destroyed)

the sanctuaries. The first passageway on the left is known as the *Gallery of the Kings* for its famous list of Seti's predecessors. Though the list is incomplete (in particular, Hatshepsut, Akhenaton, Smenkhkere and Tutankhamun are all missing, for political reasons) the 76 cartouches from Menes onwards have assisted archaeologists in determining the correct order of pharaonic succession. The list is on the right wall, upper two registers; and represented as revering their ancestors are Seti himself and his son, the future Ramses II, with youthful side-lock and holding up two papyrus prayer rolls.

Immediately behind the temple is the **Cenotaph of Seti I** or the Osireion. It stands on lower ground and was sunk within an artificial mound, an association, perhaps, with a creation myth (see Hermopolis and Medinet Habu). Funerary texts decorate the interior, and across the ceiling of the fine transverse chamber is a beautiful *relief of Nut,* goddess of the sky. But the whole place is waterlogged now.

The **temple of Ramses II** is 300 metres to the right of Seti's but is almost wholly destroyed above foundation level. The fine-grained limestone, architectural details picked out in red and black granite, and the bas-reliefs (Ramses normally employed sunk relief) suggest a standard of execution higher than was to be bothered with later in Ramses' prodigal reign.

The Worship of Hathor

The primitive roots of Egyptian religion — an animal fetishism that it never quite escaped and at the end, as seen at **The goddess of** Saqqara, retreated to — are illustrated in Hathor, the cow **love — in the** goddess, goddess of joy and love and identified by the Greeks **form of a cow** with Aphrodite, despite her bovine features. One thinks of the Dinka and other Nilotic tribes of the southern Sudan, whose entire culture is based on cattle. The cow to them is the epitome of beauty; it is tended for its milk and aesthetic satisfaction, never for its meat unless it dies. The Dinka have contempt for agriculture, the nomad's disdain for those tied to the land. Perhaps it was so with the pre-dynastic Egyptians as their grasslands were swallowed by the desert and they were forced to labour for their existence along the Nile — a yearning for a stolen way of life expressed through Hathor, one of the most ancient and revered of their gods. At any rate, the worship of Hathor at **Dendera** went back to the earliest times.

Cheops built, or rather rebuilt, here, as did numerous pharaohs throughout the Old, Middle and New Kingdoms. By Ptolemaic times the ancient cosmology had become much simplified. Deities, concepts and aspects were often assimilated to the dramatis personae of the Osiris myth. Through the incestuous working of mythology the fertility goddess Hat-Hor, literally Castle of Horus, first suckled the son of Osiris and then lay with him at Edfu in culmination of a great

Temple at Dendera: Hathoric columns

pageant issuing each year from Dendera. As it was important that each pharaoh should trace his ancestry back to Horus (see Philae), it was especially necessary that the foreign Ptolemies should stress their links with the Osirid trinity and with the wet-nurse and bed-mate of Horus. The **Temple of Hathor** at Dendera was part of this Ptolemaic assertion, and the Romans too found it expedient to contribute stones to the story.

Ptolemaic temples Cosmological simplification and single-mindedness of political purpose — and perhaps a Greek concern for harmony — gave unity to Ptolemaic temples in contrast to the sprawling accretions of earlier dynasties. The old motifs in architecture and decorations were retained to gratify the priesthood in exchange for their absorption into the machinery of Alexandrian rule, and perhaps to impress the populace — though not to include them, as the abstruseness of Ptolemaic inscriptions makes clear. Non-pharaonic nationalism was shut out, though it intruded in the protesting defacings of later centuries.

The temple *facade* is a pylon in outline, relieved by six Hathor-headed columns rising from a screen. A winged disc hovers at the centre of the huge cavetto cornice, an inscription above it, in Greek, from the reign of Tiberius — the facade and pronaos are Roman works. A central doorway admits to the *pronaos*, a great hypostyle hall, again with Hathoric columns. Its ceiling decorations include the signs of the Egyptian zodiac, the various deities traversing the heavens in their sacred boats amidst bursts of stars. The columns bear reliefs of the ankh and sceptre in alternation — life and prosperity. The grooves at the column bases were made by the insistent fingers of the faithful. The divinity reliefs on the columns were once covered with gold, and it is possible that even the floor bore a veneer of gold and silver. The successive chambers become smaller, lower, darker. The *second hypostyle hall* of six columns is decorated with scenes concerning the temple foundation rites: turning the first spadeful of earth, laying the first stone, etc. This was the Hall of Appearances where Hathor consorted joyfully with the gods and goddesses of her court before voyaging to Edfu. Beyond this is the temple proper, the sanctuary at its centre surrounded by a corridor lined with chapels. But first you pass through the Hall of Offerings and the Hall of the Ennead.

The *Hall of Offerings* marks the scene of the daily cult ritual in which offerings were laid out before the sanctuary, and from where the divine images were carried in New Year processions up the staircases to the roof to a kiosk where they made contact with the rays of Re — a spiritual emergence from darkness into light. The processions are depicted ascending and descending on both the east and west stairway walls. (See below for a description of the roof.)

The *Hall of the Ennead*, immediately before the sanctuary, contained statues of Hathor's nine consorts, these being the primal elements or deities following on the creation (eg air, moisture, earth, sky) as opposed to the pre-creation forces (see Medinet Habu) — that is, the elements of cosmic order rather than the elements of cosmic disorder.

The *sanctuary* itself would normally be bolted and in complete darkness. It was opened and illuminated by torchlight to permit the pharaoh to adore the goddess, and for her consorts to dine in communion with her. These rituals are depicted on the inner walls: on the right, the top pictorial register shows, from right to left, the pharaoh opening the door after repeating four times 'I am pure' (frames 1 and 2), meeting Hathor (frame 3) and offering libations (frame 4); the same sequence is on the left wall. The surrounding *chapels* each had their different ritual and ceremonial functions. Most interesting are the three chapels immediately behind the sanctuary: at the centre the Per-Ur, to its left the Per-Nu, and to its right the Per-Neser. The *Per-Ur chapel* was the starting point for the New Year procession and its decorations include the pharaoh offering the goddess a drink of intoxicating liquor, as Hathor was the goddess of joy. From the *Per-Nu chapel*, Hathor embarked on her annual voyage to Edfu and congress with Horus. In the *Per-Neser chapel* the goddess is

DENDERA: TEMPLE OF HATHOR

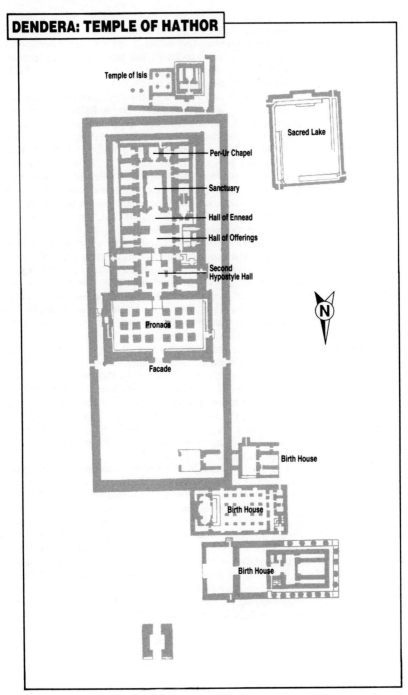

Temple of Isis

Sacred Lake

Per-Ur Chapel

Sanctuary

Hall of Ennead

Hall of Offerings

Second Hypostyle Hall

N

Pronaos

Facade

Birth House

Birth House

Birth House

represented in her terrible aspect, for example as a lioness goddess (by Ptolemaic times Hathor had assimilated the lioness goddess Sekhmet and the cat goddess Bastet, reflecting the terrible and gentle aspects of her nature). In the corridor outside the Per-Nu chapel you can descend steps to the 32 *treasure crypts* beneath the temple.

To reach the *roof* you follow the west corridor back to the Hall of Offerings, pausing first about halfway along the length of the Sanctuary to look at the *New Year Chapel* where rituals were performed preparatory to Hathor's communion with the sun. On the ceiling is a magnificent *relief of Nut* the sky goddess giving birth to the sun whose rays illuminate Hathor. The stairway, decorated with reliefs of the New Year processions, ascends to an elegant stone kiosk which was covered by a removable awning where Hathor was exposed to the sun's revivifing force. Also on the roof, but having nothing to do with the worship of Hathor, are the twin *Chapels of Osiris* (one above the west stair, the other above the east). First there is an open court, decorated with a procession of priests; then a covered court, on its ceiling a *zodiac*, unique in Egypt (the original is in the Louvre), as well as two figures of Nut (the vagina of one well worn by two millenia of fingers), with the boat of the sun shown at the different hours of night; and innermost an entirely enclosed room, representing the tomb of Osiris and decorated with resurrection scenes.

Reliefs of Cleopatra On the outside rear (south) wall of the temple colossal *reliefs* show Caesarion, son of Julius Caesar, with his mother, the great Cleopatra and the last of the Ptolemies, behind him, making offerings to a head of Hathor. The carvings are entirely conventional and in no way portraits. It is odd seeing Cleopatra in this anonymous form — for domestic consumption — when she is so much better known, or imagined, in flesh and blood, the centre-page fold-out who bedded the two most powerful Romans of her day.

The birth house is a particular feature of Ptolemaic temples and served to legitimise the dynasty through its ritual association with the birth of Horus (see Philae). At Dendera there are three **birth houses**. The *Temple of Isis,* to the rear (south) of the Hathor temple was built by Augustus and is in ruins; *a second monumental birth house,* also built by Augustus, with reliefs completed under Trajan and Hadrian, is to the front of the Hathor temple court (a *Coptic church* built of stones from this birth house is squeezed between them); *a third,* bisected by the west wall of the court, was begun during the reign of Nectanebos I (XXX Dyn) and completed under the Ptolemies.

PRACTICAL INFORMATION

For general information about travel in the valley, see the *Practical Information* section at the end of the preceding chapter.

The most convenient base for visiting Abydos and Dendera is **Luxor**. Hire a private taxi for the round trip journey after first checking at the **Tourist Police/Ministry of Tourism** office for what the rate should be. You can then go to one of the travel agencies or bargain for yourself outside one of the hotels. For an early start, make arrangements the evening before. Otherwise you can travel by train, service taxi or bus. Travel agencies in Luxor operate standard tours. Some of the boats cruising between Luxor and Aswan also come downriver to Dendera and Abydos.

Sohag (see previous chapter) and Qena can serve as bases for visits to Abydos and Dendera — at **Qena** the **New Palace Hotel** (1-star) in the station square (Midan Mahattat) should be carefully scrutinised first; it is fairly clean, though there is no hot water. There is nothing worth chancing in **Nag Hammadi** itself, but 7 km outside of town on an industrial estate is the **Aluminium Hotel** (3-star).

Abydos is 10 km from **Baliana** from where service taxis and minibuses run out to the temple. **Dendera** is 4 km from **Qena** where you can catch a service taxi or carriage. LE 2 entry fee to each temple.

Some **cruise boats** moor overnight near Dendera; in the morning it is best to disembark half an hour before the others, eschewing the coach, to enjoy the 1.5 km country walk to the temple.

North of Luxor but on the west bank (opposite Qus) is the village of **Naqada** which you might notice in passing. Crosses here outnumber crescents; about 75% of the population is Christian. There are several ruined monasteries in the desert beyond it.

LUXOR

At Luxor the Nile flows north-northeast and the town and the temples in the area take the river as their axis, but to simplify matters it will be assumed here that the river flows north and that the temples therefore lie along one or the other of the cardinal axes of the compass. The name Luxor is loosely applied by travellers to include three distinct places: the town of **Luxor**, population 75,000, on the east bank of the Nile (676 km south of Cairo), the village (suburb nowadays) of **Karnak** and its immense temple 4 km north on the same bank, and on the west bank of the river opposite Luxor and Karnak the **Theban necropolis.** A chapter is devoted to each of these places in turn. Accommodation is almost entirely in Luxor.

The Setting

The landscape all about is placid and horizontal, with a broad cultivated plain on either side of the river. The desert to the east rises gently to the Arabian plateau, while to the west a low range of hills, the Theban Mountain, interpose themselves between the cultivation and the Libyan Desert. The Nile is majestic, at sundown an implacable lava flow. By day, feluccas seem to stride upon its surface like pond insects, and distant palms rise from the level stillness, distinct and exactly outlined in the clear air and brilliant light. 'The palm — an architectural tree. Everything in Egypt seems made for architecture — the planes of the fields, the vegetation, the human anatomy, the horizon lines' (Flaubert). For the ancient Egyptians, the richness and never-failing fertility of this landscape was a source of wonder. As capital of the New Kingdom it was the focus of an architectural activity so grand, and still so well preserved, that it can lay just claim to being the world's greatest outdoor museum.

Greatest outdoor museum in the world

The Historical Background

The name Luxor derives from the Arabic *el qasr,* meaning castle or military camp (hence the Alcazar, the Moorish palace in Seville). The Arabic derived in turn from the Latin *castrum,* and may have referred to the Roman base here, though possibly to the appearance of the town to the end of the 19th C when it lay largely within the remains of the Temple of Luxor. The ancient Egyptian name for the settlement was Weset, though it is best known by the Greek name Thebes, 'where the houses are full of treasures, a city with a hundred gates' (The *Iliad*).

At the height of its glory during the XVIII and XIX Dynasties, Thebes covered all the ground of Luxor and Karnak, and may have had a population as high as one million.

During the Old Kingdom, however, when the capital was at Memphis, Thebes was only one of four humble townships in the nome — Tod and Armant to the south, Medamud to the north — each following the cult of falcon-headed Mont, a god of war. In the retreat to regional rule during the First Intermediate Period, Thebes emerged as the power binding Upper Egypt together. After a struggle it re-united the country under its administrative and religious authority, inaugurating the Middle Kingdom. Thebes repeated the pattern when following the disintegration during the Second Intermediate Period and the Hyksos invasion of Lower Egypt, it liberated the country and now also became the permanent residence of the pharaohs throughout the New Kingdom.

It is tempting to believe that apart from its prowess in war and its strategic position between the Delta and the Cataracts, Thebes achieved ascendancy over the townships of its nome and eventually over all Egypt because of the special beauty of its situation. Certainly the great pharaohs of the New Kingdom responded, sometimes sensitively, sometimes grandiosely, to the architectural possibilities of the landscape.

Orientation

The **Temple of Luxor** is on the Nile, only the corniche road, Sharia el Nil, separating it from the river. The temple and the gardens lying along its east side are the focus of the town. All

The Old Winter Palace Hotel

235

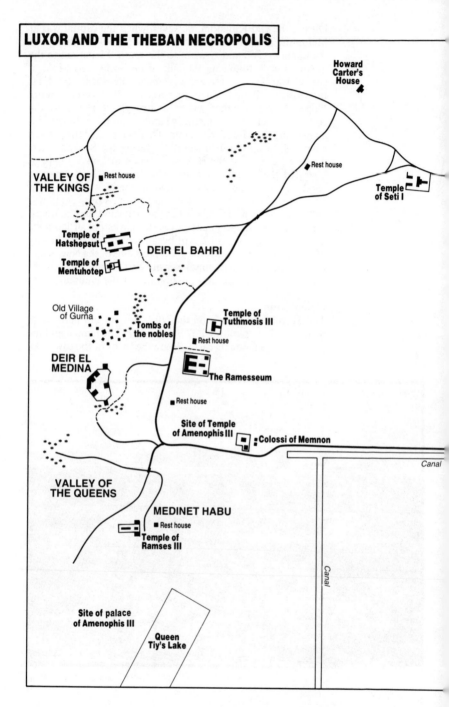

LUXOR AND THE THEBAN NECROPOLIS

Howard Carter's House

Rest house

Rest house

Temple of Seti I

VALLEY OF THE KINGS

Rest house

Temple of Hatshepsut

DEIR EL BAHRI

Temple of Mentuhotep

Old Village of Gurna

Tombs of the nobles

Temple of Tuthmosis III

Rest house

DEIR EL MEDINA

The Ramesseum

Rest house

Site of Temple of Amenophis III

Colossi of Memnon

Canal

VALLEY OF THE QUEENS

MEDINET HABU

Rest house

Temple of Ramses III

Canal

Site of palace of Amenophis III

Queen Tiy's Lake

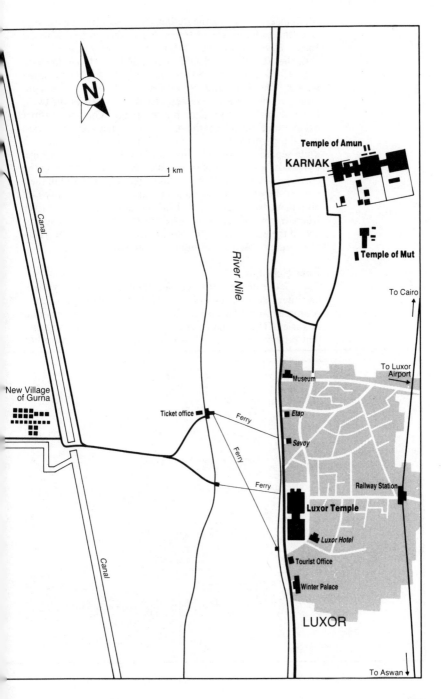

roads meet here. From the **station**, it is a short straight carriage ride (the usual means of transport) to the gardens with the Luxor Hotel on the left. A bit farther and you are on the **corniche**, the New and Old Winter Palace Hotels immediately to the south, the Savoy and Etap Hotels north of the temple. The Etap and New Winter Palace are unimaginatively modern; the others were the grand hotels of the twenties and thirties and retain an atmosphere. The town proper extends on either side of the street running between the station and the gardens; the corniche with its hotels and touts is a quite separate world. Nowhere in Egypt, except at the Giza Pyramids, are the touts so much a plague as here along the corniche — insisting that you take their carriage, sail in their felucca, buy their home-made mummified ibis or at any rate give them baksheesh — and on the other side of the river where a mob of car and donkey drivers will harrass you to accept the worst deal at the most outrageous price. The irritation comes close to spoiling Luxor altogether.

Tour Schedule
The briefest possible tour of the area requires two days, one on either side of the Nile. Three or four days are required for a comprehensive impression, though still only an impression, of ancient Thebes and its necropolis. You must bear in mind that outside the winter season, mid-afternoons get very hot

(around 40° C) and you may want to limit your excursions to the early morning and the late afternoon. On the east bank there is the enjoyment of carriage rides; on the west bank the choice is between donkey or car, the latter being infinitely preferable. Best of all for the sound of limb, and cheap, breezy and free of constraint, is to hire a bicycle in Luxor and use it on both sides of the river. Karnak and the Temple of Luxor can be visited on the same day, the latter best seen in the late afternoon as it glows in the rays of the sinking sun, or at night when it is unsparingly and intelligently floodlit. Rising as early as possible, the whole of the second day should be devoted to the west bank, and the third day too, if you have the time. A fourth day will allow you to revisit Karnak, and perhaps one or two temples or tomb clusters on the necropolis side, and will allow you greater leisure to shop in Luxor and visit the excellent museum there.

The Temple of Luxor

Close to the hotels and landing stages for the Nile cruise boats, a visit to the Temple of Luxor can be casually arranged following a more rigorously organised morning. The temple is appealing: it is well preserved, its unity clearly stated, yet there is the intriguing irregularity of its plan. The temple was built largely under Amenophis III (XVIII Dyn) on the site of an older sanctuary. He also built the Third Pylon at Karnak

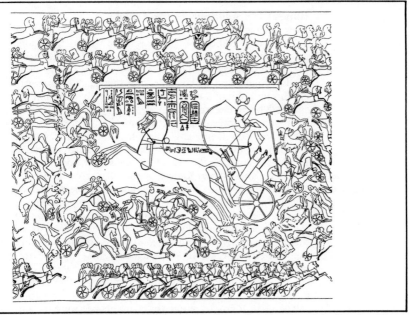

The battle of Kadesh as portrayed on the east pylon of the Temple of Luxor

and began the Hypostyle Hall there, and erected an enormous mortuary temple on the west bank of which only the Colossi of Memnon remain: he was the first pharaoh of the New Kingdom to go in for the gigantism that broadcasts the imperial pretensions of the period. He would have been delighted with the reaction of the French army in 1799: while in pursuit of the Mameluke Muradbey it rounded a bend in the Nile and came suddenly upon the temples of Karnak and Luxor. 'Without an order being given, the men formed their ranks and presented arms, to the accompaniment of the drums and bands', wrote a lieutenant.

Imperial pretensions

Since 1885 when excavations began here, the temple has been gradually cleared of the village once within it, the rubble blocking the pylon entrance, and the kom to the north which has revealed the *forecourt* and *avenue of sphinxes* leading to Karnak. It was from Karnak that Amun came during the annual Opet festival, but by water, amidst a floating procession of great splendour to this Harem of the South with his wife Mut and their son the moon god Khonsu. The forecourt wall is the work of Nectanebos I (XXX Dyn), as are the sphinxes which are set at a lower level to the excavated remains of post-pharaonic houses on either side. In the northwest corner of the forecourt is the restored *Serapeum* dedicated by the emperor Hadrian on 24 January AD 126, his birthday.

The Opet festival

Ramses II's Additions to the Temple

Now turning south to look at the **pylon**: this and the court behind it were additions by Ramses II (XIX Dyn), the pylon a gigantic billboard advertising Ramses' dubious victory over the Hittites at Kadesh in Syria. The *west (right) tower* shows the Egyptian camp within a circle of shields and Ramses on his throne holding a council of war while beneath him two spies are being interrogated by beating. In the right light, or by floodlight, you can see that Ramses has been reversed on his throne, now facing east where he once faced west. (The floodlighting also attracts bats which enjoy fluttering to rest upside-down within the deeper incisions of the drama.) The *east (left) tower* shows Kadesh on the left, surrounded by the waters of the Orontes, while to the right an heroically proportioned Ramses in his chariot is pursuing the broken enemy. In vertical lines below these scenes on both towers is the *Poem of Pentaur* (see Abu Simbel for partial translation), comparison of which with Hittite sources, and also taking into account the contemporary situation, including the superior iron weaponry of the Hittites to the Egyptian bronze, suggests that the battle was less glorious for the Egyptians than Ramses made out.

Ramses' propaganda

The *vertical grooves* along the pylon facade were for supporting flagstaffs, the apertures above to receive the braces

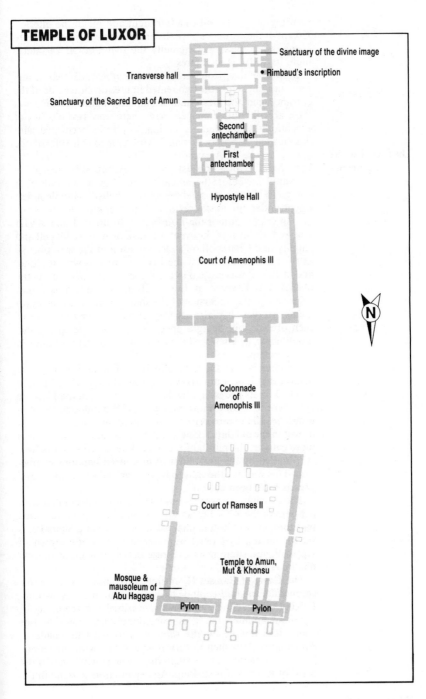

TEMPLE OF LUXOR

Sanctuary of the divine image

• Rimbaud's inscription

Transverse hall

Sanctuary of the Sacred Boat of Amun

Second antechamber

First antechamber

Hypostyle Hall

Court of Amenophis III

Colonnade of Amenophis III

Court of Ramses II

Temple to Amun, Mut & Khonsu

Mosque & mausoleum of Abu Haggag

Pylon

Pylon

securing the staffs and to admit light and air to the interior. Except at the corners above the entrance passage, the cavetto cornices are missing. Originally the pylon stood 24 metres high; its width is 65 metres.

In front of the pylon were six *statues of Ramses,* two sitting, four standing. Only the two seated figures on either side of the entrance and the westernmost standing figure remain, and these are all badly damaged. Also there were two *obelisks* of exceptionally fine detail standing on plinths decorated with dog-headed baboons in relief. Mohammed Ali offered the pair, plus one at Alexandria, to France. It is said that the French desire for an obelisk was first expressed by Josephine to Napoleon before he embarked for Egypt; 'Goodbye! If you go to Thebes, do send me a little obelisk'. Napoleon left Egypt under circumstances that denied Josephine the pleasure. In celebration of the Bourbon restoration, Louis XVIII renewed the idea. In the event, the task proved so difficult and lengthy that Champollion's identification of the west obelisk as the finest in Egypt left the French satisfied with it alone, and in 1836 it was erected in the Place de la Concorde. As the obelisk was lowered at Luxor, Ramses' name was found engraved on the underside of the shaft; his titles, his achievements, his piety had already been carved on the four sides of each obelisk, but being a great usurper of other pharaohs' monuments, he knew well the value of this secret protestation of ownership.

Standing before the temple in 1850, Flaubert wrote: 'The obelisk that is now in Paris was against the right-hand pylon. Perched on its pedestal, how bored it must be in the Place de la Concorde! How it must miss its Nile! What does it think as it watches all the cabs drive by, instead of the chariots it saw at its feet in the old days?' One hundred years later, Cocteau was more caustic: the plinth of the obelisk removed to Paris 'was surrounded by the low reliefs of dog-faced baboons in erection. This was not thought to be proper and so the monkeys' organs have been cut off'.

The *entrance passage* through the pylon is decorated with carvings of the XXV Dynasty, a period when Egypt was ruled by Ethiopian or Cushite pharaohs, one of whom, Shabaka, is shown on the east (left) wall wearing the white crown of Upper Egypt, running a ritual race in the presence of an ithyphallic Amun-Re.

The Court of Ramses II, entirely surrounded by a double colonnade of bud-capital papyrus columns, lies within. Belying the seemingly universal symmetry and regularity of Egyptian architecture, it is immediately obvious that this court does not lie on the same axis as the Colonnade of Amenophis III, which in turn is out of line with the temple proper, but these are very slight divergencies while that of the court of Ramses II is striking. An explanation is found in the

The French desire
an obelisk

northwest corner of the court, a small **temple to Amun, Mut and Khonsu** built by Tuthmosis III and Hatshepsut 100 years before Amenophis, 200 years before Ramses. The granite columns are original, while the carvings were redone by Ramses II who integrated the temple into his court, aligning his court to suit.

Sitting above the northeast corner of the court, surviving the clearance of the old village within the temple, is the **mosque and mausoleum of Abu Haggag**, a Sufi sheikh born in Baghdad, who spent the last 50 years of his life at Luxor, dying here in his 90s in 1243. The mosque, however, is only 19th C, though the north minaret is 11th C.

The interior walls of Ramses' court are adorned with reliefs. Especially interesting is the *representation of the pylon facade* at the west end of the south wall, complete with colossi, obelisks and fluttering banners. Approaching this, along the west wall, is a procession led by 17 of Ramses' sons (he fathered over 100 in his 90-odd years) and followed by priests and sacrificial oxen. The unnaturally long hooves indicate the oxen have been fattened in their stalls for the occasion, while the model of an African's head between the horns of the fifth ox and the Asiatic head with long pointed beard between the horns of the sixth symbolises the Egyptian triumph over Africa and Asia. The southern half of the court is further embellished with standing *colossi of Ramses,* while the triumph motif is repeated round the bases of the black granite seated colossi on either side of the southern doorway: the shields and bound figures of vanquished Asiatics on the east base, of Africans on the west.

Amenophis III's Temple

Passing between these last two guardians of Ramses' memory, you enter the imposing **Colonnade of Amenophis III.** The 15.8 metre high papyrus columns with calyx capitals bearing massive architraves contribute gently to the serene profile of the temple when viewed from the river. Originally, however, this columnar rhythm would have been lost behind flanking walls, the upper three-quarters of which have collapsed. The remaining courses bear fine and fascinating **Amun and** *reliefs from the reign of Tutankhamun,* a celebration of the **Tutankhamun** re-establishment of the Amun orthodoxy, depicting the god with Mut and Khonsu accompanied by the pharaoh and priests on their voyage from Karnak to Luxor at the height of the inundation period. Crowds of common folk follow by land, and there are scenes of rejoicing, of musicians and dancers, and of sacrifice. The series begins at the northwest corner with the pharaoh sacrificing to the boats at Karnak, and continues with the water-borne procession and, at the southeast corner, the arrival at Luxor. Starting at the southeast corner, the procession returns 24 days later to Karnak.

The colonnade leads into the **Court of Amenophis III,** once enclosed on east, north and west by double rows of clustered papyrus columns with bud capitals, an ensemble that appeals through its harmony. The east and west sides are well preserved and still carry their architraves. On the south side is the **Hypostyle Hall** with four rows of eight columns. On either side of its south wall are reliefs of the coronation of Amenophis by the gods. To the left of the central aisle, between the last two columns, is a Roman altar dedicated to Constantine.

You now enter the temple proper. The **first antechamber,** which once had a roof supported by eight columns, bore reliefs on its walls of Amenophis. But in the 3rd or 4th C AD the walls were thickly whitewashed and covered with paintings. One view is that this became the chapel of a Roman imperial cult; others argue that it was a church. The only evidence are the *paintings* themselves, which must once have been very fine but are badly damaged and tantalisingly inconclusive. Those on the east wall are very faint; but on the south wall to the left of the arched niche there is a much clearer group of several figures. One figure, below the third from left, seems to be a woman. Also on the south wall, and on the north wall too, the reliefs of Amenophis worshipping Amun have been laid bare. The **second antechamber** is smaller, with four columns, and as the reliefs around the walls show — Amenophis driving calves to sacrifice, offering incense and sceptres to Amun — this was the offering chapel. Beyond that is the **Sanctuary of the Sacred Boat of Amun.**

Roman paintings? Or Christian?

The sanctuary consists of a chapel open to north and south set within a chamber. The chamber walls are decorated with reliefs of Amenophis, while the chapel was rebuilt by Alexander the Great and both its exterior and interior walls bear reliefs of him before Amun and other gods. A subsidiary room with three columns to the east of the sanctuary has badly damaged scenes of Amenophis' coronation and on the north wall he is shown hunting in the marshes.

From this subsidiary room a doorway opens north onto the Birth Room with reliefs on the west wall referring to Amenophis' divine birth. At the left of the lowest register, Khnum is moulding the infant Amenophis and his ka on a potter's wheel. Moving from left to right across the middle register, Thoth foretells to Mutemuia, mother of Amenophis, the birth of her son; the pregnant Mutemuia is conducted by Isis and Khnum; her confinement; Isis presenting the infant to Amun; and Amun with the infant in his arms. The top register shows Amenophis and his ka nurtured by the gods and presented to Amun; to the far right, in the corner, Amenophis has become pharaoh.

The Divine Birth of Amenophis III

The remaining rooms at the south end of the temple have suffered considerable damage and are without antique

Alexander the Great presenting gifts to an ithyphallic Amun: Sanctuary of the Sacred Boat, Luxor Temple

245

interest. The **transverse hall** with its 12 papyrus bud columns was an antechamber or hypostyle hall leading to the three southernmost chambers, the central one a sanctuary once containing the intriguingly described 'divine image of millions of years'. It was in this transverse hall that Cocteau noticed a more recent curiosity: 'Suddenly I was struck dumb. What could that be? High up, on top of the wall, Rimbaud had carved his name. He carved it, at the height of a man, and now that the temple is cleared, it shines forth like a sunflower. It blazes out, royal and sunlike, above suspicion, dreadful in its solitude'. Rimbaud gave up poetry by the time he was 21, in 1875; for the remaining 16 years of his life he travelled in the Far and Near East and into parts of Ethiopia where no European had ever been before, variously selling coffee, girls and guns — and making a mark for French culture at the Temple of Luxor.

'A vendre les corps, les voix, l'immense opulence inquestionable, ce qu'on ne vendra jaimais. Les voyageurs n'ont pas à rendre leur commission de si tôt.'
— *Illuminations*

The area outside the temple on the east serves as a **storeyard for architectural fragments**, pharaonic, Roman and Christian. The Christian friezes, fonts, etc, presumably came from the basilica which once stood outside Ramses' great pylon.

The temple is experienced most intensely at night when the floodlights throw the carvings into deeper relief and the black night rests like a roof on the brightness of the stone, enclosing you. On the dome of the mosque of Abu Haggag, cursive green neon proclaims 'Allah'. Once a year at the saint's moulid a boat is carried in procession as was Amun's 3500 years before.

Ramadan Celebrations

At Ramadan the mosque of Abu Haggag is the focus of the nightly festivities. Hundreds of men gather in the gardens, some off to the sides playing cards, gambling, smoking hashish, many more listening raptly or dancing wildly to the drums, tambourines, ouds and violins, and to the teasing, climaxing, repeating passages of the imam's songs. They are religious songs, but passionate, or occasionally playful: a boy and girl are walking down a street hand in hand, they enter a house, they 'go to God together'. The audience laughs and shouts, but the lyrics are always secondary, and it is the narcotic beat and wailing of the music and the imam's exquisite phrasing that draws cries from the crowd. The imam twirls and sings, his eyes closed, his head shaking violently from side to side. A policeman in baggy khakis embraces him, rushes into the crowd to collect fistfulls of paper money and **Night frenzy** presses it into the imam's hands. Two or three dozen men begin to dance, arranging themselves in facing rows. First half-whirls, to the right, to the left, then hopping up and down, now jackknifing, eyes closed, bodies sweating, shouting, whirling, hopping and jackknifing in unison, beyond exhaustion. An onlooker intervenes to ask a young boy, an old man, to rest. But they all dance until they can barely stand, can merely twitch, or until they collapse.

It was less surprising that these men were killing themselves dancing than that others could resist joining the frenzy. I asked one onlooker why he did not dance. 'I am angry'. Then he showed me a photograph of himself taken five months earlier. He was bearded then. 'Now I have no beard because I am angry'. At first I thought he *was* angry, he said it with such emphasis, but he meant sad. His wife had died five months ago. 'I was happy with my wife, I loved her. I enjoyed sex with her, she washed my clothes, I gave her money to buy things.' How did she die, I asked? 'One morning I woke up and she was still in bed. I said to her, wife, you must get up and make my breakfast. But she did not get up, and I saw that she was dead.' But what did she die of? Had she been sick? 'No, she was not sick. She just died that morning.' But she must have died of something. For what reason? 'My God took her away. Maybe in two years I will look at women, but now I do not look at women. I am very angry.'

The Luxor Museum
The Museum of Ancient Egyptian Art is along the corniche to the north of the Etap Hotel; the presentation is superb, with some well chosen objects lit to best advantage. The exhibits include jewellery, furniture, pottery and stelae, but most outstanding are the stone *statues and busts.* The latter are most finely represented by granite and basalt works identified by the cartouches as Tuthmosis III, Amenophis II, Amenophis III (all XVIII Dyn) and Sesostris III (XII Dyn), any of which could stand in place of another for all they depict an individual (except for that of Sesostris with big ears). The craftsmanship is excellent, however, and the enjoyment of working with the graceful curves of crowns, necks and waists is clear. There is a marvellous alabaster statue of Sobek with crocodile's head and man's body, and one of Amenophis III, usurped by Ramses II by altering the cartouche — which shows how little the figure itself served to identify. A series of scenes in sunk relief on limestone blocks found within the Ninth Pylon at Karnak show *Akhenaton and Nefertiti worshipping Aton,* but also the most ordinary daily palace tasks. At least when Akhenaton attacked the Theban priesthood, he obliterated images of their god Amun; the post-Amarna counterrevolutionaries reverted to the traditional method of defeating a predecessor's bid for immortality: for example, *exhibit 150* is a block showing Akhenaton worshipping Aton — so clearly understandable and evidence of his heresy — yet it is defaced only to the extent that his cartouche is gouged. Always the name, the sign, rather than the idea.

PRACTICAL INFORMATION

ACCOMMODATION

During Luxor's high season (October through May) it is not advisable to show up expecting to get a room at the hotel of your choice, so it is wise then to reserve in advance.

Note that there is some no-star accommodation on the West Bank (see *The Necropolis of Thebes* chapter). However, the new Hilton at Karnak is listed below.

Four new 5-star hotels are the **Hilton** at Karnak (Tel: 384933), the **Isis** (Tel: 383366) and the **Sheraton** (Tel: 384544) some distance along a new tourist strip south of the Winter Palace, and the **Jolie Ville** (Tel: 384855) also south of town, on Crocodile Island. All are luxe places with the requisite quantity of restaurants, coffee shops, swimming pools and tennis courts, self-contained in their own gardens. Courtesy buses, even boats, take you into town. You might just feel, though, that for all the service and quality, you are staying at a dormitory suburb.

Winter Palace (5-star), Sharia el Nil. Tel: 382222. At the southern end of the corniche, this is now 2 hotels, the New Winter Palace connected to the Old Winter Palace. The latter dates back to the heyday of leisured travel earlier this century and has been refurbished and air-conditioned. At the rear, the rooms overlook a well-planted garden, while the Nile-side rooms offer beautiful views across the river and towards the Theban Mountain. Ask to be shown King Farouk's suite over the main entrance. Alas, nowadays the Old Winter Palace has been reduced to an appendage of the New Winter Palace, a characterless modern edifice; and worse, meals must be taken at the new hotel, a voluminous mess hall with third-rate food and service. There is a swimming pool, a bar, a terrace (all at the new hotel), a bank and shops, while the arcades on either side of the drive leading up to the Old Winter Palace are lined with more shops and agencies.

Etap (5-star), Sharia el Nil. Tel: 382166. Along the corniche to the north of the Temple of Luxor, this is a modern hotel in which the architect clearly attempted to recreate the claustrophobia of a pharaonic tomb — and succeeded. You will not actually bang your head on the lobby ceiling, and perhaps because the area is crammed with shops and a 24-hour café there is a sense of life and busyness here. The bars and restaurants are good, there is entertainment (disco, bellydancing) and a pool. In the main building, all rooms have Nileside balconies; at the annexe behind all rooms look at other rooms.

Savoy (4-star), Sharia el Nil, between the Temple of Luxor and the Etap. Tel: 382200. Like the Old Winter Palace and the Luxor, the Savoy also dates from the grand days of travel. Its large, high-ceilinged rooms have recently been renovated; those overlooking the Nile have balconies and beautiful views. In the garden are a number of bungalows. Pool. The terrace on either side of the main entrance is a convivial gathering place for afternoon tea or drinks at night.

Luxor (4-star), in its own grounds facing the Temple of Luxor. Tel: 382011. Another of the old hotels, gutted and rebuilt in 1989 so that many of the 1920s art deco interior features have been lost. The overall style is Moorish, with ablaq arches and columns along the verandah. Large rooms with balconies. Pool. Though the hotel is set back in its gardens from the Nile and so lacks river views, its great asset is its verandah and gardens, wonderful for late afternoon tea and evening drinks.

Egotel (3-star), immediately south of the Luxor Hotel. Tel: 383321. New, clean and dull. Air-conditioned rooms with balconies, private bathrooms, TV. No pool.

Windsor (3-star), in a small street running north off Sharia Nefertiti which runs off the corniche just north of the Etap. Tel: 382847. A good air-conditioned place, popular with tour groups. No pool.

Philippe (2-star), Sharia Nefertiti, off the corniche north of the Etap. Tel: 382279. A new hotel, clean and friendly, with a good reputation. There is a downstairs restaurant and bar and a rooftop garden. All rooms air-conditioned; those to the front, with a glancing view of the Nile, have small balconies.

Horus (1-star), right off Sharia el Mahatta (the road running down from the station) as it reaches the Temple of Luxor. Gaudy from the outside, simple and decent within, the Horus offers a range of rooms and prices, so you should ask to be shown a few first. A restaurant serves basic meals.

New Karnak (1-star), on the railway station square (Midan el Mahatta). Best of the bottom-end hangouts. Hot water but no air conditioning.

There is also a **youth hostel** on Sharia el Karnak (go down the main street from the train station; at the Temple of Luxor turn right — it is quite a distance. Reasonably clean but a lonely exile.

EATING PLACES AND ENTERTAINMENT

Atop the Tourist Bazaar building next to the New Winter Palace is the **Marhaba Restaurant** with beautiful views, air conditioning in summer and moderate prices. The menu is Egyptian, a change from Western fare at the hotels.

The **Amun Restaurant** on Sharia el Markaz (near Abu el Haggag mosque) is more authentic as is the lack of alcohol. No Nile views either.

A good light meal can be had at the **Etap's lobby café**.

The verandahs of the **Luxor** and the **Savoy** hotels are very pleasant places to while away the late afternoon or late evening with a drink or other light refreshment.

The **swimming pools** at the 5- and 4-star hotels are usually open to non-guests for a fee.

There is a certain earnestness about Luxor: so many antiquities lying on either side of the river, requiring early risings to see them before the day grows too hot, and so visitors go to bed early too. The 5-star hotels have oriental floorshows and discos, but they are not late-night raves.

SHOPPING

The principal market street in Luxor is **Sharia el Birka**, to the right off Sharia el Mahatta (the station road) as it comes to the gardens behind the Temple of Luxor. Galabiyys, spices, etc, can be purchased here.

Along the front of the Old Winter Palace are arcades of agencies and shops selling the usual souvenirs. Next to the New Winter Palace is the **Tourist Bazaar**. Here you will now find **Aboudi's shop** (see *The Necropolis of Thebes* text), selling clothing, jewellery, souvenirs, etc, but alas not his guide. Arcades in the Etap have bright **boutiques**.

Touts on both sides of the river will importune you *ad nauseam* with their phoney pharaonic relics. If you want one of these, be sure to knock the price right down, offering no more than one-tenth of what is asked. Decent replicas of **antiquities** are on sale in the arcades by the Old Winter Palace, and sometimes even the real thing — but be sure the shop has a licence from the Department of Antiquities and is prepared to offer a certificate of authenticity for what you buy. Genuine antiquities cost less in Luxor than in Cairo.

OF INTEREST

Temple of Luxor, opens 6am winter and summer, closes 9pm in winter, 10pm in summer. LE2. It is very much worth seeing when floodlit.

Luxor Museum, open evenings only, 5 to 10pm in both winter and summer. LE2. Well presented.

Dr Ragab's Papyrus Museum (as in Cairo), on a boat tied up near the museum. Open 9am to 2pm, 4 to 10pm. Free.

Hot-air balloon flights over Luxor, Karnak and the Valley of the Kings. Daily ascent at 7am, flying time about 1½ hours. Pricey but breathtaking. Operated by the Airship and Balloon Company (owned by Richard Branson of Virgin), bookings can be made at travel agencies in Luxor or beforehand.

INFORMATION

The first thing to do is to go to the **Tourist Police/Ministry of Tourism** at the Tourist Bazaar next to the New Winter Palace, and there determine the official rates for car, carriage and donkey hire on both sides of the Nile, the cost of taking the tourist ferry and the people's ferry, and the up to date entry fees for all temples, tombs, etc. You will then be fully armed against the touts.

Misr Travel, Thomas Cook and **Ameri-**

can **Express**, all in the arcades by the Old Winter Palace, can also provide a variety of information and assistance.

TRAVEL

The most pleasant way to get about Luxor, and to Karnak, is by **carriage** (caleche). The rates are posted by law on the side of the carriages, though the driver will try to hide them. Within Luxor: LE1.25; to Karnak: LE2; to Karnak son et lumiere, waiting and returning: LE5; to the museum, waiting and returning: LE3.

Bicycles can be hired for about LE3 per day. Try along the street running down from the station.

Ferries to the West Bank cost LE2 for the tourist ferry, 25PT for the people's ferry (see *The Necropolis of Thebes* chapter).

A very pleasant time can be had by sailing about the Nile in a **felucca**. Bargain with any of the boatmen along the river (get advice on rates first by checking with the Ministry of Tourism; also you might be able to arrange it all through Misr Travel). You can sail all the way up the Nile to Aswan, though you will probably get a better price coming downstream from Aswan (see *Aswan*).

Another way of covering the distance between Luxor and Aswan, with the possibility of sightseeing along the way, is to take a **service (shared) taxi**. These depart from the north end of the gardens behind the Temple of Luxor. You can go from Luxor to Esna, Esna to Edfu, Edfu to Kom Ombo and Kom Ombo to Aswan, each leg costing about LE2 and usually requiring a change of taxi.

Trains and **planes** link Luxor with Cairo and Aswan, and Luxor Airport (very user-friendly) now also handles direct flights from London. The **Egyptair** office is in the arcade by the Old Winter Palace.

Also here are **Jolley's, Eastmar, Misr Travel, American Express** and **Thomas Cook** — all of these offer tours, though these are geared mostly to groups. You can often join a group tour by going to one or the other of these agents the evening before and asking if there is space.

One tour worth singling out is a **day-cruise** to Dendera.

For a **Luxor–Aswan cruise** you should already have made arrangements in Cairo or from abroad, though possibly one of the above agents can help you out. For the Sheraton and Hilton cruises, contact their hotels here.

What about floating over Luxor, Karnak and the Valley of the Kings in a **hot-air balloon?** See *Of Interest*.

KARNAK

A carriage ride

Take a carriage along the corniche to the First Pylon of the main temple at Karnak, but when leaving ask the driver to return you to Luxor by the road which passes the Gateway of Euergetes and which continues past pastel facades, offering you a glimpse of village life too easily missed in bustling from one ancient site to another. Somewhere deep beneath this present roadway of your return journey lies the old *sacred way*, lined with sphinxes that joined the temples of Karnak and Luxor, visible now only at either end, where it leaves Eurgetes' gateway, and where it enters the forecourt of the Temple of Luxor.

The Karnak site covers an enormous area, sufficient to accommodate ten European cathedrals. The Hypostyle Hall alone is large enough to contain Notre Dame. At least two half-day visits are required to see the entire complex; if you can manage only one, then you will have to be content with walking through the main temple, that of Amun. A return can be made at night for the *son et lumiere*. The size and complexity of the site, the arrangement of its structures on both an east–west and north–south axis, the multiple extensions to several of these structures by successive pharaohs, and in some areas its ruinous state, contribute to the lack of unity

The processional avenue of rams at Karnak

and proportion at Karnak. But this has probably always been so, even in its days of completeness. Karnak astounds, but does not awaken the sensibilities. When Egypt stood at the height of empire, when Thebes ruled over Egypt, and when Amun was supreme over all, his temples here possessed 81,000 slaves and their families, 240,000 head of cattle, 83 ships, and from 65 cities and towns their vast annual tribute in gold, silver, copper and precious stones. 'Every breath that wanders down the painted aisles of Karnak seems to echo back the sighs of those who perished in the quarry, at the oar, and under the chariot wheels of the conqueror' (Amelia Edwards). It is a grandiloquent and over-bearing monument to power without spirit.

Thirteen Centuries in Stone

Apart from its size, Karnak represents a vastness of historical time. The main Temple of Amun, from the foundations of the original Middle Kingdom temple to the First Pylon built (probably) during the XXV Dynasty, saw construction over 1300 years. Comprehension of the site requires a brief historical review.

Although the war god Mont, associated with Thebes during the Old Kingdom, continued to be worshipped at Karnak, Amun achieved pre-eminence by the beginning of the Middle Kingdom and was honoured during the XII Dynasty by a series of temples facing west, the principal orientation throughout subsequent periods. All that remains of these are the alabaster foundations of what was to become the most venerable part of the extended Temple of Amun, and limestone blocks belonging to the White Chapel of Sesostris I, recovered from the foundations of the Third Pylon and re-erected in the 'open air museum' to the north of the Great Court.

With the expulsion of the Hyksos from Egypt and the elevation of Amun to victorious national god, the early pharaohs of the XVIII Dynasty set about turning Karnak into the principal sanctuary of their kingdom. Amenophis I and his son Tuthmosis I built chapels around the Middle Kingdom temple, while in front of it (to the west) the latter built the Fourth and Fifth Pylons and erected a pair of obelisks. Hatshepsut added two further obelisks between those of her father, chambers with carved decorations in front of the original temple, and initiated the north–south axis of the complex by building south. Her nephew Tuthmosis III continued building along the north–south axis with the Seventh and Eighth Pylons, and constructed the Festival Hall behind (to the east of) the Middle Kingdom temple.

In the century that passed between the Asian conquests of Tuthmosis III and the reign of Amenophis III, artistic and architectural restraint gave way to an overblown imperial style, expressed at Karnak by the Third Pylon built by Amenophis and his start on the great Hypostyle Hall. Empire introduced foreign influences and new wealth to the country, required an enlarged bureaucracy, and upset the status quo. Amun, who had lent his sword to pharaoh's victories, saw the coffers of his priesthood and of the old aristocracy from which it was drawn swell with tribute, and so their power grew. But **Divisions between** another class, which owed its very existence to empire, grew **Amun and** up around the pharaoh. Tuthmosis IV married an Asian prin- **pharaoh's court** cess, and her son Amenophis III married Tiy, an Egyptian commoner. Tiy was given unusual artistic prominence along- side her husband, and her parents, Yuya and Tuyu, were buried in splendour in the Valley of the Kings. Pharaoh and temple no longer represented identical interests. Before de- camping to Amarna with his court of parvenus, Amenophis IV (Akhenaton as he became) did some building at the east of Karnak, where several of his statues now in the Cairo Museum were found, while some blocks now in the Luxor Museum were re-used in the foundations of later pylons and the Hypostyle Hall.

But the Amarna revolution did not survive the death of Akhenaton, and the reign of Tutankhamun marked the begin- ning of the counterrevolution which proceeded with a ven- geance. The power of Amum was reaffirmed, and as though to sweep away all memory of heresy, internal conflict and the diminution of empire associated with the last pharaohs of the XVIII Dynasty, Seti I of the XIX Dynasty declared his reign the era of 'the repeating of births', literally a renaissance. Both he and his son Ramses II outdid all that had gone before, both in architecture and in military propaganda, to make good any deficiencies in this assertion. Between them they completed the Hypostyle Hall. It remained only for later dynasties to build the Great Court and the First Pylon for Karnak to assume the form it has today. The Ptolemies embellished, and the Copts cut crosses in stones.

The XIX Dynasty made its peace with Amun, but the cost in **Amun dominates** sacrificed wealth was greater than could be borne for long **Egypt** without the pharaoh becoming a mere creature of the priest- hood. The Hypostyle Hall, the Ramesseum, Abu Simbel, may all have glorified Ramses II, but only through Amun who long survived that long-lived pharaoh. By the time Ramses IV (XX Dyn) came to the throne, that is 200 years after Akhenaton's resistance and only 60 years after the death of Ramses II, the Temple of Amun owned at least seven percent of the population of Egypt and nine percent of the land, with some estimates trebling those percentages, while the family of the high priest of Amun directly controlled the collection of pharaoh's taxes and management of pharaoh's lands. Pharaoh had become no more than an instrument of a ruling oligarchy, and Karnak was its juggernaut.

Touring the Temple of Amun

You approach the maw of the beast along a short **processional way** (1) lined with ram-headed sphinxes with figures of Ramses II in mummy wrappings between their forelegs. This exactly expresses the new enveloping relationship between god and pharaoh, for the ram was identified with Amun. A now filled-in canal once linked the temple with the Nile, giving egress during the Opet festival for gods, priests and pharaoh aboard their boats. The **First Pylon**, 113 metres wide and 43 metres high, is the largest at Karnak and nearly twice the size of the entrance pylon at the Temple of Luxor. It was probably built during the XXV (Ethiopian) Dynasty, a trumpeting echo of XIX Dynasty bombast, but left unfinished, the south tower higher than the north and neither bearing any decoration. The north (left) tower can be climbed for magnificent *views* over Karnak and the surrounding countryside.

The massive outer pylons

The **Great Court** (2) was built by the rulers of the XXII Dynasty but encloses earlier structures. Columns with papyrus bud capitals line the north and south sides of the court, while a tall doorway in the southeast corner leads to the south end of the **Second Pylon** on which is cut a scene commemorating the victory of Sheshonk I (Shishak of the Bible) over Rehoboam, son of Solomon. The pylon itself was built by Horemheb, an XVIII Dynasty general who became military dictator and finally last pharaoh of the dynasty he had served. Like the Ninth and Tenth Pylons, also built by Horemheb, the Second Pylon made use of blocks that had once formed temples to Akhenaton's god, Aton. Continuing the palimpsest of politics, Ramses I and II cut their names on the pylon over that of Horemheb, and Ramses II had two *colossal figures* of himself in pink granite stand on either side of the pylon entrance. Of the one on the left hardly anything remains; nor does that sector of the avenue of rams which once ran through the area that became the court, to continue beyond the First Pylon towards the Nile. Instead, at the centre of the court Taharka (XXV Dynasty) built a **kiosk** (3) with ten enormous columns 21 metres high with papyrus calyx capitals, only one still standing. In the northwest quadrant of the court is the **Temple of Seti II** (4), a simple arrangement of three chapels facing south, the one at the centre to hold the sacred boat of Amun, those to the left and right to hold the boats of Mut and Khonsu, during preparations for the Opet festival. The **Temple of Ramses III** (5) intersecting the south wall of the court similarly served as a station chapel during processions and is a fine example of a simple pharaonic temple. Its pylon, facing north, is decorated with the obligatory triumphal scenes on the outside and with jubilee scenes, assuring the pharaoh a long life, on the inside. An open court leads to a pronaos of four columns and then to a hypostyle hall of eight columns beyond which are the three boat chapels, Amun's at the centre.

A doorway on the north side of the court leads to an *outside staircase* at the north end of the First Pylon for views from the top.

Also through this doorway you come to the **Open Air Museum** (6) where statues, blocks and architectural fragments from around the site were once gathered for private study but are now on public display (additional fee). The finest thing here is the **Alabaster Shrine**, reconstructed in the 1940s from blocks found reused in the Third Pylon. It dates from the reigns of Amenophis I and Tuthmosis I (XVIII Dyn), and apart from the pleasing gleam of the alabaster itself it is notable for the very fine style of the hieroglyphics and portraits of Amenophis, and for the oldest complete representation of the sacred ark of Amun inside.

Through the Hypostyle Hall

Spectacular forest of stone

Passing through the Second Pylon, you enter the **Hypostyle Hall** (7), certainly one of the most spectacular sights in Egypt. It is the height and massiveness of the columns that is overwhelming rather than spaciousness or even rhythm or repetition of form, for on either side of the central aisle the columns are packed tightly together in overgrown forests of stone. The eye is permitted no perspective and is incapable of taking in more than a glimpse of the whole at any one moment. It is best to come early in the morning or late in the afternoon when the effect of the columns is heightened by the black diagonals of their shadows. Tourists wander round the column bases as priests and pharaohs once wandered, like ants, and the idiot in us all is enthralled. An American woman is told by a guide that the columns are fitted drums, no mortar. She pushes against a drum to observe that the column does not fall — 'Wow!' she says.

The *columns* are in fact composed of semi-drums, the 12 along the central aisle (probably originally 14) rising to 23 metres and with a girth of 15 metres. It requires six men with outstretched arms to span one of these columns. Like the papyrus columns forming the Colonnade of Amenophis III at the Temple of Luxor, these also have calyx capitals and were probably erected as a processional way. But Seti I and Ramses II elaborated on the plan by adding a further 122 columns with bud capitals, creating extensive wings on either side. The entire hall was roofed over and the 10-metre difference in height between the central and wing columns was accounted for by raising *stone lattice windows* from the architraves of the wing columns closest to the nave, providing lateral support for the higher central roof otherwise resting on the taller columns. Several of these windows, in a better or worse state of preservation, remain in place.

The central columns are richly painted and cut in sunk relief with standard temple themes, most often pharaoh

255

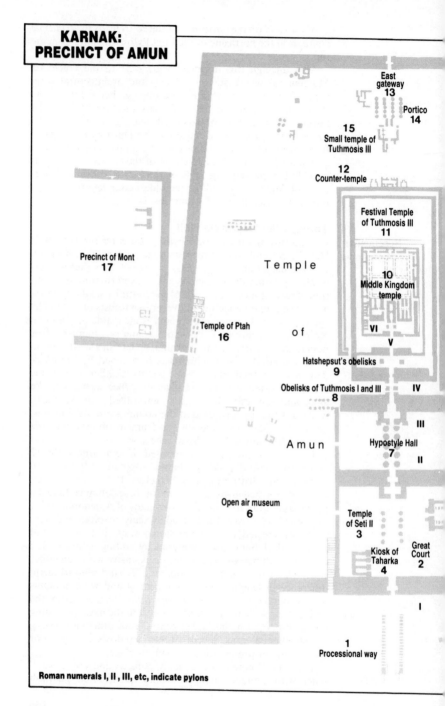

KARNAK: PRECINCT OF AMUN

East gateway
13

Portico
14

15
Small temple of Tuthmosis III

12
Counter-temple

Festival Temple of Tuthmosis III
11

10
Middle Kingdom temple

VI

V

Precinct of Mont
17

T e m p l e

Temple of Ptah
16

o f

Hatshepsut's obelisks
9

Obelisks of Tuthmosis I and III
8

IV

III

Hypostyle Hall
7

II

A m u n

Open air museum
6

Temple of Seti II
3

Great Court
2

Kiosk of Taharka
4

I

1
Processional way

Roman numerals I, II, III, etc, indicate pylons

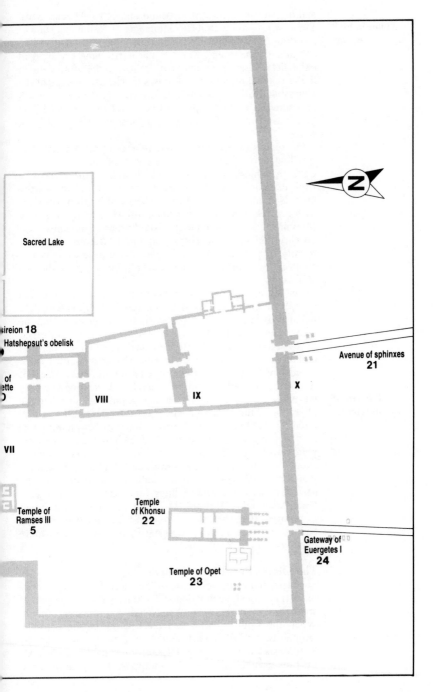

Sacred Lake

sireion 18

Hatshepsut's obelisk

of
ette
)

VIII

IX

X

Avenue of sphinxes
21

VII

Temple of
Ramses III
5

Temple
of Khonsu
22

Temple of Opet
23

Gateway of
Euergetes I
24

making various offerings to Amun and other Theban gods.

Amun in high
profile

These *cult scenes*, with recurrent images of Amun in a state of erection (ithyphallic), are continued on the phallus-like columns of the wings, those in the north wing executed in bas-relief during the reign of Seti I, those in the south wing in the sunk relief preferred by Ramses II. The inside walls of the Hypostyle Hall are similarly decorated, but the *outside walls* proclaim the military exploits of Seti I in Palestine and Libya (north wall) and of Ramses II against the Hittites (south wall).

Of some romance in the study of ancient history is a *stele* standing upright against the west wall of the Court of the Cachette which runs into the south wall of the Hypostyle Hall: it records a treaty between Ramses II and the Hittite king. Not only is it one of the earliest codifications of international relations, but its cuneiform version (now in the Museum of the Ancient Orient, Istanbul) was found inscribed on clay tablets at the Hittite capital, Hattuşaş, across the Mediterranean and when independently translated served to confirm the accuracy of the labours of philologists in the two languages.

The intimate relationship between the structure of the Temple of Amun and the development of the Egyptian state has already been outlined. It is worth noting the irony that the great columns of the Hypostyle Hall stood on bases formed of re-used blocks from the time of Akhenaton (since removed and replaced mostly by concrete) and that these in turn stood on no firmer foundation than sand. Pretension was careless of the future, though a century of archaeological engineering

Pattern of
Egyptian temples

has made good the past. Yet though grandiosity so suited the pharaohs of the XIX Dynasty, it is arguable that it was dictated by the temple itself. It was a canon of Egyptian temple architecture that as you approached the innermost sanctuary, perspective should narrow — that pylons and columns should get smaller, ceilings lower, and that even the temple platform should rise so that you walked upwards towards the sanctuary as walls and ceilings funnelled in around you. Once Amenophis III decided to build his Third Pylon, it had to be larger than the one before, and the Hypostyle Hall, the Second Pylon and finally the First Pylon had to grow more massive still.

The Oldest Part of the Temple

A constricted *court* lies between the **Third Pylon** of Amenophis III and the **Fourth Pylon** of Tuthmosis I, a narrow gap of space and time between traditional and imperial Egypt. When the Fourth Pylon still marked the entrance to the temple, two pairs of **obelisks** (8) were erected before it by Tuthmosis I and Tuthmosis III. Only one obelisk survives. Of the pink granite pair raised by Tuthmosis I, originally tipped

The Hypostyle Hall at Karnak

with electrum (a natural alloy of gold and silver), one fell as recently as the 18th C, some of its parts lying nearby, and the other leans a little but is still stable. Beyond the Fourth Pylon the outline of the temple becomes difficult to follow. The successive pylons are closely set, and the buildings have undergone repeated alterations and suffered extensive damage. But many beautiful details reward your exploration, and the absence of both overwhelming architecture and overwhelmed tourists encourages tranquil reflection.

The numerous columns in the open space behind the Fourth Pylon suggest that this, at least in part, was a hypostyle hall. It was built by Tuthmosis III and may have been **The quarrel** part of his extraordinary attempt to disguise the existence of **between** Hatshepsut's two magnificent **obelisks** (9). The lower shaft of **Tuthmosis III and** one of these remains on its base, the upper shaft lying near the **Hatshepsut** northwest corner of the Sacred Lake where you can closely examine its inscriptions. The second obelisk is *in situ*, the tallest completed obelisk in Egypt and of ancient obelisks second in height only to the Lateran obelisk in Rome. It stands 29.5 metres high and was covered in electrum not only at the pyramidion but also down half its shaft, so that as its inscription tells, 'Hatshepsut made as her monument for her father Amun two great obelisks of enduring granite from the south, their upper parts, being of electrum of the best of all lands, seen on the two sides of the river. Their rays flood the two lands when the sun-disc rises between them at its appearance on the horizon of heaven'. Step-mother to Tuthmosis III and originally regent to the young pharaoh, Hatshepsut soon proclaimed herself pharaoh and relegated Tuthmosis to the shadows for the remainder of her life. He later showed his resentment by chopping out her name wherever he found it, and here at Karnak went to the absurd length of building a now removed sandstone structure around her obelisks to a height of 25 metres.

The **Fifth Pylon** was also built by Tuthmosis I and leads almost immediately to the badly ruined **Sixth Pylon**, the smallest of all, built by Tuthmosis II. In the *court* beyond it **Symbols of Upper** he erected two tall pink granite *pillars*. Carved in high relief **and Lower Egypt** on their north and south sides are three lilies (south pillar) and three papyrus flowers (north pillar), the heraldic plants of Upper and Lower Egypt, beautifully stylised. At the north end of the court are two colossal sandstone *statues* of Amun and his 'grammatical consort' Amonet in the likeness of Tutankhamun. Farther along the main axis of the temple, on the spot where Hatshepsut's Red Chapel once stood (its quartzite blocks engraved with scenes of the procession of the sacred boats are in the Open Air Museum), is the granite **The Sanctuary** **Sanctuary of the Sacred Boats** built by the half-witted half-brother of Alexander the Great. The interior decorations in bas-relief and the exterior ones in sunk relief are finely worked and vividly coloured in yellow, red and blue. High though the standard is, however, its mock-traditional Egyptian terms were adopted by the Ptolemies for political expedience and are sadly inferior to the terms governing the greatest period of Greek art only 100 years before.

On the north side of the sanctuary, where there was much rebuilding, a *wall* erected by Hatshepsut was found concealed behind a later wall of Tuthmosis III, thus preserving the original freshness of its colouring. The wall has now been removed to a nearby room, and shows Amun, his flesh painted red and with one foot in front of the other, and also Amun in the guise of ithyphallic Min, a harvest god often amalgamated with Amun, his flesh painted black. The wall of **Battle of** Tuthmosis, known as the **Wall of Records**, was erected after **Armageddon** the battle of Megiddo (Armageddon) in northern Palestine, fought in April 1479 BC. James Henry Breasted wrote of Tuthmosis that 'he was the first to build an empire in any real sense; he was the first world-hero. He made not only a worldwide impression upon his age, but an impression of a new order' (*A History of Egypt*). Political history, insofar as it tells the story of territorial imperialism, began that April day when Tuthmosis, instead of destroying his enemies, organised the vanquished into agencies of tribute and annually recorded on this wall the share that was due to Amun.

The original The open space beyond the sanctuary marks the site of the **temple** original **Middle Kingdom temple** (10), its plan suggested by the remaining alabaster foundation stones.

To the east of the original temple is the **Festival Temple of Tuthmosis III** (11), and running north–south within it the Festival Hall of many columns and pillars where Tuthmosis celebrated his jubilees, those reinvigorations of temporal power and divine spirit (see Saqqara). The pillars form a rectangular cloister around a central and taller colonnade. The two rows of ten columns are unique in Egypt, affecting the form of tent poles or upturned tree trunks (as in Minoan Crete), broader above than below. The capitals, like bells or inverted calyxes, are incised and painted in patterns of overlapping leaves or of vertical stripes. The architectural suggestion is of an outdoor tent or, as echoed in stone at the Heb-Sed Court at Saqqara, of a temporary timbered building. Early in the Christian era the hall was converted into a church, and the occasional haloed saint may be discerned on its columns.

A chamber at the southwest corner of the hall contained, until taken to the Louvre, the *Table of Karnak*, a list of 57 predecessors of Tuthmosis. It is probable that statues of ancient pharaohs carried in procession were also kept here. From the northwest corner of the hall, an antechamber leads into a corridor lined with fine *reliefs* of Tuthmosis in the presence of Amun. Without the hall but in the northeast area of the Festival Temple is a small room with four papyrus bundle columns with bud capitals still supporting the architraves, though the roof is gone. This is popularly known as the *Botanic Garden* for its bas-reliefs of plants and animals seen in and perhaps brought from Syria by Tuthmosis.

Towards the East Enclosure Wall

A footbridge leads east across the remains of *enclosure walls*, and against this wall, on the axis of the main temple, is a *counter-temple* (12) facing east. Beyond this is the **east gateway** (13) to the Karnak complex, set in an outer wall of mud brick and built by Nectanebo I (XXX Dyn). From the avenue of rams before the First Pylon to this gateway, it is half a kilometre. Before exploring the breadth of the complex, have a look at the two structures standing between the counter-temple and the east gateway. The one to the east is a ruined **portico** (14) built by the same Taharka who built the kiosk in the Great Court; he placed similar structures at the north and south ends of the site, so covering the four cardinal points. Adjacent to this to the west is a small **temple** (15) built by Tuthmosis III. On the centre line of this temple is a large square base on which once stood the world's largest obelisk, the *Lateran obelisk* in Rome.

The Lateran obelisk   It was a considerable achievement for the French to get the 22.5-metre high obelisk of Ramses II from the Temple of Luxor to the Place de la Concorde in the 1830s, yet the giant 32.3-metre obelisk that stood at this small temple at Karnak was removed by order of the emperor Constantine in the 4th C AD, consigned originally to Constantinople but having its course changed upon the emperor's death and delivered to Rome instead where it was erected in the Circus Maximus in AD 357. It fell or more probably was toppled some centuries later, but in 1588 was re-erected in the Piazza San Giovanni in Laterano. Hieroglyphics on its shaft state that Tuthmosis III 'made as his monument for his father Amun-Re, Lord of the Thrones of the Two Lands, the setting up for him of a single obelisk in the Upper Court of the Temple in the neighbourhood of Karnak, on the very first occasion of setting up a single obelisk in Thebes'. It is stressed that the erection of a single obelisk was unusual, and it is probable that the Lateran obelisk comes from the same quarry of pink granite as that in which the great unfinished obelisk at Aswan still lies, and that the unfinished obelisk, until faults in the stone were discovered, was intended to complete the pair.

The North Complex Area

The Temple of Ptah and the Precinct of Mont at the north end of the Karnak complex are reached by a winding parth that leads from the north wall of the Great Court of the Temple of Amun. The ground is overgrown and barely excavated.

Against the north enclosure wall and shaded by palms, the **Temple of Ptah** (16) is approached through an east–west series of five doorways. If the inner doorway is locked, call to what looks like a sentry tower atop the mud brick wall. Shout. The keeper is probably asleep and will have to put on his galabiyya before coming down to let you in. Each of the doorways is carved with scenes and texts of the Ptolemaic period. The fifth doorway leads into a columned vestibule; to the rear is a small pylon marking the entrance to the temple proper. Beyond the antechamber are three chapels dating from the reign of Tuthmosis III, and most unusually the *cult state of Ptah* (with head missing) is still in the middle chapel; while in the chapel to the right is the startling apparition of *Sekhmet*, her bare-breasted body surmounted by the head of a lioness. The keeper will close the doors to enhance the eerie effect of the single shaft of sunlight from an aperture in the roof casting a greenish glow within.

Eerie cult statues

A gateway (also often locked) leads through the enclosure wall to the **Precinct of Mont** (17), god of war, its structures largely dilapidated and only of specialist interest. The main temple, totally ruined, was built by Amenophis III.

The South Complex Area

Exploration of the south end of the Karnak complex can begin at the **Sacred Lake**, restored and cemented. A grandstand at its east end is where visitors sit for the culmination of the *son et lumiere*. Near the northwest corner is a giant *scarab* dedicated by Amenophis III to Atum, the god of the rising sun. Also here is the base with underground chambers of an **Osireion** (18) built by Taharka, and the broken-off top of Hatshepsut's other **obelisk** (19). On the pyramidion a kneeling Hatshepsut is being blessed by Amun; his figure was recut by Seti I within the gouge caused by Akhenaton's attempt to obliterate the god of his priestly opponents.

At the south ends of the Third and Fourth Pylons of the Temple of Amun begins the second (north–south) axis of the Karnak complex, a *processional way* consisting of a series of open courts bounded by walls along their east and west sides and separated from each other by pylons. The Seventh and Eighth Pylons led originally to a Middle Kingdom temple and a temple of Amenophis I which both stood in what is now the Court of the Cachette. The temples were taken down by Tuthmosis III, but not before he had erected the Seventh Pylon. A large votive pit in the **Court of the Cachette** (20) was excavated early this century and found to contain several thousand bronze statues and 800 of stone. The best are on display in the Cairo Museum.

Considerable restoration work is being carried out along the north–south axis and the pylons may be closed off to the public. Nevertheless, the keepers will not hesitate to show you around for some baksheesh, and will lead you up the inner stairways to the tops of the pylons, or encourage you to follow them as they leap like goats across deep gaps in the towers and walls.

Seven *statues of Middle Kingdom pharaohs* stand or sit before the north face of the **Seventh Pylon**, while on its south side are the remains of two *colossi of Tuthmosis III*. On the outside of the east wall between this and the Eighth Pylon is an interesting **relief of the high priest of Amenophis**, his arms raised as though adoring Ramses IX (XX Dyn), who extends his palm in a reciprocal gesture. The very presence of the high priest, adoring or not, is unusual, but it is revealing that the priest is as large as the pharaoh and is even the focus of the composition. The relief is a vivid illustration of how much priestly power and arrogance had grown within a century after the reign of the great Ramses II.

Evidence of priestly power

The **Eighth Pylon** was built by Hatshepsut and, though the oldest part of the north–south axis, is well preserved. On its south side a *relief* shows Amenophis II slaughtering his enemies, while of the original six *colossi* on this side of the pylon, four remain, the figure of Amenophis I, on the left, the most complete.

The **Ninth and Tenth Pylons** were built by Horemheb in part with blocks from buildings erected by Akhenaton in honour of Aton. In front of the north side of the west tower is a *stele* erected by Horemheb proclaiming the restoration of the Amun orthodoxy. On the east side of the court between the Ninth and Tenth Pylons is a small **temple** built by Amenophis II, probably for his jubilee, with a graceful portico of square pillars. The fine bas-reliefs inside the hall, some of their colouring well preserved, show Amenophis before various deities. On the *interior wall of the court* between this temple and the Tenth Pylon, Horemheb is shown in relief leading captives from Punt bearing gifts for the Theban triad, and to the right of this he appears with fettered Syrian captives. Both claims of foreign triumph are almost certainly false, at best mere conventions, for Horemheb is known to have spent most of his energies imposing law, order and the old religion on post-Amarna Egypt, while there is no evidence at all that he led his armies abroad.

From the Tenth Pylon on **avenue of sphinxes** (21) runs for several hundred metres to the **Precinct of Mut**, still not entirely excavated and all the more picturesque for its ruins rising from the overgrown scrub. Consort of Amun and originally a vulture goddess, Mut was depicted during the New Kingdom with the skin of a vulture on her wig. Approached through a propylaeum cut with Ptolemaic cartouches, her badly ruined temple, built by Amenophis III, consists of two courts, a hypostyle hall and sanctuary. All around it, rising from the scrub, are *figures of Sekhmet*, the

Goddesses in the grass

lion goddess, beautifully worked and with care taken to use the pink veins in the bluish granite to highlight certain features such as the *ankh* sign or the goddess's breasts. A *sacred lake* enwraps the temple and across it, to the west, is a *temple of Ramses III*. Another *temple, of Amenophis III*, is in the northeast corner of the precinct.

But still within the main Karnak enclosure in the southwest corner, is the **Temple of Khonsu** (22), the moon god son of Mut and Amun. It faces south towards the Gateway of Euergetes and so towards the avenue of rams which disappears beneath village houses before emerging again before the entrance pylon of the Temple of Luxor. For the most part in a good state of preservation, its simplicity and clarity of layout make it a classic of New Kingdom architecture. It was started by Ramses III, though possibly completed and certainly almost entirely decorated by his successors down to Herihor (XXI Dyn), who like Horemheb rose from the army to seize power as pharaoh, and went one better by making himself high priest of Amun as well (see Gurna). The *pylon* is small but well proportioned, and decorated with a variety of religious scenes. On the *rear wall of the first court*, to the right, is a carving of the temple facade, banners flying. To the left is Herihor performing rites before the boats of the Theban triad. Beyond this is a small transverse hypostyle hall leading to the dilapidated sanctuary. Walking through its centre chapel once containing the sacred boat of Khonsu, you come to a small hall of four columns with reliefs of Ramses IV, but also, on either side of the entrance, Augustus. From the southeast corner of the sanctuary a staircase leads up to the roof, from which there are good views of the ruins.

Immediately to the west is the smaller **Temple of Opet** (23), a hippopotamus goddess and mother of Osiris. It was left unfinished by Euergetes II, though otherwise finely decorated throughout the Ptolemaic period and into the reign of Augustus.

Ptolemaic exit   You can now leave the Karnak site through the **Gateway of Euergetes I** (24), its concave cornice adorned with a winged sun disc.

PRACTICAL INFORMATION

For **accommodation**, see the *Practical Information* section of the previous chapter.

A **carriage** to Karnak should cost around LE2 and a bargain can be struck for having the driver wait for your return (LE5 or so). Go one way along the corniche, return along the back road which traces the old sacred way.

An **abbreviated tour** should cover the Temple of Amun, ie from the First Pylon to the Sixth Pylon and the Sanctuary.

The Karnak temples complex is open from 7am to 5pm and costs LE3. The Open Air Museum is LE1 extra. Both tickets must be bought at the kiosk outside. The **Son et Lumiere** (LE10) lasts 90 minutes and starts at 6pm and 8pm in winter, at 8pm and 10pm in summer.

The performances are in varying languages:
Sunday: French, then German
Monday: English, then French
Tuesday: French, then English
Wednesday: English, then German
Thursday: Arabic, then English
Friday: French, then English
Saturday: English, then French

The best part is the walk deeper into the temple — the lights and voices lead you on and it hardly matters what is being said. The impression is magnificent and will enhance your earlier (or later) daytime visit. But the bit around the Sacred Lake, when you are stationary and the vista does not change — and you are obliged to listen to the confused commentary — goes on far too long and is anticlimactic. When in the Hypostyle Hall, take the opportunity to wander off to one side or the other, deep and alone within the faintly illuminated columns — that is the most enjoyable.

Last but not least, there are **toilets** by the grandstand at the far end of the Sacred Lake.

THE NECROPOLIS OF THEBES

Visiting the west bank Because of the intense heat of the afternoon, it is usual to cross over to the west bank of the Nile very early in the morning and to complete your explorations by about one o'clock. If you do not mind the heat, there is no reason not to stay until the tombs close at 4pm in winter, 6pm in summer. Certainly you will have fewer fellow tourists to contend with, and if pedalling your own bicycle the breeze and dry air will evaporate the heat away. The disadvantage of a bicycle is the long incline to the Valley of the Kings, and then not being able to walk over the escarpment and down to Deir el Bahri, the Temple of Hatshepsut. So that expedition is best done by car: the driver will leave you at the Valley of the Kings and collect you later at Hatshepsut's temple. All the rest of the west bank should be covered by bicycle if you are up to it; it leaves time on your hands and frees you from the impatient harrassment of your driver. Distances can be long and donkeys are recommended only for those seeking the perversely picturesque.

In the bad old days, when donkeys were the only means of getting about the west bank, there was a wonderful Cook's dragoman called Mohammed Aboudi, who later opened a shop in Luxor and published a near to useless and vastly entertaining guide. Alas, neither is extant. But for a while Aboudi was private secretary to Cole Porter both in Europe and in Egypt, and it was perhaps this connection which encouraged Aboudi to leaven his guide book with his own poetry. It deserves what further lease on life I can provide; for example:

> O East is East and West is West in Luxor or in
> London town;
> But Aboudi, our faithful Aboudi, will never let
> us down.
> Through all the plagues of Egypt, donkey-boys,
> the flies, the sand,
> This trusty modern Moses leads us towards the
> Promised Land.
> Weird tales of long dead ages come tripping
> from his tongue,
> With him through tombs and temples we pass in
> wondering throng.
> And when foot and brain are weary with the
> sights we've come to see,
> He calls our patient donkeys up to bear us home
> to tea.
> Surely in future ages the tourists all will stand,
> An unabridged edition of Rosetta in each hand,

And read the hieroglyphics which proclaim how
  Pharaoh's Cook,
By his henchman, great Aboudi, mighty hosts
  through Egypt took!

There's one thing more, if you can stick it:
The law of this land is very intricate.
At each temple gate is an Arab picket,
So please don't forget your little ticket;
  And galloping donkeys is not allowed!

Ferries, and car and donkey hire

Before leaving the east bank, it is a good idea to ask at the Ministry of Tourism office about the going rate for car and donkey hire on the other side to prepare yourself for the bargaining that is to come. The 'tourist ferries' leave from the corniche opposite the main hotels and disembark you at the ticket kiosk downstream on the west bank. If you take what the locals call the 'people ferry', you will be landed near a village a bit upstream from the kiosk. Either way, you will have to decide as soon as you land what tombs and temples you want to see and purchase the appropriate tickets by the river bank: you cannot buy them at the sites. While you are doing this, you will be accosted by every car driver and donkey-boy in sight. Strike what you know to be a fair bargain, and do not pay until your visit is complete.

Outline of the tour

A tour of the necropolis involves following a north-south arc, starting at either end. If you want to follow the path from the Valley of the Kings to Deir el Bahri, you should start at the north, visiting first the Temple of Seti I, continuing to the Valley of the Kings, Deir el Bahri, the Tombs of the Nobles, the Ramesseum, Deir el Medina, the Valley of the Queens, Medinet Habu and back to the river via the Colossi of Memnon. This guide describes the tour in that order.

And dangers enroute

While not wishing to inhibit the curiosity of travellers, it is worth mentioning that care should be taken at excavations and you should not get off the beaten track if exploring on your own. I cite a newspaper report: 'The mystery of a Canadian woman's disappearance 2 years ago at Luxor was unravelled this week when police located her remains in an archaeological ditch. Before dying she had scribbled on a post card that she fell inside the labyrinth after losing her way, and she was preparing herself for death from thirst and hunger. The police located her skeleton this week, her clothes still on, in a distant area behind the pharaonic temples where archaeological digs were underway'.

The New and Old Villages of Gurna

From the west bank landing stage the road runs to the **new village of Gurna** and continues on past the Colossi of Memnon towards the Theban Mountain. At the village another road runs north towards the Temple of Seti I.

New Gurna was built in the late 1940s by the Egyptian architect Hassan Fathy. Employing the almost forgotten art of forming vaults and domes in mud brick without the use of timber centring, his aim was to reintroduce 'a way of building that was a natural growth in the landscape, as much a part of it as the palm tree'. He died in 1989, disappointed in his hope that traditional methods could solve urgent housing needs in the Third World, avoiding extravagant and climatically unsuitable Western technology. In his famous testament, *Architecture for the Poor*, he wrote that 'the work of an architect who designs, say, an apartment house in the poor quarters of Cairo for some stingy speculator, in which he incorporates various features of modern design copied from fashionable European work, will filter down, over a period of years, through the cheap suburbs and into the village where it will slowly poison the genuine tradition'. Fathy also objected to the bastardisation of Arab architecture as applied to recent hotel design and the interior decoration of restaurants and nightclubs.

Though the project was commissioned by the government, bureaucratic red tape and the erratic provision of funds ensured that new Gurna was never entirely finished. Nor has it ever been entirely occupied, though the houses all have plumbing, and a theatre and recreation centre were provided. One reason for this lies in Luxor's oldest profession. Over the past 3000 years or more, easy access to the Theban tombs has provided villagers on the west bank with an extra source of income. It was partly to check this that the new village was built, and for this same reason that new Gurna is so much resented. Old Gurna at the foot of the Theban Mountain has not yet been entirely abandoned, nor entirely has been tomb robbing.

Modern tomb robbing There are at least 900 tombs built into the rock. The authorities say all have been checked and locked. But there are constant rumours of secret finds beneath the houses and even the wall paintings in known tombs are occasionally removed. The modern heyday for tomb robbers was a century ago with the explosion in Europe and America of archaeological and tourist interest in ancient Egypt. Luxor saw a roaring trade in tablets, statuettes and scarabs, both real and faked — home-made scarabs were fed to turkeys to 'acquire by the simple process of digestion a degree of venerableness that is really charming', wrote one visitor. Mummies were dragged out of their tombs and unrolled, stripped of their valuables, broken up and left to crumble in the sands. In earlier centuries, mummy cases were chopped up for firewood, and from at least the 13th C through to the 19th C 'mummy' was highly regarded in Europe for its medicinal properties, the export demand sometimes proving so great that Egyptians often substituted modern corpses. In *The Innocents Abroad*, Mark Twain wrote of the Egyptian railways: 'The fuel they use for the locomotive is composed of mummies three thousand years old, purchased by the ton or by the graveyard for that purpose. . . . Sometimes one hears the profane engineer call out pettishly, "Damn these plebeians, they don't burn worth a cent — pass out a king"'.

Not that the humble quest for loot has always been without its larger benefits, or that even the poorest Egyptians have not sometimes shown respect for the objects of their peculations. In an effort to save their royal masters from contemporary tomb robbers, priests in the XXI Dynasty removed the mummies from their tombs in the Valley of the Kings and stacked them, 30 in a shaft, in a nearby rocky cleft. In 1875, Abdel-Rasul, sheikh of Gurna, found the cache and kept it secret for six years, selling off bits and pieces as he needed money. Archaeologists traced these clues to their source, and the mummies are those until recently on display in the Mummy Room of the Cairo Museum. As these long-dead pharaohs sailed down the Nile by steamer, fellahin lined the banks at village after village, the women ululating in lament, the men firing their rifles in homage.

A case of looting in pharaonic times Under the powerful pharaohs of the XVIII and XIX Dynasties local officials were closely supervised and tomb looting kept in check. But under the weaker rulers of the XX Dynasties tombs were robbed. A picture of surprising detail can be built up from surviving necropolis papyri of the necropolis workers enduring food shortages and late payments of wages, of riots, pay disputes and strikes. There are also documented accounts of bribery and collusion amongst workers, priests and officials. One papyrus describes a major Theban law case during the reign of Ramses IX (XX Dyn) in which the mayor of Thebes brought to the vizier's attention stories of tomb robbing at the necropolis. The matter was investigated by the chief of the necropolis police and the stories denied; the vizier then ensured that the mayor of Thebes was disgraced for making malicious and politically inspired accusations. Some years later, however as the tomb robbings continued, the case was reopened and it became clear that both the vizier and the chief of police were up to their eyeballs in corruption. Examined by birch and screw, the stonemason Amun-pa-nefer admitted tunnelling into a royal tomb and stripping the pharaoh and his queen of gold, silver and precious stones. 'And we made the gold which we had found on these two gods — from their mummies, amulets, ornaments and coffins — into eight shares. And two kilos of gold fell to each of us'.

Amun-pa-nefer then described the chain of corruption: 'We then crossed over to Thebes. And after some days, the agents

At Gurna: this householder has made the pilgrimage to Mecca

of Thebes heard that we had been stealing in the west, so they arrested me and imprisoned me at the mayor of Thebes' place. So I took the two kilos of gold that had fallen to me as my share, and gave them to Kha-em-Opet, the District Clerk of the harbour of Thebes. He let me go, and I joined my companions, and they made up for me another share. And I, as well as the other robbers who are with me, have continued to this day in the practice of robbing the tombs of the nobles and people of the land who rest in the west of Thebes. And a large number of the men of the land rob them also'. Presumably the bribe was shared out amongst other officials higher up the ladder, though no share falling to the mayor of Thebes who was either an honest man or complained because he was being cut out of the action.

The case has its anecdotal interest, but it throws light too on the causes underlying the enfeeblement of the New Kingdom from the XX Dynasty on. In describing Karnak it was mentioned how an ever greater proportion of the nation's wealth went to the priesthood; much gold and silver was also literally buried underground in the tombs, taken out of circulation. Yet it was precisely at this time that the world was shifting from the Bronze Age to the Iron Age, and while Egypt had copper mines, she had no iron — the essential metal for

Iron Age economic crisis

271

weapon superiority. Under the Empire, iron could be expropriated abroad; as the rule of the pharaohs weakened and the Empire shrank, Egypt was forced to buy iron abroad, payment to be made in gold and silver. The value of these precious metals rose during the period 1160 to 1110 BC (Ramses V through Ramses X, approximately). Food shortages and wage delays followed; the necropolis workers struck and many of them turned to tomb robbing. The bonanza of precious metals and stones they clawed back from the tombs and put into circulation — however corrupt the channels might have been — soon relieved the situation. By that time, however, the Empire was finished, the moral authority of the administration had been sapped, and power fell to Herihor, a general who became military dictator, assumed the high priesthood of Amun and made himself pharaoh and founder of the XXI Dynasty. His power extended only over Upper Egypt however; Lower Egypt was ruled by merchant princes at Tanis and the country was never long united again.

Renaissance and Retreat
Even more so than Karnak, the tombs and mortuary temples of the Theban necropolis tell of the rise and fall of the New Kingdom and the Egyptian Empire.

Very fine reliefs

The **Mortuary Temple of Seti I** (XIX Dyn) lies off the road to the Valley of the Kings and is usually bypassed by tourists in haste. This in itself should recommend it; also that the works of Seti's reign — famously his temple at Abydos — are amongst the finest and most restrained of the New Kingdom. The temple was founded in honour of Amun, but also devoted to the worship of Seti's father, Ramses I. The first two pylons and courts have been destroyed; what remains is the temple proper and a tour of it is made both at ground level and, the better to see certain reliefs, by leaping goatlike after the resident guide, from architrave to broken architrave.

A colonnade facing east towards the Nile admits, through a central door, to a *hypostyle hall* with six columns decorated with reliefs of Seti and Ramses II making offerings to divinities. On either side of the hall are small *chapels* with very fine reliefs of Seti, his ka, his sacred boat, Thoth and Osiris, as he offers sacrifices and performs ceremonies enroute to the afterlife. The *sanctuary*, once containing Amun's sacred boat, lies beyond. Reliefs show Seti offering incense before the boat. To the left (south) of the hypostyle hall is the *chapel of Ramses I*. On the side walls of the central chamber, Seti is again depicted offering incense to Amun's boat, and anoints a statue of Ramses I with his finger. The chambers on either side were given inferior reliefs by Ramses II. The right (north) side of the temple is ruinous; a larger hall, dedicated to Re-Herakhte, was built by Ramses II and decorated with crude reliefs.

The obsessive appropriations of Ramses II and their inferior quality stand out amongst the works of Seti I who
consciously sought a renaissance in taste and values. But then
Seti's own reliefs suffer from the New Kingdom preoccup-
ation with gaining access to the afterlife: they are reassuring
encounters with the gods at death, but do not concern themselves with the quality of life. If not yet in empire, certainly in
spirit Egypt was in retreat.

To the Valley of the Kings

The flat alluvium suddenly quits and it is utter desert to the
Valley of the Kings. On a barren hill where the road from
Seti's temple is joined by the road from Deir el Bahri sits a
large domed boulder of a **house where Howard Carter lived**
during his search for the tomb of Tutankhamun. The road
climbs towards the oven of white sand and sun that is Biban el
Muluk — the 'Gates of the Kings'. Unblinking tomb entrances stare vacantly from the close valley walls. Each ramp is
cut and swept, each doorway numbered in order of discovery.
The most exclusive suburb in the world, where the mightiest
dead once lay in silent, motionless expectation of awakening.
Anxious priests, covetous archaeologists, and robbers caring
more for life than life after, carried them away. Anubis and
Osiris remain, paintings on the wall.

Burials at the **Valley of the Kings** date from the XVIII
through the XX Dynasties, with Tuthmosis I being the first to
select the site. Though the pharaohs and, rarely, certain exalted but non-royal personages were entombed here, offerings to the dead were made at the mortuary temples built on
the plain. The tombs therefore were entirely private recepta-
cles for the sarcophagus, and their decoration concentrated
exclusively on the formulae efficacious in transferring the
deceased from this world into the next. The tombs and their
decorations can be impressive, and their contents of course
were staggering, but they do not speak of life, of humanity, or
even of personal death and resurrection — they are monuments of state and of ideology, and less vivid, less revealing
than the tombs of the lesser dead elsewhere in the Theban
necropolis.

Tomb
construction and
decoration A similar pattern of construction and decoration is
followed in each of the tombs. Three corridors lead to an
antechamber giving onto the main hall with its sunken floor
for receiving the sarcophagus. The tombs were cut into the
soft limestone by two teams of 25 men working alternating
ten-day shifts. They normally lived at Deir el Medina, but
when on shift stayed in huts within the valley. Construction of
a tomb began at the beginning of a reign and never took more
than six years to completion. Once the interior surfaces were
prepared, the designs and inscriptions were sketched in black;
the designs filled in, the hieroglyphics outlined in red; the

decorations carved and finally painted. In some tombs, notably that of Horemheb (57), these various stages of decoration are evident.

Decorative themes   The dead pharaoh, absorbed in the sun god, sailed through the underworld at night in a boat, with enemies and dangers to be avoided along the way. This is the recurrent theme of the decorations, the inscriptions being extensive quotations from the Amduat or Book of the Underworld and the Book of the Gates which provide instructions for charting the course. Pictorially, there are three registers, the middle one showing the river of passage, the top and bottom registers depicting the shores with their inhabitants of deities and demons. The registers are divided into 12 sections for the 12 hours of the night. The Book of Day and Night is also sometimes employed: after this nocturnal voyage the naked body of the goddess Nut gives birth each morning to the sun. This is beautifully represented in the sarcophagus hall of the tomb of Ramses VI.

Visiting the Tombs of the Pharaohs
In all, 62 tombs are known in the Valley of the Kings. A few of these were known and visited by tourists in Ptolemaic times as indicated by Diodorus and Strabo and the occasional Greek and Latin graffiti. Most are of little interest except to scholars and are closed to the public. Only tombs 2, 6, 8, 9, 11, 16, 17, 34, 35, 57 and 62 have electric lighting, and most visitors will be content to see those of Tutankhamun (62), Ramses VI (9), Seti I (17) and Ramses IV (2), and then possibly the tombs of Tuthmosis III (34), Amenophis II (35) and Horemheb (57). Not all of even these tombs will necessarily be open when you visit. The identity of all 62 tombs is given on the accompanying map, but only those electrically lit are described below.

Tomb 2: Ramses IV (XX Dyn). Only electrified and therefore made more accessible to the public in 1983, the bright and excellent lighting of this tomb contributes towards a favourable impression — for though the decorations are third rate the overall effect is entirely enjoyable. There is much Ptolemaic and Coptic graffiti throughout, though particularly by the entrance — on the right, two haloed saints raise their arms in prayer. Robbed in antiquity, Ramses' body never found, the tomb remained long open to the curious. Steps and then three high white corridors descend gently in a straight line to the sarcophagus chamber. The ceiling here is decorated with the goddess Nut in duplicate. The huge sarcophagus of pink granite is covered with texts and magical scenes, while Isis and Nephthys on the lid were meant to protect the hijacked body — the empty sarcophagus has been retrieved from the tomb of Amenophis II where the priests had hidden it. Throughout the chambers and corridors of the tomb, against all the whiteness, are small patterns of red, blue, yellow and

Ramses IV: brilliantly lit

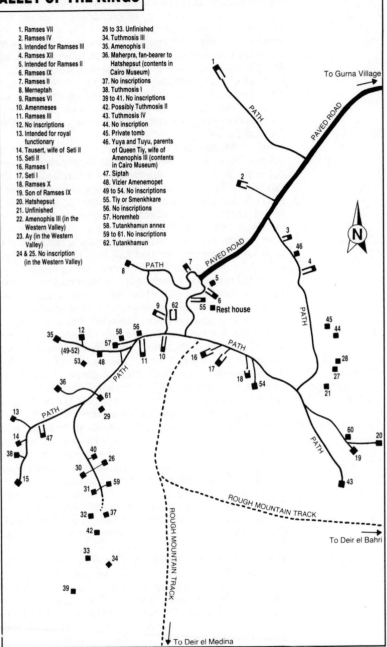

VALLEY OF THE KINGS

1. Ramses VII
2. Ramses IV
3. Intended for Ramses III
4. Ramses XII
5. Intended for Ramses II
6. Ramses IX
7. Ramses II
8. Merneptah
9. Ramses VI
10. Amenmeses
11. Ramses III
12. No inscriptions
13. Intended for royal functionary
14. Tausert, wife of Seti II
15. Seti II
16. Ramses I
17. Seti I
18. Ramses X
19. Son of Ramses IX
20. Hatshepsut
21. Unfinished
22. Amenophis III (in the Western Valley)
23. Ay (in the Western Valley)
24 & 25. No inscription (in the Western Valley)

26 to 33. Unfinished
34. Tuthmosis III
35. Amenophis II
36. Maherpra, fan-bearer to Hatshepsut (contents in Cairo Museum)
37. No inscriptions
38. Tuthmosis I
39 to 41. No inscriptions
42. Possibly Tuthmosis II
43. Tuthmosis IV
44. No inscription
45. Private tomb
46. Yuya and Tuyu, parents of Queen Tiy, wife of Amenophis III (contents in Cairo Museum)
47. Siptah
48. Vizier Amenemopet
49 to 54. No inscriptions
55. Tiy or Smenkhkare
56. No inscriptions
57. Horemheb
58. Tutankhamun annex
59 to 61. No inscriptions
62. Tutankhamun

To Gurna Village

PATH
PAVED ROAD
PATH
PAVED ROAD
PATH
Rest house
PATH
PATH
PATH
PATH
ROUGH MOUNTAIN TRACK
ROUGH MOUNTAIN TRACK
To Deir el Bahri
To Deir el Medina

some green pastels and this is pleasing, despite the poor carving and line and the sloppy application of colour. Indeed this slapdash effect has a quality of gaieté, as though the whole affair was a French reproduction.

Tomb 6: Ramses IX (XX Dyn). A flight of steps on either side of an inclined plane leads you down to the tomb door, its lintel decorated with the solar disc, the pharaoh worshipping it on both sides. Behind him stands Isis (left) and Nephthys (right). The tomb is of near-model design: three corridors, an antechamber, but then a pillared hall and short passage before the final sarcophagus chamber. The decorations are similar to those in Tomb 9.

Tomb 8: Merneptah (XIX Dyn). Possible pharaoh of the Exodus, Merneptah's tomb descends steeply through corridor steps. Such descents are typical of XVIII and XIX Dynasty tombs; those of the XX Dynnasty are shallower. Over the entrance, Isis and Nephthys worship the sun disc, while the entrance corridors are decorated with scenes from the Book of the Gates and other texts. In the small antechamber is the huge granite lid of the outer sarcophagus; a further flight of steps leads down to a pillared hall with barrelled roof containing the pink granite lid of the inner sarcophagus. Carved on the lid is the recumbent figure of Merneptah as Osiris.

Tomb 9: Ramses VI (XX Dyn). Though decorated in sunk relief of workmanship inferior to that of the previous dynasty, the colouring remains fresh. The tomb was originally constructed for Ramses V and ended with *Chamber E*. On the left walls of this part of the tomb is the complete text of the Book of the Gates with a summary of the creation of the world on the left part of the rear wall of *E*. Another text, the Book of Caverns, decorates the right walls, while the ceilings of *C, D* and *E* are decorated with the Book of Day and Night. *Corridors F* and *G* show the hours from the Amduat on their walls. In *Chamber H* are portions of the Book of the Dead; on the left wall is the negative confession. The admission of any transgression would have prevented entry into the afterlife, and so the 'confession' was a series of denials ('I have not done this or that'). The pillared *Chamber I* contains fragments of the great granite sarcophagus. Its vaulted ceiling is splendidly painted with the Book of Day and Night, the sky goddess Nut appearing twice, back to back, framing the Book of Day on the entrance side, and on the far side the Book of Night.

Ramses VI: extensive funerary texts

Tomb 11: Ramses III (XX Dyn). One of the largest tombs in the valley, the second half is ruinous and not illuminated. Once again the decorations are inferior sunk relief, but they are exceptionally varied and remain freshly coloured. This is sometimes called the 'Harpers' Tomb' after the two harpers playing to divinities in the last of four small chambers opening off the left-hand side of the second corridor. This

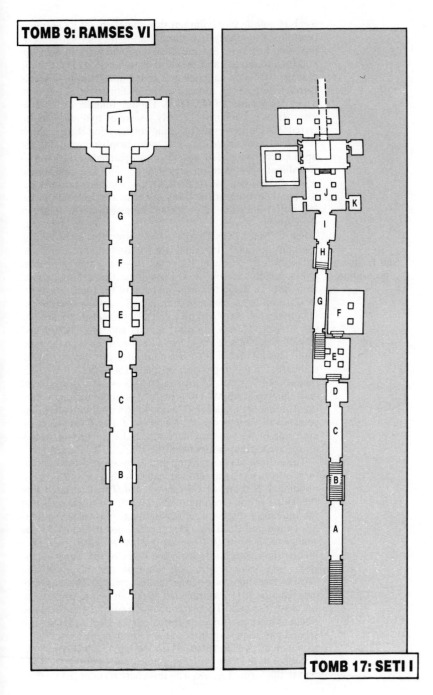

TOMB 9: RAMSES VI

TOMB 17: SETI I

277

tomb is unique in having ten side-chambers off its entrance corridors; where they do occur in tombs, they were for receiving tomb furniture. Beyond these the tomb turns to the right and then to the left and the third chamber along is a sloping passage with side galleries and four pillars: the perspective through here to the rooms beyond is impressive.

Tomb 16: Ramses I (XIX Dyn). Though founder of his dynasty, Ramses I reigned for only a year or two and was interred in a simple tomb. A sloping corridor and steep flight of steps leads to a single almost square chamber containing the open sarcophagus. The decoration — painted, not carved — is brilliantly coloured on grey ground. The pharaoh is variously shown with Maat, Ptah, Osiris, Anubis and other deities, and portions of the Book of Gates are depicted (on the left wall, notice the 12 goddesses representing the hours of the night).

Tomb 17: Seti I (XIX Dyn). At 100 metres, this is the longest tomb in the valley. Its reliefs are wonderfully preserved and so beautifully executed that they rival the famous decorations in Seti's temple at Abydos. Beneath a ceiling painted with vultures flying towards the back of the tomb, the walls of *Corridor A* are decorated on the left with Seti before the falcon-headed Re-Herakhte, god of the morning sun. The sun in other forms, as disc, scarab and ram-headed god follows, and the text of the Sun Litany continues on the right wall. This and other texts are continued in *Corridor B* with staircase. On the upper part of the recess in the left wall are represented 37 forms of the sun god. *Corridor C* is decorated with the fourth (right) and fifth (left) hours of the night from the Amduat. In *Chamber D* Seti is shown on four walls in the presence of various deities. *Chambers E and F* show Seti on each side of the square pillars with a deity. The wall decorations are various hours from the Book of the Gates.

Seti I: superb decorations

The pattern of construction and decoration of the tomb so far is now in a general sense repeated, with *G, H* and *I* corresponding to *B, C* and *D*. *Corridors G and H* are decorated with the Ritual of the Opening of the Mouth which ensured that the mummy's organs were functioning, particularly to permit eating and drinking. The decorations in *Chamber I* are similar to those in *D*. *Chamber J* is in two parts, the first a pillared hall with hours from the Book of the Gates on the walls, the second with the Amduat on the walls and astronomical figures on the vaulted ceiling. The northern constellation here was intended to permit Seti to orient himself with the sun. The sarcophagus (now in the Sir John Soane Museum, London) rested in the depression in this second part; a passage behind runs for 46 metres, apparently to nowhere. A side room, *K*, to the right, is known as the Chamber of the Cow for its representation of the sky goddess Nut in the form of a cow. The texts here recount the myth of

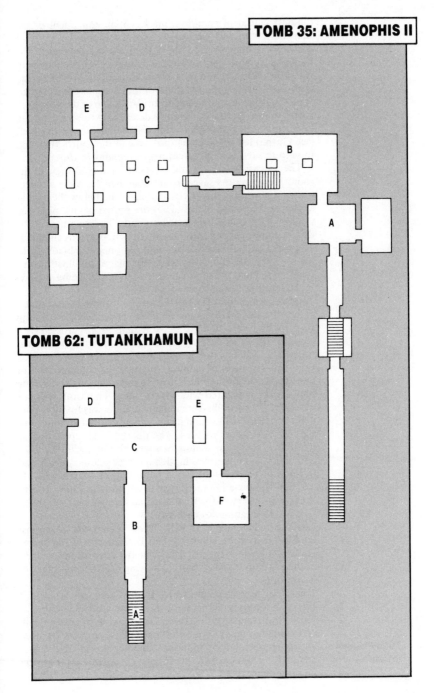

the destruction of mankind, the Egyptian equivalent of the Mesopotamian and Biblical story of the Flood.

Tomb 34: Tuthmosis III (XVIII Dyn). At the far end of the rising valley and requiring a steep climb up wooden steps to reach the entrance, and then a steep descent within, this tomb is unusual for the rounded shape of the sarcophagus chamber. A pit that you now cross by footbridge in one of the approach corridors was probably meant to deter tomb robbers, though later the priests removed Tuthmosis' mummy to a rocky cleft (see Gurna) for safekeeping; it is now in the Cairo Museum, though the red granite sarcophagus remains *in situ*.

The tomb is worth visiting for its unusual paintings. In the room preceding the sarcophagus chamber the walls are decorated with a repeating pattern of stars, and below them what appear to be potted plants. They *are* potted plants: papyrus, symbol of the south, being grown in pots. The spareness of the decorations is carried through into the sarcophagus chamber. The walls are painted in black and red only; the black stick-figures have the stylishness of 1930s magazine illustrations. Note on the first pillar you come to Tuthmosis being suckled by his mother in the form of a tree.

Tomb 35: Amenophis II (XVIII Dyn). This tomb is unadorned except for the sarcophagus chamber, approached by a long corridor and steep flight of steps. A shaft at *A* is crossed by a modern gangway leading to *Chamber B* with unfinished walls. The walls of the *Sarcophagus Chamber C* are painted yellow in imitation of papyrus and bear the complete text of the Amduat as though inscribed on a continuous scroll. The blue ceiling is painted with yellow stars. The tomb was not discovered until 1898. Amenophis' mummy was found *in situ*, a floral garland still round its neck, and was only removed to the Cairo Museum in 1934. The quartzite sarcophagus was left in the tomb. Three mummies were found in side room *D*, and nine royal mummies, hidden there by priests, were found in room *E*. These last included Tuthmosis IV, Amenophis III and Seti II, now all in the Egyptian Museum in Cairo. It is to the late discovery of the tomb that the survival and identification of these mummies is owed.

Tomb 57: Horemheb (XVIII Dyn). The plan is almost identical to that of Tomb 17 (Seti I) and some of the decorations are finely executed. The principal interest, however, is in the partially finished work, showing the various stages of decoration.

Tomb 62: Tutankhamun (XVIII Dyn). This most famous of Egyptian tombs is neither large nor impressively decorated. It bears all the marks of hasty burial following the early death of Tutankhamun in about his nineteenth year. Even its fabulous contents, seen by millions of people around the world, cannot have compared to the funerary treasures of far greater pharaohs entombed in the valley. This relative lack of impor-

Tutankhamun: treasures of a nobody

tance of a briefly reigning puppet pharaoh of the Amun priesthood's counterrevolution probably assisted in the long secrecy of the tomb's existence and whereabouts. Also, nearly above it, was the entrance to the grander tomb of Ramses VI (Tomb 9), the debris from which early on covered the entrance to the young pharaoh's tomb.

The tomb was discovered on 4 November 1922 by Howard Carter and opened by him and his patron Lord Carnarvon on 26 November in the presence of experts from New York's Metropolitan Museum of Art — or so the official story went. But in a last great irony in the history of looting at the Valley of the Kings it has recently been revealed by Thomas Hoving, ex-director of the Metropolitan Museum, in his book *Tutankhamun, the Untold Story* that between discovery and public entry, Carter and Carnarvon sneaked into the tomb, stole 35 items, and then walled it up again.

The door at the bottom of the entrance stairway *A* was found walled up and sealed with the royal seal. The entrance corridor *B* was found filled with stone debris through which a tunnel had been dug soon after interment in an unsuccessful attempt to rob the tomb. The undecorated *Chambers C, D* (now walled up) *and F* contained most of the funerary objects now on display at the Cairo Museum. *Chamber E*, originally walled off from *C* and at a lower level, contained the four gilded wooden shrines, one inside the other, within which lay the rectangular stone sarcophagus, then three mummiform coffins, the innermost of solid gold, and then finally the mummy of Tutankhamun himself. The wall has now been replaced by a railing beyond which visitors cannot venture.

From here you can view what remains in the tomb: the sarcophagus, the largest of the mummiform coffins within it, and, unseen within that, the badly decayed mummy of Tutankhamun. This chamber was the only one decorated, its paintings betraying signs of haste. (The paintings are suffering damage, perhaps from visitors' humid exhalations.) On the right wall, the coffin is transported on a sledge. To the rear from right to left, Ay, the young king's successor, performs the rite of the opening of the mouth (note a suggestion of the Amarna style); Tutankhamun sacrificing to Nut; again the young pharaoh, this time with his ka, before Osiris. On the left wall is the sun god's boat, while on the all but impossible to see entrance wall, Tutankhamun, accompanied by Anubis and Isis, receiving life from the goddess of the West.

There is nothing to see in **Tomb 46 of Yuya and his wife Tuyu** (its contents are in Room 13 of the Cairo Museum), but it is

Jehovah's witness

worth a mention all the same. Though not apparently of noble birth, Tuyu became the highest official in the land during the reigns of Tuthmosis IV and Amenophis III, and his daughter became Amenophis' remarkable wife Tiy. Yuyu was therefore grandfather of Akhenaton. In *Stranger in the Valley of the Kings* by Ahmed Osman it is argued that Yuyu, whose non-Egyptian appearance, judging from his mummy, has long been noted by some scholars, was in fact Joseph of the Bible: 'And Pharaoh said unto Joseph . . .Thou shalt be over my house, and according unto thy word shall all my people be ruled: only in the throne will I be greater than you' (Genesis 41:39–40). In other words, the reasoning goes, the origin of Akhenaton's disembodied and quasi-monotheistic Aton is to be found in his grandfather's talk of Jehovah. It is one of those engaging speculations which almost certainly lie beyond proof.

To Deir el Bahri

You can leave the Valley of the Kings by the road you came, that same ancient road along which the bodies of the pharaohs were drawn here on sledges. Or you can leave on foot, climbing the *path* to the right of Tomb 16, opposite the rest house. As it gains the ridge, there is usually a donkey boy waiting but the donkeys should be declined. Almost certainly, a guide will fasten himself on you in hope of baksheesh. He can be useful for those who are not foot sure, but otherwise he is not necessary either. On the ridge, the path divides. One heads south, rising slowly over the mountain; the other runs to the left and level along the ridge. The first leads to Deir el Medina and is the same path the workmen used when returning home from their shift at the tombs. There are sweeping views of Nile valley, magnificent in the afternoon with the sun in the west. The second path soon creeps high along the edge of the amphitheatre of Deir el Bahri and offers changing angles and elevations of Hatshepsut's temple, and views towards the Nile. You continue along until you are above the old Cook's rest house at Deir el Bahri and then pick your way down, to be met by your driver after visiting the temple. Both walks are highly recommended, but the second (about 30 minutes) is a must for a full appreciation of Hatshepsut's architectural achievement.

The **mortuary temple of Hatshepsut** at Deir el Bahri is the finest building in Egypt. Elegant, revolutionary, it satisfies and provokes in whole and in detail. Along with the Parthenon, the Taj Mahal, the interiors of Chartres and Hagia Sophia, it is one of the great buildings of the world. Not that the temple has received its fullest due: though far older than the others, it was unknown in modern times until Mariette made preliminary excavations in the third quarter of the 19th C. The temple was only entirely cleared in 1894–96 and since then has undergone sporadic restoration, still in progress today.

Hatshepsut's Reign

Interpretation of the events following the death of Tuthmosis I (XVIII Dyn) is marked by controversy amongst archaeologists which mimics, even if it does not rival, the original dynastic struggle played out between Hatshepsut, his daughter, and Tuthmosis III, his grandson. By any interpretation, Hatshepsut emerges as one of the most formidable figures in Egyptian history, only the third woman to rule as queen, the first to rule as king. In the ruthlessness and romance the story implies, and the high policy at stake, parallels between the reigns of Hatshepsut and Elizabeth I easily suggest themselves to the imagination.

Hatshepsut married her father's son and successor, Tuthmosis II, and during the lifetime of her husband her full titles were 'pharaoh's daughter, pharaoh's sister, god's wife and pharaoh's great wife'. But Tuthmosis II died before Hatshepsut could bear him a child, and it was one of her husband's secondary wives who became 'pharaoh's mother' to Tuth-

The struggle with Tuthmosis III

mosis III. But for her sex, Hatshepsut's claim to the throne through her father was at least as good as Tuthmosis III's and through her mother she was descended from the Ahmose family who had thrown the Hyksos out of Egypt. But as Tuthmosis was later to advertise, his future as pharaoh was proclaimed by no less a god than Amun who while Tuthmosis I was sacrificing at Karnak stood the young prince in the place usually occupied by the sovereign. This conveniently has Tuthmosis III designated heir in the lifetime of his own father, but betrays the more pedestrian likelihood that the priests of Amun eventually sided with the army in its support of Tuthmosis and his imperial designs against Hatshepsut and her party in the civil service who preferred a peaceful domestic policy.

Tuthmosis III, when finally he became sole pharaoh well into his manhood, launched Egypt upon her period of conquest abroad and bloated magnificence at home so often celebrated in stone at Thebes. Yet as powerful a pharaoh and warrior as he was to become, Tuthmosis was no match for Hatshepsut in her prime. In the first few years following her husband's death, Hatshepsut reigned as widow-queen, but she soon took the momentous step of assuming the title of pharaoh, co-reigning with but entirely overshadowing her stepson. She went so far as to pose and dress as a man — at least on reliefs — and to wear the pharaonic beard. In this way she ruled for about 20 years.

Hatshepsut's favourite, Senmut

Elizabeth I had her Essex; Hatshepsut had her Senmut, a man of modest birth who rose to occupy a score of high offices, including steward of Amun, probably giving him control over the vast wealth of the Karnak temple, and minister of public works, with the suggestion that he was the architect at Deir el Bahri. As such favourites often do, Senmut overstepped the mark. He used his royal mistress's temple for his own purposes, introducing reliefs of himself in niches that would be concealed behind opening doors, and though building himself a tomb at Gurna, planned secretly to be buried within the great court at Deir el Bahri. Most of his reliefs were hacked out and his sarcophagus smashed, yet in his secret tomb the name of Hatshepsut was left untouched, suggesting the destruction was wrought not by Tuthmosis III, who in malice destroyed so much that was Hatshepsut's, but by Hatshepsut herself in rage at this attempt to extend familiarity into the eternal. The last record of Senmut comes about five years before the end of his mistress's reign. In those last years she was alone.

How Hatshepsut's reign ended is not known. Perhaps she fell victim to a coup d'etat, or merely died a natural death. In any case her inward-looking peace policy was suddenly eclipsed and Tuthmosis III, obliterating her name and her image wherever he found them, within 75 days of her death was leading his army into Palestine (see Karnak).

Conception of Hatshepsut's Temple at Deir el Bahri

Into the rugged eastern flank of the Theban Mountain nature has cut an immense amphitheatre facing Thebes. Its sheer golden walls embrace the site like the wings of some mighty hovering solar disc. Just off centre, to the left and rising from the cliffline, is a pyramidal peak. A magnificent backdrop, it invites a performance, and would condemn any but the most brilliant to insignificance before it. The Middle Kingdom pharaoh Mentuhotep II (XI Dyn) built a temple here; you can see its *ruins* to the south of Hatshepsut's. What impression it made cannot fairly be judged from its remains. Like Hatshepsut's temple, it rose in terraces but then was surmounted by a pyramid, a Memphite legacy perhaps. Mentuhotep II and III were both entombed here. But a pyramidal structure set against the pyramidal peak seems superfluous, and any structure vying with the cliffs for height can only have been overwhelmed.

Mentuhotep's temple was already in ruins when 500 years later Hatshepsut was drawn to the holy site. (Whether out of convenience or some similar feeling of awe, Hatshepsut's temple was taken over by early Christians as a monastery: *Deir el Bahri*, the Northern Monastery). She was obviously influenced by the earlier temple, and in all probability would have replicated it on a larger scale: the foundations suggest a pyramid was intended. One purpose of a pyramid is to protect the tomb, but her father Tuthmosis I had abandoned this idea for the greater security of discreet entombment in the Valley of the Kings. It remained necessary therefore to build only a mortuary temple at which the appropriate ceremonies would be performed. At some point Hatshepsut decided to build wide instead of high.

If it is true that circumstances dictated this decision, or suggested that the alternative was now pointless, it is no less

Mentuhotep's earlier design

true that the new form was seized upon with conviction and executed with genius. The terraces of Hatshepsut's temple emphasise the stratification of the cliff behind and the line between rock and sky. At the same time, the bold rhythm of the pillared colonnades, vertical shafts of light-reflecting stone framing and contrasting with the shadowed ambulatories, reflect the dark gashes of gullies and fissures in the cliff face itself. Even the peak seems brought into the conception: a pyramid offered by nature. The temple mediates between the wildness of the mountain and the cultivation of the valley. The power and contradiction of the landscape is gripped and tamed with a confidence and elegance that is breathtaking, and then played throughout the structure so that as you walk round the temple you feel it, never too much, but to a measure that insists on the spiritual nature of man.

Tour of Hatshepsut's Temple

The Lower Terrace. The main temple complex may originally have been preceded by a valley temple near the Nile; if so, it has been lost beneath the tilled alluvium. From this temple ran a promenade lined with sphinxes to the Lower

Terrace, a zone of transition between the profane and the sacred. This was a garden with myrrh trees and fountains, as though a foretaste of that life which endures in the desert of

Hatshepsut's temple: at grips with the landscape

the other world. (The stumps of some trees are visible on the Lower and Middle Terraces.) A pair of *lions* (the left-hand one survives) stood at the bottom of the ramp leading up to the Middle Terrace and another pair (the right-hand one survives) stood at the top. These were at once guardians of the temple and witnesses to the rising sun, proof of rebirth. **Colonnades** are on either side of the ramp, to the north and to the south. On their pillars are simple devices stating a variation of Hatshepsut's name surmounted by the solar falcon wearing the double crown. Within the colonnades, the retaining walls of the Middle Terrace are decorated with vividly coloured *reliefs*. Not all of the original courses have survived, and where they have, the decorations have suffered deliberate defacement, first by Tuthmosis III, later by Akhenaton. Representations of Amun were restored at the counterrevolution, but Hatshepsut remains obliterated; the pharaoh seen is Tuthmosis III, who, as co-ruler, had been included in the original decorations. The carvings within the **North Colonnade** depict an idealised country life, continuing the theme established by the gardens of the Lower Terrace. Of the greatest delicacy are the scenes (right) of water birds being caught in nets. The reliefs within the **South Colonnade** depict the transport down the Nile of two obelisks cut at Aswan at Hatshepsut's order. At the far ends of the colonnades stood large Osiris statues of Hatshepsut (the north one imperfectly restored).

The Middle Terrace. The lower ramp leads up to the Middle Terrace. At its centre rises a second ramp to the Upper Terrace. Again, at the rear of the Middle Terrace and on either side of the second ramp are colonnades and at their farthest ends, pressing against the rock of the cliff face, are the Chapels of Anubis (north) and Hathor (south). Along the north side of the terrace is an unfinished colonnade.

The north and south colonnades of the Middle Terrace have double rows of square pillars, simple but well-proportioned and achieving a modest grace. On the walls of the **Birth Colonnade** (north) *are reliefs depicting Hatshepsut's divine parentage:* Amun has assumed the form of her father who sits facing Ahmosis, her mother, on a couch. The couple gaze at one another, their knees touching in a scene at once conventional and reserved and yet sensitively conveying their ardour. Queen Ahmosis is led to the birth chamber, accompanied by strange deities, a smile of suffering and delight playing on her lips. The child, conventionally shown as a boy, is fashioned by Khnum on his potter's wheel, and also its ka. Just as Tuthmosis III justified his claim to the throne with the story of Amun's selection of him at the Temple of Karnak, so these reliefs serve the same purpose for Hatshepsut. Not that we should think that either pharaoh was simply

Hatshepsut
asserts her divine
birth

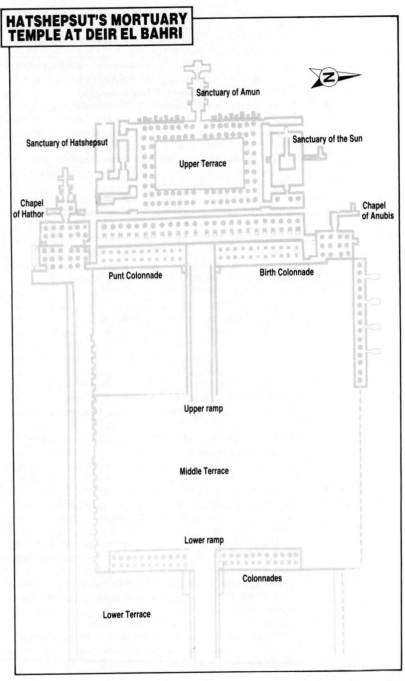

HATSHEPSUT'S MORTUARY TEMPLE AT DEIR EL BAHRI

Sanctuary of Amun

Sanctuary of Hatshepsut

Sanctuary of the Sun

Upper Terrace

Chapel of Hathor

Chapel of Anubis

Punt Colonnade

Birth Colonnade

Upper ramp

Middle Terrace

Lower ramp

Colonnades

Lower Terrace

cynical; overriding the political propaganda was probably a sincere belief in their divine birth, and these beliefs certainly have all the delicacy and feeling of a belief honestly integrated in Hatshepsut's character, sustaining her in her rule. On the lateral faces of the pillars, Tuthmosis is shown with Amun; on front and back it is Hatshepsut (defaced) with Amun.

The facade of the **Chapel of Anubis** continues the line of the colonnade, but with *columns* (fluted, with simple capitals, like Doric columns). From a distance, the columns are indistinguishable from the pillars, but stand in the northwest corner of the terrace and look along the facades towards the ramp: that almost unnoticed variation creates a subtle yet entirely harmonious contrast. There is a touch of Greece here, and in the discreet widening of the distance between the central columns as if inviting the visitor into the sanctuary within. The *walls* of the hall are brilliantly coloured and show the co-rulers (Hatshepsut hacked out), Anubis, protector of the dead, and facing each other at either end, the falcon-headed sun god (north wall) and his wife Hathor (south wall). Cut into the rock in a series of right angles are several **chambers** with vaulted roofs of brick, though lacking the wedge-shaped keystones of true weight-bearing vaults which do not appear in Egypt until the 8th C BC (and not universalised until taken up by the Romans).

On the south side of the ramp is the **Punt Colonnade**, named for the *decorations on its rear wall* of the expedition to the land of Punt (probably the coastal region of the modern Somali Republic) instigated by Hatshepsut. Amun had told her: 'It is a glorious region of god's land, it is indeed my place of delight; I have made it for myself in order to divert my heart'. Hatshepsut's ancestors had often sent expeditions there to procure the precious myrrh necessary for the incense in temple services, but now, as she recorded, Amun desired her 'to establish a Punt in his house'. So the purpose of the expedition was to obtain for the first time living myrrh trees; to plant the terraces of this temple dedicated to Amun with them.

Journey to the land of delight

The walls illustrate and relate the story. After presumably crossing the desert to a Red Sea port, the expedition sailed southwards in five ships. The Egyptians are shown being greeted on the shore by the chief of Punt and his extraordinarily corpulent wife — a rare instance of humorous caricature, the rolls of fat from her body reaching right down to her ankles. In exchange for gifts, the beached ships are laden 'very heavily with marvels of the country of Punt; all goodly fragrant woods of god's land, heaps of myrrh resin, of fresh myrrh trees, with ebony and pure ivory, with green gold of Emu, with cinnamon wood, with incense, eye cosmetic, with baboons, monkeys, dogs, with skins of the southern panther, with natives and their children. Never was the like of this brought for any pharaoh who has been since the beginning'.

Back at Thebes, Tuthmosis III and Hatshepsut are shown offering incense to Amun's sacred boat, his offering paltry compared to hers. But later he had Hatshepsut defaced; Tuthmosis' portrait, however, is beautifully carved, his individuality realised in a way lacking in the idealised representations on the pillars.

At the far south end of the colonnade it is the **Chapel of Hathor** that continues the facade. This time there are pillars, not columns, but still, and unnoticed from any distance, they differ from the rest in having the cow-eared head of Hathor serve laterally as capitals. Beyond the first pillared chamber, and then the second, decorated with a procession of boats along the Nile, is the **Sanctuary of Hathor** with vaulted roof. After all the hacking out of Hatshepsut's figure you yearn to see one intact and here, in the farthest recess of the sanctuary, that desire is satisfied. Either because the room was sealed or because at least here in Hathor's sanctuary Tuthmosis respected Hatshepsut's right to some modest remembrance, she survives, albeit in stylised and masculine form. She meets Amun, she suckles regenerating milk from Hathor, and above a recess in the left wall she and Tuthmosis III are shown kneeling, she to the left with an offering of milk, he to the right with wine. Also within this chamber, in a little alcove on the right and towards the floor, is a portrait of Senmut, Hatshepsut's favourite.

Rare portraits of Hatshepsut and Senmut

The Upper Terrace. The second ramp leads to the Upper Terrace, badly ruined and currently being restored (it may be closed). A portico of Osiris pillars stood a short distance from the edge; their restoration is well underway. On what remains of the rear wall are *reliefs* of boats accompanied along the Nile banks by a festive procession of soldiers, and of the Festival of the Valley during which Amun visited the necropolis.

Passing through the last wall against the cliffs is a granite doorway leading into the **Sanctuary of Amun** hewn out of the rock. The walls are decorated as elsewhere in the temple but are blackened with smoke. In Ptolemaic times the sanctuary was cut deeper and was dedicated to the healing cults of Imhotep, counsellor to Zoser, and Amenhotep, son of Hapu, counsellor to Amenophis III.

At the left (south) end of the Upper Terrace is the **Sanctuary of Hatshepsut**. The *reliefs* are of high quality and show processions of priests and offering-bearers. At the right (north) end of the terrace is the **Sanctuary of the Sun**, an open court with an altar in the centre. A flight of steps on its west side permitted a priest to mount the *altar* gaining a magnificent view of the valley and river below and the rugged horizon to the east, and to await the rising of the sun.

The Noble Tombs

Over 400 private tombs have been discovered at the Theban necropolis, dating from the Old Kingdom through the Ptolemaic period. These include the Workmen's Tombs at Deir el Medina (see later), and the Tombs of the Nobles (in fact nobles, priests and officials) found in clusters from near the Temple of Seti I at the north end of the necropolis to Medinet Habu at the south end. The noble tombs are interesting **Scenes of the** because they often give a vivid picture of contemporary life **living past** instead of the impersonal ritual decorations of the royal tombs. The artists have been more free to express themselves and the sensitivity of their work has been greater. The limestone on this side of the mountain is of poor quality, generally not suited to cutting reliefs; usually the decorations are paintings on stucco walls of white, grey or yellow ground. The tombs are, strictly, mortuary chapels; a filled-in shaft led to a deeper chamber containing the sarcophagus.

Seven of the most outstanding Tombs of the Nobles are described here, all XVIII Dynasty, all near the **old village of Gurna** (Sheikh Abd el-Gurna). They are signposted from the Ramesseum and fall into three groups (ticket for each group): Rekhmire (100) and Sennufer (96); Menna (69) and Nakht (52); and Ramose (55), Userhat (56) and Khaemhat (57).

To visit all seven tombs would take two hours or so. For a good sample of differing types of tomb, you should visit Rekhmire (100), Sennufer (96), Nakht (52) and Ramose (55).

Tomb 100: **Rekhmire** was vizier under Tuthmosis III and Amenophis II, and the decorations therefore concentrate on foreign policy, and matters of justice and taxation. The tomb is cruciform, ie a transverse chamber extending far to left and right, and a long corridor leading straight ahead, its ceiling steadily rising to 5.5 metres at the far end where there is a false door. *Left arm of transverse chamber*: on the far left wall Rekhmire is shown being installed as vizier; on the far right wall tribute is brought to Egypt. This is delightful: from the top register the tribute is shown from Punt, Crete and the Aegean, Nubia, Syria and Cush (on the western shore of the Red Sea), including a wonderful procession of African beasts and goods. *Right arm of transverse chamber*: on the left wall scenes of hunting, fowling and the treading of grapes; on the near right wall taxes and offerings; on the far wall Rekhmire's ancestors. *Corridor*: on the near left, Rekhmire is shown inspecting the workshops of Amun; centre left, the voyage to Abydos (see Abydos); right wall, the afterworld, with trees and lake, and a funerary feast.

Tomb 96 (up the hill from Rekhmire's tomb): **Sennufer** was mayor of Thebes and overseer of the gardens of Amun during **Dead drunk** the reign of Amenophis II. It is likely that he was also chief vintner, and you wonder whether his tomb is not his last laugh on that theme. You go down steep steps to an *ante-*

chamber, the highly irregular surface of its ceiling seeming to give deliberate relief to a painted arbour with vines and grapes. But when you step into the *chamber beyond*, you see that everything — ceiling, walls, pillars — wobbles before your eyes as though you were drunk. It is possible that the rock here was difficult to cut. It is also possible that Sennufer said what the hell. In either case the effect is extremely pleasing. The walls in both chambers are painted with religious scenes, Sennufer repeatedly depicted with his daughter, his sister and his wife.

Tomb 69 (this and 52 are across the road from one another): **Menna** was an estate inspector under a mid-XVIII Dynasty pharaoh, and so the decorations emphasise country life. The paintings are finely executed and excellently preserved. In the *entrance passage*, Menna, his wife and daughter are shown worshipping the sun. In the left wing of the *first chamber* are a variety of rural scenes, while the right wing depicts various ceremonies, with the dead man and his wife receiving offerings, Anubis facing Osiris, Re and Hathor. A lively hunting and fishing scene occupies the centre of the right-hand wall of the *second chamber*, though generally mourning and burial scenes are depicted.

Tomb 52 (across the road from 69): **Nakht** was a scribe and astronomer of Amun in the middle of the XVIII Dynasty. A short passage leads to a *transverse first chamber*, the only decorated part of the tomb. The paintings are well preserved and brilliantly coloured, and like those of Menna depict country life: the supervising of field labours by Nakht; the deceased and his wife banqueting and making offerings. Note that Nakht is frequently defaced, his eyes gouged, even the upper part of his body destroyed; also the name of Amun is everywhere obliterated — acts committed, presumably, during Akhenaton's reign. The chamber beyond, as was the custom, contained a statue of the dead man with his wife: it was shipped to America but the boat sank. A shaft here runs down to the sarcophagus chamber.

Tomb 55 (to the south of 69 and 52; to the east of 100): a relatively grandiose structure with wall carvings, the unfinished tomb of **Ramose** is one of the most fascinating in the necropolis. Ramose was governor of Thebes and vizier in the early years of Amenophis IV's reign and took pains to honour himself with two hypostyle chambers (only the first is open) decorated in the most exquisite classical style.

From an open court you enter the first chamber and follow the decorations from the near wall of the right wing: *classical reliefs* show Ramose and his wife in several offering ceremonies. These scenes are continued along the near wall of the left wing. The groups of seated figures are friends or relatives of the dead man. Continuing clockwise, the south wall bears a painting of the procession to the tomb with bearers of offerings, mourning women and priests; to the right, the dead man and his wife worshipping Osiris; and below, four representations of the dead man before his tomb. The west wall in the left wing resumes the reliefs and shows Ramose four times offering flowers to Amenophis IV seated under a canopy with the goddess Maat. At the very south (left) end of this wall you can see that prior to cutting the relief the figures were drawn in black outline over a red grid, suggesting the usual artist's concern to transfer the scene in the same detail and proportions as it appeared on the (perhaps smaller) original sketch.

Contrast between classical and Amarna styles

Now passing across the closed entrance to the second chamber you come to the north end of the west wall and suddenly the style has changed from the classical to the *Amarnan*. The explanation is that while Ramose was working on his tomb, Amenophis IV had become Akhenaton, introducing both Aton and a new art. Ramose never did finish his tomb here because he followed Akhenaton to Amarna. This wall shows Akhenaton and Nefertiti at their palace window under the rays of Aton, receiving homage from Ramose. In sketch form you can see Ramose receiving a decoration (a gold collar, as at Ay's tomb at Amarna) and acclaimed by courtiers and representatives from Nubia, Libya and Asia, and also Ramose receiving bouquets in the temple. It is interesting to compare these new-style portraits of Ramose to his classical portrait at the north side of the east wall. And it is significant to note that not only Akhenaton and Nefertiti are depicted with elongated heads, but now Ramose (though not quite so much) is too — in some measure countering the argument that Akhenaton and his family were portrayed in this way because they were afflicted by some deforming disease or gene.

Tomb 56 (immediately south of Ramose's tomb): **Userhat** was a royal scribe and tutor during the reign of Amenophis II. The walls and ceiling are finely painted, and there are some interesting scenes of barbers cutting hair and of Userhat hunting gazelle from a chariot, and fowling and fishing in the marshes. The tomb was later used by Coptic hermits who here and there added their own curious creatures and crosses.

Coptic graffiti

Tomb 57 (adjacent to 56): **Khaemhat** was a royal scribe and inspector of granaries in Upper and Lower Egypt under Amenophis III. His is another carved tomb, as fine and even firmer in style than that of Ramose. In the *entrance court*, to the right of the doorway, are reliefs showing the complete set of instruments employed in the opening of the mouth ceremony, while to the left is Khaemhat adoring Re. The *first chamber* presents scenes of country life and, particularly, aspects of Khaemhat's official life: unloading of boats, an amusing market scene, cattle herds, the harvest. The *second chamber* shows the funeral procession and ceremonies in honour of Osiris. The *chapel* beyond contains several statues

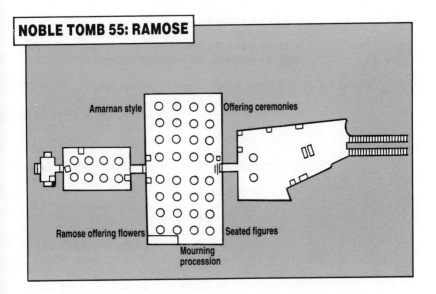

NOBLE TOMB 55: RAMOSE

Amarnan style

Offering ceremonies

Ramose offering flowers

Seated figures

Mourning procession

with finely modelled heads; in the left wing, on the right-hand wall, the dead man in the act of worship; in the right wing, on the right-hand wall, the cast of a portrait of Khaemhat.

A coffin was traditionally carried through a banquet, giving the lie to an unending feast of life. Macabre it might seem to us; to the Egyptians it must have carried with it some promise against time: 'You live again, you live again for ever, here you are young once more for ever' — the final benediction of the priests as the dessicated mummies of these titled dead were interred in their tombs.

The Ramesseum

The Ramesseum, the **mortuary temple of Ramses II**, is part of a still larger rectangular complex enclosed by its original brick wall. The area was filled with vaulted brick storehouses, now entirely ruinous, which were once invaded, as is known from an extant papyrus, by desperate tomb workers who had not been paid for two months: 'We have reached this place because of hunger, because of thirst, without clothing, without oil, without fish, without vegetables! Tell pharaoh, our good lord, about it, and tell the vizier, our superior. Act so that we may live!' So that the great Ramses should live forever this grandiose temple was built, and enough of its stones remain piled atop one another to remind us of *his* hunger. Diodorus was impressed. Coming upon the granite colossus of Ramses he fancifully interpreted its inscription, corrupting the pharaoh's praenomen, User-maat-Re, as he went: 'I am Ozymandias, king of kings. If any would know how great I am, and where I lie, let him excel me in any of my works'. To which Shelley offered time's reply:

Shelley's Ozymandias

I met a traveller from an antique land
Who said: Two vast and trunkless legs of stone
Stand in the desert ... Near them, on the sand,
Half sunk, a shattered visage lies, whose frown,
And wrinkled lip, and sneer of cold command,
Tell that its sculptor well those passions read
Which yet survive, stamped on these lifeless things,
The hand that mocked them, and the heart that fed.
On the pedestal these words appear:
'My name is Ozymandias, king of kings:
Look on my works, ye Mighty, and despair!'
Nothing beside remains. Round the decay
Of that colossal wreck, boundless and bare
The lone and level sands stretch far away.

You approach the temple at its north flank and so to reach the **First Pylon**, measuring 67 metres across, you must turn left through the ruined **First Court**. The outer wall of the pylon is as intelligible as a quarry face, but on the pylon wall facing the court there are excellently carved *reliefs*, albeit of Ramses' all too familiar exploits against the Hittites (see the Temple of Luxor). A double colonnade on the south side of the court formed the facade of the **royal palace** of which little remains. A colonnade of Osiris pillars runs along the north side of the court. At the far (west) end a flight of steps leads to the Second Court; on the left, as you ascend, is the fallen **Ozymandias**. Weighing more than 900,000 kilos and once standing at 17.5 metres this was one of the largest free-standing statues in Egypt, surpassed by the Colossi of Memnon only by virtue of their pedestals. The index finger alone is a metre long.

The inner surface of the north tower of the **Second Pylon** is decorated, again, with the battle of Kadesh, though the top register more peacefully portrays the festival of the harvest god Min. The front and back of the **Second Court** is lined with Osiris pillars, and where three stairways rise to the west portico, another *granite colossus*, not quite so large as the first, lies in fragments, the head in good condition with only the nose smashed. On a nearby throne, next to the name of Ramses,

Human pyramid

Belzoni carved his name. An Italian artist and one-time seminarian, in the early years of the 19th C Belzoni appeared on the stage of Sadler's Wells and elsewhere in England with his famous human-pyramid act, 'bearing on his colossal frame, not fewer, if we mistake not, than 20 or 22 persons'. He later turned serious explorer and succeeded in removing from the

The fallen Ozymandias, photographed in 1857

Ramesseum the giant bust of Ramses II now in the British
Museum.

On the rear wall of the **portico** (reached by stairways at the
rear of the Second Court) between the central and left-hand
doorways, are three rows of *reliefs*: the bottom register shows
11 of Ramses' sons; the middle shows Ramses with Atum (a
Heliopolitan god) and falcon-headed Mont who holds the
hieroglyph for 'life' to the pharaoh's nose, while to the right
Ramses kneels before the Theban triad and Thoth inscribes
the pharaoh's name on a palm branch; the top shows Ramses
sacrificing to Ptah, and to the right offering incense to an
ithyphallic Min. Against the outside north wall of the portico
and the Great Hypostyle Hall are the scant remains of an
earlier *temple of Seti I*, its alignment probably accounting for
the overall alignment of the Ramesseum which accordingly
skews to the south instead of fitting squarely within the rectangular walls of the complex.

The **Great Hypostyle Hall** had 48 columns of which only 29
still stand. It was similar to the one at Karnak (to which
Ramses II made a major contribution), a higher ceiling over
the central aisle allowing illumination through windows set
upon the architraves of the adjoining row of shorter columns.

The **First Small Hypostyle Hall** of eight papyrus bud columns still retains its ceiling, decorated with astronomical signs. Only four out of eight columns survive in the **Second Small Hypostyle Hall**, while of the *shrine* beyond nothing remains.

Here, as elsewhere beneath the glaring sun of Egypt, the columns, the reliefs, the sculptures are streaked with white. Ramses boasted and Shelley cut him down to size; and Flaubert dispassionately observed: 'Birdshit is Nature's protest in Egypt; she decorates monuments with it instead of with lichen or moss'.

The Workmen's Village and the Valley of the Queens

From the Valley of the Kings there was a mountain path that led down to Deir el Bahri, or if you had continued along the crest southwards it would have brought you to the village of the ancient tomb workers, **Deir el Medina**. This is more usually reached by road, travelling 700 metres or so west from the Ramesseum. There are rows of humble *houses*, 70 in all, mud brick walls rising on stone foundations along straight and narrow alleys. They had a second storey or at least a living area on the roof, reached by stairs. Some have simple wall decorations inside. The men who worked at the Valley of the Kings (which they called The Place of Truth) were not mere labourers but artisans and freemen whose food was delivered to the village by serfs, and whose houses were swept by slaves.

Tomb workers' tombs

They fashioned their own tombs, and decorated them not so much with scenes of the everyday as did the nobles but with the afterlife, borrowing from their experience in the pharaonic tombs. And over their tomb entrance they would construct a man-size pyramid. Several of the tombs, which like the village date from the XVIII to XX Dynasties, can be visited. A favourite is **Tomb 1 of Sennedjem** (contents in the Cairo Museum), a vaulted chamber down steep steps, with reliefs and paintings on religious themes including a fine funeral feast and a nicely observed cameo of a cat killing a snake under the sacred tree. Also worth visiting is **Tomb 3 of Peshedu** (in the burial chamber note Peshedu praying beneath the tree of regeneration) and **Tomb 217 of Ipy** (unusual for its scenes of everyday life).

Deir el Medina means the 'monastery of the town', for the workmen's village and the small **Ptolemaic temple** just north of it were occupied by monks during the early years of Christianity. Dedicated to Maat and to Hathor whose head adorns the pillars between the outer court and pronaos, this elegant temple is worth a look if you have the time, though other more considerable Ptolemaic temples await you upstream at Edfu, Kom Ombo and at Philae.

Tombs of the lesser royals

Beyond, in the **Valley of the Queens**, Biban el Harem, there are over 70 tombs of queens, princes and princesses of the

XVIII though mostly XIX and XX Dynasties. These dead, however, were not gods and so their tombs were not built on the same scale as those of the pharaohs. Nor did the friable limestone at this end of the Theban Mountain permit much carved decoration; the tombs are more often only painted, though many were left unfinished and have merely the appearance of caves.

Tombs 43, 44 and 55 belong to sons of Ramses III. A smallpox epidemic towards the end of Ramses' reign killed several of his sons, and in **Tomb 55 of Prince Amun-her-khopshef** in the *hall* at the bottom of the entrance steps it falls to the father to introduce his son to the gods. The *sarcophagus chamber* at the end of the corridor contains a mummiform sarcophagus and, in the far right corner, in a glass case, a six-month-old foetus. It is perhaps the foetus that makes this tomb so popular, though its real interest is the well preserved colours of the paintings, and you can have the benefit of this with fewer tour groups getting in the way by visiting **Tomb 44 of Prince Khaemweset**. **Tomb 52 of Queen Titi**, wife of one of the Ramessid pharaohs, is one of the few queens' tombs that can be visited without special permission, but the rooms are small and low, the painting faded.

The outstanding tomb in the valley is **Tomb 66 of Nefertari**, the wife of Ramses II celebrated in stone at Abu Simbel and elsewhere, but owing to damage caused by salt deposits it is closed except by special permission. There are several striking portraits of Nefertari; one, on the left wall of the antechamber, shows her beneath a canopy playing a board game, her wig covered with the skin of a vulture, the protective symbol of Maat. Above the door to the corridor leading to the burial chamber is Maat herself, wings extended in protection about the cartouche of the queen.

Medinet Habu

Though built by Ramses III of the XX Dynasty, the temple complex of Medinet Habu is in the great building tradition of the XIX Dynasty pharaohs and has many points of similarity with the Ramesseum and is better preserved. Not long after the reign of Ramses III, the power of the pharaohs declined and Egypt herself became divided once more. Medinet Habu **The last great** is the last major architectural work of the pharaonic period. **pharaonic temple** Though Egypt was threatened by foreign invaders early in Ramses' reign and a palace conspiracy against him and the succession of his son was uncovered, the greater part of his 30-odd years of rule seems to have passed in peace. A papyrus, probably part of the palace archives here, declares: 'I caused the woman of Egypt to walk freely wheresoever she would unmolested by others upon the road. I caused to sit idle the soldiers and the chariotry in my time, and the Sherden and the Kehek [Sardinian and Libyan prisoners, or their

297

children, who were recruited to the royal bodyguard] in their villages to lie at night full length without any dread'.

In nomen and praenomen, Ramses III imitated his great predecessor of the XIX Dynasty and the designers of Medinet Habu freely borrowed from the Ramesseum. They sometimes cut reliefs celebrating triumphs by Ramses III over Asian foes who had either long since perished on the field of history, or who since the reign of Ramses II lay beyond the enfeebled might of Egypt. This motif is echoed in the lofty **gatehouse**, a unique feature in Egyptian architecture, through which you enter the site. It was meant to resemble one of those Syrian fortresses which the Egyptian armies had met with so often in their Asiatic campaigns, but here the purpose was not military, the upper storeys serving as a resort where the pharaoh could amuse himself with the women of the harem. The carved heads of captured prisoners enlivened the view from the east window above, reached now by a staircase on the south (if this is closed, offer baksheesh). Scenes inside the *top apartment* show Ramses waited on by harem girls, their bodies bared of even their transparent dresses once suggested by a light wash of paint. To the left of the west window the pharaoh is stroking one of the girls under her chin.

Pharaonic erotica

To the north (right) of this gateway is an earlier **XVIII**

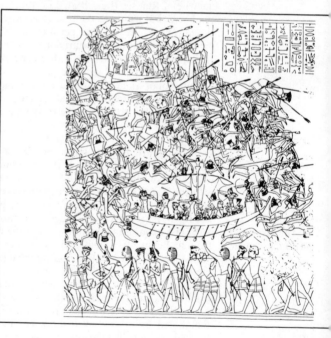

Dynasty temple built and partly decorated by Hatshepsut. Her image and name were obliterated, as elsewhere, by Tuthmosis III; Akhenaton scratched out all reference to Amun but Horemheb and Seti I replaced them; and Ramses III then decorated the north and south walls to suit his own purposes.

The primeval hill This temple stood on one of the most sacred spots in Egypt, the primeval hill which first rose clear of the receding waters of Chaos. An inscription identifies it as the burial place of the four primal pairs — Ocean and Matter, the Illimitable and the Boundless, Darkness and Obscurity, and the Hidden and Concealed ones — who preceded even the creator god, Re-Atum. While preserving this older temple, Ramses III levelled the ground behind to build his own mortuary temple dedicated to 'Amun united with Eternity', and a palace and other structures, set within gardens, surrounded by walls, and linked to the Nile by a canal.

Through the gateway and to the south (left) are the **mortuary chapels of the Divine Adorers**, princesses who were the chief priestesses of Amun at Thebes. The chapels are late additions, dating from the XXIII through the XXVI Dynasties.

Straight ahead (to the west) is the **First Pylon of Ramses' mortuary temple**. The pylon would have almost the same

Ramses III repelling the invasion of the Sea Peoples as depicted on the outer north wall of Medinet Habu

dimensions as that at the Temple of Luxor except that it has lost its cornice. A stairway at the north end leads to the top for an excellent *view* across the temple towards the Theban Mountain. The pylons, columns and chambers are smaller as you gaze westwards; the platforms at each stage of the temple are higher; an architectural funnel pointing towards the final sanctuary — as at Karnak, and with Egyptian temples generally. The *reliefs* on the pylon towers depict campaigns against the Nubians and Syrians, campaigns never fought by Ramses III and probably copied from the Ramesseum.

Battle with the Sea Peoples But in the eighth year of his reign, Ramses III was in desperate struggle with the Sea Peoples, a coalition of northerners including Sardinians, Cretans, Philistines and others, not all of whom have been identified, who by sea and by ox-carts carrying their women and children overland were bent on permanent settlement in the rich Delta pasturelands. One group, whom the Egyptians called the Danu, the Danaoi of the *Iliad*, here emerged into history for the first time. The invasion is recorded in dramatic detail by **reliefs along the north wall** of the mortuary temple (walk round to it before passing through the pylon) and should not be missed. It is the only Egyptian relief portraying a sea battle. An inscription graphically describes the outcome: 'A net was prepared for them to ensnare them, those who entered into the rivermouths being confined and fallen within it, pinioned in their places, butchered and their corpses hacked up'. In a single sweeping picture the artist has combined the various phases of the engagement: the Egyptians stand on their decks in steady order; an opposing vessel is held fast with grappling irons, the enemy in confusion, many of them falling into the water; while from the shore Ramses standing upon the heads of captives joins with his archers in shooting volleys of arrows at the invaders. In places, deep grooves have been cut into the wall by ancient visitors seeking to obtain stone dust from this sacred place for use in magical charms.

The **First Court** was the scene of ceremonies and entertainments which would have included sword fights and wrestling. The *east wall* celebrates Ramses' victory in his eleventh year against the Libyans: trophies of enemy hands and genitals are counted by scribes and soldiers are rewarded for their valour. The pharaoh himself might have distributed rewards from the window in the south wall, decorated on either side with reliefs of prisoners' heads. This was the facade of the **royal palace**; its central hall surrounded by six columns was for holding audiences; the private apartments were on the south side.

The mortuary temple continued in use for only 200 years, though the smaller temple of Hatshepsut remained a place of worship right through Ptolemaic times. In the Ptolemaic and Roman periods, the First Court was filled with houses and a monastery, the **Second Court** with the principal church of what was now a town of some size. *Traces of the church* can still be seen, for example the base of an octagonal font on the south side. Osiris figures against the pillars along the east and west sides were removed in building the church, and the central pillar on the north side was removed to make way for the apse. A few of the Osiris figures remain at the north end. Along the *west colonnade*, which is also the facade of the temple proper, the colours on the reliefs are especially bright. In the central register on either side of the doorway, Ramses is shown variously with Atum and Mont entering the temple; being crowned in the presence of the Theban triad; and being purified before receiving the emblems of his rank from the gods of Heliopolis. In the lower register on either side, Ramses' name is written in alternation with figures of his sons. None of their names, however, is inscribed as there appears to have been some uncertainty over the succession. On the architrave over the doorway is a brightly painted winged solar disc.

Beyond is the **First Hypostyle Hall**, roofless now but once with a raised ceiling over the central aisle as at the Ramesseum and Karnak. To the right are a series of *sanctuaries*, the first for the cult of the living pharaoh. To the left are *treasure chambers*, still with their original roofs. The central chamber of these shows the weighing of gold on its south wall; sacks of gold on the west wall; and precious stones on the east wall. Off to the left of the **Second Hypostyle Hall** is the *funerary chamber* of Ramses III with Thoth represented on the south wall inscribing the pharaoh's name on the sacred tree of Heliopolis. In the **Third Hypostyle Hall**, on either side of the central aisle, are statues of Ramses with Maat and with

Thoth. At the west end of this hall are three *sanctuaries*; to the right, that of Mut; to the left, Khonsu; between them, the sanctuary of Amun, once finished with electrum, its doorway of gold, the doors themselves of copper inlaid with precious stones. The granite pedestal, now to one side of the sanctuary but originally at its centre, supported Amun's sacred boat.

You should now walk back through the temple to the First Pylon and turn to the right to view the reliefs along the *outer south wall*. Above, Ramses is shown hunting various desert animals; below, most vividly, he is shown impaling with his hunting spear writhing bulls in a marsh.

The Works of Amenophis III

The remaining sights on the west bank of the Nile are associated with Amenophis III (XVIII Dyn) who ruled over Egypt at the height of her prosperity. He began the penchant for the grandiose, and though it later served pharaonic bombast, in the works of Amenophis there is always a more tolerable touch of grandeur and opulence. It is unlikely that he was ever personally engaged in any military exploits, though some inscriptions make this claim by way of convention; rather he comes across as a man who enjoyed life to the full, and had the means to enjoy it more fully than any other man of his times. A smile of contentment plays upon his lips as he sits with Queen Tiy in the colossal group at the Cairo Museum; a stela found at Amarna and now at the British Museum shows him in later years, his weary frame and jaded expression suggesting that he had known pleasures beyond even his ability to enjoy them.

Though the ancient Egyptians built their temples of stone, their homes and even their royal palaces were built merely of mud brick and so have barely survived the millenia. **Amenophis' palace** lies about a kilometre south of Medinet Habu. Though badly ruined and rarely visited, it is one of the few royal residences in Egypt of which substantial portions remain. The palace contained living and state apartments for Amenophis, a separate residence for Tiy, a large festal hall built for the pharaoh's jubilee and quarters for courtiers and for the harem. When excavated, traces of plastered walls were found, bearing lovely paintings of birds and water plants prefiguring the art of Akhenaton. These have now disappeared.

House of Joy   Though Tiy clearly enjoyed her husband's love and confidence, and was often represented as his equal in size, Amenophis did not deny himself the delights of an extensive harem. The dowry of a Hittite princess whom Amenophis married as a secondary queen included 317 damsels for most of the other nights of the year. Another text shows that having already married the sister of a Babylonian king, he was now clamouring for the king's daughter as well. And in his old age Amenophis is known to have married one of his own daughters by Tiy. Little wonder he called his palace the 'House of Joy'.

To the east of his palace Amenophis shared his bounty by digging for Tiy an enormous **lake**, 370 metres broad by 1940 metres in length, whereon the imperial couple might sail in the royal barge named 'Aton Gleams' — again suggesting that in spite of his indulgence Amenophis played some role, insensible though he might have been of the effect, in raising his son to Aton and bringing religious revolution to Egypt. (See Tomb 46 of Yuya and Tuyu in the Valley of the Kings.) Amenophis claimed, improbably, that the lake was dug in 15 days, though signs of haste are apparent in the mounds of excavated earth still lying along its western boundary.

Amenophis also built a *mortuary temple* which has now vanished beneath ploughed fields between the Ramesseum and Medinet Habu. Responsibility for its principal destruction lies with Merneptah, possible pharaoh of the Exodus, who used it as a quarry for building his own temple immediately to the north. All that remains are the two famous **Colossi of Memnon** which once guarded its outer gates. The

The vaulted ceiling in the tomb chamber of Ramses VI in the Valley of the Kings, showing the goddess Nut

Colossi are along the road leading back to the new village of Gurna and are visible from some distance. They are in fact gigantic statues of the enthroned Amenophis himself, rising 19.5 metres from the plain. At one time they wore the royal crown and were even higher. Both are damaged and are lacking their faces; the one on the right (north) broke at the waist during an earthquake in AD 27 and was later crudely repaired, the top having been sawn into blocks. Cocteau described them as victims of rainless thunder storms: 'Crucified, sitting against great crosses; the lightning has left nothing untouched except their legs'.

If it was lightning that crucified them, it was Greek and Roman tourists who cut graffiti into the legs of the figure on the right. The inscriptions reach as high as a man can stretch and were usually cut by visiting notables, including eight Roman governors. The Colossi had early on been accorded the wonder due to the divine, perhaps because of their imposing size, perhaps because Amenophis was recognised as both pharaoh and god. But their cult status was too elaborate: a commoner, Amenophis, son of Hapu, was architect of his pharaoh's mortuary temple and raised the Colossi. The vast undertaking impressed both king and public, and like Imhotep at Saqqara, he was divinised. In Ptolemaic times the Colossi this son of Hapu erected and the wise sayings attributed to him attracted followers throughout the Graeco-Roman world. All memory of Amenophis III was forgotten, and the Greeks decided the statues were of Memnon, son of Tithonus, a legendary king of Egypt, and Eos, the Dawn, who went to fight in defence of Troy and was slain by Achilles.

The singing Colossus

But it was the north Colossus that eventually attracted so much curiosity, for after it was shattered by the earthquake it would sometimes emit a musical note as the sun rose over the eastern mountains. The emperor Hadrian came in AD 130 with his wife and a large retinue, and camped for several nights at its feet to hear the phenomenon. He was at last rewarded with three performances on a single morning and was declared to have been exceptionally favoured by the gods. The association with Memnon was expanded to account for the sound: fallen at Troy, he now greeted his mother Eos with a sweet and plaintive sound when she appeared at dawn, and she in turn wept tears of dew upon her beloved child. Nowadays it is thought that the rapid change in temperature as the sun rose caused splittings off of quartzite particles which resonated within the fractures. Certainly, once the Colossus was repaired in AD 199, it cried out no more.

The last time I visited the Colossi I climbed upon the pedestal of the northern one to get a closer look at the inscriptions. As I stood knee high to the diminutive figures of Amenophis' mother Mutemuia on the left and Queen Tiy on the right, a voice began to sing. Hadrian may have heard a few squeaks, but this was a beautiful and passionate love song, and I recognised the voice of Oum Khalsoum, until her death Egypt's greatest singer. The appearance from around the other side of a young Egyptian with a portable radio revealed the source of this singing Memnon. After days of wandering around the tombs and temples of the necropolis, I realised that with the possible exception of Hatshepsut's temple at Deir el Bahri, I would rather hear that marvellous voice than see all the stones of Thebes.

PRACTICAL INFORMATION

There is some no-star **accommodation** on the west bank; **Habu**, near the entrance to Medinet Habu; **Sheikh Ali** (known also as the Mersam Hotel), opposite the Department of Antiquities at the intersection behind the Colossi of Memnon; the **Memnon Hotel**, across the road from the Colossi themselves; the **Abul Kasem Hotel**, near the Temple of Seti I; and the **Wadi el Malouk Hotel** (Tel: 382798), which is reached by heading east from the Abul Kasem Hotel and over the canal, then turning right (south). There are good rural views over the Theban plain from its rooftop restaurant. All these hotels are small and very simple. Inspect your room first; often they are better on the upper storey.

You can also **hire bicycles** at the Abul Kasem Hotel.

Sites on the west bank are open from 5am to 4pm in winter, 6pm in summer. It is often said that you should start early to avoid the crowds. But the crowds all have the same idea. My advice is to start late. **Tickets** are required for the major sites and must be purchased in advance from the ticket kiosk at the tourist landing on the west bank. Fees are:

Mortuary Temple of Seti I	LE1
Valley of the Kings (Biban el Muluk)	LE5
Mortuary Temple of Hatshepsut (Deir el Bahri)	LE2
Tombs of the Nobles (Sheikh Abdul Gurna) — there are 4 areas per area	LE1
Mortuary Temple of Ramses II (Ramesseum)	LE1
Deir el Medina (3 tombs)	LE1
Valley of the Queens (Biban el Harem)	LE1
Mortuary Temple of Ramses II (Medinet Habu)	LE2

Photographs may be taken in tombs for LE10 per tomb. Like site tickets, photo tickets must be purchased in advance at the west bank kiosk. Site and photo tickets are date-stamped and good only on the day of purchase.

Note: This may be your last chance to visit a real royal tomb. They are being so damaged by tourism that reproduction tombs may soon be built in the Valley of the Kings and the Valley of the Queens, those of Tutankhamun, Tuthmosis III and Nefertari being the first to swallow up the public— perhaps as early as 1993.

If you are with a tour, you will probably board the **tourist ferry** in front of the Winter Place or Savoy. However, just by the Temple of Luxor is the more frequent **people ferry** (as the locals call it, carefully distinguishing themselves from mere tourists). The tourist ferry costs LE2, the people's ferry 25PT.

The people ferry will land you a couple of hundred metres south of the tourist landing and ticket kiosk, but smack admidst the taxi drivers and donkey boys. You negotiate a price (see *Practical Information*, under *Information*, at the end of the *Luxor* chapter), travel to the kiosk to buy your tickets, and you are off.

The number of people that can fit in a **taxi** is 5 to 7 and the fare per full 8-hour day therefore varies accordingly. Also a taxi can be hired as private, ie it sticks with you throughout the day, or not private, ie the driver zooms off in search of passing custom while you are down a tomb or whatever and catches you up when you need him. You can imagine the variations in rates all this produces. However, for a private taxi, expect to pay LE20 for half a day (4 hours); for a non-private taxi, LE10.

Also you can try your luck on odd journeys, hiring a taxi to the Valley of the Kings, walking over the ridge to Deir el Bahri, catching a taxi from there to somewhere else.

Donkeys cost about LE10 for the whole day, to all the sites. They are uncomfortable and, unless you are possessed by some masochistic nostalgia for pre-internal combustion engine forms of transport, should be avoided. In any case, donkey boys can be bastards: they have a habit of agreeing to a price, then increasing it as you trot along, and tossing you off the donkey if you do not give in. My first time at the necropolis I was de-donkeyed 3 times enroute to the Valley of the Kings, finally agreed to an extortionate price, and when I got back to the Nile leapt onto the ferry and left the donkey boy screaming on the west bank for his money. Possibly he is now the taxi driver who gives me such a hard time.

Whether by donkey or taxi, always agree clearly on the price beforehand and do not pay a single piastre until the boy or driver has fulfilled his side of the bargain.

Bicycles, hired for about LE3 per day in Luxor (or can be hired on the west bank at the Abul Kasem Hotel; see above — but check first), are the best way to get around — if you are fit. As you peddle along past tombs and temples you are surprisingly cool and sweatless in the dry air (though beware of sunstroke); the instant you stop the sweat pours off you in buckets. Bring water.

The one disadvantage of a bicycle (apart from heart attacks and sunstroke) is not being able to **walk** from the Valley of the Kings to Deir el Bahri — this is highly recommended.

Refreshments and **toilets** are found at the resthouses at the Valley of the Kings, near the Ramesseum and at Medinet Habu. Soft drinks are sold here and there, eg at Deir el Bahri.

If you are **shopping** for souvenirs there are any number of touts at the landing stage willing to oblige, with scarabs, mummified ibises, their grandmother's big toe and God knows what else. If you really must buy this rubbish (all phoney), offer no more than one-tenth the asking price: it will be accepted with alacrity. However, I admit to being very pleased with the purchase of a reproduction ancient oil lamp. An original was used to form a mould from which copies were made; and as this was how originals were made in ancient times, I choose to regard mine as an original too, if rather late off the production line. For an interesting selection of alabaster bowls, figurines, etc, there are **workshops** (eg by the Abul Kasem Hotel and elsewhere) where you can watch these things being made (it can take 5 days to make an alabaster bowl) — the prices are, yes, one-tenth of those asked by the hawkers at the landing stage. The people here are continuing in the line of their ancient forefathers, churning out artefacts which are in a sense no less authentic. You can imagine pharaonic craftsmen working with a bit more belief, perhaps, but no less a mercenary spirit. Notice also on some of the houses of old Gurna, as elsewhere in Egypt, the paintings depicting visits to Mecca, successors to paintings in the noble tombs below.

An **abbreviated itinerary** should include, at the very least, the Valley of the Kings and Hatshepsut's mortuary temple at Deir el Bahri.

The Ramesseum is more popular (associations with Ramses II and Shelley) but Medinet Habu, a near copy and more complete, is more interesting. If not going to Abydos, go to the Temple of Seti I here.

A RIVER JOURNEY

It is godly to cruise the Nile through Egypt. Before the roads and the railways there was only this river and as the pharaohs and the hoi polloi sailed upon it and watched their world unroll it cannot have helped making a special impression on them all. The echoing silence of the deserts spoke of the void beyond the grave. But here along the river was the rhythm of bright green fields perpetually tender, small brown figures absorbed in their patch, fishermen like spikey water insects poling through the reeds. A flap of egret wings as you glide by, distant, breeze-blown, upon the artery of life itself. It is like the most beautiful murals in the ancient tombs, too sweet not to carry into eternity.

Ptolemaic tentacle
Like a string of citadels extending Alexandrian power towards Nubia, the Ptolemies built temples along the Nile at Esna, Edfu and Kom Ombo. Cruise boats ply between Luxor and Aswan throughout the year and offer an agreeable way of enjoying the lush valley scenery and visiting the temples enroute. The experience can only be improved, for the more adventurous, by hiring a felucca and entrusting yourself to the power of the current and the winds.

Esna

A short walk up from the quayside through the constricting streets of Esna (54 km from Luxor) and beside an awning-shaded market is the temple, squatting in a pit. It had been covered over with houses; now it is partly laid bare behind railings and you descend a staircase into the excavations. Ptolemy VI rebuilt this **Temple of Khnum**, the god who fashioned man on his potter's wheel, over the ruins of earlier structures, but almost all that remains to see is the later *hypostyle hall* begun by the Emperor Claudius in the 1st C AD. The carvings within are of a poor standard, but the roof is intact and supported by 24 columns with 16 different capitals, bearing their original colours well. It is these you come to see. It is best to stand here, slowly revolving, looking upwards

Forest of columns
at the myriad palm and composite plant capitals, arranged without order or symmetry, but with the most pleasing effect, as though you were standing amongst trees, admiring the subtle and powerful architecture of a forest.

In the forecourt of the temple there are several blocks from an early Christian church, recalling a time when Esna was an important centre of Christian activity. Notice the *lion-headed font* carved from an ancient block bearing fine hieroglyphics on the reverse. The Emperor Decius (reigned 249–51) decreed that all Christians should sacrifice to the Roman gods or suffer death — his is the last cartouche carved on the temple walls, but he is commemorated too in a sense by **Deir Manaos**

An almeh, or 'learned woman'

wa al-Shuhada 6 km southwest of town, the Monastery of the Three Thousand Six Hundred Martyrs, whose 10th C church is one of the most beautiful in Upper Egypt.

Esna was once a terminus for caravans picking their way from oasis to oasis across the desert from the Sudan, but this trade virtually expired with the passing of the last century. It remains though a merchant town and weaving centre, and can be interesting to wander about.

It is worth walking south a bit through the **covered market street**, where lengths of fabric are sold or made up into clothing, and then back along it (north), passing the temple, into a **quarter of old houses** with fine brickwork and mashrabiyya screens. Where the street opens up into a little square, turn right towards the Nile and look in on the Coptic church. Along the corniche, north of the church, are more fine old houses. A **barrage** crosses the Nile here, built in 1906; it is busy with trucks and carts trundling from one side of the river to the other, and in the morning with barges and cruise boats waiting to pass through its locks. Back at the **stone quay** along that part of the corniche nearest the temple, notice the carved cartouches of the Emperor Marcus Aurelius.

It was perhaps here that Flaubert landed in 1850, though his interest was not antiquarian: by an edict of Mohammed Ali's in 1834 prohibiting prostitution and female dancing in Cairo, the *almehs* (literally 'learned women') of Egypt had concentrated in Qena, Esna and Aswan. Flaubert entertained a mystique about prostitution: 'A meeting place of so many elements — lust, bitterness, complete absence of human contact, muscular frenzy, the clink of gold — that to peer into it deeply makes one reel. One learns so many things in a brothel, and feels such sadness, and dreams so longingly of love!'

The learned women of Esna

At Esna he was propositioned aboard his boat by an *almeh* followed by her pet sheep, its wool spotted with yellow henna. He went with her to the house of Kuchuk Hanem, 'a tall, splendid creature, lighter in colouring than an Arab; she comes from Damascus; her skin, particularly on her body, is slightly coffee-coloured. When she bends, her flesh ripples into bronze ridges. Her eyes are dark and enormous, her eyebrows thick, her nostrils open and wide; heavy shoulders, full, apple-shaped breasts'. She danced the Bee, which required that the musicians be blindfolded, and slowly removed her clothes. 'When it was time to leave I didn't leave. I sucked her furiously — her body was covered with sweat — she was tired after dancing — she was cold — I covered her with my pelisse, and she fell asleep with her fingers in mine. As for me, I scarcely shut my eyes. Watching that beautiful creature asleep (she snored), my night was one long, infinitely intense reverie — that was why I stayed. I thought of my nights in Paris brothels — a whole series of old memories came back — and I thought of her, of her dance, of her voice as she sang songs that for me were without meaning and even without distinguishable words. That continued all night. At three o'clock I got up to piss in the street — the stars were shining ... As for the *coups*, they were good — the third especially was ferocious, and the last tender — we told each other many sweet things — towards the end there was something sad and loving in the way we embraced' (*Flaubert in Egypt: A Sensibility on Tour*).

Back in France, while he was writing *Madame Bovary*, he wrote to Louise Colet, his jealous mistress: 'You tell me that Kuchuk's bedbugs degrade her in your eyes; for me they were the most enchanting touch of all. Their nauseating odour mingled with the scent of her skin, which was dripping with sandalwood oil. I want a touch of bitterness in everything —

always a jeer in the midst of our triumphs, desolation even in the midst of enthusiasm'. And he reminded Louise that 'you and I are thinking of her, but she is certainly not thinking of us. We are weaving an aesthetic around her, whereas this particular very interesting tourist who was vouchsafed the honours of her couch has vanished from her memory completely, like many others. Ah! Travelling makes one modest — you see what a tiny place you occupy in the world'.

Continuing Upriver to Edfu

30 km south of Esna on the east bank of the Nile, right on the water's edge, is **El Kab**, the ancient Nekhab, important from Pre-Dynastic through Ptolemaic times. A massive mud brick *enclosure wall* surrounds the ruins, 11.5 metres thick and pierced by gates approached by ramps on the north, east and south. Of the two temples here, the finest is the small *Temple of Nekhbet*, the work of Amenophis II and later Ramses II, and next to it, also within an inner enclosure, a *Temple of Thoth* built by Tuthmosis III. Nekhbet was the white vulture goddess, the 'mistress of the valley' and cult goddess of Upper Egypt. The importance of the site as a national shrine is evidenced by the fact that the innermost mud brick wall was rebuilt at least ten times.

On the west bank of the Nile, equidistant from Luxor and Aswan (105 km), **Edfu** is spread upon the mound of an ancient city. The **Temple of Horus** is on the western outskirts of the present town, at a spot where Horus and Seth met in titanic combat for the world (see Philae). The temple, the second largest in Egypt after Karnak, is suitably monumental and the best preserved in Egypt. Construction began under Ptolemy III Euergetes and it was completed, down to its decorations, by the mid-1st C BC. It is therefore hardly a century or two older than the many technically superior imperial ruins in Rome. But you forget this and applaud the Ptolemies' phoney archaic style, for this is pure theatre. Remembering Justinian's boast that with Hagia Sophia he had surpassed Solomon's temple, at Edfu despite a mouthful of popcorn you cry out, 'Cecil B DeMille, they have outdone you!'

Hollywood spectacular

On the *pylon towers* Neos Dionysos, in New Kingdom gear, snicker-snacks amongst the Bandersnatch, while in the *colonnaded court*, against the elaborate floral columns of the pronaos, is the Jabberwock itself — one of a pair of granite falcon-Horuses which stood on either side of the entrance (the other, headless, has keeled over in the dust). You walk through a series of ever smaller, ever darker halls and chambers to the *sanctuary* of the god, weirdly illuminated through three small apertures in the ceiling by a dim green Nilotic light. The reliefs on the next to lowest row on the right-hand wall within correspond to those at Dendera, in this case showing Philopator entering the sanctuary and worshipping

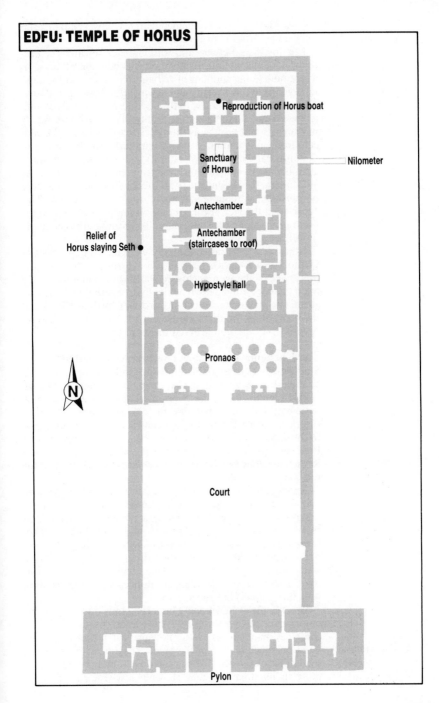

EDFU: TEMPLE OF HORUS

Reproduction of Horus boat

Sanctuary of Horus

Nilometer

Antechamber

Antechamber (staircases to roof)

Relief of Horus slaying Seth

Hypostyle hall

Pronaos

N

Court

Pylon

Horus, Hathor and his deified parents. His pendant arms indicate an attitude of reverence.

Leaving the sanctuary and walking back towards the pronaos, you enter an antechamber, off which, to the left (east), is a vestibule (a fair amount of red and blue paint on the capitals) giving on to (north) an elegant little *New Year Chapel* decorated on the ceiling with the goddess Nut, pale green with a blue skirt of stars. She is beautifully shaped, with unusually fine breasts and profile, as though here there is a Greek concern for beauty and not just conventional form. Returning to the antechamber you pass (south) to a second, outer antechamber with a staircase on either side leading to the roof. As at Dendera, the residing deity required at least an annual dose of sunshine, a reimpregnation of soul from the sun. This occasioned the New Year procession up to the roof, and the decorations along the staircase walls reproduce the ceremony in full detail.

Other rites celebrated annually were the conjugal visit of Hathor (see Dendera); the triumph of Horus over Seth (see the inner face of the west enclosure wall); the coronation in the main court of a live falcon as the living symbol of Horus on earth; and the re-enactment of the divine birth of Horus and the pharaoh at the Birth House outside the pylon (with episodes of the ceremony carved on its walls).

The Changing Landscape Towards Kom Ombo

Southwards beyond Edfu the palms and cultivation on the east bank give way to the Arabian Desert and at **Silsileh** (145 km from Luxor) the Nile passes through a defile, now with only hills on either side but thought once to mark a cataract. The rock bed of Egypt changes here from limestone to the harder sandstone used in almost all New Kingdom and Ptolemaic temple building. During the reign of Ramses II the Silsileh quarries were worked by no fewer than 3000 men for the Ramesseum alone.

Above Silsileh the mountains again recede from the river and the desert is kept at bay by canals. Irrigation and the fallahin bring harvests of cane and corn to the fields. The reclaimed land on the east bank around **Kom Ombo** (164 km from Luxor, 46 km from Aswan) supports a large Nubian population displaced from their homeland by the rising waters of Lake Nasser. The village is on the Luxor–Aswan road; nearby is a sugar refinery supplied by barges landing near the temple 4 km to the west.

The **Temple of Sobek and Horoeris** stands on a low promontory overlooking the Nile. Its elevation, its seclusion, the combination of sun and water flowing past as though in slow but determined search for the Mediterranean, at last suggests something of Greece. It has ruined well, and there is something in its stones of that Hellenic response to light, the

A suggestion of Greece

312

The Jabberwock at Edfu

uncompromising noonday glare, the soft farewell to the setting sun without fear of night.

The usual Ptolemaic (and Roman) appeasement of the fossilised Egyptian preisthood is apparent, however, as soon as you abandon mood for detail — even Marcus Aurelius must stoically appear on an outer corridor wall in pharaonic garb offering a pectoral to Sennuphis, divine wife of Haroeris. The naos was begun by Ptolemy VI Philometor; the hypostyle hall and pronaos were added by Neos Dionysos; and Augustus added the court, the outer enclosure wall and the now destroyed pylon. It is a symmetrically twin temple, the left side dedicated to falcon-headed *Horoeris* (the older Horus), the right to *Sobek*, the crocodile god. The two parts of the temple are only physically divided, however, at the two sanctuaries.

Two temples in one

The temple faces more or less west, towards the Nile. You approach from the south, past a massive ruined *Gateway* built by Neos Dionysos. In front of you, between an ancient brick wall and the outer temple wall, is a small *chapel of Hathor*, the gift of a wealthy Roman woman. Through its gratings you can see sarcophagi and the piled up mummies of crocodiles — not belonging here, merely tossed in after being dug up in a nearby cemetery.

Only a few courses of the temple *pylon* remain, and the stumps of the 16 columns once surrounding the *court* — at its centre is the stone altar used in sacrifices. Except for the three centre columns framing the dual passageways leading to the twin sanctuaries, the *pronaos* facade has lost the upper parts of its columns where they rise above the screen. But there is no loss of effect. The surviving columns burst in floral capitals, and above them, across the remaining section of the cavetto cornice, are two winged discs emphasising again the duality of the divine presence here. Within the pronaos the ceiling is decorated with flying vultures and the supporting capitals proclaim the unity of Upper and Lower Egypt, some the lily, some papyrus — and one eccentrically a palm. On this side of the screen are *reliefs* of various Ptolemaic pharaohs receiving the blessings of Egypt's high gods and the double crown of the Delta and the valley.

In the hypostyle hall beyond, and in the three rising antechambers after that, are more *reliefs*. One, between the doors into the sanctuaries, shows Ptolemy Philometor and his sister-wife before Sobek, Haroeris and Khonsu who inscribes the pharaoh's name on a palm stalk, the equivalent of St Peter confirming entry into heaven. Philometor wears a full Macedonian cloak, a rare exception to the traditional guise. Little is left of the *sanctuaries*, but they are all the more revealing for that. Between them, at a lower level, is a crypt which communicates with a chapel to the east. The crypt is now exposed but was once covered with a sliding slab. It is not

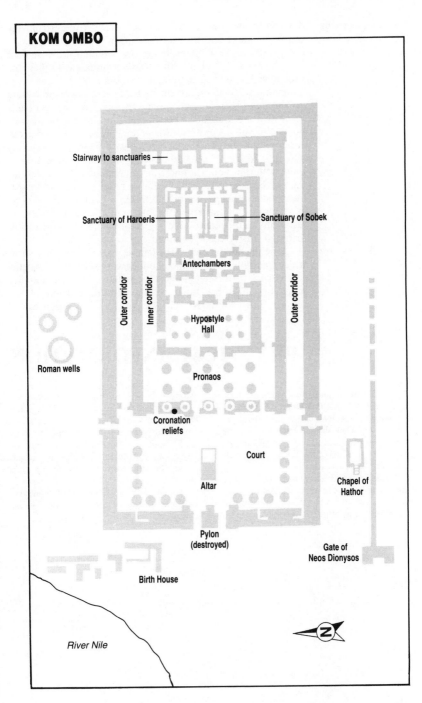

KOM OMBO

Stairway to sanctuaries

Sanctuary of Haroeris — — Sanctuary of Sobek

Antechambers

Outer corridor

Inner corridor

Outer corridor

Hypostyle Hall

Roman wells

Pronaos

Coronation reliefs

Court

Altar

Chapel of Hathor

Pylon (destroyed)

Gate of Neos Dionysos

Birth House

River Nile

N

difficult to imagine someone creeping down there from the chapel to make spectral noises at appropriate moments — the priests to fool pharaoh, or one of pharaoh's men to fool the priests? Probably the priests fooling each other, the Ptolemies having the last laugh.

Beyond the rear wall of the naos are seven *chapels* leading off the *inner corridor*. A stairway in the centre chapel leads upwards for a view over the temple. The chapels are at various stages of decoration. An *outer corridor*, entered from either end of the court, is decorated with Roman reliefs. It is here, just to the left of dead centre along the north section of outer wall that you will find Marcus Aurelius. To the left, in the northeast corner, is a display in relief of medical instruments; suction cups, scalpels, retractors, scales, lances, bone saws, chisels for surgery within the skull, dental tools, etc — testimony to the remarkable degree of medical sophistication in Egypt nearly 2000 years ago.

Along the north flank of the temple are two *Roman wells* in which, perhaps, the sacred crocodiles were kept. At the northeast corner of the temple is what is left of the *birth house*, much of which has fallen, along with its portion of the terrace, down to the Nile. It is Egypt reclaiming her own.

PRACTICAL INFORMATION

The only **accommodation** enroute is at Edfu, at the **El Medina Hotel** off the main square, very much a no-star place, without hot water. You should base yourself in Luxor or Aswan. See the *Practical Information* sections of the *Luxor* and *Aswan* chapters for **travel** details.

Esna, Edfu and Kom Ombo (LE1 fee at each) can be seen in a day if you hire a car with driver at either base, arriving at evening at the other. If relying on train, share taxi or local bus, count on seeing only two temples enroute, returning to the third from your new base — though you may find you are able to manage all 3.

El Kab can be reached by road, or by taking a train to El Mahamid, 2.5 km from the site. Most cruises do not stop here.

Faced with an **abbreviated itinerary**, Edfu is probably the place you would most kick yourself for missing.

ASWAN

Aswan (210 km from Luxor, 886 km from Cairo) is where the valley closes upon the river, no more buffer of cultivation on either side, instead a universe of desert sundered by the pulsing Nile flowing out of Africa. At this point the Nile is only 87 metres above sea level, so low a height for so massive a river, you would think it would disdain the 87-metre inducement to go farther, but there is a continent of water behind, urging it on through the cataract above Aswan, and the current is strong. The layer of sandstone covering Upper Egypt from Edfu southwards is ruptured here by the thrust of underlying granite which the river has hewn into the rocks and islands of the First Cataract. Even before construction of the British dam at the turn of the century and the giant hydroelectric dam in the 1960s, this is where traffic on the Nile stopped. Camels transported cargoes round the rocks while lightened boats took their chances through the granite passage. The more intrepid passenger might stay aboard: 'We see

Racing the rapids   the whole boat slope down bodily under our feet. We feel the leap — the dead fall — the staggering rush forward. Instantly the waves are foaming and boiling up on all sides, flooding the lower deck, and covering the upper deck with spray. The men ship their oars, leaving all to helm and

Approaching the Old Cataract Hotel on a dying breeze

317

current; and, despite the hoarse tumult, we distinctly hear those oars scrape the rocks on either side' (Amelia Edwards).

Frontier Outpost

Aswan is where Egypt ends. Beyond lie Nubia and the Sudan, and the traditional routes of invasion and trade. The ancient Egyptians garrisoned the 500-kilometre stretch of river to the Third Cataract, and the fleet patrolled the Nile between the First Cataract and the Second at Wadi Halfa. An uprising or an attack on a caravan, and signal fires relayed the summons for help to Aswan. Two thousand years and more later, Aswan marked the southernmost margin of the Roman world, and when Juvenal fell into disfavour at Rome for writing satirical verses against the emperor's court, it was to Aswan that he was posted, to guard the empire he had mocked. It is the High Dam that accounts for the modern military presence. Its breach would send a tidal wave down the whole length of the Nile Valley and inundate half of Cairo. But that presence and the object of its protection lie out of sight some kilometres south of the town, which for all of its growth and the influx of workers in recent years retains an atmosphere of remoteness and tranquillity.

Over the centuries the Tropic of Cancer has shifted slightly to the south, but in classical times it fell across Aswan, proved by a famous well into which the sun's rays plunged perpendicularly at midday during the summer solstice, leaving no shadow. Hearing of this, Eratosthenes (276–196 BC) of the Mouseion at Alexandria concluded that the earth was round and had a diameter of 12,560 km — an error of only 80 km. A triumph of constructive thought inspired by a place whose genius lies in the inducement to idle contentment. Fol-

Idle contentment lowing the day's fierce sun and dry desert heat, there is the beauty at evening of sand, sky and water fading imperceptibly through deepening violet, a lift of breeze on the Nile, a movement of palms, a flight of hoopoes, and the graceful glide of swallow-tailed feluccas. The final pleasure is to know that when morning comes at Aswan there is so little to do. Those who insist on doing it can easily do it all in a couple of days. Those who want to do nothing will want to stay far longer.

Long favoured as a winter resort with daytime temperatures around 23° to 30°C, the increase and changing style of tourism in Egypt has led greater numbers of travellers to challenge the summer heat which usually ranges from 38° to 42°C during the day, though it can climb much higher. Air conditioning and a siesta during early afternoon, and the low humidity, make even the hottest July and August days bearable.

Orientation

The **station** is at the north end of the town, some distance back from the river. The temperature, often 10°C higher at Aswan

318

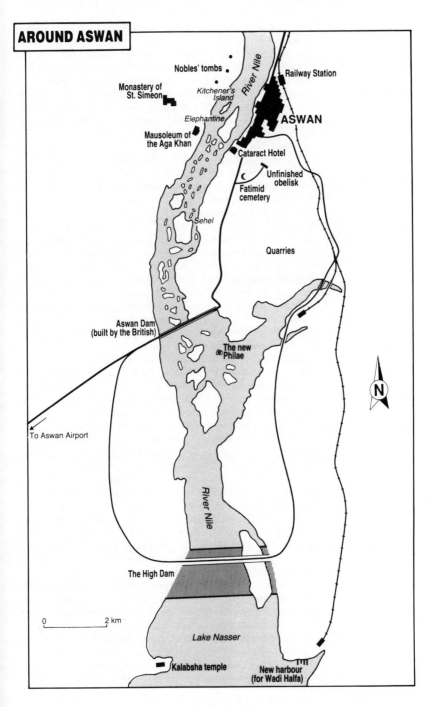

AROUND ASWAN

Nobles' tombs

River Nile

Railway Station

Monastery of St. Simeon

Kitchener's Island

ASWAN

Elephantine

Mausoleum of the Aga Khan

Cataract Hotel

Unfinished obelisk

Fatimid cemetery

Sehel

Quarries

Aswan Dam (built by the British)

The new Philae

N

To Aswan Airport

River Nile

The High Dam

0   2 km

Lake Nasser

Kalabsha temple

New harbour (for Wadi Halfa)

319

than in Cairo, hits you as you step off the train, and darker skins, lighter builds, introduce you to the tropics. You may also notice Nubian spoken, if not here then when you are floating on a felucca and hear the boatmen calling to one another. A taxi, or better yet a carriage, will take you to your hotel and provide you with your first glimpse of the setting. As you emerge onto the corniche, you see a bare hill rising from the opposite bank and cut into its face the small dark openings of the ancient **tombs** of Aswan's governors and princes.

The facades at this end of the **corniche** are new and concrete, but the sweep of the Nile is impressive. The older town lies behind. A few streets back, running parallel with the corniche, is the best **bazaar** outside Cairo, alive with Arabs and Nubians and blacks trading in gum, spices, ivory, ebony and other exotic prizes out of Africa, as well as local weaves and **African bazaar** manufactured goods. Although Aswan is not the crossroads of trade it once was, and the days of the caravans are gone, the flavour remains and the imagination recalls magnificently shawled and turbaned guards, huge scimitars dangling at their sides, accompanying a hundred camels laden with elephant tusks out of Ethiopia, driving the dust before them in clouds. The picturesque inner town deserves exploration, especially at evening. There are a few simple but good restaurants, and a large Coptic church.

In ancient times this area on the east bank was known as Syene and famous for its nearby quarries of pink granite, but it was always secondary to the main commercial and administrative settlement of Yebu, which stood at the southern end of the long palm-covered island on your right. Yebu was Egyptian for elephant, and the island today bears the Greek translation, **Elephantine**. Perhaps in the earliest millenia of their history, before the desert had crept down to the Nile, the Egyptians first encountered elephants here, though it is more likely that Yebu owed its name and much of its importance to the ivory trade from the south. The most obvious feature at this northern end of Elephantine is the unfortunate bulk of the Aswan Oberoi Hotel, like a control tower without an international airport. On the far side of Elephantine, and largely obscured by it, is **Kitchener's Island**; it was from Aswan that Kitchener set out to conquer the Sudan in 1896–98 and the island is a botanical garden begun by him.

All along the corniche, cruise boats are tied up at the **quayside**, and towards the north end many feluccas too, while midway along it the Aswan Oberoi's ferry, designed to look like a pharaonic barge, makes frequent crossings to the hotel. At the south end of the corniche is a roundabout with the Egyptair office; it is here that the road from the airport enters town. Ferries leave from here to the southernmost Nubian village on Elephantine, and there is also a ferry to the Amun

Island Hotel in mid-river. Feluccas for hire concentrate here too. One arm of the Nile runs through the narrow channel between the massive embankments of ancient Yebu and the great doughlike outcrops of pink granite on the east bank, the road rising round the shaded public gardens that overlook the river here. Surmounting the outcrop is the Old Cataract Hotel.

Murder on the Nile

Devotees of nostalgia must make a pilgrimage to the **Old Cataract Hotel**, a russet pile atop a loaf of pink granite, surrounded by gardens, with beautiful views along the Nile in either direction and across the tip of Elephantine to the **Mausoleum of the Aga Khan** and against the distant desert horizon the old **Monastery of St Simeon**. John Fowles in *Daniel Martin* describes the interior as it was in the early 1970s: 'Pierced screens, huge fans, tatty old colonial furniture, stone floors, silence, barefooted Nubian servants in their red fezzes; so redolent of an obsolete middle class that it was museum-like' — it has since been refurbished, though not spoilt. The exterior features in the film of Agatha Christie's *Death on the Nile*; the terrace, cocktail in hand, amidst the calm, is the perfect place to plot an elegant murder.

Elephantine

The purposeful excuse for visiting Elephantine Island is to see the scant ruins, the ramshackle museum and the ancient nilometer. The **nilometer** is under a sycamore tree, a few boat-lengths north of embankments bearing *inscriptions* from the reigns of Tuthmosis III and Amenophis III (XVIII Dyn) and Psammetichus II (XXVI Dyn). Its square shaft can be entered directly from the river or down steps from above. Though probably dating from an earlier period, it was rebuilt by the Romans, the scales marked in Greek. It was restored in the last century, when Arabic and French inscriptions were added. Strabo records that 'on the side of the well are marks, measuring the height sufficient for the irrigation and other water levels. These are observed and published for general information. This is of importance to the peasants for the management of the water, the embankments, the canals, etc, and to the officials on account of the taxes. For the higher the rise of water, the higher are the taxes'. The High Dam put an end to the annual inundation, and under Nasser this ancient basis of taxation was abolished. The more modest fluctuations in the level of the Nile are still measured, however. In 1984 the US Agency for International Development granted Egypt $4.5 million to install a satellite communications system that will tell irrigation engineers in Cairo the level of every waterway in the country.

Nilometer in space

The ancient town of **Yebu** stood at the southern end of the island. Its mound is being picked clean of debris by archaeologists, revealing mud brick structures of successive levels of occupation. Excavations began at the beginning of this century after the discovery that there had been a sizeable Jewish colony here in the 6th C BC with its own temple to Yahweh (Jehovah). From a military order of

Jewish garrison

King Darius II in 419 BC permitting his Yebu garrison to celebrate the Passover, it is clear that the Jews here served in defence of the Persian Empire's southernmost border. The continuing excavations have revealed the existence of several temples, amongst them, to the west of the nilometer, a **Temple of Khnum** built during the XXX Dynasty and, to the north of the museum, a New Kingdom **Temple of Satet**, the female counterpart of Khnum. At the southern tip of the island by the water's edge the fragments of a small **Ptolemaic temple** have been reassembled with the aid of much yellow brick.

The island was home to Khnum, a ram-headed god of the cataracts who was said to have fashioned man on a potter's wheel. Rams sacred to the god were mummified, and the sarcophagus of one, with mummy, is in the **museum**. Originally the villa of Sir William Willcocks, designer of the first Aswan dam, this is a verandahed old house on high ground overlooking the ruins and set in well-kept gardens. On view are a golden bust of Khnum with brown peaceful eyes, and an assortment of jewellery, pots, granite statues of island governors, weapons, bronze mirrors and beautiful slate palettes for cosmetics in the form of fish, birds, buffalo and hippopotamus — all of them local finds dating from the predynastic through Byzantine periods, and labelled in English and Arabic.

The greatest pleasure of the island, however, is to follow the pathways which wander off through the fields and luxuriant palms to the three **Nubian-speaking villages** of the island. The houses are pale yellow or brilliant blue, the eyes of the young girls alluringly black. A brass woman's hand serves as a door knocker, a ring on one finger. Some doorways are carved with crocodiles at the foot, fish in the middle and a man on top, the woman's hand between fish and man, a statement of ideal proximities. The Kaaba, the sacred black cube

Those who have been to Mecca

at Mecca, is painted on some housefronts to show that its owner has been on the hajj, and sometimes to show how he got there a boat will be added, or fancifully a single-engined propeller plane with open cockpit, or more likely a wide-bodied chartered jet.

At the north end of the island is that big hotel again, behind a 3-metre high cordon sanitaire, erected I first thought to keep the Nubians out, but on second thought almost certainly to keep the air-conditioned people in.

Botanical Gardens

On the way to **Kitchener's Island**, Aswan disappears behind Elephantine Island and you could be almost anywhere along the Nile, except that few stretches of the river are as lovely as this. Kitchener was presented with the island when he was Consul-General in Egypt and here he indulged his passion for flowers, ordering plants from India and all over the Middle and Far East. You should allow a guide to attach himself to you; he will skip about like one of Peter Pan's boys amongst the trees and plants in his sandals and galabiyya, picking leaves, flowers and fruits and crushing these in his fingers for you to smell, awakening all the pungency and variety of your surroundings. The island attracts birds of remarkable pattern and colour, and at the south end there is the odd sight of hundreds of white ducks paddling about in a closed-off cove, a research station for duck breeding.

The Noble Tombs

Interred in the noble tombs on the west bank of the Nile opposite the north ends of Elephantine and Kitchener islands were the governors, princes and priests whose lives revolved around the control of the Nubian trade. Though more modest than those at Beni Hasan, the tombs are similar in style, and like them date mostly from the end of the Old Kingdom through the First Intermediate Period and the Middle Kingdom. They can be reached by ferry from near the tourist office in Aswan or as part of a felucca cruise or by camel or on foot from St Simeon's monastery.

Princes of the Nubian trade

A slog up a sandy path from the landing stage brings you to the line of tombs cut into the cliff face. The tombs were originally approached by those steep **ramps** you see etched into the hillside, with steps on either side and a channel at the centre for dragging up the sarcophagi. Those ramps that are exposed are nevertheless sometimes partly sanded over; the more nimble visitor can afterwards pick and slalom his way back down to the Nile pretty quickly.

The tombs are numbered in ascending order from south to north. The path brings you up to the northern (high-numbered) tombs; after working your way south you can then zip down a ramp, or otherwise retrace your steps and return to the river by the path.

No. 36 is the **tomb of Sirenput I**. It is about 60 years older than that of his namesake in No. 31, though both are XII Dynasty. These are the two finest tombs. Sirenput I was governor and overseer of the priests of Khnum and Satet. A limestone doorway leads to a six-columned courtyard decorated with the makings of a contented afterlife: a large figure of the deceased followed by his sandal bearer and two dogs; another of his bow bearer, dog and three sons; and other

Tomb of Serenput II: note the elephant, upper left

paintings of fishing, women bringing flowers and two men gambling.

Tomb 31 of Sirenput II, who was also a governor, is one of the largest and best preserved. It was constructed at the apogee of the Middle Kingdom, when Egypt extended its power beyond the Second Cataract. Beyond a six-pillared hall without decoration is a corridor with three niches on either side with Osiris statues of the deceased cut from the rock. The dead man appears with his son in a brightly coloured painting to the left of the first niche; he appears again on each of the four pillars in the small hall beyond, the artist's grid lines for setting out the pictures still visible on some. At the back of this hall is a *recess with good paintings on stucco and very fine hieroglyphics.* On the left wall Sirenput is shown with his wife and son; on the right wall his mother sits at a table while he stands to the right. On the centre wall Sirenput sits at a table and his son stands before him clutching

flowers. Notice the wonderfully coloured and detailed
hieroglyphics here, particularly of birds and animals, including (upper left) an elephant.

Tombs 25 and 26 of Mekhu and his son Sabni date from the
VI Dynasty, a period of decline, and are crude both in
construction and decoration. It is the entrance of No. 26
that is noteworthy, for an inscription on it states that Sabni,
governor of the South, mounted an expedition against the
Nubians who had killed his father; that he recovered the
body which was then mummified by embalmers sent by the
pharaoh; and that Sabni went to Memphis to thank him and
offer presents. Apart from instancing an occasion of Yebu's
military role on Egypt's southern border, the inscription
shows how much importance was attached to the outpost by
Memphis.

The summit of the hill is crowned with the **Kubbet el Hawa**,
the shrine of a local sheikh and holy man, and commands a
magnificent *view* of the Nile valley, the cataract and the
desert that more than compensates for the difficult climb. A
path runs from here across the desert to St Simeon, about 45
minutes by foot.

The Mausoleum of the Aga Khan

An easier way of reaching St Simeon is by landing below the
Mausoleum of the Aga Khan. The walk from here is about 20
minutes, though you can hire a camel. But first you should
visit the mausoleum, principally for the view, built above the
Aga Khan's white *villa* where until his death in 1957 he spent
the winter months and where for three months of the year the
Begum still does. Apart from its beauty, I have heard a story
that he associated himself with the spot after he found a cure
here for his leg trouble by immersing himself up to the waist
in the sand. The restrained proportions and the granite and
sandstone of the domed mausoleum are entirely in keeping
with the surroundings. The tomb within is of white Carrara
marble, beautifully carved in Cairo with geometric patterns
and Koranic inscriptions in high relief. Each morning in
winter the Begum lays a red rose on the tomb, and the ritual is
taken over in summer by the gardener. There is another story
that one July not a single rose was to be found in Egypt and
on six successive days a red rose was flown in by private plane
from Paris.

The Aga Khan is spiritual leader of the Ismailis, a Shi'ite
sect (as were the Fatimids) centred on India but with large
communities in East Africa and elsewhere. Aga Khan III,
buried here, was a man of considerable bulk and was of such
wealth that on his diamond jubilee in 1945 he was weighed in
diamonds, which were distributed to his followers. His play-
boy son Ali predeceased him, and he was succeeded by his
more earnest grandson Karim, Aga Khan IV.

Fortress of God

The **Monastery of St Simeon** (Deir Amba Samaan) with its towers and walls looms like a Byzantine fortress on a ridge at the head of a desert valley once cultivated with fields and gardens down to the Nile. Built in the 7th C and rebuilt in the 10th, it is the finest example of an original Christian monastery in Egypt, and is highly evocative. Little is known of St Simeon — he was not the Stylite — and in any case the monastery was first dedicated to Anba Hadra, a bishop of Aswan and saint of the late 4th C, who the day after his marriage encountered a funeral procession and decided to give up the world for a desert cave. The saint's tomb may have been here, a pilgrims' rest and monastery growing up afterwards. Fearful that the monastery might serve as a refuge for Christian Nubians during their forays into southern Egypt, Saladin destroyed it in 1173.

Christian city in the desert St Simeon was built on a grand scale, with dressed stone walls 10 metres high. A small city lay within the walls, with cells for 300 resident monks and dormitories for several hundred pilgrims, as well as bakeries and workshops to support the community. The hills and desert roundabout offered solitude and godly communion for probably thousands of monks and hermits.

The lower storeys of the monastery are stone; the upper are mud brick and it is these that have most fallen into decay or vanished altogether. You enter the *portal*, and before you, on a height, is the three-storey *keep*, open to the sky, cells on either side of the long corridors. Stucco seems to have been applied throughout the monastery, and on it, in the apses of the *basilica* to your left, are badly damaged paintings. There is a Christ Pantocrator in the central apse; on the sides, the faces of saints have been cut out. Names are carved right into the paintings by Arabs and tourists alike — it is not only time that has taken its toll. The monastery has never been systematically excavated, and repairs have been slight; it is largely a confusion of vaults, staircases, walls, workshops and quarters. From the tops of the *walls* there is a glimpse of Aswan, of green, but around 350 of the other degrees there is only the desert sea, luridly red at sundown. Yet there is an evening breeze, and amidst the gardens and within the shadow of the towering walls it must have been cool. It is strange to wander round these arches, vaults and apses of familiar shape and significance; and even before the Arabs came it must have been like that, this comforting bastion against the fierce landscape.

Women and camels On the way back, my camel was grunting and snorting and emitting high-pitched complaints, and with the Nubian chiding and crying at her, it was like a dialogue, a dialogue of those inarticulations of a man and woman in bed. I would guess that there is an extensive woman-as-camel (or vice versa) folklore in the East.

Sailing on the Nile

By now you have become addicted to sailing in a felucca on the Nile, and the only cure is to have more of it. The longer journey upstream to the island of **Sehel** is recommended. The current is against you but the prevailing wind is in your favour and the gaff is extended upwards giving great height and grace to the sail. Sehel is just below the First Cataract, and even at the north end of the island the boat is shoved about by turbulent whirlpools. Hawks hovering above the cliffs wheel and dive for fish.

The First Cataract

You land on the east side and walk southwards over the sands to a granite outcrop streaked with bird droppings and covered with *inscriptions* from the IV Dynasty to the Ptolemaic period. Up top and towards the south is one of the most interesting (No. 81), Ptolemaic in date but depicting Zoser and the god Khnum. The inscription relates to a famine lasting seven years through Zoser's reign. Zoser asks the governor of Aswan why the Nile has not flooded and is told that it is in the power of Khnum to whom Zoser then erects a temple. From here there is a *view* of the rocks and swirling waters of the cataract, but the pounding Nile and foam passed into history with the construction of the British dam. It is cool as you sail upon the river, though the sun can be dangerous; on

St Simeon: Christian bastion in the desert

327

the island there is no mistaking its ferocity. You need to be well shod, for the sand and piles of rock are blisteringly hot. A *Nubian village* lies off to the west and here you may be invited into a house and invited to enjoy a refreshing cup of mint tea. The walls are thick and insulating, and the barrelled or domed roof reflects the heat at every angle; it is very cool inside.

The felucca tacks back down the Nile, taking advantage of the current. The round trip to Sehel is about 3 hours. The boatmen drink directly from the Nile, pointing out that there is no bilharzia above Esna and certainly not in the middle of

Drinking from
the Nile

the river where the current flows swiftly. It is said that to drink from the Nile is to ensure your return, so I drank; a fresh and slightly organic taste. Nor, with bilharzia no nearer than Esna and the crocodiles held at bay by the High Dam, could I resist plunging into the river altogether and opening my eyes on the almost impenetrably green water. Afterwards, you smell like the Nile, but a shower admits you once again onto the terrace of the Old Cataract. Just as they are designed to catch the slightest breeze, so in the last faint blue of sunset the felucca sails catch that glimmer of light off the horizon, and like crescent moons glide among the rocks in the Nile below.

Outlying Sights

Early another morning you are collected by your hired car and are driven round the outlying sights. A road leading off the roundabout by the public gardens turns south towards the **Fatimid cemetery** with its domed mausolea of holy figures, some local, others — such as Sayyida Zeinab, Ali's daughter and granddaughter of the Prophet — more widely revered. A turning to the left brings you to the **ancient granite quarries** and the *unfinished obelisk*. Roughly dressed and cut nearly free from the surrounding bedrock, in its finished state it would have weighed over one million kilograms (2.3 million pounds) and would have been the largest piece of stone handled in history. But work stopped after a flaw was discovered in the stone (see Karnak, the Lateran obelisk).

Back on the road south and 5 km from town you come to the old **Aswan Dam**, built by the British between 1898 and 1902. The road passes over it and across the cataract; the water swirls round the jagged stones, plays white, but has lost its boil. The height of the dam was twice raised to increase irrigation and its hydroelectric capacity was multiplied, but Egypt's fast growing population and the need both further to increase her cultivable land area and to provide vast new supplies of power for a necessary industrialisation pro-

The Low and
High Dams

gramme led to work beginning in the mid-1960s on the High Dam 6 km upriver. The road linking the two runs through disturbed desert on the west bank, a giant disused sand pit it seems; you cannot imagine that this is the shore of an uncharted sand ocean going on forever. Numerous electricity pylons add to the impression of it being a manmade litter ground. At the west approach to the dam there is a giant lotus-shaped monument commemorating Russian-Egyptian co-operation. The police here take the opportunity to check your papers and impose a charge.

The High Dam

The High Dam has commanded world attention. Its construction became a political issue between East and West. Its sheer size, its effect on the economic potential of the country, and the sudden attention it forced on the Nubian antiquities threatened by the rising waters of Lake Nasser, have all been extraordinary.

The dam was completed in 1971 and since then the water contained by it has reached a height of 182 metres and has backed up 500 km to the Second Cataract within the Sudan. Evaporation from the artificial lake amounts to 5000 million cubic metres annually (about seven percent of the lake's volume) and is causing unusual clouds and haze in the surrounding area, and even occasional rain. But the lake also retains the silt that once renewed Egypt's fields. Chemical fertiliser plants running off the dam's hydroelectric power are filling that gap, while it is estimated that in 500 years' time the silt will have filled the lake. By then, however, some other means of water conservation may have become available, or the wasteland to the south may have reverted to the lushness of long distant millenia. The water table beneath the Sahara has already risen noticeably as far away as Algeria.

Though Egypt's population explosion and mistakes in economic policy have in some measure offset the dam's immediate benefits, it has already averted catastrophe. The drought that has brought starvation to Ethiopia and the Sudan has seen the Nile fall to its lowest level in 350 years, and the same scenes of famine would have been repeated in Egypt had it not been for the High Dam. The British dam regulated the flow of the Nile during the course of the year; the High Dam can store surplus water over a number of years, balancing low floods against high and ensuring up to three harvests a year. The god Khnum has answered Zoser's prayer.

The structure that achieves this contains the equivalent in material of 17 pyramids the size of the Great Pyramid of Cheops, and enough metal has been used in its gates, sluices and power plant to build 15 Eiffel Towers. The *road* runs across the top back to the east bank. In merely driving along, somehow the hugeness of the enterprise is lost upon you, and because it is not ancient, and because it is functional and it works, it is easy not to be impressed. It is even possible for some to complain that it was not worth the drowning of so many Nubian monuments. The same was said when the

British built their dam, to which Churchill replied: 'This offering of 1500 millions of cubic feet of water to Hathor by the Wise Men of the West is the most cruel, the most wicked and the most senseless sacrifice ever offered on the altar of a false religion. The state must struggle and the people starve, in order that the professors may exult and the tourists find some place to scratch their names'.

'The most cruel, the most wicked and the most senseless sacrifice'

Some feeling for the controlled energy of the place is realised at the *viewing platform* over to the eastern end of the dam. The green water rises in eddies, like large bursting bubbles from somewhere below the visible tops of the sluices. The generators hum as the river is put through its paces. Scores of lesser pylons flick currents of electricity towards the larger pylons striding across the desert, and bound by thick cables this energy is delivered into Egypt. Downstream, the Nile slips its harness and runs free beneath a glassy surface.

New Kalabsha

The newly created archaeological site of New Kalabsha is a kilometre south of the High Dam on the west bank of the Nile. Three temples were removed here to save them from the rising waters of Lake Nasser, but considering the effort that went into the project, little encouragement is given to visiting these stone-by-stone reconstructions. This is a military area (the fear in essence is that somebody might pull the plug out of the High Dam and drown all Egypt) and special permission is required. That must be done in Aswan and will take about an hour; then you are free to make your way here by taxi.

The original site of the **Temple of Kalabsha** was 50 km farther into Nubia. It was built during the reign of Augustus to the familiar blueprint of his Ptolemaic predecessors, though as the temple was being dismantled, evidence of earlier structures dating from the time of Amenophis II and Ptolemy IX was found. Considered to rank second only to Abu Simbel as the finest monument south of Philae and enjoying a harmony of proportion, nevertheless the temple was never completely adorned with reliefs and inscriptions, and the reliefs are generally of poor workmanship. Dedicated to Mandulis, a Nubian god associated with Isis, the Kalabsha temple later became a Christian church.

An imposing causeway of dressed stone leads westwards to the *pylon* which is slightly askew to the axis of both the causeway and temple. This admits first to an open *court* and then a *hypostyle hall* (the roof has fallen in), both with columns bearing elaborate floral capitals. *Three chambers* lie beyond, the last being the sanctuary. All three are decorated with *reliefs of Augustus* making offerings to just about every god in the Egyptian pantheon, which would have made him laugh had he ever come here to see for himself — after defeating

Augustus and the bizarre

Cleopatra and Antony, Octavian (as he then was) was content to gaze at Alexander's preserved corpse (accidentally knocking off its nose, it is said), but refused to visit any Egyptian temples, dismissing native beliefs and practices as bizarre. But you, earnest traveller, can admire here the nicely preserved colours on these propaganda reliefs of Augustus.

Within the first two chambers, stairways on the left lead up to the roof and walls for the wonderful *view* across the vast blue of Lake Nasser.

Also at New Kalabsha are the **Kiosk of Qirtasi**, a Ptolemaic edifice from 40 km upriver, and the **Temple of Bayt al-Wali** rescued from near the original site of the Kalabsha temple. Bayt al-Wali is Arabic for House of the Governor, and the temple was built by the Viceroy of Cush for Ramses II.

Philae: Island of Isis

Before the construction of the British dam, you could winter at Aswan and visit the Temple of Isis standing proud on its sacred island. But the dam all but submerged the temple for half the year, during the winter at that, and Philae became a name only, hardly a place to visit. Yet there was romance in that visit, a romance, once established, far greater for some than any satisfaction gained from seeing the Temple of Isis raised again on new and profane ground. In *Daniel Martin*, John Fowles records the experience many travellers have enjoyed this century: 'Then they drove to see the temple of Philae; a long row out into the lake, followed by the slow gondola-like tour round the submerged columns, shadowy shafts in the translucent green water. An exquisite light shimmered and danced on the parts that rose into the air. They and the guide were rowed by two old men, with scrawny wrists and mummified bare feet. Every so often, on the long haul, the pair would break into a strange question-and-answer boating-chant, half sung, half spoken. Work on transporting the temple to its new site, the guide proudly told them, would begin within the next few months; very soon sunken Philae would be abusimbelized. They didn't argue with him, but voted it a vulgarity, the whole project, over lunch'.

Saving Philae's temples The annual rise and fall of the Nile, elevated behind the British dam, slowly wore on the inscriptions and reliefs of the temple and eventually, though perhaps after only hundreds of years, would have brought the whole thing down. But then the High Dam was built and the Temple of Isis, between the two, was permanently almost completely submerged, and worse, where it rose just clear of the river, suffered swift daily tide-like movements that would have destroyed it (and Philae's other monuments) far sooner. With Hathor doubly gratified, it has now been the turn of professors and tourists to avenge Churchill's words.

Now Philae has been recreated. The nearby island of **Agil-qiyyah** has been carved and sliced to replicate the original island, so that it is 450 metres long and 150 metres across, and the Temple of Isis, as well as the Temple of Hathor and the Kiosk of Trajan, have been placed in positions corresponding as nearly as possible to their previous relationship. (The plan shows the disposition of monuments on the original island of Philae, but those at the northern end of the island, in particular the Roman gate and the ruined Temple of Augustus, and also two Coptic churches and the remains of a monastery, were left where they stood. The intention is to transfer them later.) The present site was opened to the public in 1980.

Approaching the Temple of Isis

The logical starting point for a tour of the **Temple of Isis** is the **Vestibule of Nectanebos I** (XXX Dyn) at the southwest corner of the island (the landing stage is just below). The temple it once led to was washed away by the Nile, but this vestibule was rebuilt by Ptolemy II Philadelphos. Nearly every other monument on the island dates from the Ptolemaic and Roman periods, and Herodotus, who visited Elephantine c.450 BC, seems to have found no reason to make any mention of Philae, though it is probable that older temples stood on the island then. Northwards extends the *outer temple court*, the first pylon of the Temple of Isis at its far end, colonnades on either side. The *East Colonnade* is unfinished, with many of the columns only rough-hewn; the *West Colonnade* follows the shoreline, its columns bearing reliefs of Tiberius offering gifts to the gods, the capitals of varying plant motifs, no two alike.

Ptolemaic prowess

The **First Pylon**, 18 metres high, 45 metres wide, consists of two massive towers with a gateway between them. The towers were begun by Ptolemy II Philadelphos and completed by Euergetes I, though the decorations were carried out over a long period. On the front of the right or eastern tower, Ptolemy XII Neos Dionysos is shown in the traditional pharaonic pose of seizing his enemies by the hair, about to bash their brains out with a club; Isis, Hathor and the falcon-headed Horus of Edfu look on placidly. Above and to the right, Neos Dionysos offers the crowns of Upper and Lower Egypt to Horus the child. On the left or western tower, Neos Dionysos is again sacrificially braining his foes while above he appears before Unnefer (the name given to Osiris after his resurrection) and Isis, and before Isis and Harsiesis, a form of Horus. The reliefs have been severely damaged by the Copts. The vertical grooves on the towers were for holding flagstaffs. The *main gateway* was built earlier by Nectanebos and bears reliefs of his as well as Coptic crosses and, as you pass through, a French inscription on the right commemorating the victory of General Desaix over the Mamelukes in 1799 ('L'an 6 de la République').

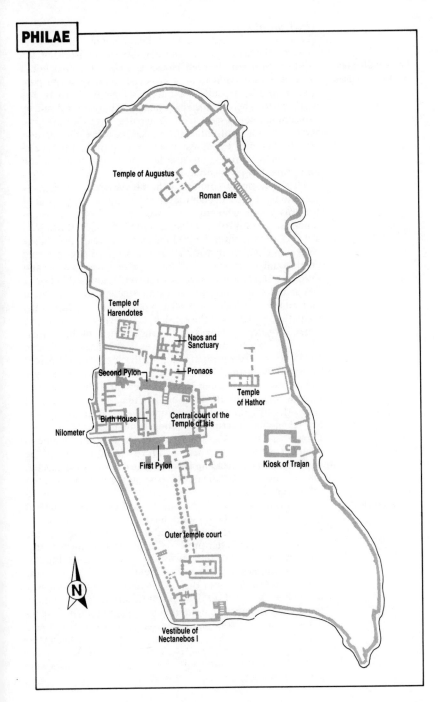

PHILAE

Temple of Augustus

Roman Gate

Temple of
Harendotes

Naos and
Sanctuary

Pronaos

Second Pylon

Temple
of Hathor

Birth House

Central court of the
Temple of Isis

Nilometer

Kiosk of Trajan

First Pylon

Outer temple court

N

Vestibule of
Nectanebos I

The Cult of Osiris

The significance of birth houses

The gateway through the First Pylon admits to the *fore-court* of the temple, with the colonnaded quarters of the priests to the right, the **Birth House** to the left. The birth house became an essential feature of Ptolemaic temples, its purpose similar to Hatshepsut's depiction at Deir el Bahri of her divine birth. There, Hatshepsut justified her temporal rule by proclaiming her descent from Amun-Re; with the spread of the Osiris cult until under the Ptolemies it became the universal religion of Egypt, each pharaoh legitimised his accession by demonstrating his descent from Horus, first pharaoh and prime law-giver in the land.

There are many strands to the Osiris legend, and many accretions to the story and levels of meaning. Osiris, son of Re, was a king who ruled and was greatly loved in distant times. Isis was his sister and wife, Seth his brother. When Seth killed Osiris and dismembered his body, Isis searched out the pieces and put them together again, wondrously restoring Osiris to life in the underworld where he reigned as judge and king. Isis' son Horus was secretly raised to manhood in Lower Egypt and after a long and desperate struggle overcame Seth and established order over all Egypt. Historically, this may recall the subjection of the south by the north in pre-dynastic times. Mystically, Horus is the incarnation of his father, while Isis is the agent of both resurrection and reincarnation. Celebration of the rites relating to the legend, and in particular to the birth of Horus, took place at these birth houses, the pharaoh proclaiming his legitimacy through his involvement in them. The Birth House at Philae is surrounded on four sides by colonnades and round their walls and columns are reliefs and inscriptions dating from Euergetes II, Neos Dionysos, Augustus and Tiberius. In the last (northernmost) chamber within are reliefs of Horus as a falcon in the marshes, and Isis suckling Horus in the marshes of the Delta. On the west shore of the island, beyond the Birth House, is a nilometer.

Defacements

The **Second Pylon** is at an angle to the first and not quite so large. Again, Neos Dionysos is shown before the deities, this time offering animal sacrifices and incense; the reliefs on the eastern tower are better preserved than those on the western. Shallow steps lead to the *gateway* between the two. Figures here of Euergetes II and deities are greatly defaced; on the right there is an inscription to Bishop Theodoros, in whose name, most likely, much of the defacement occurred. It is testimony to the sheer quantity of antiquities in Egypt that through 4000 or more years, with one pharaoh defacing the work of another, Christians defacing the work of pagans, Muslims defacing the work of Christians and tourists defacing the work of everybody, there still remains so much to be defaced by those who can find the time and excuse for doing so.

Isis suckling a young pharaoh

The Cult of Isis

Entering the
temple of the
goddess

It is through the Second Pylon that you enter the **pronaos** of the Temple of Isis proper. Pharaohs might have justified themselves at the Birth House, but this would have been the all-important goal of select pilgrims not only from Egypt but from all over the Mediterranean right through to the mid-6th C AD. For Isis was the hinge upon which the Osiris legend hung, and through her suffering and her joy the goddess offered an emotive identification so powerful and satisfying that she became identified too with all other goddesses of the Mediterranean, whom she finally absorbed. Isis was the Goddess of Ten Thousand Names, Shelter and Heaven to All Mankind, the House of Life, the Great Mother of All Gods and Nature, Victorious over Fate, the Promise of Immortality, Sexuality and Purity, the Glory of Women — when all else failed, she still could save. She was passionately worshipped by men and women alike. Cleopatra deliberately identified herself with Isis, and called herself the New Isis, casting Antony as Dionysos, the Greek equivalent of Osiris, so that on earth they affected the already existing cosmological bond.

Isis and
Christianity

Christianity, with its male-orientated antecedents in the Judaic and Greek religions, may never have given the prominence it did to the Virgin Mary had not a figure been needed to absorb in turn the great popularity and success of the rival Isis cult. It was a rivalry that continued well into the Christian era. In spite of the edicts of the Roman emperor Theodosius I, which succeeded in terminating the Olympic Games after a thousand years in the 4th C AD, pagan Philae continued as a centre of Isis worship till the reign of Justinian in the 6th C, while farther into Nubia the worship of Isis probably persisted until the Arab Islamic conquest.

The walls of the pronaos are covered both outside and inside with reliefs of Ptolemies (Philadelphos, Euergetes II, etc) and Roman emperors (Augustus, Tiberius, Antoninus) performing the customary ceremonies in the guise of pharaohs. Christian services were celebrated in the court and pronaos, of which the numerous Coptic crosses chiselled in the walls are memorials. In the doorway of a room to the right is another Greek inscription to Bishop Theodoros, claiming credit for 'this good work'.

The three antechambers of the **naos** lead through to the **Sanctuary** with two small windows and a pedestal on which stood the sacred boat with the image of Isis. On the left wall is a relief of a pharaoh facing Isis whose wings protectively embrace Osiris; on the right wall (above) Isis enthroned suckles the infant Horus, and (below) Isis standing, her face gouged out by Christians; suckling a young pharaoh. Of course these pharaohs were Ptolemaic kings in pharaonic guise.

Dahabeah moored under Trajan's Kiosk: 19th C photo of the original Philae

West of the Temple of Isis

West of the second pylon is **Hadrian's Gateway** (which can be reached by leaving the naos of Isis' temple through a west doorway). It is preceded by a badly ruined *vestibule* which nevertheless preserves an interesting relief on the inside of its north wall (second register from the top), depicting the source of the Nile: the Nile god, entwined by a serpent, pours water from two jars. This relates to the ancient belief that the source of the Nile was at the First Cataract. The waters so swirled and seemed to flow in different directions that it was thought the river rose here from underground, flowing north to the Mediterranean and south into Africa. The belief hinged, as most beliefs do, on laziness and the desire not to spoil a good story: the most cursory examination of the river's flow at any point south of the First Cataract would have revealed, as no doubt it did reveal a thousand times, that the Nile always flows north. Herodotus, who enjoyed a good story himself, nevertheless dismissed the notion expressed in this relief. He

Speculations on the source of the Nile

337

traced the northerly flow of the Nile back deep into Africa, and even reported a theory, based almost certainly on lost knowledge, that the source of the Nile, and the cause of its floods, lay in distant snowfalls — a theory he rejected (though 2000 or so years later it was proved right) because he could not imagine high snow mountains somewhere in the hot interior of Africa. North of Hadrian's Gateway are the foundations of the **Temple of Harendotes**, built by the emperor Claudius.

East of the Temple of Isis

Off to the east of the Second Pylon is the **Temple of Hathor**, comparable to the Greek Aphrodite despite the usual convention of cow's ears, built by Ptolemy VI Philometor and Euergetes II. The colonnade was decorated during the reign of Augustus with amusing carvings of music and drinking — apes dancing and one playing a lute, dwarfish Bes beating a tambourine, while Augustus offers a festal crown to Isis.

To the south stands the unfinished **Kiosk of Trajan**, a rectangular building of 14 columns with beautifully carved floral capitals. On the only two screen walls between the columns to have been completed are scenes of the emperor Trajan offering incense and wine to Isis, Osiris and Horus. The elegance of the kiosk has made it the characteristic symbol of the island.

As you return to the landing stage, look south at the larger island of **Bigah**: this was supposedly the burial place of Osiris.

PRACTICAL INFORMATION

ACCOMMODATION

Like Luxor, Aswan's high season is from October through May and it would be best then to make reservations in advance if you are choosy. Summer can be slack, however, though the heat should not deter you — it is a dry heat, and all but the cheapest places will have air conditioning.

Cataract, Sharia Abtal el Tahrir, at the south end of the corniche. Tel: 323222 for both Old and New Cataract. Like Luxor's Winter Palace, this is now 2 hotels, the New Cataract (run by PLM) and the Old Cataract (run by Pullman). Both are 5-star. The Old stands apart, on higher ground, with the most magnificent view in Aswan, and for my money is the finest place to stay in Egypt. The Old (built in 1902) has been well restored to the splendour of its early days. Its outstanding amenity is its terrace; the New has shops, bank, a hairdresser, etc, and there is an Olympic-size pool for all Cataract guests. Whether staying at the Old or the New, insist on a Nile-side room. All guests, whether at Old or New, dine at the New Cataract.

Aswan Oberoi (5-star), on Elephantine Island. Tel: 323455. Owned by the same company as the Mena House at the Pyramids, this modern and slightly tacky hotel looks like an airport control tower rising absurdly from the north end of the island. It is reached by regular ferries designed like ancient Egyptian royal barges (free for guests and the curious alike). Deplorable though its concrete monumentality is, the Oberoi offers some fine views, particularly westwards at sundown from the rear terrace across to Kitchener's Island. There are a bank, bookshop, hairdresser, café, nightclub, pool, boutiques and other trappings. Egyptair has a branch here.

Amun (4-star), Amun Island. Tel: 322555. The island is beautifully and peacefully situated just south of Elephantine and is reached by launches by the public gardens near the Egyptair office. The hotel, run by Club Med, is fairly small, which contributes to the atmosphere of remove and intimacy. After the Old Cataract, this is my favourite. There is a swimming pool. Rooms, all with bathrooms and air conditioning, overlook the gardens and the Nile.

Abu Simbel (2-star), Corniche el Nil. Tel: 322888. You come to this hotel soon after reaching the corniche from the train station; it is surrounded by tree-shaded gardens. The bar and restaurant are over the lobby and have a view of the Nile. Rooms are simple but are air conditioned; TV available. There are good views of the Nile from room balconies.

Ramses (1-star), Sharia Abtal el Tahrir, at the north end near the train station. Tel: 324119. All rooms with private bath and air conditioning. TV available.

Aswan's **youth hostel** is on Sharia Abtal el Tahrir at its station end. A horrible place, only for the desperate.

EATING PLACES AND ENTERTAINMENT

Apart from dining at the hotels, there are several Egyptian restaurants along the corniche, tables outside. Better than these, however, is **El Masri**, tucked away in the centre of town just off the main market street, Sharia el Souk. Ask and you will be directed.

The **Oberoi, New Cataract** and **Kalabsha** hotels have nightclubs with Western and Nubian music, perhaps a belly dancer too, though the dancing is usually Nubian and worth seeing. In winter the **Aswan Cultural Centre** between the Abu Simbel and Philae hotels present Nubian dancing.

Non-residents can swim in the **Cataract hotel's pool** for a payment. And of course you can swim in the Nile — no crocs or bilharzia, just find a pleasant spot (or swim off a felucca).

SHOPPING

The **Aswan Cultural Centre**, on the corniche between the Philae and Abu Simbel hotels, sells Nubian handicrafts.

A couple of blocks back from the river, however, is Sharia el Souk, Aswan's sinuous market street, the best **bazaar** outside Cairo, with an atmosphere still and an array of goods suggesting trade with Africa deeper south. Woven blankets and rugs are particularly good here and cheaper than elsewhere in Egypt; also there is silver, turquoise, ebony, spices, galabiyyas and much else. As you wander along, have a glass of pressed cane juice.

OF INTEREST

On **Elephantine Island** is the museum, admission LE1, open in winter from 9am to 5pm (Fridays to 1pm), and in summer (1 May-31 October) from 8.30am to 1.30pm daily. There is also the nilometer, the site of the ancient town of Yebu, and the pleasant walk through Nubian villages. Small ferries cross to the island from the corniche (about 25PT return trip). You cannot get to the rest of Elephantine from the Oberoi compound at the north end of the island.

Kitchener's Island (also known as **Botanical Island**) can be reached only by felucca, and you may wish to include it in a tour of west bank sites. Small entry fee; refreshments available.

On the west bank the **tombs of the nobles** can be reached by ferry from the corniche in front of the Tourist Office. Or by felucca. Or on foot or by camel from St Simeon's Monastery. Entry fee LE1.

Apart from crossing the sands from the nobles' tombs, you must take a felucca to reach the west bank landing for the **Aga Khan's Mausoleum** (free; open 9am to 4pm) and **St Simeon's Monastery** (LE1; open 9am to 6pm). At a corral by the landing stage you can hire a camel for St Simeon's (about LE4); otherwise it is no more than a 20-minute walk. A paved path runs between the mausoleum and the monastery, but a wall has been erected across it at the mausoleum end by the churlish Begum.

A felucca for these visits can be hired

along the corniche or below the Old Cataract Hotel. Expect to pay (after bargaining) no more than LE20 for 4 hours, and then expect to be hit for baksheesh later. Your bargaining position will be stronger in summer and if you do not seek a felucca by the Old Cataract.

Apart from feeling your way by bargaining, you can check first at the Tourist Office to find out what the official rates are for felucca and camel hire.

A visit to the granite **quarry**, the **old Aswan Dam** and the **new High Dam**, as well as a trip out to **Philae**, can be done in a morning starting early.

You should arrange for a taxi the day before through your hotel or a travel agent. Sometimes an agent will know of other interested people with whom you can share, so reducing the cost per person. There are small fees for the quarry with its unfinished obelisk and for the High Dam; Philae entry is LE3 and the motorboat there and back is about LE4. There is a **son et lumiere at Philae**, 2 shows nightly in various languages. Check at the Tourist Office for up-to-date details.

Visiting **New Kalabsha** will require an hour or two of preparation as permission must be obtained beforehand. At the police station towards the southern end of the corniche you will have to present, for each foreigner making the journey, a statement in duplicate saying you want to make a tourist visit to Kalabsha and giving your name, nationality and passport number. Additionally you will have to obtain from the Post Office taxi stamps for each person, including your driver. Confirm the details of this paperwork at the police station first; it is open from 8am to 2pm and from 7 to 9pm. Or better yet, first check at the Tourist Office where they can also tell you the cost of the taxi there and back.

For **Kom Ombo**, **Edfu**, **Esna** and **Luxor** you can set out by train or by local bus (from behind the Abu Simbel Hotel); or hire a taxi or take a seat in a service taxi (also behind the Abu Simbel Hotel); or go by felucca or take a tour (Thomas Cook offers half-day tours to Kom Ombo and Edfu and back, and full-day tours to Kom Ombo, Edfu and Esna, dumping you in Luxor). Some agents will make the felucca or taxi arrangements for you, ensuring a good price and reliability.

For **Abu Simbel**, see the following chapter.

The best **abbreviated itinerary** for Aswan is to do nothing but sit on the terrace of the Old Cataract Hotel. The best table for this is mine, at front right, but you will have to move when I come along.

INFORMATION AND OTHER THINGS

The **Tourist Office** is along the corniche 2 blocks north of the Abu Simbel Hotel. It is open from 9am to 2pm and 6 to 8pm Sunday to Thursday, from 10am to noon and 6 to 8pm on Fridays. Here you can obtain in advance the official prices for taxis, carriages and felucca trips.

The **Post Office** is on Sharia Salah el Din, one block in from the centre of the corniche, nearly opposite the Oberoi Hotel.

The **police station** is towards the south end of the corniche.

There are several **banks** along the corniche where you can change money.

TRAVEL

Apart from visiting the Tourist Office for information, it can also be useful to make enquiries at the various travel agencies. Sometimes they can fix things up for you on an ad hoc basis, or they might have a tour which will suit your purposes. **American Express** is in the Old Cataract, **Wagons-lits** is in the New Cataract and **Thomas Cook** is in the Aswan Oberoi. There are also various agencies along the southern end of the corniche, eg **Misr**, **Eastmar**, **Wagons-lits** and **Thomas Cook**.

The **airport** is 16 km southwest of Aswan beyond the High Dam. **Egyptair** runs buses back and forth; its office is on the roundabout at the south end of the corniche, with another at the Aswan Oberoi. Or take a taxi.

The **train station** is at the north end of the town, several blocks back from the corniche. A taxi or carriage from the station to, say, one of the Cataract hotels will cost about LE2.

Buses and **service (share) taxis** are located behind the Abu Simbel Hotel towards the north end of the corniche. By service taxi it is quite practicable to visit Kom Ombo, Edfu and Esna in a day, ending up in Luxor, though a change of taxi is required at the end of each leg.

If you want a **private taxi** for Kom Ombo, etc, or Philae, etc, try a bit of negotiating to get a feel for prices; but you could also try making arrangements through one of the agents along the corniche, eg Misr Travel or Wagons-lits.

The most enjoyable way of visiting places between Aswan and Luxor is by **felucca**. It is better to sail downriver from Aswan than upriver from Luxor as you will have the current with you. It can take 4 days at about LE50 per day for the boat plus LE6 per day per person for food. Either strike a bargain direct with the boatman or arrange things through an agent. Make sure there are plenty of blankets aboard, as it gets chilly at night (in winter it can get very cold) and that there is sufficient bottled water for drinking and cooking (though I have found drinking from the Nile down as far as Esna to be perfectly all right).

For travel to **Abu Simbel**, see next chapter.

To reach the **Sudan** you can **fly from Cairo or from Aswan** to Khartoum. Or you can **sail from Aswan** (in fact from Sadd el Ali, the port near the High Dam). The voyage lasts for about 20 hours up the length of Lake Nasser to Wadi Halfa at the Sudanese border, from where a connecting train takes you in 24 hours to Khartoum. Sailings from Sadd el Ali are between 11am and 3pm on Mondays, Thursdays and Saturdays. Thursday sailings should be avoided, as they bring you to Wadi Halfa on Friday when Sudanese offices are closed all day and you will not be permitted to disembark until Saturday. In fact these schedules are for the amusement of those enchanted by such things: the boat may not leave on time, or on that day, and it will certainly arrive at Wadi Halfa late. The train will wait, however, but will then take 36 hours to reach Khartoum instead of 24, assuming it does not fall off the tracks. (I have seen a train fall off the tracks in the Sudan, and I also narrowly missed a boat from Wadi Halfa to Aswan which caught fire and sank, most of its passengers burnt to death, drowned or eaten by crocodiles. It was in the middle of the night, and the captain and crew were the first to abandon ship.)

Tickets can be purchased at the **Sudanese Maritime Office** near the Tourist Office on the corniche, or at Ramses Station in Cairo (where it is also called the Nile Navigation Office). Both first and second class tickets consign you to uncomfortable seats in a stuffy enclosed atmosphere; as soon as you get on board, stake out a position on deck (have a sleeping bag; it gets cold at night). You can get tea on board, but the supply of food is erratic; bring your own. For the Wadi Halfa-Khartoum train journey, make sure you are travelling first class.

The boat makes no stops between Sadd el Ali and Wadi Halfa. Whether or not you see Abu Simbel enroute will depend on the erratic scheduling.

Remember that you will need a **visa** for the Sudan, obtainable in Cairo or abroad.

ABU SIMBEL

Originally, the rock-temples of Abu Simbel (280 km south of Aswan, 40 km north of Wadi Halfa on the Sudanese border) stared from sandstone cliffs which rose like gigantic pylons over the narrow Nile. In 1812, John Lewis Burckhardt, the first European since classical times to visit Abu Simbel, was not immediately impressed; he had come upon the cliffs from above, and only as he gained the river and turned upstream was he struck by the four colossal statues of Ramses II. 'Could the sand be cleared away', he said, 'a vast temple **Before the crowds** would be discovered.' The sand was repeatedly cleared away during the 19th C. There is a remarkable photograph taken in 1850 by Maxime du Camp, Flaubert's travelling companion, of the sand rising over the faces of the two right-hand colossi. On Holy Thursday, Flaubert noted, 'We began clearing operations, to disengage the chin of one of the exterior colossi'. It was only later in the century, with the coming of the British, that Abu Simbel and so many other monuments were properly cleared. Then, usually by Cook's steamer, tourists came. Laid bare in all their glory, and enhanced by the unique and striking beauty of the setting, the temples of Abu Simbel excited the enthusiasm of early visitors. Baedeker allowed himself a large adjective: they 'are among the most stupendous monuments of ancient Egyptian architecture'; and he went on to say: 'the temples produce a very grand effect by moonlight or at sunrise. The interior of the great temple is illuminated at night by electricity provided from the steamer'. Those were the days.

There is no railway to Abu Simbel, tourist steamers no longer make the voyage, and the Sudan ferry, if it does not actually sink enroute, usually passes at night and never lands. There is now a road, and you can make the return journey from Aswan in a day. But otherwise you fly. The pilot **Jetting there** may swoop back and forth before the temples so that first, unlike Burckhardt, you see the facades. But the colossi are small from the air, and further lose all advantage of proportion by having to outstare the vastness of Lake Nasser. Once the plane lands, you bumble along a desert road by bus, disembark behind the artificial mounds, tread round to the front, gaze upon Ramses in quadruplicate, and say, 'So what'. That is what I said, anyway, though the journey itself, and the phoniness of the climax, were in their way worthwhile.

The flight is a mixture of sensations: orbiting round the moon; going on a school outing. The latter because you know everyone else on board is going exactly where you are going, will stay as long as you are staying, will look at what you are looking at, and that you will appear in a thousand of their photographs and they on a roll of yours. The former because the landscape enroute is spectacularly alien, a rippling sand plateau interrupted by sharpended buttes, perhaps the cores of eroded ancient volcanoes which later from ground level will occasionally look like pyramids; and Lake Nasser, peculiar and varying in its colours, a giant drifting oil slick upon the desert sea.

Rescuing the Temples

As the waters of Lake Nasser rose during the mid-1960s, the original site of the temples was protected momentarily behind a coffer dam while the friable sandstone was injected with synthetic resin and then hand-sawn into 1050 blocks. The first block was cut in spring 1965; by autumn 1967, block had been replaced upon block at the new site 210 metres from the old one and 61 metres higher up. The $42 million operation was organised and funded by UNESCO. The temples were saved, the dam was breached, and the sacred site, which had known human activity since prehistoric times, was swallowed by the lake.

Spirit of place   If there is such a thing as spirit of place, it now lies behind you and below you somewhere beneath the waters as you stand facing the colossi of Ramses. The reconstruction has been impeccable; you knock your knuckles against Ramses' foot and are assured it is stone, not plaster; you look for the filled-in joins in the torsos but cannot detect them; and if you are there at dawn you will see that the sun's rays fall flat upon the pharaonic faces and, if the temple door is open, penetrate to the innermost sanctuary. Everything is as it was before, except that it is here and not where it used to be, and that greatly weakens the force of the new Abu Simbel. The genius of the place lay in working with the living rock, the temple facades set into cliff faces seemingly prepared by nature for the purpose, the colossi of Ramses at the south temple, those of Nefertari at the north temple, seeming to step out from the mountain, liberated from the imprisoning rock by the divine force of the rising sun. But when the cliffs are themselves reconstructions, that dramatic relationship between architecture and topography, and that mystical emergence of man from nature, is lost. To have left those ancient and powerful links intact would have meant surrendering the temples to the waters. Instead, it was decided to save the body and lose the soul. We now examine the carcass.

Purpose of the Temples

The temples stand on the west bank of the lake, the more southerly Temple of Re-Harakhte, with its colossi of Ramses II, facing east, the smaller and more northerly Temple of Hathor, with its colossi of Nefertari, Ramses' wife, angled slightly towards the south. Before the lake, the temples overlooked a bend in the Nile and must have dominated the land-

scape. This in part explains their purpose. Travellers into
Africa would first have seen the imposing colossi of Ramses, a
proud spur to Egyptians, a warning of Egypt's might to any
fractious Nubians. On the return, Hathor, in the guise of
Nefertari, would welcome Egyptians and Nubians alike to
the embrace of a great civilisation. Also, the temples would
have served as a convenient store for the gold and other riches
exacted from Nubia as tribute, just as nearly a thousand years
later the Parthenon served as the Athenian treasury. But
the political and strongbox functions of Abu Simbel would
have relied greatly on the religious character of the temples,
and that the architects addressed themselves to religious symbolism of magnificent scale and quality there can be no
doubt.

Exploring Ramses' Temple

You come first upon the **Temple of Re-Herakhte,** its
trapezoidal *facade* crowned by a corvetto cornice surmounted
by baboons worshipping the rising sun. The falcon-headed
sun god stands within the niche above the entrance door.
Arranged in pairs on either side of the entrance are the four

enthroned *colossi of Ramses* wearing the double crown. Each
figure is 20 metres high, taller than the Colossi of Memnon at
Thebes, and hewn from the cliff face. Between and beside the
massive legs are smaller figures of members of the royal
family. The feet and legs of the colossi are crudely carved, as
though deliberately inchoate, but the work grows finer up
through the torsos (the head and torso of the second colossus
from the left fell sometime in the past and has been left that
way), and the heads are excellently executed. This is most
true of the first head on the left, of which Burckhardt remarked, 'a most expressive, youthful countenance, approaching nearer to the Grecian model of beauty than that of any
ancient Egyptian figure I have seen'. The sides of the thrones
on either side of the entrance are decorated with Nile gods
symbolically uniting Egypt, while below are fettered
prisoners: those to the left, black Africans; those to the right,
Syrians.

Also to the left of the entrance, on the nearest colossal leg,
notice the Greek inscription which reads, 'When King Psammetichus came to Elephantine, this was written by those who
sailed with Psammetichus the son of Theocles, and they came
beyond Kerkis as far as the river permits. Those who spoke
foreign tongues were led by Potasimto, the Egyptians by
Amasis'. The reference is to the Nubian campaign of Psammetichus II (XXVI Dyn), but the point is that already in
the 6th C BC Greeks were operating in Egypt, albeit as
mercenaries. At sea, however, they were in control of the
Egyptian navy. With the arrival of Alexander 260 years later,
they would be in control of Egypt itself.

The left-hand colossus of Ramses II

Entering the temple, the first room is the **Hypostyle Hall,** corresponding to an open court with covered colonnades. There are four pillars on either side, against which and facing the central aisle are 10-metre high *Osiris-type figures of Ramses,* though this is Ramses alive, not dead, in an athletic near-nudity showing a process of heroisation at work. The best is the fourth figure in the north row. Heroic martial deeds are depicted in *sunk relief around the walls.* If you face the entrance you will see on the left (north) entrance wall a vigorous account of the battle of Kadesh in the fifth year of Ramses' reign. It was a battle Ramses endlessly boasted about, and boast he needed to do as it was no more than a Pyrrhic victory. Ramses cut himself out of a Hittite trap, but he failed to take Kadesh. Above Ramses is a vulture, and behind him his ka, who acted as guardian angel in the struggle. On the right (north) entrance wall a corresponding

Poem of Pentaur

scene shows Ramses in the presence of Amun-Re, to whom the king appealed at his most desperate moment: 'What ails thee, my father Amun? [Amun was absorbed in Amun-Re.] Is it a father's part to ignore his son? Have I done anything without thee, do I not walk and halt at they bidding? I have not disobeyed any course commanded by thee ... What careth thy heart, O Amun, for these Asiatics so vile and ignorant of God? ...What will men say if even a little thing befall him who bends himself to thy counsel?'

Facing again the interior, the left (south) wall of the hall bears an epic masterpiece depicting (below the top five reliefs showing Ramses making offerings to the gods) Ramses in his chariot storming a Syrian fortress, at centre the pharaoh piercing a Libyan with his lance, and to the right his triumphal return from battle with black captives. On the opposite (north) wall are further scenes from the Hittite campaign while on the rear wall Ramses is shown leading Hittite and black captives. *Lateral chambers* leading off from this top end of the Hypostyle Hall were probably used for storing the Nubian tribute.

In the next **hall of four pillars,** reliefs on the left (south) wall show Ramses and Nefertari before the sacred boat of Amun, and on the opposite (north) wall a similar scene before the boat of Re-Herakhte. Three doors lead from here into a transverse chamber from which in turn three doors lead off, the central one into the **Sanctuary.** Four seated mutilated figures are carved out of the rear wall: Ptah, god of Memphis, Amun, god of Thebes, the divinised Ramses, and Re-Harakhte, god of Heliopolis. Before them is a stone block on which would have rested the sacred boat. The symbolism is one of unity, the pharaoh and gods of Egypt's three greatest cities as one; but there is also Ramses as the living and visible god, perhaps again to awe the Nubians. The entire temple leads to this central message: Ramses as conqueror, hero and then god, the awesome progression enhanced by the heightened perspective of ever-smaller chambers, ever-smaller doorways, and at the dawns when the sun rose exactly opposite the temple, a brilliant shaft of light pointing to the sacred boat and Ramses with his fellow gods in the sanctuary. Leaving the temple you should stand before the facade again, before the entrance with its falcon-headed sun god, and imagine that effect.

The power of Allah
You now walk on to the Temple of Hathor. On the edge of the forecourt there are some trees and welcome shade. When I was last here, and perhaps now too, there was a low rectangle beneath these trees, hardly more than an outline on the ground with a gap at one end, a niche at the other. It was a mosque, just broad enough for two prostrate figures, so great a contrast to the massive temples, so great a witness to the immanence and power of Allah.

Exploring the Temple of Ramses' Queen
The **Temple of Hathor** is secondary and complementary to the larger Temple of Re-Harakhte, and in some ways more symbolically satisfying. Hathor was wife to the sun god during his day's passage and mother to his rebirth. As Ramses is identified with the god of the first temple, so his wife Nefertari is identified with the goddess of this, and so god, goddess, pharaoh and wife are each mated with one another at Abu Simbel. The *facade* is again a pylon, though the cavetto cornice has fallen. A series of buttresses rise into the cliff, and between them six *colossal statues* of Ramses and Nefertari. You should get up close to them. There is here the uncanny impression that they are emerging from the rock, that they are forming and will at any moment stride out towards the sunrise. The royal children stand knee-high in the shadows.

Delightful Nefertari
Inside the **Hypostyle Hall** with its crudely carved heads of Hathor on the six pillars, turn to examine the entrance wall. Ramses is smiting his enemies; Nefertari's hands are raised, perhaps as part of the ritual, though she seems to be seeking to moderate her husband's fury. In any case, she cuts a delightful figure, a slender form in flowing dress, appealing, graceful, dignified. The side walls show Ramses before various gods, while the rear wall shows Nefertari before Hathor (left) and before Mut (right). Three doors lead to a *transverse chamber*. On either side is a further chamber above the entrance to which are Hathor's cow in her boat. In the **Sanctuary**

A surprising cow
there is the startling sight of the *divine cow* emerging from the rear rock wall, a suggestion of the world beyond where her milk brings life to the souls of the dead.

The Bubble of Reality
By now you are parched and you discover a small door leading into the rock face to the right of Re-Harakhte's temple. The atmosphere is suddenly air-conditioned and there is a man

selling cold drinks and postcards. You climb some stairs at the back and with even more surprise then seeing a cow coming at you from a stone wall you enter a vast echoic *dome*. It is the bubble that surmounts the major temple and over which fill has been dumped and shaped to recreate the contour of the original bluff. A walkway runs right round the inside where there are abandoned displays and sheets of data explaining how it was all done. There is much to be said for this bubble. It is the one thing at Abu Simbel that is real.

PRACTICAL INFORMATION

Abu Simbel can be reached by **air** direct from Cairo, Luxor or Aswan. You should reserve a seat at the earliest opportunity, even from abroad if you can plan that far ahead, but it is always worthwhile trying at the last moment. It is better to go in the morning when the sun is full on the temple facades. A 2-hour stay at Abu Simbel is sufficient, and indeed you are usually issued with tickets timed to that assumption.

If you are flying from Aswan, the flight will take 25 minutes. Add to that the need to check in early and the likelihood that the flight will be delayed, and you can reckon that the expedition will take 5 hours in all.

A bus will take you to the temples from the airport and back, and you will be offered a guided tour of the site, the cost included in your entrance ticket.

Thomas Cook offers inclusive **air tours** from Aswan.

A road was opened to Abu Simbel in 1985, so you can now go by **bus** (or even take a **taxi**). The bus is operated by Misr Travel in Aswan and departs at 8am, arriving back at 5pm, giving you 2 to 3 hours at the temples plus time for lunch at the Nefertari Hotel. At a cost of about LE80 you get the ride, your lunch, a guide and your entrance fee paid for. This is about a third of the price of an air ticket, and when you think about the time spent in getting to and from Aswan airport, going by bus is not so much longer. The buses have air conditioning, toilets and a video — on which the driver watches his favourite Egyptian films. You also get to stop at a featureless spot in the desert which, you will be assured, is precisely the Topic of Cancer. Seats should be booked the day before.

Unless included in your air tour or bus tour, **entrance** to the temples costs LE8.

Accommodation is at the **Nefertiti** (3-star). Enquire at the Tourist Office in Aswan (or wherever) for booking details — reservations are a necessity. The hotel, with air-conditioned rooms, plus pool and tennis courts, is halfway between the airport and the temples, ie in the middle of nowhere.

Or there is the dreadful clutch of bungalows called **Pharaoh's Village**, with a Tutankhamun Tourist Centre and a Ramses Supermarket.

I have not discovered who is stupid enough to stay at any of these places. The only excuse for doing so is having more time at Abu Simbel, though the best thing for that is to bring a sleeping bag and without making yourself conspicuous to sack out right at the temples. It can get very windy, but the dawn is magnificent.

THE WESTERN DESERT

Egypt is a land of pairs — arranged as opposites, as complementaries, as identities. There is this life and the afterlife; the river and the sky; the cultivated land and the desert; and there is the desert and the sea. It is the desert and the sea, described in this and subsequent chapters, that bound Egypt, protect it, preserve it, sometimes suddenly change it, and with the Nile determine its fortunes.

The deserts and the sea have always provided Egypt with her security, but have provided her conquerors with avenues of attack. It has generally been the forces of the West that have come by sea or at least secured themselves by Mediterranean routes of supply. Alexander marched into Egypt from Gaza, but founded his city by the sea, his Ptolemaic successors governing from Alexandria. The Crusaders landed repeatedly at Damietta. The French and British came by sea and prized Egypt less for herself than for her strategic positon on the route to India. They underlined this by building and operating the Suez Canal, and as recently as 1956 fought in vain along with Israel to keep it under their control. The Germans attacked across the desert and met defeat at El Alamein, one of the most important battles of the Second World War; they had come in tanks to break British naval power in the Mediterranean, and that naval power broke them in turn.

In its effects, the greatest desert attack on Egypt came in AD 640–41 when Amr swept across the sands under the banner of Islam. He had with him only 3500 men. Today hardly more than a tenth as many men are waging from the deserts a *jihad* of another kind: in the world's oldest monasteries they are leading Christianity in Egypt towards a spiritual renaissance.

Alexander's Journey to Siwa

There is the strange story of Alexander's visit in 331 BC to Siwa, an oasis in the Western Desert, 550 km from Cairo as the crow flies, 300 km from the sea. After founding Alexandria, he made the long and dangerous journey, attended only by a small number of men, to consult the Oracle of Ammon,

Strange pilgrimage

a ram-headed Libyan god associated with Egyptian Amun and Greek Zeus. Only twice in Alexander's career did his route diverge from strategic dictates; the first time he went to Troy, the site of his hero Achilles' glory; the second he went to Siwa.

Writers ancient and modern have adduced a variety of reasons why Alexander should have made the journey, but there is the recurring theme that he went to seek confirmation that he was the son of Zeus. Alexander himself never explained his motive, nor did he ever reveal what he had asked the oracle, nor what he had been told, though from that time on he was shown on coins with the horns of a ram.

Before entering Egypt, Alexander had defeated Darius at the battle of Issus, appropriating the fleeing King's 365 concubines. After Egypt, Alexander would strike at the heart of the Persian Empire, march to the Indus, and appropriate the world. In doing so, he would combine East and West, and the journey to Siwa may have been an early example of this policy of amalgam. Alexander the son of Ammon; the son of Amun; the son of Zeus. It is a usefully embracing pedigree for a young man on the threshold of universal domination.

Even today on an asphalt road the journey to Siwa takes eight hours or more from Mersa Matruh on the Mediterranean coast, 230 km west of Alexandria.

Alexander and his guides and companions took eight days to cover the distance from the coast, getting lost in a sandstorm and after four days exhausting their water; then clouds gathered and a sudden storm broke, 'not without the help of the gods', and they were able to refill their leather water bottles. They travelled by night along a chain of hills, their way rising and falling through valley after valley and into a final pass which wound down a ravine to the sandy plains beyond. In this pass, beneath the light of the moon and desert stars, the ground was covered with shells which reflected the moonbeams till the whole road sparkled. Bayle St John, a 19th C traveller, followed Alexander's route and described it at this point: 'A gorge black as Erebus lies across the path, and on the right stands a huge pile or rocks, looking like the fortifications of some vast fabulous city . . . There were yawning gateways flanked by bastions of tremendous altitude; there were towers and pyramids and crescents and domes and dizzy pinnacles and majestic crenellated heights, all invested with unearthly grandeur by the magic beams of the moon but exhibiting, in wide breaches and indescribable ruin, that they had been battered and undermined by the hurricane, the thunderbolt, the winter torrent and all the mighty artillery of time'.

<aside>A landscape blasted by 'all the mighty artillery of time'</aside>

Here Alexander lost his way again, but was rescued by a pair of crows, some writers say also by a pair of talking snakes, who set him on the proper track. Bayle St John also saw crows here, and the valley is still known to the Berbers of the region as the Pass of the Crow.

Arrival at Siwa

Gazelles are seen along the way, until the last blinding 15 km of whitened sand and land hardened with natural salt; and then suddenly there is **Siwa Oasis**, a vastness of date palms, of olive and fruit trees, streams and meadow grasses, quail and falcons, and the remains of the Temple of Ammon. For both Alexander and the people of the oasis, the sudden arrival must have been momentous. Alexander had survived the phantasms and perils of the desert and was lucky to be alive; the natives had never seen a pharaoh, but here was a Macedonian conqueror. Desert caravans and the occasional pilgrim were its only link with the outside world, and after the oasis was visited by Pausanias in AD 160, it was not visited by a European again until 1792. Its local customs, including homosexuality to the point of all-male marriage, survived into this century, and the language spoken by its population of 5000 is as often Berber as Arabic. There is a feeling of the Sahara, of the African land mass; though most of the population is Berber, there is a significant Sudanese minority, the descendants of slaves. Egypt is distant, though Siwa's dates and olives find their way around the country and have the reputation for being the finest. Women still live secluded lives, kept often indoors, emerging wearing the veil and long robes. But their heads, their necks, their arms and legs are decorated in enormous amounts of silver jewellery, some sold at Khan el Khalili in Cairo. Amidst these unusual and gradually vanishing scenes, and innovations and new building, the old village of Siwa, its mosques and houses built of mud brick with blank and windowless facades, contributes still to the mood of isolation.

The original habitation was at Aghurmi, but in the 13th C the townspeople moved to a rocky outcrop a kilometre to the west where they built fortified houses. With the incorporation of the area into Mohammed Ali's new Egypt early in the 19th C, the people felt secure enough to move down to the base of the hill. This is the present **town of Siwa**.

The XXVI Dynasty **Temple of Ammon** stands fairly well preserved at Aghurmi. Alexander entered into the innermost shrine, a small room about 3 metres wide and 6 metres long, and put his questions directly to the god. As at Kom Ombo in Upper Egypt you can still see here — can see more than Alexander knew — the means by which the god replied: a narrow passage ran behind the right-hand wall and was linked to the shrine by a series of small holes. Through these the priest could speak as though the god were answering in person. But it was on the temple steps, as Alexander entered **Alexander's** or departed, that the words which came to establish **divinity** Alexander's divinity were spoken. Accounts and interpretations differ. Alexander had come to Siwa via Memphis and Alexandria, and the priest in welcoming him may simply have called him 'son of Amun', that is 'Pharaoh', and this translated into Greek would have been 'son of Zeus'. Another story is that the priest, who would not have known much Greek, addressed Alexander as 'my boy', but saying '*o paidios*' for '*o paidion*'. To Alexander and his Macedonians this would have sounded like the two words '*pai dios*', 'son of Zeus'. In any case, Greeks attached great significance to slips of the tongue, so even if they realised the error it would happily have been taken as a truth. What is historically important is not what was said that day, but what was believed in the four years between Siwa and the Indus, and it is true that Alexander did come as close as any mortal might to being the son of Zeus.

The Inner Oases of the Western Desert

A road something over 1000 km in length loops far out into the Western Desert from Giza, at first southwest to Bahariya and Farafra oases, continuing southeast to Dakhla Oasis and then due east to Kharga Oasis, finally turning northeast to join the Nile Valley near Assiut. The distance between each stage is about 200 km, except between Giza and Bahariya where the distance is about 350 km. The entire journey can be done by ordinary car or, sometimes erratically, by public bus. But it is the stretch between Farafra and Dakhla that is least served by any form of transport, so in practice the oases are best visited from two directions: Bahariya and Farafra direct from Cairo; Kharga and Dakhla from Assiut (or from Cairo via Assiut). Also, Kharga is served by air from Cairo.

Ninety-three percent of Egypt lies on either side of the valley and the Delta and overwhelmingly this is desert wasteland. No more than one percent of the country's population inhabits these regions, and the oases, found only in the Western Desert, are home to the majority. The four inner oases mark the line of a prehistoric branch of the Nile and in 1958 the government decided to bring this area back to life to **The New Valley** create a New Valley in parallel with the present Nile Valley. Power stations, factories, packing plants and housing estates have been built and the intention is to extend Egypt's agricultural land by many thousands of square kilometres. For the most part, however, the way of life remains simple and traditional, and, Kharga excepted, the oases are hardly visited by tourists for whom in any case there are few facilities.

Reaching Kharga and Dakhla

Kharga and Dakhla, being closest to the Nile valley, have been under greater control by the central authority and this is reflected in the number of monuments and relative prosperity of these areas.

The ancient Egyptians were in full control of **Kharga Oasis** from the XVIII Dynasty; it was an area of exceptional fertility, and the Greeks and Romans called it the Great Oasis. Decline set in during the Middle Ages, though Kharga remained an important centre on the Darb el Arba'in, the Forty Days Road named for the time it took camel caravans to reach the Nile from Darfur in the Sudan. Today attempts are being made to raise the water table and wells, some of them

Dome of a 4th–5th C Christian chapel at Baqawat

1.5 km deep, have been drilled. The water is estimated to have been in the ground 25,000 years, the time it has taken to percolate through from Lake Chad. The New Valley project has proved more difficult and costly than anticipated, and the intended mass transfer of population, mostly landless fellahin from the Delta and the 'Old' Valley, too ambitious. Nevertheless, at Kharga Oasis there is a population of around 20,000, model villages have been built, new roads laid, electricity (which often blacks out) installed. Kharga is not the most romantic of the oases, but it is the easiest to get to and there is much of interest roundabout.

In the town itself is a **museum** containing finds ranging from VI Dynasty stelae to 12 C Islamic pottery from Dakhla and Kharga. Just to the north of Kharga, on the west side of the Assiut road, lie the ruins of the ancient town of **Hibis**. The site has not been excavated except for the central **Temple of Amun**, dedicated to the god by Darius I, he whose soldiers met defeat at Marathon and whose namesake Alexander would thrash 150 years later. It has been reconstructed and makes a picturesque scene amidst groves of date palm, in contrast to the edge of desert situation of so many temples along the Nile. On a ridge one kilometre north is the **Christian necropolis** of al-Baqawat. The mud brick mausolea, some surmounted by domes, were painted inside with symbolic figures or biblical themes, a few well preserved.

It is a four-hour journey from Kharga to Dakhla with spectacular scenery enroute — cliffs, wadis and crescent dunes. The dunes in the northern end and western parts of the desert form in long continous ridges or 'swords' (*seif*), but here in the southeast are the crescent (or *barchan*) dunes — the two are never found together. The barchan is a remarkable phenomenon, weighing up to 450 million kilos, standing perhaps 30 metres high and advancing forward in the direction of its horns which may be as much as 365 metres apart. The two

**The sex life of
sand dunes**

widely separated horns always remain exactly level with one another, and the dune keeps its simple crescent shape intact with extraordinary persistence even while it is on the move, and while it is passing over such large obstacles as rocks, small hillocks and villages. It is seemingly an organism existing in a slow elementary way, and there is evidence that it is capable of a sort of reproduction whereby baby dunes are formed in the open a hundred metres or so downwind of the horn of a fully grown parent. (As to how dunes form, why they assume one shape and not another, and for details of their sex lives generally, see *The Physics of Blown Sand and Desert Dunes* by R A Bagnold; also there is his *Libyan Sands: Travel in a Dead World.*)

Dakhla Oasis is visited for the sheer beauty of the place, its peace, its pleasant walks and the kind-heartedness of its people. For this reason it is enough to arrive at **Mut**, one of the two main towns of the oasis, and sit around in the spacious central square. There are a few ruins in the area but you need

**The most
beautiful oasis**

not trouble yourself with these; every other building in Mut contains a coffee house where men sit playing backgammon and smoke waterpipes and the muezzin wails to the sudden Saharan darkness from his crenellated mosque. There are springs nearby at **Mut Talata**, one above blood temperature, the other a little cooler, where you can join the local people for a pitch-dark wallow under the desert stars. Still within the oasis, 27 km to the west, is the other principal town, **al-Qasr**. This is the original fortified settlement, silent and ageless, where the Mamelukes rebuilt the main mosque on Ayyubid foundations and its misshapen domes rise over low mud brick and white plaster houses. A kilometre southwest of al-Qasr there is a Roman cemetery, and 2 km further, at **Deir al-Hagar**, there is a picturesque ruined Roman temple dedicated to Amun, Mut and Khonsu, the Theban Triad.

Visiting Bahariya and Farafra

Despite New Kingdom inscriptions found in the Nile valley referring to both of these oases, the oldest sites at Bahariya date only from the XXVI Dynasty, while there are no ancient remains at Farafra at all.

In the near rainless environment of **Bahariya Oasis**, dates, olives, citrus fruits and onions of high quality are grown. The administrative centre is **Bawiti**, a village of white-walled houses decorated with patterns in blue and red, and with a 6th C Coptic church. A ridge overlooking Bawit to the southwest, called Qarat al-Farargi (Ridge of the Chicken Merchant), contains **subterranean galleries** of bird burials, mostly hawks and ibises, the detritus of a Thoth and Horus cult which flourished here from the XXVI Dynasty through to Roman times. The locals, who these days raise turkeys, imagined the galleries were filled with chicken bones. Farther southwest at a separate community called Qasr al-Magisbah there is a **Temple of Alexander the Great** with reliefs of the conqueror. Leaving Bahariya along the main road south you pass through an attendant oasis, **al-Hayz**, with a Coptic church. The dunes here are blackened with stones containing ferrous oxides.

The scenery soon becomes spectacular, with weirdly eroded sandstone outcrops enroute and then the sight of the vast 'white desert'. Unlike the other oases, **Farafra** does not give the impression of sitting in a depression but of instead standing on an endless plain of light coloured limestone rocks. The impression is owed to the fact that of all the major oases Farafra is the smallest, yet it sits within one of the largest depressions in the Western Desert. From the south the descent is hardly noticeable, but there are steep cliffs along the northwest rim. The limestone landscape all round dazzles, and much of the depression is filled with blown sand which here forms seif dunes. The one village of mud brick stands on an island rising out of the surrounding desert flatness. It is pleasant to follow its narrow streets to the olive groves and gardens. There is nothing else to do: the one café closes during the height of day and in the evening does not remain open after 8pm. That is when you gaze upwards and the black sky transfixes you with its milliard stars.

The white desert

The road continues round to Dakhla and Kharga, but you may wait a very long time for something to come by.

Monasteries of the Wadi Natrun

Many of the fundamental doctrines of Christianity were first shaped within gaze of the sea at Alexandria. For about 250 years, from the end of the 2nd C AD to the break between Egypt and the wider Church at the Council of Chalcedon in AD 451, Alexandria was the great centre of theological learning and controversy. At first Greek in outlook, a part of the wider Mediterranean world, Alexandria's voice was heard throughout the Roman Empire.

With the translation of the Bible into Coptic during the 3rd C, Christianity spread beyond the metropolis and other Greek-speaking communities to the native population

355

throughout Egypt. It was a century and more of persecution, beginning in 202 under Septimius Severus, continuing in 250 under Decius, and reaching its most awful climax under Diocletian from AD 303. Nowhere in the Roman Empire suffered more than Egypt, where hundreds of thousands were martyred in the final holocaust. 'So many were killed on a single day', wrote Eusebius, an eyewitness, 'that the axe, blunted and worn out by the slaughter, was broken in pieces, while the exhausted executioners had to be periodically relieved. No sooner had the first batch been sentenced, than others from every side would jump on to the platform in front of the judge and proclaim themselves Christians. They paid no heed to torture in all its terrifying forms, but undaunted spoke boldly of their devotion to the God of the universe and with joy, laughter and gaiety received the final sentence of death'.

A few sought refuge in the desert, but it was only after Constantine's Edict of Toleration in 313 when the need to flee had passed, that the great exodus began. Martyrdom had offered a direct route to God; now the way would be found in the desert. This was a peculiarly Egyptian response, for the first solitaries and monks were natives nearly to a man. In an astonishing act of anarchy, Egyptians in their thousands, rejecting any interference by the hierarchy of state or church,
deserted the towns and cultivation for the barren wilderness with the aim of shedding all worldly possessions and distinctions, wishing if possible even to shed their sense of self, the better to unite with God. Through them Christianity explored another dimension, as they strove to embody eternity in their lives. St Antony said, 'Let no one who hath renounced the world think that he hath given up some great thing. The whole earth set over against heaven's infinite is scant and poor'. That quiet voice from the Egyptian desert which said that each living moment carried its eternal freight, was to have as profound an impact on the Western imagination as all the Greek sophistication of Alexandrian thought.

It is in that place once known as Scetis or Scete, now the **Wadi Natrun**, that asceticism first most widely flourished, its famous monasteries standing as citadels of the Coptic faith through all the adversities of the past 1700 years. A pilgrim's account of the late 4th C is found in the *Historia Monachorum*: 'The place called Scete is set in a vast desert, and the way to it is to be found or shown by no track and no landmarks of earth, but one journeys by the signs and courses of the stars. Water is hard to find. Here are men made perfect in holiness, for so terrible a spot could be endured by none save those of austere resolve and supreme constancy'.

Now the 200-km Desert Road between Cairo and Alexandria, completed in 1936, passes within sight of the Wadi Natrun, and it is only a 90-minute drive from either city. A

Deir el Suriani riding a desert wave in the Wadi Natrun

depression 35 km long running southeast–northwest and never more than 8 km wide, the wadi takes its name from the salt lakes lying 6 metres below sea level; drying up in summer, they leave a deposit of sodium carbonate (natron), once used in mummification and glass making.

From Cairo, the Desert Road is gained by turning off the Pyramid Road just before the Mena House Hotel. The Rest House (95 km) about halfway to Alexandria marks the point where you turn left into the wadi. Entering a village, you keep right for the northernmost of the monasteries, Deir el Baramous, or you go left for Deir Anba Bishoi and Deir el Suriani. The signs may not be obvious and you might have to ask. The southernmost monastery, Deir Abu Maqar, can be reached from the last two, though it is easier to turn left off the Desert Road 13 km before the rest house — a road runs straight to the gate.

As you approach, the monasteries give the impression of enormous arks for the faithful sailing in a desert sea. But their high walls were raised only in the 9th C to protect them from Bedouin raids. The original communities, at one time about 50 in all, were much humbler foundations. St Macarius the Great, a disciple of St Antony, retreated here c. 330 and soon had his followers. About ten years later, on the site of Deir el

Evolution of the monastic communities

357

Baramous, they established the first laura, that is an un-enclosed settlement of scattered cells around a central nucleus, each nucleus providing a church for monks and hermits to visit on Sundays and feast days, a bakehouse and common eating place, and perhaps a hostel for pilgrims. This pattern reflected the individualistic approach of St Antony and his followers to the ascetic life, and stands in contrast to the highly regulated coenobitic monasticism which Pachom instituted from the start in Upper Egypt (see Sohag). There the need for each community to possess a wall was laid down in the Pachomian rules, its purpose probably to reinforce the sense of community as excavations at the White Monastery reveal that it would have had only limited defensive capabilities. In the Wadi Natrun, as at the Red Sea monasteries of St Antony and St Paul, the centripetal attraction of each nucleus, abetted by the need for defence, in time drew the communities together and gave them their present aspect. As well as the eventual walls, fortifications included a central keep (*qasr*), the earliest extant that of Baramous dating possibly from the 7th C, followed by the 9th C keep at Suriani, and those at Bishoi and Maqar in the 11th or 12th C.

The monasteries today

The monasteries have compromised with the encroaching world to varying degrees, none more so than Deir Abu Maqar, followed by Deir Anba Bishoi. For the greatest sense of their earlier isolation, Deir el Suriani and Deir el Baramous should be visited. The Desert Road, and now the surfaced roads which lead up to all four monasteries, have made change inevitable. But change has been deliberate as well, instigated by Pope Shenouda III, enthroned in succession to St Mark the Evangelist as 117th Patriarch in 1971. Responding to a renaissance in Coptic consciousness during this century, Shenouda (who was himself a monk at Deir el Suriani and for several years lived the life of a solitary in desert caves) has encouraged monastic involvement in parish life. The days when monks were characterised by their anti-intellectualism and occasionally even gross ignorance are over: today they are recruited from the universities and the professions, many of them having been doctors, chemists, engineers, architects, etc. If anything, however, there has been an increase in spiritual discipline, and it is as though, even here in the Wadi Natrun with its Antonian origins, the Pachomian Rule has taken new hold. Shenouda is responsible too for the revival of the traditional black cowl embroidered with 12 crosses representing the 12 apostles. A stitched-up tear running from the crown to the forehead recalls St Antony's expulsion of the devil. The design of the stars is different for each monastery. Only one monastery resists the cowl; that is Maqar, where the monks wear a simple round cap.

The Monastery of St Macarius

Until recently Deir Abu Maqar was the poorest of the four and had suffered most from Bedouin pillaging and destruction. In 1969 its walls and buildings were near collapse and it was inhabited by only six monks; today there are more than 100 monks and the monastery has seen a full-scale rebuilding and modernisation programme. Much was pulled down and 150 new cells built, a refectory, library, guesthouse, bakery, printing press and garages added. Great tracts of desert land have been reclaimed and cows, sheep and poultry are raised. For the monks and the church it is wonderful; to the visitor it looks something like a Club Méditerranée.

However, a great deal of prestige attaches to the Maqar monastery, which has supplied more patriarchs than any other, subsequently reclaiming ten of their bodies for interment in the Church of St Macarius. With them lie the bones of Macarius himself (who is said to have founded this monastery after Baramous) as well as remains discovered in 1978 and *The bones of John* felicitously identified by the monks as those of John the *the baptist* Baptist.

After entering the courtyard of the monastery, you pass beneath a pointed arch down steps to the earlier level. Straight ahead is the much rebuilt **Church of St Iskhirun**, what is left of the original dating from the 14th C, and to your right is the **Church of the Forty-Nine Martyrs**, commemorating those monks who in 444 freely submitted themselves to death at the hands of Bedouin rather than hide. Wider than it is long, it is a church without a nave and may once have been a western extension of the Church of St Macarius, which from the arch is on your left.

Though the **Church of St Macarius** too has been extensively rebuilt, it is clear that it was once a magnificent structure. There were marble columns and decorations of fine stucco work and painted frescoes, though now the pillars are of brick, and plaster covers everything. The site may well have been the nucleus of the original laura; the central sanctuary of St Benjamin and to its left the sanctuary of John the Baptist are the oldest survivals, dating from the 7th to 9th C. The *central sanctuary* deserves a close look for its large dome and on a squinch beneath it the winged cherub surrounded by the four creatures of the Apocalypse. This is probably 11th C, and of similar date to the finely painted medallions on the wooden frame of the arch at the entrance to the sanctuary, the first illustrating the embalming of Christ, the second showing his body being carried to the tomb, the third with the heads of Christ, St Peter and possibly St John the Evangelist, and the fourth showing Christ and another figure.

Beyond the churches is the three-storey **keep**, entered at second-storey level across a drawbridge from an adjacent building. Over 20 metres square and 16 metres high, it is a massive crenellated structure with inward sloping walls pierced occasionally by small windows. At almost every monastery you go to, you will be told that the keep is Justinian, ie 6th C, and in every case they are wrong. At Maqar they go one better and claim 5th C origins; in reality it is 11th or 12th C. As you enter you notice the recess in the outer wall for receiving the drawbridge, and above it, within the keep, the winch for raising it. On the ground floor were oil and wine presses, a mill and access to a deep well. On the first floor is the **Church of al-Adra** (the Virgin) of recent date, though the *screen* is perhaps 12th C. As is the case in almost every monastic keep, the top storey (ie the second floor here) has a **Church of the Archangel Michael**; it is at the north end nearest the stairway, and possesses a beautiful 14th or 15th C *screen*. But the church is especially notable for its *paintings*:

on the north wall St Michael, on the south wall a gallery of saints martyred under Diocletian. Next along the corridor is the **Church of SS Antony, Paul and Pachom**, founders of the eremetic and monastic life, with their paintings along the north wall. Last is the **Church of the Hermits**, with *portraits* of nine on the walls, amongst them the exceptionally hirsute Anba Nofer who during the 4th C wandered the desert for 60 years, covering his nakedness with his beard.

Paintings in the keep

The Monastery of St Bishoi

At Deir Anba Bishoi lies the uncorrupted and unwithered body of the monastery's 4th C founder, reported to extend its arm to shake the hands of true believers. St Bishoi, in turn, had once washed the feet of Christ when the Saviour appeared before him, and was permitted to drink the water afterwards. Next to him in the **Church of St Bishoi** (dating to the 9th C but thoroughly restored in 1957) lies the body of his friend, Paul of Tamweh, who achieved a reputation for sanctity after seven times carrying his ascetic practices to the point of death. Six times he was restored to life; on the seventh he was left to rest in peace. Otherwise the monastery is unremarkable, with much new building and an air of administrative bustle. For what it is worth, the monks have moved on to the lesser miracles of the Amstrad computer recently installed in their library, though there is hardly anything worth cataloguing. The entire monastery has been so often restored as to be without interest, and almost all the iconography is blandly modern; the oldest paintings are of the 12 apostles in the **Church of St Michael** at the top of the **keep**.

The Pope in exile

Deir Anba Bishoi became famous when Pope Shenouda III was incarcerated here by President Sadat in September 1981, its gates sealed and guarded by soldiers. Sadat had been facing growing dissent against his rule; now he arrested over 3000 people, mostly rank and file Muslim fundamentalists, but also leading lawyers, journalists, politicians and religious figures from whatever quarter. A month later Sadat was assassinated by Muslim fundamentalists. Only in January 1985 did President Mubarak allow Shenouda his freedom, though the pope's attachment to the place has since been evident and he often comes here on retreat. The number of monks has increased to about 100, additional cells have been built, new chapels opened in the keep, conference facilities and administrative offices built, and guest rooms refurbished. After Deir Abu Maqar, Deir Anba Bishoi has become the Wadi Natrun monastery most visited by Copts.

The Monastery of the Syrians

Deir el Suriani was founded later than the other monasteries of the Wadi Natrun, in the 6th C, after a quarrel within Deir Anba Bishoi in which the greater number of monks adopted the Gaianite heresy which undermined the human nature of Christ. This in turn reflected on the status of the Virgin Mary, for her popular devotional title of Theotokos, Mother of God, depended on Christ taking his human flesh from his human mother.

The minority decamped and established their opposing monastery half a kilometre to the northwest, stressing their orthodoxy by calling it the *Theotokos* Monastery of St Bishoi. Later, when their cause had won through, they returned to their original monastery; in the 7th or 8th C the Theotokos

A Coptic monk at Deir Anba Bishoi

monastery was purchased by a Syrian for the use of his devout countrymen, hence its familiar name, though its association with the Virgin Mary remains close.

It is Deir el Suriani that most suggests a desert ship, its undulating ochre walls riding a wave of sand. Domes, towers and crosses make the superstructure, and palms wag within like prizes bound for Kew. Unfortunately, the graceful line of the northern wall has been spoilt at its western end by the abutment of a tatty block of guest rooms built in the 1980s. You pass through this northern wall by a small doorway into a forecourt, then left into the courtyard before the 10th C **Church of the Virgin**, al-Adra, remarkable for its doors across the choir and central sanctuary, and the frescoes in the semi-domes of the choir.

During all periods of Egyptian history wood has been a precious commodity, and has nearly always had to be imported. The doors here at al-Adra are ebony and have been further enriched with ivory inlay. Inscriptions date the doors to the early 10th C; the work is probably Egyptian. Along the top row of the four *door panels leading on to the choir* are holy figures, from left to right St Paul, the Virgin, Christ and St Mark. The *sanctuary doors* have six panels, Christ and the Virgin on the central pair, St Mark the Evangelist and St Ignatius (representing Alexandria and Antioch) on the second and fifth panels, while on the first and sixth panels, badly damaged, are the patriachs Dioscorus of Alexandria (444–454) and Severus of Antioch (512–518), champions of the monophysite cause.

The *frescoes in the choir semidomes* are also 9th C, but are probably Syrian work. In the south semidome the theme is the Annunciation and Nativity, the colours as striking as in an illuminated manuscript. Gabriel is shown approaching Mary who stands within the doorway of a building. The Virgin is then shown reclining on a couch, the Christ Child wrapped in swaddling clothes in a manger, though in an unusual feature his legs are bare. Joseph is seated pensively below, while roundabout are angels, shepherds and the Three Kings. The theme in the north semidome is the Dormition of the Virgin, badly damaged in places and, unlike the pleasing distribution of figures in the Nativity, stilted in its rigidly symmetrical composition. The apostles are arranged on either side of the bier, while Christ stands behind, holding a swaddled infant representing his mother's soul.

At the west end of the south aisle is a grotto, said to have been the *cell of St Bishoi* long before the church was built; supposedly a tunnel leads from here to Deir Anba Bishoi. I was shown a hook in the ceiling here where the saint attached himself by the hair to keep him upright through four days of prayer until he saw Christ and washed his feet. Also, during my first visit to al-Adra some time ago, a monk called

Painting of the Nativity in al-Adra church, Deir el Suriani

The hair of Mary Magdalene

Iphlogios showed me an ebony reliquary, containing, he said, bits and pieces of Dioscuros and Severus, numerous Desert Fathers, somebody's teeth (I forget whose, he was rattling the names off so fast) and the hair of Mary Magdalene. This last I especially wanted to see, but when I tried to peer in, Iphlogios snapped the lid shut. I have looked for the box since, but I think it has been tucked away.

The **Church of the Forty-Nine Martyrs** abuts al-Adra but is of no interest; farther east is the **Church of Sitt Mariam**, the Cave Church, with good icons; while as usual the **keep** has a **Church of the Archangel Michael** on the top storey. It was in this keep that Lord Curzon, a visitor to Suriani in 1837, discovered a number of ancient manuscripts now in the British Museum.

Seeking permission to explore the keep, Curzon resorted to strategem: 'Next to the golden key, which masters so many locks, there is no better opener of the heart than a sufficiency of strong drink. I have always found it invincible; and now we sat sipping our cups of the sweet pink rosoglio, and firing little compliments at each other, and talking pleasantly over our bottle till some time passed away, and the face of the blind abbot waxed bland and confiding; and he had that expression on his countenance which men wear when they are pleased with themselves and bear goodwill towards mankind in general.'

At last the key was turned, and on the top floor Curzon discovered 'a superb manuscript of the Gospels, with commentaries by the early fathers of the church; two others were doing duty as coverings to a couple of large open pots or jars, which had contained preserves, long since evaporated'. Curzon broached the subject of money. '"Ah!" said the abbot. "Another cup of rosoglio" said I; "help yourself". "How much will you give", asked the abbot? "How much do you want?" said I; "all the money I have with me is at your service". "How much is that?" he enquired. Out came the bag of money, and the agreeable sound of the clinking of the pieces of gold or dollars, I forget which they were, had a soothing effect upon the nerves of the blind man, and in short the bottle and the bargain were concluded at the same moment' (*Visits to Monasteries in the Levant*).

Gospels and jam jars

Pope Shenouda III was a monk at Deir el Suriani. In fact, for a while he was the librarian.

The Monastery of Baramous

About 14 km west of the Desert Road Rest House is Deir el Baramous, the oldest monastery of the Wadi Natrun. Baramous is Coptic for 'the two Romans', Maximus and Domitius, sons of the emperor Valentinian, who came to Scetis to find God. In their cave they ate little and prayed all day, and indeed hardly slept, praying through the night as an angel with a sword of fire fought off demons darting round the younger brother's head like flies. As they sang the Psalms, flames rose to heaven from their mouths. Achieving perfection first, the older brother died; for the younger the battle was waged three days longer, then he too died. St Macarius witnessed their fearful struggle, and it was for these two young Roman 'martyrs without blood', as he called them, that Baramous was named.

SS Maximus and Domitius are said to be buried beneath the **Church of al-Adra**, parts of which date to the 9th C. Recent restoration has meant large areas of the church being covered with new plaster, though as layers of old plaster are removed in the nave ancient frescoes are being laid bare. Parallel to the church is the old **refectory**. There are four other churches too, one of St Michael in the 7th C **keep**, but none are much of interest.

What is special about Baramous is its atmosphere. From the parapet along its 11-metre high **walls** there is the contrast of views, down into the monastery with its central courtyard shaded beneath a vine arbour, and out into the vastness of the surrounding desert.

The monks rise at four in the morning for five hours of chanting and liturgy before beginning the day's work, some of them in the fields they have brought to life near the monastery walls. It is only then, late in the afternoon, that the monks are free. Some return to their cells for personal devotions, others sit talking and smoking beneath the grapes, as accomplished in idleness as they are in the discipline of prayer. You do not realise it at first, but they are like soldiers only momentarily resting on their swords.

A monk called Abd al-Masih, Servant of the Messiah, showed me a shirt emblazoned with blood, dotted here and there with unmistakeable crosses. A troubled man had come to the monastery, and approaching the altar — 'the womb of Mary' — he shrank back in horror. In a strange voice he cursed the monks, who anointed him with oil on his wrists and head ... and then witnessed the devil erupt from his body, splattering the shirt with blood as he went. 'I saw this', said Abd al-Masih, the shock and struggle made real by his trembling words.

It is wonderful to be a child and to be told incredible bedtime stories. It is even more wonderful to be an adult and to sit beneath a vine trellis sipping tea within ancient walls as the sun falls into the Western Desert and to hear the incredible from a bearded man in a long black robe with a starry cowl pulled over his head.

With Abd al-Masih I then walked 2 km out into that desert to the **cave** of Shenouda's predecessor, Pope Kyrillos VI. It is now something of a shrine, marked by wooden crosses and adorned inside with icons. It stands on the edge of an escarpment, where Abd al-Masih, his black robe flapping in the desert wind that rises before nightfall, pointed westwards into the featureless void. 'We have five hermits out there, 15 km to 20 km into the desert, each one out of sight of the other. They are very holy; they speak with scorpions.' I thought of those demons flitting about the head of the young Roman 1600 years ago, the fiery sword, the Psalms flaming from the brothers' mouths. 'It is very beautiful out there, very spiritual', said Abd al-Masih, and I knew he was not talking about the view, but about those solitaries he had pointed to, lifetimes spent alone in caves where apart from scorpions there is nothing to talk to except God and the devil. 'Would you become a hermit?' I asked him. 'To live with yourself in the desert and to find God you must have humility. I am trying.'

Behind us the monastery was sinking rapidly into the darkness and with a momentary shiver I felt how desperately my detachment depended on something to cling to. I turned to go, and at Baramous I pushed some money into Abd al-Masih's hand. He gave it back and reproved me: 'We do not ask for money'. 'You didn't ask; I'm just giving', I replied, but he would not take it. 'Money comes to us by miracles; God provides for us.' I wondered how consciously disingenuous this was and thought of the farm equipment and the water pumps which even Abd al-Masih would not have told me were delivered from heaven down a pillar of flame. And then I thought also why I had offered it — in payment, I suppose, to balance the account between my world and his, and I saw the impossibility.

The City of St Menes

Farther along the Desert Road to Alexandria, at Bir Abu Hush, a turning (west) is signposted in English and Arabic for the **Monastery of St Menes**, that is Deir Abu Mina. About 30 km northwest the modern Coptic monastery with its two belfry towers hoves into view. Built in 1959, the relics of St Menes were transferred here three years later. The monastery sits within high stone walls, its building concrete and ugly though luridly decorated inside. But it is not for this that you come, rather for the early Christian site near by.

Menas was a young Egyptian officer who was martyred in 296 during his service with the Roman army in Asia Minor because he would not abandon Christ. When his legion moved back into Egypt his friends brought his ashes with them, but at this spot the camel carrying the burden refused to go farther. Menes was buried and forgotten, but later a shepherd noticed that a sick lamb that crossed the spot became well. Then a sick princess was healed. The remains were exhumed and a church built (350) over the grave. The church was incorporated into the great Basilica of the Emperor Arcadius, added at the beginning of the 5th C, and soon houses, walls and cemeteries were built, a city in the desert. The secret of this rapid growth was water; there were springs in the limestone that have since dried up. But in its heyday the cult was carried by caravans across the deserts (Menas is always shown between two camels) and extended throughout the Mediterranean, pilgrims coming from as far as Italy and France for 'the beautiful water of St Menas that drives away pain'. Souvenirs of these pilgrims' visits, little earthenware flasks with the saint depicted between the camels, have been found all over Europe and Africa — and even in the Thames at Windsor.

As the water gave out, the city declined, though in the 11th C the Arab geographer El Mekri could still describe 'superb and beautifully constructed palaces' and 'the Cathedral of St Menes, an enormous building ornamented with statues and the most beautiful mosaics ... Over the church is a dome covered with paintings which, they say, represent the angels ... The whole countryside round about is planted with fruit trees which produce excellent fruit and there are also many vines which are cultivated for wine' — this when water was already scarce. A century later, when the wells finally did dry up, the city and its vineyards simply disappeared beneath the sands. For nearly a thousand years El Mekri's description was regarded as the fantasy of an Oriental

The lost city that seemed an Oriental fantasy

geographer, until, in 1905, the site was excavated almost single-handedly, by Monsignor Kaufmann.

Since then Menes has enjoyed a revival. In 1943, the Coptic pope issued an encyclical letter ascribing the saving of Egypt from invasion at the Battle of El Alamein to 'the prayers to God of the holy and glorious martyr Menas, the wonder-worker of Egypt' — which was something else Rommel never counted on. Menes has been, in fact, a very practical saint. A paralytic man and a dumb woman both happened to implore his help at the same time. During the night, the saint came to the man in a vision and said, 'Do not be afraid, but **Miracle of the** fasten your lips to the dumb woman's. Then get into bed with **dumb woman and** her and you will be cured'. Although astonished, the para-**paralytic man** lytic followed instructions: the dumb woman awoke and screamed; the paralytic, alarmed at being caught, fled.

The remains of the **City of St Menas** appear at first as slight mounds and clearings a few hundred metres beyond the monastery. The ground is littered with fragments of marble paving, granite and basalt columns and shards. The foundations of the primitive church and the encompassing basilica are clear, though little rises to any height.

The *crypt* in which St Menes was buried is down a marble staircase in the original **church** which is incorporated into the portico of the **Basilica of Arcadius**. A **baptistry**, octagonal within a square, its walls standing to 14 metres with a font in the central courtyard, is to the west. North of the basilica are the **hospice** and **sacred baths** with hot and cold cisterns. Surrounding the whole area are the remains of the pilgrims' town. Most of the artefacts and decorations found during excavations can now be seen at the Graeco–Roman Museum in Alexandria.

To the Mediterranean
From the City of St Menes it is worth following the country roads northwards to the sea. Southwest of Bahig is the model village of **Burg el Arab**, built by an Englishman early this century like a miniature medieval Italian town, circular and fortified. Hard by the carpet factory outside the walls the president of Egypt has a villa. the village is on a rise and beyond it to the north runs another, the extension of that same limestone ridge on which Alexandria stands. Between the two is **Lake Mariout** (ancient Mareotis), expiring here at its west-**Crossing Lake** ern extremity in marshes, brilliant with wildflowers in spring. **Mariout** As the road crosses the lake bed you may notice (right) traces of the *causeway* that connected ancient **Taposiris** with the desert. Its name is preserved in the modern **Abusir**; its ruins are indifferent—except for its tower and its temple. Taposiris was contemporary with Alexandria, though little is known about it. Like Alexandria it worshipped Osiris, and on the limestone ridge stand the enclosure walls of its **Temple of Osiris**. The

The ancient lighthouse at Taposiris, one-tenth the height of Alexandria's Pharos

innards of the temple have disappeared, though at the east end of the enclosure are the foundations of a *church*. But the *walls* are impressive and there are *pylon towers* to climb for fine views over the delicate greens of the Mariout marshes to the south and to the north the sea astonishingly turquoise, a burning blue against the burning white of coastal sand. A few hundred metres to the east a solitary tower (*Burg el Arab*, the Arab tower) is in fact a **Roman lighthouse** rising in three stages of honeyed stone, one of a chain that stretched from the Alexandrian Pharos all along the North African coast to Cyrene. It was modelled on its gigantic predecessor, but only one-tenth its size.

Below, on the littoral, there are plans to build a holiday complex which will ruin the place forever.

Along the Mediterranean Coast

West from Alexandria at 106 km is **El Alamein**, scene of that series of battles which from July to November 1942 halted

Rommel's thrust to the Delta and reversed the tide of war in northern Africa. On 1 July as the Afrika Korps arrived at Alamein, the British fleet left Alexandria and withdrew through the Suez Canal into the Red Sea; clouds of smoke rose from the chimneys of the British military headquarters in Cairo as their files were hastily burned; Cairenes, certain that the British were fleeing Egypt, beseiged the railway station in a rush to get away; and the outside world took it to mean that Britain had lost the Middle East. But Rommel was over extended, his men exhausted, and the majority of his supplies consigned by the British Navy to the bottom of the sea.

The battles of Alamein General Auchinleck coolly gauged the situation. 'On 17 July 1942, Auchinleck had won a historic battle. It had been as desperate, difficult and gallant as Wellington's repulse of Napoleon at Waterloo ... He saved the Middle East, with all that this implied for the general course of the war. It was the turning point' (General J F C Fuller, *Decisive Battles of the Western World*). Later, Montgomery took command of the Eighth Army: 'a man of dynamic personality and of supreme self-confidence ... a past-master in showmanship and publicity; audacious in his utterances and cautious in his actions ... He was the right man in the right place at the right moment', and during 23 October–5 November decisively defeated the Germans and put Rommel on the run. Within little more than six months the Germans and Italians were cleared from Africa altogether.

There is a **museum** at Alamein, with tanks, heavy artillery and other debris left behind after the battles, while to the east of the town is the starkly beautiful **British Cemetery**.

Beautiful beaches The drive along the coastline is startling, the desert on the left, broad scallops of fine white sand beaches on the right and the brilliant turquoise of the Mediterranean beyond. There is no transition, just sharp jumps in colour and texture. The road is good all the way to Mersa Matruh, the beaches beautiful, cooled by sea breezes and still only occasionally developed — though the Egyptian government is aware of their tourist potential and has drawn up plans. At present there are modest resort facilities at **Sidi Abdel Rahman** (20 km past El Alamein), where there are a hotel, villas and camping, as well as **cenotaphs** to the Greek, Italian and German war dead, and at **Mersa Matruh** (291 km from Alexandria), with a number of hotels along the corniche. Here too is Rommel's Cave, a hideout of the Desert Fox, now a museum containing, *inter alia*, Rommel's own armoury, donated by his son, while along the beach is the so-called Bath of Cleopatra, a sea-scoured basin at the foot of a 60-metre high cliff:

> This blue halfcircle of sea
> moving transparently
> on sand as pale as salt
>
> (*Mersa*, Keith Douglas).

PRACTICAL INFORMATION

THE OASES

All the oases can be reached by paved road and are served by bus. But the road between Bahariya and Farafra, and particularly between Farafra and Dakhla, does get potholed and sandswept; the bus service can be erratic, and if driving your own vehicle, check on road conditions in advance.

If going by **car** to any of the oases, at least two vehicles should travel together, with adequate supplies of water and petrol. Petrol is available at Siwa, Kharga, Dakhla and Bahariya, but there is no petrol between Mersa Matruh and Siwa, nor any between each of the inner oases, nor any at Farafra. If you break down, stay put by the road and someone will come along; do not go wandering off in the heat. 4-wheel drive vehicles can be hired with driver/guide, but an ordinary 2-wheel drive car will do unless you want to camp off in the desert.

However you travel, allow one week for the circuit from Cairo through the inner oases to Assiut and back to Cairo or vice versa. Or content yourself with either the round-trip from Cairo to Bahariya and Farafra, or the round-trip from Cairo via Assiut to Kharga and Dakhla.

You may well find a **service taxi** willing to take you to any of the oases. For Siwa, go to Midan el Gumhuriya in Alexandria; for the inner oases, go to Midan el Tahrir, Ramses Station, or the Kulali or Ahmed Helmi depots near Midan Ramses in Cairo.

For the inner oases there is a governorate tax of about LE5, usually payable at Dakhla; keep the receipt to show at each oasis.

SIWA

Siwa can be reached in about 12 hours by **bus** direct from Alexandria (Midan Sa'ad Zaghloul by the Cecil Hotel), or from Mersa Matruh.

There is a **rest house** in Siwa town and small new **hotels** are being built. A **campsite** lies just outside town. (For accommodation in Mersa Matruh, see below.)

KHARGA

From Cairo (via Assiut), **buses** depart from the Upper Egypt Bus terminus between Midan Ataba and Sharia Port Said (ie going towards the al-Azhar Mosque from Ezbekieh Gardens). It is not easy to find; the entrance is on the right-hand side and the sign is high up on the wall. The journey can take up to 12 hours.

Also from Cairo there are **flights** to Kharga (New Valley) at least twice-weekly.

In Assiut the **bus** terminus is a couple of blocks south from the train station. Journey time: 5 hours. Also from Assiut's bus depot you can catch a **service taxi**. Journey time: 3–4 hours.

The **El Kharga Oasis Hotel** (2-star) at the north end of town (ie the end at which you enter from Assiut) is the best. Reservations can be made at the Victoria Hotel, Cairo. You can also **camp** in its grounds and use the showers. Its restaurant is the best place to eat. The **Hamed Allah Hotel** is also clean and comfortable. Rest houses are easy to find.

DAKHLA

To Mut from Cairo or Assiut by **bus** (see Kharga). Add 3 hours to the journey time. Also **service taxis** go to Mut from both Assiut and Kharga. Mut Talata is reached from Mut by taxi or van in 5–10 minutes, or it is a 40-minute walk.

There is a **rest house** in the centre of Mut where the bus stops, and there is a very attractive one at Mut Talata (**camping site** also) where pools have been constructed at the spring. Neither rest house provides food, but there are 2 restaurants in Mut.

BAHARIYA

Direct from Cairo by **bus**, same terminus details as for Kharga (above). Journey time: 5 hours.

The **Hotel Alpenblick** in Bawiti sits on a small hill and is nicely kept, with a pleasant garden and a verandah (for those alpine views). Its restaurant provides basic meals, or you can cook your own. It is a good idea to bring at least some food.

FARAFRA

From Cairo by **bus** via Bahariya in 8 hours (same terminus as for Bahariya, etc). This service can be a bit erratic and to get back to Bahariya for Cairo you may have to arrange something amongst the locals (no real problem). More erratic is transport between Farafra and Dhakla. The scenery is spectacular.

There is one **hotel**, clean but no hot water. The only place serving food and drink is the local café, but meals are likely to be limited to potatoes and rice and will have to be asked for in advance as somebody's mother prepares them at home. Breakfast here is bread, jam and tea. The café is open from 10am to noon and from 3 to 8pm. There are two shops selling canned foods. It would be a good idea to bring your own food and a fat novel.

WADI NATRUN

Permission is not required to visit any of the monasteries, and each of them is open to both men and women. Neither shorts nor too-revealing clothes should be worn by either sex. Though there is a good chance of simply showing up and being allowed to **stay overnight**, to be on the safe side (about this and all other details) you should enquire first at the Coptic Patriarchate, Cathedral of St Mark, 222 Sharia Ramses, in the Abbassia district of Cairo, 2.5 km east of Ramses Station. Tel: 820681 or 831822.

The Coptic Church goes in for a great deal of fasting and a monastery may be closed or partly closed during a fast. In the recent past the Suriani (which has been stricter than most about such things) did not admit women at any time, and did not admit men during the 43 days preceding Coptic Christmas (7 January), the 3 days commemorating Jonah in the Whale (the Monday, Tuesday and Wednesday of the second week before the Fast of Heraclius) and the 55 continuous days of the Fast of Heraclius and Lent (the one runs into the other); and neither from Pentecost (seventh Sunday after Easter) to 12 July nor for the 15 days (7–22 August) commemorating the Assumption of the Blessed Virgin Mary. I know that they now admit women but I do not know if they have loosened up on the fast closures.

Apart from staying at the monasteries themselves, there is the **Rest House** (3-star)

along the Desert Road, 90 km from both Cairo and Alexandria. There is a restaurant and café here too, while along the roadside are many stands selling fruit, sweets, drinks, etc.

Service taxis plying between Cairo and Alexandria can drop you at the Rest House; I have been able to get a taxi to the monasteries from there, but several people travelling together would find it makes more sense to hire a **taxi** in Cairo or Alexandria and make a half or full day of it.

CITY OF ST MENES AND ABOUSIR

There is no public transport to St Menes; you will have to hire a **taxi** in Alexandria or see if an agent like Thomas Cook or Misr Travel will tailor-make something for you. There is a train from Alexandria to Bahig and on westwards, but it takes ages and I have no idea what you would do from Bahig. **Buses and service taxis** run along the coast road to points west of Alexandria; you could ask to be put down at Abousir (not that anyone will have the slightest idea that there is a temple near by; it is just before the road which turns left, ie south, for Bahig).

EL ALAMEIN AND WEST TO MERSA MATRUH

From Alexandria a slow and grotty **train** runs west to El Alamein and Mersa Matruh (8 hours). From Midan Saad Zaghloul by the Cecil Hotel **buses** run to Mersa Matruh in 4–5 hours. From Midan el Gumhuriya outside Mahattat Misr (Alexandria's central railway station) **service taxis** depart frequently to points along the coast (about 4 hours to Mersa Matruh). Thomas Cook in Alexandria does a full-day tour to El Alamein and Sidi Abdel Rahman.

If departing **from Cairo**, ask amongst the **service taxis** at Midan el Tahrir, or make arrangements at your hotel, or go first to Alexandria.

At **El Alamein** there is an inexpensive **Rest House** with restaurant. At **Sidi Abdel Rahman** there is the **hotel** (4-star) of that name right on the beach; additionally it has villas and hires out tents.

At **Mersa Matruh** almost all hotels are along the corniche: **Beau Site** (3-star), **Arous el Bahr** (2-star), **Rommel House** (2-star), plus several lower category places.

THE CANAL AND THE RED SEA

In days gone by, many visitors to Egypt were not more than passers-through the Suez Canal, disembarking from their ship at one end, racing to Cairo to see the Pyramids, then racing back to board ship as it reached the other end of the canal. Today, the process is reversed and visitors who have flown into Cairo will sometimes take a day-trip to the canal to watch the ships sail through.

The Suez Canal

The idea of a Suez canal is by no means a modern conception. The earliest authenticated attempt to connect the Red Sea with the Nile, and thereby with the Mediterranean, was made by Necho (XXVI Dyn). Herodotus says that 120,000 Egyptians perished while engaged in the work which was abandoned when an oracle warned that only the Persians would profit by it. And indeed it was Darius I (he of Marathon) who completed it a century later, c. 500 BC. Tradition, however, reports a canal as early as the reign of Tuthmosis III (XVIII Dyn). Darius' canal (which ran from the Red Sea to the Great Bitter Lakes and then westwards to Bubastis, modern Zagazig) was maintained by the Ptolemies and improved by Trajan. It was later restored by Amr, the Arab conqueror of Egypt, in order to supply Arabia with corn, but was abandoned 100 years later to starve out Medina which had risen in revolt against the caliph. The Venetians, the Ottomans and the French under Louis XIV all contemplated its renewal. It was during Napoleon's sojourn that for the first time a canal was proposed direct from the Red Sea to the Mediterranean, but his engineer wrongly calculated a difference of 10 metres between their two levels and the plan was dropped.

At its narrowest, the **Isthmus of Suez** is 144 km long and apart from dividing the two seas is also the divide between two ancient patriarchal sees, those of Alexandria and Jerusalem, the one becoming ultimately Coptic, the other remaining within the Greek Church — which explains why St Catherine's Monastery in Sinai is, unlike all those Egyptian monasteries west of the canal, Greek Orthodox.

The present **canal**, at 167 km, is the third longest in the world and the longest without locks. Its construction is owed to Ferdinand de Lesseps, formerly French consul in Cairo, who obtained a *firman* from the Khedive Said (whence Port Said) granting a concession to run 99 years after the canal's completion. Work began in 1859, two-thirds of the finance coming from private investors, one-third from the new khedive, Ismail (after whom Ismailia was named). Twenty thousand Egyptians dug the canal and many thousands died

The ancient canal

Construction of the modern canal

from cholera and accidents. The official opening took place on 17 November 1869 amidst much fanfare, the empress Eugénie the principal attraction after the ditch itself. The expense of the canal contributed largely to Ismail's bankruptcy, his shares purchased by the British government in 1875, and Egypt falling under the authority, in effect, of British and French bankers. It was this event which led Ismail to speak the words which serve as an ironic commentary on the significance of the canal: 'My country is no longer in Africa; we are now part of Europe. It is therefore natural for us to abandon our former ways and to adopt a new system adapted to our social conditions'.

The Suez Canal crisis Nasser's nationalisation of the Suez Canal Company in July 1956 was a reaction to the continued manipulation of Egypt by the West. Nasser wanted to build a new dam at Aswan which would increase farming land by one-third, and went to Britain, France and the United States for loans. These were refused because of Nasser's willingness to deal with both East and West. Nationalisation was intended to prevent canal revenue from draining to the West; instead it would help finance the High Dam. In response, Israel, France and Britain invaded Egypt in October, Sir Anthony Eden for one deluding himself that Egypt's rejection of imperialism was a replay of Hitler's reoccupation of the Rhineland. World opinion was outraged and the invaders were forced to withdraw. Nasser was left with both the canal and a considerable moral victory.

The Six Day War in 1967 closed the canal for eight years. This time the British, French and American governments proved more cooperative and aided in its dredging. But meanwhile the canal towns were impoverished by the closure and devastated by Israeli shelling, Suez even being entirely evacuated.

In 1975 President Sadat officially re-opened the canal. As many as 90 ships pass through every 24 hours with an average transit time of 15 hours. They carry with them 14 percent of the world's trade. There are plans to double the canal's width, and the Egyptian-Israeli peace has permitted the canal cities to get back on their feet.

Visiting the Canal Towns
From Cairo the most direct route to Ismailia is across the desert (128 km), though in one direction it is worth taking the slower road via Bilbeis, following the course of the **Ismailia Canal** (which in part follows Darius' ancient canal) through well-cultivated countryside for fascinating glimpses of Delta life. This was the Biblical land of Goshen. About 50 km along the desert road is **Medinet Ramadan** (Ramadan City), one of the new desert cities intended to relieve the capital's overpopulation. It is a good example of the inanity of city

planners. Where traditional architecture would be cheap, familiar and insulating against the fierce heat, here amidst the desolate expanse are pointless highrises. One knows that the lifts will break down, the air conditioners will fail, and these poor pioneers will have to sweat their way to the uppermost storeys, there to roast alive in their oven-like rooms. Farther along, on the right a **tank monument** indicates the farthest advance of the Israeli counterattack during the 1973 war. Now outside Ismailia where the eucalyptus begin there is the Sixth October Restaurant, a breakfast halt for the Cairo to Tel Aviv bus.

Along the main street through **Ismailia**, Sharia Mohammed Ali, where Sharia Ahmed Orabi runs down from the train station, is **De Lesseps's house**, a small villa now encompassed by a larger one used as a government rest house — you will have to talk your way in through the side entrance. His carriage is in the garden, and one small room contains his effects — a bed, desk, cross and picture of the empress Eugénie. In the entrance hall bookshelves there is a complete *Description,* that famous survey of Egypt published by Napoleon's savants. Ismailia stands on the edge of Lake Timsa and the canal, and in these favoured waterside quarters are the suburban villas of a tropical England. Here amongst the neat gardens, the clean and silent streets, drawn shutters keep time at bay, as though the English were still inside, drinking tea and gin. There is a **museum** among these streets, designed like a Ptolemaic temple. On the canal is a **swimming club** with refreshments, a sand beach and the opportunity to dodge the passing supertankers for a swim to Asia and back. A plume of black smoke rises from behind a ridge of sand, then you see the bridge of a ship and slowly its vast form slides into view; the constant procession is hypnotic.

Swimming across the canal

Only when looking across the canal at the steep sand embankments on the other side do you realise what a bold achievement it was for the Egyptians to have overrun the Israeli positions in 1973. Even with surprise and meticulous preparation it would seem suicide. I was told a story here, that the Egyptians had ordered from America powerful water cannon for the Cairo fire department. The Bar Lev line was least well defended at those points where the embankments were steepest, and against these sand slopes the Egyptians trained their hoses, carving gullies up which they scrambled.

Port Said, 80 km from Ismailia at the north end of the canal, flourishes owing to its status as a duty free port. Visitors arriving from inland must show their passports. It is very much a canal city with a plain grid pattern, though there is a touch of the picturesque along Sharia el Gumhuriya where there are many beautiful old wooden buildings with balconies dating from the last century and reminiscent of the French Quarter in New Orleans. Perhaps the most famous

Sunbathing along the Suez Canal at Ismailia

building, known to many sea travellers, is the **Suez Canal Building** on Sharia Filastin, its two-storey gleaming white colonnade crowned with three brilliant green domes. There is good swimming along its Mediterranean beaches. But it is the farthest of the canal towns from Cairo and not really worth the trek.

Suez is at the southern end of the canal and like Ismailia is easily reached from Cairo (134 km, or from Ismailia 88 km). It was the worst affected by the 1967 and 1973 wars and the sporadic shelling in between; three-quarters of the town was razed and has since been rebuilt. Suez is now an industrial centre producing cement, fertiliser and petrochemicals. It offers very good views of ships passing through the canal and also more distant views of Sinai stretching away to the south. A **tunnel** here takes you underneath the one and over to the other, and this, when you think about it, is bizarre. Normally a tunnel is dug beneath or through some natural obstacle, but in this case you must journey through a hole in the desert to avoid a trench in the desert which has been filled with water so that ships can sail through the desert. You hold your breath and hope that a ship filled with sand bound for Saudi Arabia does not come sinking through the ceiling.

Along the Red Sea Coast

Where the continents are tearing apart

The **Red Sea** is part of a great rip in the Earth's surface extending from the Jordan Valley in the north to East Africa's Rift Valley in the south. Sinai divides the sea into the Gulf of Suez which opens on to the Red Sea proper only just to the north of Hurghada (395 km south of Suez) and the Gulf of Aqaba with its apex at Eilat in Israel. At its southern end the Red Sea is constricted by the Bab el Mandeb (Gate of Lamentation), a strait 26 km wide, which gives access on to the Gulf of Aden and the Indian Ocean. From Suez to the Bab el Mandeb the Red Sea is 2240 km long, while its greatest width is 355 km. Being so enclosed, the Red Sea is considerably saltier than other seas; also its water temperature is high, the climate hot and dry, and the surrounding landscape barren. (During winter the prevailing north wind can make the Gulf of Suez clear down to Hurghada distinctly cooler, however.) It first acquired its appellation 'red' in Roman times, but the reason is not certain; some say it is from the colour of the mountains, sometimes 2000 metres high along this coast. They and the stretches of sandy beaches offer whatever interest the otherwise largely unindented coastline holds, though beyond Zafarana I find the coast road dull. The road runs 1100 km south from Suez to the border with Sudan, deteriorating halfway along at Quseir. In fact the traveller is unlikely to go farther than Port Safaga where a road heads off across the Eastern Desert to Qena in the Nile valley. The real attractions lie beneath the surface of the Red Sea, for scuba divers, or back within the mountains.

At 55 km south of Suez is **Ain Sukhna**, meaning Hot Springs, a developing resort with a good sandy beach where the desert plateau comes close in to the sea. (It can also be reached direct from Cairo by a good road which touches the coast just to the north.) The mountains continue to press against the sea all the way to **Zafarana** (120 km from Suez), a nondescript port marked by a lighthouse at the mouth of the Wadi Araba. A road runs east from here, rising onto the plateau and meeting the Nile valley at El Wasta (badly potholed in places, it is manageable by car but four-wheel drive would be safer), while another branch reaches the Nile farther south at Beni Suef. From Zafarana it is 30 km west along this road that a now paved turning on the left brings you after 10 km or so to St Antony's Monastery.

The Monastery of St Antony

From the base of the shorn flank of the desert plateau, here rising to 1500 metres, Deir Anba Antunius looks out across the broad flat Wadi Araba. It is a dramatic situation, best appreciated by climbing up to St Antony's cave or from the parapet of the 12-metre high walls, 2 km in circumference, which enclose what could almost be a village in some more hospitable part of Egypt, with gardens and palms watered by a spring flowing out of the rock. Until the beginning of the 20th C the monastery's only contact with the outside world was the monthly camel caravan carrying food and other necessities for the monks from the Nile valley. That journey took three or four days, with only two wells along the way. At that time too, visitors were hoisted into the monastery by a windlass which you can see above the present entrance. Even after the coast road south from Suez was built in 1946, very few visitors came; over a five-year period in the mid-1950s the total was less than 500. Now coachloads of Copts and tourists draw up before the walls.

St Antony and the origins of monasticism

St Antony would have been familiar with the problem, though on a lesser scale. A well-to-do young man living on the banks of the Nile (see Beni Suef), it was during the 3rd C that St Antony heard in church the gospel words, 'If thou wilt be perfect, go and sell that thou hast, and give to the poor, and thou shalt have treasure in heaven' (Matthew 19:21). At first he retired to the bottom of his garden, but then withdrew to a more distant tomb. There he attracted the devout and the curious, and so joined a caravan bound eastwards across the desert, and by the beginning of the 4th C he was living in a cave above the rock spring, the first historically documented Christian hermit. Even here he was pursued by followers, who after his death in 356 (at the age of 105) founded the monastery that bears his name. It is often said that this is the oldest monastic settlement in the world, though Deir el Baramous in the Wadi Natrun, founded by a disciple of Antony's, would dispute the claim. What is certain however is that it was St Antony's life which inspired the monastic movement, and so in a sense it did begin here from where it spread not only throughout Egypt but within a very few years was taken by Egyptians to Ireland and was from there carried to Britain and across northern Europe, implanting Christianity even beyond the bounds of the Roman Empire.

Appropriately, in view of his founder's act of renunciation, the monk who showed me round had once worked in a New York City bank. 'I returned to Egypt', he told me, 'to be with God', as though for God too this was home ground. When I asked him what he thought of these invasions of his monastery, he politely misunderstood my question, answering that

A cross to bear

several times St Antony's had been overrun by Arabs, Mamelukes and Bedouin. 'We Copts, you see, have suffered. It is the cross we bear. But it is the monasteries that keep Christianity alive in Egypt; here suffering does not lead to despair but to spirituality. Our people come to us, to learn of their heritage, and to find God here. But to be honest I prefer peace and prayer, and I hate that road which now brings the world to our door.' I suggested that visitors like myself were also his cross. 'You goddit in one', he replied in fluent New Yorkese. 'but after the cross comes the resurrection'.

Duly abashed, you can now look round the monastery. Once within the 10th C **walls** (rebuilt and strengthened in the 16th and 19th C), you see at the end of the north-south street ahead of you the 16-metre high **keep** of four storeys with a Church of St Michael at the top. The lower courses are of rough stone, the upper courses of mud brick bound with timber; the original was probably built in the 10th C but the present structure dates from the 16th C. In fact it is likely that there is nothing within the monastery, except the **Church of St Antony** next to the keep, that is older than the 16th C, for the reason you discover in its sanctuary. It is blackened with smoke. One night late in the 15th C, Bedouins who lived and worked within the walls (Muslim slaves iniquitously purchased, goes one version) turned against the monks and killed them all, setting up a kitchen here in the church and fuelling their fires with ancient scrolls from the library. The devastation was general and the loss is brought home when you read the words of a 14th C French traveller who described St Antony's as 'even more beautiful than the Monastery of St Catherine'.

The church is entered through the north wall of the nave, so that to your left is the choir giving on to the sanctuary with two side chapels, while to your right is the narthex off which is

Paintings in St Antony's church

a small chapel with an apse. There are paintings throughout, dating from pre-13th C to 16th C. The paintings in the *small chapel* all date to before the 13th C and include Christ enthroned and Mary with her hands slightly raised in wonderment. Around her are the four creatures of the Apocalypse (man, lion, ox and eagle). In the *narthex* the figures on the north and south walls are difficult to make out; on the north wall the beardless, haloed figure wearing a red cloak and riding a white horse may be St George. On the west wall are four warrior saints, Claude, Victor, Menas and Theodore. Note the camels between the legs of St Menas' horse (see the City of St Menas). All these figures date from the 16th C. In the *nave* are a series of monastic figures and a bishop. The archway leading into the *choir* has a painting of the Archangels Gabriel and Michael, thought variously to be 10th C, in which case they are amongst the oldest of Coptic frescoes, or 14th to 15th C. On the south wall of the choir is the one painting carrying a date, that of St Macarius, AD 1233. On either side of the arch leading into the chamber containing the *sanctuary and side chapels* are paintings relating to the Resurrection; they show three women coming to anoint Christ's body (Mark 16:1), and the two Marys with the risen Christ at the tomb. These are 15th C. On the south wall of the right-hand chapel are four patriarchs, while on the arch of the central sanctuary are busts of Jeremiah, Eli, Isaiah, Moses,

David and Daniel. All these are pre-13th C, as are the busts of St Mark and St Anastasius in the far left and far right corners of the central sanctuary, and the depiction of Abraham sacrificing Isaac on the right side of the dome.

Claims have been made that the **refectory** to the northwest of the church is 7th C, but it cannot be dated accurately. In the same building is a **Church of the Holy Virgin** (recent). Amongst other churches within the monastery are the **Church of the Apostles**, east of St Antony's Church, and the **Church of St Mark** towards the east enclosure wall. Both are 18th C. The new **library and museum** is against the northwest enclosure wall. Against the south enclosure wall is the **spring of St Antony** which provides 100 cubic metres of water daily, until recently the monastery's sole source; a spring of St Mark has now been revealed near by.

The saint's eyrie

Around the west side of the monastery a path begins its gradually stiffening ascent up to the **Cave of St Antony** (a climb of 270 metres over 2 km) where, it is said, the saint spent the last decades of his life, trudging down for water, beans and dates, and trudging up again for God and the magnificent view.

The Monastery of St Paul

Deir Anba Bula is reached by continuing 25 km south along the coast from Zafarana. There a road winds northwestwards for 15 km through the narrow Wadi el Deir to the monastery, snug within a mountain cirque. For all the remove of St Antony's in the past, you feel it always kept one eye on those caravans crawling along the Wadi Araba; but St Paul's is truly an outpost in the wilderness, at once hostage and challenge to the imposing landscape. You have in fact driven almost in a circle, for if you were to climb over the mountains behind the Monastery of St Paul you could look down into the Monastery of St Antony.

St Paul, St Antony and the crow

This, in reverse, is what Antony did at the age of 90. There had come suddenly into his mind the proud thought that there was no better hermit in the desert than he, and almost as suddenly the humbling dream that he was wrong. After three days of aimless wandering, it was at this spot that he discovered Paul, aged 113, living in a cave and waiting for him. The story is told by St Jerome, who describes how a crow, which for 60 years had brought Paul a half-loaf of bread each day, now brought a full loaf for the two. Crows fly about the monastery, attracted by its gardens amidst the desolation, but notwithstanding a crow appearing in almost every icon of their founder saint, the monks shoo them away. Also a pair of lions are associated with him, for no sooner had the two hermits met than Paul died: Antony was 'very unhappy', says Jerome, at the prospect of having to walk back over those mountains to fetch a spade, but the lions appeared, 'wagging their tails', and scratched out a grave with their paws. A modern scholar has written that Paul 'is at best a symbolic figure and at worst a pious fraud', but the word has not yet travelled up the Wadi el Deir where the saint's cave and his remains are as tangible as the faith of the monks.

St Paul's is only a seventh the size of St Antony's, which further heightens its sense of being an enclosed village. To the left of the present-day gate is the rope and pulley in use till early in the 20th C to hoist visitors into the walls. If anything, St Paul's is more pleasingly antique, though this is because it is more decrepit. It too suffered from the Bedouins late in the 15th C and was rebuilt by monks from Deir el Suriani — and then had to be reconstructed again in 1701 after lying desolate for over 100 years. Remoteness and poverty have probably been as much its enemies, yet perhaps they have contributed to the friendly atmosphere you encounter here. Visitors are not so many, and a novice will make you sweet mint tea while a monk is found to show you round.

Unusually, the four-storey **keep** has a **Church of the Virgin** rather than of St Michael on the top floor. Near by is the old **refectory**, adjacent to the triple-domed 17th C **Church of St Mercurius** or Abu Saifain, with a good sanctuary and indifferent icons.

Almost below this is the **Cave Church of St Paul**. As you go down the steps a *dome* above you is painted with warrior saints on horseback. These are 18th C. Below, to the east, are three sanctuaries marking an enlargement of faith over time. The farthest is dedicated to St Paul and is indeed meant to be the very *cave* in which St Antony found him. Near it is a modern marble *sarcophagus* containing, you are told, his remains. The central sanctuary, dedicated to St Antony, is perhaps 8th C, possibly as late as 13th C. The nearest sanctuary was built of stone in the 18th C and is dedicated to the Twenty-Four Elders of the Apocalypse. The paintings in the older portions of the church may well have dated originally from the 13th C, but most were repainted, according to a French pilgrim here in 1716, by a monk who 'informed us that he had never learnt to paint. His work is evident proof of that'. And it is true that he seems to have painted with a sure touch for the stilted and bland. On the *west wall* are four archangels, Raphael, Suriel, Zaqiel and Sathiel; also Shadrach, Meshach and Abednego in the fiery furnace. But I confess to my pleasure at the grotesquely prawnlike cherubim on either side of the Virgin and Child, and to delighting in the composition decorating the *left-hand sanctuary,* the Elders with what appear to be half a gigantic moustache each, Christ Pantocrator amidst a swirl of Fauvist colour (the monk ground up the local rock to make his paints) from which peep the cubistic heads of the four creatures of the Apocalypse — all tenth-rate Braque, perhaps, but it would not have been out of place seen from the very back row as a backdrop to a Diaghilev ballet.

Farther into the monastery is the 17th C **Church of St Michael** containing an icon of the Virgin painted, you are assured, by St Luke in AD 40, and an extraordinary icon of the head of John the Baptist staring at you horizontally from a dish, dated 1760. (St Luke's more famous icon of the Virgin, painted it is said from life, was lost at the fall of Constantinople in 1453. John the Baptist has been more fortunate; his head is kept at Venice, Aleppo, Damascus and the Monastery of St Macarius in the Wadi Natrun.)

Towards the western end of the monastery is the **spring of St Paul** with a meagre outflow of 4 cubic metres of water daily (compared to St Antony's 100 cubic metres).

South to Hurghada and Beyond

All down the coast after the turning for the Monastery of St Paul the mountains stand well back from the sea and the road runs through featureless desert on both sides, offering no more than distant views of occasional offshore oil rigs. Only at Hurghada do the mountains close in again around the bay.

Off the coast road 30 km north of Hurghada a track runs back into the Eastern Desert to **Mons Porphyrites**, the porphyry quarries, where at terrible human cost the Romans

The keep and garden within the walls of St Paul's monastery

ment of their basilicas, baths and private houses. The ruins of a settlement and unfinished Ionic temple of Hadrian's reign can be seen here, but you will need a four-wheel drive vehicle.

Once a fishing village, **Hurghada** (395 km from Suez or 214 km from Qena on the Nile) has become the centre of Egypt's Red Sea oil operations, which are second in importance only to those in Sinai. This and tourist development occasioned by the attraction of nearby coral reefs and islands set in turquoise waters have contributed to making Hurghada ugly and squalid. It is a familiar story, but here amidst a vacant landscape the intrusion is all the more offensive. The converse of the traditional Egyptian genius for building civilisation out of mud is their modern talent for contaminating much that is not mud with the rubbish of civilisation.

Avoiding the worst

Near the town the sea is too polluted with sewage and oil to swim in. Instead you must check into one of the resort hotels several kilometres south of town for their clean beaches and ostrich views (the Sheraton has built a small mountain between it and Hurghada, partly to provide pressure for its water supply which is stored in a tank on top, more importantly to shut out the landward blot). From there you can hire a boat out to the reefs and deserted islands and submerge yourself in crystalline waters to enjoy a brilliantly coloured submarine world. At the **Oceanographical Institute**, 10 km north of Hurghada, a sampling of what you might find beneath the sea has been collected in its aquarium — including sharks.

Port Safaga (65 km south of Hurghada) would no doubt be offensive if it could muster a pretention to being anything more than a road junction. Here you can turn west for Qena on the Nile (160 km); then at about 40 km enroute to Qena you can follow a newly paved road northwest to within 2 km of the ancient **Mons Claudianus** where through the reigns of Nero to Hadrian condemned prisoners were set to work to provide the prized Claudian granite for Rome's public buildings. As at Mons Porphyrites, the remains of a settlement and temple are evident, and a number of unfinished columns and blocks are lying about. Alternatively you can continue south along the coast, in 85 km reaching **Quseir**, a small inlet sheltered by a coral reef, but in medieval times a flourishing port through which Egypt exported wheat from the Nile valley and imported precious Eastern wares. Until the 19th C it was the favoured transit point for pilgrims to Mecca, and a number of caravanserais serving this traffic survive. The Suez Canal destroyed its trade. A 16th C Ottoman fortress dominates the harbour, and there is the interest of local Bedouin life, a souk, and boat trips on the Red Sea.

Passing through **Marsa Alam** (145 km south of Port Safaga), a fishing village with good offshore coral reefs, you come to **Berenice** (375 km from Port Safaga) on the same latitude as Aswan. Founded by Ptolemy II and named for his mother, it handled trade with Arabia, East Africa and India throughout the Graeco-Roman period, disappearing from history in the 5th C AD and rediscovered only in 1818 by the amazing Belzoni (see the Ramesseum). There is the ruinous Temple of Serapis, built under Trajan during Graeco-Roman times, and offshore the island of Topazos which gave its name to topaz, once abundant here. **Bir Shalatayn**, 75 km south, is the administrative border with Sudan.

Topaz island

PRACTICAL INFORMATION

THE CANAL CITIES

Trains depart from Ramses Station in Cairo for Ismailia (2½ hours) and Port Said (4 hours); but for Suez (2½ hours) trains depart from Limoun Station (adjacent to Ramses Station).

Buses to the Canal cities are operated by the East Delta Bus Company (Sharq el Delta) and depart Cairo from the al-Kulali terminal near Midan Ramses; they knock at least half an hour off the train times. From the Canal cities you can continue into Sinai or along the Red Sea coast by frequent buses or service taxis.

Port Said. As Port Said is a duty-free area, you must pass through customs on your way in and out, and must have your **passport** with you. On entering, be sure to declare any cameras, lenses, recorders, etc, in your possession to avoid paying duty when departing. Port Said (population 300,000) is the busiest of the canal cities owing to its **duty-free shopping** (from drink to video recorders) and its situation at the junction of the Suez Canal and the Mediterranean. There is some reasonable swimming off its sea beaches, a few fine buildings from its earlier heyday (much of the city was destroyed during the wars with Israel and has been rebuilt) and good views of ships passing through.

The most notable structure is the gleaming white colonnaded **Suez Canal Building** with its three green domes; this is right on the canal, a short walk from the **railway station (service taxis** adjacent).

Buses arrive by the **Farial Gardens**, a few blocks in from the canal at the centre of town. The **Tourist Office** is on the canal just to the north of the Suez Canal Building. On Sharia 23 July (the date of Nasser's coup in 1952; Farouk abdicated on 26 July), running back west from the canal, is the small **Military Museum**. The best place to perch yourself for ship-watching and a fish meal is **Maxim's**, on the corner of the Old Corniche (which runs east-west a block back from the sea) and Sharia Gumhuriya (the main north-west street just back from the canal).

Accommodation includes the **Etap** (4-star), New Corniche (Tel: 8823), overlooking both the canal and sea, with private beach; the **Palace Hotel** (3-star), 19 Sharia Gandhi (Tel: 20710), with private beach; the **Holiday Hotel** (3-star), Sharia Gumhuriya (Tel: 20710); the **Vendome** (2-star), 37 Sharia Gumhuriya (Tel: 20802); the **Abu Simbel** (2-star), 15 Sharia Gumhuriya (Tel: 21590), a clean and quiet family hotel; and the **Regent** (1-star), 27 Sharia Gumhuriya (Tel: 23802).

Ismailia. This is the most agreeable of the canal cities, at least towards the canal where you will find the old and well-tended European quarter; on the other side of the railway line is the broken down and fetid part of town where the greater number of Ismailia's 500,000 people live.

The **bus and service taxi stations** are opposite one another on Sharia Gumhuriya in the shabby part of town not far from the railway station. Immediately opposite the **railway station** is Sharia Ahmed Orabi which leads straight down to Sharia Mohammed Ali.

At the intersection of Sharia Mohammed Ali and Sharia Ahmed Orabi is **De Lesseps' house**. Sharia Mohammed Ali parallels the **Ismailia or Sweetwater Canal** (dug in the 19th C and successor to Darius' ancient canal) through town; with the canal on your right after leaving De Lesseps' house, you pass the Governorate (**Tourist Office** inside); a bit farther, and on your left is Sharia Sultan Hussein with **Groppi's** patisserie on one side and **George's** restaurant (good fish) opposite. Continuing along Sharia Mohammed Ali, the Ismailia Canal veers off to the right, as does a road which brings you to the Etap and several **beach clubs** on the Suez Canal; if instead you continue straight on, you soon come to the interesting **museum** (pharaonic and Graeco-Roman, with exhibits concerning Darius' canal), and in front of it the **Garden of the Stelae** (describing Darius' conquest of Egypt and the digging of his canal between the Nile and the Red Sea).

Accommodation includes the **Etap** (4-star), Forsan Island (Tel: 768322), with pool and private beach; the **Crocodile Inn** (3-star), 179 Sharia Sa'ad Zaghloul at the intersection with Sharia Sultan Hussein (Tel: 377); and the **Nefertari** (2-star), 41 Sharia Sultan Hussein (Tel: 2822).

Suez. This was the worst damaged of the canal cities during the wars; rebuilding is apace, but it is very much an industrial centre (population 450,000) and the only reason for being here is to overnight to or from Sinai via the nearby tunnel. Suez is dry; no alcohol to be had.

The **Arba'in bus and service taxi station** is just off Sharia Salaam (El Gaish), 1 km west of the White House Hotel. The **train station** is between Suez and Port Tewfiq. The **Tourist Office** is at Port Tewfiq.

The best **accommodation** is the **Red Sea Hotel** (3-star), 13 Sharia Riad (Tel: 23339), at Port Tewfiq, on an island at the mouth of the canal and connected by a causeway to Suez; otherwise accommodation in Suez includes the **White House Hotel** (3-star), 322 Sharia Salaam at the intersection with Sharia Sa'ad Zaghloul; and the **Beau**

Rivage (2-star), 32 Shari Sa'ad Zaghloul, near the White House Hotel.

THE MONASTERIES OF ST ANTONY AND ST PAUL

There is no **public transport** to the monasteries. You could hire a taxi for the day from Suez or Cairo, or arrange something through Misr Travel.

Visitors should not wear shorts or too-revealing clothes. Note that monasteries sometimes shut themselves off from the world during fasts, and that certainly St Paul's is closed to visitors from 25 November through 7 January (pre-Christmas fast); check first at the Coptic Patriarchate (see below).

There is a good chance that you can just show up and **stay overnight** at the monasteries, but bring your own food. At St Paul's women must stay in the guesthouse outside the walls. (New guest rooms are in any case being built outside the walls of both monasteries for both men and women.) If you do want to stay overnight, you should first enquire (about this and other details) at the Coptic Patriarchate in Cairo, Cathedral of St Mark, 222 Sharia Ramses, 2.5 km east of Ramses Station. Tel: 820681 or 831822.

HURGHADA

Ghardaka, as it is known in Arabic, is useful as a place to overnight between the monasteries and the Nile in Upper Egypt, and there is the bonus of a refreshing splash at one of the resort hotels. Tours to the Roman quarries can also be arranged. Otherwise only those dedicated to sticking their head underwater and keeping it there for the duration would want to spend more than a few hours of daylight here.

Between them, Egyptair, Air Sinai and Zas Passenger Service have daily **flights** from Cairo, while Egyptair has a couple of flights a week from Luxor. **Buses** run at least twice a day from the Upper Egyptian Bus Company's Ahmed Helmi terminal near Midan Ramses in Cairo (in 7 hours), and from Suez and Luxor.

Boat trips can be arranged and **snorkeling and scuba diving equipment** hired at the Magawish resort village, the Sheraton or at various dive shops in town.

There is agreeable **accommodation** at the

Sheraton (4-star), 7 km south of town (Tel: 40253), with pool, private beach, all watersports and tennis; and at the **Magawish** (4-star), 11 km south of town (Tel: 40253 in Hurghada, or contact Misr Travel in Cairo, Tel: 3930010), with pool, private beach, watersports, gym, tennis and squash courts. Otherwise there is a variety of cheaper accommodation in town.

SINAI

After Egypt's reocccupation of the whole of Sinai in 1982, Cairo ministries quickly unleashed scores of plans for the peninsula's rapid exploitation. The good news is that some of this development has gone ahead — and that most of it certainly will not for some time yet.

The government hopes to settle two million immigrants here from the Nile valley by the year 2000. Foreign experts doubt that Sinai's population will be more than a quarter of that by the end of the century. El Arish on the Mediterranean coast and El Tor on the Gulf of Suez are the new administrative centres of north and south Sinai; urban development is being concentrated here. Manganese, copper, phosphates and offshore oil and gas are intended to provide the industrial base, while fishing and agriculture are also being encouraged. But all this requires heavy capital investment; it is cheaper and quicker to attract tourism, and along the Gulf of Aqaba at Sharm el Sheikh, Dahab and Nuweiba the Egyptians have added to the ready-made resort facilities purchased from the evacuating Israelis. These pinpoints of activity around the three coasts of the Sinai triangle, and the attraction of St Catherine's Monastery in the southern interior, are helping to make the peninsula more accessible to travellers without spoiling what remains for the most part one of the least touched places in the world.

Another Country

When you cross the Suez Canal into Sinai there is the sense of having crossed a border. By geographical convention you have entered Asia, but that means little. Certainly you have left behind the placidity that characterises so much of the Egyptian landscape; here in the Sinai peninsula mountains rise in violent revolt. Nor is there that sense as along the Nile of the land and people being one; only 250,000 people inhabit an area the size of Sicily, most of them huddled along the coasts with their backs to the forbidding interior. Bedouin account for 50,000, eking out a tenuous existence by growing dates or scratching the barren foothills with their flocks.

Curiously, Hathor was anciently worshipped here, but that must have had less to do with her bovine qualities than with her association with the sky; it was on a mountain top that Moses rendezvoused with God. In Sinai neither man nor deity seem quite to touch the ground.

Sinai has long been a holy place, and its most fixed inhabitants for fifteen hundred years have been those neither born here nor permitted to procreate — the monks beneath Moses' mountain at the Monastery of St Catherine. And

Landscape in revolt

being ethnic Greeks (mostly from Crete and Cyprus), they remind you of another border crossed, into the patriarchal See of Jerusalem, created at the Council of Chalcedon in 451 when Alexandrian monophysitism was declared a heresy. At St Catherine's you leave behind the battered fortunes of Coptic Egypt and enter one of the most magnificent strongholds of Byzantine Orthodoxy.

Across Northern Sinai

There is a cultivable strip along the Mediterranean coast, but behind this are broad sand valleys rising towards the limestone plateau of central Sinai. Across this undulating northern half of the peninsula, migrants, caravans and armies have passed since before recorded time.

The main east-west thoroughfare is the coastal road, usually reached by going first to Ismailia and then crossing the Suez Canal to the north at Qantara. There is speculation, as yet unpublished, that **Qantara Sharq** (East Qantara, ie on the Sinai side of the canal) is the site of Ramses II's Delta capital Pi-Ramses, the Biblical Raamses from which Moses led the Israelites out of Egypt (but see also *The Delta* chapter). In the late 1980s the remains of a fortress city were discovered, 400 metres square, with initial excavations undertaken by the Egyptian Antiquities Organisation indicating a temple and palace, and 12 gigantic granaries.

In any case, from here you are following the ancient Horus Road, the military route taken by Tuthmosis III and Ramses II as they marched towards Armageddon and Kadesh (see Karnak and the Temple of Luxor respectively). At about 30 km northeast of Qantara where the road draws near the sea are, just north, the rubble mounds called Tell el Faramah, the ancient **Pelusium**. Founded as a frontier town and port in the 6th C BC, it was abandoned in the 8th C AD when the easternmost (Pelusiac) branch of the Nile on which it stood dried up. Known as the 'key to Egypt', here Alexander received the Persian surrender in November 332 BC, and here too in AD 640 Amr marshalled his Muslim horsemen before entering Egypt to end a thousand years of Western rule.

El Arish (158 km from Qantara) is the largest town on the peninsula. Until recently merely a Bedouin settlement surrounded by groves of date palms and making a living too from the sea, some industry has now been established and tourists accommodated in new luxury hotels along its magnificent beach. But to be banished in Ptolemaic times to Rhinocolura, which once stood here, was to suffer the ultimate loss of face: the name means severed nose, the mark by which its prisoners were distinguished.

At 48 km east of El Arish the road enters the **Gaza Strip**, occupied by Israel continuously since 1967.

Mediterranean beach

387

Into Southern Sinai

A great granitic massif dominates the southern part of the peninsula, an eruption of jagged peaks with remarkably convoluted and mineral-coloured veins. Gebel Musa (Mount Moses or Mount Sinai) at 2285 metres and Gebel Katerin (Mount St Catherine) at 2642 metres, both overhanging St Catherine's Monastery, are the highest mountains in Egypt and can be capped with snow in winter. The journey to the monastery introduces you to this wild and chaotic landscape, with its ever changing views and the surprise of green as you pass through the Feiran Oasis between mountain walls along the way. The road is perfectly suitable for ordinary vehicles, but to venture up the remoter wadis in the footsteps of those ancient Egyptians who from the I Dynasty onwards searched for copper and turquoise requires a four-wheel drive vehicle or a camel.

Just north of Suez at El Kubri the **Ahmed Hamdi Tunnel** passes beneath the canal and puts you on the coast road running south. 25 km after the tunnel, on the right side of the road, are the **Springs of Moses** (Ain Musa) which tradition associates with the Children of Israel's successful escape across the Red Sea (Moses' song, Miriam's dance, in Exodus 15) — mere stink holes, in fact, turbid and littered with plastic mineral bottles. At 115 km beyond the tunnel, the **Mountain of Pharaoh's Bath** (Gebel Hammam Faraun) is another wretched place, where sulphurous hot springs dribble into the sea and people come to swim and make a mess.

Abu Rudeis (166 km from the tunnel) has the look of a broken-down military camp; it is in fact a settlement founded by an oil company for its workers. For the passer-by it has the virtue of a concrete shop where you can get a cold drink and, round the side, find a toilet; also, it stands at the mouth of the Wadi Sidri which leads to ancient turquoise mines.

Off-Road Adventure

The **Wadi Magara turquoise mines** are reached by following an ancient track eastwards up the Wadi Sidri from Abu Rudeis. At 25 km the Wadi Magara opens off to the north and it is then a short distance to the mines. They are round the final leftwards bend, 40 metres above the valley floor on the left. The mines were worked as early as the I Dynasty, and as you walk deep into the valley wall you sometimes notice small turquoises, though these are of little value. If you climb up higher you come to **carvings** on the rock face depicting IV and V Dynasty pharaohs. Directly across the valley on the hill opposite are the remains of **workshops, workers's houses and a fort**, all pharaonic. Back down on the sandy wadi floor you can picnic beneath the shade of an acacia tree; the acacia survives in these most arid parts of Sinai by sending down roots as deep as 100 metres.

Inscriptions and pictures on stone in the Wadi Magara

Back in the Wadi Sidri and following it southeastwards for a few kilometres, there is a choice of following wadis north or south. Heading along the northwards track for about 50 km you come to the larger turquoise mines of **Serabit el Khadim**. (These can also be reached by turning off the coast road north of Abu Zenima into the Wadi el Homur: go east for 21 km, then south for 4 km, then east again for 7 km where a track south brings you to Serabit el Khadim in 5 km.) Here there is a rock-cut XII Dynasty **sanctuary to Hathor** with inscriptions to Hatshepsut and Tuthmosis III. But the great importance of this site is that it lays claim to being the place where the alphabet was invented. Inscriptions using hieroglyphics but serving to write some other language, probably Semitic, have been found here. Only 30 signs are used, indicating an alphabetic system. Found frequently are a set of modified hieroglyphic signs bearing a resemblance to Hebrew, Phoenician and Greek letters, and which can be read as 'Baalat', the Mistress, the name always given by the Semites to the Egyptian goddess Hathor who was worshipped here.

If instead of heading north to Serabit el Khadim you take the wadi running southwards, you enter the broad Wadi Moqattab, the **Valley of Inscriptions** — Nabataean and Greek mostly, but also Coptic and Arabic, dating from the 1st to 6th C AD, as well as more recent Hebrew inscriptions telling of the Israeli advances in Sinai in 1956 and 1967. Most

Origins of the alphabet

delightful are the presumably Nabataean depictions of various creatures and horsemen, and the somewhat later inscription, 'Mozart'.

The Wadi Moqattab runs south into the Wadi Feiran.

The Road to the Feiran Oasis and St Catherine's

The Wadi Feiran with magnificent mountain scenery along
the way has a good paved road which is normally joined by
turning off the main road at 32 km south of Abu Rudeis. At
22 km along the Wadi Feiran road is the Wadi Moqattab to
the left (see above), while continuing straight on the valley
walls narrow and rise to imposing granite peaks. In 30 km
more you enter the **Feiran Oasis** (84 km from Abu Rudeis,
250 km from the tunnel).

Oasis of early Christianity

The largest oasis and most fertile area in the whole of Sinai,
the Feiran Oasis offers the most pleasant scenery of the entire
journey. It is a secret garden of amazing lushness, filled with
palms, tamarisks and wheat. The Alexandrian geographer
Ptolemy mentions a town here, Pharan, in the 2nd C AD, and
later it became a great centre of Christian eremetic life, antedating the community beneath Gebel Musa (site of St Catherine's Monastery). The remains of monasteries and hermit
cells are evident both in the valley and on the rocky slopes of
Gebel Serbal, at 2070 metres the third highest mountain in
Sinai. At the Council of Chalcedon in 451 Pharan became the
seat of an archbishop subject to the patriarch of Jerusalem,
but late in the 7th C, following repeated Bedouin attacks and
the Muslim conquest, the town was abandoned. A **plantation**
belonging to St Catherine's was established here in 1898;
amidst it is a chapel dedicated to Moses, approached by an
avenue of column drums and capitals salvaged from ancient
buildings. A handful of nuns (often from the Greek community in Egypt) have lived here since 1978 in quarters built
partly of stones taken from the 4th C bishop's palace, the
ruins of which you can see behind; and so they tend to palms
and prayers.

The golden calf

The road climbs steadily (800 metres to 1500 metres)
through the Wadi el Sheikh, over the granite-flanked Watiya
Pass, and onto the plain of Raha. On the left a white **chapel** on
a small mound marks the place where the Israelites are said
to have worshipped the golden calf; just beyond this, running
off to the southeast, is the Wadi el Deir and, a kilometre
within it, **St Catherine's Monastery** (133 km from Abu
Rudeis, 299 km from the tunnel). The site of the monastery is
explained by early Christian tradition: it lies against the flank
of Gebel Musa, claimed as the Mt Sinai of the Bible.

The Travels of Mt Sinai

On that plain where the Children of Israel are said to have
camped the Egyptians have thoughtfully built a tourist com-

plex of small chalets, somebody's idea of Bedouin tents in stone. The view is up the Wadi el Deir, with two mountainous shoulders on either side. The scene seems pure Cecil B De-Mille and is familiar. Then you realise it is familiar because it *is* Cecil B DeMille: here Charlton Heston came down from the mountain clutching the Ten Commandments. For once a gigantically imposing set did not have to be built; the location chosen by God and Moses for their famous encounter had satisfied a Hollywood film producer's demand for spectacle.

But it may be that the mountain came to the monastery rather than the monastery to the mountain. Some historians have argued that an earlier Christian tradition claimed Gebel Serbal in the Feiran Oasis as Mt Sinai, and that Pharan became a Christian centre for that reason. Driven away from the oasis by Bedouins and Muslims, what remained of the community retreated here. The emperor Justinian had founded a church dedicated to the Virgin part way up Gebel Musa, and at the base of the mountain built a fortress which gradually drew the monks and hermits of Gebel Serbal, and along with them the early Christian legends. Yet another scholarly squib denies the site of the Ten Commandments to the Sinai peninsula altogether, saying that the fire and smoke and quaking on Mt Sinai (Exodus 19:18) must refer to the activity of now extinct volcanoes in the northern Hejaz on the eastern side of the Red Sea.

The Greek Orthodox Monastery of St Catherine
However, here you are and here is the tradition. And at a distance up the Wadi el Deir you notice St Catherine's Monastery, Deir Sant Katerin, overwhelmed by its surroundings. As you near, you pass up through a terraced garden of cypresses and flowers which bloom in March and April. Here too is the **Charnel House** heaped with piles of monkish bones, sorted into skulls, arms, legs, hands and feet, while more collectedly sits St Stephen the Porter, a 6th C monk, dressed in a purple robe and holding a staff in his skeletal hand. The monks are buried in the cemetery near by: as the latest corpse goes under, the oldest is exhumed and his bones transferred to the ossuary. This is common Greek practice, for the laity too, and saves space where good land is scarce.

It is worth having a walk round the fortress-like granite **walls**, 12 to 15 metres high, before entering the monastery. Those on the west (through which you enter) and south date from the original founding in c. AD 530: the north and east walls were destroyed by an earthquake early in the 14th C and later rebuilt. Here and there along the walls are ancient Christian symbols in relief. Until recently, access to St Catherine's was by basket and pulley into an elevated doorway in the west wall, above the sealed up gate with its massive lintel. Now you enter through the small postern to the left.

Entering St Catherine's

The Church of the Transfiguration

Ahead of you and dominating the other buildings within the monastery is the Church of the Transfiguration (its original name, though later dedicated to St Catherine). Apart from the Chapel of the Burning Bush, which it encloses, the basilica is the oldest structure within the walls and stands 4 metres below present-day ground level. It was built of massive granite blocks in the mid-6th C by Justinian in memory of his wife Theodora. You enter the **narthex**, added in the 10th or 11th C. through carved wooden *11th C doors;* then through *6th C Byzantine doors* magnificently carved from cedar from Lebanon with crosses, birds, date palms and other designs, you pass into the main body of the church.

Granite columns with richly decorated foliage capitals mark the aisles off from the exceptionally high **nave** which is illuminated by clerestory windows. Against each of the 12 columns is a *calendar icon* portraying the saints venerated within each month. The patterned marble floor and chandeliers are 18th C, as is the flat wooden ceiling. This last now hides the original trusses which support the roof, though you can see their 6th C *bracing beams,* elaborately carved with animals, plants, cherubs and scenes of life along the Nile.

Suspended from the ceiling are *ostrich eggs,* seen in Greek, Coptic and Muslim places of worship alike. The explanation is given that the ostrich is remarkable for the ceaseless care with which she guards her eggs, and this, becoming proverbial, reminds the believer that his thoughts should be fixed on spiritual things.

The **choir** is separated from the nave by a gilded *iconostasis* adorned with large icons of John the Baptist, Mary, Jesus and St Catherine, all Cretan work of 1612. Behind the iconostasis, to the right and beneath a marble canopy, is the *reliquary of St Catherine,* said to contain her skull and left hand (see Gebel Katerin).

Magnificent mosaic

In the **apse** is the 6th C **mosaic of the Transfiguration**, one of the finest works of Byzantine art. It is exceptional too for having survived the destructions of the iconoclasts (the figurative mosaics of Constantinople are 9th C or later) and for being untouched by restorers. (Part of the effect of a mosaic is the subtle way in which it refracts light, whether the moving beams of light entering through windows or the flickering of candlelight, which is achieved by setting the individual tesserae at random angles. Restoration involving the removal of the mosaic with its plaster backing tends to flatten the angle of the tesserae and reduce their refractive quality.) The Transfiguration is notable too for the painterly manner of its execution, unlike the more graphic style of its mosaic contemporaries at Ravenna.

The subject of the mosaic is taken from Matthew 17:1–3,

The Byzantine mosaic of the Transfiguration at St Catherine's monastery

after Jesus asks his disciples who they think he is: 'And after six days Jesus taketh Peter, James, and John his brother, and bringeth them up into a high mountain apart. And was transfigured before them: and his face did shine as the sun, and his raiment was white as the light. And behold, there appeared unto them Moses and Elias talking with him'. To the left of Christ are Elias and St John, to the right Moses and St James, while kneeling below is St Peter. The gold ground is surrounded by 31 portraits of saints, apostles and prophets, while above the arch are medallions of John the Baptist (left) and the Virgin (right) and a pair of angels. On either side of the windows at the top are scenes of Moses taking off his sandals before the Burning Bush (left) and receiving the Ten Commandments (right).

'Put off they shoes from off they feet, for the place whereon though standest is holy ground' (Exodus 3:5). Which is what God said to Moses at the Burning Bush and what you must do when you pass behind the apse and down to the very earliest and lowest level within the monastery, and so enter the **Chapel of the Burning Bush**. Though it goes against all logic, not to mention spiritual ecology, the altar has been placed above the roots of the bush, but in order to do so the bush itself had to be yanked out. But it is an accommodating bush and has allowed itself to be transplanted a few metres off (but outside the church) where, with your shoes back on, you can look at it flourishing if not flaming.

The Icon Gallery and the Library

To do that you have walked back through the church and out through the nave which, recently anyway, has served as the **icon gallery** (though a new Icon Gallery is next to the library at the southeast corner of the monastery). Wherever you find them, the icons should be looked at closely: they are a sampling of the 2000 icons in the monastery's collection and are wonderful. One is of St Peter, 5th-6th C, in encaustic, that same melted coloured wax technique of the Fayyum portraits seen in the Egyptian Museum in Cairo, and indeed of a similarly striking realism. In the same technique is a 7th C Christ Pantocrator, the New Testament in his left arm, his right hand raised in benediction and, weirdly, one eyebrow raised as though he might be peeping through a crack in the universe.

A feast of icons

In the **Library**, with a collection second in importance only to that of the Vatican, are 5000 books and 3000 manuscripts, the rarest of the manuscripts once in its possession being the 4th C Codex Sinaiticus. Borrowed by a German scholar in the 19th C, it was given to the Czar of Russia and never returned; the Communist government instead sold it on to the British Museum. Understandably the monks are reticent about showing their manuscripts to all and sundry, and what you see and when you are allowed to see it will be limited. I did get a look at the Library's most valuable remaining possession, the 5th C Codex Syriacus, the monk obligingly turning over the pages, each time licking his thumb.

Returning from the Library, pass behind the church towards the transplanted Burning Bush; near it is the medieval **Refectory,** on its east wall a 16th C painting of the Last Judgement by a Cretan artist, and its wooden furnishings incised with mostly 15th C graffiti.

The Monastery's Protectors

From Justinian's time St Catherine's Monastery has enjoyed the special protection and patronage of rulers. The monastery possesses what it claims is a copy of a document from Mohammed granting security; later the Crusaders took St Catherine's into their care, as did the Ottoman sultans, the Russian czars (who saw themselves as the inheritors of Byzantium) and Napoleon during his Egyptian expedition. Since 1782 the monastery has enjoyed autonomy within the Greek Orthodox Church and today its archbishop is normally resident in Cairo. Though it is sometimes said that St Catherine's is the oldest continuously inhabited monastery in the world, in fact it was sacked in the 10th C and abandoned for some time in the 15th C when relations with the Mamelukes were bad. Generally, however, it has been respected both as a refuge for wayfarers — including those making the hajj — and as a protector of shrines holy to the religions of the book. So it is not surprising that opposite the narthex of the church is what was a hospice built in the 6th C for pilgrims, but converted to a **mosque** in 1106. The free-standing *minaret* was added in the 12th C. From here you can look up at the northwest corner of the church and see its *bell tower,* built by a monk in 1871, its bells gifts of the czar of Russia.

Dawn on Moses' Mountain

It is worth walking up *Gebel Musa* (the Mount of Moses), claimed as the Mt Sinai of the Bible, to be there like Moses **Timing your** for dawn. Later with the sun up the way will be hotter and the **climb** colours flatter. At the autumnal equinox (21/22 September), which happens to be when I went up, the sun rises at about 6.30am, though the sky begins turning light a good half hour before that. So depending on the season you should time your arrival a bit earlier or later, bearing in mind that in Egypt there is only about an hour's difference between a summer and winter sunrise. Also, before a September dawn it gets pretty chilly on the top. Allow about two hours to get up, and keep at least half an hour in hand to ensure a good position. You will not be alone. Some people camp out on the peak for the night, and others begin the ascent at 2am.

The mountain is 2285 metres high, but the monastery is already at an altitude of 1500 metres. There are two ways up. The shorter and more difficult, established perhaps as early as the 6th C, is 3750 *rock steps* built by the monks and starting immediately to the south of the monastery. The easier and longer route follows the *road* cut by the Egyptian government in the last century: this passes alongside the monastery and loops off behind it in a gradual ascent until, near the top, you must follow the ancient way for the final few hundred steps. This route is perfectly easy to follow in the dark, though sometimes you might trip over a camel. The Bedouin lie in wait, hoping you will hire their beast. And there are little stalls along the way, selling coffee, mint tea and biscuits. If I were expecting to meet God, I would feel shamefaced with all these indulgences; as it is, I thought, I will take what I can get. The not so wicked could go up by the road and down by the steps.

At dawn there is first a gentle seepage of blue into the black sky and the stars go out. The surrounding mountain forms go mauve. The sun slips up from behind the horizon like a levitating egg yolk. It is very good, and there is a scattering of applause, the occasional shout of 'Do it again!' The jagged peaks run through a violent range of reds and oranges. There is the silvery glint of the Red Sea and Gulf of Aqaba far in the distance. From within the *chapel,* built in 1934 on 6th C foundations, there are the sounds of a mass.

The argument between God and man

What came to mind as I watched the dawn up here was not so much the handing over of the Ten Commandments as the extraordinary exchange between God and Moses beforehand (Exodus 32). For 40 days and 40 nights, Moses had been on the mount, receiving God's detailed instructions for the construction of the tabernacle, the clothing of the priests, the dedication of the altar, etc. But the people below, believing they had been abandoned, came to Aaron who made for them the golden calf, round which they sang and danced naked. 'Go, get thee down', God says to Moses, 'for thy people have corrupted themselves. Let me alone, that my wrath may wax hot against them, and that I may consume them'. To which Moses replies: 'Wherefore should the Egyptians speak, and say, For mischief did he bring them out, to slay them in the mountains, and to consume them from the face of the earth? Turn from thy fierce wrath, and repent of this evil against thy people'. Considering that God had already once drowned the world and had promised the fire next time, you have to admire Moses' audacious attempt to shame God into forgiveness. And it works, for 'the Lord repented of the evil which he thought to do unto his people'. It is the great theme that develops through the Bible, this covenant, this civilising relationship, between God and man, and between man and man, and it is on the mount that it takes its first step forward. It was, as I said, an impressive dawn.

The Travels of St Catherine

Gebel Katerin or St Catherine's Mount, at 2642 metres, is the highest mountain in Egypt and requires greater exertion. From the monastery to the summit via the Plain of Raha it is a five-hour walk, ascending a path marked out by cairns. Camels are available for going up, but you will have to walk down. Effort aside, you appreciate the difference 357 additional metres of height can make when you find snow lying in crevices about its summit well into summer. Carry something warm. The view extends as far as the mountains of Arabia.

The story is that 500 years after her martyrdom in Alexandria during the Diocletian persecutions, monks found St Catherine's body glowing on the summit (notice the depressions in the rock by the chapel). Beautiful, high-born and learned, she had publicly protested her Christian belief to the emperor, who responded by sending 50 pagan philosophers to point out the error of her ways. Instead it was she who converted them to Christ, for which the emperor had them burnt alive. He then asked to marry her but was refused. Thrown into a dungeon and tortured, she converted 200 of the imperial guard. These were beheaded. Put on a spiked wheel,

A persistent woman

it fell apart, killing several onlookers. Finally when her head was chopped off, milk flowed from her veins. Angels carried her away, no one knew where, until in the 9th C she was discovered atop this mountain, whence she was placed in a casket within the Monastery of the Transfiguration, renamed St Catherine's in the 11th C. There her bones oozed sacred oil, and to this day, say the monks, 'the sweet fragrance of her sacred remains is a continuous miracle'.

That 11th C date of the renaming of the monastery is significant. E M Forster writes in *Alexandria*: 'St Catherine of Alexandria is said to have died under Diocletian, but it is improbable that she ever lived; she and her wheel were creations of Western Catholicism, and the land of her supposed sufferings has only recognised her out of politeness to the French'. It was indeed precisely at the time of the First Crusade, when the monastery found itself with new protectors, that it took on St Catherine's name: certainly the story made a great impression on the Crusaders, mostly French, who carried it back to Europe. St Catherine is recognised by churches of the Greek and Latin rites, but she does not appear in the early martyrologies. She was probably invented by some Greek writer who intended her life as an edifying romance. The Copts ignore her.

St Catherine's in morning shadow during the descent from Mt Sinai

Along the Gulf of Aqaba

From St Catherine's you can head east to the Gulf of Aqaba, turning south for **Dahab** or north for **Nuweiba** (79 km and 126 km from St Catherine's respectively). Either make convenient alternatives to spending the night in accommodation near the monastery. Both are beach resorts set against striking mountain scenery and offer wonderful coral reefs to dive down to. Nuweiba is the more popular but apart from the scenery is unattractive; the Dahab resort is 3 km from the preexisting friendly Bedouin village of palms and grass huts.

Sharm el Sheikh is near the very bottom of the Sinai peninsula (370 km from the canal tunnel along the Gulf of Suez road, 171 km from St Catherine's, and 240 km down the Gulf of Aqaba from Eilat in Israel). Together with **Na'ama Bay** 6 km to the north, it marks the beginning of an outstanding stretch of underwater scenery, attracting divers from all over the world. The submarine spectacle climaxes at **Ras Mohammed**, the southernmost point of the peninsula, where also there are superb views across the Gulf of Suez to the Red Sea Mountains and across the Gulf of Aqaba to Arabia.

Submarine climax

At the extreme top end of the Gulf of Aqaba and right next door to Eilat in Israel is the beach resort of **Taba**, handed back to Egypt early in 1989. Offshore is **Geziret el Faraun** (Pharaoh's Island), bearing along its crest the ruins of a *Crusader castle.* Built roughly and in haste in about 1115 by King Baldwin I of Jerusalem, this castle on what the Franks called the Isle de Graye marks the farthest point of Crusader expansion.

PRACTICAL INFORMATION

TRAVEL TO SINAI
Flights from Cairo to St Catherine's are by Air Sinai and Zas Passenger Service: additionally Air Sinai serves El Tor and Sharm el Sheikh.

From Cairo (Sinai Terminal, Midan Abbassia, 2.5 km east of Midan Ramses) the Shark el Delta (ie East Delta) Bus Company (Tel: 2611882) runs at least one **bus** a day to El Arish (5 hours), Rafah (7 hours) and Tel Aviv (9 hours), El Tor (5 hours), St Catherine's (6 hours), Sharm el Sheikh and Na'ama Beach (6 hours), Dahab and Nuweiba (8 hours), and Taba (8 hours).

Service taxis for Sinai leave from the al-Kulali station near Midan Ramses, Cairo.

Misr Travel, American Express, etc, offer **tours** to St Catherine's and the Gulf of Aqaba resorts.

Four-wheel drive safaris can be arranged in Cairo through American Express; Isis Travel, 48 Sharia Giza, just south of the Cairo Sheraton (Tel: 3484821); or Acacia Adventure Travel, 27 Sharia Libnan, Mohandiseen (Tel: 3474713).

EL ARISH
There is a story told me by a friend from Dublin. Arriving at Cairo Airport, he presented his passport emblazoned with a harp on the cover to the immigration officer, who flipped through it several times, reading the entries inside which are

in Gaelic, English and French. In puzzlement he asked my friend where he was from. 'Ireland', he said. The puzzlement grew, and he was asked again. 'I'm Irish.' 'Ah', said the immigration officer, 'you are from El Arish!'

Apart from a small **museum** devoted to the natural and human history of Sinai, and a Bedouin **souk** on Wednesdays, the sole attraction of El Arish is its watersports, which you can best enjoy by staying at the **Egoth Oberoi Hotel** (4-star) on the Mediterranean (Tel: 341018). All rooms overlook the beach, and facilities include fresh and salt water pools, a health club, tennis and squash courts, windsurfing, waterskiing and fishing trips.

ST CATHERINE'S MONASTERY

Accommodation is at **St Catherine's Tourist Village** (2-star), 1 km from the monastery (in Cairo, Tel: 830242), or at **El Salaam Hotel** (2-star), St Catherine's airport (in Cairo, Tel: 2402832).

ALONG THE GULF OF AQABA

For **information** on the resorts, contact the Sinai Hotels and Diving Clubs company, 32 Sharia Sabri Abu Alam, Cairo. Tel. 770200.

There is camping at **Ras Mohammed**, but no hotels, nor fresh water, food, shade or petrol. Access is by private vehicle or boat only. The best diving in the Red Sea is here, and includes rocky, sandy and reef dives. Services are at Sharm el Sheikh.

At **Sharm el Sheikh** there is the **Fayrouz Village** (5-star), on Na'ama Bay (Tel: 769400); the **Aquamarine** (4-star), Na'ama Bay (Tel: 270474); and the **Cliff Top Village Hotel** (3-star), in Sharm proper (Tel: 7702001). There is a **youth hostel** by the Cliff Top Village Hotel.

Sharm has three **dive shops and boat rentals**; its many diving spots include Ras Umm Sid for dolphins and turtles, The Tower for barracuda, Na'ama Bay for turtles, and the Near, Middle and Far Gardens for sea fauna.

At **Dahab** there is the **Dahab Holiday Village** (3-star) (Tel: 770220 in Cairo). Dahab has several **dive shops and full facilities**.

At **Nuweiba** there are two 3-star places, **Nuweiba Holiday Village** (Tel: 770200 in Cairo) and **El Sayadin Tourist Village** (Tel: 757398). There are several **dive shops and full facilities**. The diving here is easy, good for novices.

At **Taba** (only recently returned to Egypt) there is what was the ultra-luxurious Sonesta Beach Hotel, perhaps now under another name.

THE DELTA

From the beginning of the dynastic period through Ptolemaic times, the Delta played a role of gathering importance, politically, economically and culturally. Already by the New Kingdom the draining of the Delta marshes had provided Egypt with an area of cultivation double that of the entire Nile valley. But whereas the course of the Nile from the First Cataract down to Cairo has remained almost unchanged throughout recorded history, the play of the river across the alluvium of Lower Egypt has erased history itself.

The ancient arms of the Nile In antiquity the Nile had seven arms, from east to west the Pelusiac, the Tanitic, the Mendesian, the Phatnitic or Bucolic, the Sebennytic, the Bolbitine and the Canopic. Now it has only two, one (the ancient Phatnitic) flowing into the sea at Damietta, the other (the ancient Bolbitine) at Rosetta. As arms dried up or changed course, cities were abandoned; often they disappeared; and even today, when Egyptologists discover a site, the arguments rage over its identification, unhelped by the shifting topography.

A Great but Vanished Past

The wealth of its soil and the Delta's proximity to the Mediterranean and nearby coastal lands attracted foreign settlement, both peaceful and by force. From their capital in the eastern Delta the Hyksos ruled over the whole of Egypt during the Second Intermediate Period, and in the eastern Delta too was the Land of Goshen mentioned in Genesis and Exodus. The Sea Peoples, recorded on the wall of Ramses III's funerary temple (see Medinet Habu), fought to establish themselves in the Delta estuaries, and in the 7th C Naucratis in the western Delta became a flourishing Greek trading centre. The Ramessids had their roots in the Delta and Ramses II built his capital, Pi-Ramses, here. Throughout the first millenium BC the Delta dominated the affairs of Egypt. The XXI Dynasty came from Tanis; the XXII Dynasty was founded at Bubastis; the XXIII Dynasty came also from Tanis; and the XXIV, XXVI and XXVIII Dynasties all came from Sais. Its importance became all the greater when the Ptolemies built their capital, Alexandria, between the Delta and the sea.

Yet the Delta, for all its rich and cosmopolitan past, its important sanctuaries and great cities, almost entirely lacks the historical survivals of the deserts and the valley. Where the aridity and limited cultivation of the south has preserved the past, in the north the shifting Nile, the fanning mud, abundant harvests, repeatedly ploughed fields and Mediterranean rainfall have all but obliterated it.

The Delta often built in limestone and granite, but the blocks had to be brought great distances from the deserts and the valley. It was common already in pharaonic times for the stone of earlier structures to be reused in later ones rather than to go to the far-off quarries for more. The disassembling of the past was even more intense during the Middle Ages when the Delta people would plunder ancient buildings, burning the limestone in their kilns and using the granite for foundations or grindstones. Right up until recent decades the sebakhin (see Medinet el Fayyum) would work the tells (or *koms*, to use the particularly Egyptian word for those great mounds of debris marking the sites of ancient settlements) for fertiliser, so that some that were 10 metres high in Napoleon's time are near-level today. In any case, mud brick was more often used, and where these remains have been excavated, they have immediately begun to suffer weathering. Finds from the famous sites of the Delta have been taken away to the museums of Cairo, Alexandria or abroad, and what remains *in situ* does no justice to their historical renown.

Green and Watery Landscape

Whatever your interest in the ancient sites, there is the fascination of a drive or train ride through the Delta landscape — its extraordinary flatness and vast fields of cotton, rice and

Delta fellahin who still play a role in making the past disappear

401

maize; buffalo with sleek oily coats and down-turned horns like large floppy ears, grazing or ploughing or turning wheels for grinding or pumping; also sheep, donkeys, camels and huge dovecotes like Cambodian temples. High clouds blow in from the Mediterranean, a reminder that here in the north during the winter months it is advisable to have a raincoat, and along the coast a warm sweater for evening breezes throughout the year. And spectacle though it is to see a tanker seemingly plough through the desert at Suez, it is enchanting to see the sails of feluccas billow across fields furrowed with canals — the effect of Norman church towers at stages across the watery flatness of the East Anglia landscape.

You get a sense of all this even if you simply travel between Cairo and Alexandria, taking the Agricultural Road (not the Desert Road) or the railway, which parallel one another, passing through Benha, Tanta and Damanhur.

Ancient Sites in the Eastern Delta
The most significant ancient sites in the eastern Delta are Bubastis near Zagazig (85 km northeast of Cairo), the sites claimed as Avaris and Pi-Ramses adjacent to one another at Tell el Daba and Qantir (just beyond Faqus and 45 km northeast of Zagazig) and Tanis near San el Hagar (74 km northeast of Zagazig). The first two would probably be of little interest to the non-specialist.

Zagazig, founded only in the 1820s, is a chief centre of the corn and cotton trade. It stands on the Muweis Canal, once the Tanitic arm of the Nile. At 3 km south along the road to Bilbeis is Tell Basta, the site of **Bubastis**, one of the most ancient cities in Egypt. Bubastis means House of the Goddess Bastet, represented as a lioness, later as a graceful domestic cat. Below the southwest side of the tell is her much ruined **temple**, founded during the Old Kingdom but given its final form by the pharoahs of the XXII Dynasty, who resided here — the *festival hall*, dating from this last period, is the most evident feature of the temple. Where now there are only some granite blocks and columns to see, some with inscriptions and reliefs, and a few statues, Herodotus said that of all the temples of Egypt, this gave the greatest pleasure to look at, both for its own merits but also because the city all round it had been raised to a higher level, so you could look down upon it where it stood amidst shade trees on almost an island formed by two embracing canals which stopped short without meeting.

Near by are **underground galleries** for the burial of cats, where many fine bronzes of cats or of Bastet have been found.

A licentious festival was held here. 'They come in barges, men and women together, a great number in each boat', wrote Herodotus. 'On the way, some of the women keep up a continual clatter with castinets and some of the men play flutes,

City of the cat

while the rest, both men and women, sing and clap their hands. Whenever they pass a town on the riverbank, they bring the barge close inshore, some of the women continuing to act as I have said, while others shout abuse at the women of the place or start dancing, or stand up and hitch up their skirts. When they reach Bubastis they celebrate the festival with elaborate sacrifices, and more wine is consumed than during all the rest of the year. The numbers that meet there, are, according to a native report, as many as 700,000 men and women'.

The Pi-Ramses Problem

Avaris was the Hyksos capital and Pi-Ramses was the Delta capital of Ramses II. But though it has long been accepted that Pi-Ramses stood on or near the site of Avaris, their location has been disputed since the beginning of modern Egyptology. For much of that time, Tanis was favoured; but then starting with Egyptian excavations at **Qantir** in the 1920s and 1950s, and culminating with Austrian excavations just south of it at **Tell el Daba** in the 1960s and 1970s, opinion has swung round to accepting the former as the site of **Pi-Ramses** and the latter as the site of **Avaris**. Both are situated along the ancient course of the Pelusiac arm of the Nile.

City of the Exodus?   What has always given this question a heightened interest is the mention of Pi-Ramses in Exodus 1:11 and 12:37 as the city built for the pharaoh by the afflicted children of Israel and, under Moses' leadership, their point of departure out of Egypt. (But see Qantara Sharq in the *Sinai* chapter.)

In fact the excavations look like an exposed underground car park, and as a recent report on the sites says, 'The old splendour of the two cities has vanished completely because of quarrying, plundering and later land reclamation'.

Late Dynastic Period Capital

The site of **Tanis**, for all its fall from Biblical grace, is the most outstanding in the Delta from the layman's point of view. It is a huge kom, 3.5 km from north to south, 1.5 km broad and rising to 35 metres above sea level. A number of excavations since 1825 have still only turned up a small portion of the whole, revealing structural remains from the XXI Dynasty through Ptolemaic times. But also a great quantity of stone, originally statues, stelae, carvings and blocks from the time of Ramses II and frequently bearing his cartouche, have been found incorporated into later buildings or littered about. It was on this basis that the French excavators here from 1927 to 1956 argued that this was Pi-Ramses — and certainly as much statuary has been found here as anywhere else in Egypt except Thebes, causing it to be known as the 'Thebes of the North'.

Several points went against its identification with Avaris and Pi-Ramses, however; one being that it was too far inland, on the Tanitic rather than on the Pelusiac arm of the Nile, and therefore too far from the edge of the Delta to have been a suitable military base for incoming Hyksos or an outward bound Ramses II; another, more importantly, being that for all its Ramessid statuary, the earliest structural level belonged to the XXI rather than to the IXX Dynasty. In fact what seems to have happened is that in building Tanis, Pi-Ramses was pilfered of its stones.

From the road a track leads up to the excavation headquarters from where there is a good view of the walled **temple precinct** and the rubble mounds beneath which a great deal of the city still lies. The completely ruined **Temple of Amun** is nevertheless spectacular for its fallen colossal statuary and architectural fragments, though the most important pieces have been taken to the Egyptian Museum in Cairo, along with the splendid gold masks, inlaid jewellery and silver sarcophagus found at the royal necropolis towards the southwest of the enclosure. Discovered in 1939, these XXI and XXII Dynasty **royal tombs** were at least as important a find as that of Tutankhamun's. The coming war, however, overshadowed the discovery and it received little public attention at the time. The best preserved tomb is No.3 of Psusennes I (XXI Dyn). A sacred lake and the remains of two other temples are evident within the enclosure walls.

A treasure to rival Tutankhamun's *(marginal note)*

Damietta and the Crusades

Dumyat (210 km northeast of Cairo), as Damietta is known in Arabic, lies 15 km from the Mediterranean on a narrow strip of land between the Nile (the ancient Phatnitic arm) and Lake Manzala. It is a thriving port and industrial centre, and has some interesting **housing of the Ottoman period** comparable to those at Rosetta (which being near Alexandria is much easier to visit).

Damietta's heyday was before the revival of Alexandria and the opening of the Suez Canal when it was a prosperous Arab trading city. But its fame rests in its struggle against the Crusaders, and *that* Damietta stood farther north, to be razed to the ground in 1250 by Shagarat al-Durr's Mamelukes after the site had yet again proved its vulnerability to foreign attack. (See Cairo, *To the Northern Walls* chapter.) The old port was taken in 1218, principally by Germans, and abandoned again in 1221, but not before its townspeople were sold into slavery. Its inhabitants fled when in 1249 St Louis landed near by, but Damietta was returned to Egypt a year later as part of St Louis' ransom.

One of those amongst the besiegers of Damietta in 1218 was St Francis of Assisi. Seeing that the attack was at first going badly, he courageously crossed the enemy lines to confront Sultan Kamil in person. He informed the sultan that he had come to convert him and his people to Christ, apparently unaware that Kamil was surrounded with Coptic advisors and fully familiar with the Christian faith. St Francis offered to enter a fiery furnace on the condition that should he come out alive, Kamil and his people would embrace Christianity. The sultan replied to the saint with a lesson in humanity and common sense, saying that gambling with one's life was not a valid proof of one's God, and saw St Francis on his way with Oriental courtesy and lavish gifts.

Between **Lake Manzala** and the sea a narrow spit of land carries a poor road to Port Said (66 km). Pelicans, storks, flamingos and egrets inhabit its brackish waters and southern marshes. The lagoon was caused by the subsidence of the northern Delta; from the time of Augustus the Mediterranean began its incursion, destroying good land and disrupting the drainage system (the Mendesian and Tanitic mouths were once here), a process completed by the end of the 4th C AD.

Modern Miracles and Ancient Sites in the Western Delta

The Cairo-Alexandria railway and Delta Road parallel one another all the way, passing through Benha, Tanta and Damanhur. **Tanta's** claim to fame is its **Mosque and Tomb of Said Ahmed el Badawi** (died 1276), which I visited in the company of an Armenian Christian woman. She owned a cinema in Alexandria but had experienced some legal complications over its sale, and was told that if she bribed a certain official as well as prayed to el Badawi, the sale would go smoothly. So the bribe was paid in Alexandria and we came to Tanta for the prayer. El Badawi, though a Muslim saint, is clearly both ecumenical and efficacious, for the Armenian woman crossed herself before his tomb several times, and immediately afterwards sold her cinema. This sort of thing is quite common in Egypt; I have for example seen Muslim women wanting to become pregnant implore the Virgin Mary at Deir el Muharraq.

So little remains of antiquity in the western Delta that it is not worth visiting except as a passerby between Cairo and Alexandria.

Sais is to the northwest of Tanta; once a royal capital, it was sacred to the goddess Neith who protected the embalmed bodies and entrails of the dead and is often depicted on sarcophagi and at the entrances to tombs. **Buto** lies to the east of Desuk and is most conveniently reached via Damanhur; its deity was the cobra goddess Wadjet, represented as the uraeus on the pharaonic crown. **Naucratis** was founded in the 7th C BC as a Greek trading city, and until the founding of Alexandria three centuries later was the preeminent commercial centre in Egypt. It is now a level and desolate patch of ground to the left of the Tanta-Damanhur road. **Damanhur** stands on the site of the Roman **Hermopolis Parva**, no remains of its past surviving.

Rosetta (Rashid) and Abu Qir (ancient Canopus) are covered later as excursions from Alexandria.

PRACTICAL INFORMATION

There is almost no **accommodation** above the no-star category in the Delta. At **Tanta** there is the **Arafa** (3-star), by the train station (Tel: 26952) — and that is it, unless you stay (summer only) at the Mediterranean resorts of **Res el Bar** (numerous 1-star hotels) and **Gamassa** (3-star **Amoun**, and lesser hotels) near Damietta.

Unless you arrange something through a travel agency, hire your own car or go by service **taxi** (all the Delta towns are served from the Ahmed Helmi terminus near Midan Ramses, Cairo), your travels into the eastern Delta will have to depend on **buses**. The East Delta Bus Company has frequent daily services to Zagazig, Faqus, Mansura, Damietta, Ras el Bar (summer only), etc, from the Kulali terminal near Midan Ramses, Cairo. The western Delta is served by the **railway** to Alexandria, which stops at Benha, Tanta and Damanhur.

ALEXANDRIA: CAPITAL OF MEMORY

Alexandrian facades have the same dull brown colour as those of Cairo. Possibly a little lighter, the rooftops almost white and gleaming in the morning sun. Instead of brushed by desert sand, frosted perhaps by the salt air of the Mediterranean. When open to the sea, playing a role in the broader life of the Mediterranean, receiving into her the Greeks, the Jews and others, the milieu has been intoxicating and Alexandria has thrived. But like the desert, the Arabs encroached upon the sea, they stood with their backs to it, and Alexandria (in Arabic, Iskandariya) withered. The meteorological fact of the prevailing northern breeze driving the sea against the rocks along the Corniche reminds you of the city's past and possibilities.

The founding of Alexandria

When Alexander the Great entered Egypt in November 332 BC he marched straight to Memphis. But early in 331 he sailed northwards down the Nile, as though one last time to gaze upon the uncertain Hellenic sea, and on the site of a small fishing village made his most lasting contribution to civilisation. He did not stay long enough to see a single building erected, and instead made his mysterious visit to Siwa and then back across the desert to Memphis before committing his life to the conquest of Asia. Eight years later, at the age of 33, he was dead. His body was brought to Memphis but the priests refused it, saying 'Do not settle him here, but at the city he built at Rhakotis, for wherever this body must lie the city will be uneasy, disturbed with wars and battles'. So he descended the Nile again, wrapped in gold and enclosed in a coffin of glass, and he was buried at the centre of Alexandria, by her great crossroads, to be her civic hero and tutelary god. Memphis has slipped into the mud. Alexandria after many battles survives.

Once flying to Egypt it was nighttime and all below was black. I did not know if it was the Mediterranean or the desert. And then the captain said that we had crossed the coast, were approaching Cairo over the Western Desert, and that to the left you could see Alexandria. And there she was, far away, bright with lights — and unmistakable. No other city in the world has such an unmistakable and enduring form. Amr or Cleopatra could have recognised her, and perhaps even Alexander himself: the island of Pharos attached to Rhakotis by the causeway that has silted up.

On the edge of two worlds

The causeway, now a thickened neck of land, joins two limestone ridges running parallel to the coast. The inner ridge holds Alexandria fixed against the shifting alluvium of Egypt; the outer breaks the waves and gives Alexandria her harbours. It is a unique feature in Egypt, and Alexandria, never wholly Egyptian, yearns for the wider vistas of the Mediterranean.

Immortal in form, ambiguous in her situation, Alexandria is a curiously drifting city. Memories were stirred a few years ago by a wedding near the crossroads where Alexander was buried. The ground opened beneath the bride and she was never seen again. For all the commonplace surface of the modern town, Alexandria is haunted by the past. If more survived it would haunt you less. Unlike Rome or Athens with their monuments extant, Alexandria is all intimation: *here* (some spot) is where Alexander lay entombed, *here* Cleopatra committed suicide; *here* the Library, the Serapeum, etc ... and there is nothing physically there — a stone, a broken column, an unsuspected chamber, but nothing substantial to root her phantom personages to their place, and they wander through Alexandria's streets, intruding on your waking thoughts.

History of the City

When Alexander died, one of his Macedonian generals made Egypt his portion of the divided empire and Alexandria his capital, ruling as Ptolemy I Soter, and founding a dynasty that was to end with the suicide of Cleopatra VI — 'It is well done and fitting for a princess/Descended of so many royal kings.' Under Cleopatra and Antony, the city very nearly supplanted Rome which both strategically and culturally was Alexandria's inferior.

The Ptolemaic dynasty

During the reign of the Ptolemies Alexandria became a resort of artists, poets and scholars, and was outstanding particularly in its mathematicians and scientists. Amongst these were Euclid, who in his theories of numbers and plane and solid geometry demonstrated how knowledge can be derived from rational methods alone; Eratosthenes (see Aswan) who determined the earth's diameter; Aristarchus of Samos, who, anticipating Copernicus by 1800 years, was author of the heliocentric theory; and Erasistratus, who came close to discovering the circulation of blood and first made the distinction between motor and sensory nerves. Later, in Roman times, philosophy flourished too; so that here between desert and sea, men enquired into the problems of the universe in a way unknown before in Egypt, though unlike some of their predecessors in Greece never doubting the existence of God.

Christianity and its persecution

It was Alexandria which raised Christianity, until then addressed to the poor and unlearned in Palestine, to the level of philosophy, and Egypt which provided it with many of its images: the resurrection of Osiris; Isis with Horus her child — we can recognise these in Christ and the Virgin — while the pharaonic *ankh* appears unaltered on some early Christian tombstones as a looped cross and slightly altered on others as a cross with a handle. These early Christians suffered heavily for their faith: early in the 4th C Diocletian demolished all churches, demoted all Christian officials and enslaved the rest, also killing 60 a day over five years, according to the Coptic Church.

It was Diocletian who divided the Roman Empire into four administrative regions, an emperor each for East and West, each emperor assisted by a caesar; and it was Diocletian who began the caesaropapism, albeit in pagan form, that later marked the rule of the Christian emperors of Byzantium. His persecutions made such an impression on the Egyptian Church that it dates its calendar from his accession in 284, and his reign is known as the Era of the Martyrs. It is understandable that in Egypt this struggle between Christianity and paganism should have given rise to a kind of nationalism — indeed Copt means Egyptian — and that it should have continued even after the emperors at Constantinope were Christians themselves, for whatever the religion of the Empire, it was still a foreign (now Greek) oppressor.

The monophysite controversy It was this undercurrent of nationalism that fuelled a divisive debate on the nature of Christ. The Council of Chalcedon in 451 decided that Christ had two natures, the human and the divine, and that these were unmixed and unchangeable but at the same time indistinguishable and inseparable. This is the view of almost all Christian Churches to this day, but the Alexandrian theologians, while not denying the two natures, put emphasis on their unity at the Incarnation. For this they were called monophysites (*monophysis*, single nature), and

The Cecil Hotel along the corniche in the 1930s

were charged with the heretical belief that Christ's human nature had been entirely absorbed in the divine, a charge which the Copts deny.

What exactly the parties to the dispute meant when they talked of the nature of Christ was affected by shades of language and culture, and these were taken to the limits of contrast by opposing political ambitions. The three great apostolic sees had been Rome, Antioch and Alexandria, with Alexandria preeminent amongst them. With the founding of Constantinople, the lesser see of Ephesus was translated to the new imperial capital, which at Chalcedon (conveniently across the Bosphorus) sought to achieve supremacy along with Rome, and to humble Alexandria.

The Christological issue may not seem terribly important, or even comprehensible, but it provided the slogans by which two political groupings denounced one another, provoking the schism by which Christian Egypt was lost to the wider world.

In a new spirit of ecumenism the whole shadowy business is coming to be accepted as a misunderstanding, and by means of agreements such as the following (signed in 1988 at Deir Anba Bishoi in the Wadi Natrun by Pope Shenouda III and the Roman Catholic Nuncio) the Copts are being reintegrated into the wider fold: 'We believe that our Lord, God and Saviour Jesus Christ, the Incarnate-Logos, is perfect in His Divinity and perfect in His Humanity. He made His Humanity One with His Divinity without Mixture, nor Mingling, nor Confusion. His Divinity was not separated from His Humanity even for a moment or a twinkling of the eye. At the same time, we Anathematise the Doctrines of both Nestorius [the original proponent of two separate natures in the Incarnate Christ] and Eutyches [the original proponent of "two natures before, but only one after, the Union", which is what true monophysitism means]'.

The Arabs welcomed   The hatred between Constantinople and Alexandria was so intense that when in 641 the Arab general Amr rode into Egypt with his 3500 Bedouin horsemen, the Alexandrians signed an armistice and in the following year admitted him into their city as a lesser evil than the evacuating Greeks. The city was still recognisably that of its glorious past; colonnades of marble lined Amr's triumph along the Canopic Way; the Tomb of Alexander rose to his left, the Pharos to his right. Amr reported back to the caliph in Arabia: 'I have taken a city of which I can only say that it contains 4000 palaces, 4000 baths, 400 theatres, 1200 greengrocers and 40,000 Jews'. E M Forster writes: 'There was nothing studied in this indifference. The Arabs could not realise the value of their prize. They knew that Allah had given them a large and strong city. They could not know that there was no other like it in the world, that the science of Greece had planned it, that

410

it had been the intellectual birthplace of Christianity. Legends of a dim Alexander, a dimmer Cleopatra, might move in their minds, but they had not the historical sense, they could never realise what had happened on this spot nor how inevitably the city of the double harbour should have arisen between the lake and the sea. And so though they had no intention of destroying her, they destroyed her, as a child might a watch. She never functioned again for over 1000 years'.

In fact, and it must be held to their eternal credit, the Arabs did absorb much of what Alexandria offered, creating with its help a civilisation for many centuries incomparably more beautiful, more intelligent, more humane than existed in Europe, storehousing, adding to and then passing on to the world the learning of the ancients. But Alexandria herself did suffer, and eventually Egypt too relapsed. By the time Napoleon landed Alexandria was no more than a fishing village once again. What brought her back to life was the construction of the Mahmudiya Canal by Mohammed Ali, giving her access to the vital Egyptian hinterland, and bringing Egypt again face to face with the Mediterranean. During the 19th C the Greeks returned and the Jews, and also came the French, the English, the Italians, and all of central Alexandria and the coast stretching out to Montaza was a European town. 'Alexandria was the foremost port of Egypt, and a hive of activity for the country's cotton brokers ...with wide streets flanked by palms and flame trees, large gardens, stylish villas, neat new buildings, and above all, room to breathe. Life was easy. Labour was cheap. Nothing was impossible, especially when it involved one's comfort' (as Jacqueline Carol remembers in *Cocktails and Camels*).

The modern city

Post-war and post-Suez nationalism meant the ejection of the Jews, Greeks and other foreigners and for some years the Arabs were again in possession of no more than a skeleton, a city 'clinging to the minds of old men like traces of perfume upon a sleeve: Alexandria, the capital of Memory' (Lawrence Durrell, *Justine*).

There is a nostalgia about the city, but also lately something of her former sparkle. Alexandrian women are attactive and often smartly dressed. They are of a wide range of colour and beauty, reflecting a cosmopolitan ancestry. At restaurants, cafés, patisseries — Alexandria has a reputation for the best food in Egypt — you are often served by women (almost unheard of in Upper Egypt and not all that common in Cairo), and they are pleasant, self-assured, chatty, even flirtatious. (There is much to be said for judging a place by the rapport you can have with the opposite sex.) Alexandria, with a population of three million, is cleaner, less congested than Cairo, not desperate. There are slums, but on the whole the city does not have Cairo's problems. There is a sense of well-being; Alexandrians stream about the streets late into the night, shopping or simply walking, sitting at cafés talking. And there is the breeze that licks sudden plumes of water against the Corniche and carries an Aegean tang and freshness into Africa. This much has not changed since Alexander ordered his Greek metropolis to be built on this Egyptian shore.

Orientation

The old Turkish quarter

That part of Alexandria which juts out into the Mediterranean is the old, rundown and interesting area called **El Anfushi**. But this was once the island of Pharos, and prophetically it was a Greek who gave a first account of it: 'There is an island in the surging sea, which they call Pharos, lying off Egypt' (The *Odyssey*); it was here that Menelaus was becalmed on his way home from Troy. Towards the western tip of the headland is the Ras el Tin Palace; at the eastern tip Fort Qaytbay, which stands on the foundations of Alexandria's ancient lighthouse, the Pharos, which was one of the Seven Wonders of the World.

The island was connected to the mainland by a causeway 7 stades long, the Heptastadion. Silting has made it a permanent broad neck of land. Along this neck runs Sharia Faransa (Rue de France). This runs south into **Midan el Tahrir**, the former Place Mohammed Ali; at the southern end of the midan was, approximately, the former mainland coastline and the fishing village of Rhakotis.

The harbours

To either side of the Heptastadion were the two ancient harbours, the Eunostos or Harbour of Safe Return to the west, the Great Harbour to the east. Their roles have been reversed in modern times; Mohammed Ali developed the **Western Harbour** for commerce and it can be difficult to get to for all its docks and warehouses, but under the Ptolemies it was the less important of the two. (A third harbour, on Lake Mareotis to the south, took the Nile traffic and was said to clear a bigger tonnage than even the sea harbours.) The **Eastern Harbour** makes a graceful sweep and with its long **Corniche**, Sharia 26 July, is the most pleasing attraction of the city. Fort Qaytbay marks the tip of its northern arm; the lesser promontory of **Silsileh**, hardly developed but for a military compound, forms its eastern arm. From Silsileh westwards ran the palace of the Ptolemies — some of its foundations have recently been found by an Egyptian archaeologist, lying beneath the waters of the Eastern Harbour.

Midan Saad Zaghloul is between the Ramleh tram station and the Corniche. Here Cleopatra began the Caesareum in honour of Antony and Octavian finished it in honour of himself. And it was probably here that Cleopatra committed suicide. Two obelisks from this spot, the famous 'Cleopatra's Needles', are now on London's Embankment and in New

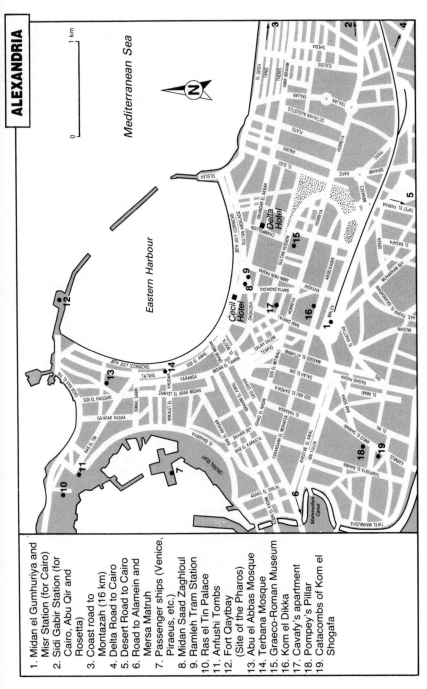

ALEXANDRIA

Mediterranean Sea

Eastern Harbour

1. Midan el Gumhuriya and Misr Station (for Cairo)
2. Sidi Gabir Station (for Cairo, Abu Qir and Rosetta)
3. Coast road to Montazah (16 km)
4. Delta Road to Cairo
5. Desert Road to Cairo
6. Road to Alamein and Mersa Matruh
7. Passenger ships (Venice, Piraeus, etc.)
8. Midan Saad Zaghloul
9. Ramleh Tram Station
10. Ras el Tin Palace
11. Anfushi Tombs
12. Fort Qaytbay (Site of the Pharos)
13. Abu el Abbas Mosque
14. Terbana Mosque
15. Graeco-Roman Museum
16. Kom el Dikka
17. Cavafy's apartment
18. Pompey's Pillar
19. Catacombs of Kom el Shogafa

413

York's Central Park. In the midan is a statue of Saad Zagh-loul, a nationalist leader who after the First World War negotiated the British withdrawal from Egypt, though they maintained a military presence in the Canal Zone. Another nationalist leader was the fellah officer Arabi who in 1882 led an uprising against the British. British warships retaliated by devastating Alexandria. Where Arabi failed, Nasser later triumphed. Arabi is remembered by a square in downtown Cairo and in Alexandria by **Midan Orabi** which extends from Midan el Tahrir to the Corniche.

Shopping and tourist facilities
The Hotel Cecil stands on the west side of Midan Saad Zaghloul, and the streets to the south of the midan and between it and Midan el Tahrir form the central shopping district of Alexandria. The most fashionable street is Sharia Salah-Salem, formerly Rue Chérif Pasha, running southeast out of Midan el Tahrir. Parallel to this and then turning south is the Rue Attarine, good for antiques. Also in this area, and around the Ramleh tram station, as well as along Sharia Horreya, are many airline offices and travel agencies.

Sharia Nebi Danyal runs nearly north to south through this area, at its southern end running into **Midan el Gumhuriya** with the train station for Cairo. About halfway along its length, Nebi Danyal intersects a street called Sharia el Mit-walli to the west, Sharia Horreya to the east. Nebi Danyal was anciently the Street of the Soma and the east-west street was the famous Canopic Way. Their intersection was once the crossroads of the world, and here was Alexander's tomb. To the west the Canopic Way left the city through the Gate of the Moon, to the east through the Gate of the Sun — by which Amr entered in triumph, Antony in final defeat after his last resistance against Octavian outside the walls. A poem by Constantine Cavafy (1863–1933), who lived not far from the crossroads, describes this moment as the god Hercules, whom Antony loved and who loved him, was heard passing away from Alexandria in mysterious music and song. It is called 'The God Abandons Antony'.

> When at the hour of midnight
> an invisible choir is suddenly heard passing
> with exquisite music, with voices —
> Do not lament your fortune that at last subsides,
> your life's work that has failed, your schemes that have
> proved illusions.
> But like a man prepared, like a brave man,
> bid farewell to her, to Alexandria who is departing.
> Above all, do not delude yourself, do not say that it is a
> dream,
> that your ear was mistaken,
> Do not condescend to such empty hopes.
> Like a man for long prepared, like a brave man,

like to the man who was worthy of such a city,
go to the window firmly,
and listen with emotion,
but not with the prayers and complaints of the coward
(Ah! supreme rapture!)
listen to the notes, to the exquisite instruments of the
mystic choir,
and bid farewell to her, to Alexandria whom you are
losing.

Eastwards   Still within the vanished lines of the ancient walls, farther east along Sharia Horreya and then a short way down a road to the left is the Graeco-Roman Museum, while at this point but to the right of Horreya are the Ptolemaic and Roman ruins being excavated at Kom el Dikka. The modern city extends 16 km eastwards in what was a string of beach suburbs, now all built up, to **Montazah**, a former summer residence of the royal family, with vast gardens and good swimming nearby.

Southwest   To the far southwest of the city, near the **Mahmudiya Canal**, is Pompey's Column and the Catacombs of Kom el Shogafa.

While this outline might already suggest a number of casual strolls through the city or excursions beyond, detailed itineraries are set out in the following chapter.

PRACTICAL INFORMATION

ACCOMMODATION

Montazah Sheraton (5-star), on the Corniche at Montazah. Tel: 969220. All rooms with balconies and sea views, colour TV and air conditioning. Restaurant, café, nightclub. Private beach, heated pool; tennis and watersports by arrangement. A well-run and friendly hotel. The great disadvantage for those who want to get the feel of Alexandria is its distance (16 km) from the centre of town.

Cecil (4-star), Midan Saad Zaghloul. Tel: 807250. (Now part of the Pullman group.) This is my favourite hotel in Alexandria. Make sure you have a room commanding the magnificent view over the Eastern Harbour. From your balcony you watch the Mediterranean splash against the Corniche; you see the site of the Pharos on the breakwater in the distance; and off to the right on the Silsileh headland you can

imagine the palace of the Ptolemies. Built in 1930, the Cecil figures often in Lawrence Durrell's *Alexandria Quartet* and he himself stayed here when he first came to the city. A generation later and it is there in Neguib Mahfouz's *Miramar*. Ask to see the visitors book, signed by royalty and the likes of Noel Coward and Somerset Maugham. A Moorish pile in the centre of town, the Cecil *is* Alexandria still. The cavernous rooms, all with balconies, have been refurbished and fully equipped; there is an art deco restaurant, a bar (Monty's), a charming tea lounge, casino, bank and Avis desk.

Delta (3-star), 14 Sharia Champollion. Tel: 4829028. Reasonably central (½ km east of the Cecil but back from the Corniche), this is a new and very good hotel for its class. All rooms with bath, air conditioning and TV. Excellent restaurant, French cuisine.

415

Metropole (3-star), 52 Sharia Saad Zagh-loul. Tel: 4821465. Recently refurbished, this is another of Alexandria's period hotels — this one owned by a Greek who has remained in the city. Most rooms with bath. Restaurant (this and the salon outside it with marvellous art nouveau/art deco friezes), bar, coffee shop. Rooms on the harbour side have a good view over Midan Saad Zaghloul and the Corniche beyond, but can be noisy with passing trams in the night.

Admiral (2-star), 24 Sharia Amin Fakhry. Tel: 32388 or 805343. Well located near (but not noisily near) the Ramleh tram terminus. Restaurant, bar, café, nightclub. The air-conditioned rooms are clean, but check the bathrooms.

Leroy (2-star), 25 Sharia Talaat Harb. Tel: 4833439. The hotel occupies the top 3 floors of a 7-storey building; the rooms are large and high, have bath and TV, and have balcony views over the city's rooftops — a good view too from the top floor restaurant.

Acropole (1-star), 1 Sharia Gamal al Din Yassin. Tel: 805980. Round the other side of the same block as the Cecil, on the 4th floor, it is very well located. Its rooms are clean, some offering views over the harbour.

There is a **youth hostel** at 32 Sharia Port Said, also known as el Geish (the eastward continuation of the Corniche) at Chatby. Tel: 75459. Take tram No 2 from Ramleh Station to Chatby Beach.

EATING PLACES

Alexandria's **restaurants** are rarely expensive (if you take Cairo as the comparison), and the range includes French, Italian, Greek, Middle Eastern and Chinese, with an emphasis too on seafood. Most are open for lunch (usually noon-4pm) and dinner (7 or 8pm till at least 11pm). See also under *Entertainment* below. A number of places that can loosely be described as **cafés** are also included, where over coffee, beer or wine and a bite to eat it can be very pleasant to let time pass.

Tikka Grill, on the seaward side of the Corniche about halfway along from the Cecil to Fort Qaytbay. The best restaurant setting in Alexandria, with a view along the full sweep of the Eastern Harbour. The menu is varied (Oriental and Western, grills, seafood and salads) and the food good.

Santa Lucia, 40 Sharia Safiya Zaghloul, towards Sharia Horreya. One of Alexandria's older popular restaurants. European menu.

Restaurant Denis, 1 Sharia Ibn Bassam, a short street between Midan Ramleh (Olympic Airways on the corner) and the Corniche. Salads and fresh seafood by weight.

Delta Hotel Restaurant, 14 Sharia Champollion, a 10-minute walk east from Ramleh Station. Excellent French cuisine. Bar.

Hassan Bleik, 12 Sharia Saad Zaghloul. Good, simple, inexpensive Lebanese.

El Ekhlaas, 49 Sharia Safiya Zaghloul. Very good Oriental cuisine.

Elite, 43 Sharia Safiya Zaghloul. One of the old Greek places, the menu French, Greek and Egyptian.

Chez Gaby, 22 Sharia Horreya. A new and popular restaurant. Western cuisine.

La Pizzeria, 14 Sharia Horreya. Popular and inexpensive, but the truth is that the Egyptians are incapable of making a good pizza.

San Giovanni, 205 Sharia El Geish (the eastwards continuation of the Corniche), at Stanley Bay. The restaurant at the hotel is very good, with a view out over the bay. Seafood, Oriental and Western. Also here is the 24-hour La Sirene Coffee Shop.

New Chinese Restaurant, in the Hotel Corail, 802 Sharia El Geish at Mandara Bay, hard by Montazah. Hong Kong chefs.

Sea Gull, at Mex, going west out of Alexandria on the way to Agami (the direction indicated by No 6 on the map). A huge castle affair specialising in seafood. Open all day till late.

Zephyrion, at Abu Qir (24 km east of Alexandria). Reservations advisable (Tel: 5601319). With its terrace overlooking the Mediterranean, this is Alexandria's most famous seafood restaurant, a Greek-run place where you choose your own fish and say how you want it done.

Trianon, Midan Saad Zaghloul, where Sharia Safiya Zaghloul runs off southwards. One of the old cafés (also a formal restaurant deeper within), beautifully decorated in art nouveau, recently refurbished. Coffee, beer, light meals. Open all day till late. This was once a favourite of Cavafy's; above it, within what is now the Metropole Hotel, was the Third Circle of Irrigation where he worked. Forster described Cavafy waiting at the corner, 'standing at a slight angle to the universe'. In his imagination and his poetry, Cavafy ranged freely over the Hellenistic world, but if you want to trace the limits of the man's physical world you need only walk the short distance from the Trianon up Sharia Safiya Zaghloul and then right into Estanbul for Sharia Sharm el Sheik — about 700 paces. In the mundane sense, he rarely travelled farther.

Athineos, Midan Ramleh, diagonally opposite the Trianon. Another old Greek café and patisserie, but alas this place has been refurbished to the extinction of almost all charm.

Pastroudis, 39 Sharia Horreya. Restaurant, patisserie and indoor/outdoor café. Founded in 1923, it is along with the Cecil the Alexandrian institution most frequently mentioned in Durrell's *Alexandria Quartet*.

Baudrot, 14 Sharia Saad Zaghloul. Bar, café, patisserie. In his introduction to E M Forster's *Alexandria: A History and a Guide*, Durrell describes it as once 'twinkling with light and music', which like so much of Alexandria it does not anymore, but it remains pleasant to sit out in the summer garden at the rear.

Cap d'Or — I have always got to this place by instinct and have failed to notice the street name (probably because it has been removed). Going down Sharia Salah Salem towards Midan el Tahrir, you turn right (before Sharia el Bosta unless it *is* Bosta I am thinking of) into a narrow street, probably Sharia Borsa el Qadima (Rue de l'Ancienne Bourse — though as the Bourse has been torn down, perhaps even the Arabised street name has been changed). The Cap d'Or is on the left, a quiet monument to Alexandria's past, all art nouveau. An agreeable place to sit with a bottle of wine.

ENTERTAINMENT

You would expect Alexandria to have a lively **nightlife**. It does not. Belly dancing is uncommon, and almost all the old Greek bazouki joints have gone the way of the old Greeks. The **Santa Lucia**, 40 Sharia Safiya Zaghloul, has a nightclub, while **Athineos** (not the café) and **Crazy Horse** are nightclubs on Midan Ramleh. Otherwise, you have to rely on the nightclubs in the major hotels. **El Phanar Nightclub** at the Montazah Sheraton, the **Layali Nightclub** at the Cecil and **Alexander's** (summer only) at the Ramada Renaissance at 544 Sharia El Geish, Sidi Bishr, are all dining places with live entertainment including belly dancer.

As for **cultural events** — forget it. What little of this there is is organised mostly by the foreign cultural institutes, eg the **British Council**, 9 Sharia Batalsa (Tel: 4829890), the **French Cultural Centre**, 30 Sharia Nebi Danyal (Tel: 4922503), the **American Cultural Center**, 3 Sharia Pharana (Tel: 4821009), the **Goethe Institute**, 10 Sharia Batalsa (Tel: 4839870).

OF INTEREST

See the following chapter for the *Of Interest* listings.

INFORMATION

The principal **Tourist Office** and the **Tourist Police** are in Midan Saad Zaghloul (Tel: 807611) near Sharia Nebi Danyal. There is also a Tourist Office at the port.

Alexandria Night and Day is a free booklet listing hotels, etc, which you can pick up at the Tourist Office or at your hotel, but the information is skimpy, the map almost useless. The newspapers *Egyptian Gazette* and *Egyptian Mail* and the monthly magazine *Cairo Today* carry some listings of events, entertainments, restaurants, etc, in Alexandria.

TRAVEL

Central Alexandria is best covered **on foot**.

Buses and trams are very cheap and can get you to some of the more distant sights. Buses 120, 220 and 320 ply the Corniche as far out as Montazah, while bus 129 goes from Midan Orabi to Abu Qir. Tram 16 from Midan Orabi goes to Pompey's Pillar. Tram 15 from Ramleh Station goes to Fort Qaytbay. Also from Ramleh Station, trams 1 and 2 both go eastbound to Al-Nasr College (the former Victoria College) at Sidi Bishr, but tram 1 takes a somewhat inland route via Bacos, while tram 2 goes via Glymenopoulo (Glym), close to though not within sight of the sea. This loop could be followed for the hell of it.

Taxis, which are orange and black, are inexpensive, especially as you stand a somewhat better chance of running on the meter than in Cairo. Otherwise, LE2 is adequate for anywhere within the area shown on the map — except from the main railway station to a central hotel (eg the Cecil) when, as the driver has been waiting, and he has you over a barrel, you will pay a premium. In any case, as a tourist you will always pay more. Along the Corniche between the centre of town and all the way out to Montazah it is worth flagging down any taxi you see, regardless of whether it is already carrying a passenger. This is almost like a service taxi route, with drivers picking up and letting off people along the way.

Carriages are the most delightful way of being transported about the city. Hail them on the trot; also they can be found waiting at the main railway station (Mahattat Misr) and outside the Cecil Hotel. The fare has to be bargained over but is in line with taxi fares.

Car hire, with or without driver, is available from **Avis** at the Cecil Hotel in Midan Saad Zaghloul (Tel: 807532 and 807055). **Budget Rent a Car** is at 59 Sharia El Geish (Tel: 5971273). Outside the Cecil is a good place to hire a **taxi for excursions** (usually big Peugeots), eg to Rosetta, Abu Mina, Alamein, Wadi Natrun and even to Cairo.

Alexandria's **airport** (6 km from the centre, 13 km from Montazah) has flights to Cairo (though these are hardly worth it as the train and bus services are so frequent and quick, and are also more reliable — flights are occasionally cancelled) as well as a few international flights. The taxi to or from the airport should not cost more than LE7 to LE10.

Airline offices are centrally located, eg British Airways, Olympic and Egyptair in Midan Ramleh.

The main **railway station**, Mahattat Misr, is at Midan el Gumhuriya at the south end of Sharia Nebi Danyal. There are frequent trains to Cairo (3 hours) via Sidi Gabir (a secondary station in the eastern part of Alexandria), Damanhur, Tanta and Benha. Trains also leave here (or from Sidi Gabir) to Rosetta in the east and Mersa Matruh in the west, but it is a slow, uncomfortable, non-air-conditioned second- or third-class journey and is not recommended (go by bus or service taxi instead).

Frequent and fast luxury **bus services to Cairo** (Giza, Midan el Tahrir, Cairo Airport) via the Desert Road depart from Midan Saad Zaghloul and take about 3 hours. Tickets should be bought some hours, preferably a day, in advance and are sold at the kiosk in the square near the Cecil.

Long-distance buses and service taxis generally leave from Midan el Gumhuriya in front of the main railway station (Mahattat Misr). A few bus services may depart from Midan Saad Zaghloul.

There is a year-round **ferry** service between Alexandria, Heraklion (Crete), Piraeus and Venice operated by Adriatica. The agent is **Menatours**, Midan Saad Zaghloul, next to the Cecil Hotel (Tel: 808407).

For **tours**, etc, **Thomas Cook** is at 15 Midan Saad Zaghloul (Tel: 4827830).

The best all-round **travel agent** is **Annie Travel**, 30 Sharia Ahmed Orabi, also known as Sharia Tewfiq, which runs parallel with Sharia Salah Salem (Tel: 4830007/8). With courtesy, efficiency and reliability, they can fix up flights, Wagons-Lits tickets, cruises, excursions, you name it.

OTHER THINGS

You can **change money** at the major hotels and at **Thomas Cook**, 15 Midan Saad Zaghloul, and **American Express**, 26 Sharia Horreya.

There is a 24-hour **telephone office** for domestic and international calls (much cheaper than from the hotels) in Midan Ramleh.

To register (if this has not been done by your hotel) or to renew your visa, go to the **Passport Office**, 28 Sharia Talaat Harb (Tel: 4824366).

The **British Consulate** is at 3 Sharia Mena, Roushdi (Tel: 847166); the **American Consulate** is at 110 Sharia Horreya (Tel: 4911911).

For **medical care**, ask your hotel. Your consulate or the Tourist Police can also advise. Recommended is the **University Hospital** in Chatby (Tel: 4201573). For **urgent help** of any sort, telephone 123.

For a city so famous in literature it is remakable that Alexandria possesses so few **bookshops** these days, let alone the chance of finding Shakespeare's *Antony and Cleopatra*, Cavafy's poetry, Forster's *Alexandria: A History and a Guide* or his *Pharos and Pharillon*, Durrell's *Alexandria Quartet* or Mahfouz's *Miramar*. The feeble best is **Al Ahram**, 10 Sharia Horreya (at the crossroads with Sharia Nebi Danyal), and sells English- and French-language books, magazines and newspapers. There are bookshops also in the Montazah Sheraton and Ramada Renaissance hotels.

DISCOVERING ALEXANDRIA

'If a man make a pilgrimage round Alexandria in the morning, God will make for him a golden crown, set with pearls, perfumed with musk and camphor, and shining from the East to the West' (Ibn Duqmaq). Today even the most determined seer of sights will be able to catch the evening train back to Cairo. A Roman odeon, Pompey's Pillar, the catacombs at Kom el Shogafa; these and a medieval fortress squatting on the foundations of the Pharos lighthouse are the principal but paltry remains of Alexandria's resplendent past. Some will see nothing in her. Others will voyage through the phantom city and listen to her voices and her music.

From the Crossroads to Kom el Dikka
From Midan Saad Zaghloul you should walk south along Sharia Nebi Danyal and where it meets Sharia Horreya you should pause. This is the **crossroads of the city**, and has been for more than 2300 years. From east to west ran the Canopic Way (Horreya), from the Gate of the Sun to the Gate of the Moon. From north to south ran the Street of the Soma (Nebi Danyal). Standing on this rather ordinary-looking corner you might need this description by Achilles Tatius, a 5th C bishop, to assist your imagination: 'The first thing one noticed in entering Alexandria by the Gate of the Sun was the beauty of the city. A range of columns went from one end of it to the other. Advancing down them, I came in time to the place that bears the name of Alexander, and there could see the other half of the town, which was equally beautiful. For just as the colonnades stretched ahead of me, so did other colonnades now appear at right angles to them'.

Continue south along Sharia Nebi Danyal till you are nearly at the large square before the train station. On the right is a mosque set back from the street and with **four antique columns** serving as gate posts. This is the typical way you encounter the past, if you encounter it tangibly at all, in Alexandria — a dwindling number of remnants used in building after successive building, their original purpose only to be guessed at. It is possible that the Mouseion once stood here and that these columns once adorned its facade. Founded by Ptolemy Soter, the Museion was the great intellectual accomplishment of his dynasty, a vast complex of lecture halls, laboratories, observatories, a library, a dining hall, a park and a zoo. It was like a university, except that the scholars, scientists and literary men it supported were under no obligation to teach. It would have been here that Euclid and Eratosthenes worked.

The Museion

Directly opposite is the **Mosque of Nebi Danyal** (named for Mohammed Danyal al-Maridi, a venerated sheikh who died

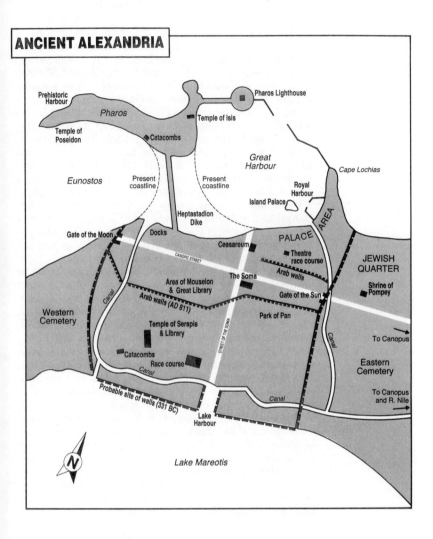

ANCIENT ALEXANDRIA

Prehistoric Harbour

Pharos

Pharos Lighthouse

Temple of Isis

Temple of Poseidon

Catacombs

Great Harbour

Cape Lochias

Eunostos

Present coastline

Present coastline

Royal Harbour

Island Palace

Heptastadion Dike

PALACE AREA

Gate of the Moon

Docks

CANOPIC STREET

Ceasareum

Theatre race course

JEWISH QUARTER

The Soma

Arab walls

Shrine of Pompey

Area of Mouseion & Great Library

Gate of the Sun

Arab walls (AD 811)

Canal

Park of Pan

STREET OF THE SOMA

Western Cemetery

To Canopus

Temple of Serapis & Library

Catacombs

Race course

Canal

Eastern Cemetery

Probable site of walls (331 BC)

Canal

To Canopus and R. Nile

Lake Harbour

N

Lake Mareotis

Alexander's tomb?

in 1407) on the supposed site of Alexander's tomb, the Soma, where he and some of the Ptolemies lay. (Its entrance is set back from the street, nearly hidden between two buildings.) If you go in you can gaze down upon a cruciform *crypt* where Danyal and an uncertain figure called Lukman the Wise lie. It is easy to imagine a still deeper crypt where Alexander himself still lies, for the cellars and foundations of the mosque have never been properly examined.

The body is thought to have been destroyed in city riots of the late 3rd C AD, but in the absence of any certain knowledge rumour has flourished. In 1850 a dragoman from the Russian Consulate said that down in the cellars through a hole in a wooden door he saw 'a human body in a sort of glass cage with a diadem on its head and half bowed on a sort of elevation or throne. A quantity of books or papyrus were scattered around'. (I have climbed down and looked around, but short of breaking through the walls there is nothing to see.) Suetonius tells a good story of Octavian's (later Augustus) visit here: 'When Alexander's sarcophagus was brought from its shrine, Augustus gazed at the body, then laid a crown of gold on its case and scattered some flowers to pay his respects. When they asked if he would like to see Ptolemy too, 'I wished to see a king', he replied, 'I did not wish to see corpses'.

If you now continue southwards to the top of Rue Nebi Danyal so that Midan el Gumhuriya (the square in front of the railway station) is ahead of you, and turn left so that you are walking beside a high wall, you come shortly on your left to the entrance to the **Kom el Dikka** site.

It is likely that a great deal of Alexandria's past could be uncovered, and the work here, begun by the Polish Centre of Mediterranean Archaeology in 1959, marks a start. Layers of Muslim tombs were found, dating from the 9th to 11th C, and a large complex of 3rd C AD **Roman baths**. The spur to further and intensive excavation came in 1964 with the unearthing of a small **Roman odeon**, a covered theatre for musical performances, with seating for 700 to 800. Inscriptions suggest it was used also for wrestling contests. It is pretty, the area around it landscaped, which is all very well, but it possesses none of the excitement of an excavation in progress.

That is provided by the deep broad trenches still being dug to the northeast of the odeon. The dusty walls of the trenches are layered with extraordinary amounts of potsherds, and as you peer down several metres from the surface of the kom you can see substantial stone walls and the remains of brick houses. Best of all is to climb down. You walk along **Ptolemaic streets** lined with shopfronts. If Cleopatra ever went shopping, then here you can say to yourself is where Cleopatra walked. It is a sensation of immediacy rare to Alexandria.

You can now leave the Kom el Dikka excavations by the way you came in, but turning left (east) to walk counterclockwise round the perimeter of the site, so that you will turn left again (north) at the first street you come to, in a few moments coming to Sharia Horreya. The Amir Cinema is on the corner, and next to it is Pastroudis, an old Greek place (Egyptian-run now), where it is pleasant to sit with a drink, a coffee, a rich pastry — there is also a restaurant — and let time pass.

It was at Pastroudis that Darley and Nessim, and Balthazar for an arak, would gather — those fictional inhabitants of Lawrence Durrell's Alexandria.

In *The Alexandria Quartet,* Lawrence Durrell refers to 'the city's exemplars — Cavafy, Alexander, Cleopatra and the rest', giving pride of place to the poet who inspired E M Forster and Durrell himself to discover the dream-city Alexandria. Cavafy lived nearby, at **10 Rue Lepsius** as it was early this century, now 4 Sharia Sharm el Sheikh — typical of Alexandria to disguise the whereabouts of even this part of her past. You get there by heading west along Sharia Horreya (in Forster's time the Rue Rosette, in Durrell's the Rue Fuad) to the crossroads and there turning right (north) into Sharia Nebi Danyal. You take the second right off this into Sharia Sultan Hussein (also called Sharia Estanbul); then off this street to the right is first a foot-alley, then a narrow street which is Cavafy's.

Here the literary apotheosis of Alexandria began. On the second floor of what is now the Pension Amir but was once a more impressive building, Constantine Cavafy passed the years of his poetic maturity. A dusty plaque in Arabic and Greek reads, 'In this house for the last 25 years of his life lived the Alexandrian poet Constantine Cavafy (1863–1933)'. (Cavafy's apartment has been recreated as a **museum** on the top floor of the Greek Consulate, 63 Sharia Iskandar el Akbar.)

Constantine Cavafy

Forster, who had already written *A Room With a View* and *Howards End* (but was still struggling with *A Passage to India*), was working for the Red Cross in Alexandria during the war when he first met Cavafy in 1917: 'It never occurred to him that I might like his work or even understand it ... and I remember the delight to us both, one dusky evening in his flat, when it appeared that I was "following". When he was pleased he would jump and light a candle, and then another candle and he would cut cigarettes in half and light them and bring offerings of mastica with little bits of bread and cheese, and his talk would sway over the Mediterranean world and over much of the world within'. In *Pharos and Pharillon* and *Alexandria: a History and a Guide,* Forster introduced Cavafy to the English-speaking world. Years later Forster remarked, 'I did a little to spread his fame. It was about the best thing I did'.

E M Forster

On the ground floor of 10 Rue Lepsius was a brothel. 'Poor things!' Cavafy said to a friend who had accompanied him to his door one night. 'One must be sorry for them. They receive some disgusting people, some monsters, but' — and here his voice took on a deep, ardent tone — 'they receive some angels, some angels!' His English friends called the street the 'Rue Clapsius', though indeed the entire quarter was ill-famed. Cavafy satisfied his homosexuality by picking up boys in the cafés along the Rue Missala (now Sharia Safiya Zagh-loul). With the Greek Hospital opposite and the patriarchal church round the corner, Cavafy was fond of saying, 'Where could I live better? Below, the brothel caters for the flesh. And there is the church which forgives sin. And there is the hospital where we die'. He did die in that hospital, his funeral service took place at St Saba, and his body buried in the Greek Cemetery at Chatby.

'Radiating out like the arms of a starfish from the axis of the founder's tomb' (*Clea*), the streets of this part of the city housed most of Durrell's characters. Darley and Pombal shared a flat in the Rue Nebi Daniel; Clea's studio was in the Rue St Saba; Justine and Nessim lived in a town house set back from the Rue Fuad — and Balthazar lived in the Rue Lepsius, in 'the worm-eaten room with the cane chair which creaked all night, and where once the old poet of the city had recited "The Barbarians"' (*Clea*). The Cervoni's house, where at the carnival ball Narouz drove a hat pin through Toto de Brunel's skull, thinking he was killing Justine, was not far from the Greek Patriarchate; both Cohen and Melissa died in the Greek Hospital; and like you, many of them would find themselves sitting at the tables at Pastroudis.

East Along the Canopic Way

If you are sitting at Pastroudis on Sharia Horreya, a block east of Sharia Nebi Danyal and the ancient crossroads of the city, you can now stroll a few blocks east along the Canopic Way (Horreya). The Rue de la Musée (Sharia el Mathaf) on your left runs along the entrance to the **Graeco-Roman Museum** (see below).

But continuing east you come, after nearly a kilometre, to the **Shallalat Gardens**. Here stood the Gate of the Sun, while remaining still are ruined segments of the **Arab wall** (north side of gardens). About 3 km southeast, by the Mahmudiya Canal, are a series of gardens. The northernmost is the **Zoo**; in the middle are the **Nouzha Gardens**, originally planted for the Khedive Ismail with specimen trees; the southernmost are the **Antoniadis Gardens**, early this century the grounds of a wealthy Greek family, rather formal and planted with statues. In the area of these gardens Amr and his cavalry camped before entering the city.

Gardens

The Graeco-Roman Museum

East along Sharia Horreya and then turning north (left) into the Rue de la Musée (Sharia Mathaf), is the Graeco-Roman Museum which fills the historical gap between the Egyptian Museum in Cairo and the Coptic Museum in Old Cairo. It is a fascinating period, when a familiar Western culture overlaid and sometimes incorporated the native Egyptian world; and the museum itself, while not large, is spacious and arranged around a central garden, an invitation to pleasurable lingering.

Many of the exhibits are from in and around Alexandria; the rest are from the Delta, the Fayyum and Middle Egypt. In a very loose sense the collection runs chronologically, beginning (as does the following tour) to the left of the entrance

Serapis with a bushel on his head: the most successful god made by a man

vestibule with Room 6 and continuing clockwise to the Christian period in Rooms 1 to 5. But the collection is also arranged by subject, so that some rooms are devoted to pottery, others to glass, still others to sculpture, etc, and this can cut across the chronological arrangement.

Note that the rooms are numbered but the exhibits are not always numbered, or their numbers are hard to find. Nor is everything labelled, though usually the most important exhibits are. Furthermore there has been some rearranging recently. In short, take what follows with a sense of adventure.

To the left of the entrance vestibule is *Room 6,* and at its centre is a fine diorite statue of the Apis bull, erected at the time of Hadrian and found towards the end of the 19th C at Pompey's Pillar. It had probably been buried there when a Christian mob sacked the Serapeum in 391. Against the left-hand wall is a statue of Serapis (22158), a great jolly fellow like Dickens' Ghost of Christmas Past, and one of Isis.

The cult of Serapis

Serapis was the only god ever successfully made by a modern man. Egyptians at Memphis had worshipped Osiris in his Apis form as Osarapis; Ptolemy I combined this deity with Dionysos and made what was in effect a new god. The intention, probably, was to unit Greeks and Egyptians in a common worship, but the Egyptians would not accept him and he became the Greek god of Alexandria. His cult statue (this is a contemporary copy) of white marble was painted blue, his gilt head and jewelled eyes gleaming from the darkened recess of its shrine, the Alexandrian Serapeum. His worship spread throughout the Aegean, his cult established at Athens and particularly at Delos, though he was venerated as far away as India. His importance can be gauged by the fact that when Bishop Theophilus destroyed the Serapeum and its statue in 391, it was taken by the world as the definitive triumph of Christianity.

Cleopatra identified herself with Isis, that still greater deity, and so naturally, and with useful effect, Antony was identified with her consort Serapis, or at least with Dionysos. This may have assisted Roman propagandists (from whom Shakespeare took his cue) in depicting Antony as a debauched Bacchic figure — more a measure of Roman methods and philistine contempt for Greek culture (and fear of Antony's alliance with Greek Alexandria) than any true reflection on Antony the man. Romans admired and copied *things* Greek, but Greeks themselves, and those like Antony who immersed themselves with genuine understanding in Greek culture, were despised. There was a ready Roman audience for a 'scheming' and 'treacherous' Cleopatra, a 'cowardly' and 'besotted' Antony, and history, particularly the Battle of Actium, was easily distorted to provide proof for the slanders.

Room 7 has a statue of a Hyksos pharaoh (Second Intermediate Period) at the centre. It was appropriated by Ramses

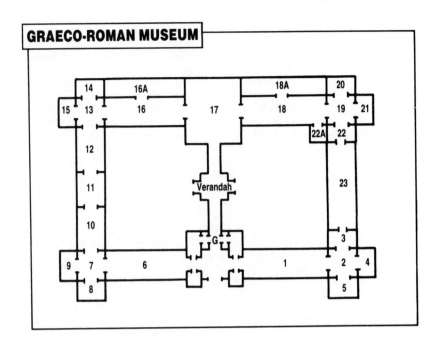

II and on its shoulder appears Ramses' daughter Hout-Ma-Ra, traditionally the princess who found Moses in the bulrushes.

Room 8 contains several mummies, one of the Roman period with an encaustic portrait mask, elaborate diamond-pattern wrapping and a glimpse of toes. (See the reference to the Fayyum portraits at the end of *The Fayyum* chapter; the best are in Room 14 of the Egyptian Museum in Cairo).

In *Room 9* is a wooden stretcher bearing a mummified crocodile. The room illustrates the Ptolemies in their Egyptian aspect, and here it is crocodile worship in the Fayyum. Because of such mummified crocodiles as these, found wrapped in and stuffed with papyri, we know more about Graeco-Roman Egypt than about any other past time or place (see Omm el Borigat, ancient Tebtynis, in the Fayyum). There are the remains of the chapel (19678–81) of a crocodile god with the wooden door of the first pylon and the coffin and beir of the sacred animal (2nd C BC). The entire chapel has been reconstructed in the North Garden of the museum.

Room 10 is the Antoniadis Collection of various objects. Most strange is the mummy of a baby. Apart from its smallness, no concession is made to its babyness, eg the face mask is the usual stereotype. Once here, though I could not find it last time, was a headless, sensuous piece, a fragment of diorite breast (3221), similar to a statue of Queen Arsinoë, wife of Ptolemy II Philadelphos, in the Vatican. I mention it because it was magnificent.

Room 11 has objects in which the Greek and Egyptian influences mingle — never very well. There are some curious blocks with footprints, votive offerings to Isis and Serapis.

Alexander and Cleopatra

At the centre of *Room 12* is a dull statue of Marcus Aurelius; a sea-worn marble head of Alexander is on the left, as is a limestone head of Cleopatra VII (21992) in Egyptian guise — though this may be a misattribution. Compare this to the Cleopatra head nearby (3239) in which she appears in her Greek guise and bears a resemblance to her coin portraits, albeit sucked by the sea like a jujube.

Rooms 13 and 14 contain miscellaneous sculptures: bodies without heads, heads without bodies, including Julius Caesar, Augustus, Tiberius, Hadrian, Vespasian, Claudius and Septimius Severus.

In *Room 15* is a portion of tomb wall, late Ptolemaic period or early Roman, painted with a rural scene of oxen turning a *sakiya* or waterwheel.

Room 16 is devoted to sculpture. Against the wall at the far end is the repulsive Mithras (24407), sun god of the Persians, his virile cult carried by the legions to the corners of the Roman Empire during the early centuries AD. This statue comes from near Minya. He is lion-headed, cloven-hoofed and winged, with hairy legs, and is draped with snakes. The foundations of one of his temples lie exposed along Queen Victoria Street in the City of London.

Hellenistic sculpture

In *Room 16A* are the finest pieces of Hellenistic sculpture in the museum. The large torsos at the left end of the room are particularly impressive: two unclothed male torsos (3923 and 3925); and a female torso (3924) wearing a light tunic.

In *Room 17* is the largest known statue (5934) carved from a monolithic block of porphyry; some authorities say he is Diocletian, others that he is Christ Pantocrator — about as wide a split as you could hope for. Among the six marble sarcophagi is one (17927) showing the sleeping Ariadne surprised by Dionysos on Naxos.

Room 18 has pottery, terracotta and funerary urns. In the centre is an urn (16152) from the Chatby necropolis which still retains its wreath of artificial leaves and berries, bright green and gold (4th C BC). Also in the centre is a caseload of bronze wreaths, their flowers gilded. These are ugly and were probably more ugly at the time, but they are impressive for being so old. In Case X against the wall is a crude terracotta oil lantern in the shape of the Pharos. Also in various wall cases are terracotta figurines, and these are mostly stupid and vulgar.

But in *Room 18A* are the finest objects in the museum:

Exquisite figurines miniature Tanagra terracotta figures of great delicacy and charm. These come from Alexandrian cemeteries, late 4th to early 2nd C BC, and occur only in tombs of children, adolescents or young women. The best are the figurines of women in Cases K, L, M, N and O, full of detail and dignity. These works were prompted by the sadness of death in youth; they are entirely sincere and noble, and they live. On the opposite side of this room is a statuette of Isis-Aphrodite (23936), her dress hitched up to reveal her bounty.

Rooms 19, 20 and 21 contain more terracottas and pottery, including much from the Chatby and Ibrahimiya necropolises in Alexandria.

Room 22 displays some beautiful examples of glass vases, plates and all manner of pots and vials for perfumes, wines, etc — mostly Graeco-Roman, but also belonging to the Islamic period.

Rooms 23 and 3 contain coins, jewellery and assorted treasures. The most beautiful items are the torso of Aphrodite (24042) in silver and the silver gilt goblet (24201) decorated with cupids gathering grapes. The most important, however, are the foundation plaques (8357–66 and 9431–40) in gold, silver, bronze, Nile mud, green faience and opaque glass, carved with Greek and hieroglyphic inscriptions, each recording Ptolemy III's dedication of the Temple of Serapis. Only when these were found in 1943–45 was it established with certainty that the Serapeum had stood on the plateau where Pompey's Pillar stands.

At the centre of *Room 2* is a Christian capital; in *Room 4* are delightful fragments of Coptic textiles, with rabbits, centaurs and dancing women, full of movement and sensuality; in *Room 5,* in painted stucco, are Christian designs and saints from the environs of Alexandria.

In *Room 1* there is the surprise of a Christian mummy, a two-way bet on immortality: note the black cross painted at his neck. In wall cases there are many objects associated with St Menes (see Abu Mina, the City of St Menes), including little souvenir flasks (13953 and 13922) once filled with oil and taken by departing pilgrims all over the Christian world. Note the recurrent motif of the saint between two camels.

Christian sensuousness As in their textiles, so in their carving, the Egyptians of this period were capable of great delicacy and sensuousness. You see this for example in the case containing bone and ivory pieces with their exquisite female forms, most definitely not the Virgin Mary, for decorating furniture and weapons. (Though identified as 'Christian period', clearly not everyone was yet a Christian, while some who were, like that mummy in the centre of the room, also had their fingers in other pies.) And you see it with less technical finesse but in the almost Indian style of the limestone relief (14145) of two women sitting in the shade of a tree with a basket of fruit between

429

them. But then look at the two architectural fragments in high relief (23779 and 23776): these are definitely Christian work, from Bahnasa, which is the modern name for Oxyrhynchus, the great monastic centre. There is that same lusciousness in their vine motifs, even while in 23776 the leaves form a cross within the encircling vine. Also from Oxyrhynchus is the low relief fragment of plant and cross motif (23565), the cross in this case very much based on a pharaonic ankh, the sign of life.

Now from the vestibule you can enter the gardens encircled by the museum. To the right is the *South Garden* with two reconstructed rock-cut tombs. One (21004) of the 3rd C BC contains a sarcophagus in the form of a bed. The other (20986) of the 1st C AD has an arched entrance with shell decoration in relief. To the left is the *North Garden* with the three recon- structed pylons and chapel of the crocodile god whose fur- nishings you have already seen in Room 9. Against the far wall is a head, supposedly of Mark Antony, though the attri- bution is unlikely. A composite capital sprouts from the grass like a giant flower, its top surface hollowed out to serve as a baptismal font.

The Heptastadion
From the ancient crossroads of the city, that is from the inter- section of Sharia Nebi Danyal and Sharia Horreya, you should now walk along the western extension of Sharia Horreya, called Sharia el Mitwalli. A block along and leading diagonally off to the right is Sharia Salah-Salem, formerly Rue Chérif Pasha, once Alexandria's most fashion- able shopping street but not as smart as it was. Nothing in Alexandria is.

At No. 30 on the right is the National Bank of Egypt, once the Banco di Roma (the wolf of Rome can still be seen over the left doorway). A modified **copy of the Palazzo Farnese** in Rome, Forster thought this the finest building in the city. During the Second World War the British Information Office was lodged round the side and in a letter to Henry Miller, Lawrence Durrell wrote: 'I am in charge of a goodish-sized office of war-propaganda here, trying to usher in the new washboard world which our demented peoples are trying "to forge in blood and iron". It's tiring work. However, it's an office full of beautiful girls, and Alexandria is, after Hollywood, fuller of beautiful women than any place else. Incomparably more beautiful than Athens or Paris; the mix- ture Coptic, Jewish, Syrian, Egyptian, Moroccan, Spanish gives you slant dark eyes, olive freckled skin, hawk lips and noses, and a temperament like a bomb'.

At the end of Sharia Salah-Salem, on the left as it issues into Midan el Tahrir, was the Bourse, once housing the Cotton Exchange. 'The howls and cries that may be heard here of a morning proceed not from a menagerie but from the

wealthy merchants of Alexandria as they buy and sell'
(Forster). It was set alight and gutted during food riots in 1977
and has since been demolished.

European eclipse Midan el Tahrir (Liberation Square) was formerly Place
Mohammed Ali and was laid out by him in 1830 as the centre
of his new city. Once attractively planted with trees and gardens, it now roars with traffic and is filled with fumes. This
was the European centre of the city, flanked on the left (west)
by the Mixed Tribunals which mediated between foreigners
and natives (these are now the **Law Courts**), and on the right
(east) by the Anglican **Church of St Mark**, commemorating
inside the British regiments which saw action against Arabi.
At the centre of the square is a fine **equestrian statue of
Mohammed Ali**. In Ptolemaic times all this was under the sea.

In the wake of political fortune the streets of Alexandria
have suffered many changes in name. The locals however are
usually a revolution behind and so the old Rue de France
(Arabised into Sharia Faransa) which starts at the northeast
end of Midan el Tahrir is still familiarly known as such. If
some general, sheikh or politician has appropriated the
street, he has so far failed to impress either me or the neighbourhood with his name.

Here you are walking along the Heptastadion through
what is very much an Egyptian quarter of the city, often
picturesque. There are several mosques along the way; the
most interesting is the **Terbana Mosque**, dating from 1684. Its
exterior is pale yellow except for its high doorway of brick,
painted red and black in Delta style (there is much more of
this at Rosetta), with occasional courses of wood and a Kufic
inscription: 'There is no God but God' and 'Mohammed is the
Prophet of God'.

Alexandrian Before going in, have a look at the entrance to the cellars
pastiche round the left-hand side of the building. The columns are
ancient. Now go up the steps of the main entrance, arriving at
an open air terrace with two great Corinthian columns of
granite. The entire building seems to have been made out of
Alexandria's antique past; there are more ancient columns
propping up the interior and painted gloss white. You will
probably be shown round, the gloss paint and similar refur-
bishments pointed out with pride. Tiles decorate this upstairs
entrance to the mosque, but they are in a bad state, the enamel
dropping off, but fine where they survive. There are excellent
tiles too in the mihrab inside, predominantly blue, though
some green; the larger tiles with white daisies are inferior
modern work.

The Turkish town As you continue north along Sharia Faransa from the
Terbana and cross a main intersection, the street becomes
narrower and winding with several overhanging balconies in
the Turkish style. This is landfall for the island of Pharos.
Continue north along Sharia Tatwig; it runs into a square

dominated by the large **Mosque of Abu el Abbas Moursi**. It was built in 1943 but stands on the site of a 1767 mosque built by Algerians over the tomb of the 13th C saint. At the end of the square where two tall palm trees rise is the little Mosque of Sidi Daoud with his tomb. This was the main square of the Turkish town, the reduced settlement, its population 4000, to which Alexandria had shrunk when Napoleon landed in 1798. Between the Abu el Abbas Mosque and the harbour is the **Bouseiri Mosque,** its own square illuminated with white lights visible from anywhere along the Corniche at night. From this mosque there is a view of Fort Qaytbay and fishing boats, their nets stretched along the harbour wall.

To the Pharos

From the old Turkish quarter, first follow Sharia Ras el Tin westwards to the **Tombs of Anfushi** near the end of the tram line. These are Ptolemaic, their decorations principally Greek but with Egyptian elements. They have been cut into the limestone ridge that was the island of Pharos; there are four of them, arranged in pairs, each pair sharing an atrium. Their walls are painted to simulate marble, or alabaster blocks, or tiles; archaeologists call this the First Pompeian Style, with all the shoddiness that suggests. In the tomb farthest to the right are scenes of a felucca and a warship of the sort Cleopatra may have sailed in to Actium. The keeper rubs the felucca with his moistened thumb to show that it will not come off — it does not, but is covered with smudgy thumb prints. Also in this tomb are Greek scribblings left by a work-man of the period named Diodoros, who immortalises his friend Antiphiles. How innocent these ancients were in their graffiti; we know by what signs our present period would instantly be recognised by archaeologists of the future. The attempt in all these tombs of simulated materials is poor. They are very much bourgeois tombs; their inhabitants paid the going rate for an eternity of tastelessness.

Farouk's abdication   Farther towards the western tip is the **Palace of Ras el Tin**, built by Mohammed Ali, though altered this century. Here on 26 July 1952 King Farouk abdicated and sailed away to Italy aboard his yacht. It is now the Admiralty headquarters. You cannot get in.

Now walk eastwards along the seafront towards **Fort Qaytbay**. There is a poor beach and a fish market enroute. The fort is at the end of a breakwater and has been restored since the British shelling in 1882. It was built in 1480 by Sultan Qaytbay on the site and partly from fragments of the Pharos lighthouse, the wonder of the ancient world.

The Pharos was built during the reign of Ptolemy Philadel-phos, its architect Sostratus, an Asiatic Greek. 'The sensation it caused was tremendous. It appealed both to the sense of beauty and to the taste for science — an appeal typical of the

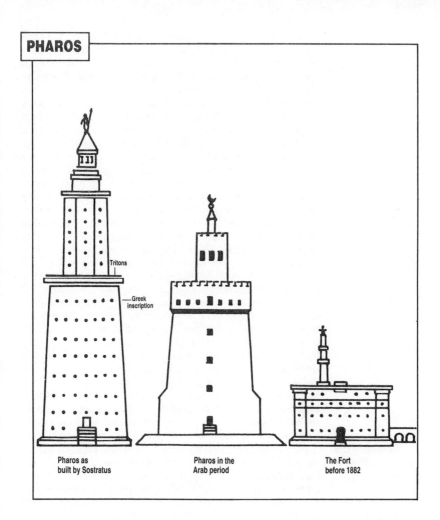

Pharos as
built by Sostratus

Tritons

Greek
inscription

Pharos in the
Arab period

The Fort
before 1882

age. Poets and engineers combined to praise it. Just as the Parthenon had been identified with Athens and St Peter's was to be identified with Rome, so, to the imagination of contemporaries, the Pharos became Alexandria and Alexandria became the Pharos. Never, in the history of architecture, has a secular building been thus worshipped and taken on a spiritual life of its own. It beaconed to the imagination, not only to ships at sea, and long after its light was extinguished memories of it glowed in the minds of men' (Forster).

One of the Seven Wonders of the Ancient World

The Pharos exceeded 125 metres in height and might possibly have touched 150 metres. Its square bottom storey was pierced with many windows and contained perhaps 300 rooms

433

where the mechanics and attendants were housed. A double spiral ascent ran through the centre and hydraulic machinery was used for raising fuel to the top. At its cornice were tritons and an inscription by which Sostratus dedicated the Pharos 'to the Saviour Gods; for sailors', the gods being Castor and Pollux who protected mariners, but an allusion to Ptolemy Soter and Berenice, whose worship their son Philadelphos was promoting. Above this was an octagonal second storey, then a circular third storey, and finally the lantern.

The workings of the lantern were mysterious. Visitors spoke of a mirror, perhaps of polished steel for reflecting the sun by day, the fire by night; though others described it as made of glass or transparent stone, and declared that a man sitting under it could see ships at sea that were invisible to the naked eye. It might have been a lens, and it is not at all impossible that Alexandrian mathematicians did discover the lens and that their discovery was lost and forgotten when the Pharos fell.

The Pharos retained its form and functions up to the Arab conquest in 641. About 700 the lantern fell, and perhaps at the same time but certainly soon after the two top storeys fell also — the tale is that the Byzantine emperor, frustrated in his ambitions against Egypt because of the early detection of his ships, put it about that the Pharos stood upon Alexander's treasure, whereupon the caliph commenced demolition. The first storey survived intact and Ibn Tulun restored the octagonal storey around 880, but an earthquake around 1100 destroyed his work and its place was taken by a mosque. Finally the bottom storey was ruined by a final earthquake in the 14th C. Interestingly, the four stages of the Pharos — square, octagon, round and summit — are exactly reproduced in the minaret of Qaytbay's Mausoleum in Cairo's City of the Dead.

Traces of the Pharos Here on this promontory, Qaytbay built in part at least from the debris of the Pharos and you can see where bits of it have been incorporated into his structure. The *enclosure walls* describe an irregular pentagon and as you approach, with the open sea to your left, you can make out some granite and marble columns in the northwest section. The seawall of the Pharos probably diverged slightly from the present walls and where these meet the sea it laps over what might have been ancient foundations. There are numerous column sections in the facade of the *keep,* and within its entrance are five great monolithic pillars of red Aswan granite. Inside is the **Naval Museum.**

While approaching the fort along the causeway you passed the **Hydrobiological Museum** and the **Marine Life Institute** (aquarium) — and missed nothing.

To Rhakotis

What Alexander flattened he in this case immortalised. Who would know of this obscure Egyptian fishing village had his town planners not built upon it the capital of the Hellenistic

Cleopatra returns to Alexandria, at the Amir cinema along the Canopic Way

Acropolis of the Ptolemies
world? To reach what was once the citadel of Rhakotis, later the acropolis of the Ptolemies, you must today travel about 1.5 km southwest from the Corniche, perhaps along Sharias Salah al-Din and Amud el Sawari, in any case through less salubrious parts of the city where impressions in paint, in mud, of children's hands against the walls of squalid streets avert the evil eye.

The landmark attraction on the mound is **Pompey's Pillar,** wrongly named such by the Crusaders. It was raised in honour of Diocletian at the very end of the 4th C AD; he had come to Egypt to defeat a rival, and averted a famine by revictualing Alexandria after it had been under siege. The Arabs called it El Amud el Sawari, Column of the Horseman, and an equestrian statue of the emperor may have pranced on top when Amr entered the city. Within a few years of the column's erection, Diocletian was making a less favourable impression, torturing and slaughtering Christians in their thousands. The column with its base and Corinthian capital rises 27 metres; the shaft has a circumference of 9 metres and is of pink Aswan granite. The assemblage is entirely uninteresting, but being the tallest ancient thing in Alexandria it attracts attention. Immediately south of Pompey's Pillar are two pink granite **sphinxes** of the

435

Ptolemaic period; they were not original to this exact spot but were found near by. Here too is a **statue of Isis** found in 1961 in the sea near Fort Qaytbay; her temple had once stood on the island of Pharos and perhaps this comes from it.

Following the gaze of the sphinxes several metres farther south and off the height of the mound is the partly excavated site, marked by a few broken columns and a sign, where the foundation plaques of the **Serapeum**, the Temple of Serapis, were found (see Rooms 23 and 3 in the Graeco-Roman Museum). Presumably the temple spread over the entire mound; this and some *tunnels* cut into the rock to the north-west of Pompey's Pillar are all that remain. The Serapeum incorporated a library established by Cleopatra. The destruction of the complex was wrought, originally, in 391 when the Patriarch Theophilus led a mob against it in the final triumph of Christianity. Paganism was overthrown, as was learning. The belief that the older 'mother' Library, part of the Mouseion, was burnt when Julius Caesar fought to maintain himself in the city is now discredited.

The most interesting thing I have seen here is Egyptians catching pigeons. An orange beetle is used to bait a small wire trap hidden in the dry powdery soil.

A short distance south are the **Catacombs of Kom el Shogafa**, the largest Roman funerary complex in Egypt and run by a syndicate for the benefit of non-Christians. The catacombs date from the 2nd C AD and are decorated in a curious blend of classical and Egyptian styles. They are a sort of underground Forest Lawn.

Roman-Egyptian weirdness

The catacombs are on three levels, the lowest usually flooded and inaccessible. A winding staircase leads up to a *rotunda* encircled by chambers with sarcophagi and niches for funerary urns. The large room to the left was the *banqueting hall* where relatives of the deceased saw him out with a feast. The table in the middle, probably of wood, has disappeared, but cut out of the limestone are the three couches where they reclined on mattresses.

From the rotunda a stairway goes down to the second level. You are now at the *central tomb*. The decorations are composite, not to say weird. Bearded serpents adorn the vestibule wall at the entrance to the inner chamber. Each holds the suggestive pine cone of Dionysos and the serpent wand of Hermes, and also wears the double crown of Upper and Lower Egypt, while above them are Medusas in round shields. In the *tomb chamber proper* are three large sarcophagi, cut out from the rock. Their lids do not open, for the bodies would have been introduced from the passage which runs right round the chamber with accommodation for 300 mummies. In the niche over each sarcophagus is a relief in Egyptian style. Turning round and facing the entrance, on either side of the door are two extraordinary figures. On the right is Anubis, with a dog's head, but dressed up as a Roman soldier, with sword, lance and shield; on the left is Sobek who, despite being a crocodile, is also shoved into a military costume, with cloak and spear. 'Perhaps the queer couple were meant to guard the tomb, but one must not read too much into them or into anything here — the workmen employed were only concerned to turn out a room that should look suitable for death, and judged by this standard they have succeeded' (Forster).

Along the Coast East to Abu Qir

There are numerous public beaches along the city's seafront between the Eastern Harbour and Montazah — Chatby, Sporting, Ibrahimiya, Cleopatra, Stanley, Glym, San Stefano (also a private beach, small fee, belonging to the hotel of that name), Sidi Bishr, Miami, Asfara and Mandara; the public beaches are free but usually crowded and often dirty. There are 47 sewerage discharge pipes between Qaytbay's Fort and Montazah, emptying only 40 metres out to sea, making for some strange encounters. Also there is a dangerous undertow if you go much beyond the shore. At Montazah itself, and beyond, the pollution becomes negligible.

Jewellery and royal palaces

Along the way you could visit the **Royal Jewellery Museum**, housed in the palace of Princess Fatma el Zahraa in the Zizinia district (between Glym and San Stefano), with a glittering collection from the rise of Mohammed Ali to the fall of King Farouk.

At **Montazah** (16 km from the Eastern Harbour) is the former summer residence of the royal family. Farouk was there when the 1952 coup occurred in Cairo — he fled to Ras el Tin. The *palace* was built in Turko-Florentine style by the khedive Abbas II around the turn of the century; he also built the *Salamlek* nearby, overlooking a cove, in the style of a chalet for his Austrian mistress. These are set within extensive grounds planted with pines imported from Europe and palms.

The next bay east is Maamoura with a long fine beach (fee). In the distance you can see the long limestone spur running out to Abu Qir.

Battle of the Nile

Abu Qir (or Aboukir), 24 km east of central Alexandria, is most famous for the two battles fought here in 1798 and 1799. The first was the Battle of the Nile at which Nelson surprised Napoleon's anchored fleet and over the course of two days (1 and 2 August) annihilated it. Though still in control of the country, Napoleon was cut off from France by sea and eventually had to abandon his army and his dreams of Eastern dominion. The circumstances were similar to Antony's at Actium, except that Napoleon's star was still rising. A year later, in July, he personally commanded a battle here against a Turkish force of 15,000 landed by British ships. Napoleon had raced down from Cairo with Kléber and Murat, and with 10,000 men, mostly cavalry, drove the Turks back into the sea, drowning a third of them. That same year he returned to France and overthrew the Directory.

Today Abu Qir is built-up and unattractive, its beaches filthy, though Alexandrians will drive here for its seafood restaurants. Nearby is the site of ancient **Canopus,** once one of the most important cities in Egypt owing to its position on the Canopic mouth of the Nile, since dried up. There is little to see. Hadrian liked to stay here, and tried to recreate its pleasures in the garden of the Villa Hadriana at Tivoli, near Rome.

To the Rosetta Mouth of the Nile

The excursion to Abu Qir (which could be skipped) and on to Rosetta will take about half a day. **Rosetta** (Rashid) is 63 km from Alexandria and stands on the now westernmost (the ancient Bolbitine) branch of the Nile near the sea. Its name is associated most famously in the West with the discovery here of the Rosetta Stone, inscribed in ancient hieroglyphics, demotic Egyptian and Greek, enabling the eventual decipherment of the pharaonic language by Champollion. It is testimony to Napoleon's expedition, which included numerous savants and a well-informed soldiery, that when a Captain Bourchard was shown the stone, turned up by one of his men while restoring Fort Rashid, he immediately recognised its significance.

The Rosetta
Stone

The town is visited, however, for other reasons. Founded in the 9th C, it flourished while Alexandria faded and declined again as modern Alexandria prospered. It reached its apogee in the 17th and 18th C, when it was the most important port in Egypt, and there are still some fine houses dating from this period, built in red and black brick, their facades decorated in the Delta style illustrated, though not nearly so well, by the Terbana Mosque in Alexandria. Many, too, incorporate ancient stones and columns, and have delicately carved mashrabiyyas. The oldest and finest of these is the **House of Ali el Fatairi,** 17th C, just off the main street which runs south, parallel with the Nile, from the train station. This street is fascinating in itself, a market for much of the way, covered by awnings. Other houses are the **Arab Keli,** 18th C, now a museum; and **El Amaciali,** early 19th C. At the bottom of the main street is the most important building in town, the **Mosque of Zaghloul.** This is really two mosques, the eastern one smartly painted white, arcades with handsome arches running round a glaring courtyard. The western one, founded in 1600, is more interesting however, partly because it is under a few feet of water and crumbling but mostly for its wonderful forest of columns, as though rising out of a swamp.

Fine Delta
architecture

Rosetta makes an interesting footnote to Alexandria's

history. Its fortunes were built on the default of the greater city. The coast of Egypt here is delta, the shifting sediment of a senseless river. Rosetta can have no sea harbour, the lime-stone ridges that created the two great harbours of Alexandria do not continue eastward of Abu Qir. Alexander saw this potential, that his city could hold its own against land and sea. When the broad political will is there, Alexandria is willing. Meanwhile she is waiting.

Leaving Rosetta by the north, numerous high chimneys mark brickworks along the Nile; here even at the very end of the river's 5440 km journey from its source at Lake Victoria its mud was pressed into service — until 1988 when building with mud brick was banned. Since the building of the High Dam at Aswan, the Nile hardly lays down silt: mud has become a finite commodity in Egypt. A few kilometres along there is a spit of land, the river washing up on one side, the sea washing up on the other. At the very point there is a small yellow mosque; inside I saw two men praying. The sea and the river are rising up through its foundations, curling the paint off its walls, the whole thing disintegrating and tipping towards that line where the blue steady Nile is pounded by the light green waves of the Mediterranean.

The mosque at the end of the Nile

A soldier came up to me: 'Have you come to save the land from the sea?' It seems that the lack of mud means that the Nile no longer pushes the Delta out into the Mediterranean. Those waves were nibbling away at Egypt at the rate of a metre or so each year. The mosque will soon tumble and be drowned. The soldier stood on lonely station, guarding in vain against his country's retreat.

Ecologists come, I suppose, sent by international organis-ations, and offer him some comfort. I said nothing, and with an idiot's fascination I stood there watching the Mediter-ranean grow imperceptibly larger.

PRACTICAL INFORMATION

OF INTEREST

If you want to explore the city thoroughly, the best book is E M Forster's *Alexandria: A History and a Guide*, published by Michael Haag Limited, London, and Oxford University Press, New York. You may be able to pick one up in an Alexan-drian bookshop, though more likely in Cairo.

Not all the places mentioned in the text are listed below, rather only those where some further information, eg hours of

opening, is helpful. Also a few additional places of interest, not mentioned in the text, are listed in passing.

The **Graeco-Roman Museum** is off Sharia Horreya, its collection covering the period 300 BC to AD 300. LE1, students 50PT, camera LE5. Open 9am to 4pm daily except Fridays when it is closed from 11.30am to 1.30pm.

Kom el Dikka, the site of excavations into Alexandria's Ptolemaic and Roman past, is entered from the south off Midan el

Gumhuriya LE1, students 50PT. Hours as for the Graeco-Roman Museum.

The **old Opera House** (now the Sayed Darwish Theatre), is discovered through an archway on the north side of Sharia Horreya between Sharias Nebi Danyal and Safiya Zaghloul. Now used it seems for popular farces, once carriages rolled up here and the audience took its seats beneath the dome where still, absurdly, hover the names Berlioz, Wagner, Verdi, Gounod, Mozart, Bizet, Gluck and Rossini.

Cavafy's apartment is at what is now 4 Sharia Sharm el Sheikh, two flights up. You can knock and will kindly be admitted in to rooms let to students. They know why you have come, but are uncomprehending of your interest in one of the century's greatest poets. Like his rooms, Cavafy's Alexandria has changed hands. 'Then, sad, I went out on to the balcony,/ went out to change my thoughts at least by seeing something of this city I love,/ a little movement in the streets, in the shops' (*In the Evening*). The **Greek Consulate**, 63 Sharia Iskandar el Akbar (ie Alexander the Great Street, of course), in a rare and moving gesture recreates on its top floor the poet's apartment: his desk, books, some interesting photos, etc. They keep consular hours, and it might be a good idea to phone them first to make sure they are open (Tel: 4922318).

The **Synagogue**, 69 Sharia Nebi Danyal, near Midan Saad Zaghloul, is open 10am to 1pm daily, 8am to 10am Saturdays. In Ptolemaic times perhaps as many as 400,000 of Alexandria's 1 million inhabitants were Jews, and they also represented an important part of the community in more recent times until the wars with Israel. Now they cannot rouse enough men (10) to form a *schul*.

The **Coptic Orthodox Patriarchate** is reached through a narrow passage of Sharia Nebi Danyal almost opposite the Synagogue, or by turning left into the Rue de l'Eglise Copte after a short walk west from Sharia Nebi Danyal along Sharia Saad Zaghloul. In fact the seat of the Patriarchate is in Cairo, at St Mark's Cathedral, Abbassia, but the Pope remains the Patriarch of Alexandria and the See of St Mark. This is *not* (whatever the Copts might tell you) the site of the original church supposedly founded by St Mark (that Church, founded by the Evangelist or otherwise, was by the sea just east of Silsileh at Chatby; and it was there that Arius was deacon — see the Rue Attarine, below). But certainly it is impressive to read on the plaque here the names of all the patriarchs, including the great Athanasius, and to recall that Alexandria was once the most important city in the Christian world.

The **Rue Attarine,** which intersects Sharia Sidi el Mitwalli (the western extension of Sharia Horreya), is interesting for its numerous junk and antique shops. The triangular **Attarine Mosque** at the intersection stands on the site of the church dedicated to St Athanasius soon after his death — the Church of St Theonas where Athanasius preached, stood farther west near the Gate of the Moon. Between Athanasius on the Western Harbour and Arius at Chatby, the two Alexandrians tore the Christian world apart during the 4th C, until in 325 the Council of Nicaea issued its Creed declaring Arianism a heresy, anathematising 'those who say that there was a time when the Son of God was not, and that he was not before he was begotten, and that he was made from that which did not exist; or who assert that he is of other substance or essence than the Father, or is susceptible of change'.

The **Anfushi tombs** lie east of Ras el Tin Palace. LE1, students 50PT. Opening hours as for the Graeco-Roman Museum.

Fort Qaytbay, site of the Pharos, has vaulted passages and stores to explore outside and beneath the inner keep on the seaward side, while from the outer walls there are fine views over the whole of the Eastern Harbour. LE1, students 50PT. Opening hours as for the Graeco-Roman Museum.

Pompey's Pillar at the site of the Serapeum costs LE1, students 50PT, to enter. Opening hours as for the Graeco-Roman Museum. Fee and hours are the same for the **Catacombs of Kom el Shogafa** near by.

The **Chatby tombs**, 500 metres east of Silsileh, are the oldest in the city and similar to those at Anfushi. Entrance is 50PT, 25PT for students; hours as for the Graeco-

Roman Museum. If you walk back from here up towards the **Shallalat Gardens** (site of the Gate of the Sun and with sections of the Arab walls), you pass the city's more **recent cemeteries**, Coptic, Greek Orthodox, Protestant, Catholic and Jewish, fascinating and sometimes startling, as when a date on the gravestone of some scion of a great Jewish or Greek family is only a few days prior to Nasser's coup which spelt the end of their fortunes and presence in Alexandria.

The **Museum of Fine Arts**, to quote from *Alexandria Night and Day*, 'is one of the quietest beaches in Alexandria, and an excellent area for fishing'. This is very true. You will find it at 18 Rue Menasce (Sharia Mahmoud Bey Salama) in the Moharrem Bey area, just south of the railway lines from the Shallalat Gardens. Open daily 8am to 2pm, closed Fridays. Free. Concerts and exhibitions are also sometimes held here.

The **Nouzha Gardens and Zoo** are about 4 km southeast of Midan Saad Zaghloul and are open from 8am to 4pm, 10PT for the zoo, 15PT for the gardens. Immediately south on the Mahmoudieh Canal and opposite the airport are the **Antoniadis Villa and Gardens**, owned originally by a wealthy Greek family (and important benefactors of the Graeco-Roman Museum). The villa is used for state affairs, but the gardens (with some ancient tombs) are open from 8am to 4pm and can be enjoyed for 25PT.

The **Royal Jewellery Museum**, 27 Sharia Ahmed Yehia, Glym, is open daily from 9am to 4pm, closed Fridays from 11.30am to 1.30pm, and costs LE2, students LE1.

The **Montazah Palace and Gardens** are at the eastern extremity of the corniche road (16 km from Midan Saad Zaghloul, and across the road from the Montazah Sheraton). The gardens are open 24 hours and cost LE1. There is decent swimming at the cove by the vulgar Palestine Hotel; there is better swimming at **Maamoura**, the next bay along.

The palace is closed to the public, but notice the letter F which appears as a motif on the outside. A fortune teller had told King Fuad that the letter F would bring his family luck, so he named his daughters Fawzia, Faiza, Faika and Fathia, and his only son Farouk who in turn renamed Safinaz, his first wife, Farida, by whom he had three daughters, Ferial, Fawzia and Fadia. In 1951 Farouk married Narriman, neglecting to change her name, and in January 1952 she bore him his only son, the letter F relegated to second place in Ahmed Fuad. Six months later and Farouk was out of a job.

Abu Qir is not worth visiting except for a meal, but it is certainly worth visiting **Rosetta** (though nobody ever does), and the best way to get there is to hire a taxi. The town has been the subject of a major restoration project by the Egyptian Antiquities Organisation since 1985 and possesses some of the finest examples in Egypt of Islamic domestic architecture outside Cairo.

If you can manage only an **abbreviated itinerary**, take a carriage ride along the Corniche to Fort Qaytbay, then to the catacombs at Kom el Shogafa, and finally to the Graeco-Roman Museum. If you are staying a night, then from the balcony of your room at the Cecil overlooking the harbour try to resurrect in your mind's eye the Alexandria that was. Sit at a café, and in the evening walk about aimlessly. She is less a city you come to for seeing specific sights than a city which might just come to you.

441

PLACE INDEX

The following index is in two parts, the first covering Cairo, the second covering the rest of Egypt.

Note that the Arabic prefixes *el* and *al* have not been taken into account for the purpose of alphabetisation.

MAP AND PLAN INDEX

The following index is arranged alphabetically by place, ie sites at *Abydos* first, at *Thebes* last.